THE
REACHES

Baen Books by David Drake

The RCN Series
With the Lightnings
Lt. Leary, Commanding
The Far Side of the Stars

The General Series
Warlord with S.M. Stirling
(omnibus)
Conqueror with S.M.Stirling
(omnibus)
The Chosen with S.M. Stirling
The Reformer
with S.M. Stirling
The Tyrant with Eric Flint

Hammer's Slammers
The Tank Lords
Caught in the Crossfire
The Butcher's Bill
The Sharp End
Paying the Piper

The Belisarius Series
with Eric Flint
An Oblique Approach
In the Heart of Darkness
Destiny's Shield
Fortune's Stroke
The Tide of Victory

Independent Novels and Collections
The Reaches Trilogy
Seas of Venus
Foriegn Legions, edited by David Drake
Ranks of Bronze
Cross the Stars
The Dragon Lord
Birds of Prey
Northworld Trilogy
Redliners
Starliner
All the Way to the Gallows
Grimmer Than Hell
The Undesired Princess and The Enchanted Bunny
(with L. Sprague de Camp)
Lest Darkness Fall and To Bring the Light
(with L. Sprague de Camp)
Armageddon
(edited with Billie Sue Mosiman)
Killer
(with Karl Edward Wagner)

THE
REACHES

DAVID DRAKE

THE REACHES

Introduction copyright © 2004 by David Drake; *Igniting the Reaches* copyright © 1994; *Through the Breach* copyright © 1995; *Fireships* copyright © 1996; all by David Drake.

A Baen Megabook

Baen Publishing Enterprises
P.O. Box 1403
Riverdale, NY 10471

ISBN: 0-7434-7177-6

Cover art by Stephen Hickman

Distributed by Simon & Schuster
1230 Avenue of the Americas
New York, NY 10020

Production by Windhaven Press, Auburn, NH
Printed in the United States of America

CONTENTS

Introduction 1

Igniting the Reaches 5

Through the Breach 267

Fireships 561

INTRODUCTION:
The One That Got Away

I'm a very organized writer—insanely organized, one might say, and we'll get back to that in a moment. I take extensive notes before I start plotting, and I do very detailed plots (usually in the range of 5–15,000 words per plot, though a few have been much longer).

Occasionally I hear a writer say something along the lines of "My hero went off in a direction I didn't expect." I shake my head: *my* heroes don't do anything of the sort. It turned out, however, that they could still surprise me.

I got the notion of using the Age of Discovery as the background for a series of space operas. I'd bought a set (eight volumes) of Hakluyt's *Voyages* (the 1598 edition, which adds a great deal of material but drops David Ingram's very interesting account from the 1589 edition) while I was still an undergraduate and dipped into it frequently. When I chose that world for my setting, I read and took notes of the whole work. I then started plotting.

The life of Francis, later Sir Francis, Drake lent itself to development into a trilogy: his first voyages to the Caribbean, which made him an enemy of Spain and gained him a name; the round the world voyage of 1580–1, which brought him great wealth and a knighthood; and finally the climactic struggle against the Armada. I actually followed Drake's life quite closely, but especially in the second book I wove in events which happened to some of his contemporaries.

Though Drake was my model, I didn't attempt to tell the stories from his viewpoint. He's a very attractive man in many ways. His luck was in great measure the result of careful planning. For example, he didn't lose a man to scurvy, the deficiency disease which nearly wiped out Magellan's crew during the only round the world voyage preceding Drake's. Anson, a century and a half later, was still losing large numbers of crewmen to scurvy. Drake had figured out something that the greatest navigators before and after him did not, to their great cost.

Furthermore, in a cruel age and under brutal conditions, Drake wasn't himself cruel and didn't allow those under him to practice cruelty. This is truly remarkable, more remarkable than readers who haven't been in hard places themselves can imagine. Drake, suffering a painful wound from an Indian ambush, prevented his men from bombarding the Indian village. He said, probably correctly, that the Indians mistook him for a Spaniard—but the man who could do that after an arrow has been pulled from his face was humane in the best sense of the word.

But.

Drake was a religious fanatic and a fanatical patriot. He had sufficient reason—Philip II of Spain was a tyrant from the same mold as later provided the world with Hitler—and Drake's behavior was almost invariably within what now are accepted civilized norms. (The one instance of a war crime in modern terms involved hanging a hostage priest and promising to hang more if the Spaniard who'd murdered an envoy under a white flag weren't surrendered for punishment.)

But if what Drake did is acceptable, what he *was* is not. I don't say that I couldn't get into the mind of a fanatic, but the world and *my* world wouldn't be better places if I did so. I told the story—the stories—from the point of view of fictional sidekicks who, though men of their times, took a detached attitude toward the great issues of their day. Men, in short, who weren't very different from me.

I won't say that was a mistake, but I think it *is* the reason that the wheels came off my careful plan. Those viewpoint characters turned out to have minds of their own: my mind. And as a result, the novels weren't at all what I'd intended them to be.

That's the background to *The Reaches*. I'll now offer three ... well, call them caveats regarding the books themselves.

1) I postulated a future in which war had brought Mankind to the brink of extinction. The civilization that returns is based on individual craftsmanship, not mass production (although that's clearly on its way back by the end of the series). Some readers, faced with stories in which the characters fly starships but fight (some of them) with single-shot rifles, were not only baffled but infuriated.

2) Though I didn't use ideologues for my viewpoint characters, the period itself was fiercely ideological. I didn't attempt to hide that reality by inventing characters with modern sensibilities to exclaim with horror at situations which everyone of the day took for granted. Thus the books are deeply steeped in ideology that readers may find not only foreign but distasteful.

3) Finally, I'd intended *The Reaches* to be light space opera, the sort of thing I later did in the RCN series. Space opera they are, but they're very hard, *harsh* books. *Through the Breach* in particular is a more realistic view of what war does to a citizen/soldier than *Redliners* was. I'm more self-aware now than I was when I wrote the series, but I'm honestly not sure whether more than chance was involved in my choosing to write *Through the Breach* in first person, which is nearly unique in my fiction.

There's no single Truth in my world, but there are lots of little truths. There are several of those woven into *The Reaches*, but they're not all of them the truths that make me happiest in the hours before dawn.

Dave Drake
david-drake.com

IGNITING THE REACHES

To Rana Van Name
Who first heard about this one
when we were all going off to dinner;
And who is special.

1

Above Salute

Piet Ricimer stood out like an open flame on the crowded, cluttered bridge of the *Sultan* as she orbited Salute. Stephen Gregg was amused by the young officer's flashy dress.

Well, Ricimer was no younger than Gregg himself—but Gregg, as a member of a factorial family, was mature in ways that no sailor would ever be. More sophisticated, at any rate. Realizing that sophistication and maturity might not be the same made Gregg frown for a moment until he focused on the discussion again.

"I suppose it *might* be Salute," mumbled Bivens, the navigator. Gregg had already marked Bivens down as a man who never saw a planetfall he liked—or was sure he could identify.

"Look, of course it's Salute!" insisted Captain Choransky, commander of the *Sultan* and the other two ships of the argosy. "It's just this tub's lousy optics that makes it hard to tell."

His vehemence made the landfall seem as doubtful as Bivens' concern had done. This was Gregg's first voyage off Venus, much less out of the solar system. He was too young at twenty-two Earth years to worry much about it, but he wondered at the back of his mind whether this lot would be able to find their way home.

Besides the officers, three crewmen sat at the workstations controlling the forward band of attitude jets. The *Sultan* had been

7

stretched by two hull sections after her first decade of service as an intrasystem trader. That had required adding another band of jets.

The new controls and the sprawl of conduits feeding them had been placed on the bridge. They made it difficult for a landsman like Gregg to walk there under normal 1-g acceleration without tripping or bruising himself against a hip-high projection. Now, with the flagship floating in orbit, Gregg had even worse problems. The spacers slid easily along.

The most reassuring thing about the situation was the expression of utter boredom worn by every one of the crewmen on the control boards. They were experienced, and they saw no reason for concern.

"Sir," said Ricimer, "I'll take the cutter down and find us a landing site. This is Salute. I've checked the star plots myself."

"Can't be sure of a plot with these optics," Bivens muttered. "Maybe the *Dove* got a better sighting than I could."

"I'll take the six men who came with me when I sold *The Judge*," Ricimer said brightly. "I'm pretty sure I've spotted two Southern compounds, and there are scores of Molt cities for sure."

Ricimer was a short man, dark where Gregg was fair. Though willing to be critical, Gregg admitted that the spacer was good-looking, with regular features and a waist that nipped in beneath powerful shoulders. Ricimer wore a tunic of naturally red fibers from somewhere outside the solar system, and his large St. Christopher medal hung from a strand of glittering crystals that were more showy than valuable.

"Might not even be Molts here if it isn't Salute," Bivens said. "Between the twenty-third and twenty-ninth transits, I think we went off track."

Choransky turned, probably as much to get away from his navigator as for a positive purpose, and said, "All right, Ricimer, take the cutter down. But don't lose her, and *don't* con me into some needle farm that won't give me a hundred meters of smooth ground. The *Sultan*'s no featherboat, remember."

"Aye-aye, sir!" Ricimer said with another of his brilliant smiles.

"I'd like to go down with the boat," Gregg said, as much to his own surprise as anyone else's.

That drew the interest of the other men on the bridge, even the common sailors. Piet Ricimer's face went as blank as a bulkhead.

Gregg anchored himself firmly to the underside of a workstation with his left hand. "I'm Stephen Gregg," he said. "I'm traveling as supercargo for my uncle, Gregg of Weyston."

"I know that," Ricimer said, with no more expression in his voice than his face held.

"Ah—Ricimer," Captain Choransky said nervously. "Factor Gregg is quite a major investor in this voyage."

"I know that too," Ricimer said. His eyes continued to appraise Gregg. In a tone of challenge, he went on, "Can you handle a boat in an atmosphere, then, Gregg?"

Gregg sniffed. "I can't handle a boat anywhere," he said flatly. "But I'm colonel of the Eryx battalion of the militia, and I'm as good a gunman as anybody aboard *this* ship."

Ricimer's smile spread again. "Yeah," he said, "that might be useful."

He reached out his hand to shake Gregg's. When he saw the landsman was afraid to seem awkward in reaching to take it, Ricimer slid closer. He moved as smoothly as a feather in the breeze. Ricimer's grip was firm, but he didn't make the mistake of trying to crush Gregg's hand to prove that he was as strong as the bigger man.

"Maybe," Ricimer added over his shoulder as he led Gregg out through the bridge hatch, "we can give you some hands-on with the boat as well."

2

Above Salute

"Tancred!" Ricimer shouted as he slid hand over hand past crewmen in the bay containing the other two sets of attitude-jet controls. "C'mon along. Leon, get Bailey and Dole from the main engine compartment. We're taking the cutter down!"

"Bloody well about time!" agreed Leon. He was the *Sultan*'s bosun, a burly, scarred man. Leon picked his way with practiced skill through a jungle of equipment and connectors toward a back passage to the fusion thrusters.

"Lightbody and Jeude are already in Cargo Three with the boat," Ricimer said as he plunged headfirst down a ladderway toward the cargo holds.

Gregg tried to go "down" feetfirst as he would on a ladder under gravity. The passage, looped with conduits, was too narrow for him to turn when he realized his mistake. Tancred, following Gregg the proper way, was scarcely a boy in age. His face bore a look of bored disgust as he waited for the landsman to kick his way clear of obstacles he couldn't see.

Though the *Sultan* wasn't under thrust, scores of machines worked within the vessel's hull to keep her habitable. Echoes in the passage sighed like souls overwhelmed by misery.

Three crewmen under Leon were readying the eight-meter cutter when Gregg reached the hold. Tancred dogged the hatch closed, then joined the others with a snorted comment that Gregg chose not to hear.

Ricimer was at the arms locker, handing a cutting bar to a wiry spacer. "Here you go, Gregg," Ricimer called. The hold's empty volume blurred and thinned Ricimer's tones. "What do you want to carry?"

Gregg looked over the selection. The bridge had a separate arms locker, but the larger cabinet was here in Cargo Three, whose outer hatch provided the *Sultan's* main access—except, presumably, when the hold was full of cargo.

The locker held a dozen breech-loading rifles, each with a bag of ammunition sized to that weapon's chamber. Two of the rifles were repeaters, but those would be even more sensitive to ammo variations than the single-shots.

True standardization had ended a millennium before, when hit-and-run attacks during the revolt of the outer colonies wrecked automated factories throughout the human universe. Billions of people died in the Collapse that followed.

Humanity had recovered to a degree. Mass production was technically possible again. The horror of complex systems that could be destroyed by a shock—and bring down civilization with them—remained. It was as much a religious attitude as a practical one.

Most of the locker was filled with powered cutting bars, forty or more of them. Venerian ceramic technology made their blades, super-hard teeth laminated in a resilient matrix, deadly even when the powerpack was exhausted and could not vibrate the cutting edge. Apart from their use as weapons, the bars were useful tools when anything from steel to tree trunks had to be cut.

There were also three flashguns in the locker. These had stubby barrels of black ceramic, thirty centimeters long and about twenty in diameter, mounted on shoulder stocks.

Under the right circumstances, a flashgun's laser bolts were far more effective than shots from a projectile weapon. The flashgun drained its power at each bolt, but the battery in the butt could be replaced with reasonable ease. Under sunny conditions, a parasol accumulator deployed over the gunner's head would recharge the weapon in two or three minutes anyway, making it still handier.

But flashguns were heavy, nearly useless in smoke or rain, and dangerous when the barrel cracked in use. The man carrying one was a target for every enemy within range, and side-scatter from the bolt was at best unpleasant to the shooter. They weren't popular weapons despite their undoubted efficiency.

Gregg took a flashgun and a bandolier holding six spare batteries from the locker.

Piet Ricimer raised an eyebrow. "I don't like to fool with flashguns unless I'm wearing a hard suit," he said.

Gregg shrugged, aware that he'd impressed the sailor for the first time. "I don't think we'll run into anything requiring hard suits," he said. "Do you?"

Ricimer shrugged in reply. "No, I don't suppose so," he said mildly.

Carrying two single-shot rifles, Ricimer nodded the crewman holding another rifle and three cutting bars toward the boat. He followed, side by side with Gregg.

"You owned your own ship?" Gregg asked, both from curiosity for the answer and to find a friendly topic. He didn't care to be on prickly terms with anybody else in the narrow confines of a starship.

Ricimer smiled at the memory. "*The Judge*, yes," he said. "Captain Cooper, the man who trained me, willed her to me when he died without kin. Just a little intrasystem trader, but she taught me as much as the captain himself did. I wouldn't have sold her, except that I really wanted to see the stars."

Ricimer braked himself on the cutter's hull with an expert flex of his knees, then caught Gregg to prevent him from caroming toward a far corner of the hold. "You'll get the hang of it in no time," he added encouragingly to the landsman.

The interior of the boat was tight for eight people. The bench down the axis of the cabin would seat only about five, so the others squatted in the aisles along the bulkheads.

Gregg had heard of as many as twenty being crammed into a vessel of similar size. He couldn't imagine how. He had to duck when a sailor took the pair of rifles from Ricimer and swung, poking their barrels toward Gregg's eyes.

Ricimer seated himself at the control console in the rear of the cabin. "Make room here for Mr. Gregg," he ordered Leon, who'd taken the end of the bench nearest him. The burly spacer gave Gregg a cold look as he obeyed.

"Hatch is tight, sir," Tancred reported from the bow as he checked the dogs.

Ricimer keyed the console's radio. "Cutter to *Sultan*'s bridge," he said. "Open Cargo Three. Over."

There was no response over the radio, but a jolt transmitted through the hull indicated that something was happening in the hold. The boat's vision screen was on the bulkhead to the left of the controls. Gregg leaned forward for a clearer view. The double hatchway pivoted open like a clam gaping. Vacuum was a nonreflecting darkness between the valves of dull white ceramic.

"Hang on, boys," Ricimer said. He touched a control. An attitude jet puffed the cutter out of the hold, on the first stage of its descent to the surface of the planet below.

3

Salute

"Got a hot spot, sir," Leon said, shouting over the atmospheric buffeting. He nodded toward the snake of glowing red across the decking forward. The interior of the cutter was unpleasantly warm, and the bitter tinge of things burning out of the bilges made Gregg's eyes water and his throat squeeze closed.

"Noted," Ricimer agreed. He fired the pair of small thrusters again, skewing the impulse 10° from a perpendicular through the axis of the bench.

The spacers swayed without seeming to notice the change. Tancred grabbed Gregg's bandolier. That was all that prevented the landsman from hurtling into a bulkhead.

"Thanks," Gregg muttered in embarrassment.

The young spacer sneered.

Ricimer leaned over his console. "Sorry," he said. "I needed to yaw us a bit. There's a crack in the outer hull, and if the inner facing gets hot enough, we'll have problems with that too."

Gregg nodded. He looked at the hot spot, possibly a duller red than it had been a moment before, and wondered whether atmospheric entry with a perforated hull could be survivable. He decided the answer didn't matter.

"Do you have a particular landing site in mind, Ricimer?" he asked, hoping his raw throat wouldn't make his voice break.

"Three of them," Ricimer said, glancing toward the vision screen. "But I don't trust the *Sultan*'s optics either. We'll find something here, no worry."

The cutter's vision screen gave a torn, grainy view of the landscape racing by beneath. A few cogs of the scanning raster were out of synch with the rest, displacing the center of the image to the right. Ragged green streaks marked the generally arid, rocky terrain.

Gregg squinted at the screen. He'd seen a regular pattern, a mosaic of pentagons, across the green floor of one valley. "That's something!" he said.

Ricimer nodded approvingly. "There's Molts here, at least. Captain Choransky wants a place where the Southerns have already set up the trade, though."

The Molts inhabited scores of planets within what had been human space before the Collapse. Tradition said that men had brought the chitinous humanoids from some unguessed homeworld and used them as laborers. Certainly there was no sign that the Molts had ever developed mechanical transport on their own, let alone star drive.

It was easy to think of the Molts as man-sized ants and their cities as mere hives, but they had survived the Collapse on the outworlds far better than humans had. Some planets beyond the solar system still had human populations of a sort: naked savages, "Rabbits" to the spacers, susceptible to diseases hatched among the larger populations of Earth and Venus and virtually useless for the purposes of resurgent civilization.

Molt culture was the same as it had been a thousand years ago, and perhaps for ten million years before that; and there was one thing more:

A few robot factories had survived the Collapse. They were sited at the farthest edges of human expansion, the colony worlds which had been overwhelmed by disaster so swiftly that the population didn't have time to cannibalize their systems in a desperate bid for survival. To present-day humans, these automated wonders were as mysterious as the processes which had first brought forth life.

But the Molts had genetic memory of the robot factories humans had trained them to manage before the Collapse. Whatever the Molts had been to men of the first expansion, equals or slaves, they were assuredly slaves now; and they were very valuable slaves.

Gregg checked his flashgun's parasol. Space in the boat was too tight to deploy the solar collector fully, but it appeared to slide smoothly on the extension rod.

Two spacers forward were discussing an entertainer in Redport on Titan. From their description of her movements, she must have had snake blood.

The thrusters roared, braking hard. "So . . ." said Ricimer. "You're going to be a factor one of these days?"

Gregg looked at him. "Probably not," he said. "My brother inherited the hold. He's healthy, and he's got two sons already."

He paused, then added, "It's a small place in the Atalanta Plains, you know. Eryx. Nothing to get excited about."

The edge of Ricimer's mouth quirked. "Easy to say when you've got it," he said, so softly that Gregg had to read the words off the smaller man's lips.

The thrusters fired again. Gregg held himself as rigid as a cary-atid. He smiled coldly at Tancred beside him.

Ricimer stroked a lever down, gimballing the thrusters sternward. The cigar-shaped vessel dropped from orbit with its long axis dis-played to the shock of the atmosphere. Now that they'd slowed sufficiently, Ricimer slewed them into normal flight. They were about a thousand meters above the ground.

"You know, I'm from a factorial family too," Ricimer said with a challenge in his tone.

Gregg raised an eyebrow. "Are you?" he said. "Myself, I've always suspected that my family was really of some no-account in the service of Captain Gregg during the Revolt."

His smile was similar to the one he had directed at Tancred a moment before. "My Uncle Benjamin, though," Gregg continued, "that's Gregg of Weyston . . . He swears he's checked the genealogy and I'm wrong. That sort of thing matters a great deal—to Uncle Benjamin."

The two young men stared at one another while the cutter shud-dered clumsily through the air. Starships' boats could operate in atmospheres, but they weren't optimized for the duty.

Piet Ricimer suddenly laughed. He reached over the console and gripped Gregg's hand. "You're all right, Gregg," he said. "And so am I, most of the time." His smile lighted the interior of the vessel. "Though you must be wondering.

"And there . . ." Ricimer went on—he hadn't looked toward the vision screen, so he must have caught the blurred glint of metal out of the corner of his eyes—"is what we're looking for."

Ricimer cut the thruster and brought the boat around in a slow curve with one hand while the other keyed the radio. "Ricimer to *Sultan*," he said. "Home on me. We've got what looks like a Molt compound with two Southern Cross ships there already."

"And we're all going to be rich!" Leon rumbled from where he squatted beside the bow hatch. He touched the trigger of his cutting bar and brought it to brief, howling life—

Just enough to be sure the weapon was as ready as Leon himself was.

4

Salute

The *Preakness,* third and last vessel of Captain Choransky's argosy, spluttered like water boiling to lift a pot lid as she descended onto the gravel scrubland. Her engines cut in and out raggedly instead of holding a balanced thrust the way those of the *Sultan*'s boat had done for Ricimer.

Compared to the *Sultan* herself, the little *Preakness* was a model of control. Choransky's flagship slid down the gravity slope like a hog learning to skate. Gregg had been so sure the *Sultan* was going to crash that he'd looked around for some sort of cover from the gout of flaming debris.

The flagship had cooled enough for the crew to begin opening its hatches. It had finally set down six hundred meters away from the boat, too close for Gregg's comfort during the landing but a long walk for him now.

The roaring engines of the *Preakness* shut off abruptly. The ground shuddered with the weight of the vessel. Bits of rock, kicked up from the soil by the thrusters, clicked and pinged for a few moments on the hulls of the other ships.

"Let's go see what Captain Choransky has in mind," Ricimer said, adjusting the sling of the rifle on his shoulder. He sighed and added, "You know, if they'd trust the ships' artificial intelligences, they could land a lot smoother. When the *Sultan* wallowed in, I was ready to run for cover."

Gregg chuckled. "There wasn't any," he said.

"You're telling me!" Ricimer agreed.

He turned to the sailors. Two were still in the boat, while the others huddled unhappily in the vessel's shadow. Venerians weren't used to open skies. Gregg was uncomfortable himself, but his honor as a gentleman—and Piet Ricimer's apparent imperturbability—prevented him from showing his fear.

"The rest of you stay here with the boat," Ricimer ordered. "Chances are, the captain'll want us to ferry him closer to the Southern compound. There's no point in doing anything until we know what the plan is."

"Aye-aye," Leon muttered for the crew. The bosun was as obviously glad as the remainder of the crew that he didn't have to cross the empty expanse.

"And keep a watch," Ricimer added. "Just because we don't see much here—"

He gestured. Except for the Venerian ships—the crews of the *Sultan* and *Dove* were unloading ground vehicles—there was nothing between the boat and the horizon except rocky hummocks of brush separated by sparse growths of a plant similar to grass.

"—doesn't mean that there isn't something around that thinks we're dinner. Besides, Molts can be dangerous, and you know the Southern Cross government in Buenos Aires doesn't want us to trade on the worlds it claims."

"Let them Southerns just try something!" Tancred said. The boy got up and stalked purposefully around to the other side of the boat, from where he could see the rest of the surroundings.

Gregg and Ricimer set out for the flagship. The dust of landing had settled, but reaction mass exhausted as plasma had ignited patches of scrub. The fires gave off bitter smoke.

"Do you think there's really anything dangerous around here?" Gregg asked curiously.

Ricimer shrugged. "I doubt it," he said. "But I don't know anything about Salute." He stared at the white sky. "If this really *is* Salute."

From above, the landscape appeared flat and featureless. The hummocks were three or four meters high, lifted from the ground on the plateaus of dirt which clung to the roots of woody scrub. Sometimes they hid even the *Sultan*'s 300-tonne bulk from the pair on foot.

The bushes were brown, leafless, and seemingly as dead as the gravel beneath. Gregg saw no sign of animal life whatever.

"How do you think the Southerns are going to react?" Ricimer asked suddenly.

Gregg snorted. "They can claim the Administration of Humanity gave them sole rights to this region if they like. The Administration didn't do a damned thing for the Gregg family after the Collapse, when we could've used some help—didn't do a damned thing—"

"Don't swear," Ricimer said sharply. "God hears us here also."

Gregg grimaced. In a softer tone, he continued, "Nobody but God and Venus helped Venus during the Collapse. The Administration isn't going to tell us where in God's universe we can trade now."

Ricimer nodded. He flashed his companion a brief grin to take away the sting of his previous rebuke. Factorial families were notoriously loose about their language; though the same was true of most sailors as well.

"But what will the Southerns *do*, do you think?" Ricimer asked in a mild voice.

"They'll trade with us," Gregg said flatly. He shifted his grip on the flashgun. It was an awkward weapon to carry for any distance. The fat barrel made it muzzle-heavy and difficult to sling. "Just as the colonies of the North American Federation will trade with us when we carry the Molts to them. The people out in the Reaches, they need the trade, whatever politics are back in the solar system."

"Anyway," Ricimer said in partial agreement, "the Southerns can't possibly have enough strength here to give us a hard time. We've got almost two hundred men."

Choransky's crew had uncrated the three stake-bed trucks carried in the *Sultan*'s forward hold. Two of them were running. As Ricimer and Gregg approached, the smoky rotary engine of the third vibrated into life. Armed crewmen, many of them wearing full or partial body armor, clambered aboard.

Captain Choransky stood up in the open cab of the leading vehicle. "There you are, Ricimer!" he called over the head of his driver. "We're off to load our ships. You and Mr. Gregg can come along if you can find room."

The truck bed was full of men, and the other two would be

packed before the young officers could reach them. Without hesitation, Ricimer gripped a cleat and hauled himself onto the outside of Choransky's vehicle. His boot toes thrust between the stakes which he held with one hand. He reached down with the other hand to help Gregg into a similarly precarious position, just as the truck accelerated away.

Gregg wondered what he would have done if Ricimer hadn't extended a hand, certain that his companion wanted to come despite the risk. Gregg didn't worry about his own courage—but he preferred to act deliberately rather than at the spur of the moment.

He looked over his shoulder. The *Sultan*'s other two trucks were right behind them, but the *Dove*'s crew were still setting up the vehicle they'd unloaded. The *Preakness* was just opening her single hatch.

"Shouldn't we have gotten organized first?" Gregg shouted into Ricimer's ear over the wind noise.

Ricimer shrugged, but he was frowning.

5

Salute

The general rise in the lumpy terrain was imperceptible, but when the trucks jounced onto a crest, Gregg found he could look sharply *down* at the ships three kilometers behind him—

And, in the other direction, at the compound. Neither of the Southern vessels was as big as the *Preakness,* the lightest of Choransky's argosy. The installation itself consisted of a pair of orange, prefabricated buildings and a sprawling area set off by metal fencing several meters high. The fence twinkled as it incinerated scraps of vegetation which blew against it.

There was no sign of humans. Squat, mauve-colored figures watched the Venerians from inside the fence: Molts, over a hundred of them.

Captain Choransky stood up in his seat again, aiming his rifle skyward in one hand. The truck rumbled over the crest, gaining speed as it went.

"Here we go, boys!" Choransky bellowed. His shot cracked flatly across the barren distances.

A dozen other crewmen fired. Dust puffed just short of the orange buildings, indicating that at least one of the men wasn't aiming at the empty heavens.

"What are we doing?" Gregg shouted to Ricimer. "Is this an attack? What's happening?"

Ricimer cross-stepped along the stakes and leaned toward the cab. "Captain Choransky!" he said. "We're not at war with the Southern Cross, are we?"

The captain turned with a startled expression replacing his glee. "War, boy?" he said. "There's no peace beyond Pluto! Don't you know anything?"

Choransky's truck pulled up between the two buildings. Gregg squeezed hard to keep from losing his grip either on the vehicle or the heavy flashgun which inertia tried to drag out of the hand he could spare for it. The second truck almost skidded into theirs in a cloud of stinging grit. The third stopped near the Southern starships.

Gregg jumped down, glad to be on firm ground again. The smaller building was a barracks. Sliding doors and no windows marked the larger as a warehouse.

Gregg ran toward the warehouse, his flashgun ready. Ricimer was just ahead of him. They were spurred by events, even though neither of them was sure what was going on.

Ricimer twisted the latch of the small personnel door in the slider. It wasn't locked.

The warehouse lights were on. The interior was almost empty. A man in bright clothing lay facedown on the concrete floor with his hands clasped behind his neck. "I surrender!" he bleated. "I'm not armed! Don't hurt—"

Gregg gripped the Southern by the shoulder. "Come on, get up," he said. "Nobody's going to hurt you."

"I got one!" cried the spacer who pushed into the warehouse behind Gregg. He waved his cutting bar toward the prisoner.

Ricimer used his rifle muzzle to prod the blade aside as he stepped in front of the Venerian. "*Our* prisoner, I think, sailor," he said. "And take off your cap when you address officers!"

The man stumbled backward into the group following him. One of the newcomers was Platt, another member of Choransky's command group. Platt wore a helmet with the faceshield raised. In addition, he carried a revolving pistol belted on over body armor.

"Who else is here?" Gregg asked the Southern he held. He spoke in English, the language of trade—and the tongue in which the fellow had begged for mercy.

"What's going on?" Platt demanded.

Ricimer shushed him curtly. He stood protectively between Gregg and the newcomers, but his face was turned to catch the Southern's answers.

"Nobody, nobody!" the prisoner said. "I was in here—all right, I was asleep. I heard a ship landing, I thought it was, so I went out and all the bastards had run away and left me! All of them! Taken the trucks and what was I supposed to do? Defend the compound?"

"Why didn't you defend the compound?" Gregg asked. "I mean, all of you. There's the crews of those two ships as well as the staff here."

Around them, Platt and a score of other Venerians were poking among bales of trade goods, mostly synthetic fabrics and metal containers. The warehouse was spacious enough to hold twenty times the amount of merchandise present.

"Defend?" the Southern sputtered. He was a small man, as dark as Ricimer, with a face that hadn't been prepossessing before a disease had pocked it. "With what, half a dozen rifles? And there wasn't but ten of us all told. The local Molts bring us prisoners and we buy them. We aren't soldiers."

"We should've landed right here in the valley," said Platt, who'd drifted close enough to hear the comment. "Cap'n Choransky was too afraid of taking a plasma charge up the bum while we hovered to do that, though."

"And so would you be if you had the sense God gave a goose!" boomed Choransky himself as he strode into the warehouse. "You got a prisoner, Mr. Gregg? Good work. There wasn't anybody in the house."

The captain rubbed his cheek with the knuckles of his right hand, in which he held his rifle. "Like a pigsty, that place."

"He says his fellows drove off in a panic and left him when they heard the ships landing, sir," Ricimer said.

Choransky stepped closer to the prisoner. "Where's the rest of your stock?" he asked.

"You can't just come and take—" the Southern began.

Choransky punched him, again using his right hand with the rifle. The prisoner sprawled backward on the concrete. His lip bled, and there was a livid mark at the hairline where the fore-end struck him.

"We've got pretty much a full load," the Southern said in a flat voice from the floor. He was staring at the toes of his boots.

He touched the cut in his lip with his tongue, then continued,

"There's a freighter due in a week or so. The ships out there, they don't have transit capability. The freighter, it stays in orbit. We ferry up air, reaction mass, and cargo and bring down the food and trade goods."

Choransky nodded. "Maybe we'll use them to ferry the water over and top off our reaction mass. Those ships, they've got pumps to load water themselves?"

"Yes," the Southern muttered to his toes.

Platt kicked the side of the prisoner's head, not hard. "Say 'sir' when you talk to the captain, dog!"

"Yes sir, Captain," the Southern said.

"All right," Choransky said as he turned to leave the warehouse. "Platt, get the Molts organized and march them to the ships. Ricimer, you think you're a whiz with thrusters, you see if you can get one of those Southern boats working. I'll tell Baltasar to put an officer and crew from the *Dove* in the other."

He strode out the door. Platt followed him, and the rest of the spacers began to drift along in their wake.

"Right," said Ricimer. He counted off the six nearest men with pecks of his index finger. "You lot, come along with me and Mr. Gregg. I'm going to show people how to make a ship hover on thrust."

He shooed them toward the doorway ahead of him with both arms. The chosen crewmen scowled or didn't, depending on temperament, but no one questioned the order.

"You don't mind, do you?" Ricimer murmured to Gregg as they stepped out under an open sky again. "They haven't worked with me before. You won't have to do anything, but I'd like a little extra authority present."

"Glad to help," Gregg said. He looked at his left hand. He'd managed to bark the knuckles badly during the wild ride to the compound. "Besides, I wasn't looking forward to those trucks again."

Ricimer chuckled. His dark, animated face settled. Without looking at his companion, he said, "What do you think about all this, anyway? The way we're dealing with the Southerns."

Gregg glanced around while he framed a reply. Venerians had unlocked the gate in the electrified fence and were herding out the Molts. Some crewmen waved their weapons, but that seemed unnecessary. The Molts were perfectly docile.

The wedge-faced humanoids were a little shorter than the human average. Most of them were slightly built, but a few had double the bulk of the norm. Gregg wondered whether that was a sexual distinction or some more esoteric specialization.

Viewed up close, many of the Molts bore dark scars on their waxy, purplish exoskeletons. A few were missing arms, and more lacked one or more of the trio of multijointed fingers that formed a normal "hand."

"I'm my uncle's agent," Gregg said at last. "And I can tell you, nothing bothers my Uncle Ben if there's profit in it. Which there certainly is here."

Ricimer nodded. "I'm second cousin to the Mosterts," he said.

One of the crewmen he'd dragooned showed enough initiative to run ahead and find the hatch mechanism of the nearer ship. It sighed open.

"Really, now," Ricimer added with a grin to his companion. "Though what I said about a factorial family, there's evidence."

Gregg laughed.

"All three ships are Alexi Mostert's," Ricimer continued. "In the past, my cousin's made the voyage himself, though he sent Choransky out in charge this time. I'm sure this is how Alexi conducted the business too."

They'd reached the Southern Cross vessel. It weighed about 50 tonnes and was metal-hulled, unlike the ships of the Venerian argosy. Metals were cheap and readily available in the asteroids of every planetary system; but ceramic hulls were preferable for vessels which had to traverse the hellish atmosphere of Venus. Besides, the surface of the second planet was metal-poor.

Survival after the Collapse had raised ceramic technology to a level higher than had been dreamed of while Venus was part of a functioning intergalactic economy. After a thousand years of refinement, Venerians sneered at the notion metals could ever equal ceramics—though the taunt "glass-boat sailor!" had started fights in many spaceports since Venus returned to space.

"Some of you find the water intakes and figure out how to deploy them," Ricimer ordered as he sat at the control console.

The interior of the vessel stank with a variety of odors, some of them simply those of a large mass of metal to noses unfamiliar with it. The control cabin could be sealed. The rest of the ship was a single open hold.

"What do *you* think of what we're doing?" Ricimer said to Gregg. Then, before the landsman could reply, he added in a crisp voice, "All hands watch yourselves. I'm going to light the thrusters."

"I think . . ." Gregg murmured as Ricimer engaged the vessel's AI, "that it's bad for business, my friend."

6

Near Virginia

Choransky and Bivens muttered, their heads close above a CRT packed with data. The navigator grimaced but nodded. Choransky reached for a switch.

Ricimer turned from where he stood in the midst of the forward attitude-control boards he now supervised. "All right, gentlemen," he said. "We're about to transit again."

He winked at Gregg.

Gregg clasped a stanchion. He kept his eyes open, because he'd learned that helped—*helped*—him control vertigo. There wasn't anything in his stomach but acid, but he'd spew *that*, sure as the sun shone somewhere, if he wasn't lucky.

The *Sultan* lurched into transit space—and lurched out again calculated milliseconds later. The starship's location and velocity were modified by the amount she'd accelerated in a spacetime whose constants were radically different from those of the sidereal universe.

They dropped in and out of alien universes thirty-eight times by Gregg's count, bootstrapping the length of each jump by the acceleration achieved in the series previous before they returned to the sidereal universe to stay—until the next insertion. The entire sequence took a little more than one sidereal minute. Gregg's stomach echoed the jumps a dozen times over before finally settling again.

"There!" cried Captain Choransky, pointing to the blurred starfield that suddenly filled the *Sultan*'s positioning screen. "There, we've got Virginia!"

"We've got something," Bivens said morosely. "I'm not sure it's Virginia. These optics . . ."

Dole, at one of the attitude workstations, yawned and closed his eyes. Lightbody took out his pocket Bible and began to read, moving his lips. Jeude, at the third workstation, appeared to be comatose.

Two officers came in from aft compartments. They joined Choransky and Bivens at the front of the bridge, squabbling over the *Sultan*'s location and whether or not their consorts were among the flecks of light on the positional display. It was obviously going to be some minutes, perhaps hours, before the next transit.

Gregg maneuvered carefully through the cluttered three meters separating him from Ricimer. The landsman was getting better at moving in freefall. He'd learned that his very speed and strength were against him, and that he had to move in tiny, precisely-controlled increments.

Ricimer grinned. "These were easy jumps," he said. "Wait till the gradients rise and the thrusters have us bucking fit to spring the frames before we can get into transit space. But you'll get used to it."

"Where are we?" Gregg asked, pretending to ignore the spacer's comments.

He spoke softly, but the combination of mechanical racket, the keening of the Molts—they didn't like transit any better than Gregg's stomach did—and the increasingly loud argument around the positional display provided privacy from anyone but the trio at the attitude controls. Those men were Ricimer's, body and soul. They were as unlikely to carry tales against him as they were to try to swim home to Venus.

"The Virginia system," Ricimer said. "Both the captain and Bivens are pretty fair navigators. We're about a hundred million kilometers out from the planet; three jumps or maybe four."

"Why are you sure and they aren't?" the landsman asked.

Jeude turned his head toward the officers. He was a young man, fair-haired and angelic in appearance. "Because Mr. Ricimer knows his ass from a hole in the ground, sir," he said to Gregg. "Which that lot"—he nodded forward—"don't."

"None of that, Jeude," Ricimer said sharply. His expression softened as he added to Gregg, "I memorized starcharts for some of the likely planetfalls when I applied for a place on this voyage."

"But . . . ?" Gregg said. He peered at the flat-screen positional display, placed at an angle across the bridge. It would be blurry even close up. "You can tell from *that?*"

Ricimer shrugged. "Well, you can't expect to have a perfect sighting or a precise attitude," he said. "You have to study. And trust your judgment."

"I'd rather trust *your* judgment, sir," Jeude said. When he spoke, it was like seeing a dead man come to life.

"I think that'll do for me, too," Gregg agreed.

"Right, it's Virginia and I don't want any more bloody argument!" Captain Choransky boomed. "We'll do it in four jumps."

"I'd do it in three," Ricimer murmured. His voice was too soft for Gregg to hear the words, but the landsman read them in his grin.

7

Above Virginia

"If they don't make up their mind in the next thirty seconds," Ricimer said in Gregg's ear, "we'll lose our reentry window and have to orbit a fourth time."

"All right," Choransky said, as though prodded by the comment that he couldn't have heard. "That's got to be the settlement. We're going down."

He threw a large switch on his console, engaging not the main thrusters directly but rather the AI which had planned the descent two and a half hours earlier. The thrusters fired in a steady 1-g impulse quite different from the vertiginous throbs required by navigation through transit space.

Gregg's legs flexed slightly. It felt good to have weight again.

Attitude jets burped, rocking the *Sultan* as they counteracted the first effects of atmospheric buffeting. Lightbody spread his fingers over his control keys.

"Keep your hands off those, sailor!" Ricimer said sharply. "When I want you to override the AI, I'll tell you so."

Such images as had been available on the positioning display vanished behind curtains of light. The *Sultan*'s powerplant converted reaction mass, normally water, into plasma accelerated to a sizable fraction of light speed. When the thrusters were being used, as now, to brake the vessel's descent into an atmosphere, she drove down into a bath of the stripped ions she herself had ejected.

"Shouldn't we have told the *Dove* and the *Preakness* we were going down?" Gregg said. He pitched his voice low, not only to prevent the captain from hearing but because he didn't want to interfere with Piet Ricimer's concentration if the young officer was busier than he appeared to Gregg to be.

Ricimer pursed his lips. "One could say . . ." he replied. His eyes darted from one of the workstations to the next, checking to be sure his men were alert but not acting where silicon decisions were preferable. " . . . that Baltasar and Roon will see us going down, and that we need to land first anyway because the *Sultan* is such a pig. But one also could say that . . ."

"Communication doesn't hurt," Gregg said, not so much putting words in the spacer's mouth as offering his own opinion.

Ricimer nodded.

The *Sultan* began to vibrate unpleasantly. Gregg wasn't sure whether it was his imagination until Ricimer scowled and called out, "Sir, that harmonic is causing trouble with my controls. Can you give me—"

Choransky swore and thumbed a vernier on his console. The increment to the AI's calculated power was minute, but it kept the hull from resonating with sympathetic vibration.

Gregg frowned at the three workstations, trying to see anything different about them. "What was wrong with the controls?" he asked after a moment.

Ricimer grinned, then mouthed, "Nothing," with the back of his head to the captain and navigator. "She would've shaken to bits in time," he said, amplifying his statement in a scarcely louder voice. "And I don't know how *much* time."

He glanced at Choransky, then turned again and added, "He doesn't trust the AI for navigation, when he ought to; but he won't overrule it for something like that, harmonics that a chip can't *feel* so a man's got to."

Gregg watched as the display slowly cleared. The *Sultan* had scrubbed away her orbital velocity. Now she descended under gravity alone, partially balanced by atmospheric braking. The AI cut thruster output, so there was less plasma-generated interference with the optics which fed the screen.

Virginia was slightly more prepossessing than Salute had been.

The landmass expanding beneath the starship was green and gray-green with vegetation.

The planet's main export was cellulose base, useful as a raw material in the solar system albeit not a high-value cargo. The few pre-Collapse sites on Virginia provided a trickle of artifacts which current civilization could not duplicate. There were no caches of microchips on Virginia or automated factories like those which made some planets so valuable.

About thirty kilometers of slant distance away, metal glittered in the center of an expanse of lighter green. That was Virginia's unnamed spaceport, from which drones lifted mats of cellulose into orbit for starships to clamp to the outside of their hulls. Gregg squinted at the settlement, trying to bring it into focus.

The display vibrated in rainbow colors. Something slammed the *Sultan.*

"Plasma bolt!" Gregg shouted in amazement.

Captain Choransky disconnected the AI with one hand and chopped thruster output with the other. For an instant, the starship hesitated as gravity fought the inertia of earlier thrust. Gregg's stomach flip-flopped.

Ricimer reached past Dole and mashed a control button on his workstation. "Gregg!" he shouted. "Get aft and tell the other two bands to give us side-impulse! Only Jet Two on each bank!"

A bell on the navigational console clanged. Red lights were flashing from Dole's workstation. Gregg didn't know what the alarms meant—maybe the *Sultan* was breaking up—and he didn't understand Ricimer's words.

He understood that he had to repeat the command to the sailors controlling the other two bands of attitude jets in the next compartment sternward, though.

Gregg sprinted through the rear hatch. The starship was nearly in freefall as Choransky tried to drop out of the sights of the Federation gunners. Ricimer wanted to slew the vessel sideways as well, but the impulse from his forward attitude jet was being resisted fiercely by the crewmen at the other two bands who didn't have a clue as to what was happening on the bridge.

The *Sultan* yawed. Gregg jumped over a squat power supply and through the hatch like a practiced gymnast, touching nothing on the way. "Those Federation heathens are shooting at us!" someone bleated behind him.

The next compartment was even more crowded than the bridge. The double bank of attitude-control workstations, each with an officer standing in the middle of three seated crewmen, was against the starboard bulkhead. Platt and Martre were on duty.

The port side was usually rolled hammocks and a table for off-duty men to do handwork. Now it was stacked with rations for the Molts—fungus-processed carbohydrate bricks that stank almost as bad now as they did when the aliens excreted the residue. Half a dozen men clustered around the crates for want of anywhere better to be.

Overhead a tannoy blurted fragments of Choransky's voice. The *Sultan*'s intercom system worked badly, and the captain was nearly incoherent at the moment anyway.

"What's going on?" Platt demanded. Gregg's appearance caught him leaving his station to go to the bridge.

"Fire Jet Two, both bands!" Gregg shouted. "Not the others!"

"You heard him!" Martre said, pointing to one of his team. Choransky had dropped the men on the central and rear attitude controls into an unexplained crisis when he switched off the artificial intelligence. Martre was delighted to have someone— anyone—tell him what to do.

"What in *hell* is going on?" Platt repeated. The *Sultan* began to yaw as the attitude jets fought one another.

Ricimer came through the hatch behind Gregg and darted for Platt's control set. Platt tried to grab him. Gregg put his right arm around Platt's throat from behind and clamped hard enough to choke off the officer's startled squawk.

Platt's team members jumped up from their seats—to get out of the way rather than to interfere. Ricimer slid one control up. Tancred, off duty in the compartment a moment before, sprawled over a workstation in order to drop its slide and that of the third to the bottom of their tracks.

Lights flickered. Gregg felt hairs lift on his arms.

"*Missed* us, by the mercy of God," Ricimer said, and there was no blasphemy in his tone. He seated himself properly at the workstation he'd taken over. "But not by much."

Bivens stuck his head through the hatch from the bridge. "Stand by for braking!" he warned in a shrill voice.

Gregg released Platt.

The smaller man turned and croaked, "You whoreson!" He

cocked a fist, then took in Gregg's size and the particular smile on the young gentleman's face.

Platt turned away. Leon, who'd popped up from one of the lower compartments, judiciously concealed what looked like a length of high-pressure tubing in his trouser leg. The bosun nodded respectfully to Gregg.

The thrusters cut in again with a tremendous roar, slowing the massive starship after her freefall through the line-of-sight range of the Federation guns. The braking effort was an abnormal several Gs, slamming men to the decks and causing some shelves to collapse. Gregg kept his feet with difficulty.

On the bridge, the men at the forward attitude controls were bellowing "Onward, Christian Soldiers" in surprisingly good harmony.

8

Virginia

The *Sultan*'s long cigar shape lay on its side with the landing legs properly deployed and all three cargo hatches open. The ground beneath the thrusters fizzed and snapped as heat-stressed stones cooled.

Gregg hunched in his hard suit and wondered whether he ought to drop the thick visor as well. That would mean using bottled air and seeing out through a slit, but at least it would keep the *wind* off him.

Virginia's breezes slapped harshly against skin used to the weatherless corridors of Venus. The *Sultan*'s thrusters had ignited pungent fires as she roared in to land, and miniature leaves blew from the scorched trees surrounding the starship. They were hard-shelled, and their tips were as sharp as shards of glass.

More by luck than planning, Choransky had brought the *Sultan* down at the edge of a natural clearing. The ground was so thin-soiled that only ankle-high moss grew on it. That was fortunate, because the trees beyond the clearing were thirty or forty meters high, with trunks so thin and closely spaced that they resembled a field of giant wheat.

Starships' plasma exhaust could clear landing sites in almost any vegetation, but the blazing, shattered trunks would form an impassable barrier. The debris would have locked the crew and cargo within the *Sultan* as surely as hard vacuum had during the voyage.

A Molt stumbled off the ramp and bumped a guard. "God damn your crinkly soul to Hell!" shouted the spacer as he lashed out with his boot. The chitinous alien tried to back away, but one of its legs flailed spastically. It fell toward the human again.

Piet Ricimer grabbed the crewman by the collar and jerked him backward. "You!" Ricimer said. "If I hear you blaspheme that way again, you'll swab out all three holds alone! Do you think God no longer hears us because we're off Venus?"

"Sorry, sir," the sailor muttered. Gregg had expected more trouble—and was moving closer in case it occurred. Ricimer's fierce sincerity shocked the man into quiet obedience.

Navigator Bivens appeared at the edge of Cargo One. He cupped his hands before his mouth as an amplifier and shouted, "Watch out, boys. There's aircraft coming, the radar says."

"Hell *take* them!" Gregg snarled, meaning life in general. He was glad an instant later that he hadn't spoken loudly enough for his new friend Ricimer to hear.

And after all, the spacer was right. They were going to need the Lord's help here in the outer reaches of his universe at least as much as they did among the familiar verities of home.

Captain Choransky was on the radio, trying to raise the *Sultan's* consorts and whoever was in charge of the Federation settlement. Ricimer, Gregg, and about two dozen armed crewmen shepherded the cargo of Molts onto the surface so that the holds could be washed down. So far as the men aboard the starship were concerned, Ricimer's task was the more important.

They'd loaded ninety-eight Molts aboard the *Sultan* on Salute, a slight majority of the total, with the rest split between the smaller Venerian ships. Ninety-two had survived thus far, but many of them were on their last legs, and in a confined space they stank like death itself.

A single air system served the entire starship. The *Sultan's* human complement had been breathing the stench throughout a voyage of seventeen days.

Men checked their weapons. Only a few of those guarding the Molts had brought rifles: cutting bars were lighter and more effective, both for use and as threats. More riflemen and another flashgunner in a hard suit appeared at the lip of Cargo One a moment after Bivens called his warning.

"Don't shoot unless I tell you to," Ricimer shouted to the men spread in a loose perimeter around the Molts. "Remember we aren't here to fight. We're traders!"

"Hope *they* remember that," said Jeude as he spun his cutting bar for a test. His tone undercut the words.

Gregg thought he heard the faint *pop-pop-pop-pop* of motors. He glanced at the cloud-streaked sky. The sound didn't have a clear direction.

"Which way is the settlement?" he called to Ricimer.

Ricimer turned from the Molt he'd helped over the coaming at the bottom of the ramp. The alien was the last to leave the *Sultan*. It was either sick or very old, and the ramp's four-centimeter lip had stopped it like a slab of bedrock.

"That way," Ricimer said, pointing across the clearing toward south-southwest based on sun position. "Five klicks, a hair less. Once a ship the size of the *Sultan* commits to landing, you don't maneuver much."

Someone hammered within the starship's hull, freeing a stuck latch. One, then five more meter-square hatches swung open along the *Sultan*'s hull. The muzzle of a plasma cannon poked through the nearest opening.

Ricimer looked at the Molts, milling slowly in the midst of the crewmen. Some of the aliens were rubbing their torsos with wads of moss they'd plucked. "Move them into the woods," Ricimer ordered. "Now! Nobody'd better be in the clearing if the heavy ordnance fires."

Gregg focused in the direction of the settlement. The sound of motors was very close, though nothing was visible over the trees at the edge of the clearing. He aimed his flashgun at the expected target and shouted, "Don't fire until Master Ricimer orders!" to prevent anyone from mistaking his intent.

The *Sultan* carried ten plasma cannon, but she was pierced with over forty gunports so that the heavy weapons could be moved to where they were needed. Even in weightlessness, the weapons' mass made them difficult to shift through the strait confines of the vessel. When the crews were working here on the ground, they'd be lucky if scrapes and bruises were the only injuries before the start of the fighting.

If there was going to be fighting.

Two aircraft crossed the edge of the clearing and banked in opposite directions. They were one- or two-place autogyros, moving at 100 kph or slower.

Nobody fired at them, but one of the crewmen screamed, "Federation dog-mothers!" and waved his cutting bar. Leon grabbed the man's arm and growled at him before Ricimer could react.

The first aircraft vanished beneath the treetops again. Three more autogyros appeared. One of them settled into the clearing. It bounced twice on the rocky soil but came to a halt within fifteen meters. Its four consorts began to circle the starship slowly at a hundred meters.

Choransky, Bivens, and several other officers stamped down the Cargo Three ramp. They were all armed. Martre wore the helmet and torso of a hard suit and carried another flashgun. He nodded as Gregg fell in step to one side of the command group and Ricimer joined on the other.

The autogyro's four-bladed support rotor slowed to a halt. The passenger getting out of the tandem seat to the rear was male, but Gregg noticed with distaste that the pilot was a woman. Gregg wasn't a religious zealot, but the way the North American Federation put women in positions of danger—women even served in the crews of Federation starships—would be offensive to any decent man.

The autogyro was powered by an air-cooled diesel. Gregg didn't realize how noisy it was until the passenger shouted an order and his pilot shut the clattering motor off.

"What do you mean shooting at us?" Captain Choransky shouted while he was still twenty meters from the aircraft. "Look at that!"

He pointed over his shoulder in the general direction of the *Sultan*. Through air at such long range, the plasma bolt had only scoured away a patch of yellow-brown corrosion the Venerian atmosphere had left on the starship's white hull. Even such a relatively light weapon could have been fatal if it hit the thrusters during the descent, or if the *Sultan*'s hull was crazed by long vibration.

"You have no right to be here!" the Federation envoy said shrilly. "The Administration of Humanity has awarded exploitation of this sector to America!"

The envoy was a tall, thin man with a full beard but almost no hair above the line of his ears. He wore a gray tunic over blue trousers, perhaps a uniform, with gaudy decorations on his left breast. His holstered pistol was for show rather than use, and he looked extremely apprehensive of the heavily-armed Venerians.

"Brisbane's authority is a farce!" Choransky said. He stopped directly in front of the envoy and stood with his arms akimbo, emphasizing the breadth of his chest. "The Secretary General can't *fart* unless President Pleyal tells him to."

The envoy swallowed. He met Choransky's glare, but Gregg had the feeling that was to avoid having to admit the presence of the other murderous-looking Venerians surrounding him. The Fed's courage wasn't in doubt.

"Whatever President Pleyal may be to you," the envoy said, "he is my head of state. And his orders are that his domains beyond Earth shall have no dealings except with vessels of the North American Federation."

Choransky poked the envoy's chest with one powerful finger. "Balls!" he said. "Captain Mostert turned over his whole cargo on Virginia last year. I'm *from* Captain Mostert. Don't you recognize the damned ship?"

The Federation envoy made an angry moue with his lips. "Port Commander Finchly, who dealt with your Captain Mostert," he said, "was arrested and carried back to Earth last month to stand trial. His replacement, Port Commander Zaloga, arrived with the orders for his predecessor's arrest."

Choransky seized the grip of the cutting bar dangling from his belt. He also wore a slung rifle. The envoy shut his eyes but didn't move.

"God grind your stupid bones to meal!" the captain said, his voice low-pitched but sincere. Then he went on in a grating but nearly normal tone, "Look, you tell your Commander Zaloga this. I'm bringing my other ships down, because they stink worse 'n sewers with the Molts we're carrying. And you bastards *need* Molts!"

The envoy's eyelids quivered.

"Then we'll come talk to Zaloga, and talk like sensible people. If he's looking for a little something for himself to clear this, well, I guess something can be arranged. But no more shooting!"

The envoy nodded, then opened his eyes. "I'll tell the commander," he said, "and I'm sure he'll talk with you himself. But as for your business—"

For an instant there was something more than fear and formality in the Fed's voice. "Gentlemen, you *know* President Pleyal. It's as much as a man's life is worth to cross him."

Choransky gripped the envoy by the shoulder, gently enough, and turned the man back toward his autogyro. "Pleyal's a long way away," the Venerian captain said. "I'm here, and believe me, I'm not taking these stinking Molts back to Venus with me."

Ricimer stepped in front of the envoy. "Sir," he said. "Without trade your colony will die, and without outside resources the homeworlds—even Earth in her present condition—will die also. No orders that restrict trade can be in keeping with the will of God for mankind to survive."

The Federation officer stared as Ricimer moved out of the way again. "Does President Pleyal recognize a god beyond himself?" he asked, half a taunt. He got into the aircraft.

"And no shooting!" Choransky repeated in a loud voice as the Fed pilot restarted her motor.

9

Virginia

The roar of the vessels landing made bones quiver. The glare of the thrusters was so intense that Gregg felt the bare backs of his hands prickle. He'd lowered his visor to protect his sight.

They'd had to reload the Molts temporarily. With luck, the other ships could manage to avoid the *Sultan* when they landed around the edges of the clearing, but there was no way to safely mark the location of off-loaded cargo among the trees. The aliens moaned as they were forced back aboard the vessel.

From the *Sultan*'s open hatchways Gregg, Ricimer, and a score of other crewmen and officers watched their consorts land. Partly because of his filtered vision, partly due to simple unfamiliarity with the fine points of starship construction, it wasn't until the vessels were within fifty meters of the ground that Gregg understood what was wrong.

"That's not the *Preakness* with the *Dove*," he bellowed to Ricimer. The spacer couldn't possibly hear him—and had no doubt known the truth within seconds of the time the starships came in sight, making a rare and dangerous simultaneous landing. "That's some Earth ship! She's got a metal hull!"

Whatever the vessel was, she landed neatly in the clear area. The *Dove* came down in an orange fireball fifty meters within the margin of the forest, blasting splinters in every direction.

Virginia's vegetation didn't sustain flames very well when it was green. The fire wouldn't be dangerous, but it would smolder and reek for days or longer. Ricimer, his face screened by the rosy filter which pivoted down from inside the brim of his cap, shook his head in disgust at the *Dove*'s awkwardness.

The strange vessel was about the 150 tonnes of the *Dove*. The hull was more smoothly curved than that of a Venerian ship, but there were a dozen or more blisters marring the general lines. Some of the blisters were obviously weapons installations.

Metal was easier to form into complex shapes than mold-cast ceramics. It was also easier to tack this or that extra installation onto a metal hull later, instead of getting the design right the first time.

The *Preakness* had started her landing approach. Radio was useless when a starship's thrusters were swamping the RF spectrum with ions. Gregg didn't expect to learn anything until all the vessels were down.

A personnel hatch on the newcomer's belly curve opened. The rock beneath still glowed white from the landing, distorting the vessel's appearance with heat waves.

A man—a very big man—wearing a silver hard suit jumped out of the ship and ran heavily toward the *Sultan*. He must have heard the *Preakness* coming in, but he ignored the chance that the Venerian ship would crush his plasma-fried ashes to the rock.

Gregg's lips pursed. He risked raising his visor for a moment to be sure. The stranger carried a repeating rifle, as ornately splendid as his metal hard suit. The suit, at least, was functional. It had just protected its wearer across a stretch of stone so hot it was tacky.

Gregg knew better than most what it took out of you to run in a hard suit, and how easy it was to trip with your helmet visor down. He strode down to the bottom of the ramp and offered the stranger a hand—a delicate way of warning the fellow of the raised lip.

The stranger caught his bootheel anyway and shouted curses in German loud enough to be heard above the *Preakness*' approach. With his left gauntlet in Gregg's right hand, they clomped into Cargo Three. It wasn't often Gregg met somebody bigger than he himself was.

Molts packed themselves tighter against the bulkheads to keep clear. The aliens understood human orders, even without the kicks that normally accompanied the words. Supposedly their mouth parts permitted them to use human speech, but Gregg hadn't heard one do so yet.

The ramp/hatchcover began to rise before Gregg and the stranger were fully clear of it, lowering the noise level abruptly. Piet Ricimer was at the control box.

The stranger opened his helmet. "So!" he said in Trade English. "I am *Kapitän,* that is Captain Schremp of Drillinghausen. My *Adler* has been here in orbit for a week, but the Federation bastards, they even shot at us when we tried to land. And you are?"

"The *Sultan* out of Betaport, Captain Choransky commanding," Ricimer said easily. "I think the captain—"

United Europe had not been involved in reopening the stars. Even now, the North American Federation and the Southern Cross were the only regions of Earth which showed a governmental interest in interstellar trade. Private ventures from the Rhine Basin were not uncommon, though.

From the rumors, the Germans' approach to trade was rough-and-ready, even by the standards Captain Choransky applied.

Choransky appeared at the ladder from the mid-deck. "What in God's name do you think you're playing at, landing at the same time as my *Dove,* you poxy bastard?" he roared at Schremp.

"I thought it was better to stay close to one of your ships until I had time to explain," Schremp said without embarrassment. His full beard was blacker than seemed natural for a man whose appearance otherwise was that of a fifty-year-old. "Explain that we are to be allies, yes? If we stay together, the pussies will be *glad* to deal with us, I'm sure!"

He smiled. The expression made Gregg think of the stories about German "trade."

10

Virginia

The orange berm of stabilized soil protecting the settlement was in sight, half a kilometer away. A uniformed Fed stood on it to watch the Venerians and Germans approach. He had either binoculars or an electronic magnifier.

Piet Ricimer knelt and teased a thorny plant loose from the margin of the grainfield surrounding the Fed settlement. "Stephen?" he said to Gregg. "Do you ever wonder what life was like before the Collapse?"

"What?" Gregg said. "Oh, you mean everybody rich with electronics? Well, sometimes."

He'd thought he was losing his fear of open spaces. Now that they'd left the dark trunks of the native forest for the cleared area supplying food for the settlement and the vessels that touched on it, he wasn't quite so sure.

Well, it wasn't really fear, just discomfort. And God knew that there was plenty of other discomfort, wearing armor and carrying a flashgun and still managing to lead a five-klick march.

"No, I meant . . ." Ricimer said. "See this? It's not a native plant, and I doubt the Feds brought it with them in the rediscovery."

The other spacers were coming up slowly, but nobody else was within a hundred meters of Ricimer and Gregg. The whole sixty or so in the party probably stretched a klick back into the forest.

"A thornbush?" Gregg said in puzzlement.

Two more Feds had joined the observer on the berm. One of them carried a megaphone. Despite its greater access to pre-Collapse sites on the outworlds, the North American Federation wasn't overall more technically advanced than Venus.

"Not a thornbush," Ricimer said. His finger carefully freed a full yellow bloom from the native foliage concealing it. "A rose."

"Stay where you are!" called the Fed with the megaphone. "Don't come any closer or we'll fire!"

"Right," said Leon, wheezing with the exertion of keeping up—almost—with the leaders. "And if that was the worst I had to worry about, I'd still die in bed."

"What you got, sir?" Tancred asked, squatting down beside Ricimer. "Hey! Artifacts!"

The young spacer carried a rifle. He used the barrel of the weapon to sweep back the vegetation. Underneath was half of a shallow porcelain bowl. Varicolored birds sang on a white field. The material had survived its millennium of exposure well enough, but Gregg didn't think it was up to the quality of current Venerian manufacture.

"Nothing valuable, though," Tancred said in disappointment. "You know, when I signed on, I kinda thought I'd, you know, pick up handfuls of chips when we got out-system."

"I think they're moving guns up behind the berm," Gregg said. "I can't see over, but there's some sort of commotion back there."

Two autogyros *pop-popped* in slow circles overhead. A line of diesel-powered ground vehicles rounded the edge of the ravelin shielding a gap in the berm. The spacers hadn't bothered to unload the trucks their vessels carried, because the forest was trackless and the tree boles averaged less than a meter and a half apart.

Choransky, Schremp, and a dozen men from each party joined the score of spacers who'd clustered around Ricimer and Gregg. As many more straggled along behind.

"I heard them shout," Choransky said. "What was it?"

"They told us not to come closer, sir," Ricimer said.

Schremp snorted. "Why should we want to do that?" he said. "When they're coming to us, and they don't have to walk like dogs."

The German leader wore only the torso and helmet from his hard suit. The face beneath his lifted visor was sweaty and bright red with exertion.

Gregg eyed the German's armor speculatively. The metal's bright finish—it appeared to be silver-plated, not just highly polished—would reflect energy better than Gregg's suit, and if the core was titanium alloy, it might be lighter as well. The metal couldn't be as effective a heat sink as Venerian ceramic, though, and Gregg was willing to bet his armor's higher hardness against metal's ability to deform under extreme stress instead of shattering.

Schremp glanced at Tancred. "Find anything valuable, kid?" he asked.

Tancred's face tightened. Before he could speak, Ricimer said, "Just the remains of somebody's garden, from a long time ago."

Schremp nodded and turned his attention to the oncoming vehicles that the other spacers were watching.

Rather than trucks, the Feds approached in three tracked, open-topped tractors, each towing a flatbed trailer in which forty or so figures rode. Figures, not "men," because half of the personnel were Molts and many of the humans wore coarse, bark-fabric clothing.

Though humans survived after a fashion on many outworlds, civilization did not. The men in indigenous dress were Rabbits, feral remnants of the pre-Collapse colonies.

The Rabbits and Molts were armed with cutting bars and even manual axes. None of them wore armor. There were half a dozen troops in Fed uniform on each vehicle. Not all of them had fire-arms, and only two wore head and torso armor.

"Huh!" said Jeude, scratching his neck with the edge of his cutting bar. "Those trucks're slower than glass flowing. I could walk as fast as that."

"They haul mats of timber processed at field stations," Ricimer explained. "They don't need to be fast."

"They're riding," Gregg guessed aloud, "because they want to show they've got vehicles and we're on foot."

"They got plasma guns in the fort," Leon said, eyeing the berm opposite the party of spacers. Metal glinted there without being raised quite high enough to make identification certain. "Them I'm willing to worry about."

Gregg spread and raised his flashgun's parasol. The meter-square solar cell swayed awkwardly in the breeze, making the weapon harder to control.

He didn't need to deploy the charger for any practical reason. He was carrying six extra batteries, and it was much faster to replace than recharge them in a firefight. The Feds weren't the only ones who could make silent threats, however.

Ten meters from the spacers, the tractor-trailers swung broadside and halted. A man wearing a white uniform and a number of medals got out of the cab of the leading tractor. He waited for two more officers, one of them female, and a pair of guards armed with rifles to get off the trailer behind him. With them in tow, he strode toward the spacers.

The whole party of Venerians and Germans surged forward across the wheat.

"Not so many!" the Fed leader cried, waggling his hand. He wore a pair of pistols completely swallowed by their cross-draw holsters. At careful inspection his uniform, though fancy enough, was frayed at the cuffs and noticeably dingy.

Choransky and Schremp muttered to one another for a moment. Choransky looked around. "You lot stay where you are!" he ordered. The two captains, accompanied by Platt and two Germans—as choice a pair of cutthroats as Gregg remembered seeing in his life—met the Feds between the waiting lines.

Choransky seized the initiative by blustering, "I want to know who you think you are, shooting at peaceful traders?"

"*I* am Port Commander Zaloga," the Fed leader blustered back, "and there'll be no trade with illegal interlopers like yourself on this planet or any planet of the North American Federation."

"North America is a thousand light-years away," said Captain Schremp in a surprisingly calm voice. "We are here with cargo your people need, slaves from my Venerian fellows there and the highest quality sauces and dairy solids aboard my *Adler*. Surely you must be tired of eating the bland mush you grow here, not so?"

"Your predecessor gave Captain Mostert a want list when he landed on Virginia last year," Choransky put in. "We brought our Molts here at your orders."

"My predecessor," Zaloga said, "was arrested for his treasonous dealings with interlopers like your Captain Mostert. You're not here at my orders. *My* orders are that you leave the planet at once. And as you see—"

He pointed toward the settlement. Half a dozen soldiers had lifted a small plasma cannon onto the top of the berm. The crew wore helmets, gauntlets, and padded coveralls against the effects of their own weapon.

"—I can enforce those orders!"

"Can you?" Schremp said with a sneer in his voice. "Take them," he added flatly.

Each of the Germans with him grabbed a Fed officer. Schremp himself caught Zaloga by the throat with his scarred left hand and squeezed hard enough to choke the port commander's protests into a startled bleat.

Choransky grasped the rifle of a Fed guard and prevented the man from lowering his weapon. Platt tried to do the same with the remaining guard, but he wasn't strong enough to overpower the fellow. They struggled for a moment.

Schremp, holding his repeater in one hand like a huge pistol, socketed the muzzle in the guard's ear and blew his brains out. The Fed's skull sagged sideways like a fruit dropped against concrete. Bits of colloid sprayed the female officer and the German who held her. She began to scream and kick hysterically.

"Stephen!" Ricimer shouted. His grip on Gregg's shoulder was as firm as a C-clamp. He pointed toward the plasma cannon with his rifle. He didn't bother to shoot because it was hopelessly out of his range. "Stop them!"

The half-armed militia on the trailers were too shocked by the violence to react, but the crew of the plasma gun were traversing their weapon squarely onto what had been the negotiating party. A bolt from that weapon—three or four centimeters in bore—would incinerate both command groups and probably a score of other spacers besides. The gunners might or might not fire—

But Piet Ricimer was right. The choice couldn't be left to them.

Gregg clashed his visor down and swore as the world blurred amber. The flashgun had a simple, four-post optical sight. He could only wish now that he'd checked the collimation, made sure that the point of aim was aligned with the point of impact, because at five-hundred meters you didn't have to be out by much to miss by a country klick.

The parasol swayed, twisting against the stock to which it was connected. One of the Feds on the berm raised his arm.

Gregg fired. The air snapped like the string of a powerful cross-bow letting go. The line of the bolt was too sudden to see, but it left dazzling purple afterimages despite the filtering visor.

Light haloed the plasma cannon. Metal sublimed from the

trunnion Gregg hit, flashing outward in a shockwave that ignited as it expanded. The ball of fire threw down the four crewmen on that side and behind the weapon. They lay where they fell. The remaining pair, untouched, vanished behind the berm.

Gregg lifted his visor. The air smelled burned. Half the members of the Fed militia had jumped behind the trailers. Those still visible had thrown down their weapons.

Gregg's flashgun whined as it started to recharge. The sound cut off when he opened the compartment in the stock and removed the discharged battery.

He thought he was fine, but his fingers fumbled and dropped the battery. He took a fresh charge from his side pocket and snapped it into the gun.

"That was necessary," Piet Ricimer murmured beside him. "Not this, what these *folk* are doing. But what you did, if we were to survive."

"Right!" said Captain Choransky. "Now, we're all going to trade like reasonable people. Isn't that right, Zaloga?"

Schremp transferred his grip to the port commander's shoulder. Zaloga was white-faced. He didn't attempt to speak, but he nodded agreement.

"That was easy, not so?" Schremp said cheerfully.

With the visor raised, Gregg could see a haze lift from the crew of the plasma cannon. Blazing metal vapor had ignited their clothing.

11

Venus

The probe dangling a hundred meters below the *Sultan* recorded the change in wind direction as it dipped into the third and final set of Hadley Cells layering the Venerian atmosphere. Warning bells clanged on the forward attitude-control workstations and, slightly distorted, from the stations in the next compartment.

"Oh, put a sock in it," Jeude muttered to his alarm.

"Think of it as welcoming us home, Jeude," Piet Ricimer said cheerfully. "This old girl could pretty well con herself into dock from here."

The *Sultan* twisted like a leaping fish when her hull passed through the discontinuity. Gregg felt a vague mushiness through his boots as the vessel continued her descent. Atmospheric density at this level was itself enough to slow a falling object appreciably.

The upper reaches of Venus' atmosphere roared from west to east at 450 kph, transferring heat from the sun-facing side of the planet to the cooler dark. Ships had to take wind direction and velocity into account during reentry.

But the top layer of sun-heated convection cells bottomed out and reversed course well above the planetary surface. Friction from the high-altitude cells formed an intermediate pattern of contra-rotating winds in the mid-atmosphere, but at much lower velocities.

When the convection pattern reversed again near the surface, completing the sequence of Hadley Cells, average wind velocity had dropped to 30 kph. That was scarcely a noticeable breeze to a craft which had managed to penetrate the crushing high-altitude violence.

"You know, Stephen, we should thank the Lord more often for our atmosphere," Ricimer said.

He was smiling, but Gregg knew Ricimer too well to think that anything the spacer said referencing God was a joke.

"As a warning of the Hell that awaits those who deny him?" Gregg suggested.

"For saving us during the Collapse," Ricimer explained. "All of the settlements on Venus were underground, so raiders didn't have any easy targets. And very few outplanet captains chose to hit us anyway. They knew that defensive vessels couldn't prevent hit-and-run attacks—but that if their ship attacked Venus, the planet herself would fight them. And the planet would win, as often as not, against inexperienced pilots."

"People died anyway," Gregg said. "Nine in ten died. Venus colony almost died!"

The harsh edge in his voice was a surprise even to him—especially to him. Many factorial families had their own records of the Collapse, and the journals of the Eryx County Greggs were particularly detailed. Stephen Gregg had found that reading about the deaths of your kin and ancestors by starvation, wall fractures, and manufacturing processes which desperation pushed beyond safe limits was not the same as "learning history."

Ricimer nodded. There was a tic of wariness though not fear in his expression. "Yes," he said, "the Lord scourged us. It had been easier to import some of our needs. When trade stopped, life almost stopped before we were able to expand food production sufficiently for the population."

"The surviving population," Gregg said. His voice was very soft, but it trembled.

Piet Ricimer rested his fingertips on the back of Gregg's right hand. "Never again, Stephen," he said quietly. "Trade must never fail. The tyrants who would stop it, President Pleyal and his toadies in Brisbane—the Lord won't let them stop free trade."

Gregg laughed and put his arm around the smaller man's shoulders. "And we're the instruments of the Lord?" he said, only half gibing. "Well, I don't usually think of myself that way, Piet."

As he spoke, Gregg realized that Piet Ricimer *did* usually think of himself as a tool of God. The odd thing from Gregg's viewpoint was that the holy types he'd met before always struck him as sanctimonious prigs, thoroughly unlikable . . .

"Prepare for landing," called Captain Choransky, hunched over a CRT loaded with scores of data readouts, each one crucially important in the moments of touchdown.

The vessel was coming down nearly empty since her main cargo, nearly 1,000 tonnes of cellulose base, had been unloaded in orbit. The mats had to be armored with a ceramic coating before purpose-built tugs brought them down through an atmosphere which would have consumed them utterly in their unprotected state.

The *Sultan* vibrated as the shockwaves from her thrusters echoed from the sides of the landing pit. Choransky chopped the feedlines, starving the thrusters an instant before the artificial intelligence would have done so.

The *Sultan* hit with a ringing impact. Gregg staggered but didn't fall against the workstations around him.

"Not really dangerous," Ricimer murmured, to Gregg and to himself. "The lower hull may want some reglazing . . . but after a long voyage, the torquing of so many transits, that'd be a good idea anyway."

Vibration continued even with the *Sultan*'s powerplant shut off. A huge dome rolled to cover the landing pit. When the pit's centrifugal pumps had dumped the Venerian atmosphere back into the hell where it belonged and the hull had cooled sufficiently, conveyor belts would haul the vessel into a storage dock. Betaport was a major facility with six landing pits, but the volume of trade she handled required that the pits be cleared as soon as possible.

The men at the attitude controls stood up and stretched. "C'mon, c'mon, c'mon," Jeude said toward a bulkhead. "Get that personnel bridge out here."

"I *got* my pay," Dole singsonged, "and I *want* somebody to spend it with. I do want that."

Lightbody looked at Dole. Ostentatiously, he took his Bible out of the pocket where he'd placed it on landing. He began to read, his lips forming the words as his right index finger traced the line.

The bridge console beeped. The CRT, blanked when Choransky shut down, filled with characters.

"What?" the captain demanded. "Are we getting hard copy of this?"

Bivens squinted at the screen. "This is message traffic from Captain Mostert," he said as he watched the data scroll upward.

"I know what it is," Choransky said angrily. He opened a cabinet beneath the CRT and threw a switch with no effect. "Are we getting hard copy of it, that's what I want to know?"

The duty of a ship's crewman was to do whatever a superior ordered him to do. It wasn't clear that a gentleman like Gregg *had* any superior aboard the *Sultan;* but he knew a great deal more about office equipment than anybody else on the ship did, and he didn't care to sit on his hands.

Gregg stepped past Choransky, knelt to study the installation for a moment, and reconnected the printer. It began spewing out copy as soon as he switched it on.

"There you go," he said to the captain. "Somebody probably got tired of the way it clucked every time the board switched mode." To the best of Gregg's knowledge, the printer hadn't been used at any previous point in the voyage.

The *Sultan* rocked.

"About d—" Jeude began. He caught Ricimer's eye. "About time the personnel bridge got here," he finished.

The vessel shuddered softly as ground staff evacuated the seal which clamped the enclosed walkway to the starship's hull.

"That message," Gregg said to Ricimer quietly. "Captain Mostert is summoning Choransky and his top officers to a meeting and party at his house in Ishtar City tomorrow morning. He's going to have potential investors for a larger voyage present. Some of them may be from the Governor's Council."

"Are you going?" Ricimer asked.

Gregg looked at him. "I suppose Uncle Benjamin will already have a representative chosen," he said. "If he's interested, that is."

"I doubt my cousin Alexi would leave you on his doorstep, though," Ricimer said.

A hatch sighed open. The air pressure increased minutely. Crewmen—none of them on the bridge—shouted "Yippee!" and "Yee-ha!"

"Why are you asking?" Gregg said. "Are you going yourself?"

"I'm not sure Alexi really expects me . . ." Ricimer explained. His grin flashed. "Though he *is* my cousin. I'm pretty sure his servants wouldn't bat an eyelash if I came with the nephew of Factor Benjamin Gregg, though."

Gregg began to laugh. He put his arm around Ricimer's shoulders again. "I'll tell you what," he said. "We'll go see my uncle. He's in Ishtar City and I need to report anyway. Then we'll play it by ear, just as we've been doing"—he gestured upward—"out there."

Gregg wondered as he spoke whether the reality of high-level politics would be as far from his expectations as the reality of trade in the Reaches had been.

Ricimer must have been thinking something similar, because he said, "In Ishtar City, they won't be trying to shoot us, at least."

12

Venus

Ricimer was darkly splendid when he emerged from the men's room outside the Western Rail Station in Ishtar City. The close-coupled spacer wore a tunic and beret of black velvet, set off by a gold sash and band respectively. His trousers were gray, pocketless and closely tailored. They fit into calf-height boots of natural leather, black and highly polished.

"I don't see why you had to waste time changing," Gregg said sourly.

Ricimer tucked a small duffel bag into the luggage on the porter's cart, then snugged the tie-down over it. "Why?" he asked. "We're not late, are we?"

The traffic of Ishtar City buffeted them without so much as a curse. Pedestrians; battery-powered carts like the one holding their luggage; occasionally a passenger vehicle carrying someone who chose to flaunt his wealth by riding, despite the punitive tax intended as much as a morality measure as it was for traffic control, though traffic control was necessary, especially here in the center of the Old Town. West Station served not only Betaport but the whole complex of hamlets and individual holds in Beta Regio and the plains southwest of Ishtar Terra.

The rail links were built before the Collapse, close beneath the surface. During the recovery, Ishtar City grew from the

56

administrative capital of a colony to the heart of a resurgent, independent Venus. Housing and manufacturing expanded both downward and—much later, as ceramic techniques improved and fear of devastating war receded—into domes on the surface.

Rail communications across the planet were improved progressively rather than by a single, massive redesign. The traffic they carried continued to enter and leave the growing capital at the near-surface levels, creating conditions that were as crushingly tight as the living quarters of a starship on a long voyage.

Gregg had been raised in an outlying hold. He knew that the discomfort he felt in this crowding was making him irritable.

"No, it's not the time," he said, stolidly breasting the crowd, though his flesh crept from the repeated jarring on other humans. He knew the way to his uncle's house, so he led; it was as simple as that. "It's getting dressed up as if Uncle Ben was—" He started to say "God Almighty," but remembered his listener in time to twist the words into "—Governor Halys."

Ricimer laughed. "You're going to see Uncle Ben, my friend. I will meet Factor Gregg of Weyston—and no, before you say, 'Do you think you'll fool him that you're not the jumped-up sailor *I* know you are?'—no. But he'll recognize that I'm showing him the respect which is his due . . . from such as me."

Gregg grimaced. He was glad Ricimer couldn't see his face. "I never said you were a jumped-up sailor, Piet," he said.

"You both humored me *and* guarded our baggage while I changed, my friend," Ricimer said. "This is important to me. Important to God's plan for mankind, I believe, but certainly to me personally. I appreciate everything you're doing."

Many wealthy men, the Mostert brothers among them, now lived in the domed levels of Ishtar City where the ambience was relatively open. Uncle Ben's great wealth was a result of his own trading endeavors, but he had a conservative affection for the Old Town where the rich and powerful had lived when he was growing up. His townhouse was within a half kilometer of West Station.

By the time they'd made half that distance through twisting corridors cut by the first permanent human settlements on Venus, Gregg wished he was in armor and lugging his flashgun ten times as far in the forests of Virginia. The trees didn't shove their way into and past pedestrians.

"Stephen?" Ricimer said, breaking into Gregg's grim reverie.

"Uh?" Gregg said. "Oh, sorry." As he spoke, he realized he was apologizing for thoughts his friend couldn't read and which weren't directed to him specifically, just at cities and those who lived in them in general.

"When Captain Schremp spoke to the Federation officials, he referred to our cargo as slaves. Do you remember?"

There was a ceramic patch at the next intersection, and the dwellings kitty-corner across it were misaligned. When Gregg was a boy of three, there'd been a landslip that vented a portion of Ishtar City to the outer atmosphere. An error by a tunneling contractor, some believed, but there was too little left at the heart of the catastrophe to be sure.

Over a thousand people had died, despite Ishtar City's compartmentalization by corridor and the emergency seals in all dwellings. Uncle Ben had been able to pick up his present townhouse cheap, from heirs who'd been out of town when the disaster occurred.

"Schremp!" Gregg said in harsh dismissal. "The Molts aren't even human. They *can't* be slaves."

He pursed his lips. "The way the Feds treat the indigs, the Rabbits—maybe they're slaves. But that's nothing to do with us."

"Yes, well," Ricimer said. "I suppose you're right, Stephen."

Gregg looked back over his shoulder. His friend threw him a smile, but it wasn't a particularly bright one.

The facade of Uncle Ben's townhouse was glazed a dull slate-gray. The style and treatment were similar to other gray, dun, and russet buildings on the corridor, but it was unusually clean. The four red-uniformed attendants outside the doorway kept loungers and graffiti-scribblers away from the Factor's door.

The attendants straightened when they saw Gregg, suddenly conscious that he'd been on a train for twenty hours from Betaport, striding toward them. One of the men recognized the Factor's nephew and pushed the call button.

"Master Stephen Gregg!" he shouted at the intercom. He focused on Ricimer and the luggage, then added, "And companion."

There was no external door-switch. The valve itself was round, shaped like a section of a cone through the flats, and a meter-fifty in diameter across the inner face. If the Venerian atmosphere flooded the corridor, its pressure would wedge the door more tightly sealed until emergency crews could deal with the disaster.

Burt, a white-haired senior servant wearing street clothes of good quality, bowed to Gregg in the anteroom. Two red-suited under-lings waited behind him to take the luggage from the porter.

"*Sir,* the Factor is expecting you and Mr. Ricimer in his office," Hurt said. "Will you change first?"

"I don't think that will be necessary," Gregg said grimly. *For God's sake! This was Uncle Ben, who up until a few years ago traveled aboard his intrasystem traders on the Earth-Asteroids-Venus triangle to check them out!*

"Very good, sir," Burt said with another bow.

Uncle Ben had redone the anteroom mosaics since Gregg had last been to the townhouse. These were supposed to suggest a forest glade on Earth before toxins released during the Revolt finished what fifteen millennia of human fire-setting had begun.

Gregg thought of tramping through the woodlands of Virginia. He smiled. Uncle Ben, for all his wealth and success and ability, was in some ways more parochial than the young nephew who until recently hadn't been out of the Atalanta Plains for more than a week at a time.

Another liveried servant bowed and stepped away from the open door of the Factor's office.

In Old Town, corridors and dwellings were all as close to three meters high as the excavators could cut them. Ceilings were nor-mally lowered to provide storage space or, in poorer housing, to double the number of available compartments. Gregg of Weyston's office was full height, paneled in bleached wood with a barely perceptible grain. The material was natural, rather than something reprocessed from cellulose base.

"Good to see you, Stephen," the Factor said. Through a tight smile he added, "I see you've had a hard journey."

Gregg glared at his uncle. "I'll change here, Uncle Ben," he said. "For G—for *pity*'s sake, I could have sent my dress suit by a ser-vant to report to you, if that's what's important."

"My brother never saw much reason to dress like a gentleman either, Stephen," the Factor said. "That's perfectly all right—if you're going to bury yourself in the hinterlands with no one save fam-ily retainers to see you."

Gregg began to laugh. "May I present Mr. Ricimer, Uncle," he said. "An officer of Captain Choransky's company and a cousin of the Mosterts." He paused. "He gave me the same lecture on our way from the rail station."

Benjamin Gregg laughed also. He got up and reached over his broad desk to shake first his nephew's hand, then that of Piet Ricimer.

Gregg of Weyston was dark where his brother's side of the family, the Greggs of Eryx, were mostly fair, but he was as big as his nephew and had been both strong and active till back problems slowed him down. Even now, the weight he'd gained was under control except for a potbelly that resisted anything short of the girdle he wore on formal occasions.

The Factor gestured the younger men to chairs of the same blond wood as the paneling—as uncomfortable as they were obviously expensive—and sat down heavily again himself. "I've seen your report, Stephen," he said with a nod toward the sheaf of printouts on his desk. "It's as careful and precise as the accounts of Eryx always are. I'm impressed, though not surprised."

He pursed his lips. "Now," he went on, "what is it that you and Mr. Ricimer feel you need to add in person to the written account you transmitted when you landed at Betaport?"

"The Mosterts are giving a matinee this afternoon to launch plans for a larger expedition to the Reaches," Gregg said. "I suppose you've already made arrangements to be represented, but we'd like—I'd like—to be there on your behalf also, with Mr. Ricimer."

He flicked his eyes to his companion. Ricimer was seated in his chair with the poised, unmoving alertness of a guard dog.

The Factor nodded. "And why do you think I should be represented, Stephen?" he asked.

The question took Gregg aback. "What?" he blurted. "Why—for the profit, Uncle Ben. You're a merchant, and there are huge profits to be made in out-system trade."

The walls of the office were lined with books—hard-copy ledgers, some of them almost five decades old—and with memorabilia from the Factor's years of intrasystem trade. One of Gregg's earliest memories was of his uncle handing him a bit of clear crystal with waxy inclusions and saying that it was a relic of life from the asteroid belt before Earth had even coalesced as a planet.

But this was a different Uncle Ben. He lifted his nephew's itemized report. "Yes," he said. "Profit. One hundred twelve percent on my investment on Captain Choransky's voyage."

"Possibly a little less," Gregg said in a desire to be precise. "I'm assuming a low valuation for tariff purposes, in the belief that

Governor Halys will want to minimize the amount of her invest-ment profits that pass through the Exchequer. I may be wrong."

The Factor laughed. "You're not wrong, lad," he said. "If any-thing, you're overconservative. And in any event, over one hun-dred percent compares favorably with the thirty-three to thirty-five percent margin I try to run within the system."

Gregg nodded, allowing himself a wary smile while he waited for the hook.

"Until you factor in risk," Gregg of Weyston added, slapping the report down on his desk.

The Factor looked sharply at Ricimer. "Mr. Ricimer," he said crisply. "I can see you're a spaceman. How do you assess the possibility that one or all of Captain Choransky's vessels would have been lost on the voyage just completed?"

Ricimer lifted his chin to acknowledge the question. His eyes were bright.

"In-system, landings are the most dangerous part of a voyage," he said in a tone as cold and sharp as the blade of a cutting bar. "The risk varies from ship to ship, but say . . . three percent per vessel on the voyage in question because of the greater frequency of landings. Transits—again, that varies, but obviously the greater number of entries increases the possibility of system failure and of being caught in a pattern of rising gradients in which a vessel shakes its hull apart in trying to enter transit space."

The spacer tapped his right index finger on his chair arm while his eyes stared at a point beyond the Factor's ear. "I would say," he continued as his eyes locked with those of his questioner, "five per-cent on a well-found vessel, but I'll admit that the *Sultan* wasn't in the best condition, and I can't claim to have full confidence in the ship-handling abilities of the *Dove*'s officers."

Ricimer smiled bleakly. "You'll pardon me for frankness, sir," he said.

"I'll pardon you for anything except telling me damned lies, lad," the Factor said, "and there seems little risk of that. But—what about the Federation and the Southern Cross, then? I've had more reports of the voyage than this one, you know."

The older man brushed the sheaf of hard copy with his fingers. "It's all over Betaport, you see. My Stephen there"—he nodded, Uncle Ben again for the instant—"acquitted himself like a Gregg, and that surprises me no more than his accounts do. But one lucky bolt from a plasma cannon and there's your thrusters, your ship . . . and all hope of profit for your investors, lad."

His eyes were on his nephew now, not Ricimer. "And families at home to grieve besides."

Gregg jumped to his feet. "Christ's *wounds*, Uncle Ben!" he shouted. "Do you think I'm a, I'm a—" He shrugged angrily. "Some kind of a damned painting that's so delicate I'll fade if I'm put out in the light?"

"I think," the Factor said, "that I'm an old man, Stephen. When I die, I don't choose to explain to my late brother how I provided the rope with which his son hanged himself."

"I'll not be coddled!"

"I'm not offering to coddle you!" the Factor boomed. "Come and work for me, boy, and I'll grind you into all the hardest problems Gregg Trading falls against. *If* you can handle them, then—well, my brother had sons, and I have Gregg Trading. What I *won't* do is send you to swim with sharks."

Piet Ricimer stood up. He put his hand in the crook of Gregg's elbow. "Let me speak, Stephen," he said in a quiet, trembling voice.

Gregg turned his back on his uncle.

"Sir," Ricimer said. "You say you don't mind frankness, and I don't know any other way to be."

The Factor nodded curtly, a gesture much like that with which Ricimer had acknowledged the question a moment before.

"You'll survive and prosper if you hold to the in-system trade," the spacer said. "So will your heir and very likely his heir, if they're as able as you. What won't survive if you and the other leading merchants who respect you turn your backs on it is trade from Venus to the stars."

"Assuming that's true," Gregg of Weyston said carefully, "which I do *not* assume except for discussion—what of it? When humanity was at its height before the Collapse, ninety-eight percent of the humans in the universe were within the solar system. There'll always be trade for us here."

"There were twenty billion people on Earth before the Collapse," Ricimer replied evenly. "If there are twenty million today, I'll be surprised. Earth is a poisoned hulk. Venus is—the Lord put us on Venus to make us strong, sir, but nobody can think our world is more than a way station on the path of God's plan. The other in-system colonies breed men who are freaks, too weak for lack of gravity to live on any normal planet. We *need* the stars."

Gregg faced slowly around again. He was embarrassed by his outburst. If there had been a way to ease back into his chair, he would have done so.

"Man needs the stars, I accept," the Factor agreed with another nod. "And man is retaking them. Now, I don't accept Brisbane's dividing the Reaches between America and the Southerns, either— as a matter of principle. But principle makes a bad meal, and war makes for damned bad trade, in-system as well as out. Let them have it if they want it so bad. They'll still need manufactures from Venus, and it'll be Venerian ships that dare *our* atmosphere nine times in ten."

Ricimer nodded with his lips pursed, not agreeing but rather choosing his words. The skin was stretched as tightly over the spacer's cheeks as it had been when he warned Gregg to shoot on Virginia.

"The Southerns will do nothing, sir, as they've always done nothing with their opportunities," he said. "The Feds, now . . . the Feds will continue to strip the caches of microchips they find in the Reaches. They'll try to run the few factories they find still operable, but they won't do the work themselves, they'll put Molts to it. And the Molts will do only what their ancestors were taught to do a thousand years ago."

The Factor opened his mouth to speak. Ricimer forestalled him with, "What they do get from the Reaches, they'll use to strengthen themselves on Earth. They've been fighting the rebels on their own west coast for a generation. Perhaps the wealth they bring from the Reaches will permit them to finally succeed. And they'll fight Europe, conquer Europe I shouldn't doubt, because the Europeans can never conquer them and President Pleyal won't stop while he has a single rival on Earth."

"Venus can't be conquered," the Factor said, leaping a step ahead in the argument and denying it harshly.

"Perhaps not," the spacer agreed. "But all mankind can stagnate while President Pleyal forges an empire as rigid and brittle as the one that shattered in the Collapse. And if we fall back from the stars again . . . I don't believe the Lord will give us a third chance."

The two fierce-eyed men stared at one another for a long

moment. The Factor shuddered and said in a surprisingly gentle tone, "Stephen? What's your opinion of all this?"

Gregg touched his lips with his tongue. He smiled wryly and seated himself as he'd wanted to do for some while. "I'm not a religious man, Uncle," he said, kneading his fingers together on the edge of the desk and staring at them. "I don't like transit, and I don't like"—he looked up—"some of the ways trade's carried on beyond Pluto." The starkness of his own voice startled him. "But I think I could learn to like standing under an open sky. And I'm sure I'm going to do that again."

His lips quirked. "God willing," he added, half in mockery. Gregg's expression lost even the hint of humor. "Someone will ship me, Uncle Ben. It doesn't have to be an expedition in which Gregg Trading has invested."

The Factor glared at him. "Your father, boy," he said, "was as stubborn as any man God put on Venus."

Gregg nodded. "He used to say the same of you, Uncle Ben," he said.

Gregg of Weyston burst out laughing and reached across the desk with both hands, clasping his nephew's. "Then I suppose it runs in the family, lad. Go to your damned meeting, then—I'll call ahead. And when you come back, we'll discuss what you in your *business* judgment recommend for Gregg Trading."

Piet Ricimer stood formally, with his heels near together and his wrists crossed behind his back. There was the slightest of smiles on his lips.

13

Venus

Gregg hadn't met Councilor Duneen before—he'd never *expected* to meet the head of the Bureau of External Relations—but there Duneen was at the side of Alexi Mostert, nodding affably and extending his hand. Siddons, by two years the elder Mostert brother, didn't appear to be present.

"So . . ." Duneen said. He was short and a trifle pudgy, but there was nothing soft about his eyes. "You'd be Gregg of Eryx, then?"

Gregg shook the councilor's hand. Duneen was only forty or so, younger than Gregg had expected in a man whom many said was Governor Halys' chief advisor. "That would be my brother, sir," he said.

"Mr. Gregg's here representing his uncle, Gregg of Weyston," Mostert put in quickly. "A major investor in the voyage just returned, and we hope in the present endeavor as well."

The Mostert brothers, Alexi and Siddons, had inherited a bustling shipping business from their father. They themselves had expanded the operations in various fashions. The politically powerful guests at this party were examples of the expansion as surely as the out-system trading ventures were.

"Allow me to introduce my friend Mr. Ricimer, Councilor," Gregg said. He noticed that Mostert's jaw tightened, but there was nothing the shipper could do about it. "One of Captain Choransky's officers on the recent voyage, and one of the major reasons for our success."

"A sailor indeed, Mr. Ricimer?" Duneen said approvingly. "I shouldn't have guessed it."

He nodded minusculy toward the bar. The captains and navigators from the recent voyage clustered there like six sheep floating amongst shark fins. The spacers were dressed in a mismatch of finery purchased for this event combined with roughly serviceable garb that would have been out of place in a good house in Betaport, much less Ishtar City.

Ricimer's turnout was stylish in an idiosyncratic way. For the party he'd kept the black tunic and boots, but he'd changed into taupe trousers and a matching neckerchief. His St. Christopher medal dangled across his chest on its massy chain, and he wore a ring whose similar metalwork clamped what was either a fire opal or something more exotic.

"Yes sir," Ricimer agreed promptly. "A sailor proud to serve a governor who understands the value of out-system trade to God's plan and the welfare of Venus."

Duneen shifted his feet slightly to close the conversation with Ricimer. Gregg started to put his hand out to his friend, but Ricimer already understood the signal and stepped away.

"A keen lad, Mostert," the councilor said. "We'll have use for him, I shouldn't wonder."

"Very keen indeed," Mostert replied with a touch of irritation.

Gregg glanced around the gathering. About half the forty or so present were gentlemen—or dressed like it. He didn't recognize them all. Most of the others were identifiably from the shipping trade: a mix of middle-aged men like Mostert himself and younger fellows, acting as Gregg was for a wealthy principal.

Councilor Duneen might have his own interests, but he was certainly here to represent Governor Halys as well. Out-system trade was a matter of state so long as President Pleyal claimed it infringed the sovereignty of the North American Federation.

The meeting room had ceilings three and a half meters high. The additional half meter wasn't functional; it simply proved that the Mosterts' mansion made use of the greater freedom permitted by buildings in the new domed quarters.

Out-system vegetation grew in niches along three of the walls. None of it was thriving: varied requirements for nutrition and light saw to that. Still, the display showed the breadth of the Mosterts' endeavors, which was probably all that it was intended to do.

Mostert stepped to a dais and rang a spoon in his glass for attention. "Councilor Duneen," he said, "gentlemen. As you all know, Mostert Trading is about to embark on a voyage promising levels and percentages of profit greater even than those of the voyage just returned under my subordinate, Captain Choransky. I've called you together as interested parties, so that all your questions can be answered."

"All right, Alexi," said a soberly-dressed man in his fifties; probably a shipper in the same order of business as the Mosterts, though Gregg didn't recognize him. "Are you talking about going to the Mirror this time, then?"

"No," Mostert said. "No, Paul, the time isn't right for that just yet. We'll be penetrating other portions of the Reaches for the first time, though—planets that aren't well served by the Feds themselves. We'll be able to skim the cream of the trade there."

"The cream," Paul rejoined, "is microchips, and that means going to the Mirror."

"The Feds won't trade for chips anywhere," somebody else objected morosely. "Pleyal knows how good a thing he's got there."

"We're talking about planets like Jewelhouse, Heartbreak, Desire," Mostert said loudly as he tried to get the discussion back on the track he desired. "Planets with valuable products of their own *and* the remains of extensive pre-Collapse colonies being discovered every day. There weren't microchip factories there, no, but those aren't the only ancient artifacts that can bring huge profits."

"The mirror worlds, all their settlements have forts and real soldiers," Captain Choransky said with the air of a man trying to explain why humans can't breathe water. "If we sashayed up to Umber, say, they'd just laugh at us."

"If they didn't blow our asses away," Bivens added, shaking his head in sad amazement. "That's what they'd do, you know."

Mostert grimaced. "We all know the orders President Pleyal has sent to his colonies," he said in brusque admission. "That won't last—it can't last. The colonies can't depend on Rabbits for labor. They need Molts to expand their operations, and they *want* to buy them from us. But—"

"They want to buy if there's a gun to their head," interjected Roon, who'd commanded the *Preakness*.

"But that means we don't go where they've got guns of their own," Bivens said.

"They want to do most *anything* with guns to their heads," Roon added with a giggle.

Mostert's face was naturally ruddy, so the best clue to his mental state was the way he suddenly flung his glass to the side with a fierce motion. The vessel clinked against the wall but didn't break.

The clot of ships' officers, all of whom had drunk more than was good for them because they were nervous, grunted and looked away.

Gregg smothered a smile. Alexi Mostert had used better judgment when he bought tumblers for this gathering than when he made up the guest list.

Piet Ricimer swept the room with his eyes. "The best way to break the monopoly on out-system trade which the Feds and Southerns claim," he said in a clear voice, "will be for Venus to develop our own network of colonies, trading stations—perhaps our own routes across the Mirror or around it in transit space. But that will take time."

He stepped closer to the dais though not onto it. His back was to Mostert but he held the eyes of everyone else. Gregg watched their host over Ricimer's head. Mostert's expression was perfectly blank, but his fingers were bending the spoon into a tight spiral.

"For now," Ricimer continued, "we need to gain experience in out-system navigation in order to carry out what I'm convinced is God's plan. But—"

His smile was as dazzling as the ring on his finger. "—God doesn't forbid us to help ourselves while carrying out His will. The investors in the voyage just completed are wealthier by more than a hundred percent of their investments. Our mistress, Governor Halys"—Ricimer nodded to Duneen—"included. No one who's served with Captain Mostert can doubt that an argosy he commands in person will be even more successful."

Gregg began to clap. He was only slightly surprised when light applause ran quickly across the room, like fire in cotton lint.

"For you gentlemen who don't know him," Mostert called from the dais, "this is my relative Captain Ricimer. He'll be commanding one of the vessels in the new endeavor."

There was another flurry of applause. Gregg raised an eyebrow. Ricimer acknowledged with something between a deep nod and a bow.

A servant entered the room carrying a round package nearly a meter in diameter. He scanned the crowd, then homed in on Ricimer.

"One moment, gentlemen," Ricimer said loudly to cut through the buzz of conversation following his speech and Mostert's.

He took the package and ripped the seal on the thin, light-scattering wrapper. All eyes were on him.

"Councilor Duneen," Ricimer continued, "we've spoken of the artifacts to be found beyond Pluto. I ask you to take this to Governor Halys, as my personal token of appreciation for her support of the voyage just ended."

He reached into the package and removed the fragment of porcelain birdbath Gregg had last seen in a garden on Virginia. Though carefully cleaned, the broad bowl was only half complete—and that badly worn.

There was a general gasp. Gregg's skin went cold. A flick of Mostert's wrist sent the spoon to follow the glass he'd thrown.

"And this as well," Ricimer continued loudly. His left hand shook the wrapping away. He raised a copy of the birdbath in its perfect state, the scalloped circuit whole and the colors as bright as Venerian ceramicists could form them.

Ricimer waved the ancient artifact in his right hand. "The past—" he cried.

He stepped onto the dais and waved his right hand. "And the glorious future of Venus and mankind! God for Venus! God for Governor Halys!"

Stephen Gregg clapped and cheered like everybody else in the meeting room. His eyes stung, and a part of him was angry at being manipulated.

But tears ran down the cheeks of Piet Ricimer as well, as the young spacer stood clasped by both Mostert and Duneen on the dais.

14

Above Punta Verde

"Featherboat *Peaches* landing in sequence," Ricimer said. "*Peaches* out."

He cradled the radio handset and engaged the artificial intelligence. "Hang on," he added with a grin over his shoulder, but even Gregg was an old enough sailor by now to have cinched his straps tight.

The thrusters fired, braking the 20-tonne featherboat from orbit, the last of Captain Mostert's argosy to do so. The deep green of Punta Verde's jungles swelled beneath them, though their landing spot was still on the other side of the planet.

The screens dissolved into colored snow for a moment, then snapped back to greater clarity than they'd managed in the stillness of freefall. Gregg swallowed his heart again.

Leon sat beside Gregg in the constricted cabin. He patted an outer bulkhead and muttered, "Silly old cow."

"You know, Piet," Gregg called over the vibration, "I never did ask you how you got that replica birdbath made so quickly."

"A friend in the industry," Ricimer replied without turning. "My, ah . . ."

He looked back at Gregg. "My father preaches in the Jamaica hamlet outside Betaport," he said. Gregg had to watch his friend's lips to be sure of the words. "But there were ten of us children, and now the new wife. He has a ceramic workshop. Mostly thruster nozzles for the port, but he can turn out special orders too."

Ricimer's voice grew louder. "He's as good a craftsman as you'll find on Venus. And that means anywhere in the universe!"

"Yes," Gregg said with a deep nod. "I was amazed at the high quality of the piece."

That was more or less true, but he'd have said as much if the bath looked like somebody'd fed a dog clay and then glazed the turds. A Gregg of Eryx understood family pride.

"You might," Gregg continued, changing the subject with a smile, "have parlayed it into something a little bigger than the *Peaches*. Your cousin really owed you for the way you put his voyage over with the investors. Councilor Duneen was impressed too, you know."

For a moment the featherboat trembled unpowered as her remaining velocity balanced the density of Punta Verde's atmosphere. The thrusters resumed firing at low output, providing the *Peaches* with controllable forward motion. The featherboat was now an atmosphere vessel. At best, the larger ships were more or less terminally-guided ballistic missiles.

"Ah, this is the ship to be in, Stephen," Ricimer said, no less serious for the laughter in his eyes. "Isn't that right, boys?"

"Beats the *Tolliver,* that's G-g-heaven's truth," Tancred agreed. "Leaks like a sieve, that one does. Wouldn't doubt they were all on oxygen bottles by now."

The featherboat could accept twenty men or so in reasonable comfort, but the six men from Ricimer's intrasystem trader were more than sufficient for the needs of the vessel. Gregg wondered if that was why his friend had accepted the tiny command when he might have pushed for the 100-tonne *Hawkwood* or even the slightly larger *Rose*. Piet Ricimer was a first-rate leader, but the business of *command* as opposed to leadership didn't come naturally to him.

"We ought to be coming up on a Molt city," Ricimer said, returning his attention to the viewscreen. As he spoke, the uniform green blurred by the featherboat's 200 kph gave way abruptly to beige. The Molts of Punta Verde used the trunks of living trees to support dwellings like giant shelf fungi. The smooth roofs underlay but did not displace the uppermost canopy, giving the city an organic appearance . . .

Which was justified. The Molts, though not indigenous to any of the worlds they were known to occupy, formed stable equilibria wherever man had placed them.

"We're coming up on the landing site," Ricimer warned. "It'd be nice if they'd cleared a patch for us, but don't count on it."

Plasma engines made communication between vessels during a landing impractical. The *Desire,* the argosy's other featherboat, had barely shut down when Ricimer went in, so the *Peaches* crew could only hope that matters had gone as planned in orbit.

Ricimer overrode the AI, holding the *Peaches* in a staggering hover. The *Tolliver,* 500 tonnes burden and owned by the government of Venus, was spherical rather than cigar-shaped. Her dome stood as high as the canopy beyond the area her thrusters had shattered. The 300-tonne *Grandcamp* was a good kilometer away, while gaps in the jungle between the big ships probably marked the *Rose* and *Hawkwood.*

At least none of the bigger ships had crashed. That wasn't a given in the case of the *Tolliver,* eighty years old and at least twenty years past her most recent rebuild. The big vessel was intended to be serviced in orbit, but the state of her hull was such that she leaked air faster than it could be ferried up to her by boat.

The *Tolliver's* size and armament were valuable additions, though. The fact that the ancient vessel came from Governor Halys made it a claim of official support—

As well as a difficult gift to refuse.

"We're going in," Ricimer said curtly as he reduced power and swiveled the main thrusters. Leon and Dole, operating without orders from their captain, pumped the nose high with the attitude jets.

The *Peaches* lurched, balanced, and settled down on trees smashed to matchsticks when the *Tolliver* landed a hundred meters away. An instant before touchdown, the featherboat was wobbling like a top about to fall over, but the landing was as soft as a kiss.

"Nice work, Cap'n," Lightbody grunted.

"Only the best for my boys," Ricimer said with satisfaction.

The viewscreen provided a panorama of the *Peaches'* surroundings, though not a particularly crisp one. Heavily-armed men disembarked from the flagship. One man, apparently closer than he cared to have been when the featherboat landed, hurled a fruit or seedpod at the *Peaches.* Gregg heard a soggy impact on the hull.

Leon and Bailey undogged the main hatch topside. The *Peaches* had a forward hatch as well, but that was little more than a gunport for the light plasma cannon.

Gregg frowned. "Shouldn't we let her cool?" he asked—aloud but carefully avoiding eye contact with the vessel's more experienced personnel.

"Aw, just watch what you grab hold of, sir," Tancred explained. "Featherboats like this, we braked on thrust, not friction pretty much."

"Will you pass the arms out as each man disembarks, Stephen?" Ricimer said. "You're the tallest, you see."

And also the most likely to grab a handgrip that would sear him down to the bone, Gregg thought. Having a gentleman dispensing the weapons was good form, but the only reason arms were segregated aboard the *Peaches* was to keep them from flying about the cabin during violent maneuvers.

Ricimer took another look at what was going on outside. A truckload of men seemed about ready to pull out, and additional crewmen were boarding two other vehicles.

"Leon, bring a rifle for me, will you?" Ricimer said sharply. He moved from the control console to the hatch and out in three lithe jumps. The viewscreen elongated the figure of the young officer bounding swiftly toward the flagship.

"He'll sort them out," Tancred said.

"Anybody who'd ship aboard a chamber pot like the *Tolliver*," Leon muttered, "hasn't got enough brains to keep his scalp inflated. And the *Grandcamp* isn't much better."

Gregg took his place beside the locker in the center of the ship. As each crewman hopped from the edge of the storage cabinet beneath the hatch—there was a ladder, but nobody used it—to the featherboat's outer hull, Gregg handed up a weapon.

Tancred took a rifle; there were cutting bars for the remainder of the crewmen. Besides his bar and the second rifle, Leon carried the torso and helmet of the captain's hard suit. He reached down from the hull to help Gregg.

Gregg wore his faceplate raised, but the chin bar still reduced his downward vision. He jumped into a mass of vegetation that smoldered and stank but was thankfully too wet to burn. The remainder of the crew had followed their captain, but the bosun solicitously waited for Gregg.

"I'm all right!" Gregg snapped.

"It's the flashgun and you wearing armor, sir," Leon said. He scuffed his feet in the mat of leaves, bark, and splintered wood. "That's a bad load in muck like this."

"Sorry," Gregg said sincerely. He knew that he'd spoken more sharply than he should have, because he *hadn't* been sure he was all right.

Piet Ricimer was having a discussion with Mostert and a group of other officers beside the leading truck. They had to speak loudly to be heard over the air-cooled rotary engine. The need to shout may have affected tempers as well. Platt, who'd been aboard the *Sultan,* hung out of the vehicle's cab with an angry expression on his face.

"But we can reconnoiter with the *Peaches,*" Ricimer protested. "This isn't a planet we know anything about except its coordinates—"

"*And* the fact it's full of Molts, which is what the hell we're here for, Ricimer!" Platt snarled. Gregg suspected that Platt thought he rather than Ricimer should have been given a ship to command, though the officers hadn't gotten along particularly well during the previous voyage either.

"I just don't think we should jump in without investigating," Ricimer said. "There's no sign of Southerns here and—"

"Calm down, both of you," Alexi Mostert said in obvious irritation. His helmet and breastplate were gilded and engraved, and he carried a pistol as well as a repeating rifle. Sweat ran down the furrow between his thick eyebrows and dripped from his nose.

"We're not looking for Southerns, we're looking for Molts!" said Cseka of the *Desire.*

"Only the ones of us who've got balls," Platt added.

Gregg put his big left hand on Ricimer's shoulder. "I've got balls, Mr. Platt," he said in a deliberate voice that was loud enough to rattle glass. "And I think it's a good idea to know what we're doing before we do it."

Actually, a quick in-and-out raid seemed reasonable to Gregg. He'd have backed Ricimer in the argument if his friend said he thought they'd landed in a desert.

"Look, buddy!" Platt shouted. "You just sit back here on your butt if you want to. I don't have a rich daddy to feed my family if I'm too chicken to earn a living."

Captain Mostert stepped onto the running board of the cab and thrust, not shook, his fist under Platt's nose and moustache. "That's enough!" he said.

Platt jerked back, his face twitching nervously.

Mostert turned to look at the remainder of the officers around him. "This group goes now," he said. "Three trucks. Quile's sending fifty men from the *Grandcamp,* so we'll take the Molts from both sides. Surprise is more important than poking around."

He jumped down from the running board and glowered at Ricimer. "We *know* where the bloody city is, man," he added harshly.

Gregg still had a hand on his friend's shoulder. He felt Ricimer stiffen; much as Gregg himself had done when Platt suggested he was a coward.

The lead truck accelerated away, spewing bits of vegetation from its six driven wheels. The forest's multiple canopies starved the undergrowth of light, opening broad avenues among the boles of the giant trees. The other two truckloads of men followed. There were several officers besides Platt in the force, but it wasn't clear to Gregg who was in charge.

Piet Ricimer clasped his hand over Gregg's on his shoulder and turned around slowly.

"Come on, come on!" Mostert shouted. "Let's get the rest of these trucks set up."

"I wonder how surprised these Molts are going to be," Ricimer murmured to Gregg, "when they've heard six starships land within a klick of their city?"

15

Punta Verde

The jungle drank sound, but the clearing itself was bedlam.

The loudest portion of the racket came from the *Tolliver*'s pumps, refilling the old ship's air tanks. There was plenty of other noise as well. Piet Ricimer supervised a team probing for groundwater between the *Peaches* and the flagship. The rotary drill screamed through the friable stone of the forest floor. Nearby, crewmen argued as they loaded three more trucks to follow the lead element of Molt-hunters.

Gregg was only twenty meters from the featherboat. Even so, it wasn't till he turned idly and noticed Dole waving from the hatch that he heard the man shouting. "Sir! Get the captain! Platt, he's stepped on his dick for sure!"

Gregg opened his mouth to ask a question—but realized that whatever the details were, Ricimer needed to hear them worse than he did. He lumbered toward the drilling crew, feeling like a bowling ball with the burden of his weapon and armor.

Gregg felt out of place, both in the lush greenery surrounding the landing site and, at a human level, while watching knowledgeable sailors refit the vessels for the next hop. If he'd been among the crews off to snatch Molts for the ships' holds, Gregg would have a person of importance: better equipped and more skillful than the men around him, as well as being a leader by virtue of birth. He had no place in the argosy's peacetime occupations.

Rather than join the raiders on the second set of trucks, Piet Ricimer had pointedly taken charge of the drilling. The equipment was carried in the flagship's capacious holds, but Ricimer operated it with his own crew. A cable snaking from one of the *Tolliver*'s external outlets powered the auger's electric motors.

The ceramic bits had reached the subsurface water levels. The tailings, crumbly laterite somewhere between rock and soil, lay in a russet pile at the end of the drill's ejection pipe a few meters away. The crew—including Ricimer himself, Gregg was surprised to see—now manhandled sections of twenty centimeter hose to connect the well with the *Tolliver*'s reaction-mass tanks.

It struck Gregg that he could have stood radio watch, freeing Dole to help with the drilling, or he could have laid down his weapon for the moment and carried sections of hose. Because he was a gentleman, no one had suggested that . . . and the thought hadn't crossed *his* mind until now.

"Piet!" he called. "Dole's got something on the radio. There's been trouble with the raid."

Other operators than Dole had caught an emergency signal. As Gregg spoke, one of the ships distant in the forest honked its klaxon. The siren on top of the *Tolliver*'s dome began to wind up, setting nerves on edge and making it even more difficult to hear speech in the clearing below.

The raiding party had blown a gap in the tangle of trunks which the flagship knocked down on landing. Ricimer looked up at the curtain of foliage overhanging that, the only route by which the vehicles could return to the ships. Not so much as a leaf twitched in the still, humid air.

"Stephen," Ricimer said, "can you get four more rifles from the *Tolliver*? If I send one of the men, they'll be refused." He looked back from the jungle and made eye contact. "And I need to get the *Peaches* ready."

"Yes," Gregg said. He set off for the flagship's ramp at something between a long stride and a jog. The sweat soaking his tunic and scalp was suddenly cold, and his muscles trembled with the adrenaline rush.

"Bailey and Jeude, go along to carry," he heard Ricimer call behind him. "But *don't* get in his way. The rest of you, come on!"

Gregg had never been aboard the *Tolliver* before, but the men milling at the central pillar of the lower hold drew him to the arms locker. Incandescent bulbs in the ceiling left the rest of the enormous room dim by comparison with the daylight flooding through the open hatch behind Gregg. The air smelled sour, reeking with decades of abuse.

The *Tolliver* carried a crew of a hundred and sixty on this voyage. About half the men had joined the initial raiding party, but scores waited uncertainly about the arms locker and the trucks being assembled in the clearing.

Captain Mostert was neither place. He must have climbed six decks to the bridge when the alarm sounded.

Two sailors were handing out cutting bars under the observation of an officer Gregg didn't know by name. "You there!" Gregg said to one of the sailors. "I'm Gregg of Eryx and I need four rifles now!"

"But—" the sailor said.

"There aren't any rifles left, sir," said the other attendant, the man Gregg hadn't addressed.

"There may be some unassigned firearms still on the bridge, Mr. Gregg," the overseeing officer put in.

"May there indeed!" Gregg exploded. "Who in hell do you think I am, my man?"

He wasn't angry, but the soup of hormones in his blood gave his voice a trembling violence that counterfeited towering rage. Gregg was a big man in any case, the tallest in the hold. With the bulk of his helmet and body armor, he looked like a troll.

He looked at the men around him. The nearest started back from the gentleman's glare.

"You!" Gregg said, pointing to a man with a repeater. His eyes were beginning to adapt to the interior lights. "You—" another rifleman. "Y—" and the third man was holding out his breechloader to Gregg before the demand fully crossed his lips. Jeude and Bailey collected the weapons and bandoliers of sized ammunition without orders.

None of the other crewmen present held firearms.

Gregg focused on the officer. "You, you've got a rifle too. Quick, man!"

The man clutched the repeating carbine slung over his shoulder. "But I own this!" he protested.

"God strike you dead!" Gregg roared, raising the massive flashgun in his right hand as though he intended to preempt the deity. "We've got a battle to fight, man! Go up to the bridge if you need a gun!"

Jeude stepped to the officer's side and silently lifted the weapon by its sling. The man opened his mouth, then closed it again.

"Oh, for *God's* sake!" he blurted. He ducked so that Gregg's two subordinates could remove both the carbine and the belt of cartridges looped in groups of five to match magazine capacity.

"Come along, you two!" Gregg said. He spoke to keep control of the situation. Bailey and Jeude were already ahead of him, silhouetted against sunlight. "There isn't much time!"

It occurred to Gregg as he spoke that there might not be much time, but he personally didn't have a clue as to what was going on. That didn't bother him. He'd carried out *his* task.

16

Punta Verde

A jet of foul steam spouted from around the *Peaches* as Gregg and his helpers lumbered toward the vessel. The thrusters had fired, barely enough to rock the hull. Leon and Dole were locking the bow hatch open to the outside hull. The muzzle of the 50-mm plasma cannon had been run out of the port.

"What's going on?" Bailey shouted to the visible crewmen.

A projectile struck the featherboat's bow hard enough to make the hull ring over the siren's continuing wail. Dole and Leon jumped back. Neither was injured, but there was a greenish smear across the ceramic.

The shot had come from above. Gregg paused, scanning the trees a hundred meters away at the clearing's edge. He couldn't see anything—

Bailey and Jeude had stopped when he did, looking nervous but waiting for orders. Another missile *whicked* into the matted vegetation between them at a 45° angle. The body of the shaft was smooth wood, thumb-thick and perhaps a meter long. An integral filament grew from the end of the shaft, stabilizing the missile in place of fletching.

"Get aboard!" Gregg shouted to the crewmen. "Now!"

He still couldn't see anyone in the high branches from which the projectiles must have come, but the foliage quivered. Gregg lowered his visor, aimed the flashgun, and fired.

Vegetation ripped apart in a blast of steam. Gregg threw up his visor to be able to scan for targets better as his hands performed the instinctive job of reloading. His mind was cold as ice, and his fingers exchanged batteries with mechanical crispness.

After ten or fifteen seconds, something dropped from the place where the laser bolt had scalloped the vegetation. Gregg couldn't make out a figure, but a flicker of mauve suggested the color of the Molts they'd loaded on Salute. The falling body made the second canopy, then the undergrowth, quiver.

Two more missiles snapped from the curtain on the other side of the trucks' passage. Gregg saw them, foreshortened into black dots as they sailed toward him. One missed his shoulder by a hand's breadth as he aimed the flashgun again.

He didn't have time to close the visor. He froze the sight picture, squeezed his eyes shut, and fired. The dazzle burned through the veils of mere skin and blood vessels and left purple afterimages when he tried to see what he'd accomplished.

"Mr. Gregg!" a voice called. "Mr. Gregg, *please,* get aboard, the captain says!"

Gregg ran back toward the *Peaches.* A projectile struck the hull in front of him and glanced away in two major pieces and a spray of splinters from the center of the shaft where it broke. He wondered if the arrows were poisoned.

He grabbed one of the handholds dished into the featherboat during casting and hauled himself up. Leon and Tancred aimed rifles out of the hatch. As Gregg rose above the curve of the hull, Tancred fired at the jungle behind him.

Bits of jacket metal and unburned powder bit Gregg's face like a swarm of gnats. He shouted, "God flay you, whore—"

A Molt projectile slammed into the middle of Gregg's back and shattered on his body armor. His breastplate banged forward into the hull, driving all the breath out of his lungs. Leon let his rifle fall into the featherboat's interior so that he could lean forward and catch the gasping gentleman's wrists.

"Take the flashgun," Gregg wheezed.

Tancred worked the bolt of his repeater and fired again. "Stubborn bastard," the bosun snarled, probably meaning Gregg, but he lifted the flashgun with one hand and dropped it behind him down the hatch while he supported Gregg with the other.

The *Peaches* lifted a meter or two with a wobbly, unbalanced

motion. She rotated slowly about her vertical axis. Gregg saw
another projectile as a flicker of motion in the corner of his eye,
but it must have missed even the vessel.

Leon gave a loud grunt and hauled the gentleman up with a
two-handed grip. Gregg managed to find a foothold and thrust
himself safely over the hatch coaming with no more grace or
control than a sack of grain. Bailey and Dole were waiting inside
to catch him.

Ricimer was at the controls. Lightbody and Jeude were hunched
forward, wearing helmets. Leon hopped down from the hatch to
pick up his rifle again.

The plasma cannon fired and recoiled. Vivid light across and
beyond the visual spectrum reflected through the gunport and the
open hatch. The thunderclap made the featherboat lurch as though
Ricimer had run them into a granite ledge.

"That'll make the bastards think!" Jeude crowed from the bow.
He opened the ammunition locker and took out another round
for the plasma cannon, though it would be minutes before the
weapon cooled to the point it could be safely reloaded.

The egg-shaped shell was a miniature laser array with a deuterium pellet at the heart of it. When the lasers fired, their beams
heated and compressed the deuterium into a fusion explosion. The
only way out in the microsecond before the laser array vaporized
was through the gap in the front of the egg, aligned with the
ceramic bore. The deuterium, converted to sun-hot plasma by the
energy of its own fusion, ripped down the channel of the barrel
and devoured everything in its path.

Gregg got to his feet. He found the flashgun and loaded a fresh
battery from the pack slapping against his chest.

"The Molts ambushed the trucks before they ever got to the city,"
Leon shouted in explanation. "The buggers are up the trees, Platt
says."

"I noticed," Gregg said grimly as he stepped onto the storage locker again. A sharp pain in his ribs made him gasp. His
mouth tasted of blood, but he thought he must have bitten his
tongue when the arrow knocked him forward. Tancred stood
head and shoulders out of the hatch, trying awkwardly to reload
his rifle.

The *Peaches* was fifty meters above the ground, wobbling greasily
and moving at the speed of a fast walk. The plasma bolt had blown

a huge crater in the foliage. A dozen tree trunks, stripped bare of bark and branches, blazed at the edge of the stricken area.

Piet Ricimer kept the featherboat rising a meter for every meter it slid forward. By the time the Venerians reached the edge of the original clearing, they were high enough that their thrusters seared the topmost canopy into blackened curls and steam.

Gregg stepped to the front of the long hatch and nudged Tancred aside. The young spacer grimaced but didn't protest aloud. Leon and Bailey, each holding a rifle, climbed onto the locker as well.

There were no targets. Indeed, from the topside hatch, nothing was visible over the bow save an occasional giant tree emerging from the general "landscape." Massed blooms added splotches of yellow, brown, and eye-catching scarlet to the normal green.

Accelerating very slightly, the *Peaches* proceeded in the direction the raiders' trucks had followed through the jungle. If there were Molt warriors beneath, they fled or died in the vessel's superheated exhaust.

Somebody tugged at the thigh of Gregg's trousers. He looked down.

"Sir," called Dole over the waterfall roar of the thrusters. "The captain, he needs you." He jerked his head toward Ricimer, facing forward over the control console.

Gregg knelt and stepped down into the featherboat's bay. He didn't duck low enough; his helmet cracked loudly against the hatch coaming, no harm done but an irritation. Between armor and the big flashgun in his arms, he was clumsy as a blind bear.

Despite the open hatch and gunport, the vessel's interior was much quieter than the outside. "Stephen," Ricimer said, "we're getting close to the vehicles. If I overfly them, they'll be broiled by our thrusters."

Ricimer's eyes were on the viewscreen. His hands moved as two separate living creatures across the controls, modifying thrust and vector. Dole seated himself at one of the attitude-jet panels, but from the rigidity of the crewman's face, he was afraid to do anything that might interfere with Ricimer's delicate adjustments.

"The only way I can think to break our people loose is to go down into the canopy and circle," Ricimer continued in a voice that was controlled to perfect flatness, not calm. "The men on the ground don't have any targets, but the Molts aren't camouflaged from their own level or a little above."

"Right," Gregg said. "Take us down." He turned.

"Stephen!" Ricimer said.

Gregg looked back. Ricimer risked a glance away from the viewscreens so their eyes could meet. "It will be very dangerous," Ricimer said. "And I have to stay here."

"Do your bloody job, man!" Gregg snapped in irritation. "Leave me to mine."

He climbed onto the locker again and moved Tancred aside. "Get ready," he ordered his fellow gunmen as he lowered his visor. "We're going down. Everybody take one side."

The *Peaches* shuddered and lost forward way for a moment. The stern dipped. The featherboat dropped into the canopy with its bow pitched up 20°, advancing at barely a fast walk. An arrow clanged against the underside.

Shadows and the faceshield's tint came dangerously close to blinding Gregg. He saw movement over the *Peaches*' bow, three Molts on a platform anchored where a pair of branches crossed between trunks. A catwalk of vine-lashed poles led into the green curtain to either side.

One Molt was cocking a shoulder-stocked weapon with a vertical throwing arm. Another fired his similar weapon at the featherboat's bow, not the men above the hatch. A crewman's rifle spoke.

Gregg squeezed off. The carapace of the Molt cocking his launcher exploded. The blast of vaporized flesh threw both his/her companions off the platform.

The *Peaches* nudged into a tree bole and crushed it over, tugging out the distant roots. The catwalk separated and fell away. Gregg saw poles flying from another walkway, unguessed until the moment of collapse. All his men were shooting, and he thought he heard muffled gunfire from the ground.

The laser was the wrong weapon for a close-quarter firefight like this. He couldn't see well enough with the visor down to react. "Give me a rif—" he shouted as he fed a fresh battery into the flashgun's stock.

The plasma cannon fired. The shockwave threw Gregg backward. If the *Peaches* hadn't bucked at the same time, he might have fallen flat. The directed thermonuclear explosion bored a cone of radiant hell hundreds of meters through the mid-canopy. Foliage to either side of the path withered and died.

Gregg saw a Molt plunging toward the ground like a flung torch. The aliens wore no clothing, but the creature's entire body had been ignited by the discharge.

Ricimer guided the featherboat along the ionized track. Molt constructions showed vividly where the leaves were burned away.

Gregg saw an alien clinging to the poles of a catwalk whose farther end had vanished. Instead of shooting the Molt he saw, he aimed at the high crotch where the poles were still attached. The flash of his bolt illuminated a pair of Molts crouching in the darkness. They hurtled to either side, while their fellow dropped in the tangle of his poles.

The featherboat nosed to starboard. Ricimer needed to encircle the site in order to free the raiders pinned down below. He or Dole had corrected the attitude to lower the bow. A gnarled, wrist-thick branch struck Gregg hard enough on the head to make his eyes water despite the helmet.

At least a dozen Molts fired a simultaneous volley. All the missiles were aimed at the gunmen this time. An arrow struck just in front of the hatch coaming and glanced upward into Gregg's chest. The impact stabbed daggers through his ribs.

A crewman screamed behind him. A pair of Molts reloaded on a catwalk only twenty meters ahead of the *Peaches*. The bow would throw them down in a moment. Gregg fired anyway and saw the bodies cartwheel away, one of them headless.

He flipped up his visor and turned. "A rifle!" he shouted. "Give me a—"

Leon was trying to keep Bailey from climbing out of the hatch. An arrow had plunged into Bailey's right eye and down, pinning his face to his left shoulder. The crewman gobbled bloody froth. His remaining eye was wild.

Tancred bellowed wordlessly as tears streamed down his cheeks. He didn't appear to be physically injured. He worked the bolt of his repeater and pulled the trigger, but the weapon's magazine was empty.

"Get down, all of you!" Gregg ordered. He dropped his flashgun and gripped the repeater at the balance. Tancred resisted momentarily. Gregg punched the boy in the pit of the stomach. He crumpled. Gregg snatched the bandolier and broke the strap free with the violence of his tug.

Bailey suddenly collapsed. Leon straightened and brought up

his breechloader. Molt projectiles crossed in the air between Gregg and the bosun. "Get *down!*" Gregg repeated as he thumbed cartridges into the integral magazine.

The *Peaches* rocked into a series of tree trunks in quick succession. One splintered at the point of impact. The other trees pulled out of the thin soil and tilted crazily, half-supported by vines and branches interlocking with those of their neighbors. As the featherboat passed over the tangle, her superheated exhaust devoured those impediments and sent the trunks crashing the remainder of the way to the ground.

A Molt aimed his weapon down at the hatch. Gregg shot the creature through the body. Recoil brought a sharp reminder of the injured ribs. He chambered the next round, rotated to his left where motion shimmered in the corner of his eye, and smashed the triangular skull of an alien seventy meters away.

Leon fired. A projectile grazed the back of Gregg's helmet, making his vision blur.

"God rot your bones in Hell!" Gregg screamed in the bosun's face. "Get down and load for me! I've got armor!"

As he spoke, he fired the last round in his magazine. A Molt dropped his weapon to one side of a catwalk and fell to the other. He managed to grasp a guy rope of braided vine and cling there for the instant's notice Gregg had to give anything that wasn't immediately lethal.

He dropped the repeater. Tancred offered him a loaded rifle, stock-first, from the featherboat's bay. Leon ducked down as ordered. Either the words or the sense or the naked fury in Stephen Gregg's face had penetrated the bosun's consciousness.

With his visor up, Gregg felt like a god. He could see *everything*, and he couldn't miss. The *Peaches* was unstable at low speed even without grinding her hull into huge trees, which themselves weighed tonnes. It didn't matter. Gregg and the gunsights and each Molt were one until the *flash/shock* signaled the need to seek another alien target.

Two more arrows hit Gregg—on the right side and in the back, squarely over the smear where he'd been struck while boarding the featherboat. He was aware of the impacts the way he saw the black and green of vegetation—facts, but unimportant when only the mauve smudges of Molt bodies mattered.

He didn't bother to look down when he'd emptied a rifle, just dropped it and opened his hand to take the fresh weapon a crewman would slap there. The carbine from the *Tolliver*'s officer had a five-round magazine and was dead accurate. Gregg used it to shoot the eye out of a Molt warrior at least a hundred meters away.

A corner of Gregg's mind noted two trucks glimpsed where the *Peaches* had cleared a sight line to the ground. Men huddled beneath the vehicles and behind nearby trees. A few of them waved. Molt projectiles stood out from the thin panels of the truck bodies like quills on a porcupine, and from sprawled men as well.

The featherboat yawed uneasily as Ricimer brought her bow onto a new heading. Gregg hadn't fired for—he didn't know how long. There weren't any targets, though occasionally he glimpsed an empty platform or catwalk.

The *Peaches* nosed onto the track her thrusters had cleared on the way to the ambush site. Over the bow Gregg saw the trucks again, all three of them, retreating toward the ships. They jounced over the buttress roots of trees at the best speed they were capable of. He realized he couldn't hear anything, not even the roaring thrusters, though he felt the vibration through his feet and the hatch coaming against which he braced his belly.

The clearing the *Tolliver* had blasted was a bright splotch without the shadow-dappling of the jungle beyond. The flagship had run out several of her big plasma cannon. Men rose from hasty barricades to greet the returning trucks.

"That's okay, sir," said a voice close to Gregg's ear. "We'll take over now."

A wet cloth dabbed at his forehead. He wasn't wearing his helmet anymore.

"Jesus God! What happened to his head?"

"Arrow must've hit right over the visor. Jesus!"

The last thing Gregg saw was the worried face of Piet Ricimer, framed by the hatch opening above him.

17

Punta Verde

Gregg didn't recognize the ceiling. He turned his head. A wave of nausea tried to turn his stomach inside out. Nothing came up except thin bile, but the spasms made his rib cage feel as though it was jacketed in molten glass.

Piet Ricimer leaned over him and gently mopped the vomit away with a sponge. "Welcome back," he said.

"I feel awful," Gregg whispered.

Ricimer shrugged. "Cracked ribs, a concussion, and unconscious for three days," he said. "You *ought* to feel awful, my friend."

"Three *days?*"

"I was beginning to worry a little," Ricimer said without emphasis. "The medic thought most of it was simple exhaustion, though. You were operating"—he smiled wryly—"well beyond redline, Stephen."

Gregg closed his eyes for a moment. "Christ's blood, I feel awful," he said. He looked up again. "Sorry."

"You've had quite a time," Ricimer said. "The Lord makes allowances, I'm sure."

"Where are—" Gregg began. He broke off, winced, and continued, "Just a bit. I'm going to sit up."

"The medics—" Ricimer said. Gregg lurched up on his right elbow and gasped. Ricimer slid an arm behind his friend's back but followed rather than lifted Gregg the rest of the way up.

The gentleman sat with his eyes closed, breathing in quick, shallow breaths. At last he resumed, "Where are we?"

"The argosy hasn't moved, if that's what you mean," Ricimer said. "You and I are in a cabin on the *Tolliver*."

His smile had claws of memory. "They were going to put you in the sick bay," he added. "But I didn't think you ought to be disturbed by the other wounded men."

"I don't think I'm going to stand up just yet," Gregg said deliberately. He opened his eyes and saw the worry on Ricimer's face melt into a look of studied unconcern. "We're *going* to lift off, aren't we?" he pressed. "Mostert can't possibly think we can capture enough Molts here to be worth the, the cost."

"As a matter of fact . . ." Ricimer said. Gregg couldn't be sure of his tone. "The village we attacked—city, really, there are thousands of Molts living in it. The Molts were impressed. They've dealt with the Southerns before, but they'd never met anything like us."

Looking at a corner of the ceiling, Ricimer went on, "Leon's in the sick bay, you know. Splinters through the shoulder from an arrow that hit the hull beside him."

Gregg pursed his lips, remembering flashes of the way he'd shouted at the bosun. "I didn't know that," he said.

Ricimer shrugged. "He'll be all right. But I heard him telling a rating from the *Tolliver* in the next bed, 'Our Mr. Gregg, he's a right bastard. He went through them bugs like shit through a goose. As soon kill you as look at you, Mr. Gregg would.'"

"Lord, I'm sorry," Gregg whispered with his eyes closed. "I was . . ."

"He's proud of you, Stephen," Ricimer explained softly. "We all are. *Our* Mr. Gregg. And the Molts were so impressed that they want us to help them against their neighbors forty klicks away. In return, we get the prisoners."

"Well, I'll be damned," Gregg said.

"Not for what you did three days ago," Ricimer said. "Eight of the men with the trucks were killed, but none of them would have made it back except for us. Especially for you."

"Especially for you," Gregg corrected. He met his friend's eyes again. "Bailey?" he asked.

Ricimer shook his head minusculy. "No. But that's not—anyone's fault."

"When do we . . ." Gregg said. "The raid, the attack. When is it?"

"Three days from now," Ricimer said. "The Molts are getting their army, I suppose you'd call it, together. But Stephen, I don't think—"

"I'm going," Gregg said. He set his lips firmly together, then held out his hand toward his friend. "Now," he said. "Help me stand . . ."

18

Punta Verde

Because the four men stationed at the *Peaches'* hatch all wore body armor and helmets, Gregg knocked elbows when he twisted to either side. Even so, the hatchway was less crowded than the featherboat's bay in which twenty more heavily-armed men waited.

The *Hawkwood* at three hundred meters altitude led the expedition. She wobbled across the sky, losing or gaining twenty meters of elevation in an instant and slewing sideways by twice that much. The *Hawkwood* had a good enough thrust-to-weight ratio to make atmospheric flight a possible proposition, but not an especially practical one. They were using her because Mostert needed the firepower and the hundred men he could cram into the vessel's hull.

Four lifeboats, each with a dozen or more men aboard, veed out to the *Hawkwood*'s flanks. They skimmed the treetops, buttoned up but still washed dangerously by hot, electrically-excited exhaust from the leading vessel's thrusters. Occasionally one of them, buffeted or simply blinded when the *Hawkwood* slid to the side, dipped into the forest. As yet, none of them had been noticeably damaged by such mishaps.

The featherboats closed both arms of the vee. Gregg noted with grim amusement that the *Desire* to starboard porpoised almost as badly as the *Hawkwood* did, while Piet Ricimer kept the *Peaches* as steady as if she ran on tracks.

A kilometer ahead of the expedition's leading vessel, Gregg saw an incandescent rainbow: sun catching the plume of another spaceship's thrusters. The reason the Molts had allied themselves with the Venerians was that their rivals were in league with the Southerns, trading captives for firearms.

No one would hear Gregg if he shouted. The flashgunners in the hatch had their visors locked down against the retina-crisping dazzle of the *Hawkwood*'s exhaust. That and the engine roar isolated them as individuals. The other three came from the *Rose*. Gregg wouldn't recognize any of them with their helmets off.

Anyway, it wasn't the hatch crew which had to be warned but rather the vessels' captains. Their view was even blurrier than Gregg's through his filtered visor. It was possible that the distant vessel wasn't hostile . . . but it was equally possible that pigs flew on some undiscovered planet.

Gregg aimed his flashgun at the top of the distant plume where the other vessel had to be. He tried to steady his weapon. The shot was beyond human skill, but the vivid lance across the optics of the expedition vessels would at least call attention to the interloper.

The world fluoresced with a shockwave that felt for an instant like freefall. Forest vaporized in the bolt from the *Peaches*' plasma cannon. Despite the featherboat's distant position, Ricimer had seen the target as soon as Gregg had.

The interloper appeared startled, though it was untouched by the blast. It lifted from where it lurked in the upper canopy and ripped a series of brilliant sparks toward the *Hawkwood*. It appeared to mount a multishot laser rather than a plasma weapon.

The 14-cm Long Tom in the *Hawkwood*'s bow belched a sky-devouring gout of directed energy toward the interloper. Foliage exploded. Eighty meters of a giant tree leaped upward like a javelin, shedding leaves and branches as it rose. It had been struck near the base. The target dived to vanish within the forest again.

Mostert brought the *Hawkwood*'s bow around to starboard. He ignored the danger to the cutters on that side and the *Desire* in his eagerness to bring his port six-gun battery into play. These lighter weapons, 8- and 10-cm plasma cannon, had no target by the time they bore, but the gun captains loosed anyway. Gregg could imagine Piet Ricimer white-lipped at his controls as he watched his cousin's actions.

The squadron's destination was in sight: flat mushrooms rising beneath the topmost foliage. The city's extent seemed greater than that of the one Platt had tried to attack. These domes were mottled gray instead of being beige.

The *Peaches* swung wide and dipped as the other Venerian vessels homed in on the Molt stronghold. Ricimer was waiting for the Southern vessel to reappear. Gregg tightened his grip on the flashgun, then forced himself to relax so that he wouldn't be too keyed-up to react if he had to. The featherboat's plasma cannon was still too hot to reload, so it was up to him and his fellows if the target appeared.

It didn't. The Southerns had already shown more courage than Gregg would've expected, engaging a force that was so hugely more powerful.

The *Hawkwood* lowered toward the canopy, pitching and yawing. As she neared the treetops, her starboard battery fired. Four fireballs flared across the nearest Molt dome. Farther back across the stronghold, misdirected blasts blasted another structure and the topmost fifty meters from one of the forest's emergent giants.

The squadron's leader sank into the jungle at the edge of the stronghold in a barely-controlled slide. The cutters and the *Desire* settled in beside her.

The *Peaches* swept over the outer ring of domes and into the interior of the stronghold.

Gregg glanced down. The cellulose-based roof of the nearest dome was afire where the plasma discharges had struck it. Gangs of Molts sprayed the flames with a sticky fluid. Warriors on the roof of the structure fired point-blank at the featherboat with rifles as well as indigenous weapons. An arrow that missed the *Peaches* arched high over Gregg's head.

As he took her down, Ricimer rotated the *Peaches* on her vertical axis like a dog preparing its bed. The dome they'd overflown was completely alight from the plasma exhaust. Warriors and members of the firefighting team were dark sprawls within the sea of flame.

The Molts had cut away the undergrowth and mid-level vegetation within their stronghold. The boles of emergents split and corkscrewed as the thrusters seared them. Walkways connecting the domes burned brightly. The city stretched nearly a kilometer across its separate elements.

The featherboat grounded, then sank a meter lower when what appeared to be soil turned out to be the roof of a turf-and-laterite structure covering the interior of the stronghold. An unarmed Molt clawed its way through the broken surface, shrieking until one of the flashgunners shot him.

A warrior leaned from the crotch of an emergent, aiming his rifle at the *Peaches* seventy meters below. Gregg's hasty snap shot struck a meter below the Molt. The trunk blew apart with enough violence to fling the alien in one direction while the upper portion of the tree tilted slowly in the other.

Shouting men tried to push past Gregg. He lifted himself out of the hatch and toppled to the ground when his boot caught on the coaming. Armor and the flashgun made him top-heavy. Somebody jumped onto Gregg's back as he tried to rise. Finally he managed to roll sideways, then get his feet under him again.

The interior of the stronghold was as open as a manicured park. Here and there Molts popped to the surface from the underground shelter, but none of them were armed. Occasional warriors sniped from distant trees. The featherboat's thrusters had cleared the immediate area of catwalks by which the defenders might have approached dangerously close.

More—many more—Molts boiled from the lower levels of the burning dome. They were all warriors. The domes were actually the tops of towers rising from the ground. They were connected by gray vertical walls. At a close look, the material was wood pulp masticated with enzymes and allowed to solidify into something akin to concrete-hard *papier-mâché.*

Gregg reloaded his flashgun. Men leaped from the featherboat and hesitated. Those with rifles fired at Molts, but the disparity in their numbers compared to those of the aliens was shockingly apparent. Gunfire and cries could be heard through the stronghold's wall as if from a great distance.

"Follow me!" Gregg shouted as he fired his flashgun at a closed door in the base of the burning tower. His bolt shattered the panel and ignited it, as he'd hoped. He lumbered toward the nearest stretch of wall, reloading as he ran.

Three Molts swinging edged clubs rushed Gregg from the side. One wore a pink sash.

The battery Gregg was loading hung up in its compartment. When he tried to force it with his thumbs, the connectors bent.

A sailor Gregg didn't know aimed his rifle in the face of a Molt and squeezed the trigger. Nothing happened. The sailor bawled and flattened himself on the ground.

Gregg lunged forward, stepping inside the nearest alien's stroke instead of taking it on the side of his head. The Molt caromed away from Gregg's armored shoulder. As the warrior fell, Gregg saw the creature wore a pistol holster on its sash, but the weapon was missing.

Gregg clubbed his flashgun at the second Molt as the creature swung at him. Their blows, both right-handed, described the two halves of a circle. The flashgun's heavy barrel crunched a broad dent in the wedge-shaped skull. The alien's club was wooden, but dense and metal-hard. It rang on Gregg's helmet.

His limbs lost feeling. He slipped down on his right side. He could see and hear perfectly well, but his body seemed to belong to someone else. The third Molt stood splay-legged before him, raising his weapon for a vertical, two-handed chop. The Molts of this city had a tinge of yellow in their chitinous exoskeletons, unlike the smooth mauve of the clan with which the Venerians were now allied.

A bullet punched through the thorax of the Molt about to finish Gregg. The warrior fell backward in a splash of ichor. Piet Ricimer loaded a fresh round, butt-stroked the Molt beginning to rise from where the impact of Gregg's body had flung him, and bent to Gregg.

"Leon!" he shouted. "Help Mr. Gregg—"

Gregg twisted his body violently. As though the first motion broke a spell, he found he had control of his arms and legs again.

"C'mon," he said. He tried to shout, but the words came out in a slurred croak. The bosun gripped his shoulders to help him rise. "Gotta cut through the wall from this side."

The Venerian raiders wore half-armor or at least helmets for the assault. One man lay with a pair of arrows crossing through his throat, but that appeared to be the only fatality. A rifleman fired from the featherboat's open hatch. There might be a few others inside, either left for a guard or unwilling at the crisis to put themselves into open danger.

The rest of the force, eighteen or twenty men, was coalescing into a frightened group in the open area between the *Peaches* and the stronghold's wall. Most of them couldn't have realized where

Ricimer was landing them. They'd spread momentarily when they jumped from the featherboat, but realization of how badly outnumbered they were drove the Venerians together again. Some of them were wounded.

For their own part, the Molts were equally confused by the series of events. A hundred or so warriors threatened the band of Venerians, but they didn't press closer than five meters or so in the face of gunfire. Relatively few of the aliens carried projectile weapons. Gregg suspected the shooters had been stationed high in the tower for a better field of fire. The *Peaches'* thrusters had cooked most of those, though others were bound to swarm to the point of attack from neighboring towers.

"With me!" Ricimer shouted. "We'll cut through the wall!" He waved his rifle in a great vertical arc as if it were a saber and ran forward. Gregg felt like a hippo when he moved wearing armor. His friend sprinted as though he were in shoes and a tunic.

Gregg took the jammed reload out of the flashgun's compartment and flung the battery as a dense missile at the nearest Molt. He inserted a fresh battery. "Come on, Leon," he said as he backed slowly with his face to the enemy. "I'm fine, you bet."

Leon carried a cutting bar. He swung it in a showy figure eight with the power on. The blade vibrated like a beam of coherent light. He and Gregg were the rear guard. The wall was thirty meters away. Gregg expected the Molts to rush them, but instead warriors hopped uncertainly from one jointed leg to another as the flashgun's muzzle flicked sideways.

Gregg's heel bumped something. He glanced down reflexively. An unseen marksman slammed an arrow into Gregg's breastplate. He pitched backward over the body of an alien eviscerated by a cutting bar. Thirty or forty warriors charged in chittering fury. Gregg scrambled to his feet in a red haze of pain and squeezed the flashgun's trigger.

The barrel had cracked when he used the weapon as a mace. Instead of frying the Molt at the point of aim, it blew up like a ceramic-cased bomb, hurling shrapnel forward and to all sides. None of the fragments hit Gregg, but the concussion knocked him on his back again.

Several Molts were down, though their exoskeletons were relatively proof against small cuts. The rush halted in surprise, though.

A four-shot volley from the rest of the company dropped several more aliens and turned the attack into a broken rout.

Piet Ricimer knelt beside Gregg and rose, lifting the whole weight of the bigger man until the bosun grabbed the opposite arm and helped.

"I'm not hurt!" Gregg shouted angrily. "I'm not hurt!" He wondered if that was true. He seemed to be standing a few centimeters away from his body, so that the edges of his flesh and soul didn't quite match.

The flashgun's barrel had disintegrated as completely as a hot filament suddenly exposed to oxygen. Gregg threw away the stock and picked up a repeater with Southern Cross markings. He didn't know whether it was a crewman's loot from an earlier voyage, or if a Molt had carried the weapon. There was an empty case in the chamber but two cartridges in the magazine.

A five-meter section of wall as high as a man sagged, then collapsed outward when crewmen kicked the panel to break the joins their hasty bar-cuts had left. Several armored Venerians burst through from outside the stronghold. Behind them were scores of allied Molts carrying projectile weapons and long wooden spears in place of the locals' edged clubs.

Gregg felt himself sway. He lifted his visor for the first time since he boarded the *Peaches* for the attack. He *knew* the air was steamy, but it touched his face like an icy shower. He thought of unlatching his body armor, but he wasn't sure he retained enough dexterity to work the catches.

Ricimer put a hand on Gregg's shoulder. "We did it," Ricimer croaked. "We've made the breakthrough. The Molts can carry the fight now."

He guided Gregg toward the featherboat. The tower was fully involved, a spire of flames leaping from the ground to twice the eighty-meter height of the structure that fed them. The radiant heat was a hammer. Gregg was too numb to connect cause and effect, so Ricimer led him clear.

The stronghold's defenders lay all about. Most of them were dead, but some twitched or even made attempts at connected motion. Allied Molts ripped open the ceiling of the underground chamber as soon as they were within the stronghold's walls, then disappeared from sight.

High-pitched screams came from distant portions of the city.

The cries went on longer than human throats could have sustained. There had been other breakthroughs now that the Venerians had smashed the point at which the defenders concentrated against the assault. Gregg saw flames quiver upward through the sparse interior vegetation.

The Molt Gregg had bodychecked and Ricimer then clubbed was sitting up. It followed their approach with its eyes but did not move.

Gregg presented his rifle.

"Kill me, then, human," the Molt said in high-pitched but intelligible English.

"We're not here to kill p-p-p—" Ricimer began. "We're not here to kill you, we want workers."

A band of twenty or thirty defending warriors sprinted across the clearing the featherboat had made toward a neighboring tower. Allied Molts pursued them. Both sides paused and exchanged a volley of projectiles. A few fell. The survivors continued their race. Gregg covered the action with the rifle he'd appropriated, but he didn't bother to fire.

Ricimer put his hand on the shoulder of the Molt who had spoken. "Do you yield, then?" the spacer demanded.

"I yield to you, human," the Molt said calmly. "But the Y'Lyme will kill me and all my clan. We sold them to the slavers for a brood-year. Now they will kill us all."

"Nobody's going to kill you," Ricimer said harshly.

Smoke seeped from the soil in a dozen locations. Fires had started in the underground chambers. Allied Molts—Y'Lyme—came up, driving yellow-tinged locals ahead of them. Those hidden below were juveniles or cramped with age. Y'Lyme began to spear them to death. The victims seemed apathetic.

Ricimer's captive made a clicking sound that Gregg supposed was a laugh. "The slavers called me Guillermo," he said. "I was in charge of my clan's trade with them."

Platt jogged over to Ricimer and Gregg with three crewmen from the *Tolliver*. He carried a cutting bar. It and his breastplate were smeared with brownish Molt internal juices. Behind Platt, Captain Mostert and other members of his headquarters group entered the stronghold through the gap the *Peaches*' crew had cut.

"I'll get him!" Platt cried. He stepped to Guillermo and raised his howling bar.

"Hey!" Ricimer shouted. He stepped between Platt and his would-be victim. "What do you think you're doing?"

Platt shoved Ricimer aside. "Killing fucking Molts!" he said. "Till they all give up!"

Stephen Gregg extended his repeater like a long pistol. The barrel lay across Platt's Adam's apple; the muzzle pointed past his left shoulder.

Platt bleated. One of the men accompanying him aimed a rifle at Gregg's midriff. Out of the corner of Gregg's eye he saw Tancred, Dole, and Lightbody running toward the tableau.

"Look there, Platt," Gregg said. He jerked his chin to draw the officer's gaze along the line of the rifle.

A Molt thirty meters away sat up to aim a projectile weapon. A wooden arrow pinned the creature's thighs together.

The Molt fired. The missile whacked through the bridge of Platt's nose and lifted the officer's helmet from the inside.

Platt toppled backward. Gregg fired and missed. While other Venerians shouted and fired wildly, Gregg chambered his last round. He raised the rifle to his shoulder normally and fired. The Molt collapsed, thrashing.

Piet Ricimer surveyed his surroundings in a series of fierce jerks of his head. His fingertips rested on the head of the Molt who had yielded to him. His five crewmen and a promiscuous group of Venerians, from the *Peaches* and outside the stronghold, stared at him and Gregg, waiting for direction.

"All right!" Ricimer ordered. "Start rounding up prisoners. Don't let the, the others kill them. Do what you have to, to stop the killing."

His eyes met those of Stephen Gregg. Gregg stood like a tree. He was aware of what was going on around him, but his mind was no longer capable of taking an active part in it.

"In the name of God . . ." Piet Ricimer said. "*Stop* the killing!"

In all directions, the guard towers of the captured city blazed like Hell's pillars.

19

Sunrise

When the six Venerian captains conferred by radio about the moon they were orbiting, Piet Ricimer suggested the name Sunrise because of the way sunlight washed to a rose-purple color the gases belching from a huge volcano. The name stuck, at least for as long as the argosy refitted here. The next visitors, years or millennia hence, would give it their own name—if they even bothered.

Between the sun and the moon's primary, a gas giant on the verge of collapsing into a star, Sunrise was habitably warm though on the low side of comfortable. The atmosphere stank of sulphur, but it was breathable.

Cellular life had not arisen here, nor was it likely to arise. The primary raised tides in Sunrise's rocky core and swamped the moon's surface every few years with magma or volcanically-melted water which refroze as soon as the tremors paused.

The planet-sized moon was a useful staging point in the patterns of transit space connecting the Reaches with the worlds of the Mirror, where the sidereal universe doubled itself in close detail. There would be a Federation outpost on Sunrise—

Except for storms that battered the moon's atmosphere with a violence equal to the surges in the crust itself. Landing a large vessel on Sunrise would have been nearly suicidal for pilots who had not trained in the roiling hell of Venus.

For that matter, the *Tolliver*'s landing had been a close brush with disaster and the *Grandcamp* was still in orbit. Captain Kershaw's cutter ferried him down to attend the conference in person.

There hadn't been any choice about landing the flagship. Quite apart from the need to replenish the *Tolliver*'s air supply, her disintegrating hull required repairs that could best be performed on the ground. Ricimer had hinted to Gregg that nothing that could be done outside a major dockyard was going to help the big vessel significantly, though.

"I say we head straight for home," said Fedders of the *Rose*. "We've got our profit and a dozen times over, what with the shell from Jewelhouse. The amount of risk we face if we try to move the last hundred Molts isn't worth it. And I'm talking about strain to the ships, irregardless of the Feds."

"We can't make a straight run for Venus," Kershaw protested. "I can't, at least. The gradients between transit universes are rising, and I tell you frankly—the *Grandcamp* isn't going to take the strain."

The buzz of crews overglazing the *Tolliver* provided a constant background to the discussion. Portable kilns crawled across the hull in regular bands, spraying vaporized rock onto the crumbling ceramic plates. The process returned the flagship to proper airtightness so long as she remained at rest. The stress of takeoff, followed by the repeated hammering of transit, would craze the surface anew.

"It's not the gradients—" said Fedders.

"The gradients *are* rising," Ricimer interjected quickly. "They're twenty percent above what the sailing directions we loaded on Jewelhouse indicate is normal."

"All right, they are," Fedders snapped, "but the real problem is the *Grandcamp*'s AI not making the insertions properly. And the Federation's Earth Convoy is due in the region any day now."

"That's enough squabbling about causes," Admiral Mostert said forcefully. "The situation is what's important. And the situation is that the *Tolliver* can't make a straight run home either. We're going to have to land on Biruta to refit and take on reaction mass."

Kelly of the *Hawkwood* muttered a curse. "Right," he said to his hands. They were clenched, knuckles to knuckles, on the opalglass conference table before him. "And what do we do if the Earth

Convoy's waiting there for us? Pray they won't have heard how we traded on Jewelhouse?"

"*And* Bowman," Stephen Gregg murmured from his chair against the bulkhead behind Ricimer—Captain Ricimer—at the table. The aged flagship had few virtues, but the scale of her accommodations, including a full conference room as part of the admiral's suite, was one of them. "*And* Guelph. We didn't actually blow up any buildings either of those places, but the locals did business with us because forty plasma guns were trained on them."

A particularly strong gust of wind ripped across the surface of Sunrise. The *Tolliver* rocked and settled again. A similar blast when Gregg and Ricimer trekked from the *Peaches* to the flagship had skidded them thirty meters across a terrain of rock crevices filled with ice.

"I don't suppose there'd be another uncharted stopover we could use instead of Biruta, would there?" Fedders suggested plaintively. "I mean . . ."

Everyone in the conference room, the six captains and their chief aides and navigators, knew what Fedders meant. They also knew that Sunrise had been discovered only because of the *Peaches'* one-in-a-million piece of luck. Ricimer cast widely ahead of the remainder of the argosy, confident that he could rendezvous without constantly comparing positions the way the other navigators had to do.

The voyage thus far had been a stunning success. The Venerians loaded pre-Collapse artifacts from two Federation colonies, and on Jewelhouse they'd gained half a tonne of the shells that made the planet famous. The material came from deepwater snails which fluoresced vividly to stun prey in the black depths of the ocean trench they inhabited. Kilo for kilo, the shell was as valuable as purpose-designed microchips from factories operating across the Mirror.

When the voyage began, Mostert's men were willing to take risks for the chance of becoming wealthy. Now they *were* wealthy, all the officers in this room . . . if only they could get home with their takings. There was no longer a carrot to balance the stick of danger; and that stick was more and more a spiked club as the condition of the older vessels degraded from brutal use.

"We should be ahead of the Earth Convoy," Mostert said. His heavy face was without visible emotion, but the precise way his hands rested on the conference table suggested the control he exerted to retain that impassivity. "We'll load, repair, and be gone in a few days. We can offer the authorities on Biruta a fair price for using their graving docks. They need Molt labor as badly as the other colonies."

"There's only one place to land a starship on Biruta," Fedders said with his eyes on a ceiling molding. "That's Island Able. And they'll have defenses there, the Feds will . . ."

A starship which committed to land on Biruta had no options if batteries at the port opened fire. The seas that wrapped the remainder of the planet would swallow any vessel which tried to avoid plasma bolts that would otherwise rip her belly out.

"They won't know we're from Venus," said Mostert. "I'll go in first with the guns ready for as soon as we're down."

He looked at his cousin. "Ricimer," he said. "You can bring your featherboat in at the same time the *Tolliver* lands, can't you?"

"Yes," Ricimer said softly. "We could do that. It'll confuse the garrison."

Mostert nodded. "If we give them enough to think about, they won't act. So that's what we'll do."

He looked around the conference table. "No further questions, then?" he said with a deliberate lack of subtlety.

No one spoke for a moment. The Venerians had accessed the data banks in the Jewelhouse Commandatura while they held the Fed governor and his wife under guard. The information there suggested that the annual Earth Convoy was due anytime within a standard week of the present . . .

"If there isn't any choice," Piet Ricimer said in the grim silence, "then—may the Lord shelter us in our necessity."

Gregg remembered the terror in the eyes of the wife of the Jewelhouse governor. He wondered if the Lord saw any reason to shelter the men in this room . . . including Stephen Gregg, who was of their number whether or not he approved of every action his company took.

20

Biruta

Biruta's atmosphere was notably calm. That, with the planet's location at the nearer edge (through transit space) of the Reaches and the huge expanse of water to provide reaction mass, made Biruta an ideal way station for starships staggering out from the solar system.

The *Peaches* had to come in at the worst part of the flagship's turbulence. She bucked and pitched like lint above an air vent. Ricimer and the men on the attitude jets, Leon and Lightbody this time, kept the featherboat on a reasonably even keel.

Jeude and Tancred in their hard suits hunched over the plasma cannon forward. They'd opened the gunport at three klicks of altitude, though they'd have to run the weapon out before they brought it into action.

Gregg smiled grimly as he gripped a stanchion and braced one boot against a bulkhead. He was getting better at this. And there were amusement parks where people paid money to have similar experiences.

Guillermo stood across the narrow hull from Gregg. From his first landing, the Molt rode as easily as if his jointed legs were the oil-filled struts of shock absorbers.

"Guillermo," Gregg called. "Did your genetic memory cover space flight? Landings, I mean."

"Yes, Mr. Gregg," the Molt said. "It does."

Gregg wasn't sure precisely what Guillermo's status was. So far as Mostert was concerned, Guillermo was an unsold part of the cargo loaded at Punta Verde. The larger vessels still carried fifty or sixty other Molts . . . who would be sold to the Feds here, if all went well.

To Gregg and the *Peaches* crewmen, the alien who'd taken over Bailey's duties in the course of the past four planetfalls wasn't simply merchandise. Gregg wasn't sure Guillermo had ever been merchandise to Piet Ricimer.

"What're them ships there?" Lightbody muttered as he peered at the viewscreen over his control consoles. "They're not big enough to be the Earth Convoy."

"Water buffalo," Leon said. "Liftships, laser-guided drones. The Feds' biggest ships boost to orbit with minimum reaction mass to keep the strain down. Liftships, they're just buckets to ferry water up to them."

Island Able was a ragged triangle with sides of about a kilometer each. A complex of buildings and two very small ships—featherboats or perhaps merely atmosphere vessels—were placed at the northern corner, protected by an artificial seawall.

Grounded near the eastern corner were the water buffalo, ships in the 50-to-80-tonne range. Until the bosun explained what they were, Gregg thought the vessels' simple outlines were a result of the screen's mediocre resolution.

On the third, western, corner, the Feds had built a fort with four roof turrets. Even as bad as the viewscreen was, Gregg should have been able to see the barrels of the guns if they were harmlessly lowered.

"Captain," he said, glad to note there was no quaver in his voice. "I think the fort's guns are muzzle-on to us."

"They might track the *Tolliver*, Stephen," Ricimer said, "but I don't think they'd all four track us. I don't think the turrets have their guns mounted."

As he spoke, his hands played delicately with the thruster controls. The *Tolliver* rotated slowly on its vertical axis as it dropped. One or more of its attitude jets must be misaligned. Ricimer held the *Peaches* in a helix that kept the featherboat between the lobes of two of the flagship's huge thrusters.

The *Tolliver* settled close to the administration complex in a blast

of steam and gravel. The featherboat hovered for a moment. When
the flagship's cloud of stripped atoms dissipated suddenly like a
rainbow overtaken by nightfall, Ricimer brought them in a hundred meters from the *Tolliver.* They flanked the direct path between
the bigger ship and the Federation buildings.

It was probably not chance that the line at which the featherboat
came to rest pointed her bow and plasma cannon at the fort a
kilometer away.

Gregg and the Molt undogged the roof hatch. Steam billowed
in like a slap with a hot towel. Jeude and Tancred remained at
their gun, but the remainder of the crewmen got to their feet.

Gregg glanced at the viewscreen. Two Federation trucks drove
close to the *Tolliver,* dragging hoses. "What—" he started to say.

The trucks suddenly bloomed with a mist of seawater. It paled
to steam as it cooled the landing site and the vessel's hull. The
hoses stretched to intakes out beyond the line of Island Able's gentle
surf.

"They think we're the Earth Convoy," Ricimer said. It was only
when he grinned broadly that Gregg realized how tense his friend
had been beneath his outer calm. "They don't let their admirals
sit aboard for an hour or so while the site cools naturally."

"They aren't going to bother with us, though, are they?" Dole
grumbled. "*Not* that it looks like there's much entertainment on
this gravel heap."

"I think if we suited up, Stephen," Ricimer said, "we could get
to the *Tolliver* about the time they opened up for the local greeting
party. Eh?"

"They got some platforms out a ways, fella told me on Jewelhouse," Jeude called in response to Dole's comment. "Not on the
island, though. Not enough land."

"Sure," Gregg said. He thumped his armored chest. "I'd feel
naked getting off a ship without a hard suit, the way things have
been going. The leggings won't make much difference."

Guillermo opened the armor store and sorted out ceramic pieces,
the full suit sized to Ricimer's body and the lower half of Gregg's.
Ballistic protection alone didn't justify the awkwardness and burden
of complete armor.

Piet Ricimer latched his torso armor over him, then paused. He
looked around the featherboat's bay, even glancing at the suited
gun crew behind him. In a clear, challenging voice, he said,

"Guillermo, when we get back home, I'll have a suit made to fit you. I don't like carrying crewmen who don't have a way to stay alive in case we have to open the bay in vacuum."

"Too fucking right," Dole said, responding for the crew.

"And I'll chip in on the cost," Gregg said evenly, completing the answer of the question that nobody was willing to admit had been asked.

Ricimer's smile lit the bay. "Leon, you're in charge," he said. "Stephen, let's go watch my cousin negotiate."

21

Biruta

Five meters from the *Peaches,* the shingle was cool again. Gregg lifted his visor. Another Venerian ship dropped from orbit, but for the moment it was no more than a spark of high-altitude opalescence. The thunder of its approach had yet to reach the ground.

An airboat supported by three boom-mounted ducted props lifted from the administrative complex. Gregg tapped Ricimer's shoulder—armor on armor clacked loudly—and pointed. "Look," he said, "they're sending a courier to the outlying platforms."

Instead of heading off with a message that couldn't be radioed because of interference from starship thrusters, the airboat hummed a hundred and fifty yards across the shingle and settled again before the *Tolliver's* lowering cargo ramp.

Piet Ricimer chuckled. "You wouldn't expect a Federation admiral to walk, would you, Stephen?" he said. "The locals expect high brass with the Earth Convoy, so they've sent a ride for them."

Four Federation officials descended from the airboat. They'd put on their uniforms in haste: one of them still wore grease-stained utility trousers, though his white dress tunic was in good shape.

The vehicle had only six seats. One of those was for the driver, who remained behind. Presumably some of the locals planned to walk back.

Gregg and Ricimer walked in front of the boat, following the officials to the flagship's ramp. The driver looked startled when he saw the two strangers were armed as well as wearing hard suits. Ricimer had a rifle, while Gregg carried a replacement for the flashgun that had failed at Punta Verde.

Ricimer eyed the driver through the windscreen, then raised a gauntleted index finger to his lips in a *shush* sign. The driver nodded furiously, too frightened even to duck behind the plastic bow of his vehicle.

"Administrator Carstensen?" called the leader of the local officials from the foot of the ramp. The *Tolliver's* dark cargo bay showed only shadows where the crew awaited their visitors. "I'm Port Commander Dupuy. We're glad to welcome you to Biruta. I'm sure your stay will be enjoyable."

"I'm sure it will too, gentlemen," boomed Alexi Mostert. "I'm *absolutely* sure that you'll treat me and my ships as if we belonged to your own Federation."

"What?" said Dupuy. "What?"

The man in greasy trousers was either quicker on the uptake or more willing to act. He spun on his heel and started a long stride off the ramp—

And froze. Between him and escape were the officers from the featherboat, huge in their stained white hard suits. The Fed official drew himself up straight, nodded formally to Ricimer and Gregg, and turned around again.

"I'm afraid I'll have to ask you gentlemen to be our guests for a time," Mostert continued. "We'll pay at normal rates with Molt laborers for the supplies we take, I assure you . . . but so that there aren't any misunderstandings, I'll be putting my own men in your fort and admin buildings. I'm sure you understand, Mr. Dupuy."

If the Federation official made any reply to Mostert, his words were lost in the roar of the *Hawkwood*, landing with her plasma cannon run out for use.

22

Biruta

"Easy, easy . . ." echoed Leon's voice through the fort's super-structure. Heavy masses of metal chinged, then clanged loudly together—the trunnions of a 15-cm plasma cannon dropping into the cheek pieces. "Lock 'em down!"

"Look at this," Ricimer murmured to Gregg in the control room below—and to Guillermo; at any rate, the Molt was present. Ricimer slowly turned a dial, increasing the magnification of the image in the holographic screen. "Just look at the resolution."

"Boardman, use the twenty-*four*-millimeter end, not the twenty-two!" Leon shouted. "D'ye have shit for brains?"

The bosun's twenty-man crew was completing the mounting of the fort's armament. The heavy plasma cannon had been delivered by a previous Earth Convoy. In three days, the Venerians had accomplished a job that Federation personnel on Biruta hadn't gotten around to in at least a year.

On the other hand, the Feds in their heart of hearts didn't expect to need the fort. The Venerians did.

"This is what we'll have on Venus soon," Ricimer said. "This is what all humanity will have, now that we have the stars again."

The five Venerian ships—the *Grandcamp* had vanished after the first series of transits, and only an optimist believed that she or her crew would ever be seen again—clustered together near the buildings at the north end of the island. Men were busy refitting the battered vessels for the long voyage back to Venus. They used Federation equipment as well as that carried by the argosy.

"All right," Leon ordered. "You four, torque her down tight. Loong, you and your lot are dismissed. Take the shearlegs and tackle back to the *Tolliver* with you. Anders, you're in charge here until you're relieved."

Ricimer had focused on the *Rose,* eight hundred meters across the island. At the present magnification, Gregg could identify some of the crewmen fitting new thruster nozzles beneath the vessel. The holds gaped open above them, letting the sea breeze flow through the vessel.

"We could see right into the ship if the light was a little better," Gregg agreed.

Guillermo said, "The third control from the right." His three jointed fingers together indicated the rotary switch he meant. "Up will increase light levels above ambient."

Ricimer touched the control, then rolled it upward. The edges of the display whited out with overload. Shadowed areas congealed into clarity beneath the ship, within the holds, and even through the open gunports.

"You've seen this sort of equipment before?" Ricimer asked.

The Molt flicked his fingers behind his palms in the equivalent of a shrug. "It's a standard design," he said. "My memory—"

"Memory" was a more or less satisfactory description of what amounted to genetic encoding.

"—includes identical designs."

"They'd have to be," Gregg realized aloud. "It's not as though the Feds built this. Their Molts did."

The huge advantage the North American Federation had over other states was its possession of planets whose automated factories had continued to produce microchips for years or even centuries after the Collapse. When the factories finally broke down, they left behind dispersed stockpiles of circuitry whose quality and miniaturization were beyond the capacity of the present age.

Fed electronics were not so much better than those of the Venerians as greatly more common. But Fed electronics were better also . . .

"Once Venus has its trade in hand," Ricimer said, "we'll do it properly. The Federation goes by rote—"

He nodded to Guillermo. Leon, muttering about the lazy frogspawn crewing some vessels he could name, clomped down the ladder serving the gun stations on the roof.

"—only doing what was done a thousand years ago. We'll build from where mankind was before the Rebellion—new ways through the Mirror, new planets with new products. Not just the same old ways."

"Old ways is right," Leon said as he entered the control room. "Those guns we mounted, they're alike as so many peas. Men didn't make them, Molts and machines did. The Feds just sit on their butts and let the work do itself—like people did before the Collapse."

Guillermo looked at the bosun. "Is work by itself good?" the Molt asked. "How can it matter whether you pull a rope or I pull a rope or a winch pulls the rope—so long as the rope is pulled?"

"Centralized production is sure enough *bad*," Leon said. "That's what caused the Collapse, after all. That and people having too much time to spend on politics, since they didn't do anything real."

"It's more than that," Piet Ricimer added. "Machines can't create. They'll make the same thing each time—whether it's a nozzle or a flashgun barrel or a birdbath. When my father or even one of his apprentices makes an item, it has . . ."

He smiled wryly to wipe the hint of blasphemy away from what he was about to say. "A *man's* work has what would be a soul, if the work were a man rather than a thing."

Guillermo's head moved from Leon to Ricimer, as if the neck were clicking between detents. "And my race has no soul," the Molt said. The words were too flat to be a question.

"If you do have souls," Ricimer replied after a moment's hesitation, "then in selling your fellows as merchandise, we're committing an unspeakable sin, Guillermo."

Man and Molt looked at one another in silence. The alien's face was impassive by virtue of its exoskeletal construction. Piet Ricimer's expression gave up equally little information.

Guillermo cocked his head in a gesture of amusement. "Things are things, Captain," he said. "But I'll admit that the number of things may be less important than how you use the things you have. And your Venus clan uses things very well."

The *Tolliver's* siren began to wind.

"Damn the timing!" Gregg snarled. "Leon, did the men from the *Tolliver* leave in the truck?"

The bosun pursed his lips and nodded.

"All right," Gregg decided aloud. "Piet, I'll run across to the flagship and find out what's going on. You can—"

Ricimer smiled. "I think we can learn what's happening more easily than that, Stephen," he said.

As he spoke, he tapped pairs of numbers into a keypad on the console. Each touch switched the holographic display, either to a lustrous void or an image:

An office in the island's administrative complex, where half a dozen Venerians had put down their playing cards when the siren blew;

A panorama from a camera placed a hundred meters above the empty sea;

Another office, this one empty save for a chair over which was draped the uniform jacket of a Federation officer.

"Seventeen," Guillermo suggested, pointing.

Ricimer keyed in one-seven. The screen split, with Alexi Mostert on the left half, saying to the Federation officer on the right side, "Yes, your Administrator Carstensen, if he's in charge! And don't even *think* of trying to land without my permission!"

"I thought," Gregg said softly, "that we might manage to get away before the Earth Convoy arrived."

"It's no problem, sir," Leon said in mild surprise. "If they try to land, we'll rip 'em up the jacksies while they're braking. It's suicide for ships to attack plasma batteries on the surface."

"That's not the whole question, Leon," Piet Ricimer said. The right half of the screen had gone blank. On the left, Mostert was in profile as he spoke with subordinates. The Federation communications equipment completely muted all sound not directed toward it, so Mostert's lips moved silently.

The right side of the screen solidified into an image again. This time it was a heavy-jowled man in his fifties, wearing Federation court dress. He looked angry enough to chew nails. For the moment, he too was talking to someone outside the range of the pickup.

"Federation ships with Fed crews, they'll be in much worse shape than ours were," Ricimer continued in a bare whisper. "If we don't let them land, at least half of them will be lost . . . and that will mean war between Venus and the Federation."

"I'll fight a war if that's what they want, Mr. Ricimer," Leon said. He didn't raise his voice, but there was challenge in the set of his chin.

Gregg smiled tightly and squeezed the bosun's biceps in a friendly grip. "We'll all do what we have to, Leon," he said. "But war's bad for trade."

The Federation leader faced front. "I'm Henry Carstensen, Administrator of the Outer Ways by order of President Pleyal and the Federation Parliament," he said. "You wanted me and I'm here. Speak."

The crispness of both the visual and audio portions of the transmission were striking to men used to Venerian commo. There was no sign that Federation AIs made a better job of the complex equations governing transit, though . . .

"First, Your Excellency," Alexi Mostert said unctuously, "I want to apologize for this little awkward—"

"Stop your nonsense," Carstensen snapped. "You're holding a Federation port against Federation vessels. Is it war, then, between Venus and Earth—or are you a pirate, operating against the will of Governor Halys?"

"Neither, Excellency," Mostert said. "If I can explain—"

"I'm not interested in explanations!" Carstensen said. "I have ships in immediate need of landing. If one of them is lost, if one *crewman* dies, then the only thing that will prevent the forces of Earth from *devastating* your planet is your head on a platter, Mostert. Do you understand? My ships must be allowed to land *now*."

The Venerian commander bent his head and pressed his fingertips firmly against his forehead.

"Cousin Alexi's going at it the wrong way," Ricimer said dispassionately. "With a man like Carstensen, you negotiate from strength or you don't negotiate at all."

"I'll see how they're coming on the fourth gun," Leon said abruptly. He bolted from the control room.

Mostert lifted his head. "Then listen," he said. "These are the terms on which I—"

"You have no right to set terms!" Carstensen shouted.

"Don't talk to me about rights, mister!" said Alexi Mostert. "I've got enough firepower to scour every Federation platform off the surface of this world. I can fry your ships even if you stay in orbit. If you try to come down there won't be bits big enough to splash when they finally hit the water. These are my terms! Are you ready to listen?"

"Much better, cousin," Piet Ricimer murmured.

Administrator Carstensen lifted his chin in acceptance.

"Your eight ships will be allowed to land," Mostert said. "Their guns will be shuttered. As soon as they're on the ground, the crews will be transported to outlying platforms. There will be no Federation personnel on Island Able until my argosy has finished refitting and left."

"That's impractical," Carstensen said.

"These are my terms!"

"I understand that," Carstensen said calmly. It was as though the Federation official who started the negotiation had been replaced by a wholly different man. "But some of my vessels are in very bad shape. They need immediate repairs or there'll be major fires and probably a powerplant explosion. I need to keep maintenance personnel and a few officers aboard to avoid disaster."

The Venerian commander's lips sucked in and out as he thought. "All right," he said. "But in that case I'll need liaison officers from you. Six of them. They'll be entertained in comfort for the few remaining days that my ships need to complete their refit."

Carstensen sniffed. "Hostages, you mean. Well, as you've pointed out, *Admiral* Mostert, you're holding a gun to the heads of nearly a thousand innocent men and women as it is. I accept your conditions."

Mostert licked at the dryness of his lips. "Very well," he said. "Do you swear by God and your hope of salvation to keep these terms, sir?"

"I swear," Carstensen said in the same cool tones which had characterized his latter half of the negotiations.

Carstensen stood up. His console's pickup lengthened its viewing field automatically. The administrator was surprisingly tall, a big man rather than simply a broad one. "And I swear also, Admiral," he said, "that when President Pleyal hears of this, then your Governor Halys will hear; and you will hear of it again yourself."

The convoy's side of the screen went blank.

"I'm not worried," Mostert said to the pearl emptiness. His side of the transmission blanked out as well.

Piet Ricimer turned to Gregg with an unreadable smile. "What do you think, Stephen?" he asked.

"I think if your cousin isn't worried," Gregg replied, "then he's a very stupid man."

23

Biruta

"Slow down," Gregg said to Tancred, who was driving the guards back from the fort at the end of their watch. He peered into the darkness behind the brilliant cone of the truck's ceramic headlamps and the softer, yellower gleam of lights from the Federation vessels. "That looks like—stop, it's Mr. Ricimer."

Tancred brought the vehicle to a squealing halt. "Christ's blood!" he said. "I don't care what oaths those Feds swore. This is no safe place for one of our people alone."

The Earth Convoy lay across the center of Island Able. The straggling line was as close a group as the vessels' condition and their pilots' skill permitted. The Feds were well separated from the five Venerian ships at the north end of the island, but the metal-built vessels controlled the route between there and the fort on the western corner.

Changing the guard at the fort required driving through the midst of the Federation fleet. That didn't feel a bit comfortable, even for twenty armed men in a vehicle; and as Tancred said, it was no place for a Venerian on foot.

"He's not alone," Gregg said, clutching the flashgun closer to his breastplate so that it wouldn't clack against the cab frame as he got down. "He's with me. Leon?" he added to the men in amorphous shadow in the truck bed. "You're in charge till we get back."

Ignoring the crewmen's protests, Gregg jumped to the shingle and crunched toward his friend. After a moment, the truck drove on.

The sea breeze sighed. It was surprisingly peaceful when the truck engine had whined itself downwind, toward the administrative complex and Venerian ships. Work proceeded round the clock on several Federation ships, but the uniformly open horizon absorbed sound better than anechoic paneling.

"What in the name of heaven do you think you're doing here, Piet?" Gregg demanded softly. "Trying to be the spark that turns this business into a shooting war?"

"I'm just looking at things, Stephen," Ricimer answered. "But not for trouble, no."

Though Gregg thought at first that his friend was a deliberate provocation, standing in the very middle of the ragged Federation line, he realized that except for the moment Ricimer was swept by the truck's headlights he was well shielded by darkness. The young captain wasn't going to be noticed and attacked by a squad of Federation engine fitters who objected to his presence.

"It's a good place to find trouble anyway," Gregg grumbled. "Look, let's get back to where we belong."

"Listen," Ricimer said. A large airboat approached low over the sea with a throb of ducted fans. A landing officer used a hand strobe to guide the vehicle down beside the Federation flagship three hundred meters from Gregg and Ricimer. It landed on the south side of the vessel so that the latter's 800-tonne bulk was between the airboat and the Venerian ships.

"Well, they've been bringing in supplies," Gregg said. "Taking cargo off too, I shouldn't wonder."

"*Listen,*" Ricimer repeated more sharply.

Gregg heard voices on the breeze. They were too low to be intelligible, and from the timbre the speakers had nothing important to say anyway.

But there were a lot of them. Several score of men, very likely. And they had disembarked on the north side of the airboat so that *it* blocked the view from the Venerians and the night vision equipment in the fort.

"Oh," Gregg said. "I see."

"Boats came in the same way last night," Ricimer explained. "Three loads. I thought I ought to be sure before I—told my cousin something that he's not going to want to hear."

Gregg grimaced in the darkness. "Let's get on back," he said. "Look, we leave tomorrow morning. It'll be all right."

Ricimer nodded or shrugged, the gesture uncertain in the darkness. "We'd best get back," he agreed.

"No, the admiral's still up in his cabin," said the steward who'd turned angrily from the midst of banquet preparations. The man calmed instantly when he saw that two officers and not a fellow crewman had interrupted him. "Captain Fedders is in with him and some others."

Level Four, the higher of the *Tolliver*'s two gun decks, was bustling chaos. The flagship was pierced for fifty guns and carried twenty on the present voyage. The eight on this level were run out of their ports to provide more deck space for banquet tables. Officers' servants from the three larger vessels combined on the flagship to prepare and present the celebratory dinner.

The *Tolliver*'s vertical core was taken up by tanks of air and reaction mass. The remaining space, even when undivided as now on Level Four, wasn't really suitable for a large gathering, but it was the best available aboard the ships themselves.

Fed structures on Island Able provided minimal shelter for low-ranking service personnel. No buildings could be solid enough to survive the crash of a starship, so all comfortable facilities were on artificial platforms at a distance from the island. The barracks, the only large building in the administrative complex, was a flimsy barn with no kitchen. It smelled as much of its previous Molt occupants as the holds of the Venerian vessels did.

Guests—the officers and gentlemen from the other vessels— had already drifted to the flagship's banquet area, getting in the way of the men who were trying to prepare it.

The ships had been repaired to the degree possible outside a major dockyard. The only people on duty were the stewards, a port watch on each vessel, and the guard detachment in the fort—supplied by the *Tolliver* for this final night on Biruta.

In the morning the argosy would lift for Venus, carrying cargo of enough value to make every officer rich, and every crewman popular for three days or a week, until he'd spent or been robbed of his share. The investors, Gregg of Weyston among them, would have their stakes returned tenfold. Even assuming the *Grandcamp* had come apart in the strain of forcing her way between bubble universes as the energy gradients separating them rose, the voyage had been a stunning success.

Gregg followed Piet Ricimer up the companionway to the bridge on Level Six. Behind them, coming from barracks in the administrative complex, were Administrator Carstensen's six hostages and the Venerian gentlemen watching over them. Mostert had invited the "liaison officers" to the banquet, although it had become obvious by the second day that the Feds were not nearly of the rank their titles and uniforms claimed.

Alexi Mostert, wearing trousers of red plush but still holding the matching jacket in his hand, stood in the doorway of his cabin, partitioned off from the bridge proper, and shouted, "God grind your bones to *dust*, Fedders! Don't you know an order when you hear one?"

Three officers of the flagship, Mostert's personal servant, and Fedders of the *Rose* were part of the tableau surrounding the admiral. Two crewmen, detailed to the port watch while their fellows partied on a lesser scale than their leaders, listened from behind one of the pair of plasma cannon mounted vertically in the bow.

"Don't you know danger when you see it, Mostert?" Fedders shouted back. "I tell you, they're cutting gunports in the side of the big freighter facing us. What d'ye think they're planning to do from them? Wave us goodbye?"

Unlike the other officers on the bridge, Fedders wore shipboard clothing of synthetic canvas and carried a ceramic helmet instead of dress headgear. The fact that Fedders was fully clothed and had forced himself on Mostert while changing was an implicit threat that made the admiral certain to explode, but the discussion probably would have gone wrong anyway.

Mostert clutched his tunic with both hands. The hair on the admiral's chest was white though his hair and beard were generally brown. For an instant, Gregg thought from the way Mostert's pectoral muscles bunched that he was going to rip the garment across.

Instead he deliberately unclenched his hands and said, "All right, Fedders, I'll put a special watch on what our Terran friends are doing. You. Report to your ship immediately and don't leave her again until we land in Betaport."

"Punishing me isn't going to stop the Feds from blasting the hell out of us as we lift, Mostert!" Fedders said. "What we need to do is take over their ships right now and put every damned soul of them off the island before it's too late!"

"He's right, Admiral," Piet Ricimer said, careful to stay a non-threatening distance from Mostert.

"Christ bugger you both for fools!" Mostert bellowed. He tugged at the tunic, unable to tear the fabric but pulling it all out of shape or the possibility of wearing. "Both of you! To your ships! *Now,* or God blind me if I don't have you shot for treason!"

Galliard, the *Tolliver's* navigator, was a friend of Fedders'. He took the *Rose's* captain by the elbows and half guided, half pushed him toward the companionway.

"Sir," said Ricimer, "blasphemy now is—"

"You canting preacher!" Mostert said. "I've enough chaplains aboard already. Get to your ship—and see if you can find some courage along the way!"

Ricimer's face went white.

Gregg set his flashgun down to balance on its broad muzzle. He stepped deliberately between his friend and Mostert. "Admiral Mostert," he said in a voice pared to the bone by anger. "If a man were to address me in that fashion, I would demand that he meet me in the field so that I might recover my honor."

The cold fury in the gentleman's voice slapped Mostert out of his own state. The admiral wasn't afraid of Gregg, but neither was he a mere spacer with money. There was no profit in making Gregg of Weyston's nephew an enemy.

"I assure you, Mr. Gregg," he said, "that no part of my comments were directed at you."

"Come away, Stephen," Ricimer said, drawing Gregg around to break his eye contact with Admiral Mostert.

"The *Tolliver* will lift last of the argosy," Mostert said in a gruffly reasonable voice. "We'll have our guns run out. At the least hint of trouble we'll clear the island!"

Ricimer picked up the flashgun by its butt. Gregg reached for it numbly but his friend twitched the weapon to his side.

"We've gotten this far without having trouble that the Governor, that Governor Halys can't forgive," Mostert said. He sounded wistful, almost desperate. "We're not going to start a war now!"

"You'll need to change for the banquet," Ricimer said as he directed Gregg down the companionway ahead of him. "The *Peaches* should have some representative there, after all."

24

Biruta

"To the further expansion of trade across the universe!" Alexi Mostert called from the head table. He raised the glass in his right hand. That was the only part of the admiral which Gregg could see from where he sat, a third of the way around the curve of the deck.

"Expansion of trade," murmured the gathered officers and gentlemen in a slurred attempt at unison. The night's heavy drinking hadn't begun. A combination of relief at going home and fear of another series of transits like the set which had devoured the *Grandcamp* had given some of those present a head start on the festivities, however.

The banquet was served on rectangular tables, each of which cut an arc of the circular deck space. The sixty or so diners sat on the hull side, while stewards served them from the inner curve. The *Tolliver*'s galley was on Level Three, and the two companionways were built into the vessel's central core.

The hostages were spaced out among the Venerians. The older man beside Mostert, supposedly the deputy commander of a Fed warship but probably a clerk of some sort, looked gloomy. The female Gregg could see on almost the opposite side of Level Four was terrified and slobberingly drunk. To Gregg's immediate left sat a man named Tilbury, younger than Gregg himself. He was keyed to such a bright-eyed pitch that Gregg wondered if he was using some drug other than alcohol.

Well, perhaps the hostages thought they would be slaughtered when the argosy left—or as bad from their viewpoint, carried off to the sulphurous caves of Venus.

"Sir," said a steward. "*Sir.*" To get Gregg's attention, the fellow leaned across the remains of a savory prepared from canned fruit. "There's an urgent call for you on the bridge. From your ship."

Walking would feel good. Gregg was muzzy from the meal, more drink than normal, and reaction to the scene on the bridge two hours before. He still trembled when he thought about that . . .

"All right," he muttered, and slid his chair back. The breech of a 20-cm plasma cannon blocked his path to the right. Even run out, the heavy weapons took up a great deal of space. He could go to his left and maybe creep between the corners of two tables, but that would be tight. Tilbury looked ready to explode if awakened from his glittering dreamworld to move.

Gregg ducked under the table. He knocked his head by rising too quickly and found himself on the other side with something greasy smeared on the knees of his dress trousers. They were gray-green silk shot with silver filaments, and they'd be the very devil to clean.

Cursing his stupidity, not the call that summoned him, Gregg strode to the companionway and climbed the helical stairs three treads at a time.

The bridge felt shockingly comfortable. The petty officer and two crewmen on watch had opened the horizontal gunports. The mild cross-breeze made Gregg realize how hot and crowded Level Four was.

"Here you go, sir," the petty officer said as he gave Gregg the handset. It would have been nice if they could have stripped the Federation communications system out of the port buildings . . . but this was a trading voyage.

"Go ahead," Gregg said into the handset. At least it was a dual frequency unit, so the two carrier waves didn't step on one another if the parties spoke simultaneously.

"Stephen," said Piet Ricimer's crackling voice, "I don't think the Feds are going to wait till tomorrow. Their three warships are clearing their gunports, and airboats have been ferrying more men onto the island all night."

Gregg moved to an open gunport within the five-meter length of the handset's flex. He peered out. The circular port looked south. He couldn't see the *Peaches,* but the Federation convoy bulked across the night sky like a herd of sleeping monsters.

"What do you . . ." Gregg said. He shook his head, wishing that he could think more clearly. The bridge watch watched him covertly. " . . . want me to do?"

Biruta's moon was a jagged chunk of rock. Even full, as now, it did little to illuminate the landscape. The silhouettes of Federation ships were speckled by light. The Feds were opening, then closing their gunports to be sure that the shutters wouldn't jam when the order came to run the guns out for use.

"Stephen," Ricimer said tautly, "you've *got* to convince Mostert to take some action immediately. I know what I'm asking, but there's no choice."

"Right," said Gregg. He put down the handset and glanced around for the petty officer.

He didn't know the man's name. "You," he said, pointing. "Sound the general alarm now. *Now!*"

"What?" said the petty officer. One of the crewmen threw a large knife-switch attached to a stanchion. The flagship's siren began slowly to wind.

A plasma cannon fired from one of the Federation vessels.

Gregg was fully alert and alive. "Get those guns slewed!" he cried as he jumped into the companionway. With his right hand on the rail, he took the fifteen steps in three huge, spiraling jumps and burst out onto the banquet room again.

Men were looking up, alarmed by the siren and drawn to the electric *crashTHUMP* of the plasma discharge.

"We're being attacked!" Gregg shouted. "Get to your—"

Tilbury rose from his seat, looking toward Admiral Mostert as though the two of them were the only people in all the universe. The Federation hostage lifted the short-barreled shotgun which had been strapped to his right calf.

Gregg dived over the table at him. As he did so, three guns salvoed from the *Rose*, lighting the night with their iridescence. The metal hull of the Federation flagship bloomed with white fireballs which merged into a three-headed monster.

Gregg hit Tilbury. The shotgun fired into the ceiling. Lead pellets splashed from the hard ceramic.

Gregg slammed the smaller Terran into the bulkhead hard enough to crush ribs, but he couldn't wrest away Tilbury's shotgun as they wrestled on the deck in a welter of food and broken crockery. Tilbury giggled wildly.

Gregg suddenly realized that the weapon was a single-shot. He released it, gripped Tilbury's short hair, and used the strength of both arms to slam the hostage's head against the deck until the victim went limp.

Something crashed dazzlingly into the *Tolliver*. A portion of the hull shattered. The rainbow light was so intense that it flared through the gunports open to the east, south, and west together. Gregg couldn't tell where they'd been hit.

"Stand clear!" somebody roared as he switched on the gunnery controls for the weapon Gregg sprawled under.

Gregg jumped to his feet. There was already a crush of men at the nearer companionway. Gregg fought into them. He was bigger than most, and adrenaline had already brought his instincts to full, murderous life.

A 20-cm gun, *beside* the one whose captain had given a warning, fired at the Fed convoy. The cannon recoiled, pistoning the air in a searing flash.

Under normal circumstances, plasma cannon were fired by crews wearing hard suits, in sections of the vessel partitioned off to protect nonarmored personnel from the weapons' ravening violence. There was neither time nor inclination to rig the ship for battle now.

The blast knocked down the men nearest to the gun. Ribbons and the gauze ornaments of their clothing smoldered. The other south-facing cannon fired also. Three Fed bolts raked the *Tolliver*. A red-hot spark shot up the center of the companionway.

By the time Gregg reached Level Three, there was only one officer ahead of him. That fellow stumbled midway down the next winding flight, and Gregg jumped his cursing form.

The *Tolliver*'s crewmen were running forward the Level Two plasma cannon; the shutters had already been raised for ventilation. The internal lights had gone off. A glowing hole in the outer hull showed where a Federation bolt had gotten home. The air stank of insulation, ionized gases, and burning flesh.

Gregg dropped into the hold and ran down the ramp. His hard suit and flashgun were on the featherboat. In his urge to get to familiar equipment and his friends, he hadn't thought about arming himself aboard the flagship. Now he felt naked.

Plasma spurted from the flank of a 100-tonne Federation warship. There were four bolts, but they were light ones. Two struck the *Rose*, throwing up sparks of white-hot ceramic slivers. The

Delight bucked, then collapsed into separate bow and stern fragments with only glowing slag between them.

The *Hawkwood,* lying slightly to the north of all the Venerian ships save the *Peaches,* had not been hit by the cannonading thus far. Five 10-cm plasma cannon along her starboard side volleyed. The bolts converged squarely amidships of the spherical Federation flagship. White-hot metal erupted as if from a horizontal volcano.

For several seconds, steam from blown reaction-mass tanks wreathed the vessel. The vapor was so hot that it didn't cool to visibility until it was several meters beyond the hull. A secondary explosion, either a store of plasma shells or compressed flammables, spewed fire suddenly from every port and hatchway on the huge vessel.

Gregg was running toward the *Peaches.* The concussion knocked him down. He looked over his shoulder. The Federation warship's thick hull gleamed yellow as it lost strength and slumped toward the shingle.

Gregg scrambled forward, dabbing his hands down before he got his feet properly under him. Carstensen's disintegrating flagship threw a soft radiance across the island. Most of the plasma cannon on both sides had fired and were cooling before they could be reloaded. Twin shocks from the *Tolliver* indicated the guns on the lower level had been brought into action.

Gravel spat from beneath the *Peaches;* Ricimer had lighted the thrusters. A pebble stung Gregg's thigh. "Wait for me!" he screamed. He could barely hear his own voice over the roar of the incandescent Federation flagship.

A handheld spotlight spiked Gregg from the featherboat's hatch. It blinded him, so he didn't see the rope flung to him until it slapped him in the face. "Quick! Quick!" a voice warned faintly.

Gregg braced his boot against the curve of the hull and began to pull himself upward, hand over hand. As he did so, the thrusters fired at mid-output. The *Peaches* lifted a meter and began to swing.

Two of the fort's plasma cannon fired simultaneously. A large airboat approaching from the west blew apart only a few meters above the sea, showering the surface with debris, bodies, and blazing kerosene. A second airboat, slanting down parallel to the first, ground to a halt beside the fort.

Federation soldiers, humans and Molts together, jumped out of the vehicle. Rifles flashed and spat, mostly aimed at the Venerian defenders. More Federation troops spilled from nearby cargo vessels and ran toward the fort.

Gregg flopped over the hatch coaming and into the featherboat's bay like a fish being landed. Internal lights were on, but his retinas were too stunned by plasma discharges for him to be able to see more than shadows and the purple blotches across his retinas.

"Give me my flashgun!" he cried as he tried to stand up. "And a helmet, Christ's blood!"

The *Peaches'* bow gun fired, jolting the hovering featherboat into a wild yaw. Somebody lowered a helmet onto Gregg's head, visor down. Leon said, "Here you go, Mr. Gregg," and pressed the familiar angles of a flashgun into his hands.

"Ammo!" Gregg demanded as he jumped on top of the storage locker to aim out the hatch. Even as he spoke, he realized that Leon had slung a bandolier heavy with charged batteries over the laser's receiver.

Bullets or gravel spit by other thrusters clicked against the featherboat's hull. The *Rose* was under way, swinging to bring her portside guns to bear on the Federation convoy.

Three bolts from Fed ships punched the *Rose* as she slowly rotated. Sections of ceramic hull blew out in bright showers. The third hit doused internal lighting over the forward half of the vessel. Then her six-gun port battery cut loose in a volley timed to half-second intervals.

During the truce, the Feds had mounted guns in their largest ship, a cylindrical cargo hauler of 1,000 tonnes. It was the vessel closest to the Venerian ships and its fire had been galling. Now the freighter's hull plating, thinner than that of a warship, vaporized under the point-blank salvo. The last of the six bolts blew through the ship's far side. Flame-shot gases gushed from both bow and stern.

The *Tolliver* and three surviving ships of the Earth Convoy settled into a series of punch and counterpunch. Individual bolts from the Venerian flagship's heavy guns were answered by double or triple discharges from lighter Federation weapons.

A yellow-orange spot on the hull of a Fed warship indicated where a plasma cannon had been run out again after being fired. The barrel, stellite rather than ceramic in normal Terran usage, still glowed from the previous discharge. Gregg used it as his aiming point and fired.

His flashgun couldn't damage the vessel's hull, but the laser bolt might snap through the open port. Even better, a bolt that passed down the cannon's bore would detonate the shell out of sequence, turning it into a miniature fusion bomb instead of a directed-energy weapon. That would require amazing luck under the present conditions—

But the Venerian argosy was going to need amazing luck if any of them were to survive this treacherous attack.

The *Tolliver*'s bow guns fired. Scratch crews had pivoted the weapons from vertical to horizontal gunports.

Each hit on a Fed hull belched gouts of flaming metal, but the ships continued to work their guns. Bubbles of glowing vapor flashed through the interior of the vessels. Even with partitions rigged within the compartments to limit blast effects, Terran casualties must have been horrendous.

Federation troops rushed from the two freighters toward the *Tolliver*. Harsh shadows from plasma weapons confused their numbers: there may have been a few score, there may have been over a hundred. Some were Molts, angular and thin-limbed.

Gregg fired, trying to keep his aim low. The flashgun wasn't a particularly good weapon against troops well spaced across an empty plain. A laser bolt striking in front of the ragged line would spray gravel across the attackers. That provided some hope of casualties and considerable psychological effect.

Ricimer slewed the *Peaches* eastward, keeping the featherboat's bow toward the hostile vessels. Gregg wondered if his friend was taking them out of the battle. A single plasma bolt could gut the featherboat. All that had saved them thus far was being some distance from the fighting and therefore ignored by Federation cannoneers.

Gregg fired again. Tancred was beside him with a repeater, a better choice for the task. Rifles and a flashgun flashed from the *Tolliver*'s holds where crewmen prepared to meet the Federation attack. The Venerians were badly outnumbered.

The *Peaches*' bow gun fired. Ricimer had swung the featherboat to a position that enfiladed the line of Federation troops. The plasma bolt flashed the length of the attackers, killing half a dozen of them outright and throwing the survivors back in panic. Burning bodies and the sparks of detonating ammunition littered the shingle.

One rifleman—a Molt—stood silhouetted against the blazing

freighter and aimed at the featherboat. The alien soldier was almost four hundred meters away. Gregg aimed as if the boat quivering beneath him were the bedrock solidity of a target range.

The Molt fired and missed. Gregg's laser lighted the Molt's instantaneous death. The creature's torso exploded as its body fluids flashed to steam.

Why had it fought to preserve Federation claims?

Why did anybody fight for anything?

The fort's heavy guns fired in pairs. The *Rose* flared like the filament of a lightbulb. Because the Venerian ship had risen to fifty meters, her underside was exposed. One bolt shattered half her forward thrusters.

Captain Fedders and the *Rose*'s AI tried to keep control. A quick switch of the angle of the surviving thruster nozzles kept the ship from augering in under power, but nothing could prevent a crash.

The *Rose* nosed into the shingle at a walking pace, yawing to port as she did so. Fragments of ceramic stressed beyond several strength moduli flew about in razor-edged profusion, far more dangerous than the spray of gravel gouged from the ground. The stern of the vessel came to rest in fairly complete condition, but the bow disintegrated into shards of a few square meters or less.

Light winked toward the *Peaches* from a port open onto the flagship's bridge. For a moment Gregg thought someone had mistaken them for a Fed vessel; then he realized that Mostert or one of his men was using a handheld talk-between-ships unit to communicate with the featherboat. The TBS used a modulated laser beam which wasn't affected by plasma cannon and thrusters radiating across all the radio bands.

Ricimer brought the *Peaches* in tight behind the *Tolliver*. The *Hawkwood* was already there. A line of men transferred crates and bales of goods from the flagship's holds to the lighter vessel.

The guns of the recaptured fort hammered the *Tolliver*. The plasma bolts blew pieces of the west-facing hull high above the vessel, glittering in the light of burning ships. Gregg grunted as though he'd been struck by medicine balls, even though the flagship's mass was between him and the bolts' impact.

The featherboat grounded hard. Gregg didn't have any targets because they were behind the *Tolliver*. He felt as though he'd come to shelter after a terrible storm. His bandolier was empty. He was sure there had been six spare batteries in it at first, and he didn't remember firing that many rounds.

His laser's ceramic barrel glowed dull red.

Crewmen in one of the *Tolliver*'s holds extended a boarding bridge to the featherboat. The end clanged down in front of Gregg. Tancred and Dole clamped it to the coaming. Gregg moved back, out of the way. He stumbled off the closed locker and into the vessel's bay.

Guillermo caught him; the Molt's hard-surfaced grip was unmistakable. Gregg was blind until he remembered to raise his helmet's visor. The featherboat's interior was a reeking side-corridor of Hell.

Forward, the plasma cannon's barrel threw a soft light that silhouetted the figures of the armored crewmen who were about to load a third round. The bore must still be dangerously hot, but needs must when the Devil drives.

Piet Ricimer got up from the main console. "Stephen, you're all right?" he called.

The seats before the attitude-control boards weren't occupied. Guillermo and Lightbody had run them until the *Peaches* grounded. Now Lightbody caught and stowed bales of cargo that the men at the hatch swung down to him.

"We're going to take aboard men and valuables from the *Tolliver*," Ricimer said. "She's lost, she can't lift with—"

A drumroll interrupted him. It started with a further exchange by plasma cannon and ended in the cataclysmic destruction of another Federation vessel. Light from plasma bolts reflected through the *Tolliver*'s interior and brightened the image of the flagship's holds on the viewscreen behind Ricimer.

"We're all lost," Gregg said. Ionized air had stripped the mucus from his throat. He wasn't sure he had any voice left.

"No!" Piet Ricimer cried. Perhaps he'd read Gregg's lips. "We're not lost and we're not quitting!"

Gregg pawed at a bandolier hanging from a hook. Its pockets were filled with rifle cartridges, but the satchel beneath it held more flashgun batteries. He lifted the satchel free, only vaguely aware that the bandolier dropped into the litter on the deck when he did so.

"Who said quitting?" he muttered through cracked lips.

25

Biruta

If it had been Mostert's ships against the Earth Convoy alone, the Venerians would have ruled Island Able at the end of the fight. Better crews, heavier guns, and the refractory ceramic hulls made the argosy far superior even to Carstensen's warships. The thin-skinned freighters were little better than targets. All of them were gapped and blazing by now.

But possession of the fort was decisive. Its meters-thick walls could withstand the *Tolliver*'s heavy plasma cannon, and the separately-mounted guns could be destroyed only one at a time by direct hits. The only way to take the fort was as the Feds had done, by a sudden infantry assault that ignored casualties. The Venerians had neither the personnel nor a chance of surprise to reverse the situation.

The flagship fired a plasma cannon directly over the *Peaches*. Men transferring cargo screamed as the iridescent light shadowed the bones through their flesh. Tancred wasn't wearing a helmet. He fell into the featherboat, batting at the orange flames licking from his hair.

The concussion threw Gregg forward. His mouth opened, but his bludgeoned mind couldn't find a curse vile enough for the gunner who fired in a direction where there were no hostile targets.

"Look—" Ricimer said/mouthed, and turned from Gregg to point at the viewscreen's fuzzy panorama.

One of the remotely-controlled water buffalo had lifted from the station at the far end of the island. It slid slowly toward the three surviving Venerian ships, only a few meters above the ground.

The *Tolliver* fired another 20-cm plasma cannon at the water buffalo. Though the gunport was next to that of the first weapon, the discharge seemed a pale echo of the unexpected previous bolt. At impact, steam blasted a hundred meters in every direction. Moments later the unmanned vessel emerged from the cloud, spewing water from a second huge gap in its bow plating.

The Federation drone was full of seawater, nearly a hundred tonnes of it. Guns that fired at the water buffalo bow-on, even weapons as powerful as those of the *Tolliver*, could only convert part of that reaction mass to steam. The bolts couldn't reach the thrusters, the only part of the simple vessel that was vulnerable.

The amount of kinetic energy involved in a loaded water buffalo hitting the *Tolliver* would be comparable to that liberated by a nuclear weapon.

Ricimer bent to put his lips to Gregg's ear and shouted, "Stephen, if I bring us alongside, can you hit a nozzle with—"

"Do it!" Gregg said, turning away as soon as he understood. *We'll do what we have to.*

Crewmen cursing and shouting for medical attention hunched beneath the roof hatch. Cargo, more than a dozen cases of valuables transferred from the flagship in the minutes before the gun fired overhead, choked the narrow confines. Gregg bulled his way through, treating people and goods with the same ruthless abandon.

If he didn't do his job, it wouldn't matter how badly his fellows had been injured by the ravening ions. If he did do his job, it might not matter anyway . . .

The featherboat lifted. Guillermo was alone at the attitude controls. Lightbody must have been one of those flayed by the sidescatter of ions. Nevertheless, the *Peaches* spun on her vertical axis with a slow grace that belied her short staffing.

The liftship came on like Juggernaut, moving slowly but with an inexorable majesty. It was already within five hundred meters of the Venerian ships. Plasma cannon clawed at one another to the south, but the gunfire was no longer significant to the outcome.

The *Peaches* pulled away from the flagship. The boarding bridge cracked loose, bits of clamp ricocheting like shrapnel off the featherboat's inner bulkheads. There'd been a few bales of cargo on the walkway, but the crewmen carrying them had either jumped or been flung off when the cannon fired above them.

Gregg aimed, over the barrel of his flashgun rather than through its sights for the moment. He didn't want to focus down too early and miss some crucial aspect of the tableau. He wouldn't get another chance. None of them would get another chance.

The *Peaches* swung into line with the water buffalo. Leon and Jeude fired their plasma cannon, a dart of light through Gregg's filtered visor. The featherboat's bow lit like a display piece. A line of ionized air bound the two vessels. At the point of impact, a section of steel belly plates became blazing gas.

The drone's thrusters were undamaged.

Gregg felt the *Peaches* buck beneath him. His bare hands stung from stripped atoms, but he didn't hear the crash of the discharge. His brain began shutting down extraneous senses. Cotton batting swaddled sound. Objects faded to vague flickers beyond the tunnel connecting him to his target.

"Reloads, Mr. Gregg," said a voice that was almost within Gregg's consciousness. Tancred stood beside him in the hatch. He held a battery vertically in his left hand, three more in his right.

The featherboat was on a nearly converging course with the water buffalo. Neither vessel moved at more than 8 kph.

Did the Feds think they were going to ram? That wouldn't work. The heavily laden drone would carry on, locked with the featherboat, and finish the job by driving the *Hawkwood* into the flagship in a blast that would light a hemisphere of the planet.

Three hundred meters.

Water spurted in great gulps from the drone's bow. The plasma bolts had hit low, so each surge drew a vacuum within the water tank and choked the outflow until air forced its way through the holes.

Two hundred meters. Ricimer's course was nearly a reciprocal of his target's.

The water buffalo sailed on a cloud of plasma from which flew pebbles the thrusters kicked up. The nozzles were white glows within the rainbow ambience of their exhaust.

The Fed controller kept his clumsy vessel within a few meters of the ground. He was very good, but as the *Peaches* closed he tried to lower the water buffalo still further.

One hundred meters. At this pace, the featherboat would slide ahead of the drone by the thickness of the rust on the steel plating. They would pass starboard-to-starboard.

The water buffalo grazed the shingle, then lifted upward on a surge of reflected thrust. Its eight nozzles were clear ovals with hearts of consuming radiance.

Gregg fired. He was aware both of the contacts closing within the flashgun's trigger mechanism and of the jolt to his shoulder as the weapon released.

The laser bolt touched the rim of the second nozzle back on the starboard side. The asymmetric heating of metal already stressed to its thermal limits blew the nozzle apart.

There was no sound.

Gregg's fingers unlatched the flashgun's butt, flicked out the discharged battery, and snapped in the fresh load. He didn't bother to look at what he was doing. He knew where everything in the necessary universe was.

Tancred shifted another battery into the ready position in his left hand.

The drone's bow dropped, both from loss of the thruster and because the vessel had risen high enough to lose ground effect. It was beginning to slew to starboard.

Fifty meters.

Only the leading nozzles were visible, white dashes alternately rippled and clear as water gushed over the bow just ahead of them. The drone was a curved steel wall, crushing forward relentlessly.

There was no sound or movement. The rim of the starboard nozzle was a line only a centimeter thick at this angle. The sight posts centered on it.

Trigger contacts closed.

The universe rang with light so intense it was palpable. Gunners in the fort had tried desperately to hit the featherboat but not the drone almost in line with it. They missed both, but the jet of plasma ripped less than the height of a man's head above the *Peaches*.

The water buffalo yawed and nosed in, much as the *Rose* had done minutes before. At this altitude, the Fed controller couldn't correct for the failure of both thrusters in the same quadrant.

The roar went on forever. Steam drenched the impact site, but bits of white-hot metal from the disintegrating engines sailed in dazzling arcs above the gray cloud.

Piet Ricimer slammed the featherboat's thrusters to full power. Guillermo at the attitude jets rolled the vessel almost onto her port side. The *Peaches* blasted past to safety as the ruin of the Federation drone crumpled toward her. For a moment, the featherboat was bathed in warm steam that smothered the stench of air burned to plasma.

Gregg didn't lose consciousness. He lay on his back. Someone removed his helmet, but when Lightbody tried to take the flashgun from his hands, Gregg's eyes rotated to track him. Lightbody jumped away.

There were voices. Gregg understood the words, but they didn't touch him.

We're low on reaction mass.

When the cannon's cool enough to reload, we'll choose one of the outlying platforms and top off. They must be down to skeleton crews, with all the force they threw into the attack.

Then?

Then we go back.

Gregg knew that if he moved, he would break into tiny shards; become a pile of sand that would sift down through the crates on which he lay. Hands gentle beneath their calluses rubbed ointment onto his skin. The back of Gregg's neck was raw fire. The pain didn't touch him either.

How is he?

He wasn't hit, but . . . take a look, why don't you, sir? I'll con. Stephen.

"Stephen?"

Everything he had felt for the past ten minutes flooded past the barriers Gregg's brain had set up. His chest arched. He would have screamed except that the convulsion didn't permit him to draw in a breath.

"Oh, God, Piet," he wheezed when the shock left him and the only pain he felt was that of the present moment. "Oh, God."

His fingers relaxed. Lightbody lifted away the flashgun.

"I think," Gregg said carefully, "that you'd better give me more pain blocker."

Piet Ricimer nodded. Without turning his head, Gregg couldn't see which of the crewmen bent and injected something into his right biceps. Turning his head would have hurt too much to be contemplated.

He closed his eyes. Because of where he lay, he couldn't avoid seeing Tancred. The young crewman's body remained in a crouch at the hatchway despite the featherboat's violent maneuvers. The plasma bolt had fused his torso to the coaming.

When the water baked out of Tancred's arms, his contracting muscles drew up as if he were trying to cover his face with his hands. His skeletal grip still held reloads for the laser, but the battery casings had ruptured with the heat.

Tancred's head and neck were gone. Simply gone.

26

Biruta

When the *Peaches* returned to Island Able with full tanks and her bow gun ready, the *Hawkwood* had vanished and the *Tolliver* was a glowing ruin, the southern side shattered by scores of unanswered plasma bolts. By the time the fort's guns rotated to track the featherboat, Piet Ricimer had ducked under the horizon again.

Stephen Gregg was drugged numb for most of the long transit home, but by the time they prepared for landing at Betaport, he could move around the strait cabin again.

He didn't talk much. None of them did.

27

Venus

Stephen Gregg walked along Dock Street with the deliberation of a much older man who fears that he may injure himself irreparably if he falls. Four months of medical treatment had repaired most of the physical damage which the near miss had done, but the mental effects still remained.

You couldn't doubt your own mortality while you remembered the blackened trunk of the man beside you. Gregg would remember *that* for the rest of his life.

The docks area of Betaport was crowded but neither dangerous nor particularly dirty. The community's trade had reached a new high for each year of the past generation. Accommodations were tight, but money and a vibrant air of success infused the community. The despair that led to squalor was absent, and there were nearly as many sailors' hostels as there were bordellos in the area.

On the opposite side of the passage was the port proper, the airlocks through which spacers and their cargoes entered Betaport. The Blue Rose Tavern—its internally-lighted sign was a compass rose, not a flower—nestled between a clothing store/pawnshop and a large ship chandlery with forty meters of corridor frontage. The public bar was packed with spacers and gentlemen's servants.

The ocher fabric of Gregg's garments shifted to gray as the eye traveled down it from shoulders to boots. He was so obviously a gentleman that the bartender's opening was, "Looking for the meeting, sir? That's in the back." He gestured with his thumb.

"Good day to you, Mr. Gregg!" Guillermo called from the doorway. The Molt wore a sash and sabretache of red silk and cloth of gold. His chitinous form blocked the opening, though he didn't precisely guard it. "Good to have you back, sir."

Men drinking in the public bar watched curiously. Many of the spacers had seen Molts during their voyages, but the aliens weren't common on Venus.

"Good to see you also, Guillermo," Gregg said as he passed into the inner room. He wondered if the Molt realized how cautious his choice of words had been.

There were nearly twenty men and one middle-aged woman in the private room. Piet Ricimer got up from the table when Guillermo announced Gregg. Leaving the navigational projector and the six-person inner circle seated at the table, he said, "Stephen! Very glad you could come. You're getting along well?"

"Very well," Gregg said, wondering to what degree the statement was true. "But go on with your presentation. I'm—I regret being late."

Gregg never consciously considered turning down his friend's invitation—but he hadn't gotten around to making travel arrangements until just after the last minute.

Ricimer turned around. "Mr. Gregg represents Gregg of Weyston," he said to the seated group. "Stephen, you know Councilor Duneen and Mr. Mostert—"

Siddons Mostert was a year older than his brother. He shared Alexi's facial structure, but his body was spare rather than blocky and he didn't radiate energy the way his brother did.

The way his brother did when alive. After four months, the *Hawkwood* had to be assumed to have been lost.

"Factors Wiley and Blanc—"

Very wealthy men, well connected at court; though not major shippers so far as Gregg knew.

"Comptroller Murillo—"

The sole female, and the person who administered Governor Halys' private fortune. She nodded to Gregg with a look of cold appraisal.

"And Mr. Capellupo, whose principal prefers to be anonymous.

We've just started to discuss the profits, financial and otherwise, to be made from a voyage to the Mirror."

"And I'm Adrien Ricimer," interrupted a youth who leaned forward and extended his hand to Gregg. "This voyage, I'm going along to keep my big brother's shoulder to the wheel."

Gregg winced for his friend. Adrien, who looked about nineteen years old, had no conception of the wealth and power concentrated in this little room. This was a gathering that Gregg himself wouldn't have been comfortable joining were it not that he *did* represent his uncle.

"Adrien," Piet Ricimer said tonelessly, "please be silent."

Brightening again, Ricimer resumed, "This is the Mirror."

He flourished a gesture toward the chart projected above the table. "This is the core of the empire by which President Pleyal intends to strangle mankind . . . and it's the spring from which Venus can draw the wealth to accomplish God's plan!"

The navigational display was of the highest quality, Venerian craftsmanship using purpose-built chips which the Feds had produced in a pre-Collapse factory across the Mirror. The unit was set to project a view of stars as they aligned through transit space, not in the sidereal universe.

In most cases, only very sensitive equipment could view one of the stars from the vicinity of another. For ships in transit through the bubble universes, the highlighted stars were neighbors—

And they all lay along the Mirror.

The holographic chart indicated the Mirror as a film, thin and iridescent as the wall of a soap bubble. In reality, the Mirror was a juncture rather than a barrier. Matter as understood in the sidereal universe existed in only one portion of transit space: across the Mirror, in a bubble which had begun as a reciprocal of the sidereal universe. The two had diverged only slightly, even after billions of years.

There were two ways to reach the mirrorside from the solar system. One was by transit, a voyage that took six months if conditions and the captain's skill were favorable and more than a lifetime if they were not.

The other method required going *through* the Mirror, on one of the planets which existed partly in the sidereal universe and partly as a reflected copy mirrorside. The interior of the Mirror was a labyrinth as complex as a section of charcoal. Like charcoal it acted as a filter, passing objects of two hundred kilograms or less and rejecting everything larger without apparent contact.

There was no evidence that intelligent life had arisen on the mirrorside. Human settlement there had begun less than a generation before the Collapse, and none of those proto-colonies survived beyond the first winter on their own. Because men had vanished so suddenly, they hadn't had time to disrupt the colonies' automatic factories in vain, desperate battles. Some of the sites continued to produce microchips for centuries, creating huge dumps of their products.

Some factories were designed with custom lines to tailor limited runs to the colony's local needs. Often those lines had been shut down at the time their supervisors fled or were killed, so the equipment had not worn itself out in the intervening centuries. With the proper knowledge, those lines could be restarted.

Molts carried that genetically-encoded knowledge. The Federation had begun to bring some of the factories back in service.

"That's where the wealth is, all right," said Murillo. "But President Pleyal has no intention of giving any but his own creatures a chance to bring it back."

"We need the governor's authorization to redress damages the Federation caused by its treacherous attack," Siddons Mostert said forcefully, his eyes on Councilor Duneen. "The ships, the lives— my brother's life! We can't bring back the dead, but we can take the money value of the losses out of the hides of their treacherous murderers."

Gregg's mouth quirked in something between a smile and a nervous tic. He understood perfectly well how to reduce injuries to monetary terms. Life expectancy times earnings, reduced by the value of the interest on the lump-sum payment. He'd done the calculation scores of times for the relicts of laborers killed on the family holdings.

He thought that if Administrator Carstensen appeared in person with the mulct for Tancred—and a very modest amount it would be—he, Stephen Gregg, would *chew* through Carstensen's neck if no better weapon presented itself.

"No," said Duneen. He looked around the gathering. Though a passionate man, the councilor's voice was for the moment as cold as chilled steel. "Governor Halys *absolutely* will not authorize an act of war against the North American Federation."

"But all I ask is leave to organize a trading expedition," Piet Ricimer said quietly. His index finger idly pointed from one point on the chart to another. Prize, Benison, Cauldron; Heartbreak, Rondelet, Umber. Names for a trader to conjure with. The source of the Federation's wealth, and the core of the empire President Pleyal schemed to build.

Damn him, Gregg thought. Only when startled eyes glanced around did he realize he had spoken aloud.

"I beg your pardon, gentlemen." he said. "Milady."

He nodded with cold formality, then continued, "Mr. Ricimer. Factor Benjamin Gregg, my principal, was extremely pleased on his return from your recent voyage. Despite the difficulty and losses at the end of it. I'm confident that he'll be willing to subscribe a portion of any new venture you plan."

"What are we talking about precisely?" Capellupo demanded bluntly. "A fleet? Five ships? Ten?"

"Two," Piet Ricimer said. "And they needn't—shouldn't, in fact—be large."

"Two?" Murillo said in surprise. She looked at Mostert, who sat beside her.

The shipper shrugged and made a wry face. "It wasn't my, ah, first thought either, madam. But Mr. Ricimer has very settled notions. And he's been on the scene, of course."

"He hasn't been to the Mirror," Capellupo said flatly. The agent wasn't precisely hostile, but he obviously regarded it as his duty to press the points that others might be willing to slough. The stories that returned aboard the *Peaches* made Piet Ricimer a hero in Betaport; and to the local spacefaring community, President Pleyal was Satan's brother if he wasn't the Devil himself.

"My brother's been to the gates of Hell!" Adrien Ricimer burst out angrily. "*That's* where—"

"Adrien!" Piet Ricimer said.

"I just . . ." Adrien began. He stopped, a syllable before something would have happened—an order to leave, that might or might not have been obeyed; a scuffle, with Stephen Gregg doing what had to be done if the conference were to continue.

"You're quite right, Mr. Capellupo," Piet Ricimer resumed smoothly. "Things that are true for other parts of the Reaches don't necessarily hold for Federation outposts on the Mirror. We'll reconnoiter the region before we proceed further, staging out of an undeveloped world Admiral Mostert explored on the voyage just ended."

Sunrise . . . Gregg thought. *Which Ricimer and the* Peaches *had discovered.*

"The need to keep a low profile while gathering information along the Mirror is one of the reasons I think a modest force is the best choice for this voyage," Ricimer continued. "The *Peaches,* a feather-boat which I own in partnership with Factor Mostert—"

He nodded toward Siddons. *Piet must have bought part of the little vessel with his share of the cargo packed aboard her in the last moments on Biruta.*

"—and another vessel a little larger, say fifty to a hundred tonnes. That and fifty men should be sufficient."

Factor Wiley, a stooped man known both for his piety and his ruthlessness in business transactions, frowned. "Mostert, you could fund a business this small yourself," he said. "Why is it you've called this lot together? I thought you must be planning a full-scale expedition to capture some of the planets Pleyal's heathens try to bar us from."

Councilor Duneen looked at him. "I don't know that so public a gathering—"

He glanced at the men standing around the walls of the modest room. Gregg knew that many of them or their principals were major shipping figures; in Duneen's terms, they were rabble.

"—is the best place to discuss such matters."

"This is where we are, Councilor," Murillo said with unexpected harshness. Gregg's eyes flicked to her from Duneen. There was clearly no love lost between Governor Halys' chief public and personal advisors.

Murillo jerked her chin toward Mostert in a peremptory fashion. "Go on, say it out loud. You want to compromise as many powerful people as you can, so that you'll be protected when President Pleyal asks the governor for your head."

"I want as many successful people as possible," said Piet Ricimer, speaking before Siddons Mostert could frame the answer demanded of him, "because I intend to make everyone who invests in this voyage extremely wealthy. Wealth even in the governor's terms, milady."

He flashed Comptroller Murillo a hard smile, not the joyous one Gregg had seen on his friend's face before.

"I want to bring wealth to so many of you," he continued forcefully, "because this won't be the last voyage. There'll be scores of others, hundreds of others. Voyages that you send out yourselves, because of the profit you see is waiting beyond Pluto. Voyages that no one here will be concerned in, because others will see the staggering wealth, the inconceivable wealth, and want some for themselves. And they'll find it! It's waiting there, for us and for Venus and for mankind—with the help of God!"

"Venus and God!" Duneen cried, turning toward Murillo to make his words an undeserved slap.

Hear hear/Venus and God crackled through the room. Gregg did not speak.

"And no, milady," Ricimer said as the cheers faded, "I don't expect investors on Venus to bring me safety. I saw what safety Admiral Mostert gained by being in the governor's own ship when he met Federation treachery. There'll be no safety beyond Pluto until decent men wrest the universe from President Pleyal and his murderers!"

"Which we will do!" Murillo cried as she rose to her feet, anticipating the cheers that would otherwise have been directed against her. Neither she nor her mistress would have survived in a male-dominated society without knowing how to turn political necessity into a virtue.

"Factor Mostert will discuss shares in the venture with you, milady and gentlemen," Ricimer said when the applause had settled enough for him to be heard by at least those nearest to him. "I need to talk over some personal matters with my old shipmate here, Mr. Gregg."

They stepped together into the public bar. Sailors watched them with open curiosity, while the gentlemen's liveried attendants tried to conceal their interest in the enthusiasm from the back room.

"Marvin?" Ricimer asked the bartender. "May we use your office?"

"Of course, Mr. Ricimer," the bartender replied. He lifted the bar leaf to pass them through to the combined office/storeroom behind the rack of ready-use supplies.

Part of Gregg's mind found leisure to be amused. Ricimer had set this meeting not in a townhouse but on ground where he had an advantage over the nobles who were attending.

Ricimer closed the door. "What do you think, Stephen?" he asked.

Gregg shrugged. "You have them eating out of your hand," he said. "Even though they know you're going as a raider this time, not to trade."

Ricimer lifted his jaw a millimeter. "President Pleyal can't be allowed to trap mankind within the solar system again," he said. "Nobody can be allowed to do that. Whatever God's will requires *shall* be done."

He quirked a wry grin toward Gregg. "But that isn't what I was asking, Stephen. As you know."

"Of course Uncle Ben will support this," Gregg said. As an excuse for not meeting his friend's eyes, he turned to survey the kegs and crates of bottles. The Blue Rose had its beer delivered instead of brewing on-premises, as taverns in less expensive locations normally did.

"I . . . was afraid that would be your answer," Ricimer said quietly. "When you didn't contact me after we got back. Well, I'm sorry, but I understand."

Gregg turned. "Do you understand, Piet?" he demanded. "Tell me—how many people do you think I've killed since you met me? You don't have to count Molts."

"I do count Molts, Stephen," Ricimer said. He crossed his wrists behind his back and looked directly into Gregg's angry gaze. "You killed because it was necessary to save your own life and those of your friends. We all did, whoever's finger was on the trigger."

"It was necessary because I went beyond Pluto," Gregg said. He didn't shout, but the way his voice trembled would have frightened anyone who didn't trust Gregg's control. "So I'm not going to do that again."

"I can't force you, Stephen," Ricimer said. "But I want you to know that I don't think of you as merely an investor or even as a friend. Your abilities may be necessary to our success."

"You know, Piet," Gregg said, "I don't care if you think I'm a coward. I suppose I am. . . . But what I'm afraid of is me."

"Stephen, you're not a coward," Ricimer said. He tried to take Gregg's right hand in his, but the bigger man jerked it away.

"I don't hate killing," Gregg shouted. "I like it, Piet. I'm good at it, and I really like it! The only problem is, that makes me hate myself."

"Stephen—" Ricimer said, then twisted away. He clenched his fists, opened them again, and pressed his fingertips against the wall of living rock. "The Lord won't let His purpose fail," he whispered.

Ricimer turned around again. He gave Gregg a genuine smile, though tears glittered in the corners of his eyes. "You'll be taking that troubleshooting job your uncle offered you?" he asked.

Gregg nodded. "We haven't discussed it formally," he said. "Probably, yes."

He hugged the smaller man to him. "Look, Piet," he said. "If you needed me . . . But you don't. There's plenty of gunmen out there."

Ricimer squeezed Gregg's shoulder as they broke apart. "There's plenty of gunmen out there," he repeated without agreement.

An outcry from the street redoubled when the men within the tavern took it up. Feet and furniture shuffled.

Gregg opened the office door. The sailors were already gone. The gentlemen from the back room were crowding toward the street in turn, accompanied by their servants. The bartender himself rubbed his hands on his apron as if thinking of leaving himself.

"Marvin?" Ricimer asked.

"The *Hawkwood*'s landed, Mr. Ricimer," the bartender blurted. "They're bringing the crew through the airlocks right now, what there's left of them."

"The *Hawkwood*?" Gregg said in amazement.

"Yessir," Marvin agreed with a furious nod. "But the crew, they're in terrible shape! The port warden says they loaded two hundred men on Biruta and there's not but fifteen alive!"

Guillermo followed as Ricimer and Gregg pushed out onto Dock Street. Ricimer's status as a local hero cleared them a path through the gathering mob. The gentlemen who'd attended the meeting had to fight their way to the front with the help of their servants.

The airlock serving Dock Three, directly across the corridor from the tavern, rumbled open. A whiff of sulphurous fumes from the outer atmosphere dissipated across the crowd. Port personnel carrying stretchers, some of them fashioned from tarpaulin-wrapped rifles, filled the lock's interior.

"Alexi!" Siddons Mostert cried as he knelt beside his supine brother. An ambulance clanged in the near distance, trying to make its way through the people filling the corridor. "Ricimer and I thought that avenging you was all we could offer your memory!"

Alexi Mostert lurched upright on his stretcher. He looked like a carving of hollow-cheeked Death. His skin had a grayish sheen, and all his teeth had fallen out. "Ricimer?" he croaked. "That traitor!"

Ricimer stood beside Siddons Mostert. It was only when Ricimer jerked at the accusation that Alexi's wild eyes actually focused on him.

"Traitor!" Alexi repeated. He tried to point at Ricimer, but the effort was too great and he fell back again.

Spectators looked from the *Hawkwood*'s hideously wasted survivors to the man Mostert was accusing—and edged away. Ricimer drew himself up stiffly.

Gregg had lagged a step behind Ricimer. Now he moved to his friend's side.

"What's this?" Factor Wiley demanded. "Traitor?"

"He abandoned us," Alexi Mostert said, closing his eyes to concentrate his energy on his words. "Half our thrusters were shot out before we could transit. We had only a week's food for as many people as we'd taken aboard, and only half the thrusters to carry us. He—"

Mostert opened his eyes. This time he managed to point a finger bony as a chicken's claw at Piet Ricimer. "He ran off and left us to starve!"

"No!" Stephen Gregg shouted. "No! That's not what happened!"

The crowd surged as the ambulance finally arrived. Men who'd heard Mostert bellowed the accusation to those farther back. Soon the corridor thundered with inarticulate rage.

Gregg shouted himself hoarse, though he couldn't hear his own voice over the general din. When he thought to look around for his friend, he saw no sign of either Piet Ricimer or his Molt attendant.

28

Venus

"Mr. Gregg, gentlemen," said the servant in fawn livery. He bowed Gregg into the Mostert brothers' drawing room, then closed the door behind the visitor.

"Very good to see you again, Mr. Gregg," Siddons Mostert said with a shade too much enthusiasm. He rose from the couch and extended his hand.

"And that in spades from me, Gregg," said his brother. "But I won't get up just this moment, if it's all the same with you."

A month of food and medical care had made a considerable improvement in Alexi Mostert. If Gregg hadn't seen the survivors as they were carried into Betaport, though, he would have said the shipowner was on the point of death. Alexi sat in a wheelchair with a robe over his legs. His hands and face had filled out, but there was a degree of stiffness to all his motions.

"I'm glad to see you looking so well, sir," Gregg said as he leaned over to shake Alexi's hand. "And I appreciate you both giving me this audience. I know you must be very busy."

The drawing room was spacious but furnished in a deliberately sparse fashion. Room was the ultimate luxury on Venus, where habitable volume had to be armored against elements as violent as those of any human-occupied world.

As if to underscore that fact, the room's sole decoration was the mural on the long wall facing the door. In reds and grays and oranges, a storm ripped over the sculptured basalt of the Venerian surface. In the background, a curve overlaid by yellow-brown swirls of sulphuric acid might have been either the Betaport dome which protected the Mosterts' townhouse—or the whim of an atmosphere dense enough to cut with a knife.

"Pour yourself a drink and sit down, lad," Alexi said. He gestured toward the glasses, bottles, and carafe of water on the serving table along the short wall to his left.

Gregg nodded and stepped toward the table. When his back was turned, Alexi continued, "I was planning to call on you, you know, as soon as I got my pins under me properly. I'm told that you were the fellow who saved my life by bringing down that Fed drone."

"Saved the lives of everyone who was saved," Siddons said primly. "*And* saved the cargo loaded on the *Hawkwood,* which is quite a nice amount."

He cleared his throat. "Ah, the share-out on the cargo isn't quite complete yet," he added. "But if your uncle is concerned about the delay, I'm sure . . . ?"

Gregg turned to his hosts holding a shot of greenish-gray liquor in one hand and a water chaser in the other. He sipped the liquor, then water. "Uncle Benjamin trusts you implicitly, gentlemen," he said. "We await the accounting with interest, but you needn't hurry such a complex matter on our part."

Every factory on Venus distilled its own version of algal liquor, slash, according to recipes handed down since before the Collapse. The Mosterts' sideboard contained wines and liquors imported from Earth at heavy expense, but it was slash that Stephen Gregg grew up with. This version was all right, though it hadn't the resinous aftertaste of Eryx slash that made outsiders wince.

"We were actually wondering whether it was business or pleasure that brought you to us tonight, Gregg," Alexi said carefully. "You're welcome for either reason, of course, shipmate."

There was a glass of whiskey on the arm of his wheelchair. The level didn't change noticeably when he lifted it to his lips and set it down again.

Gregg barked out a laugh. "Oh, business," he said, "indeed business. I thought I'd relax at Eryx for a time, you know, when we got back. But that didn't work very well."

"Your brother's the factor, I believe?" Siddons said.

Gregg nodded and looked at the shot glass. It was empty. "Dead soldier," he said.

He flipped the glass into a waste container across the room. Neither the glass nor the ceramic basket broke, but they rang in different keys for some seconds.

Gregg giggled. "Sorry," he apologized. "I shouldn't have done that." He rotated on his heel and poured slash into a fresh tumbler. With his back to his hosts he continued, "My brother August was very kind, but I could tell he wasn't, well, comfortable around me."

His arm lifted and his head jerked back. He put down the shot glass, refilled it, and faced the Mosterts again.

"He'd talked to my doctors, August had," Gregg said, "and they—well, you know about doctors, Admiral. I shouldn't have told them about the dreams. They don't understand. You know that."

Gregg smiled. The smile slowly softened. His eyes were focused on the mural rather than the two seated men.

"Ah . . ." Siddons said. "This is Gregg of Weyston's business that you've come to us with, Mr. Gregg?"

"No," said Gregg. "No." He gave an exaggerated shake of his head. "This is my own business."

He looked at Alexi Mostert with absolutely no expression in his eyes. "You've been getting a better perspective on what happened at Biruta, have you, Admiral? Than you had right when you docked, I mean."

"I hope nothing I may have said when I was delirious, Mr. Gregg . . ." Alexi said. The fingers of his right hand opened and closed on the whiskey glass. " . . . could have been construed as an insult directed toward you. To be honest, I don't recall anything from docking until I awakened in hospital three days later."

"It wasn't until my brother read the report compiled for Governor Halys that the details of that very confused business became clear, Mr. Gregg," Siddons said.

"Nobody insulted me, Admiral," Gregg said. "Besides, I wouldn't kill anybody just because of words. Not anymore."

He giggled. "My brother didn't like it when I said it was *fun* to kill people. He thought I was making a bad joke."

Siddons got up from the couch, then sat again before he'd reached a full standing position. "The compilation of accounts from all the survivors—including those of the *Peaches,* of course—created a degree of understanding that, ah, individuals didn't have while lost in their personal problems."

"You understand that, don't you, shipmate?" Alexi said. "It was Hell. Hell. There's no other word for it."

Gregg tossed off his shot. "I understand Hell," he said. He smiled again.

"I suspect I owe my cousin an apology," Alexi said heavily, looking at his glass. "During the whole trip home, all I could see in my mind was the featherboat running off instead of staying to help us."

"He knows now that you loaded reaction mass and came back," Siddons put in with a forced grin. "It was all a very tragic time."

"Ricimer's a friend of yours, I believe, Mr. Gregg?" Alexi said.

"Best friend I've ever had," Gregg agreed nonchalantly. "I wonder if he has the dreams, do you think, Admiral?"

He hurled the shot glass into the waste container. Both glasses and the container rang together. "Sorry, I didn't mean to do that."

Gregg turned to the serving table. "I don't think an apology really does much good," he said as he tilted the decanter of slash. "Do you, gentlemen?"

"You're here on Mr. Ricimer's behalf, is that it?" Siddons said.

Gregg glanced over his shoulder and grinned. "Nope," he said.

He looked down, raised the glass to his lips, and poured again before he faced around. "I'm here on my own. Piet, he's trying to put together an expedition still. He's having trouble even buying a featherboat, though."

"I believe one of my secretaries made problems about my cousin buying the remaining share in the *Peaches*" Alexi said. "I'll put that right immediately."

"A lot of people won't touch Piet because of the trouble when the *Hawkwood* landed, you know," Gregg said. He hadn't drunk any of the chaser since his first sip on pouring it. "Stories travel better than corrections do. You know how it is."

He threw back his head and emptied the shot glass.

"I'm not responsible for anything that happened while I was delirious!" Alexi Mostert shouted from his wheelchair.

"We're all responsible for everything we do, Admiral," Gregg said through his smile. "D'ye sometimes dream about things you haven't done yet? I do."

He looked at Siddons. "You don't have the dreams, do you, Master Siddons? You're lucky, but you're missing some interesting things, too. You know, a man's head can be there and then *poof!* gone, not an eyeblink between them. Right beside you, a man's head is just *gone*."

Alexi's glass fell onto the floor of polished stone. Both brothers jumped. Gregg chuckled and returned to the serving table.

"What do you think might be a fair recompense for the inconvenience I've caused my cousin, Mr. Gregg?" Alexi Mostert said hoarsely.

"Well, it occurs to me that a simple commercial proposition might turn out to everybody's benefit," Gregg said toward the wall.

He swung around. "For his expedition, Piet wanted a featherboat, which he could provide himself, and a bigger ship. If Mostert Trading provided an eighty tonner, with crew and all expenses—why, that'd prove the stories about Piet betraying you on Biruta were false. Wouldn't it, Admiral?"

Siddons leaned forward on the couch. He took a memorandum book from his waist pouch. "What share-out do you propose?" he asked.

"For the vessels," said Gregg, "equal shares. Officers and crewmen sharing from a single pool, with full shares for those who—"

Gregg's unfocused eyes made his grin even more horrible.

"—don't make it back."

Alexi Mostert leaned back in his wheelchair and forced a laugh. "So *that* was the business that brought you here," he said.

"Oh, no, Admiral," said Stephen Gregg. His voice was as soft as the quiver of wind against the dome far overhead. "But if this commercial transaction goes ahead, then there won't be any need for my business."

Gregg turned his chaser over. Water splashed his boots and the floor. He walked to the stone wall and twisted the tumbler against it.

The glass held for a moment. Then a scratch from the harder basalt destroyed the integrity of the man-made material. The tumbler shattered into powder and spewed between Gregg's fingers.

He looked at the brothers. "Sooner or later, they always break," he said. "Everything does, you know?"

"We accept your terms," said Alexi Mostert without expression. "Will you notify Mr. Ricimer so that we can formalize the agreement?"

Gregg dusted his hands together. Because his right palm was wet, shards too tiny to be seen except as a glitter stuck to the skin.

He shook his head. "No, gentlemen," he said, "that's for you and Piet to work out together. He doesn't have any idea that I'm here, you see. I'd like it to stay that way."

Gregg cocked an eyebrow. Siddons looked up from his notebook. Alexi Mostert nodded minusculy in agreement.

"Then I'll take my leave of you," Gregg said. "I appreciate you giving me your time."

He put his hand on the door. As soon as the panel quivered at his touch, the servant in the hall swept it fully open. "And I hope our next meeting," Gregg concluded, "will be at the share-out party when Mr. Ricimer's expedition returns."

"Mr. Gregg?" Alexi Mostert called.

Gregg turned in the hallway. "Sir?"

"Will you be accompanying the expedition yourself?"

"That's right," Gregg said. "I've decided that's where I belong. Beyond Pluto."

Mostert nodded stiffly. Gregg disappeared down the hall behind the footman.

"That's odd," Siddons Mostert said. "The level of slash in the decanter doesn't seem to have gone down as much as it should have."

"That young gentleman may not have been drunk," his brother said, "but you won't convince me that he's not crazy. Not after I saw him in action on Biruta. I think we'd best take him at his word."

"Yes," Siddons said as he rose to his feet. "I'll call Ricimer. Shall we offer the *Dalriada,* do you think?"

29

Benison

Ricimer brought the *Peaches* to a near halt a meter above the ground, then slid her forward between the boles of the broadleaf trees. The yellow-rimmed hole the thrusters seared on entering the forest would be obvious from the air. If the featherboat herself was concealed, though, an observer might assume the interlopers had taken off again.

Gregg and the new crewman, Coye, flung the main hatch open. Benison's atmosphere was sweet and pleasantly cool in comparison to the fug within the *Peaches* after a voyage of seventeen days.

"Not so very bad, Piet," Gregg said approvingly as he raised his visor. He lifted himself out on the featherboat's deck, glancing around with the nervous quickness of a mouse on the floor of a ballroom. The flashgun was a useless burden in this pastoral woodland.

"I don't see the piles of microchips, though," Coye muttered. Gregg didn't know the sailor well enough to be sure that he was making a joke, but he chuckled anyway.

As armed crewmen hopped up to join Gregg, waiting for the lower hull to cool, Piet Ricimer talked to Captain Dulcie of the *Dalriada*. When Gregg bought the remaining half share in the *Peaches'* hull from the Mostert brothers, Ricimer invested some of his capital thus freed into first-class electronics for the featherboat.

Her viewscreen and voice radio were now both enhanced to diamond clarity.

"Find a landing site at least fifty klicks from here, Dulcie," Ricimer ordered. "And stay away from the cultivated fields. There's no sign of Fed patrols, but they can't very well miss a ship the size of the *Dalriada* if it drops on top of them. Over."

"Weren't we coming in alongside the Mirror, sir?" Leon said quietly to Gregg. The bosun peered about him as if expecting to see a glittering wall in the near distance.

"I can't imagine that Mr. Ricimer didn't land us where he intended to, Leon," Gregg replied. Dulcie's reply was an inaudible murmur within the vessel. "I suppose we're here on Benison because he wants to get experience of the Mirror where it's safer to do that."

Piet wasn't forthcoming with his plans. Gregg didn't like to press, because he was pretty sure his friend wouldn't tell him anything useful anyway. It wasn't as though any of them needed to know, after all.

Adrien Ricimer had equipped himself with helmet, torso armor, and a slung cutting bar as well as the repeater he carried. He called, "The fields are that way!" and leaped to the ground. He sprawled full length, overborne by his load.

Gregg jumped down beside him. In the guise of helping the boy up, he kept a grip on him. "When your brother's finished administrative chores," he said to Adrien, "it'll be time to go exploring."

Adrien gave an angry shrug and found that it had absolutely no effect on the bigger man's grip. When he relaxed, Gregg let him go. The rest of the crew joined them, moving a few steps into the forest to get clear of ground which the thrusters had baked.

Benison was three-quarters of an Earth-like world with a diameter of 14,000 kilometers. Three-quarters, because a section centered in the planet's northern hemisphere didn't exist either in the sidereal universe or across the Mirror. The mirrorside of Benison was an identical three-quarters of a planet, orbiting an identical sun and clothed in similar though genetically distinct native vegetation.

The juncture that turned a single world into a near duplicate of itself was not in the three-dimensional universe. Benison's orbit and planetary rotation had no effect on the boundary that separated the sidereal universe from the bubble that mimicked it across the Mirror.

It had been noted, though not explained, that the apparent thickness of the boundary layer was directly proportional to the percentage of planetary mass that existed in the paired universes. It was possible to cross the Mirror on Benison, but the length of the route made it impractical to carry any significant quantity of goods from side to side that way. Umber, the 5,000-kilometer disk of a planet whose calculated diameter would have been over 12,000 kilometers, carried virtually all of the direct trade between mirrorside and the sidereal universe.

Ricimer and Guillermo jumped down from the featherboat. "Dulcie says that apart from air and reaction mass, the *Dalriada*'s in perfect condition," Ricimer explained, obviously pleased with the situation. "He'll keep his crew close by the ship and relax while we do what exploring there is."

The men stiffened, waiting for direction. Ricimer went on, "Stephen and I will cover Guillermo while he talks to field workers. Leon, you're in charge of the ship until we return. If that's more than two hours, I'll radio."

He patted the flat radio hanging from the right side of his belt, where it balanced the forty rounds of rifle ammunition on the left.

"You're leaving me under *him*!" Adrien said in amazement.

Piet looked at him. "No," he said with scarcely a hint of hesitation. "You'll come with us, Adrien . . . But leave the rifle, that's too much to carry."

Gregg nodded mentally. Adrien couldn't get into too much trouble with a cutting bar.

"Look, I'll take off my armor instead. I—"

"*Leave the rifle,* Adrien," Ricimer repeated, very clearly the captain.

Adrien's handsome face scrunched up, but he obeyed without further comment.

Benison's open woodlands were as alien to Gregg as anything beyond the corridors of Venus, but he found they had a friendly feel. The leaves overhead provided a ceiling of sorts, but they didn't have the overpowering immensity of Punta Verde's layered forests.

Small animals chirped and mewed, unseen. Sometimes the ankle-high ground cover—neither moss nor ferns, but similar to both—quivered ahead of the party.

Guillermo led, carrying a fist-sized direction finder. The Molt slung a holstered revolver from a pink sash like the one he'd worn on Punta Verde when he was captured. Piet was next in line. Twice Adrien tried to come abreast of his brother and talk, but Piet brushed him back.

Gregg brought up the rear with his flashgun and bleak thoughts. He was nervous around Adrien Ricimer. He was afraid of his own temper, afraid that one day he was going to crush the boy like a bug.

Afraid that jealousy was as much a reason for his anger as Adrien's brashness.

They came to the verge of cultivated fields a quarter klick from the landing site. Hectares of waist-high sorghum stretched for as far as Gregg could see. Stripes and wedges of native vegetation, taller and a brighter green, marked patches too wet or rocky for gang plows.

A pair of high-wheeled cultivators crawled across the fields in the middle distance. Guillermo immediately entered the open area, pushing through the saw-edged leaves with chitin-clad ease.

"Wait!" Gregg said. "Shouldn't you take your, your sash off?"

The Molt's triangular head turned almost directly backward though his torso didn't move. "Any human observer will think I'm a supervisor, Mr. Gregg," he said. "A thousand years ago, his ancestors would have thought the same."

Guillermo resumed his swift progress toward the Federation equipment. Gregg sighted on the nearer vehicle, but his laser's 1.5x scope didn't provide enough magnification to tell whether the driver was a Molt or perhaps a Rabbit.

It hadn't occurred to him until Guillermo spoke that *all* the aspects of Molt-human interaction had been set before the Collapse. The thought made him a little queasy. He had a vision of eighty generations of Stephen Greggs sighting their flashguns toward treetops full of defiant warriors . . .

"The *Dalriada*'s truly a first-class ship," Piet Ricimer murmured as the three men watched Guillermo from the forest-edge under-growth. "I suppose it's my cousins' way of making apology for the business when the *Hawkwood* landed. Though after that ordeal, nobody could blame Alexi for wild talk."

"I wanted to call him out!" Adrien snarled.

Neither of the older men spoke. Had the Mosterts bothered to respond, they would have sent servants to beat the pup within an inch of his life—or beyond. Betaport would have applauded that

handling of lower-class scum who insulted his betters by claiming the right of challenge.

A red film lowered over Gregg's eyes. He pointed the flashgun
toward the ground. He didn't want an accident because his trigger finger trembled.

Guillermo jumped off the cultivator he'd mounted and returned
toward the waiting humans. The vehicle had never paused in its
slow progress across the sorghum.

"Frankly, I did my cousins an injustice," Piet continued. "I
expected them to, well, ignore that they'd been mistaken. Instead,
well—I couldn't have hoped for a finer ship than the one they
provided. I'd hoped to involve more of the . . . upper levels of the
nation in this expedition than I've done. But that will come next
time."

"Sometimes people come through when they come right up
against it," Gregg said. "I'm glad your cousins did."

His voice was hoarse. He coughed, as if to clear his throat.

Guillermo rejoined them. The Molt's chestplate pumped with
exertion, sucking and expelling air from the breathing holes along
the lateral lines of his torso. "They'll meet us tonight," he said.

"Those will?" Adrien asked. "The workers?"

"Not them," his brother explained. "Their kindred, who've
escaped and hide along the Mirror. The only food available is what's
grown here on the plantations, so I was sure that there'd be contact
between free Molts and the slaves."

He nodded toward the *Peaches* to start the party walking back.
"I want to understand the Mirror better before I make final plans.
That means I need someone to guide me through."

30

Benison

Coye waggled Gregg's booted foot to awaken him before going on to each next man in the lean-to and doing the same. Gregg pulled his helmet on as he got up. He was already fully dressed, with the flashgun sling over his right arm.

The sky was faintly pale where it could be glimpsed through the foliage, but it did nothing to illuminate the forest floor. Even the featherboat's off-white hull was easier to sense than see in the first moments of wakefulness.

Gregg was stiff in odd places. The bed of springy boughs had seemed comfortable when he lay on it, but it had locked his body into one posture as the thin pad over the *Peaches'* decking hadn't done during the voyage. His sinuses were stuffy from pollen, either native or drifting from the nearby plantation.

And he was afraid. Clambering up the side of the featherboat was good for the fear. The massive solidity of the *Peaches'* hull soothed Gregg in a fashion that the personal weapon he carried could not.

In the hatchway Leon, who'd shared the watch with Coye, whispered to Piet Ricimer. Clipped to the coaming was the sonic scanner, another piece of hardware purchased with the profits of Mostert's disastrous voyage. Rather than magnifying sounds for the operator to classify, the scanner plotted an ambient and indicated changes above that baseline on a screen. It didn't tell the operator what a sound was, but it gave volume and vector.

Gregg glanced at the readout. He lay across the hull beside the hatch and aimed his weapon toward the line of peaks which the scanner had noted—footsteps or brush rustling past an oncoming body.

Ricimer laid his left hand across the eyepiece of the flashgun's sight. "Guillermo's out there," he whispered. "He's meeting them."

"Sirs?" the Molt called in a clear voice. "Our friends are here. We're coming in."

Gregg glimpsed the movement of several bodies. Faint light bloomed. Three strange Molts accompanied Guillermo. One of them brought a phosphorescent twig out of the pot which had covered it. In this near-total darkness, the bioluminescent sheen was as good as a magnesium flare.

The strange Molts were noticeably bulkier though not taller than Guillermo. One carried a breechloader, while the others had one-armed "bows" similar in design to those the Venerians had faced on Punta Verde.

Piet Ricimer swung his legs over the hatch coaming and jumped to the ground in front of the Molts.

"This is K'Jax," Guillermo said, dipping both forelimbs toward the rifleman in a gesture of respect. "I have told him that you need a guide through the Mirror."

"Why?" said K'Jax. His eyes and those of his fellows tracked quickly across the humans facing them, hesitating minutely at each weapon they noted.

"Because I need to know more about the Mirror in order to determine how best to take from the Federation the wealth belonging to all persons," Ricimer replied calmly. Gregg noted that his friend had left his rifle in the featherboat. "Wealth which the Feds claim as their own."

"So you want us to be your servants," K'Jax said flatly.

The Molt leader spoke unaccented English, but his intonations were as mechanical as those of a synthesizer. By contrast, Guillermo's voice couldn't be told from that of a human except that the Molt clipped his labials slightly.

"I want you to be our allies," Ricimer said. "The Feds are your enemies as well as ours. We can provide you with weapons. A few now, more after we're successful and return—though that will be sometime hence, perhaps as much as a year. But I *will* return."

K'Jax clucked. "I am the chieftain of Clan Deel," he said. "They burned my limbs when I would not work for them. I fled as others have fled."

The Molt leader glanced around, at his silent fellows and the forest which surrounded him. He had a look of rocklike solidity, a soul that could be pulverized but never changed in essence.

"If they let us grow our own crops," K'Jax continued, "we would ignore them. When we clear fields, they find us and attack, and they hunt us with planes. So we raid their fields. We kill them when we can. One day we will kill them all."

His chitinous fingers caressed his Federation breechloader, designed for human hands but adaptable to those of a Molt.

K'Jax clucked again. The sound was that of a repeater chambering the next round. "If you're the enemy of the Federation, human," he said, "then you don't have to pay me or mine for our help. When do you want to pass through the Mirror?"

"Now?" said Ricimer.

"Now," K'Jax agreed. He and his fellows turned.

Gregg jumped down from the featherboat. He was pleased and a little surprised to land squarely on his feet without stumbling. The satchel of spare batteries slapped his thigh.

"Leon, you're in charge," Ricimer said. "Guillermo and Mr. Gregg accompany me."

"I'm going too!" cried his brother, stepping forward.

"Adrien," Piet Ricimer said sharply, "you will stay with the vessel and obey Leon's directions."

The bosun tossed a rifle and bandolier from the hatch. Despite the poor light, Ricimer caught the gear in the air.

The Molts paused five meters off in the darkness. Ricimer glanced at them, then said to Leon, "If we're not back in four days, use your judgment. But we should be back."

He strode swiftly after K'Jax with Gregg and Guillermo flanking him. Gregg was glad when the local Molt covered his glowing wand, because only then could they be sure Adrien Ricimer would not be able to follow.

31

Benison

"This is the Mirror," said K'Jax.

The words brought Gregg up like a brick wall. He'd gotten into a rhythm in the darkness, tramping along close to Guillermo. The concept of distance vanished when each stride became a blind venture. The Molt's night vision was better than a human's, though occasionally Guillermo brushed a shadowed tree bole and Gregg collided with him.

Gregg edged closer with his left hand advanced. He instinctively gripped the flashgun close to his body and pointing forward, though his conscious mind realized there was no material threat before him.

His hand felt cold. He saw nothing, absolutely nothing, until the Molt uncovered the torch again. Gregg's left arm had vanished to the elbow. Only the degree of shock he felt kept him from shouting.

One of K'Jax's fellows must have gone ahead. The transition was hard to see because an image of the sidereal universe shimmered on it in perfect fidelity. The reflected forest appeared as real as the one through which Gregg had just stumbled.

"We've laid poles along the ground within," the Molt leader said. He pointed down. The crudely-chopped end of a sapling about a hundred millimeters in diameter protruded from the transition. "Touch one foot against them to keep your direction."

He clucked. The sound must be equivalent to a laugh. "Don't disarrange the poles," he added. "You can walk forever in the Mirror."

He vanished through the boundary. His fellow with the light followed, then Guillermo.

"Stephen?" Ricimer said.

"Sure," said Gregg. He stepped into nothingness, feeling as detached as he had when he aimed at the oncoming water buffalo.

The interior of the Mirror was not only lightless but empty. There was a feeling of presence everywhere in the sidereal universe, the echo from surrounding existence of the observer's being. Nothing echoed here, nothing *was* here. Gregg had to be standing on something, but there was no feeling of pressure against the balls of his feet when he flexed his body upward as an experiment.

He slid his left foot sideways, suddenly aware that he wasn't sure of direction. When his foot stopped, he knew that he must be in contact with the pole, but he couldn't feel even that.

"God our help in ages past," Gregg whispered. He shuffled forward, picking up the pace. Now that he had begun, there was nothing in life that he wanted so much as to be out of this *place*. "God who saved Eryx when the ground shook and the sky rained fire. Be with me, Lord. Be with me . . ."

There was a gap between one sapling and the next. Gregg was a vessel for another's will, the will of the man who had stepped into the Mirror seconds ago. He wasn't afraid for the instant his boot wandered unchecked, only doubtful. It was as if he were falling, painless and even exhilarating until the shock that would pulp him, bones and spirit together.

He touched the next pole in sequence and stepped on.

Gregg's skin began to prickle. He wasn't sure whether the sensation was real or, like the flashes of purple and orange that crossed his vision, merely neuroreceptors tripping in the absence of normal stimuli.

Needles of ice. Needles driving into every cell of his skin. Needles sinking deeper, probing, penetrating his bone marrow and the very core of his brain. He could no longer tell if he still carried the flashgun. He felt nothing when he patted his left palm in the direction where his chest should be.

Gregg knew now why men so rarely entered the Mirror. Part of his mind wondered whether he would have the courage to cross the barrier again to return to realside, but only part. For the most part, his intellect was resigned to spending eternity within the Hell that was the Mirror.

The shock of the tree trunk was utter and complete. Gregg shouted and grasped the coarse bark that had bloodied his lip. The air was warm and there was enough light to read by, enough light to see Guillermo reaching in surprise to steady the young gentleman who had walked straight into a tree several meters beyond the edge of the Mirror.

Piet Ricimer appeared from nowhere, his eyes open and staring. Only when he tripped on a sprawling runner and flew forward did awareness flame back into his expression. Ricimer hit the ground, wheezing and chuckling in a joy that echoed Gregg's own.

The Molts watched, Guillermo and the locals together. Their expressionless faces could have been so many grotesque masks.

"How long were we . . ." Ricimer asked as Guillermo helped him to his feet. Gregg held onto the tree with which he'd collided. He thought he would probably fall if he let go. "In there. In the Mirror."

Guillermo and the Benison Molts talked for a moment in a clicking language nothing like Trade English. "About four hours," Guillermo finally said to Ricimer. "It's nearly dawn on the other side as well as here."

Gregg tried to understand how long he'd been walking. His mind glanced off the concept of duration the way light reflects from a wall of ice. The experience had been eternal, in one sense, but— his thigh muscles didn't ache the way they should have done after so long a hike. Perhaps brain functions slowed within the Mirror . . .

"How far is the nearest Federation colony on this side?" Ricimer asked. He tried to clean away the loam sticking to the front of his tunic, but after a few pats he stopped and closed his eyes for a moment.

Gregg deliberately let go of the tree and squeezed his cut lip between his thumb and forefinger. The tingling pain helped to clear his brain of the icy cobwebs in which the Mirror had shrouded it.

"Two kilometers," K'Jax said. He pointed his free hand eastward. "They build spaceships there. There are a few mines, some crops. Most of the settlements are on the other side."

The Molt leader nodded to indicate his fellows. "We stay on the other side, because the fields there are too extensive for the humans to guard well. When they bring in extra troops and hunt us there, we cross to here."

"Let's take a look at the settlement," Ricimer said. "I think I can walk." He looked at Gregg. "Are you all right, Stephen?"

"I'll do," Gregg said. Maybe. He wasn't sure that he could walk two klicks, but his intellect realized that he'd probably be better off for moving.

He wasn't sure he could bear to reenter the Mirror, either; and perhaps that would be possible also.

K'Jax and his fellows set off without comment, as they had done earlier at the *Peaches.* To them, the decision appeared to be the act. Gregg wondered whether Guillermo's less abrupt manner was a response learned as an individual when he was liaison to the Southerns for his clan rather than a genetic memory.

Ricimer threw himself after the Molts. Guillermo hung at his side, but after the first staggering steps both humans were back in control of their limbs.

"Don't the Feds conduct combined operations?" Ricimer asked. "Hunting you on both sides of the Mirror at once?"

"They try," K'Jax replied. "Their timing isn't good enough."

"Humans don't enter the Mirror," another of the local Molts added unexpectedly. "*They* send us as couriers. Molts." He made the clucking noise Gregg had decided was laughter.

The vegetation here was nothing like that on the sidereal side of the Mirror. The trees grew in clumps from a common base, like enlarged grasses. The foliage formed a dense net overhead, but the volume beneath was divided into conical vaults rather than the cathedral aisles of a forest whose trees grew as individual vertical columns.

After a time, Gregg shifted the flashgun from his right arm to his left. The weapon was less accessible there, but he couldn't bring himself to believe they were in serious danger of ambush. He wasn't a good judge of distances, certainly not in gullied forest like this.

Everything seemed profitless: this hike, this expedition; life itself. Passage through the Mirror had blighted his mind like a field ripped by black frost. He could only pray that the effect would wear off—or that the Feds would anticipate his own sinful consideration of looking down the short, fat barrel of his laser as his thumb stroked the trigger.

"K'Jax?" Gregg called suddenly. He supposed they shouldn't make any more noise than necessary, but it was necessary for him to blast his thoughts out of their current channel. "Does the Mirror bother you Molts? Does it make you feel as if . . ."

"As if your mind had been coated in wax and sectioned for slides?" Piet Ricimer offered. It hadn't occurred to Gregg to ask his friend.

"Yes," said the Molt leader flatly.

"Does it go away?" Gregg demanded.

"Mostly," said K'Jax. He continued striding ahead, not bothering to look back as he spoke. The Molts took swifter, shorter strides than humans of similar height.

"Until the next time," said another of the locals. "We enter the Mirror only when we must, so it doesn't matter what it costs."

"But you entered it for us," said Ricimer.

"You are enemies of our enemies," the Molt explained.

From the head of the line, K'Jax stopped, knelt, and announced, "The settlement is just ahead. The humans call it Cedrao."

Gregg eased forward in a crouch to bring himself parallel with K'Jax. He noticed that one of the local Molts turned to watch their backtrail, his projectile weapon ready.

The trees grew up to the edge of a twenty-meter drop. From that point, the ground fell away in a series of a dozen comparable steps, about as broad as they were deep. The *Peaches* had overflown similar country as Piet brought her in, but it didn't lie within fifty kilometers of their eventual landing point. Divergence on the mirrorside of Benison included details of tectonics as well as biology.

Below the escarpment, the tilted remains of ancient sediments, lay a broad valley. Sunrise painted into a pink squiggle half a kilometer distant the river that had cut through the rocks over ages.

On the near bank was a straggle of two or three hundred houses. The community stank of human and industrial wastes even at this distance.

"Cedrao," K'Jax repeated.

Ricimer sighted through the hand-sized electronic magnifier which he carried. Gregg suspected that a simple optical telescope would have been nearly as effective and considerably more rugged, but Piet liked modern toys.

A steam whistle blew from a long shed at one end of the community. An autogyro was parked behind the cast-concrete building that appeared to be the Commandatura. A few pedestrians wandered the street between the river and the dwellings. All of those Gregg could see through the flashgun's sight were Molts.

Ricimer backed away from the edge of the bluff and stood up. "How many humans live in Cedrao?" he asked.

"A few score," K'Jax said. "Transients when a ship lands. And a few human slaves."

"Rabbits," Guillermo explained.

"You could capture the town by a surprise attack," Gregg said/ suggested.

"If we attacked," said the Molt watching their backtrail, "the Molts down there would fight us too. They aren't Deels. They won't hunt us in the woods, but they'll resist an attempt on *their* clan."

"K'Jax and his fellows ran away from humans and formed their own clan," Guillermo said. "Others of my folk bond to their supervisors." He clucked as the locals had done.

Guillermo himself had bonded to his supervisor—as he knew very well.

Ricimer shook himself. "We can go now," he said. "Though—Stephen, would you prefer to, ah, rest on this side before we cross the Mirror again?"

"I don't want to think about it," Gregg said in a voice as pale as hoarfrost. "If I thought about it for a day, I'd, I'd . . . It'd be harder."

K'Jax strode off in the lead as brusquely as he'd executed each previous decision of the human leader. The others fell into line behind him.

"Piet?" Gregg said.

"Um?" his friend said, grinning wryly back over his shoulder.

"Why did we come here at all?"

Ricimer looked front again and nodded his head. "Because I had to see," he said at last. "See the Mirror, and see how President Pleyal was really developing the worlds he claims."

He looked back at Gregg again. All the humor was gone from his face. "They can't be allowed to continue, Stephen," he said. "Everything here, everything on Jewelhouse and Biruta and everywhere the Federation squats—slavery, cruelty, and no chance of survival if there's the least shock to the home government. Mankind *will* return to the stars. President Pleyal and his henchmen can't be allowed to stop it, no matter what it takes."

"Oh, I know what it'll take," Stephen Gregg said, as much to himself as to his friend. His right hand rested on the grip of his flashgun, while his left gently rubbed the weapon's barrel. "And it can be arranged, you bet."

32

Near Rondelet

"We ought to go down and get them," said Adrien Ricimer. "There's probably a dozen ships on Rondelet for the taking."

He turned. Because everyone aboard the *Peaches* wore his hard suit, there was much less room than usual in the featherboat's interior. Adrien's elbow clacked against the back of Gregg's suit. For an instant, Gregg's right fist bunched. He didn't look around. After a moment, he relaxed.

"I watched the *Rose* come down with her thrusters shot away, boy," Dole said from the scanner readout. "I don't much want to watch from the inside when another drops."

The featherboat slowly orbited Rondelet at ten light-seconds distance; the *Dalriada* kept station a little less than a light-second away. Piet had narrowed the viewscreen field to the image of the planet alone, since a spherical panorama was useless on this scale, but even so Rondelet was no more than a cloud-streaked blue bead.

Radar and even optical magnifiers on the planet *could* find the ships. There was no reason to assume that would happen so long as the Venerians kept their thrusters and transit apparatus shut down. Chances were good that an incoming Federation vessel would spend a number of close orbits trying to raise an operator on the planet's surface who could supply landing information.

"Ionization track," said Dole.

Coye, crewing the plasma weapon with Leon, reacted by latching down his faceshield. There was no need for that yet, but the slap *click* startled Gregg into doing the same thing. Gregg quickly reopened his visor, embarrassed but obscurely happy to have something to do with his hands at a moment he had no duties.

"Adrien," Piet Ricimer ordered his brother, "get the *Dalriada*. We'll handle this, but they're to be ready to support us. Leon, don't run the gun out until I order. Everyone, check your suit now before we open up."

As Ricimer spoke, his fingers accessed scanner data and imported it to the AI's navigational software. The AI would set a course for interception, updating it regularly as further information came in.

Gregg peered over the console toward the viewscreen, trying to make out the target they were hunting. It might not have registered as yet on the small-scale optical display.

"I'm lighting the thrusters," Piet Ricimer said.

The featherboat shook like a wet dog as the separate engines came on-line at fractionally different moments. Ricimer held the thrusters to low output, just enough to give the *Peaches* maneuvering way.

Gregg shook his head and laughed harshly. Jeude, crouched across the central chest from Gregg, looked at him in concern. The two of them would be the boarding party, if and when it came to that.

Behind Gregg, Adrien talked excitedly to Captain Dulcie of their consort. "Don't worry about me," Gregg said. "I just want it to happen. But it'll happen soon enough."

"I'm about to engage the AI," Piet Ricimer said. His voice was clear and calm—but also loud enough to be heard throughout a larger vessel than the *Peaches*.

Gregg clamped his armored left arm to a stanchion. He held the flashgun to his chest with his right, so that it wouldn't flail around under acceleration. He should have checked his satchel of reloads again, but there would be time for that . . .

"Enga—"

Gregg's tripes everted repeatedly in a series that had by now become familiar if not comfortable. It was like watching an acrobat do backflips, only these were in four dimensions and he *was* them.

"—ging."

Rondelet vanished from the viewscreen. A fleck of light grew between intervals of transit, when grayness blinked like a camera shutter across the screen. At the sixth jump, the fleck was a ship for the instant before disappearing through transit space.

On the seventh jump, the *Peaches* and its target were parallel and so apparently close on the screen that Gregg imagined that he could pucker and spit across to the other vessel's metal hull. He closed his visor, though for the moment he left the vents open to save the hard suit's air bottle.

"I'll take the communicator, Adrien," Piet said. He lifted the handset from his brother's half-resisting grip and switched it from radio to modulated laser.

The screen blanked and cleared. The vessels retained the same alignment, though they must have shifted some distance within the sidereal universe. The featherboat's AI had locked courses with the Federation ship. For the moment, the Fed crew was probably unaware that they had company, but they had no chance now of escaping.

There were infinite possible actions but only one best solution. Given the task of predicting what another navigational computer would do, an AI with sufficient data could find the correct answer every time.

"Federation cargo vessel," Ricimer said in a voice punctuated by intervals of transit. "Shut down your drives and prepare for boarding. If you cooperate, you won't be harmed. Shut down your drives."

"Sir," said Leon. "I want to run the gun out."

"Go ahead, Leon," Ricimer agreed calmly.

The bosun activated the hydraulics which opened the bow port and slid the muzzle of the plasma cannon clear of the hull. A flexible gaiter made an attempt at sealing the gap between hull and gun tube, but it leaked so badly that Dole shut down the *Peaches'* environmental system as soon as Ricimer ordered the gun brought to battery.

Pressure in the featherboat's hull dropped abruptly. The vents in Gregg's suit closed automatically and he began to breathe dry bottled air. Sound came through his feet.

Another jump. Another. The Federation vessel was no longer on the viewscreen. Adrien swore.

Another jump and there was the target again, the four thrusters podded on its belly brilliant. At this range the *Peaches'* 50-mm plasma cannon would shatter all the nozzles and probably open the hull besides.

The Fed ship wasn't very prepossessing. Judging from hull fittings of standard size, particularly the personnel hatch, it was barely larger than the featherboat—30 tonnes burden at most. It was a simple vessel, even crude. Gregg suspected it had been built here in the Reaches in a plant like the one they'd viewed on the mirrorside of Benison.

"Take the heathens, sir!" Lightbody said from the attitude controls. The processor in Gregg's helmet flattened the voice transmitted by infrared intercom.

"Federation vessel—" Ricimer began. As he spoke, vacuum drank the target's exhaust flare. For a moment, the nozzles stood out, cooling visibly against the hull their glow lighted. The Feds vanished again; the *Peaches* jumped and they did not.

The featherboat's AI corrected. After a final, gut-wrenching motion, the *Peaches* lay alongside the target. The thrusters and transit drives of both vessels were shut down.

"Boarders away," Piet Ricimer said.

"Boarders away!" Gregg echoed as he and Dole threw the undogging levers that opened the featherboat's main hatch.

Dole stepped onto the coaming and checked his lifeline. The Federation ship hung above them, a section of its hull framed by the *Peaches'* hatch. He flexed his knees slightly and jumped.

Gregg climbed onto the hull. He couldn't see Rondelet or even the yellow sun the planet orbited. Perhaps they were below the featherboat. The metal skin of the Federation vessel was a shimmer of highlights, not a shape. He'd never been outside a ship in vacuum before.

"I'm anchored, sir," Dole's voice called. Gregg couldn't see the crewman. "Hold my line and come on."

Gregg hooked his right arm, his flashgun arm, across the end of Dole's lifeline. The multistrand fiber was white where the featherboat's internal lighting touched it. A few meters beyond the vessel, it vanished in darkness.

"I'm coming," said Stephen Gregg. He pushed off, too hard. His mouth was open. His limbs held their initial grotesque posture as though he were a dancer painted on the wall of a tomb.

The pull of the line in the crook of Gregg's arm made him turn a lazy pinwheel. The Fed ship rotated away. He saw the featherboat beneath him as a blur of grays and lightlessness.

The brilliant star beyond was Rondelet's sun. The few transits the Feds made before the *Peaches* brought them to had not taken the vessels beyond the local solar system.

Gregg hit, feet down by accident. His legs flexed to take the shock. "Good job, sir!" Dole cried as he steadied Gregg, attributing to skill what luck had achieved.

The boots of the hard suit had both electromagnets and adhesive grippers, staged to permit the same movements as gravity would. The suction system held here, as it would have done on a ceramic hull. The Fed ship was made of nonferrous alloys, probably aluminum. A plasma bolt would have made half the hull blaze like a torch. No wonder the crew had shut down as soon as they were aware they were under threat.

"Open them up, Dole," Jeude called. "They don't have suits, just an escape bubble, so they say they can't work the controls."

Jeude must have stuck his head out of the featherboat's hatch in order to use the IR intercom. Gregg thought he could see a vague movement against the straight lines of the coaming when he looked back, but that might have been imagination. He felt very much alone.

Large ships were normally fitted with airlocks for operations in vacuum. Small vessels didn't have space for them. In the case of *this* flimsy craft, cost had probably been a factor as well.

Dole twisted the wheel in the center of the hatch. It was mechanical rather than electronic. He had to spin it three full circuits before an icy twinkle of air puffed over him, shifting the hatch on its hinges at the same time.

As soon as the hatch had opened sufficiently for his armored form, Stephen Gregg pulled himself into the captured vessel behind his flashgun. He was unutterably glad to have a job he could do.

The three Fed crewmen cowered within the milky fabric of an escape bubble. Such translucent envelopes provided a modicum of protection at very little cost in terms of money or internal space. Inflated, they could keep one or two—three was stretching it, literally—persons alive so long as the air supply and CO_2 scrubbers held out.

One of the two humans in the bubble was a Rabbit. The remaining crewman was a Molt. Alone of the three, the Molt didn't flinch when the laser's fat muzzle prodded toward the bubble.

Dole scrambled in behind Gregg. "The captain's coming," he said. "Leave the hatch open."

The speaker on the vessel's control panel was useless without air to carry the sounds to the boarding party. Piet must have used radio or intercom to alert the crewman while he was still out on the hull.

The cabin of the captured ship was small. It was partitioned off from the cargo spaces with no direct internal communication. The Venerian featherboat was cramped and simple, but this ship had the crudity of a concrete slab.

A third armored figure slid through the hatchway, carrying a rough coil over his shoulder: Dole's lifeline, which Ricimer had unhooked from the *Peaches* before he launched himself toward the captive. Dole reached out and drew the hatch closed.

When the dogs were seated but the air system had only begun repressurizing the cabin, Piet Ricimer opened his visor. "Gentlemen," he announced in a voice made tinny by the rarefied atmosphere, "when you've answered my questions, I'll set you down on the surface of Rondelet where your friends can rescue you. But you *will* answer my questions."

Another man would have added a curse or a threat, Gregg thought. Piet Ricimer did neither.

Though with the flashgun aimed at the captives from point-blank range, threatening words wouldn't have added a lot.

33

Sunrise

"The meeting's in ten minutes," said Piet Ricimer, wobbling as a long gust typical of Sunrise stuttered to a lull. Though the two men were within arm's length of one another, he used the intercom in order to be heard. "Time we were getting back."

"You're in charge," Gregg said. There were no real hills in this landscape. He'd found a hummock of harder rock to sit down on. There was enough rise for his heels to grip and steady his torso against the omnipresent wind. "The meeting won't start until you get there."

A three-meter rivulet of light rippled toward them across the rocks and thin snow. The creature was a transparent red like that of a pomegranate cell. Twice its length from the humans, it dived like an otter into the rock and vanished.

Gregg's trigger finger relaxed slightly. He leaned on his left hand to look behind him, but there was no threat in that direction either.

The *Peaches, Dalriada*, and the prize Ricimer had named the *Halys* were a few hundred meters away. The ships had already gathered drifts in the lee of the prevailing winds. Temporary outbuildings housed the crusher and kiln with which the crews applied hull patches, though neither Venerian vessel was in serious need of refit.

On a less hostile world, men would have built huts for themselves as well. On Sunrise, they slept in the ships.

"What do you think, Stephen?" Ricimer asked. He faced out,

toward a horizon as empty as the plain on which he stood. Occasionally a tremble of light marked another of the planet's indigenous life forms.

Gregg shrugged within his hard suit. "You do the thinking, Piet," he said. "I'll back you up."

Ricimer turned abruptly. He staggered before he came to terms with the wind from this attitude. "Don't pretend to be stupid!" he said. "If you think I'm making a mistake, tell me!"

"I'm not stupid, Piet," Gregg said. He was glad he was seated. Contact with the ground calmed him against the atmosphere's volatility. "I don't care. About where we go, about how we hit the Feds. You'll decide, and I'll help you execute whatever you do decide."

A creature of light so richly azure that it was almost material quivered across the snow between the two men and vanished again. Gregg restrained himself from an urge to prod the rippling form with his boot toe.

Ricimer laughed wryly. "So it's up to me and God, is it, Stephen?" He clasped his arms closer to his armored torso. "I hope God is with me. I pray He is."

Gregg said nothing. He had been raised to believe in God and God's will, though without the particular emphasis his friend had received. Now—

He supposed he still believed in them. But he couldn't believe that the smoking bodies Stephen Gregg had left in his wake were any part of the will of God.

"I'm going to go back there and give orders," Ricimer continued. His face nodded behind the visor, though the suit's locked helmet didn't move. "There's a risk that my plan will fail disastrously. Even if it succeeds, some of my men will almost certainly die. Stephen, *you* may die."

"All my ancestors have," Gregg said. "I don't expect to be any different."

He raised his gauntleted hand to watch the ringers clench and unclench. "Piet," he said, "I trust you to do the best job you can. And to do a better job than anybody else could."

Ricimer laughed again, this time with more humor. "Do you, Stephen? Well, I suppose you must, or you wouldn't be here."

He put out a hand to help his friend stand. "Then let's go back to *Peaches,* since until I do my job of laying out the plan, none of the rest of you can do yours."

34

Sunrise

The command group met on the featherboat rather than the much larger *Dalriada* because of the electronics with which Ricimer had outfitted the vessel he and Gregg owned personally. The planning kernel which coupled to the AI was the most important of these toys at the moment. It converted navigational information into cartographic data and projected the result onto the *Peaches'* viewscreen.

An image of Umber, simplified into a tawny pancake marked with standard symbols, filled the screen now.

There were ten humans—the gentlemen and officers of the expedition—and two Molts packed into the featherboat's bay. John, the Molt captured aboard the *Halys*, had asked and been allowed to join the Venerians.

John's recent knowledge of Umber was an obvious advantage for the raid; Guillermo operated the display with a skill that none of the humans on the expedition could have equaled. Nonetheless, several of the *Dalriada*'s gentlemen looked askance at seeing aliens included in the command group.

"There's only one community on this side of Umber," Ricimer said as Guillermo focused the screen onto the upper edge of the pancake. "It's paired with a single community across the Mirror. The planetary surface is entirely desert on both sides, lifeless except for imported species."

From straight on like this, Umber appeared to be a normal planet with a diameter of about 5,000 kilometers. Instead, it was a section from the surface of a spheroid 12,000 klicks in diameter—had the remainder of the planet existed.

Umber's gravitational attraction was normal for the calculated size and density of the complete planet—slightly below that of Venus. There was no mass in realside, mirrorside, or *anywhere* to account for that gravity.

"Umber City is built along the Mirror," Ricimer continued. "The population varies, but there are usually about a thousand persons present."

"Both sides?" asked Wassail, the *Dalriada*'s navigator. Gregg had already been impressed by the way Wassail showed interest in new concepts. Dulcie, the *Dalriada*'s captain, was competent but as dull as his vessel's artificial intelligence.

"This side only," Ricimer said. "The community on mirrorside is much smaller and ninety percent of the residents are Molts. On realside, up to a third at any given time are human Federation personnel."

"One Venerian's worth six of those Fed pussies any day," Adrien interjected. "We'll go right through them!"

"We aren't here to fight," his brother said sharply. "We're going to take them by surprise, load with chips, and be away before they understand what's happened."

His lips pursed, then flattened into a smile of sorts. "Our task is somewhat complicated by the fact that another vessel attacked a freighter as it was starting to land on Umber two weeks ago."

Ricimer nodded toward John to source the data. "The attempt was unsuccessful—the attacker pursued into the atmosphere, and guns from the fort drove the hostile vessel off. It was sufficient to alarm the entire region, however. Umber sent couriers to neighboring planets and to Earth itself."

"A ship from Venus?" asked Bong. He was a younger son, like Gregg, but from an Ishtar City family.

"It was metal-hulled," Ricimer said. "In all likelihood Germans from United Europe."

He turned to face the screen in order to discourage further questions. "The spaceport is here," he said, pointing at the lower edge of the developed area.

The port area was bounded by four large water tanks on the

right. They held reaction mass brought from Rondelet on purpose-built tankers. Artesian wells supplied the town with drinking water, but such local reserves couldn't match the needs of the thrusters arriving at a major port.

The fort, a circle smaller than those of the water tanks, was sited below the lowest rank of dwellings. Below it in turn were the outlines of six starships, ranging from 20 to about 100 tonnes burden.

The ships, typical of the traffic Umber expected at any given time, were a symptom of a problem with the planning kernel. Its precision was a lie.

The kernel assembled data on Umber from the *Halys'* navigational files and from interrogations of two of the Fed crewmen. The third, the Rabbit, hadn't said a word from the time he was captured until Ricimer landed him, as promised, back on Rondelet.

The sum of that information was very slight. The kernel fleshed it out according to stored paradigms, creating streets and individual buildings in patterns which fit the specific data. It was easier for humans to visualize acting in a sketched city than in a shading marked DEVELOPED AREA, but that very feeling of knowledge had a dangerous side.

"The fort mounts four heavy guns," Ricimer went on. "They can be aimed and fired from inside the citadel, but there are no turrets or shields for the loading crews."

"Molts," John said.

Ricimer nodded. "The guns will certainly be manned, though two weeks without further trouble is long enough for some of the increased watchfulness to fade away.

"In the center of the community is a park fifty meters by seventy-five," Ricimer continued, "parallel to the Mirror. It's stocked with Terran vegetation, mostly grasses and shrubs. No large trees. The Commandatura faces it."

He tapped the screen. "All the colony's control and communications are centered in the Commandatura, and valuables are frequently stored in the vaults in the basement."

"Chips?" Wassail asked.

"Chips, valuable artifacts," Ricimer agreed. "They're brought across the Mirror here"—he indicated the "eastern" end of town, assuming north was up—"by a sectioned tramway laid through the Mirror. Molts push the cars through from mirrorside and back."

Guillermo murmured to John, who said, "No Molts are allowed to live west of the park. They use Rabbits for house servants." The click he added at the end of the statement was clearly the equivalent of a human spitting.

Piet Ricimer bowed his head, a pause or a silent prayer. "We'll proceed as follows," he resumed. "The *Halys* will land an hour after full darkness. Mr. Gregg will command."

Adrien Ricimer jumped to his feet. "No!" he said. "Let me lead the attack, Piet! I'm your brother!"

Everyone stared at him. No one spoke. Gregg began to smile, though it wasn't a pleasant expression.

"Adrien," Piet Ricimer said through dry lips, "please sit down. You're embarrassing me. You will be my second-in-command for the assault on the Commandatura."

Adrien's face set itself in a rictus. He hunched back into his seat.

"Stephen," Ricimer continued, "you'll have Dole as your bosun— is that satisfactory?"

"Yes."

"As well as John and four men from the *Dalriada*. Captain Dulcie, you will provide Mr. Gregg with four of your most trustworthy people. Do you understand?"

"I'll pick the men, sir," Wassail volunteered. "You'll want trained gunners?"

Ricimer nodded. "Yes, that's a good idea. Now, when the *Halys* has captured the fort . . ."

Stephen Gregg's mind wrapped itself in a crackling reverie that smothered the remainder of his friend's words. He would go over the complete plan at leisure. For now, all Gregg could focus on was the initial attack that might be the end of his involvement in the operation, and in life itself.

35

Umber

The *Halys* lurched into freefall. Dole cursed and reached for the main fuel feed.

"*Don't*," Gregg snapped, "touch that, Mr. Dole."

The thrusters fired under direction from the artificial intelligence. The vessel yawed violently before she came to balance and resumed a measured descent. John, crewing both sets of attitude controls, didn't move during the commotion.

"Christ's *blood*, sir!" Dole protested. "That's rough as a cob. I could do better than that!"

"We're here to look like Feds landing," Gregg said coolly. "That's what we're going to do"—he gave Dole a tight smile—"if it kills us. That means we let the AI bring us in, as coarse as it is and as crude as the thrusters it controls."

Gregg looked at the Molt on the attitude controls. "Is this how you would have landed if it had been you and your regular captain, John?" he asked.

"Yes," the alien said.

The *Halys*' viewscreen was raster-scanned. Synchronous problems divided the display into horizontal thirds, and the image within those segments was bad to begin with. Nor did it help visuals that a windstorm was blowing dust across Umber City as the raiders came in.

179

The four men from the *Dalriada* braced themselves against stan-chions and tried to keep their cutting bars from flopping. They seemed a solid crew. The three common sailors showed a natu-ral tendency to look to the fourth, a gunner's mate named Stampfer, when orders were given, but they'd showed no signs of deliber-ately rejecting either Gregg's authority or Dole's.

That was as well for them. Stephen Gregg might not trust him-self at piloting a starship, but he could damned well see to it that his orders were obeyed the second time.

The viewscreen's jagged images of sandy soil and the three ships already docked on Umber vanished suddenly in a wash of dust. "Hang on, boys," Gregg said. "Here it comes."

The thrusters slammed up to three-quarter power. Two of the attitude jets fired, controlling the yaw from the thrusters' asym-metry. The corrections were so harsh and violent that it was a moment before Gregg realized that the final shock had been the landing legs grounding.

He let go of the stanchion and flexed life back into his left hand. His right biceps had twinges also, from the way he'd clamped the flashgun against his chest.

He gave a broad grin. "Gentlemen," he said, "I can't begin to tell you how glad I am that's over."

For a moment, none of the crewmen spoke. Then Stampfer broke into a grin of his own and said, "Too fucking right, sir!"

Dole got up from the thruster controls. He nodded toward the hatch. "Shall I?"

Gregg switched off the *Halys'* internal lights. "Just crack it," he ordered. "Enough to check the local conditions. We aren't going anywhere for . . . fifteen minutes, that'll let them go back to sleep in the fort."

Dole swung the hatch far enough to provide a twenty-centimeter opening. The six humans instinctively formed a tight arc, shoulder-to-shoulder, to look out. One of the Dalriadans eased the hatch a little farther outward; Gregg didn't object.

Dust blew in. It created yellow swirls in the glow above instru-ment telltales. The outside light of the fort was a similar blur, scarcely brighter though it was less than a hundred meters away. Gregg couldn't see the docked ships from this angle, but they'd shown no signs of life from above.

Dole covered the breech of his rifle with a rag. Even so, the chance of the second round jamming when he tried to reload was considerable. Gregg consciously avoided checking his laser's battery, because he'd get nonconducting grit on the contacts sure as Satan loved sinners.

Well, even one shot would be too much. If a threat wasn't sufficient, they were going to need a warship's guns; and they didn't have a warship.

"I'll lead," he said, repeating the plan aloud to fill time, his and his men's, rather than because he thought any of them had forgotten it. "They'll be expecting us to register for tariff..."

The door beneath the light was steel and closed. It didn't open when Gregg pushed the latchplate. He pounded the panel with the heel of his left hand. Nothing happened.

He was terrified, not of death, but of failing so completely that he became a laughingstock for the expedition.

Dole muttered something to John. The Molt reached past Gregg, rapped the latch sharply to clear it of dust, and slammed the panel with the full weight of his body. Chitin rapped against the metal.

The door gave. Gregg pushed it violently inward with his left boot, bringing the flashgun up to his shoulder as he did so.

One of the six Molts in the room beyond had gotten up to deal with the door. He fell flat on the concrete floor when he saw he was looking down a laser's muzzle. The others froze where they sat at the desk they were using as a dining table.

Gregg jumped into the room so that his crew could follow him. "Who else?" he demanded in a harsh whisper. John chittered something in his own language.

A seated Molt pointed toward the inner door. He used only half his limb as though fearing that a broader gesture would leave his carapace blasted across the wall behind him. Things like that happened when the man at the trigger of a flashgun was keyed-up enough.

"One human," John said. "Perhaps asleep." He indicated the ladder through the ceiling. "There's no one in the gun room."

"Stampfer, check it out," Gregg whispered. "One of you, open the door for me."

He slid into position. The door panel was thermoplastic foam with a slick surface coating, no real obstacle. It opened outward.

A Dalriadan touched the handle, well aware that gobs of molten plastic would spray him if the flashgun fired *into* the panel. He jerked it open as Stampfer and two men clattered up the ladder.

Gregg pivoted in behind his flashgun. His visor was up, despite the risk to his retinas if he had to fire, but even so he couldn't find a target in a room lighted only by what spilled from the chamber behind him.

Something blurred. "What? What?" cried a woman's voice.

Dole found the light switch. A young woman, pig ugly by the standards of anyone who hadn't spent the past month in a male-crewed starship, sat up in a cot that was the only piece of furniture in the room. She looked terrified.

Gregg let out his breath in a sigh of relief that told him just how tense he had been. "Madam," he said, "you'll have to be tied up, but you will not be harmed in any way. You are a prisoner of the Free State of Venus."

"What?" she repeated. She tugged at her sheet. It was caught somewhere and tore. The hem covered her collarbones like a stripper's boa, leaving her breasts and navel bare.

"Tie her, Dole," Gregg said as he turned to leave. "And *no* problems! We're not animals."

"Of course not, sir," the bosun said. His voice was so meek that Gregg knew he'd been right to be concerned.

"While I go call down Piet and the others," Gregg added to himself. "May God be with them."

36

Umber

The *Peaches* grounded hard; Leon at the control console understood that speed was not only more important than grace, speed
was the *only* important thing.

Lightbody and Jeude threw the undogging levers, and a big
Dalriadan hurled the hatch open with a lift of his shoulders. Dirt
which the featherboat had gouged from the park as it landed
dribbled through the opening.

"Follow me!" Piet Ricimer cried. He stepped to the coaming and
pushed off in a leap that carried him clear of the plasma-blasted
ground. He sprawled onto all fours, jabbing the knuckles of his
rifle hand on a bush which exhaust had seared into a knot of
spikes. "Follow me!"

His men were following, squirting from the hatchway like somebody spitting watermelon seeds. He'd stripped the *Peaches*' interior for the operation, even shipping the bow gun onto the
Dalriada. Sixteen armed men were still a claustrophobically full
load for a landing from orbit.

The Commandatura was a stuccoed two-story building with an
arching false front to give the impression of greater height. There
were no lights on inside, but windows in neighboring structures
began to brighten. There was surprisingly little interest, given that
the featherboat had landed squarely in the center of town. The

spaceport was close enough that residents must be used to the roar of thrusters at all hours of the day and night.

The entrance doors were double glass panels in frames of baroque metalwork. Blowing sand had etched the glass into milky translucence.

Ricimer pushed the door. It didn't give.

"I got it!" bellowed the torso-armored Dalriadan who'd lifted the hatch. He hit the doors shoulder-first. Glass disintegrated into dangerous shards—

Terran ceramics! sneered a back part of Ricimer's mind.

—and the Dalriadan crashed through into a terrazzo lobby. The empty hinges clicked back and forth from the impact. They were intended to open outward.

A Molt wearing a dingy sash of office, probably a janitor, stepped from a side room, then fled back inside. A Venerian swept his cutting bar through the door and kicked the remnants aside as he and two fellows pursued.

Ricimer took the stairs to the second floor three at a time. He used his left hand to pull himself even faster by the balustrade. He fought to keep his eyes on the top of the stairs, not the step he was striding for as instinct would draw them. One of his men found the main light switch and brought the building to brilliant life.

"Somebody watch these rooms!" Ricimer called as he rounded the newel-post on the second floor and started up the black metal stairs to the communications center on the roof.

Every member of the landing party had been briefed on his job during the assault. Despite that, it was still possible that in the rush of the moment the men told off for cellars, ground-, and second-floor duties were all going to follow their commander to the roof.

The latch turned but the door at the top of the stair tower resisted. Ricimer put his shoulder against it. He was panting. The panel whipped away from him, pulled by the same strong wind that had held it closed.

The roof was a thicket of antennas and the guy wires that kept them upright. Lamps around the roof coping, ankle-height on three sides and taller than a man in front, cast a dust-dimmed illumination across the tangle. The antenna leads merged at the three-by-three-meter shed on a back corner of the roof. Ricimer ran to the structure, hopping like a spastic dancer to clear guys crossing his path.

The *Dalriada* was coming down, three minutes behind the featherboat, as planned. Gusts of wind compressed the roar of her thrusters into a throbbing pulse.

"Let me, sir," Leon cried as Ricimer reached for the door.

Ricimer nodded, knelt, and presented his rifle. The bosun leaned past him and gripped the latch in his left hand while his right held a cutting bar ready to strike. He jerked the door open.

The man inside the commo shack was asleep in his chair. His right hand trailed to the floor. A bottle had rolled away from him. Wind rattled another bottle, empty, against legs of the console.

Leon sniffed the fluid in the partial bottle and said, "Phew! I'd sooner drink hydraulic fluid!"

"Find the emergency channels," Ricimer ordered. "Start broadcasting that everyone should get into their bomb shelters immediately."

"Do they have bomb shelters, sir?" asked Marek, one of the pair of Dalriadans who had followed Ricimer to the roof as they were supposed to do.

"If they don't," Ricimer said, "they'll be even more frightened than if they do."

Leon pulled the radioman from his swivel chair and slung him out of the shack. The fellow still didn't awaken. Ricimer had heard him snore, so he wasn't dead of alcohol poisoning. Not yet, at any rate.

The lot to the east of the Commandatura was a fenced vehicle store. The building beyond it was two-story, with lines as simple as those of a concrete block. Lights went on behind the bank of curtained windows on the upper floor, but they went off again almost instantly.

Ricimer frowned. That showed an undesirable degree of alertness on somebody's part.

The *Dalriada* shook the city. The vertical glare of her eight small thrusters stood every vertical form in a pool of its own shadow. Moving with the ease of a featherboat, the 70-tonne vessel lowered beside the *Peaches,* demolishing the remainder of the park. Clods of imported dirt and the stony bedrock beneath pelted the Commandatura's facade and the other buildings nearby.

The thrusters shut off with a sucked-in *hiss,* hugely loud in the silence that followed. Guillermo handed Ricimer unasked the portable radio he could use now that plasma exhaust didn't blanket the RF spectrum.

As Ricimer put the modular unit to his mouth and ear, Leon came out of the commo shack and said, "I put Marek on the horn, sir." He thumbed toward the console. The Dalriadan had arranged three microphones before him on the ledge. He spoke earnestly into all of them at the same time. "What next?"

Ricimer opened his mouth to speak. Something glimmered on the upper floor of the building across the parking lot. "Watch—" he said.

At least a dozen rifles volleyed from the other building. Leon pitched forward, blood spraying from his mouth. Something punched Ricimer's right thigh below his body armor; another round slammed high on his left shoulder. The bullet splashed on the ceramic, but its shock threw Ricimer down. Bits of red-hot jacket metal stung his cheek.

A bullet-severed guy wire howled a sour chord. The antenna it braced fell over.

Adrien was yammering something on his radio. Ricimer's own unit was the command set. He held the radio above his face as he lay on his back and switched it to the glowing purple override setting.

"Ricimer to Dulcie!" he called. He wasn't shouting. "Hit the building across the parking lot from us. It's a barracks. Use your cannon to—"

The *Dalriada* had landed with her eight 10-cm weapons run out to port and starboard. The crash of the first gun to fire cut Ricimer's orders short.

The point-blank bolt punched low through the front of the building and blew out all the ground-floor windows. Glass and framing shotgunned in all directions, driven by a rainbow-hued fireball.

The barracks walls were thermoplastic sheathing on a metal frame. They were beginning to sag outward when a second plasma cannon fired into the upper story.

The Feds' armory exploded in a numbing blast. Chunks of roof lifted and rained down from a black mushroom cloud. The remainder of the barracks flattened across the immediate neighborhood like a crushed puffball.

Marek stumbled out of the commo shack. The secondary

explosion had wrecked the equipment and torn off three walls, but the Dalriadan seemed unhurt. Lights all over the city went out when the barracks exploded.

Guillermo examined Leon with a pencil flash. Ricimer glanced over. The bosun wasn't wearing a gorget to lock his helmet and body armor together. A bullet had drilled through the back of Leon's neck and exited where his nose had been until that instant.

Guillermo switched off the light.

It must have been instantaneous. All things were with God.

Ricimer rolled to his knees. He thought he was okay, though a double spasm shook his right thigh as he moved. He rotated the radio's control to its green setting, normal send-and-receive.

"—basement vault open," Adrien's voice was saying. *Did the boy even realize he'd been locked out of the net?* "But the real value, the purpose-built chips, they're at the tramhead. Let's go get them now. They're worth ten times the old pre-Collapse run! Answer me, Piet!"

"Ricimer to Adrien," Piet said. He stood up unaided, but he had to grasp Guillermo's shoulder an instant later when his thigh spasmed again. "Stay where you are. I'm coming down. Break. Ricimer to Dulcie, over."

"Go ahead, sir," the *Dalriada*'s captain caroled back. "Did you see how we blasted those bastards? Ah, over."

"Don't release your follow-up party until further orders," Ricimer said. He was feeling dizzy. Perhaps that was why Dulcie's delight in the—necessary, and ordered—slaughter struck him so wrong. "Ricimer out."

He released the sending key and handed the radio back to Guillermo. It would be some minutes before the ground beneath the *Dalriada* cooled enough for the second sixteen-man team to disembark, but Ricimer didn't want them scattering before he determined how best to deploy them. The expedition had only three handheld radios—his, Adrien's, and the one with Stephen's party in the fort. When the additional crewmen left the *Dalriada*, they were out of touch except by shouted commands.

"Come on," Ricimer said to Marek and Guillermo. "There's nothing more for us up here."

The Dalriadan glanced down at Leon.

Ricimer was already heading for the stair tower. Their duties were to the living. The dead were in the hands of God.

37

Umber

The Commandatura basement was divided by concrete walls into a larger and a smaller volume. The former was a jumble of general storage, unsorted and in large measure junk. The smaller room was intended as a vault, but the open door couldn't have been closed until some of the boxes piled around it were removed.

A man in Federation whites cowered against the wall outside the vault. A Dalriadan held a flashlight on him, while another waved a cutting bar close to the prisoner's face. When the Venerian saw Ricimer appear at the foot of the stairs, he triggered the bar. Its whine brought a howl of terror from the captive.

"Stop that," Ricimer ordered sharply.

His brother came out of the vault, holding a handful of loose microchips. "See Piet?" he said, waving his booty through a flashlight's beam. "They're old production here, and it'll take forever to load them with the power out. You! Heathen! Tell my brother about the new stock."

The prisoner had opened his eyes a crack when the cutting bar went off. "Sirs," he whimpered, "the latest production, they're just now being brought across the Mirror. It's only two weeks till the Earth Convoy arrives, so they're being stored in the blockhouse at the head of the tramway."

"Why?" Ricimer demanded. He shook his head to try and clear

it. His sight and hearing were both sharp, but all sensory impressions came to him as if from a distance.

"So as not to have to shift it twice, sirs," the prisoner said. His sleeve insignia marked him as a mid-level specialist of some sort, probably a clerk pulling night duty. He'd opened his eyes fully and had even straightened up a little against the wall. "The blockhouse is safe enough for a few days, surely."

"Not now it isn't!" Adrien cried exultantly. "Let's go clear it out now! Right, Piet?"

A Dalriadan crashed down the stairs so quickly that he almost bowled Ricimer out of the way. Guillermo's presence brought him at the last instant to the realization the man with his back to the stairs was his commander.

"Schmitt and Lucius got two of the trucks running, sir!" the man shouted. "The windshield's blown off, but they run. Do we go?"

Ricimer started to shake his head, still trying to clear it. He pressed his hands to his face instead when he realized the gesture would be misinterpreted. He wished he could think. He must have left his rifle on the roof, or was that one of the weapons Guillermo now carried?

"Yes, all right," he said through his hands. "I'll have the second team begin loading these as soon as they can open the *Dalriada*. I wish—"

He didn't know how he'd meant to finish the sentence.

Adrien and the Dalriadans bolted up the stairs. Ricimer wobbled as he started to follow. He got his stride under control and shook away the Molt's offered hand.

He wished Stephen were here.

Jeude met him at the ground-floor stairhead. "We're getting the navigational data out of the computers, sir," he said, waving a sheaf of flat transfer chips. "Lightbody's finishing up. We got the emergency backup running when the mains power blew. Hey, what was that bang?"

"Leon's dead," Piet Ricimer said inconsequently. "I—you two stay here, finish your work. It's important. We'll be back. Tell—"

He shook his head. "Guillermo, give him the radio. Adrien has one already. Tell Captain Dulcie to put the second team to loading the vault's contents as soon as they can. We're going after purpose-built chips at the, at the tramhead."

"Piet!" Adrien's voice echoed faintly through the wrecked doorway. "Come on if you're coming!"

"We're coming," Piet Ricimer mumbled as he staggered forward. Guillermo paced him. One jointed arm curved about the commander's waist, not touching him but ready to grasp should Ricimer fall.

Jeude watched them with a worried expression.

As the first truck roared out of the parking lot, a Dalriadan helped lift Piet Ricimer onto the bed of the second while Guillermo lifted him from behind. He was very tired. The truck driver accelerated after Adrien in the leading vehicle. The Molt had to run along behind for a few steps before he could jump aboard.

Though the wind had abated, the lead truck lifted freshly-deposited dust from the street and spun it back in the follower's headlights in a double whorl. The diffused illumination joined them as a bar of opaque yellow.

Occasionally the edges of murky light touched a Molt standing in front of a building, watching the vehicles. Once a human ran out into the street ahead, shouting and waving his arms. He jumped to safety when Adrien's truck didn't slow. The Dalriadan beside Ricimer fired at the sprawling figure but missed.

Instead of being laid out in a straight line, the street to the tramway kinked like a watercourse. The trucks, diesel stake beds, were clumsy, and even the leading driver's visibility was marginal. The modest pace, grinding gears, and frequent jolting direction changes hammered Ricimer into a kind of waking nightmare.

Something changed, but Ricimer wasn't sure what it was. Then he realized the vehicles had pulled up at a line of steel bollards. Beyond the waist-high barrier was a low building with several meters of frontage. One leaf of the front double door was open. The facade was pierced by four loopholes besides.

"Master, are you all right?" someone/Guillermo murmured in Ricimer's ear.

Men jumped out of the trucks. Adrien swung from the cab of the other vehicle and strode to the bollards. Beyond the blockhouse, the Mirror could be sensed but not seen.

"I'm—" Piet Ricimer said. He pitched sideways, off the truck bed. Guillermo tried to grab him but failed.

Ricimer knew that he'd hit the pavement, but he felt no pain.

His right leg was cold. The trousers were glued to his skin by blood from the thigh wound that he only noticed now. He couldn't make his limbs move.

A Molt wearing a Federation sash stepped out of the blockhouse. "Halt!" he ordered in Trade English. "Who are you?"

Adrien shot the alien in the head. "C'mon, boys!" he cried. "They're just Molts!"

The wall gun mounted at one of the loopholes fired a 1-kg explosive shell into Adrien's chest. Ricimer saw his brother's body hurled back in a red blast. Adrien's helmet and bits of his shattered breastplate gleamed in the flash of the second gun, which fired from the other side of the door. The round hit a Dalriadan, blowing off both legs and lifting his armored torso several meters in the air.

Guillermo knelt and lifted Piet Ricimer in a fireman's carry. The Molt had discarded his weapons to free both arms.

Rifle bullets pecked craters in the surface of the blockhouse. A Venerian jumped into the cab of the other truck. A shell struck the engine compartment and blew blazing kerosene across the men falling back in confusion. The cannons' muzzle flashes were yellow-orange, brighter than those of the bursting charges.

Guillermo jogged down the dusty street. Only the wall guns were firing. A crewman passed them, screaming, "Jesusjesusjesus!" Ricimer saw the man was missing his right arm.

That was the last thing he noticed before night stooped down on him with yellow pinions.

38

Umber

Flame burped over the roofs of the darkened city. The light was gone before Gregg could jerk his head around to watch it directly. The sound which came a moment later was hollow, *choong* rather than a bang.

"What was that, sir?" Dole called from the control room. "Was it a bomb?"

A post-mounted tannoy and omnidirectional microphone connected the unprotected gun deck on the fort's roof with the thick-walled citadel set off in a corner below. The latter had room for only the battery controls and one person, the fort's human officer.

The emergency generator had fired up without hesitation when external power failed after the explosion. It was a ceramic diesel of Venerian manufacture. Trade would have been a lot simpler.

Gregg stared at Umber City. The center of the community was a rose and magenta glow, though the flames were too low to be seen above the buildings on the southern side of town. "No," he said.

He realized that his bosun couldn't hear him. He turned and called loudly toward the microphone array, "No, it was probably a fuel tank rupturing in the heat. Don't bother us with questions, Mr. Dole."

"Watch it! Watch it!" Stampfer cried.

A cutting bar's note rose to a high scream as the gun mount twisted enough to free the sides of the blade. Gregg pressed himself against the roof's chest-high windscreen. The light metal bonged from the pressure.

A Dalriadan tugged his cutting bar hard to free it and jumped clear. A tag of metal fractured. The heavy plasma cannon sagged slowly toward the deck, restrained but not supported by the remaining mount.

"There we are!" the crewman said triumphantly. "Let 'em try to use that one as we take off."

"One down," Stampfer said, "three to go. Get at it."

He looked over to Gregg. "We're not equipped for this, sir," he added apologetically. "It's a job for a machine shop, not cutting bars."

"Do what you can," Gregg said. "Likely that the Feds'll have other things on their minds by the time we lift."

"I wish they'd tell us what was going on," one of the Dalriadans said wistfully.

"They've got their own duties!" Gregg blazed. "So do you! Get to it!"

He turned, more to hide his embarrassment at overreacting than to look at the city. He wished somebody'd tell him what was going on too. The sophisticated handheld radios Ricimer had bought for the expedition couldn't listen in on calls on the net that weren't directed to them.

When the *Dalriada* fired its main battery and the target went up in a gigantic secondary explosion, Gregg and his outlying squad spent nearly a minute convinced there'd been a catastrophe. Dulcie had finally responded to Gregg's call, but he didn't know anything about what Piet and the landing party were doing either.

Stampfer, the two crewmen on deck with him, and John changed batteries in their cutting bars and sawed at a mount of another 20-cm cannon. Gregg had expected to disable the guns as he left the fort by blasting the control room. Though the fort did have director control, the individual cannon each had a mechanical triggering system that was too simple and sturdy to be easily destroyed.

That meant they had to cut the gun mounts—properly a third-echelon job, as Stampfer said. But you did what you had to do.

Gunfire thumped from the east end of town. Gregg squinted

in an attempt to see what was happening—nothing at this distance, not even the flicker of muzzle flashes.

He glanced back at his men. They hadn't heard the shooting over the howl of their bars, and they probably wouldn't have understood the significance anyway.

The weapons firing were bigger than handheld rifles. The expedition hadn't brought any projectile weapons that big.

A car with a rectangular central headlight sped toward the fort from the west end of town. The vehicle wasn't following a road. It jounced wildly and occasionally slewed in deep sand.

"Watch it!" Gregg cried. "We've got company. Dole, Gallois, can you hear me?"

"Yessir-ir," crackled the tannoy. One Dalriadan guarded the prisoners in the ready room, while Dole kept track of distant threats in the control room. All they needed for this to become an epic disaster was for the Earth Convoy to arrive while the raid was going on . . .

"Don't shoot!" he added. "They may be our people."

They might be a party of whirling dervishes from the Moon, for all he knew. Why the *hell* didn't anybody communicate?

"Stampfer!" he said. "Cut away this fucking shield for me, will you?"

He kicked the windscreen; it flexed and rang. "It won't stop spit, but *I* can't shoot through it with a laser."

Stampfer triggered his bar and swept it through the screen in a parabola, taking a deep scallop out of the thin metal. The windscreen depended on integrity and a rolled rim for stiffening. The edges of the cut flapped inward, shivering like distant thunder.

The car swung to a halt beside the door on the fort's north side. It was an open vehicle with three people aboard, all of them human. They were armed.

"Hold it!" Gregg called, aiming the flashgun. The flat roof was three meters above the ground.

"You idiots!" screamed the woman who jumped from the left side of the car. "We're under attack! Are you blind?"

She waved a pistol in Gregg's direction.

"Drop your guns!" Gregg ordered. "Now!"

His visor was down, but the light outside the fort was good enough that he could see the woman's expression change from anger to open-eyed amazement.

The two men climbing from the other side of the car put their hands in the air. The woman fired at Gregg.

He didn't know where the bullet went. It didn't hit him. He put a bolt from his flashgun into the fuel tank of the car. The tank must have been nearly empty, a good mix of air and hydrocarbons, because it went off like a bomb instead of merely bursting in a slow gush of flame.

The shock threw the woman against the fort's wall and straightened Gregg as he groped for a reload. She was screaming. Gregg raised his visor and tried to locate the others. Somebody was running back toward Umber City. He couldn't see the remaining Fed; he was probably in the ring of burning diesel.

A bullet whanged through the north and south sides of the windscreen but managed to miss everything else. The shooter was in one of the houses, but the twinkling muzzle flash didn't give Gregg a good target.

He keyed the radio. "Gregg to Ricimer!" he shouted. "We're under attack. What is your status? Over!"

A shot winked from one of the houses only a hundred and fifty meters away. The bullet slapped the concrete and ricocheted upward.

Gregg sighted, closed his eyes because he hadn't time to fool with the visor, and squeezed. His bolt cracked through an open window, liberated its energy on an interior wall, and turned somebody's bedroom into a belching inferno.

Nobody answered him on the radio. More Feds were shooting. A bullet that glanced from one of the plasma cannon splashed bits onto Gregg's hand as he reached for his battery satchel. Pity the fort's architect had made sure the big guns couldn't be trained on the city.

Dole knelt beside Gregg, fired, and reloaded. He must have cleaned his rifle of grit while he had time.

"Stampfer," Gregg called without looking behind him. "How long to disable all the guns?"

"Jesus, sir—"

Something moved between buildings. Gregg's snap shot was instinctive. Only when the rattling explosion followed his bolt did he realize that he'd hit another vehicle. This one was loaded with enough ammunition to flatten both the adjacent structures. He blinked as if he could wipe the afterimages of his own shot from the surface of his eyes.

"—at least a fucking hour!"

"Hey!" shouted a Dalriadan. "Hey, that Molt of ours just jumped off the roof and run away!"

"So let him go," Gregg snarled. "Dole, get back to the *Halys.* Don't light her up, I don't want to lose the radio—"

It seemed he'd already lost the fucking radio, so far as everybody in the main party was concerned.

"—but be ready to go. Leave me your rifle! Stampfer, can that gun you cut loose still fire?"

"You bet!"

"Get down in the control room. Send your men off with Dole, they're no good now. Don't worry about the prisoners, the tape'll hold long enough. *Move,* everybody!"

Dole fired again toward the city. "Sir," he said, "I don't want to leave—"

A bullet struck the center of Gregg's breastplate. His chest went numb with the *whack!* The inside of both arms burned as though they'd been scraped with a saw blade.

"Get the *fuck* out, you whoreson!" Gregg screamed as he lurched to his feet. He fired into the night, without a conscious target. A figure flung its rifle away and fell from a second-story window. It was a Molt. It lay on the ground, its Federation trappings burning brightly enough to illuminate the body.

Everyone else had left the roof. Gregg ducked below the level of the windscreen, no protection but it blocked his opponents' view.

The dismounted plasma cannon was already pointed generally to the north. Gregg put his shoulder against the barrel and tried to slew it more nearly in line with the houses from which the rifle fire came. The gun wouldn't move. His boots slipped on the deck.

"*Dalriada* to Gregg!" the radio flopping against his side shrilled. The voice might have been Dulcie's, though it was an octave higher than Gregg had heard before from Dulcie's throat. "For God's sake save yourself! Mr. Ricimer's dead and—"

Two plasma cannon blasted from the center of town, backlighting rooftops like a strobe light. Even as the second blast rang out, thruster exhaust blanketed the RF spectrum.

Gregg's radio roared with static. He prodded at it with a finger, trying to find the power switch. The static pulsed as he switched bands uselessly instead. He smashed the unit with the edge of his hand, using his torso armor as the anvil to his rage.

Fragments of thermoplastic and electronic components prickled his skin.

The *Dalriada* rose on a huge billow of plasma, shaking the world. A moment later, the *Peaches* followed, dancing like lint above an air vent because of the larger vessel's exhaust.

Gregg screamed in fury, backed a step, and kicked the *twisted* gun mount with his bootheel. Metal creaked. He pushed again at the barrel, planting his hands as close to the muzzle as he could to maximize his leverage. The massive weapon slid a millimeter, then jounced across the decking for half a meter before it locked up again. The edge of the muzzle scored a bright line in the concrete.

Gregg jumped into the stairway to the ready room and hunched there. "Go ahead, Stampfer!" he shouted. He didn't have time to close the armored door above him. He'd seen figures scuttling toward the fort out of the corner of his eye. "Shoot! Shoo—"

The plasma cannon fired. The bolt, the residue of a directed thermonuclear explosion, struck the deck at a flat angle and sprayed out over a 120° arc. The portion of windscreen in the blast's path vaporized; the shockwave blew the rest of it off the fort's roof, along with everything else smaller than the other cannon. The rifle and bandolier Dole left according to orders were gone forever.

Scattered backflare seared Gregg's hands even though he huddled below roof level and clasped them against his chest. The cannon recoiled hard, shearing the remaining mount and dumping the weapon itself over the lip of the building.

Stampfer stumbled out of the control citadel. He mouthed words, but Gregg couldn't hear them. Gregg waved the gunner ahead and climbed after him to the blast-scarred roof.

The line of thirty houses facing the fort was on fire, every one of them. Some were built of concrete, but the surge of ions had ignited their interiors as surely as those of houses built of less refractory materials.

For a moment Gregg thought he was still being shot at. No bullets sparked or whined around him. Rifle ammunition was cooking off in the blaze.

There were still three mounted plasma cannon. Gregg stared at them transfixed. *He could hold the fort himself while the* Halys *lifted the rest of his party to safety.*

Stampfer seized Gregg by the hand and rotated him so that they

were face-to-face. The Dalriadan patted the nearest plasma cannon with his free hand.

"C'mon!" he said, speaking with exaggerated lip movements to
make himself more comprehensible to his half-deafened commander. "These're fucked good by the backblast. The training gear's
welded. Let's get out while we can!"

Stampfer jumped off the south side of the deck, keeping the
fort's bulk between him and the burning city.

Gregg followed. When he threw his arms out to balance him,
pain lancing across his pectoral muscles stopped the motion. He
fell on his face and had to shuffle his knees forward to rise.

He began running, ten paces behind Stampfer. The vessel's side
hatch was open, and the glow of her idling thrusters was a beacon to safety.

39

Sunrise

Dole waited poised at the controls while a gust of unusual violence even for Sunrise channeled between the hulls of the *Dalriada* and that of the metal-built ship lying parallel to her. The wind settled to 15 or 20 kph.

"There!" the *Halys'* bosun said as he shut the thrusters down with a flourish. "*That's* greasing her in!"

"I'll go see what I can learn about why we were abandoned on Umber that way," said Stephen Gregg in an expressionless voice. He reached for the hatch control.

"Sir?" Dole said, sharply enough to draw Gregg's attention back from its bleak reverie. "Ah—d'ye think you're going to need the flashgun you're carrying?"

Gregg stared at him. "That depends on what I learn," he said evenly.

"Right, right," said Dole as he rose from the console. "So wait for a minute while I get my gear on too, okay?"

Stampfer got up from the attitude controls. He laced his fingers together over his head and stretched them against the normal direction of the joints. "I guess we'll all go, sir," he said toward the bulkhead. "It was all our asses they left to swing in the breeze, wasn't it?"

"Too right," murmured Gallois, already half into his hard suit.

"Say," said another of the Dalriadans plaintively as he donned his armor, "does anybody know what that other ship's doing here with our two?"

"I don't know what it's doing," Gregg said as he waited for his men to equip themselves, "but I'm pretty sure what it is, is the *Adler.* They're Germans from United Europe."

He paused while he remembered Virginia. "The captain's a man named Schremp," he added. "I could have lived a good deal longer without seeing him again."

Dole had brought the *Halys* in between two ships lying within a hundred meters of one another. It was a form of bragging, proving how much better he could do than the *Halys'* AI.

It had also been dangerous, but Gregg felt too bloody-minded to care if misjudgment sent them crashing through the side of the *Dalriada.* Anyway, it was a short walk hatch-to-hatch in the brutal wind.

The ramp to the *Dalriada's* forward hold dropped as soon as Gregg opened the *Halys.* He and his crew started toward the larger vessel. A single man waited for them in the hold. He raised his visor as they entered.

It was Piet Ricimer.

"Good Christ!" Gregg blurted. "Piet, I—Dulcie told me you were dead."

"Thanks to the goodness of Christ," Ricimer said, a reproof so gentle you had to know him well to recognize it, "nothing happened to me that rest and a great deal of blood plasma couldn't cure."

He glanced toward the ramp. "I'm going to close the hatch now," he said, reaching for the control. "You'd better step forward, Gallois."

Gregg embraced him. Their suits clashed together loudly.

"I thought you were, were lost too, Stephen," Ricimer murmured. "When I came to, I asked where you were. They said they were sure you'd lifted off of Umber, but you hadn't joined them on the run to Sunrise."

"Them bastards took off like scalded cats!" Dole snarled. "And us in a Federation pig that thinks it's a miracle to come within four zeros of her setting on a transit. Of *course* we were going to be a couple days behind, if the bastards didn't wait up on us!"

"I've got something to discuss with Captain Dulcie," Gregg said in a voice as pale as winter dawn. He clapped his friend on the back and moved toward the companionway to the bridge.

Ricimer stepped in front of him. "No, Stephen," he said. "I made the plans, I gave the orders. The fault was mine."

"You were unconscious!" Gregg shouted.

"I was responsible!" Ricimer shouted. They were chest-to-chest. "I *am* responsible, under God, for the future success of this voyage. Me!"

Both men eased back by half-steps. They were breathing hard. "Stephen," Ricimer said softly. "What's done is done. It's the future that counts. Those mistakes won't happen again."

Gregg smiled savagely. "So, it's forgive and forget, is that it, Piet?" he said.

"No, Stephen," Ricimer said. "Just forgive." He wet his lips with his tongue. "It was good enough for our Lord, after all."

Gregg laughed. He turned to his crew. "How do you men feel about that?" he asked mildly.

Men shrugged within their hard suits. "Whatever you say, sir," Stampfer said.

Gregg put his flashgun muzzle-down on the deck. "What I say," he said, "is that we all swore an oath to obey Captain Ricimer when we signed on for this voyage. So I guess we'd better do that."

He grinned lopsidedly at his friend.

Ricimer unlatched his hard suit. "We can leave all the gear here," he said. "I'll be going back aboard the *Peaches* after the meeting myself."

"Meeting?" Gregg repeated as he began to strip off his armor also.

"Yes," Ricimer said. "You're just in time for it. Captain Schremp has a crewman who was aboard the *Tolliver* when we refitted here on the previous voyage. As a result he located us, and he wants us to join forces with him on the next stage of our operations . . ."

40

Sunrise

A dozen members of the *Dalriada* crew bent over equipment in the compartment adjoining the bridge and captain's suite. They weren't precisely lurking; even after the casualties on Umber, space aboard the 70-tonne vessel was tight. There was no question that the men's nervous attention was directed toward the meeting in the next chamber.

Besides the Dalriadans, three metal hard suits stood in pools of condensate. One of the suits was silvered, and the rifle slung from it was the ornate, pump-action repeater Gregg had seen Captain Schremp carrying.

Ricimer led Gregg onto the bridge. The ten men already there crowded it. Only Wassail among the *Dalriada*'s officers would meet Gregg's cold eyes, but the Germans nodded to the newcomers.

To Gregg's surprise, Schremp clearly recognized him. Of course, Gregg hadn't forgotten Captain Schremp . . .

"Rondelet," the German captain boomed before Ricimer had seated himself again at the head of the chart table. "There's a hundred occupied islands with Fed ships at a score of them at any given time. None of them are defended to the degree that'll be a problem to you and me together."

He waved a hairy, powerful hand. "Umber was suicide. You were lucky to get out of it as well as you did, Ricimer."

"Umber might not have been such a problem," said Stephen Gregg from where he stood by the hatch, "except some idiot had botched a raid two weeks before and roused the whole region."

One of the Germans muttered a curse and started to get up from his chair. Schremp waved him down with a curt gesture and said, "We needed a featherboat on Umber, that is so. On Rondelet your featherboat comes in low, eliminates the defense battery, and the larger ships drop down and finish the job. Together, it's easy."

"Our raid on Umber wasn't such a failure as it may have appeared to outsiders," Ricimer said coolly. "I've reviewed the pilotry data we gathered there, and it's clear that the Federation holds Rondelet in considerable strength. Each of the magnates there has an armed airship of his own . . . and as you've pointed out, Captain Schremp, there are more than a hundred of these individual fiefdoms."

"They're spread out," insisted one of Schremp's henchmen, a squat fellow with blond hair on his head but a full red beard. "We pick an island where a ship is loading, strip the place, and we're gone before the neighbors wake up."

"Or," Ricimer said, "we're a few seconds late in lifting off, and there's a score of airships circling the island, waiting to put plasma bolts into our thrusters when we're a thousand meters up. I think not."

Schremp's hands clenched on the chart table. He deliberately opened them and forced his face into a smile. "Come now, Captain Ricimer," he said in a falsely jocular tone. "There are always risks, of course, but these Principals as they call themselves—they live like kings on their little islands, yes, but they don't have armies. A dozen or so armed Molts for show, that is all. *They* won't fight."

"My late brother," Ricimer said with a perfect absence of emotion, "was saying something very similar when a Molt killed him."

Gregg's face went as blank as his friend's. *He'd wondered why Adrien wasn't present* . . . He reached over, regardless of the others, and squeezed Ricimer's shoulder.

"The Earth Convoy will top off and refit on Rondelet on its way to Umber," Wassail put in. He'd obviously studied and understood the data lifted from Umber's Commandatura also. "It's due anytime now."

"All right," snarled the blond German, "what do you propose we do? Calisthenics on the beautiful beaches outside and then go home?"

"No, Mr. Groener," Ricimer said. "My men and I are going to Benison. What your party does is of course your own affair."

"Benison?" Schremp cried. "Benison! There's nothing but local trade there. *Food* ships to Rondelet and Umber. Where's the profit there?"

"A ship itself is worth something," said Dulcie, "when you pay for it at the point of a gun." The *Dalriada*'s captain had brightened noticeably when Ricimer said they weren't going to attack another well-defended target.

Schremp stood up. His right fist pumped three times, ending each stroke millimeters above the tabletop. "Are you all cowards?" he demanded. "Did you all have your balls shot off on Umber, is that it?"

He turned and pointed at Gregg. "You, Mr. Gregg," he said. "Will you come with me? *You're* not a coward."

Gregg had been leaning against the hatchway. He rocked himself fully upright by flexing his shoulders. "My enemies have generally come to that conclusion, Captain," he said. "Neither am I a deserter, or a fool."

Schremp didn't flinch at Gregg's tone, but Dulcie stared at his hands in horror.

"So be it!" Schremp said. Everyone in the room was standing. "You will not help us, so we will help ourselves."

He led his entourage off the bridge, bumping between chairs and Venerians pressed against the bulkhead. At the hatch Schremp turned and said, "Captain Ricimer, for your further endeavors, I wish you even better fortune than you had on Umber!"

Gregg closed the hatch behind the Germans. They would be several minutes in the next compartment donning their hard suits—unless they were angry enough to face Sunrise weather unprotected as they returned to the *Adler*.

The Venerians looked at one another, visibly relaxing. "Well," said Dulcie, breaking the silence, "I think picking up the local trade on Benison is far the best idea."

Ricimer gave him a lopsided smile. "Oh," he said, "that isn't my plan at all, Captain Dulcie. Though we *are* going to Benison."

41

Benison

Lightbody would be watching the panel, but Gregg had set the sonic scanner to provide an audio signal before he let himself doze off in the featherboat's bay. The *peep-peep-peep* of the alarm wakened him instantly, even though when he came alert the tiny sound was lost in the shriek of a saw fifty meters away cutting into the frame of the *Halys.*

Lightbody, bending down to arouse Gregg, seemed surprised he was already up. "Somebody's coming from the east, sir," he whispered. "I think it must be the captain coming back."

"I think so too," Gregg said. He checked the satchel of reloads, aimed his flashgun, and then tested his faceshield's detents to be sure that it would snap closed easily if he needed the protection. Daylight through the foliage had a soft, golden tinge.

The saw stopped. Somebody cheered in satisfaction. The men were treating their work as if it were a normal shipwright's task, ignoring the fact they were on a hostile planet. Realistically, there was no silent way to remove a thruster and the transit system from a ship built as a single module; besides, five hundred meters of the dense forest would drink the noise anyway. The comfortable, even carefree manner of the men under his temporary command irritated Gregg nonetheless.

"I'm coming in," called Piet Ricimer. He was out of sight, to prevent a nervous bullet or laser bolt. "I'm alone, and I'm coming in."

"Thank God for that!" Gregg said. He jumped down and met his friend ten meters from the *Peaches*. They shook, left hand to left hand, because Gregg held the flashgun to his side on its muzzle-forward patrol sling.

"Where's Guillermo?" Gregg asked.

"With K'Jax and his, well, Clan Deel," Ricimer explained as they walked back to the featherboat. "There's fifty or sixty of them coming. I came on ahead."

"We need that many?" Gregg said.

"For portage," his friend replied. "I don't want more than one trip through the Mirror. I'll only need a few of our people, humans; specialists. Ah, I want you to remain in charge of the base party and the vessels."

They'd reached the *Peaches*. Men without specific tasks—and Dulcie, who was supposed to be overseeing work on the *Halys*—strode toward their commander along the paths trampled to mud beneath the trees.

"I want to be able to flap my arms and fly," said Gregg evenly. "That's not going to happen either."

"We've got the AI dismounted and we're almost done sectioning it for carriage, Captain Ricimer," Dulcie boomed with enthusiasm. "And the powerplant, thrusters and plumbing, that's already complete. The ship's pretty well junked, though."

Ricimer nodded absently to him. "The *Halys* wasn't a great deal to begin with," he said. "But she'll do. Stephen—"

Gregg shook his head. "There was work to be done here," he said. "Fine, I stayed while you went off to find the Molts. I'd sooner have gone, but I understood the need."

"And—" began Ricimer.

"*Now*," Gregg continued forcefully, "the operation's on the other side of the Mirror, and there's nothing to do here but wait. I'm sure Captain Dulcie can wait just as well as I could."

He nodded pleasantly at the *Dalriada*'s captain. Dulcie blinked, suspicious that he was being insulted but relieved at the implication that he wouldn't be expected to take a front rank in the coming raid. "Well, I'm sure you can depend on me to do my duty, gentlemen," he said.

"An autogyro patrolling the fields came close enough we could hear it," Gregg said. "The camouflage net over the *Dalriada* did the job. That's the *only* threat in the past three days. Don't tell me you're not going to need a shooter worse on mirrorside. Because if you do, I'll call you a liar, Piet."

Ricimer shook his head. "Well," he said, "we can't have that. I think six of the men will be sufficient. How did those with you aboard the *Halys* work out, Stephen?"

"None of them were problems," Gregg said without hesitation. "Dole and Stampfer I'd take with me anywhere."

"Then we'll take them on this operation," Ricimer said. He smiled. "I'm not sure they'll find it so great an honor after they've had personal experience with the Mirror."

Ricimer's face hardened. "I'll inspect the supplies and equipment for the operation now," he added crisply. "If possible, I'd like to leave as soon as Guillermo gets here with our allies."

"I've got them," Gregg called up to the Molt invisible in the treetop as the wicker basket wobbled down into his arms.

Gregg transferred handfuls of recharged batteries from the basket to an empty satchel, then replaced them with another dozen that had been run flat with the tree cutting and shaping. The barkfiber rope was looped around the basket handle and spliced instead of simply being tied off. Otherwise it would have been simpler to trade baskets rather than empty and refill the one.

"Ready to go!" he called. He stepped back as the Molt hoisted away.

The solar collector had to be above the foliage to work. It was easier to lift batteries up to the collector than it would have been to haul fifty meters of electrical cable through the Mirror so that the rest of the charging system could be at ground level.

"And so, I think, are we, Stephen," Piet Ricimer said, shocking Gregg as he turned without realizing his friend had walked over to him as he stared up into the tree.

"Ready?" Gregg said in surprise. He looked toward the starship in the center of the circle that had been cleared to provide the vessel's framework.

The portable kiln still chugged like a cat preparing to vomit, grinding, heating, and spraying out the sand and rock dumped into its feed hopper. The routine of work over the past week had been so unchanging that Gregg was subconsciously convinced it would never change.

"Lightbody and Stampfer are clearing the kiln," Ricimer said. He smiled wanly. "My father would never forgive me if I put up a kiln with the output lines full of glass. That can cause backflow through the feed chute the next time you use the equipment."

Side by side, the two officers walked toward the ship, which was possibly the ugliest human artifact Stephen Gregg had ever seen in his life. He was about to entrust his life to her.

The crewmen waited expectantly. The Molts who aided them when possible—Venerian ceramic technology belonged to the post-Collapse era, so it was not genetically coded into the aliens' cells—were ready to begin loading the ship with the piled equipment and supplies, but no one had given the order to begin.

"Gentlemen," Piet Ricimer said loudly. Everyone's attention was on him already.

The ship was a framework of wooden beams, covered with planks sawn from the neighboring forest with cutting bars. She was less than twenty meters long.

"We're men of action, not ceremony," Ricimer continued. "Nonetheless, I thought we should pause for a moment, to pray and to name the vessel we have built."

The rough-hewn planks were sealed and friction-proofed with a ceramic coating applied by one of the portable kilns the expedition carried to make repairs. It was the largest item the Molts had had to carry through the Mirror. Gregg couldn't imagine how K'Jax, who took the load himself, had managed.

"I considered calling our ship the *Avenger*," Ricimer said. His voice, strong from the beginning, grew firmer and clearer yet. Gregg recalled Piet mentioning that his father was a lay preacher. "But vengeance is for the Lord. Our eyes must be on the benefit to all men that will occur when our profit leads our fellows to join in breaking the Federation monopoly."

They'd installed the artificial intelligence and transit apparatus from the *Halys* in the flimsy wooden vessel. By comparison with this construction, the shoddy Federation prize was a marvel of strength and craftsmanship.

"And I thought of naming her the *Biruta*," Piet continued. "It was on Biruta that the treachery of the Federation authorities proved to us all that the Federation had to be fought and defeated if men were to live as God wills among the stars. But Biruta was the past, and we must view the future."

For power and direction, they had a single thruster from the *Halys*, gimballed with ceramic bearings held in hardwood journals. If anyone but Piet Ricimer had offered to take off in such a contraption, Gregg would have made sure to be out of the probable impact zone. Instead, he would be aboard her.

"The future is Umber—the unprotected mirrorside where Pleyal's henchmen store the chips that will launch a hundred further vessels when we return laden with them," Ricimer said. "Therefore, under God, I name this ship the *Umber*. May she bear us to triumph!"

The tanks of reaction mass were wood partitions sealed with glass, much like the hull itself. Air was a greater problem. They couldn't build high-pressure tanks, so the crew would have to breathe from bottles attached to their hard suits for the entire voyage. They were taking along all the expedition's containers. At best, it would be very close.

"Friends and allies," Ricimer concluded. "Friends! Let us pray." He bowed his head.

God help us all, thought Stephen Gregg.

42

Mirrorside, near Umber

The *Umber* trembled in the atmosphere like a bubble deforming in a breeze. Umber's tawny planetary disk shuddered past in the viewscreen. There was no sign that the ship was descending.

Guillermo was in what appeared to be a state of suspended animation. Gregg hadn't realized that Molts could slow their metabolism at will. For Guillermo, the entire voyage would be a blank filled with whatever dreams Molts dream.

For the humans aboard the *Umber*, the voyage was a living Hell.

"Get on with it!" Coye whimpered. "For God's own sake, set her *down!*"

Lightbody snicked open a knife and put the point of its ceramic blade to the throat of his fellow crewman. "Blaspheme again," he said in a voice husky with tension and pain, "and it won't matter to you if we never touch down!"

Gregg knocked up Lightbody's hand with the toe of his boot. Dole was lurching upright with his rifle reversed to club the butt. Gregg caught the bosun's eye; Dole forced a grin and sat down again.

The *Umber* bucked harder than usual. Gregg lost his feet but managed to sit with a suggestion of control by letting his hand slide down one of the poles cross-bracing the interior. He wanted to stand up; he *would* stand up. But not for a moment yet.

Ricimer bent over the control console, hunched forward from

the wicker back of his chair—the *Umber*'s sole piece of cabin furniture. Piet had to balance thrust, the slight reaction mass remaining in the tanks, and the vessel's wooden frame. At a slight excess of atmospheric braking, the hull would flex and the ceramic coating would scale off like bits of shell from a hard-boiled egg.

If the *Umber* wasn't opened to a breathable atmosphere soon, everybody aboard her was going to die from lack of oxygen.

"Oh, God," Coye moaned. He raised his air bottle to his mouth and squeezed the release vainly again. He hurled the empty container away from him. It hit Stampfer. The gunner either ignored it or didn't feel the impact.

The *Umber* tracked across the planetary surface in a reciprocal of her previous direction. Gregg hadn't felt a transition, but they had reversed at the Mirror.

The ship had slowed. The ragged settlement looked larger as it passed through the viewscreen.

Gregg stood up. His head hammered as though each pulse threatened to burst it wide open. He wanted desperately to sip air from the bottle. Instead he walked over to Coye, ducking under a brace that was in the way.

Gregg put the bottle to the crewman's lips. Coye tried to trigger the release himself. Gregg slapped away Coye's greedy hand and gave him a measured shot of air.

It was the hardest act that Gregg remembered ever having performed.

Filters scrubbed CO_2 from the jerry-built vessel's atmosphere, but that did nothing to replenish the converted oxygen. Rather than release the contents of the air bottles directly into the ship's interior, Gregg doled them out on a schedule to the individual crewmen. Human lungs absorbed only a small percentage of the oxygen in a breath, so the exhaled volume increased the breathability of the cabin air.

To a degree.

Everyone was on his last bottle. Most of them had finished theirs. It was going to be very close.

Piet Ricimer adjusted the fuel feed and thruster angle. Gregg swayed forward from deceleration. Through the cross brace, he felt the *Umber* creak with strain.

He wondered if the ship was going to disintegrate so close to their goal. Part of his mind noted that if impact with the atmosphere converted his body to flaked meat, the pain in his head would stop.

Very deliberately, he took a swig from his air bottle. The feeling of cold as gas expanded against his tongue eased his pain somewhat, even before the whiff of oxygen could diffuse into his blood . . . but the bottle emptied before his finger released the trigger.

Umber's natural surface was too uniform for Gregg to be able to judge their velocity against it. When the Federation settlement came in sight again, it was clear that Piet now had the wooden vessel in controlled flight rather than a braking orbit.

Umber City on the planet's realside wasn't prepossessing. The community here on the mirrorside was a dingy slum.

Two small freighters sat on the exhaust-fused landing field. They resembled the *Halys;* like her, they had been built in the Reaches, very possibly in the yards on Benison. Memory of the prize he had so recently commanded made Gregg dizzy from recalled luxury: the ability to fill his lungs without feeling he was being suffocated with a pillow.

There were six human-built structures. Four of them were large enough to be warehouses, constructed of sheet metal. A smaller metal building stood between the larger pairs, at the head of the tramline crossing the Mirror.

A large circular tank formed the center of the landing field. Like the similar structures on realside, it held reaction mass for the ships that landed here. Dedicated tankers shuttled back and forth between Umber and the nearest water world, replenishing the reservoir. The local groundwater was barely sufficient for drinking purposes.

A small barracks and an individual dwelling built of concrete each had a peaked metal roof while all the other structures were flat. There was no need of roof slope in a climate as dry as Umber's; someone had decided on the design for esthetic reasons, probably to differentiate human habitations from those of the alien slaves.

The Molt dwellings looked like a junkyard or, at best, a series of metal-roofed anthills. Walls of sandbags woven from scrap cloth supported sheet-metal plates. Loose sand was heaped onto the plates to anchor them against the wind.

On Punta Verde and among K'Jax' folk on Benison, Molts adapted their buildings to varied sorts of locally available raw materials. Gregg was sure that they would have occupied a neat community on Umber's mirrorside, if their human masters had allowed them basics. The sand could be stabilized by cement powder, heat-setting plastic with a simple applicator, or portable kilns of the sort any modest Venerian spaceship carried—and would trade away for a handful of microchips.

The Federation administrators weren't saving money by condemning the aliens to this squalor: they were making a political statement. Duty on the mirrorside of Umber was worse than a prison sentence for the humans involved. They felt a need to prove they were better than somebody else.

It was, in its way, a rare example of the Feds treating Molts as something other than objects. The Molts became persons for the purpose of being discriminated against.

"There . . ." Ricimer murmured. He eased back a millimeter the fuel feed. The image advancing on the viewscreen slowed still further, then began to expand. The *Umber* dropped against the pilot's precisely-measured thrust. The landing field was directly beneath the vessel.

Gregg turned from the viewscreen to the hatch. He stared at it for some seconds before the oxygen-starved higher levels of his mind responded to what his lizard brain was trying to tell him. He staggered across the bay, avoiding the frame members but tripping on Jeude's sprawled feet on the way.

The hatch was a half meter across. They'd had to bring large fittings into the *Umber* before the hull was sealed. The wooden edges of the hatch and jamb were beveled to mate under internal pressure. They were ceramic-coated and smeared with the milky, resilient sap of a mirrorside climbing vine immediately before the ship was closed for liftoff.

The square panel was wedged closed on the inside. Gregg grabbed the handle of one wedge and strained against it. It didn't move. He grunted in frustration.

"The other way, sir!" Jeude croaked. "You're pushing it home."

That's exactly what he was doing.

Dole had gotten cautiously to his feet, but he swayed where he stood. It was hard to imagine that in the recent past the crew had enough energy to fight.

Gregg didn't need help, now that Jeude had oriented him. The closures were paired, one on each of the four surfaces. Stampfer knocked them home with a mallet on Benison. Gregg used his left hand on the forward handle to anchor his pull on the wedge opposite. The right side gave, the top gave—

He switched the power grip to his left hand, because his right fingers were bleeding from pressure cuts. The forward closure pulled out. Gregg lost his balance with it and fell backward.

Dole, Jeude, and Lightbody reached over him, grabbed the hatch crossbar, and tugged inward with their combined strength. Though the bottom wedge was still in place, the hatch jumped from its jamb and tilted inward.

The air that blasted past it was dusty and tinged with ions from the thruster's exhaust. Its touch was as close to heaven as Gregg expected ever to know.

"Coming in!" said Piet Ricimer, his voice high-pitched and trembling with relief.

The *Umber* grounded in a controlled crash and immediately rolled onto her portside. She'd been launched from a cradle. Hydraulically-extended landing legs to stabilize the craft on the ground were out of the question, and fixed outriggers would have put too much strain on the hull during atmospheric braking.

The hatch was nearly overhead. Gregg stepped to a cross brace—he was still too logy to jump—and thrust his flashgun through the opening. Ricimer stroked Guillermo awake. The Molt was strapped to what now was the starboard bulkhead.

"Follow me!" Gregg cried as he crawled through the hatch. His battery satchel, slung at hip level, caught on the jamb. A crewman below gave Gregg a boost. He slid down the hull and hit Umber's mirrorside on his shoulder and chest.

He didn't care. He was breathing in deep lungfuls of air, and it would be a long time before any injuries outweighed the pleasure of that feeling.

A pair of Molts stared at the *Umber* from the open door of the warehouse two hundred meters away. Other Molts clustered near the tramhead, apparently intent on their own thoughts. Gregg didn't see any humans.

He glanced over his shoulder. Dole had squirmed through the hatch with a repeater held high to keep it from knocking the hull as he dropped to the ground. Gregg reached up to help control the bosun's fall.

The *Umber* herself was in amazingly good condition. The ceramic coating had flaked away in patches from her underside when she scraped onto the landing field, but the rest of the hull appeared intact. She could be made to fly with a little effort.

It would take much greater effort to convince any of the present complement to crew her again, though.

Piet Ricimer was the third man out. He must have used his rank to press ahead of the other men. Gregg and Dole together caught him as he slid down.

"Let's go," Ricimer said as he unslung his rifle. He grinned. Guillermo hopped easily to the ground beside them. "Since we don't have a battalion to back us up, I think we'd best depend on speed."

The four of them spread into a loose skirmish line as they moved toward the tramhead. Jeude climbed through the hatch, jumped to the ground, and fell. He brushed off his rifle's receiver as he jogged to a place between Dole and Ricimer.

The warehouses were on the left, with the Molt hovels straggling against the Mirror beyond. Gregg took the right side of the Venerian formation, toward the barracks and house. None of Umber's structures seemed to have windows. The doors to the residences were on the far side.

The wind blew hard enough to sting sand against Gregg's bare hands, but it didn't raise a pall the way the storm had during the assault on realside. At least the weather was cooperating. He really wished there'd been time to don his body armor, but there wasn't. Suits for the whole crew were stored in the *Umber*, but removing them would mean dismantling the ship.

Lightbody joined them. Gregg looked back. Stampfer was climbing through the hatch. All the men carried rifles. Besides a cutting bar, Guillermo wore a holstered pistol, but Gregg wasn't sure how serious a weapon it was meant to be.

The Molts at the tramhead watched the Venerians. Many of them turned only their heads, giving the crowd an uncanny resemblance to an array of mechanical toys.

The line reached the buildings. The Molts in the warehouse doorway had moved only their heads to track the Venerians. Ricimer turned and gestured toward Coye, running to catch up with them. "Coye!" he called, aided by the breeze. "Watch that pair!"

Gregg stepped smoothly around the corner of the barracks, the nearer of the two buildings on his end, and presented his laser. The doors in the middle of both buildings were closed tightly against the windblown sand. There were no windows on this side either.

Nothing to see, and no one to impress by pomp.

"Who is in charge here?" Ricimer called to the Molts at the tramhead.

None of them reacted until Guillermo chittered something in his own speech. One of the Molts said in English, "Our supervisors have gone across the Mirror for the celebration. Who are you?"

Guillermo continued to talk in quick, clattering vocables. The local Molts moved, slight shifts of position that relieved the Venerians' tension at the abnormal stillness of a moment before. Ricimer approached the group. His men hung back by a step or a half-step each, so that the line of humans became a shallow vee. None of the aliens was armed or appeared hostile.

Guillermo turned to Ricimer and explained, "The Earth Convoy has arrived on the realside. There will be a party in Umber City. The humans from here have crossed the Mirror to join it."

"Most of the humans," said the Molt who had spoken before. He wore a sash of office, gray from a distance but grease-smeared white when Gregg saw it closer. "Under-clerk Elkinghorn is—there she is."

The Molt pointed. Gregg was already turning. The barracks door had opened. The woman who'd started toward the tramhead had failed to latch it properly behind her: as Gregg watched, the door blew open again, then slammed with a bang deadened by the adverse wind.

"Hey!" she called. She wore uniform trousers and tunic, but she had on house slippers rather than boots. "Hey! Who are you?"

"Hold it right where you are!" Dole shouted as he aimed his rifle.

"Don't!" Piet Ricimer cried. "Don't shoot!"

The woman turned and ran back toward the door from which she'd come. A bottle flew out of the pocket of her tunic and broke on the ground. It was half full of amber liquor.

Elkinghorn was ten meters away. Gregg aimed. He was coldly furious with himself for not having continued to watch the residence buildings.

"Stephen!" Ricimer called. "Don't shoot her!"

Elkinghorn threw open the door. Gregg fired past her head, into the partition wall opposite.

Elkinghorn flung herself backward, onto the ground. The laser bolt converted paint and insulation to blazing gas. It blew the door shut and bulged the sides of the barracks.

"I think," said Gregg as he clicked a fresh battery into his flashgun, "that she'll be in a mood to answer our questions now."

43

Umber

"Not a thing!" Jeude snarled as he stamped into the secretary's residence. "Not a *damned* thing."

"There's food," said Stampfer, closing the outer door behind himself and his partner in searching the nearer warehouse. The gunner sucked on a hard-cored fruit so lush that juice dripped into his beard. With his free hand, he pulled another fruit from his bulging pocket. He offered it to Ricimer, Gregg, and the Fed captive promiscuously. "Want one?"

Gregg shook his head at Stampfer and said to Jeude, "Maybe Dole and Coye had better luck."

"It's not up to date," Elkinghorn said miserably from the outpost's central computer. "I know it shows twelve cases of Class A chips here, but as God is my witness, they've all been trucked across. All of them."

She squeezed her forehead with her right hand, then resumed advancing the manifest with the light pen in her left, master, hand. She was trembling badly.

Ricimer had refused to give the prisoner more liquor. She'd been drinking herself comatose in irritation at being left behind, "in charge", while the rest of the outpost's complement crossed to Umber City for the celebration. The laser bolt had shocked her sober, but she wasn't happy about the fact.

"That other warehouse, Dole's looking, but it's not going to do a bit of good," Jeude replied. "Supplies, machinery—trade goods for other colonies on the mirrorside, that's all there is."

Stampfer dropped his pit on the coarse rug. He began eating the fruit in his left hand.

Lightbody came in the door, carrying his cutting bar in his hand. "I got through the sidewall of the barracks," he announced, "but it wasn't any good. You torched her right and proper, sir."

He nodded to Gregg. "Fully involved. *Zip, I* cut through the wall, and *boom,* the roof lifts off because air got to the inside that had about smothered itself out."

Gregg shrugged sheepishly. "I thought she might have a gun inside," he said.

"There's no guns here," the prisoner said. "There's nothing but Christ-bitten *desert* here, so what's to shoot?"

Anger raised her blood pressure. She dropped the light pen and pressed both hands to her temples. "Oh, God, I need a drink so bad," she groaned.

Ricimer stood. "Tie her," he said to Lightbody. At the tramhead, the Venerians had found a coil of rope woven somewhere on mirrorside. The Molt laborers said they used it to bind bulky loads onto the cars. "And give her a drink, if there is one."

Jeude shrugged and took a bottle out of his sabretache.

The door opened and banged closed again. Dole and Coye came into the office with a drift of sand despite the near airlock.

"It's all outgoing stuff, sir," the bosun said, echoing Jeude of a moment before. "There's not a chip in the settlement."

He noticed the office console and pointed his breechloader at it. "Besides whatever's in that unit, I guess."

Ricimer looked at his men. Greg winced mentally to see his friend's haggard face. While the rest of them simply tried not to scream during the slow suffocation of the *Umber*'s approach, Piet brought the jerry-built vessel down softly by the standards of a manual landing on a proper ship.

"We've gotten here too late to find the chips I'd hoped," he said quietly. "Over the past week, the stockpile was taken across the Mirror in anticipation of the Earth Convoy's arrival."

He licked his lips, chapped by sand blown on the dry wind. "The chips haven't vanished. With the celebration going on, officials of

Umber City and the convoy won't have had time to complete loading the ships. They may not even have started yet."

Ricimer's voice grew louder, stronger. Gregg grinned coldly to see gray tension vanish from his friend's face and his eyes brighten again.

"To get the chips, we would have to cross the Mirror again," he said. "To return to Umber City. You all know the risks. You all know—"

His voice would have filled a room of ten times the volume of this office.

"—that I failed before, that many of our f-friends and loved ones were killed because of my miscalculation. The risks are even greater now, because the convoy and all its personnel will be in Umber City."

"Hey, it's not that dangerous," Jeude protested. "The Feds won't be expecting us this direction, right?"

Ricimer's head rotated like a lathe turret. "They didn't *expect* us before," he said harshly to Jeude. "That didn't prevent them from reacting effectively."

He scanned his assembled men. "Guillermo tells me the labor force here will help us, run the trams the way they do for their masters. He's organizing that now. In exchange, we will take every *slave* off this planet. We can't return them to their home planets, but they'll be able to live free on Benison with K'Jax."

"Gonna be tight . . ." Dole muttered. Catching himself, he added quickly, "Not that we're not used to it. No problem."

Free with K'Jax, Gregg thought. He was willing to grant that Molts were "human," whatever that meant. He hadn't seen anything to suggest they were saints, though; or that K'Jax would be considered a particularly benevolent leader of *any* race.

"I won't order you men to go to Umber City again with me," Ricimer went on fiercely. "I won't think the less of anyone who wants to stay. But I'm going across, and with the help of God I hope this time to succeed."

Stampfer dropped the second fruit pit on the floor. "I haven't come all this way to go home poor," he said.

Yeah/Sure/Count me in from the remainder of the crew.

Gregg said nothing. He was smiling slightly, and his eyes were light-years distant.

"Stephen?" Piet Ricimer said.

Gregg shook himself to wakefulness. "If the Earth Convoy's in, then so is Administrator Carstensen," he said in a trembling, gentle voice. "I'd like to meet him and discuss Biruta. For a time."

Coye, who hadn't been around Stephen Gregg as long as some of the others, swore softly and turned away from the expression on the young gentleman's face.

44

Umber

The tramcars were constructed of wire netting on light metal frames. Each car's weight and that of the Molt pushing it had to be subtracted from the potential payload.

Gregg eyed a car dubiously. "A motor wouldn't weigh as much as a, a person," he said. "If you've got tracks through the Mirror, then they'll guide the car whether or not there's somebody behind it pushing."

"Motors will not work in the Mirror," said the Molt leader. Her name was Ch'Kan.

"Electric motors?" Ricimer asked.

"Diesel, electric—even flywheels," Ch'Kan said. "None of them work in the Mirror."

She clicked her mandibles to indicate some emotion or other. "We work in the Mirror. Until we die."

The tracks ran from the warehouses to the lambent surface of the Mirror. The rails were solid and spiked deep into the surface of Umber for as far as the eye could follow them. Beyond the transition zone, the rails were laid with short gaps between ends. They weren't attached because there was no ground within the Mirror, merely a level which objects could not penetrate.

The Molts said that sometimes cars tilted off the rails. The slave pushing the vehicle could usually find his way to one end of the tramway or the other by following the tracks.

If he or she abandoned the load within the Mirror, the Federation supervisors whipped the creature to death for sabotage.

Ricimer clambered into a tramcar. It creaked under his weight.

"I'd better go in the first one," Gregg said. He climbed into a car in a siding beside his friend's. The main line split to serve both warehouses, and there were a dozen lay-bys on each branch to allow cars to pass and be sorted.

The Feds had left a dozen Molts on mirrorside for routine tasks. Most of the labor force had crossed with their masters to handle cargo for and from the Earth Convoy. Their heads rotated from one human officer to the other, waiting for clear directions. The Venerian crewmen watched in silence also.

"I'll lead, Stephen," Ricimer said with a touch of iron in his voice. The sun had set. Pole-mounted lights at the tramhead threw vertical shadows down across his face.

Gregg smiled and shook his head. "When you get a flashgun," he said, "and learn to use it the way I can use this one—"

He nodded his weapon's muzzle in the air. He handled the flashgun as easily as another man might have waved a pistol.

"Then you can lead. For now, we need as much firepower up front as we can get. And that's me, Piet—not so?"

Ricimer shrugged tightly. "Go ahead, then," he said.

The crewmen got into cars like those of their leaders. Stampfer's almost upset from a combination of his short legs and weight, but two Molts balanced the vehicle for him.

The Molt leader threw a switch lever, then stepped around behind Gregg's car and began to push it forward. He heard the wheels squeaking, a loud pulse at the end of each full turn. Gregg concentrated on that so completely that he barely started to tremble by the moment his face gleamed at him and the terrible cold turned his soul inside out.

Only the cold. Utterly the cold.

The car wheels clacked at the gaps between rails. If Gregg could have counted the jolts, he would have known the length of the trip. The tracks were no longer straight, though. They curved, and the rails were seconds clicking on a circular dial that would take him back to zero before starting again.

Only the cold.

The change was sudden and much sooner than Gregg expected. Time and space within the Mirror were not constants. However the temporal or spatial distance between realside and mirrorside was measured, it was shorter on Umber than had been the case on Benison.

The tramcar plunged Gregg into the sidereal universe. The shock was like a bath in magma. Floodlights overhead and the fireworks streaking the sky toward the center of Umber City merged with the patterns of frozen color which Gregg's optic nerves fired to his brain in the frozen emptiness.

Gregg gasped and threw himself sideways. The tramcar tipped over, as he intended. He wasn't sure he had enough motor control to climb out of the car normally.

He had to get clear of its confinement *now*.

Gregg hadn't been within a klick of the realside tramhead during the raid on Umber City, and Piet's fainting recollections of shots and chaos were of limited help for visualizing the place. Gregg hit the stone pavement, pointing his flashgun and trying to look in all directions at once.

The blockhouse was set three meters forward of the Mirror to provide space for the tracks to split and curve right and left of the building. Instead of individual switched sidings, the architect who laid out the tramway on realside used these two fifty-meter tails of trackway to store empties. At the moment, the lengths of track were nearly full of cars.

Rather than a wall, the rear face of the blockhouse was protected by a grille that was now rolled up to the roofline. The building's interior was stacked with rough wooden cases whose volume ranged from a quarter cubic meter down to half that size. There was a narrow passageway to the open door in the front wall, but Gregg couldn't tell if the loopholes to either side were blocked.

Cases of more irregular size were stacked to either side of the blockhouse. There were others between it and the bollards which formed a deadline separating the stored valuables and Umber City. Twenty or more Molts, singly or in pairs, poised to lift containers.

The diesel trucks that would normally have transported cargo to the landing field were burnt skeletons in front of the bollards. They'd been dragged out of the immediate way but not removed from where the defenders' own fire had destroyed them during the previous raid.

A human cradling a double-barreled shotgun oversaw the gang of Molt porters. Another human stood beside the back corner of the blockhouse, watching aliens work. A radio hung from the second man's belt. His weapon, a brightly decorated rifle, leaned against the wall beside him.

The shock of hitting the ground broke Gregg's mind free of the frozen constraints that bound it until that moment. The clatter as his tram toppled drew the eyes of Molts and human officials together. One of Gregg's trouser legs was caught in the wire mesh.

"_Don't move!_" he shouted. The short trip through the Mirror hadn't numbed him, but it sharpened his voice to an edge of hysteria more disquieting than the fat muzzle of his laser.

The man by the blockhouse stiffened as though he'd been given a jolt of electricity. His hip bumped the ornate rifle and knocked it down. As it rattled away from him, he threw both hands in front of his face and screamed, "Lord Jesus Christ preserve me!"

Ch'Kan called to her fellows in a sequence of liquid trills. A second car squealed out of the transition behind Gregg, but his attention had focused down on the man with the shotgun. Everything beyond the Fed's face and torso vanished behind a mental curtain as gray as a sight ring.

The fellow's uniform was white with blue epaulets instead of the yellow of Federation ground personnel. He was big, almost as tall as Gregg and much bulkier. The short-barreled weapon in his hands looked like a child's toy. His teeth were bared in a snarl in the midst of his neatly-cropped beard and moustache, and he spun to bring the shotgun to bear.

To Gregg's adrenaline-speeded senses, the Fed was turning in slow motion. Gregg felt his trigger reach its release point beneath the pad of his index finger.

The target, bathed in vivid coherent light, flipped optically into the photographic negative of a human being. The Fed's shout turned into an elephantine grunt as all the air in his lungs exploded out his open mouth. The body toppled. The head and shoulders lay at an angle kinked from that of the legs and lower chest. A smoldering tatter of cloth and flesh joined the portions.

Gregg kicked hard. His trouser leg tore. He got to his feet, keeping the flashgun pointed at the remaining Federation official while the fingers of his right hand switched the discharged battery for a fresh one.

" . . . now and at the hour of our death," the Fed mumbled. His eyes were open, but he'd only half lowered his hands. He was swaying and seemed about to fall.

Ricimer carefully got out of the cart that had brought him across the Mirror. He glanced at the rifle in his hands as though he'd never seen anything like it before, then pointed an index finger toward the corpse.

"Get that into the building and out of sight," he said in a firm, clear voice.

Two of the Molts immediately obeyed. The rest of the labor party moved slightly away from the piled crates, distancing themselves from their duties for the Federation. A car with Dole aboard shimmered through the transition layer. The bosun's face was set, and his eyes stared vacantly.

Gregg stepped over to the Fed official. The man was in his early twenties. He had fine features and blond hair that was already starting to thin. Gregg gripped the Fed's shoulder with his left hand, to immobilize the fellow and to focus his horror-struck attention.

Ch'Kan pointed to Ricimer. "Here is the man who will take us away from this place," she said. Now that the immediate crisis was past, she had switched to Trade English. "We will load the cargo on carts and take it back to mirrorside for him."

A gush of fireworks streaked above the city. The vessels of the Earth Convoy were hidden by darkness and the buildings, but some of them played searchlights with colored filters into the air.

A party of Molts trudged up the central street toward the bollards. In the uncertain illumination, Gregg couldn't spot the armed guard who he was sure accompanied the group to prevent pilferage and malingering. He squinted, holding the flashgun down at his side where its unexpected outline wouldn't cause alarm.

"Whether or not you help us," Piet Ricimer said to the Molts who stared at him, "I'll take any of you who want to go to Benison and release you with your own free fellows. If you *do* help me and my men, though, you bring closer the day that we can smash the Federation's grip on the stars and free *all* your fellows."

Not so very long ago, Gregg thought, *you and I were in the business of supplying crews just like this one. But times change, and men change . . . and maybe occasionally they change for the better.*

Coye came out of the Mirror. Stampfer's cart followed on the heels of the Molt pushing Coye. Dole's expression was one of blinking awareness, but he still stood in the car while a Molt looked on from behind.

"Dole!" Gregg called. "Come watch this guy. Tie him or something."

"You're going to be fine," he added to the prisoner. "Just don't play any games. Because I'll smash your skull all over the stones if you do."

Gregg didn't speak loudly. He knew he was very close to the edge. If he'd shouted the threat, it might have triggered his arm to move, swinging the laser's heavy butt. And anyway, he didn't need to shout to be believable.

Dole and the Molt who'd pushed him took the white-faced prisoner and began to secure him with pieces of rope from the coil they'd brought. Under Guillermo's direction, Molts were loading the empty tramcars. They concentrated on the smaller cases stenciled as new-run chips.

Ricimer patted Gregg on the back as he strode past. "I'm going to see what else is in here," he explained. "Keep a watch on that gang coming, though they don't seem in much of a hurry."

Gregg peered around the back corner of the blockhouse. "Coye," he called. "Stampfer. Keep down, will you? Behind the stacks of cases or inside the building."

It didn't much matter whether Feds saw Guillermo and the Molts reloading the cars—no one was likely to pay enough attention to note that the chips were going in the wrong direction. Too many armed humans around the blockhouse could be more of a problem.

The ground on which the blockhouse stood was slightly higher than that of Umber City and the spaceport beyond, though the slope would have been imperceptible on a surface less flat than the present one. Because the city was so full of transients, illuminated windows marked the roads though there was no streetlighting as such.

The floodlit Commandatura stood out in white glory. The park and the street between it and the building were hidden behind intervening structures. Tricolored bunting and the Federation's maple leaf emblem hung between the windows of the second floor.

Besides the fireworks at the park, occasional shots whacked the air. That could mean either "happy shooting" toward the starless sky or the quarrels of drunken sailors getting out of hand.

Whichever, it was useful cover if there was trouble with the party nearing the blockhouse.

The guard walked beside her charges, near the front but generally hidden by the line of alien bodies. Glimpses showed Gregg that she had reddish hair, no cap, and carried a weapon slung muzzle-down over her right shoulder.

"Sir," Dole said tensely. "This guy's—"

"Not now," Gregg whispered. Only the right side of his face projected beyond the corner of the blockhouse. His flashgun, muzzle-up, was withdrawn to his side so that the oncoming party wouldn't see it.

"There's a radio back there," Ricimer said as he came from the front of the building, "but the loopholes are both covered by box—"

He continued to speak for a moment. Gregg's mind turned the words into background buzz. It was no more than the hiss of the breeze and the sting of sand on his neck.

The oncoming Molts reached the line of bollards. Guillermo trilled to them in their own language. The remainder of the co-opted aliens continued to load cars. Now that all the Venerians had crossed on the single track, the Molts could begin taking chips over to mirrorside.

"Blauer?" the Fed guard called. Besides the slung carbine, she carried a quirt in her right hand. She slapped the shaft against her left palm. "Hey! Blauer!"

The Molts nearest to her flattened to the pavement. Gregg stepped around the corner and leveled his flashgun. "Don't," he said in a high, distant voice.

The woman blinked, held by the laser's sight line like a beetle pinned to a board. She dropped the quirt, then shrugged carefully to let the carbine sling slide off her shoulder without her hands coming anywhere near the weapon.

"Now come forward," Gregg ordered quietly. He nodded to Stampfer, poising behind a loaded tramcar. Stampfer ran out to pick up the carbine while Lightbody and Coye secured the new prisoner.

She didn't speak, but her eyes glared hatred at everything her gaze touched.

"Jesus!" Gregg said, letting his breath out for the first time in too long. The air stank of cooked filth, the effluvium of the torso shot into the previous guard. His hands were shaking and he almost gagged.

Molts were widening the narrow aisle into the blockhouse. Piet put a comforting hand on Gregg's arm. "I want to clear the loopholes inside," he said. "We may need them before we're done."

"Right," Gregg said. He looked down at the receiver of his flashgun. The present locked into focus again.

"Right," he repeated. "I can't believe they blocked those wall guns off. You'd think the Feds would've learned a lesson from our first raid, wouldn't you?"

"They learned they didn't have to be afraid of raiders," Ricimer said with a slight grin. "Not every lesson is the right lesson."

"There's more coming, sir," Stampfer called from the shelter to which he'd returned. "Molts, anyhow."

"We'll handle them the same way," Ricimer replied. "Maybe we won't have any real problems with this."

"Captain!" Jeude called from inside the blockhouse. "There's somebody on the radio, wondering where his cargo is."

"I'll handle it," Ricimer said, brushing past a Molt coming out of the building with a case of chips.

"Look at this, Mr. Gregg," Dole murmured, holding up their first captive's rifle. "Don't it look like it's . . . ?"

"It sure does . . ." Gregg agreed. He handed his flashgun to Dole and took the richly-carved pump gun. The chance of there being another rifle so much like Captain Schremp's wasn't high enough to consider.

The blond captive lay on his side, with his ankles and wrists tied together behind his back. Gregg knelt beside him, waggled the ornate weapon in his face, and then touched the muzzle to the prisoner's knee.

"Tell me exactly how you got this rifle," he said. His finger took up the slack on the trigger. He hadn't checked to be sure there was a round in the chamber, but they'd learn that quickly enough when the hammer fell.

"I bought it!" the Fed screamed. "From the flagship's purser! I swear to God I bought it!"

Gregg eased off the trigger very slightly. He tapped again with the muzzle. "All right," he said. "Where did the purser get it?"

"Oh, God, I just wanted a rifle," the blond man moaned. He squeezed his eyes shut, but he couldn't escape the caress of the weapon. It would blow his leg off at this range. "I don't know, I just asked around when the convoy landed. They all do a little business on the side, you know how it is, and I had a few chips saved back. Oh God oh God."

"Blauer, you make me want to puke," sneered the female prisoner unexpectedly. She turned her head from her fellow to Gregg. "You want to know where it came from? From a pirate like you!"

"Go on," Gregg said. He raised the repeater's muzzle and handed the weapon back to Dole. Threatening the woman would be counterproductive; and anyway, she had balls.

"We caught them on Rondelet," she said. "They were attacking a mansion when we came out of transit. We smashed their ship from orbit and they all surrendered. Were they friends of yours?"

Piet joined the tableau. He didn't interrupt.

"Not really," Gregg said. By habit, he checked the flashgun Dole returned to him. "What happened then?"

"Then we hanged them all," the woman said. "*After* we'd convinced them to talk. Too bad they weren't friends!"

Gregg stood up. "Well," he said mildly to Ricimer. "We know what Schremp did after he left us. I can't say I'm sorry he's gone."

Ricimer nodded. "We can get to one of the wall guns now," he said. "It's a one-kilogram. There's only a few shells for it."

Molts pushed laden tramcars into the Mirror one after the other. They moved at a measured, almost mechanical pace, a skill learned to prevent them from running up on each other's heels in the hellish void beyond the transition layer.

Ricimer stepped past Gregg to peer at the labor party trudging up from Umber City. "They'll be here in a few minutes," he said.

Gregg smiled tightly. He indicated the female prisoner with the toe of his boot. "Gag that one," he said to Dole. "Or she'll try to warn the next batch. And I don't want to kill her."

Piet Ricimer squeezed his friend's shoulder again.

45

Umber

The Umber tramway had thirty-four cars. There'd been thirty-five when the Venerians arrived, but Gregg had bent the trucks of the one that carried him when he kicked his way free. He didn't remember anything so violent occurring, but his right leg ached as though a piano'd fallen on it.

The Molts were starting a second round trip to mirrorside. Because there was only a single trackway, none of the cars could return until all had gone across. The blockhouse was nearly emptied; five bound and gagged Federation guards lay out of sight within it.

Lightbody had draped a tarpaulin over the corpse. Gregg hadn't killed anybody since that one. The sudden dissolution of the man's chest had merged with the soul-freezing trip through the Mirror in a shadowland that Gregg would revisit only when he dreamed.

The front of the blockhouse was pierced by four loopholes, though there were only two wall guns. Ricimer watched Umber City from one of the clear openings while he responded to radio traffic with a throat mike and plug earphone.

Gregg remained at the right rear corner of the structure. Ricimer looked back over his shoulder at his friend with a wan smile and tapped the earphone. "The watch officer on the *Triple Tiara*'s getting pretty insistent about where his cargo is," he said. "He doesn't get to join the party until it's delivered."

Gregg tried to grin. The result was more of a tic, and his eyes returned to the street beyond immediately. "That's Carstensen's flagship?" he said.

"Yeah. I told him I had the same problem, but once the porters left here, there wasn't a thing I could do about how fast they marched."

The fireworks had ended. Snatches of music drifted up when the breeze was right. The captured guards said there was always a banquet when the convoy arrived: a sit-down meal in the Commandatura for the brass, and an open-air orgy in the park for common sailors and the journeymen of the community's service industries.

Both sites had suffered during the previous raid. If anything, that would increase the sense of celebratory relief.

Gregg heard the ringing sound of a distant engine. A green, then a red and a green light wobbled into the sky beyond the rooftops.

"They're coming!" Gregg called. "One of the ships just launched an autogyro."

Four of the Venerian enlisted men were with Piet inside the blockhouse, crewing the 1-kaygees. Jeude squatted behind one of the shrinking stacks of boxes. Like Gregg, he wore a white jumper stripped from a prisoner. He kept out of sight because the guards with the two remaining labor gangs might nonetheless realize that he wasn't one of their number.

An autogyro wasn't a threat. One of the watch officers was sending a scout to track down the missing cargo. No problem.

Ricimer murmured to the gun crews, then handed the communications set to Dole. He strode back to Gregg and eyed the situation himself.

"Jeude," Gregg said. "Stand up—don't look like you're hiding. If he lands, we'll pick him up just like the guards. No shooting."

He looked at Piet. "Right?"

"Right . . ." Ricimer said with an appraising frown. "That would be the best result we can hope for."

The appearance of things at the tramhead shouldn't arouse much concern. The raiders had been sending excess Molt laborers back to mirrorside to load the ships under Guillermo's direction. Ch'Kan acted as straw boss here. If shooting started, Guillermo could be better spared than any of the Venerians—though Gregg wouldn't have minded the presence of K'Jax and a few of his warriors.

Piet looked over the remaining cargo and pursed his lips. "We shouldn't get greedy and stay too long," he said.

"We'll be all right for a while yet," Gregg said.

Gregg's mouth spoke for him. His mind was in a disconnected state between the future and past, unable to touch the present.

His eyes tracked the path of the autogyro, visible only as running lights angling toward the blockhouse at fifty meters altitude. Its engine and the hiss of its slotted rotor were occasionally audible. There was no place to fly on Umber, but the ships of the Earth Convoy were equipped for worlds like Rondelet and Biruta, where solid ground was scattered in patches of a few hectares each.

In Gregg's mind, humans and Molts exploded in the sight picture of his flashgun. Every one a unique individual up to the instant of the bolt: the snarling guard here, the woman beneath the fort trying to shoot him; a dozen, a score, perhaps a hundred others.

All of them identical carrion after Stephen Gregg's light-swift touch.

More to come when the present impinged again. *Lord God of hosts, deliver me.*

Ricimer touched the back of his friend's hand. "Why don't you go into the blockhouse, Stephen?" he suggested. "We shouldn't have more than two humans visible."

"I'll handle it," Gregg said. He watched as the autogyro turned parallel to the Mirror and approached the tramhead from the west. "I'm dressed for it."

He plucked at the commandeered tunic with his free hand. He held the flashgun close to the ceiling of the blockhouse so that it couldn't be seen from above.

Ricimer nodded and moved back.

The Federation aircraft zoomed overhead, its engine singing. The sweet, stomach-turning odor of diesel exhaust wafted down.

The Molts hefted cases, pretending they were about to carry them to the spaceport. The last of the tramcars had disappeared into the Mirror some minutes before, so the crew had no real work. A few of them looked up.

Jeude waved. Gregg raised his free hand, ostensibly to shade his eyes from the floodlights but actually to hide his face. Two faces peered down from the autogyro's in-line cockpits.

"Fooled them that time, Mr. Gregg!" Jeude called.

"So far," Gregg said to the men within the blockhouse, "so good."

His expression changed. "They're coming back," he added. "I think they're going to land."

The note of the diesel changed as the pilot coarsened the prop pitch. He was bringing the autogyro down, very low and slow, between the rear of the blockhouse and the Mirror.

They couldn't land there because of the tracks . . .

The autogyro swept by with its fixed landing gear barely skimming the pavement. The fuselage was robin's-egg blue, and the rotor turning slowly on its mast was painted yellow with red maple leaves near the tips. Both the pilot and the observer wore goggles, but there was no mistaking the shock on their faces when they saw the number of humans, standing and lying bound, within the blockhouse.

The diesel belched a ring of black smoke as the pilot brought it to full power. He banked hard, swinging the nose toward the city. The observer craned his head back over the autogyro's tail as he held a microphone to his lips.

"We're fucked!" Dole shouted from the blockhouse radio. "They've spotted—"

The fuselage faded to gray, but reflection from the pavement still lighted the rotor blades a rich yellow-orange. The flashgun was tight against Gregg's shoulder. Though the autogyro was turning away from him, it wasn't quite a zero-deflection shot yet. He swung through the tail surfaces and continued the graceful motion even after his trigger finger stroked with the sights centered between the forward cockpit and the glittering dial of the prop.

All he'd wanted to do was to bring the aircraft down, to punch his laser through the thin plastic hull and smash the engine block. The fuel tank was directly behind the diesel. It ruptured, hurling a ball of blazing kerosene over hundreds of square meters of the nearest buildings.

The pilot and observer were the two largest pieces of debris from the explosion. They were burning as they fell, but impact with the ground would have been instantly fatal even if they'd survived the blast.

"Now we'd better leave," Gregg said as he reloaded.

"Not yet!" Ricimer said crisply.

He clicked off the interior light, then pointed to the blond prisoner wearing ground-personnel flashes. "You! How do we turn out these area lights?" Though Ricimer was inside the blockhouse, the toss of his head adequately indicated the four pole-mounted flood-lights bathing the site.

"There's no switch!" the Fed bleated. "It's got a sensor, it goes on and off with sunlight!"

The Commandatura darkened suddenly as a Federation official had the same idea and executed it with dispatch.

Jeude stood up. He still carried the repeating carbine he'd lib-erated from a Venerian officer on Punta Verde. He shot out the first bulb, worked the bolt, and missed the second. The reflector whanged as the bullet pierced its rim.

Jeude finished the job with the remaining three cartridges in his magazine. The blockhouse and its surroundings weren't in the dark, but now the illumination came from the burning buildings fifty meters beyond the bollards.

"Why don't we go back now, Piet?" Gregg asked in much the voice that he'd have offered a cup of coffee. He had four charged batteries remaining, plus the one in the laser. His fingertip ticked over the corner of each in the satchel. He didn't touch the bat-tery contacts, because the sweat on his skin would minusculy corrode them.

The siren on the Commandatura began to sound.

"Because if we go back now . . ." Ricimer said. His voice seemed calm rather than controlled, and he spoke no louder than he needed to for Jeude and the wall gun crews all to hear him. " . . . we meet the empty cars returning from mirrorside. We have to wait until they've all come through."

"Christ's blood!" Dole said as he realized how long *that* would take.

Ricimer turned on the bosun like an avenging angel. "Mr. Dole!" he said. "I suggest that you remember that the next words we speak may be those we have on our lips when we go to meet our God. Do you understand?"

Dole swallowed and fell to his knees. He pressed his palms together, but his face was still lifted toward his captain with a look of supplication.

Ricimer shook himself and bent to lift Dole to his feet. "He'll understand," Ricimer muttered. "As He'll understand the fear that causes me to lose my temper."

A bullet, fired from somewhere within the town, slapped the

front of the blockhouse. Gregg didn't hear the shot, and he couldn't spot the muzzle flash through the glare of burning buildings either. The nearest portion of the street was lighted by the houses and scattered pools of kerosene, but beyond that the pavement was curtained in darkness.

"Madam Ch'Kan," Ricimer called to the Molt leader. "Get your people to cover. There's room for most of you in the blockhouse without affecting our ability to fight. Jeude—if you stay there to the side, you won't be as well covered when it comes time to run for the tramline."

Jeude shook his head. "Those loopholes, they're nothing but bull's-eyes. I'll take my chances here, thank'ee kindly."

He patted the waist-high breastwork of boxed microchips which hadn't been carried back to mirrorside yet.

The Molt leader chittered to her fellows. Four of them lay behind crates the way Jeude had. The rest—there were about twenty on this side of the Mirror—shuffled quickly into the blockhouse and knelt, beneath the level of the loopholes.

Another bullet sang past nearby. The sound ended abruptly as the projectile vanished into the Mirror. *At least they didn't have to worry about ricochets from behind.*

Lightbody flinched instinctively. Stampfer muttered a curse, and the frozen stillness of the other crewmen showed that they too were affected by the unseen snipers.

All of the Federation guards had carried firearms. Piet Ricimer chose a captured weapon, a long-barreled breechloader, and the owner's cross-belts with about fifty tapered cartridges in the loops. He carried the gear over to Jeude, deliberately sauntering. Gregg chuckled.

Crewmen watched Ricimer through the loopholes in the side of the blockhouse. He set the rifle beside Jeude and said loudly, "Here. I don't like to trust repeaters not to jam."

Fed soldiers volleyed. There were six or eight of them, sited on a three-story rooftop some two hundred meters away. This time a breeze parted the curtain of flame enough for Gregg to see the nervous yellow winking of muzzle flashes. The structure beneath them was dark, but Gregg knew where it must be.

"Gunners!" he shouted as he locked down his visor. "*Here's* your aiming point!"

The flashgun jolted in his hands. Smoke may have scattered the coherent light somewhat, but not to a great enough degree to prevent the bolt's impact from shattering the concrete roof coping.

White-hot lime in the cement hadn't faded below yellow when Jeude fired toward it with his carbine. Stampfer, professionally quick and angry with himself for feeling windy a moment before, was almost as fast. The 1-kg shell burst with a bright flash that hurled a Fed soldier backward.

The *whop!* of the bursting charge echoed the muzzle blast of the short-barreled wall gun. Dole, firing the other weapon of the pair a moment later, put his round a meter or two low. The aiming error was a useful one, because the shell went off within the building and set the contents of a room on fire.

Gregg stepped back into the blockhouse as he changed batteries in his laser. The breechblocks of the wall guns clanged as the gunners cammed them open, then closed again after the loaders dropped in fresh rounds. Propellant residues from the shell casings smelled like hot wax.

An empty cart emerged from the transition layer. The Molt pushing it took three steps forward, numbed by the Mirror, before he noticed the battle going on around him. He gaped.

Ch'Kan shouted to the laborer. He broke into a multijointed trot, pushing the car to the end of the branch. There it was out of the way of later comers like the one already entering realside.

A bullet struck one of the metal bollards and howled horribly away. None of the Venerians seemed to notice. The wall guns banged.

Piet and Jeude aimed out over their breastwork. The crewman fired as fast as he could work his carbine's bolt, then picked up the powerful single-shot. Ricimer watched as much as he aimed, but after a moment he fired. Gregg saw shards of glass fly into the street from a window eighty meters away.

Gregg raised his visor to scan for a worthy target. He had only four charges left, and the flashgun was too valuable a weapon to empty with indiscriminate firing. He thought of taking one of the captured rifles, but instinct told him not to put the laser down.

Movement beyond the smoke.

Something was coming around the corner where the street leading to the tramhead kinked and hid whatever preparations went on beyond it. The flashgun came up. Gregg closed his eyes over the sight picture and fired.

Actinics from the bolt pulsed orange through the skin of Gregg's eyelids. The blockhouse shuddered behind a puff of dust and smoke. The Feds had brought up a landing array from one of the ships, three 4-cm barrels on a single wheeled carriage. The shells were comparable to those thrown by the wall guns in the blockhouse.

Only one tube fired before Gregg's laser stabbed into the open magazine attached to the trail of the array's carriage.

The blast was red and went on for a considerable while, like a man coughing to clear phlegm. Some shells burst like grenades against walls and rooftops where the initial explosion hurled them. The bodies of the crew, Molts and humans both, lay around the ruined weapon. Burning scraps of clothes and shell spacer lighted them.

The Fed round hit the door in the center of the blockhouse facade and sprang it. The hinges and the staple of the closure bar held, but acrid smoke from the shellburst oozed around the edges of the armored panel. The inner face of the door bulged, and the center of the dent glowed faintly.

46

Umber

The wall guns were silent. Dole swung his out of the way to fire through the loophole with a rifle while Coye used the other opening to the left of the door. Stampfer and Lightbody took turns at the loophole on their side, but the gunner had left his 1-kg in position. He'd saved a shell back for special need, where Dole had fired off the entire stock of ammunition.

Tramcars continued to reappear from the Mirror. Ch'Kan called directions to each blinking laborer who followed a car.

Occasionally the newcomer stumbled away when his faculties warmed enough to realize what was going on around him. One Molt even plunged back into the Mirror in a blind panic that must have ended only when he starved in the interdimensional maze. Ch'Kan herself pushed abandoned cars out of the way or simply toppled them off the rails.

Molts in the blockhouse reloaded rifles for the Venerians to fire through the loopholes. Gregg saw two of the aliens, solemn as judges, using their delicate "fingers" to work loose a cartridge case that had ruptured instead of extracting from the hot breech of a repeater.

Gregg slung his flashgun. Its barrel was shimmering. If he'd laid the weapon down on the cold stone, the ceramic might have shattered. The Molts had left Schremp's rifle beside Gregg by chance or intent. He took it and let his cold killer's soul search for movement.

A bullet sparked through the wire sides of a cart being pushed toward the line of those stored on Gregg's side of the blockhouse. A second bullet shattered the head of the Molt pushing the cart. Her body continued to pace forward.

Gregg spotted the shooter at a ground-floor window of a nearby building whose roof was ablaze. He aimed through the post-and-ring sight, squeezed into the third muzzle flash, and felt the concrete explode beside his left ear as the Fed soldier fired at the glint of Schremp's silvered receiver.

Grit and bullet fragments slapped Gregg's head sideways. His helmet twisted and flew off. He knelt and patted his face with his left hand. His cheek felt cold and his hand came away sticky.

"This is the last!" Ch'Kan called in the high, carrying treble to which Molt voices rose at high amplitudes.

Piet Ricimer turned from where he crouched behind the row of crates. The breech of his rifle was open and streaming gray powder gases. "Ch'Kan!" he ordered. "Start your people through. Fast! We're safe when we're into the Mirror!"

"They're coming!" Stampfer warned.

Gregg looked toward the city. He didn't have binocular vision, but he only needed one eye for the sights. Shadows approached through the smoke, moving with the doll-like jerkiness of men in hard suits.

Stampfer's wall gun banged. A figure fell back in a red flash. Gregg pumped his rifle's action, aimed low, and fired. Maybe the Feds were wearing only head and torso armor rather than complete suits. Flexible joints might not stop a bullet at this range, and a hammerblow on a knee could drop a man even if the projectile didn't penetrate.

The target fell. The man or woman fell, but that didn't matter, wouldn't matter until the dreams came. Gregg pumped the slide again, very smooth, and dropped another Fed. Schremp had bought a first-rate *weapon,* if only he hadn't turned it into a sighting point for every hostile in the world.

The sniper who'd almost nailed Gregg from the window didn't fire again. Close only counts in horseshoes . . .

Half the attackers were down; the others crowded close to the buildings instead of advancing. The Molts who'd brought the carts through had mostly returned to the Mirror, though nearly a dozen alien bodies lay or thrashed on the pavement. There hadn't been much cover for them, and they'd been silhouetted against the Mirror for Feds who wanted soft targets. Molts in the blockhouse poised to leave under Ch'Kan's fluting direction.

Gregg shot at a Fed and spun him, though for a moment the target didn't seem willing to go down. The pump gun shucked out the empty case, but there wasn't quite enough resistance as the breech slapped home again. It hadn't picked up a fresh round because the tubular magazine was empty. Gregg reached down for the shoulder belt that came with the rifle, slung with pockets each holding five rounds.

Rainbow light erupted from the spaceport. It silhouetted buildings for an instant before the vessel rose too high. Gregg got a good view of the craft while it was illuminated by the reflection of its own exhaust from the ground. It was a ship's boat, a cutter; but a large one, nearly the size of the *Peaches*.

Gregg dropped the rifle and ammo belt to unsling his flashgun. The cutter's hull would be proof against the amount of energy the laser delivered, but if the vessel tried to overfly the blockhouse and fry the raiders with its exhaust—well, Gregg had smashed thruster nozzles under more difficult conditions.

Molts streamed from the shelter of the blockhouse at a measured trot. A part of Gregg's mind wondered about sending aliens to safety while humans remained at risk; but the Venerians were needed as a rear guard until the last instant . . . and anyway, Piet didn't think in terms of men and not-men.

Neither did Gregg at the moment. His universe was a place in which targets would appear if only he waited.

The cutter slanted slowly upward to fifty meters, turning on its vertical axis. The starboard side swung parallel to the front of the blockhouse a kilometer away. At this distance, Gregg didn't have an angle to hit a thruster no matter how steady his aim was.

A few Feds still fired from the town. Venerians shot back, but the crewmen were tensed to follow the Molts in a moment or two. Quick, scuttling movement beyond the screening smoke indicated that the Feds planned *something*, but there were no good targets just now.

"By God, we're going to make—" Jeude cried in a tone of burgeoning triumph.

Because the cutter was illuminated from below, Gregg didn't guess the existence of the vessel's large side-opening hatch until the Fed gunner opened fire with the laser mounted in the hold. It was a powerful weapon, pumped by the cutter's fusion drive. The tube tripped six or eight times a second to keep from overloading individual components.

The gunner's aim was good for line. Though he started low, the cutter was rolling on its horizontal axis and walked the burst on. A bollard blazed like a magnesium flare. Pavement between there and the blockhouse shattered into shrapnel of fist size and smaller, flying in all directions. It was no danger to Gregg at the rear corner of the structure.

The laser hit the front of the blockhouse and blew off meters of the concrete facing. The grid of reinforcing wires acted as a cleavage line, saving the inner ten centimeters of thickness, but a pulse of coherent light streamed through a loophole unhindered.

Coye blew apart in a flash of painful density. Dole, a meter away, screamed from the burst of live steam that had been his loader an instant before. Gregg felt something splash his left ankle. He didn't look down to see what it was.

It didn't matter. He had a target.

Gregg aimed as the Fed laser ripped across the last of the Molts entering the Mirror. Parts of three or more of the aliens—the destruction was too great to be sure of the number—sprayed out in a white-hot dazzle.

Shouting to encourage themselves, fifty or more Fed soldiers rose and charged the blockhouse. Piet Ricimer's rifle cracked alone to meet them.

The target was a klick away; Stephen Gregg was using a handheld weapon. He had no doubt at all that he would hit. He and the flashgun and the cutter's hatch were beads on a wire that would be straight though it stretched to infinity. He squeezed.

The hatch flared, becoming a rectangle of momentary white against the dark hull. Gregg's bolt had punched a bulkhead inside the cutter, converting an egg-sized dollop of metal to blazing gas. The shock hurled one of the weapon's crew forward, out of the hatch.

The laser slewed left and down but continued to fire. Gouts of flame leaped each time a pulse stabbed into Umber City. The Fed infantry paused, looking back at what had been their hope.

The laser's wild firing stopped after a few seconds. Reflected light glimmered as the gunner swiveled his tube back on target.

Gregg swung his reloaded flashgun up to his shoulder. *Beads on a wire.* He squeezed the trigger.

The second bolt's impact was a brief flash, followed by ropes of coruscating blue fire that grew brighter as they ate the metal away from all four sides of the hatch. Gregg had severed one of the armored conduits which powered the laser's pumping system. The generator's full output dumped into the cutter's hull through a dead short.

"Run for it!" Ricimer cried. He stood and swept his rifle's barrel toward the tramline like a cavalryman gesturing with his saber. "Stay between the rails!"

Stephen Gregg locked the lid of the butt compartment down over his last charged battery.

Jeude ran hunched over, carrying the heavy rifle in his right hand and dragging his carbine by its sling in his left. The three Venerians surviving within the blockhouse ran for the tramline also. Coye's legs to the pelvis, baked to the consistency of wood, remained standing behind them. Piet waited till his men were clear, then followed.

The Federation cutter rolled over on its back and plunged out of sight. The flash and the shockwave three seconds later were much greater than a vessel so small could have caused by hitting the ground. The cutter must have dived into one of the starships, perhaps the one which had launched it.

"Stephen!"

Gregg aimed his flashgun.

He was hard to see against the concrete, but some of the Fed soldiers had now reached the bollards. Several of them fired simultaneously. Something *hot* stabbed Gregg's lower abdomen and his right foot kicked out behind.

He squeezed. The bolt from the flashgun illuminated the figure who stood at the central window of the blacked-out Commandatura. The target existed only for the instant of the shot, high-intensity light converted to heat in the flesh of a man's chest.

Gregg turned to run. A bullet had carried away the heel of his right boot. He fell over. When he tried to get up, he found his arms had no strength.

Half a dozen Fed soldiers continued their assault even after the cutter's crash broke the glass out of all the remaining windows in Umber City. They'd ducked as Gregg leveled his lethal flashgun, but they came on again when he fell.

Gregg levered his torso off the ground. It was over. He couldn't move beyond that.

"On my *soul* you won't have him!" Piet Ricimer screamed. He held the short-barreled shotgun a Fed guard had carried. It belched twice, bottle-shaped flares of powder gases burning ahead of the muzzle. A soldier staggered backward at either shot. The unexpected flashes and roars did as much to stop the attack as the actual damage did.

Gregg felt arms around him. He knew they must be Piet's, but he couldn't see his friend for the pulsing orange light that swelled silently around him.

The orange suddenly flipped to cyan. Then there was nothing. Nothing but the cold.

47

Above Benison

"Lift the suit around me and latch it," Gregg said. "I'll be fine with it carried on my shoulders. I just don't want to bend to pick it up."

Weightlessness in orbit above Benison made his guts shift into attitudes slightly different from those of the gravity well in which he'd been wounded. The result wasn't so much painful as terrifying. Part of Gregg's mind kept expecting ropes of intestine to suddenly spill out, twisting around his shocked companions.

His left eye was undamaged. Blood from his cut brow had gummed it shut during the blockhouse fight.

"Stephen," Ricimer said, "you can't do any good in your present condition. You'll only get in the way. Besides, the mirrorside authorities don't have the strength to interfere with us and K'Jax' people together, if they so much as notice us land."

"Lightbody," Gregg said. "Pick up my body armor and latch it around me." He glared at Ricimer.

The Venerians hadn't bothered to formally name the ships they captured on Umber's mirrorside. Because you had to call them something, the other vessel was *Dum* and this one, *Dee*. Lightbody looked from Gregg to Ricimer and fingered his pocket Bible. The three of them were the only humans aboard.

Ricimer sighed. "No, I'll take care of it," he said to the crewman. He reflexively crooked his leg around a stanchion to hold him as he lifted the torso of the hard suit. "Is it just that you want to die?"

"I'm sorry," Gregg said. He stretched his arms out to his side so that Ricimer could slide the right armhole over him. The movement was controlled by his fear of the consequences. "I—if I give in to it, I will die, I think. I don't want to push too hard, really. But I can't just. Lie back."

"Okay, now lower them," Ricimer said. The backplate was solid, with hinges on the sides and the breastplate split along an overlapping seam in the middle. Ricimer closed the left half of the plate carefully over the bandaged wound.

One of the Molts from Umber was a surgeon. It was typical of Federation behavior that she and other specialists had been sent to the labor crews when there was need to carry crates to the spaceport.

Because the surgeon had survived the firefight, and because there was a reasonably-equipped clinic on Umber's mirrorside, Gregg had survived also.

When Gregg awakened halfway through the voyage back to Benison, Lightbody offered him the bullet. He'd taken the battered slug because he was still too woozy from analgesics to refuse, but now he was looking forward to tossing it away discreetly as soon as they were on a planet again.

"*Dum* has arrived," Guillermo called from the control console, where he watched the rudimentary navigational equipment. "Shall I radio her?"

He was one of the half dozen Molts awake on the two vessels together. The rest were in suspended animation. Air wasn't a problem this time, but there were limited provisions available. Besides, with all the cargo, there was no space to move around as it was.

"Yes, of course," Ricimer said. "Tell Dole that we'll set down first, but I'll wait till he's ready to follow immediately."

"If there's no trouble with the locals, Piet," Gregg said quietly, "then it won't matter whether I'm holding a rifle or not. If there *is* trouble, then I'm still the best you've got."

His lips smiled. "Even now."

Ricimer latched the strap over Gregg's left shoulder. "You never explained why you waited to fire that last shot," he said, his eyes resolutely on his work. "After you brought the cutter down."

"It was an idea I had," Gregg said. A Molt who had been

watching the proceedings without speaking handed him the helmet that replaced the one Gregg had lost beside the blockhouse. Coye hadn't worn his through the Mirror, and he had no need of one now.

"I thought that Carstensen would be watching the . . . proceedings," Gregg continued.

"You thought?" Ricimer said sharply.

"I felt he was," Gregg said. He was embarrassed to explain something he didn't understand himself. "Sometimes when, when there's . . ."

His voice trailed off. Piet met his gaze from centimeters away.

"Sometimes when I've got a gun in my hands," Gregg continued coldly, "I know things that I can't see. I saved one charge in the flashgun. And I was willing for whatever happened later if I'd sent that bastard to Hell to greet me."

He licked his dry lips. "I'm not really thinking when I'm like that, Piet," he said. "And I don't care to remember it later."

But I do remember.

"Yes," said Ricimer. "Do you want to wear the rest of the suit?"

Gregg shook his head. "This'll be fine," he said. "It's really a security blanket, you know."

"Mr. Dole reports they're ready to land," Guillermo called.

"All right," Ricimer said. "I'll take the console for landing."

He handed Gregg the breechloader and cross-belts Jeude had brought back through the Mirror because he was too single-minded to think of throwing them down.

"The Lord has mercy for all who love Him, Stephen," he added softly as he turned away.

48

Benison

Piet shut off the thrusters. The *Dum* dropped the last meter and pogoed back on the shock absorbers, simply springs rather than oleo struts, of her landing outrigger.

Gregg jounced in the hammock that was all the mirrorside builders had provided in the way of acceleration couches. Everything felt all right; though he didn't suppose there'd be nerves to tell him that the stitches holding his guts together had all let go. He got up, carefully but trying to hide his concern.

"Sorry," Ricimer said as he undid his harness. "I was getting so irregular a backwash from the ground that I shut down sooner than I cared to do."

"Any one you walk away from, sir," Lightbody said cheerfully. He stood and stretched at the rudimentary attitude-control panel. He'd let the AI do the work, wisely and at Ricimer's direction. "Not as though we're going to need these again, anyhow."

"That's not a way I like to think, Mr. Lightbody," Piet said tartly. He latched on his own body armor. The suits were too confining to wear safely while piloting.

The two Molts from Umber went into the *Dum*'s single hold to wake their fellows. Guillermo stepped to the personnel hatch in the cockpit bulkhead and undogged it.

Ricimer glanced at the viewscreen. It was almost useless. If you knew what the terrain of Benison's mirrorside looked like, you could just make out the skeletons of multitrunked trees, burned bare by the exhaust.

Gregg checked the chamber to make sure his rifle was loaded. It was a falling-block weapon. He would have preferred a turn-bolt with more power to cam a bulged or corroded case home. *Beggars can't be choosers.*

"I'm ready," he said aloud.

Guillermo dragged the hatch inward hard. Hot air surged in; heat waves rippled from the baked soil beyond. K'Jax rose into sight twenty meters away, just beyond the burned area. Both of his bodyguards now carried firearms.

"Any trouble here, K'Jax?" Ricimer called. The relief in his voice was as evident as that which Gregg felt at seeing the situation they had planned on.

A glint in the upper atmosphere indicated Dole was bringing the *Dee* down right on their heels. The nearest Federation settlement was hundreds of klicks away, so the chance of being disturbed really hadn't been very high. It was only paranoia, Gregg supposed, that had made him so fearful ever since they reached orbit.

"None here," said the Molt leader. "But across the Mirror, the humans came and attacked your ships. One was destroyed, and the other two fled."

49

Benison

"You're all right now, Mr. Gregg," said the black-bearded Federation guard whose chest was a tangle of charred bone. The corpse
gripped Gregg with icy hands. "You've passed through the Mirror, sir."

Gregg shouted or screamed, he wasn't sure which. He swung.
The butt of the rifle he was carrying struck a tree and spun the
weapon out of his hands. The Molt who'd tried to stop Gregg,
already five paces from the edge of the Mirror, ducked away from
the rifle and Gregg's flailing hands.

"Oh!" Gregg said. "Oh." He took a deep breath, closed his eyes,
and said, "I'm all right now," before he opened them again.

It was overcast on Benison's realside. Gregg had traveled enough
by now that open skies bothered him less than they once had, but
the tight gray clouds were a relief after another episode with the
Mirror.

The Molt he'd swung at was T'Leen, whom K'Jax had sent with
Ricimer and Gregg as a guide. He picked up the rifle, examined
it—a smear of russet bark on the stock, but no cracks or serious
damage. He gave the weapon back to Gregg.

"I'm sorry," Gregg said. "I don't handle the Mirror well." *And
I'm getting worse, like a man sensitized to an allergen.*

Piet sat on the stump of a tree burned off close to the ground by a plasma bolt. Guillermo stood beside him, ready to grab if his master toppled from what couldn't have been a comfortable seat.

The Mirror took it out of a fellow. Even on Umber where the boundary was shallower, what must it have been like to carry a man the size of Stephen Gregg through in your arms?

Gregg forced himself to walk toward Ricimer. He felt increasingly human with every consciously-directed step. The wound in his lower abdomen was a frozen lump, but that was better than the twist of fiery needles he'd been living with since he awakened during transit.

Piet smiled and started to get up. His face went blank. Guillermo reached down, but Ricimer managed to lurch to his feet unaided. He smiled again, this time with a mixture of relief and triumph.

"There's no sign that the Feds harmed either the *Peaches* or *Dalriada*," he said. "After all, we'd dismantled the *Halys* ourselves before we crossed to mirrorside."

A party of armed Molts appeared from the forest surrounding the blasted area. T'Leen clicked reassuringly to them. K'Jax remained on mirrorside for the moment, greeting and working out power arrangements with the newcomers from Umber.

A plasma bolt had struck the bow of the *Halys*. It came from a powerful weapon, but the depth of atmosphere between target and the bombarding vessel in orbit dispersed the effect over several square meters. An oxidized crust of thin metal plated the soil around the point of impact. Metal icicles jagged where they'd cooled on lower portions of the hull.

A dozen other bolts had vaporized chunks of forest in the immediate neighborhood. That didn't say a great deal for the Feds' fire direction, though Gregg realized there were severe problems in hitting anything with a packet of charged particles that had to pass through kilometers of atmosphere.

"How did they find us, do you think?" he asked Ricimer.

Piet clambered aboard the *Halys*. The hatch, open when the bolt hit, had crumpled in on itself like foil held too close to a flame.

He looked back. "Schremp, I suppose," he said. "Or one of his men. I said we were going to Benison to mislead them."

Ricimer grinned. "Without lying, you see. Carstensen must have sent a warship from Rondelet to check out the report."

His grin became bleak. "The next time," he said, "I'll lie."

T'Leen returned to the humans with others of the clan in tow. "Fire came from the sky," he said. "Eight days ago, in the morning. It killed two of our people."

He pointed in the general direction where the *Dalriada* had been berthed in the forest.

"Were the ships hit?" Ricimer asked.

"No, not then," the Molt said. T'Leen's voice lacked human inflections, but the vocabulary of Trade English was close to the surface of his mind, in contrast to the impression Gregg had of K'Jax.

"The fire came again, nine times," T'Leen went on. "It didn't hit any of us, or the ships. We ran into the Mirror, all but K'Jax and I and S'Tan. The large ship fired guns into the sky."

T'Leen cocked his head to one side, then the other, in a gesture Gregg couldn't read. "We have never seen guns like those used before. If we had guns like those, we would drive the humans off this world."

Gregg mentally translated "human" as "Fed" when members of K'Jax' clan used the word. At moments like this, he was less than certain that the Molts didn't mean exactly what they said.

"The fire from the sky stopped when the large vessel began to shoot," T'Leen said. "The ships took off, the little one and then the large one."

He pointed to the *Halys*. "This they left. S'Tan would have gone back to bring the clan from mirrorside, but the fire came again. Here."

His chitinous fingertips clicked against the ruined hull. "Then soldiers came on vehicles and aircraft, and we went across the Mirror too," T'Leen said. "There was nothing more here."

"Well," Gregg said. "They got away, at least. Dulcie and the crews did."

He wondered how much of the chill in his guts was physical and how much came from the realization that he might spend the rest of his life on Benison.

"It was my fault," Ricimer said as he examined the vessel's cockpit.

Though the dispersed bolt had opened the *Halys* as completely as a pathologist does a skull before brain removal, the interior of what remained wasn't in too bad a condition. That was partly because the Venerians themselves had gutted her thoroughly to create the *Umber*, abandoned on the mirrorside of her namesake.

"The fire that did this," T'Leen said. "And burned the forest. That was from guns like those on your ship?"

Gregg nodded. "Yeah," he said. "Plasma cannon. Probably bigger ones than the *Dalriada* mounts. Not so well served, though."

"We thought so," said T'Leen. "One day we will have such guns."

Gregg sighed and wiped the stock of his rifle with the palm of his hand. How many times would he have to run into the Mirror to save himself from Fed hunters?

"A ship in orbit's at a disadvantage in a fight with ground batteries," he said to divert his mind from an icy future. "The Feds didn't get lucky when they sprang their surprise, so they eased off and let our people get away."

He snorted. "I've got a suspicion the *Halys* will be promoted to a Venerian dreadnought in that Fed captain's report."

"Stephen!" Ricimer said. "Switch your radio on to Channel Three!"

"Huh?" said Gregg. The helmet radio was designed for use by men in vacuum wearing gauntlets. He clicked the dial on the right temple from Channel One, intercom, to Channel Three which the squadron used for general talk-between-ships, then pressed the dial to turn the unit on.

" . . . *to Ricimer, we've been attacked by the enemy. We'll remain in orbit for another day. Call us when you return. Dulcie to Ricimer. We've been attacked—*"

Gregg switched his radio off. The static-broken voice, a recording that presumably played in segments interspersed with dead air for a reply, was the most welcome sound he'd ever heard.

"Piet!" he said. "We're saved!"

A cold as terrible as that of the Mirror flooded back into his soul. "Except we *can't* call them," he said. "These helmet intercoms won't punch a signal through the atmosphere. Stripping the commo system out of *Dee* or *Dum* and setting it up in working order will take a lot more than a day with the tools and personnel we've got."

"Yes," Ricimer said crisply. He looked down at their Molt guide. "T'Leen," he said, "please recross the Mirror and tell the personnel there to immediately begin bringing the cargo over to this side. First of all, send across all of my crewmen. I'll need their skills for the work."

T'Leen flexed his elbow joints out in his equivalent of a nod. He stepped toward the transition layer.

"What work, Piet?" Gregg asked.

It was possible to travel from mirrorside to realside through normal transits, though it was a brutal voyage that might take years. *Dum* and *Dee* would never survive it, but they could capture a larger ship—

Six humans and perhaps a few Molt volunteers. Most of their weapons abandoned on the realside of Umber. Capturing a ship that could journey home from the mirrorside.

Right. And perhaps the angels would come down in all their glory and carry Stephen Gregg to Eryx without need for a ship at all.

"To put the *Halys* in shape to lift off," Ricimer said.

"What? Piet, we gutted her before we left. She's got three thrusters, no AI, and she's been torn to Hell besides!"

"Yes," Ricimer said. "But if she lifts me to orbit, then I think I can raise our friends with my helmet radio."

Gregg stared at the ruined vessel. They'd cut frame members to remove the thruster. "Piet," he said. "She'll twist, flip over, and come in like a bomb."

Like the Federation cutter he'd brought down on Umber.

Ricimer smiled gently. "If that's God's will, Stephen," he said, "so it shall. But if we give up hope in the Lord's help, then we're already lost."

Gregg opened his mouth. He couldn't think of anything to say, so he turned away quickly before Piet could see his tears of frustration.

50

Benison

The thrusters crashed to life. The *Halys* yawed nose-down to star-board as her stern came unstuck. The Venerians had removed the starboard stern unit to power the *Umber*. Ricimer, a suited doll in the open cockpit, seemed to have overcompensated for the imbalance.

"Forward throttle, sir!" Dole screamed. Piet couldn't hear him over the exhaust's crackling roar, and it wasn't as though the deathtrap's pilot didn't know what the problem was.

Besides, Gregg knew instinctively that Dole's advice was wrong. Gregg couldn't pilot a boat in a bathtub himself, but he knew from marksmanship that you were better off carrying through with a plan than to try to reprogram your actions in mid-execution.

You'd probably gotten it right when you had leisure to consider. Your muscles couldn't react quickly enough to follow each flash of ephemeral data. If you kept your swing and squeeze constant, the chances were that the shot and the target would intersect down-range.

If you were as good a shot as Stephen Gregg.

Ricimer was at least as good a pilot as his friend was a gun-man.

The *Halys* continued to lift with her nose low. Her bow drifted to starboard so that as the blasted vessel climbed, she also wheeled slowly.

"You've got her, Piet," Gregg whispered. "You've *got* her, you do!"

They'd rigged manual controls to the *Halys'* remaining thrusters, using what remained of the reel of monocrystal line they'd left on mirrorside after the *Umber* was complete. They couldn't fit her with a collective: they didn't have a test facility in which to check alignments and power delivery, so that a single control could change speed and attitude in a unified fashion. Flying the *Halys* now was like walking three dogs on separate leashes—through a roomful of cats.

"He's got it!" Stampfer shouted, clapping his big hands together in enthusiasm. "I didn't think—"

He didn't finish the sentence. He didn't have to. Lightbody read his Bible with his back to the launch. Jeude squatted beside him. His eyes drifted toward the book, but every time they did, he set his mouth firmly and looked away.

Cased microchips stood in neat piles just within the edge of the undamaged forest. The only Molt present was Guillermo. The aliens had shifted the cargo through the Mirror more than an hour before the Venerians finished rerigging the *Halys*. K'Jax immediately gathered both Clan Deel and the newcomers from Umber and whisked them away.

He claimed he was doing that because the spaceship's liftoff would call Feds to the site. That might well be true, but Gregg suspected K'Jax wanted to absorb the new immigrants beyond human interference. Absorb them, and assert his own dominance.

The Feds had eased K'Jax' difficulties. The cutter's weapon had caught Ch'Kan, last of her people to run for the Mirror and safety.

Gregg's momentary shiver of hatred for K'Jax wasn't fair, wasn't even sane. The clan chief hadn't created the situation from which he was profiting. He was simply a politician handed an opportunity. A single strong clan under a leader with experience of Benison's conditions was to the benefit of all the race ...

With the exception of one or two of the newcomers who would balk, and who would become examples for the rest.

Gregg stroked the fore-end of his rifle. His feelings were quite insane; but it was just as well that K'Jax, a faithful ally, was nowhere around just now.

The *Halys* rose slowly. Her nozzles were toed outward, because if they'd been aligned truly parallel Piet would have had insufficient lateral stability. Half the attitude jets had been destroyed or plugged when the plasma bolt hit. Manually-controlled thrusters were as much as one man could hope to handle anyway.

As much or more.

The *Halys* reached the cloud base and disappeared. The throb of the thrusters faded more slowly.

A patch of cloud glowed for some moments. Lightning licked within the overcast. The charged exhaust had created imbalances that nature sought to rectify.

Gregg looked at his command: a Molt and five humans, himself included. Four firearms if you counted Guillermo's pistol, and four cutting bars.

None of the personnel in perfect condition, and Gregg able to move only by walking slowly. If he'd been physically able to survive the shock of takeoff, he'd have been in the *Halys* with Piet; but he couldn't.

"Mr. Dole," he said crisply. "You, Lightbody and Jeude position yourselves at the edge of the clearing there."

Between the *Halys'* exhaust on landing and takeoff, and the plasma bolts the Feds had directed at her from orbit, fires had burned an irregular swatch a hundred meters by three hundred into the forest. Large trees spiked up as blackened trunks, but in general you could see across the area. Gregg pointed to the center of one long side.

"Stampfer, Guillermo and I will wait across the clearing," he continued. "That way we'll have any intruders in a cross fire."

Jeude glanced at the party's equipment. "Some cross fire," he muttered.

Gregg smiled tightly. He hefted the heavy rifle Jeude himself had brought back from Umber City. "I'd prefer to have a flashgun, Mr. Jeude," he said. "But if the need arises, I'll endeavor to give a good account of myself with what's available. As shall we all, I'm confident."

The smile disappeared; his face looked human again. "Let's go," he said as he turned.

He heard Dole murmur as the parties separated, "If it's him with a sharp stick and the Feds with plasma guns, Jeude, I know where *my* money lies."

51

Benison

"They're coming!" Stampfer said. He clicked his channel selector across the detents, making sure that the increasing crackle of static blanketed the RF spectrum. "Mr. Gregg, they're coming! I can hear the thrusters!"

"Mr. Dole," Gregg said, speaking loudly on intercom mode, though he knew that wouldn't really help carry his voice over the hash of plasma exhaust. "Don't show yourselves until we're sure this is friendly."

He cut off the helmet radio and looked at Stampfer—Guillermo wasn't going to run out into the middle of the clearing waving his arms. "Us too," he said. "We don't know it's Piet. We don't even know it's a spaceship."

"Aw, *sir*," the gunner said. The thrusters were a growing rumble rather than just white noise on the radio. "It couldn't be anybody else!"

He craned his neck skyward.

The vessel overflew the clearing at a thousand meters. Its speed was in the high subsonic range. It was a ship's boat. From the hull's metallic glint it was of Terran manufacture.

Perversely, Gregg's first reaction was an urge to smirk knowingly at Stampfer, who had been so sure the news had to be good. Next he wondered what they could do about it . . . and the answer was probably nothing, though he'd see.

"It may be a boat they've captured, like the *Halys*," Gregg said aloud.

"The larger settlements on Benison usually have a cutter available," Guillermo said. "This craft comes from the direction of Fianna, which is the nearest settlement."

"Or it could be from orbit," said Stampfer, as gloomy now as he had been enthusiastic a moment before. "The Fed warship that drove them away before—Dulcie may not be the only one that came back and waited for something to happen."

The sound of the thruster had died away to a shadow of itself. Now it rose again, the sharper pulses syncopating the dying echoes of the previous pass. The boat was coming back.

"I doubt a warship from the Earth Convoy has been wasting the past week and a half in orbit here, Mr. Stampfer," Gregg snapped. He wasn't so much frightened as completely at a loss for anything to do. The local Feds had noticed Piet's liftoff. They'd sent a cutter to scout the location.

The boat roared over the clearing again, this time within a hundred meters of the ground. It had slowed considerably, but not even Gregg could have hit the vessel in the instant it was visible overhead. A rifle bullet wouldn't have done any damage to a spacegoing hull, but the Feds might be concerned about laser bolts.

If only he hadn't lost the flashgun . . .

"Stampfer and Guillermo," Gregg said. "Go directly across the clearing to Mr. Dole's force and inform him that all of you are to run for the Mirror immediately. Go!"

Neither of them moved. "Hey," said Stampfer. "We can still fight."

"God's blood, you fool, there won't *be* a fight!" Gregg shouted. "They'll come over on the deck and fry us with their exhaust. Go!"

Stampfer looked at the Molt, then back at Gregg.

"His injury won't permit him to run," Guillermo said to the gunner.

"We'll help him," Stampfer said. He forcibly wrapped Gregg's left arm across his shoulders.

"No, there's not enough—" Gregg began, and then it truly was too late. The boat was coming back, very fast and traveling parallel with the clearing's long axis. The pilot wanted to get the maximum effect now that he'd identified the target by the waiting crates.

Did he know what the crates contained? Probably not, but it

wouldn't matter. Though the cargo was hugely valuable, none of it was going into the pockets of the boat's crew. They would be far more concerned about their own safety, especially if word of the bloodbath in Umber City had reached Benison by now.

"Let go of me," Gregg said. He had to shout to be heard. "I'll get one shot at least. Guillermo, you shoot too."

Gregg aimed, wondering which side of the clearing the Feds would ignite on their first pass. Either way, it wouldn't be long before they finished the job.

Guillermo took the pistol from his holster. He pointed it vaguely toward the north end of the clearing. His head rotated to stare at Gregg rather than the sight picture.

Was the pilot perhaps a Molt too?

The boat, transonic again, glinted over the rifle sight. Gregg squeezed.

The boat's hull crumpled around an iridescent fireball. The bow section cartwheeled through the sky, shedding sparkling bits of itself as it went. The stern dissolved in what was less a secondary explosion than a gigantic plasma flare involving the vessel's powerplant. The initial thunderclap knocked Gregg and his companions down, but the hissing roar continued for several seconds.

"Metal hulls," said Stampfer, seated with his hands out behind him to prop his torso. "Never trust them. Good ceramic wouldn't have failed that way to a fifty-mike-mike popgun."

The *Peaches* boomed across the clearing, moving too fast to land on this pass. Gregg saw the featherboat bank to return.

"Not bad shooting, though," Stampfer added. "Not bad at all."

Gregg didn't have the strength to sit up just at the moment. He tried to reload the rifle by holding it above his chest, but after fumbling twice to get a cartridge out of its loop, he gave that up too.

"Only the best for Piet's boys," he said, knowing the words were lost in the sound of the featherboat returning to land.

52

Venus

The personnel bridge shocked against the hull of the *Peaches*. The featherboat rocked and chattered as the tube's lip tried to grip the hot ceramic around the roof hatch. A hiss indicated the Betaport staff was purging the bridge even though they didn't have a good seal yet.

"Boy, they're in a hurry for us!" Dole said with a chuckle. "When Customs sent *our* manifest down from orbit, that got some action, didn't it?"

"What do you figure the value is, Captain?" Jeude asked. "All those chips—"

He gestured, careful both because he wore a hard suit in anticipation of landing and because of the featherboat's packed interior. They'd skimped on rations for the return voyage in order to find space for more crated microchips.

"I never *saw* so many, just here. And the *Dalriada*, it's as full as we are for all she's so much bigger."

Ricimer looked at Gregg and raised an eyebrow.

Rather than quote a figure in Venerian consols, Gregg said, "I'd estimate the value of our cargo is in the order of half or two-thirds of the planetary budget, Jeude."

His mouth quirked in something like a smile. It was amusing to be asked to be an accountant again. It was amazing to realize that he *was* still an accountant, a part of him. Humans were like panels of stained glass, each colored segment partitioned from the others by impassable black bars.

"Of course," he added, still an accountant, "the quantity of chips we're bringing is great enough that they'll depress the value of the class on the market if they're all released at the same time."

"They will be," Ricimer said, his eyes on the future beyond the *Peaches'* hatch. "To build more starships for Venus, to give them the best controls and optics as they've already got the best hulls and crews."

He looked at his men. "The best crews God ever gave a captain in His service," he said.

"What'll a personal share be then, Mr. Gregg?" Lightbody asked. His right hand absently stroked his breastplate, beneath which he carried his pocket Bible. "Ah—for a sailor, I mean, is all."

"*If* they let us keep it," Stampfer said. "You know how the gentlemen do—begging your pardon, Mr. Gregg, I don't mean *you*. But it may mean a war, and it may be they don't want that."

"It was a war on fucking Biruta, wasn't it?" Jeude said. "Nobody cared about that but the widows!"

"I cared," Gregg said without emphasis. And at the end, Henry Carstensen cared; though perhaps not for long.

"Well, we all cared," Jeude said, "and all Betaport cared. But the gent—the people in Ishtar City, they let it go by."

He gave Gregg a pleading look. "The governor, she won't give our cargo back, will she, sir?"

Gregg looked at Ricimer, who shrugged. Gregg smiled coldly and said, "No, Jeude, she won't. Her own share's too great, and the value to the planet's industrial capacity is too great. Pleyal's government will threaten, and they'll sue for recovery . . . but they'll have to sue in our courts, and I doubt they can even prove ownership."

Ricimer looked surprised.

Gregg laughed. "You're too innocent to be a merchant, Piet," he said.

He rapped a case with his armored knuckles. "How much of this do you think was properly manifested on Umber—and so subject to Federation taxes and customs? My guess is ten percent. A quarter at the outside. And they'll play hell getting proper documentation on *that*."

"And our share, Mr. Gregg?" Lightbody repeated.

"Enough to buy a tavern in Betaport," Gregg said. "Enough to buy a third share in a boat like the *Peaches*, if that's what you want to do."

Enough to stay drunk for a month, with the best friends of any man on Venus during that month. Lightbody might not be the one to spend his share that way, but you can't always guess how a man would act until he had the consols in his hands.

"I want to go out with the cap'n again," Dole said. "And you, Mr. Gregg."

Gregg gripped the back of the bosun's hand and squeezed it.

"Open your hatch," a voice crackled on the intercom. The featherboat's ceramic hull didn't form a Faraday cage the way a metal vessel's did, but sulphur compounds baked on during the descent through Venus' atmosphere were conductive enough to diffuse even short-range radio communications. "Captain Ricimer and Mr. Gregg are to proceed to the personnel lock, where an escort is waiting."

"Hey, the royal treatment!" Jeude crowed as he reached for one of the undogging levers. "Not just coming in like the cargo, *we* aren't."

"We" would do just that, enter Betaport when the landing pit cooled enough for machinery to haul the *Peaches* into a storage dock. Jeude thought of his officers as representing all the crew.

In a manner of speaking, he could be right.

Gregg started to lock down his faceshield. Ricimer put out a hand. "I think the tube will be bearable without that," he said. "Not comfortable, but bearable for a short time."

"Sure," Gregg said.

Positive pressure in the personnel bridge rammed a blast of air into the *Peaches* when the hatch unsealed. The influx must have started out cool and pure, but at this end of the tube the hot reek made Gregg sneeze and his eyes water.

The crewmen didn't seem to be affected. Gregg noticed that none of them had bothered to close up, as they could have done.

Ricimer murmured something to Guillermo and climbed into the bridge. He extended a hand that Gregg refused. An upward pull would stress his guts the wrong way.

A crewman pushed from behind, welcome help.

The two men walked along the slightly resilient surface of the personnel bridge. With their faceshields up they could talk without using radio intercom, but at first neither of them spoke.

"I don't suppose they understand," Ricimer said. "Do you think they do, Stephen?"

"That Governor Halys could find her life a lot simpler if she handed a couple of high-ranking scapegoats to the Federation for trial?" Gregg said. "No, I doubt it."

He snorted. "As Stampfer implied, sailors don't think the way gentlemen do. And rulers. But I don't think she'd bother throwing the men to Pleyal as well."

"It'll go on, what we've started," Ricimer said. The sidewalls of the tube had a faint red glow, but there was a white light-source at the distant end. "When they see, when all Venus sees the wealth out there, there'll be no keeping us back from the stars. This time it won't be a single empire that shatters into another Collapse. Man will *have* the stars!"

Gregg would have chuckled, but his throat caught in the harsh atmosphere. "You don't have to preach to me, Piet," he said when he'd hacked his voice clear again.

Ricimer looked at him. "What do you believe in, Stephen?" he asked.

Gregg looked back. He lifted a hand to wipe his eyes and remembered that he wore armored gauntlets. "I believe," he said, "that when I'm—the way I get. That I can hit anything I aim at. Anything."

Ricimer nodded, sad-eyed. "And God?" he asked. "Do you believe in God?"

"Not the way you do, Piet," Gregg said flatly. Time was too short to spend it in lies.

"Yes," Ricimer said. "But almost as much as I believe in God, Stephen, I believe in the stars. And I believe He means mankind to have the stars."

Gregg laughed and broke into wheezing coughs again. He bent to lessen the strain on his wound.

His friend put out an arm to steady him. Their armored hands locked. "I believe in you, Piet," Gregg said at last. "That's been enough this far."

They'd reached the personnel lock set into one panel of the huge cargo doors. Ricimer pushed the latchplate.

The portal slid sideways. The men waiting for them within the main lock wore hard suits of black ceramic: members of the Governor's Guard. Their visors were down. They weren't armed, but there were six of them.

"This way, please, gentlemen," said a voice on the intercom. A guard gestured to the inner lock as the other portal sealed again. "Precede us, if you will."

The guards were anonymous in their armor. They weren't normally stationed in Betaport, but there'd been plenty of time since the *Peaches* and *Dalriada* made Venus orbit to send a contingent from the capital.

Piet Ricimer straightened. "It was really worth it, Stephen," he said. "Please believe that."

"It was worth it for me," Gregg said. His eyes were still watering from the sulphur in the boarding tube.

A guard touched the door latch. The portal slid open. Gregg stepped through behind Ricimer.

Three more guards stood to either side of the lock. Beyond them, Dock Street was full of people: citizens of Betaport, factors from Beta Regio and even farther, and a large contingent of brilliantly-garbed court officials.

In the midst of the court officials was a small woman. Stephen Gregg could barely make her out because of his tears and the bodies of twelve more of her black-armored guards.

They were cheering. The whole crowd was cheering, every soul of them.

Author's Afterword: Drake's Drake

Truth is something each individual holds within his heart. It differs from person to person, and it can't really be expressed to anyone else.

Having said that, I try to write fiction about people who behave as closely as possible to the way people do in my internal version of truth. One of the ways I achieve that end is to use historical events as the paradigm for my fiction: if somebody did something, another person at least *might* act that way under similar circumstances.

In the present instance, I've built *Igniting the Reaches* on an armature of events from the early life of Francis Drake (including acts of his contemporaries, particularly the Hawkins brothers and John Oxenham). This isn't biography or even exegesis. Still, I wound up with a better understanding of the period than I had when I started researching it, and I hope I was able to pass some of that feel on to readers.

My research involved a quantity of secondary sources ranging from biographies to treatises on ship construction by naval architects. These were necessary to give me both an overview and an acquaintance with matters that were too familiar to contemporary writers for them to bother providing explanations.

The heart of my reading, however, was *The Principall Navigations of the English Nation,* the 1598 edition, edited by Richard

Hakluyt: *Hakluyt's Voyages.* I've owned the eight-volume set since I was in law school many years ago and have dipped into it on occasion, but this time I had an excuse to read the volumes straight through and take notes. The *Voyages* provided not only facts but a wonderful evocation of the knowledge and attitudes of their time.

The authors of the accounts varied from simple sailors to some of the most polished writers of the day (Sir Walter Raleigh, whatever else he may have been, was and remains a model of English prose style). I appreciated the period far better for the careful way two sailors described coconuts—because people back home wouldn't have the faintest idea of what they were talking about. (Another writer's description of what is clearly a West African manatee concludes, "It tasteth like the best Beef"; which also told me something about attitudes.)

When one views the Age of Discovery from a modern viewpoint, one tends to assume that those involved in the events knew what they were doing. In general, they didn't. It's useful to realize that Raleigh, for example, consistently confused the theatre of his activities on the Orinoco with explorations of the Amazon by Spaniards starting in the latter river's Andean headwaters. Indeed, Drake was practically unique in having a well-considered plan which he attempted to execute. (That didn't keep the wheels from coming off, much as described in this novel.)

I'll add here a statement that experience has taught me will not be obvious to everyone who reads my fiction: I'm writing about characters who are generally brave and occasionally heroes, but I'm not describing saints. Some of the attitudes and the fashions in which my characters behave are very regrettable.

I would like to believe that in the distant future, people will be perfect—tolerant, peaceful, nonsexist. Events of the twentieth century do not, unfortunately, suggest to me that we've improved significantly in the four hundred years since the time of the paradigm I've used here.

Let's work to do better; but we *won't* solve problems in human behavior if we attempt to ignore the realities of the past and present.

Dave Drake
Chatham County, N.C.

THROUGH THE BREACH

To Allyn Vogel
Most of my friends are smart, competent,
and unfailingly helpful to me when
I need it. Allyn is all those things.
She is also a gentle and genuinely good person,
which puts her in a much smaller category.

BETAPORT, VENUS

7 Days Before Sailing

"Mister Jeremy Moore," announced the alien slave as he ushered me into the private chamber of the Blue Rose Tavern. The public bar served as a waiting room and hiring hall for the Venus Asteroid Expedition, while General Commander Piet Ricimer used the back room as an office.

I'd heard that the aide now with Ricimer, Stephen Gregg, was a conscienceless killer. My first glimpse of the man was both a relief and a disappointment. Gregg was big, true; but he looked empty, no more dangerous than a suit of ceramic armor waiting for someone to put it on. Blond and pale, Gregg could have been handsome if his features were more animated.

Whereas General Commander Ricimer wasn't . . . *pretty,* say, the way women enough have found me, but the fire in the man's soul gleamed through every atom of his physical person. Ricimer's glance and quick smile were genuinely friendly, while Gregg's more lingering appraisal was . . .

Maybe Stephen Gregg wasn't as empty as I'd first thought.

"Thank you, Guillermo," said Ricimer. "Has Captain Macquerie arrived?"

"Not yet," the slave replied. "I'll alert you when he does."

269

Guillermo's diction was excellent, though his tongueless mouth clipped the sibilant. He closed the door behind him, shutting out the bustle of the public bar.

Guillermo was a chitinous biped with a triangular face and a pink sash-of-office worn bandolier fashion over one shoulder. I'd never been so close to a Molt slave before. There weren't many in the Solar System and fewer still on Venus. Their planet of origin was unknown, but their present province was the entire region of space mankind had colonized before the Collapse.

Molts remained and prospered on worlds from which men had vanished. Now, with man's return to the stars, the aliens' racial memory made them additionally valuable: Molts could operate the pre-Collapse machinery which survived on some outworlds.

"Well, Mister Moore," Ricimer said. "What are your qualifications for the Asteroid Expedition?"

"Well, I've not myself been involved in off-planet trade, sir," I said, trying to look earnest and superior, "but I'm a gentleman, you see, and thus an asset to any proposal. My father—may he continue well—is Moore of Rhadicund. Ah—"

The two spacemen watched me: Ricimer with amusement, Gregg with no amusement at all. I didn't understand their coolness. I'd thought this was the way to build rapport, since Gregg was a gentleman also, member of a factorial family, and Ricimer at least claimed the status.

"Ah . . ." I repeated. Carefully, because the subject could easily become a can of worms, I went on, "I've been a member of the household of Councilor Duneen—chief advisor to the Governor of the Free State of Venus."

"We know who Councilor Duneen is, Mister Moore," Ricimer said dryly. "We'd probably know of him even if he weren't a major backer of the expedition."

The walls of the room were covered to shoulder height in tilework. The color blurred upward from near black at floor level to smoky gray shot with wisps of silver. The ceiling and upper walls were coated with beige sealant that might well date from the tavern's construction.

The table behind which Ricimer and Gregg sat—they hadn't offered me a chair—was probably part of the tavern furnishings. The communications console in a back corner was brand-new. The ceramic chassis marked the console as of Venerian manufacture, since an off-planet unit would have been made of metal or organic resin instead, but its electronics were built from chips stockpiled on distant worlds where automated factories continued to produce even after the human colonies perished.

Very probably, Piet Ricimer himself had brought those chips to Venus on an earlier voyage. Earth, with a population of twenty millions after the Collapse, had returned to space earlier than tiny Venus. Now that all planets outside the Solar System were claimed by the largest pair of ramshackle Terran states, the North American Federation and the Southern Cross, other men traded beyond Pluto only with one hand on their guns.

Piet Ricimer and his cohorts had kept both hands on their guns, and they traded very well indeed. Whatever the cover story—Venus and the Federation weren't technically at war—the present expedition wasn't headed for the Asteroid Belt to bring back metals that Venus had learned to do without during the Collapse.

I changed tack. I'd prepared for this interview by trading my floridly expensive best suit for clothing of more sober cut and material, though I'd have stayed with the former's purple silk plush and gold lace if the garments had fit my spare frame just a little better. The suit had been a gift from a friend whose husband was much more portly, and there's a limit to what alterations can accomplish.

"I believe it's the duty of every man on Venus," I said loudly, "to expand our planet's trade beyond the orbit of Pluto. We owe this to Venus and to God. The duty is particularly upon those like the three of us who are members of factorial families."

I struck the defiant pose of a man ashamed of the strength of his principles. I'd polished the expression over years of explaining— to women—why honor forbade me to accept money from my father, the factor. In truth, the little factory of Rhadicund in Beta Regio had been abandoned three generations before, and the family certainly hadn't prospered in the governor's court the way my grandfather had hoped.

Piet Ricimer's face stilled. It took me a moment to realize how serious a mistake I'd made in falsely claiming an opinion which Ricimer felt as strongly as he hoped for salvation.

Stephen Gregg stretched his arm out on the table before Ricimer, interposing himself between his friend and a problem that the friend needn't deal with. Gregg wasn't angry. Perhaps Gregg no longer had the capacity for anger or any other human emotion.

"About the manner of your leaving Councilor Duneen's service, Moore," Gregg said. He spoke quietly, his voice cat-playful. "A problem with the accounts, was there?"

I met the bigger man's eyes. What I saw there shocked me out of all my poses, my calculations. "My worst enemies have never denied that their purse would be safe in my keeping," I said flatly. "There was a misunderstanding about a woman of the household. As a gentleman—"

My normal attitudes were reasserting themselves. I couldn't help it.

"—I can say no more."

The Molt's three-fingered hand tapped on the door. "Captain Macquerie has arrived, sir."

"You have no business here, Mister Jeremy Moore," Gregg said. He rose to his feet. Gregg moved with a slight stiffness which suggested that more than his soul had been scarred beyond Pluto; but surely his soul as well. "There'll be no women where we're going. While there may be opportunities for wealth, it won't be what one would call easy money."

"Good luck in your further occupations, Mister Moore," Ricimer said. "Guillermo, please show in Captain Macquerie."

Ricimer and his aide were no more than my own age, 27 Earth years. In this moment they seemed to be from a different generation.

"Good day, gentlemen," I said. I bowed and stepped quickly from the room as a squat fellow wearing coveralls and a striped neckerchief entered. Macquerie moved with the gimballed grace of a spacer who expects the deck to shift beneath him at any moment.

I knew that arguing with Ricimer and Gregg wouldn't have gained me anything. I knew also that Mister Stephen Gregg would *literally* just as soon kill me as look at me.

There were more than thirty men in the tavern's public room—and one woman, a spacer's wife engaged in a low-voiced but obviously acrimonious attempt to drag her husband away. The noise of the crowd blurred whenever the outer door opened onto Dock Street and its heavy traffic.

I pushed my way to one corner of the bar, my progress aided somewhat by the fact I was a gentleman—but only somewhat. Betaport was more egalitarian than Ishtar City, the capital; and spacers are a rough lot anywhere.

The tapster drew beer and took payment with an efficiency that seemed more fluid than mechanical. His eyes were sleepy, but the fashion in which he chalked a tab or held out his free hand in a silent demand for scrip before he offered the glass showed he was fully aware of his surroundings.

I opened my purse and took out the 10-Mapleleaf coin. That left me only twenty Venerian consols to live on for the next week, but I'd find a way. Eloise, I supposed. I hadn't planned to see her again after the problem with her maid, but she'd come around.

"Barman," I said crisply. "I want the unrestricted use of your phone, immediately and for the whole of the afternoon."

I rang the coin on the rippling blue translucence of the bar's ceramic surface.

The barman's expression sharpened into focus. He took the edges of the coin between the thumb and index fingers of his right hand, turning it to view both sides. "Where'd *you* get Fed money?" he demanded.

"Gambling with an in-system trader on the New Troy run," I said truthfully. "Now, if you don't want the coin . . ."

That was a bluff—I needed this particular phone for what I intended to do.

The tapster shrugged. He had neither cause nor intention to refuse, merely a general distaste for strangers; and perhaps for gentlemen as well. He nipped up the gate in the bar so that I could slip through to the one-piece phone against the wall.

"It's local net only," the tapster warned. "I'm not connected to the planetary grid."

"Local's what I want," I said.

Very local indeed. The tool kit on my belt looked like a merchant's papersafe. I took from it a device of my own design and construction.

The poker game three weeks before had been with a merchant/captain and three of his officers, in a sailors' tavern in Ishtar City. The four spacers were using a marked deck. If I'd complained or even tried to leave the game, they would have beaten me within an inch of my life.

The would-be sharpers had thought I was wealthy and a fool; and were wrong on both counts. They let me win for the first two hours. The money I'd lived on since the game came from that pump priming. Much of it was in Federation coin.

The captain and his henchmen ran the betting up and cold-decked me, their pigeon. I weepingly threw down a huge roll of Venerian scrip and staggered out of the tavern. I'd left Ishtar City for Betaport before the spacers realized that I'd paid them in counterfeit—and except for the top bill, very poor counterfeit.

I attached to the phone module's speaker a contact transducer which fed a separate keypad and an earpiece. The tapster looked at me and said, "Hey! What d'ye think you're doing?"

"What I paid you for the right to do," I said. I pivoted deliberately so that my body blocked the tapster's view of what I was typing on the keypad—not that it would have meant anything to the fellow.

On my third attempt at the combination, the plug in my ear said in Piet Ricimer's voice, ". . . not just as a Venerian patriot, Captain Macquerie. All *mankind* needs you."

The communications console in the private room was patched into the tavern's existing phone line. The commands I sent through the line converted Ricimer's own electronics into a listening device. I could have accessed the console from anywhere in Betaport, but not as quickly as I needed to hear the interview with Macquerie.

"Look, Captain Ricimer," said an unfamiliar voice that must by elimination be Macquerie, "I'm flattered that you'd call for me the way you have, but I gave up voyaging to the Reaches when I married the daughter of my supplier on Os Sertoes. Long runs are no life for a married man. From here on out, I'm shuttling my *Bahia* between Betaport and Buenos Aires."

"We mean no harm to the Southern Cross," said Stephen Gregg. "Your wife's family won't be affected."

With Macquerie, there was obviously no pretense that the expedition had anything to do with asteroids. Os Sertoes was little more than a name to me. I vaguely thought that it was one of the most distant Southern colonies, uninteresting and without exports of any particular value.

"Look," said Macquerie, "you gentlemen've been to the Reaches yourself. You don't need me to pilot you—except to Os Sertoes, and who'd want to go there? It's stuffed right in the neck of the Breach, so the transit gradients won't let you go anywhere but back."

"Captain," said Ricimer, "I wouldn't ask you if I didn't believe I needed you. Venus *must* take her place in the greater universe. If most of the wealth of the outworlds continues to funnel into the Federation, President Pleyal will use it to impose his will on all men. Whether Pleyal succeeds or fails, the attempt will lead to a second Collapse—one from which there'll be no returning. The Lord can't want that, nor can any man who fears Him."

A chair scraped. "I'm sorry, gentlemen," Macquerie said. His voice was subdued, but firm. Ricimer's enthusiasm had touched but not won the man. "If you really need a pilot for the Reaches, well— you can pick one up on Punta Verde or Decades. But not me."

The door opened at the corner of my eye. The Molt standing there stepped aside as noise from the public bar boomed through the pickup on my earpiece. Captain Macquerie strode past, his face forming into a scowl of concern as he left the Blue Rose.

"No one just yet, Guillermo," called Piet Ricimer, his words slightly out of synchrony as they reached my ears through different media.

The door closed.

"I could bring him along, you know," Gregg said calmly in the relative silence.

"No," said Ricimer. "We won't use force against our own citizens, Stephen."

"Then you'll have to feel your way into the Breach without help," Gregg said. "You know we won't find a pilot for Os Sertoes at any of the probable stopovers. There's not that much trade to the place."

"Captain Macquerie may change his mind, Stephen," Ricimer replied. "There's still a week before we lift."

"He won't," snapped Gregg. "He feels guilty, sure; but he's not going to give up all he has on a mad risk. And if he doesn't— what? The Lord will provide?"

"Yes, Stephen," said Piet Ricimer. "I rather think He will. Though perhaps not for us as individuals, I'll admit."

In a brighter, apparently careless voice, Ricimer went on, "Now, Guillermo has the three bidders for dried rations waiting outside. Shall we—"

I quickly disconnected my listening device and slipped from behind the bar, keeping low. If Ricimer—or worse, Gregg—saw me through the open door, they might wonder why I'd stayed in the tavern after they dismissed me.

"Hey!" called the barman to my back. "What is it you think you're doing, anyway?"

I only wished I knew the answer myself.

BETAPORT, VENUS

6 Days Before Sailing

The brimstone smell of Venus's atmosphere clung to the starships' ceramic hulls.

Betaport's storage dock held over a hundred vessels, ranging in size from featherboats of under 20 tonnes to a bulk freighter of nearly 150. The latter vessel was as large as Betaport's domed transfer docks on the surface could accommodate for landings and launches.

Many of the ships were laid up, awaiting parts or consignment to the breakers' yard, but four vessels at one end of the cavernous dock bustled with the imminence of departure. The cylindrical hulls of two were already on roller-equipped cradles so that tractors could drag them to the transfer docks.

I eyed the vessels morosely, knowing there was nothing in the sight to help me make up my mind. I'd familiarized myself with the vessels' statistics, but I wasn't a spacer whose technical expertise could judge the risks of an expedition by viewing the ships detailed for it.

I supposed as much as anything I was forcing myself to think about what I intended to do. I rubbed my palms together with the fingers splayed and out of contact.

A lowboy rumbled slowly past. It was carrying cannon to the

expedition's flagship, the 100-tonne *Porcelain*. The hull of Ricimer's vessel gleamed white, unstained by the sulphur compounds which would bake on at first exposure to the Venerian atmosphere. She was brand-new, purpose-built for distant exploration. Her frames and hull plating were of unusual thickness for her burden.

The four 15-cm plasma cannon on the lowboy were heavy guns for a 100-tonne vessel, and the Long Tom which pivoted to fire through any of five ports in the bow was a still-larger 17-cm weapon. The *Porcelain*'s hull could take the shock of the cannons' powerful thermonuclear explosions, but the guns' bulk filled much of the ship's internal volume. The most casual observer could see that the *Porcelain* wasn't fitting out for a normal trading voyage.

I ambled along the quay. Pillars of living rock supported the ceiling of the storage dock, but the huge volume wasn't subdivided by bulkheads. The sounds of men, machinery, and the working of the planetary mantle merged as a low-frequency hum that buffered me from my surroundings.

The *Absalom 231* was a cargo hulk: a ceramic box with a carrying capacity as great as that of the flagship. She was already in a transport cradle. Food and drink for the expedition filled the vessel's single cavernous hold. Lightly and cheaply built, the *Absalom 231* could be stripped and abandoned when the supplies aboard her were exhausted.

The expedition's personnel complement was set at a hundred and eighty men. I wondered how many of them, like the hulk, would be used up on the voyage.

A bowser circled on the quay, heading back to the water point. Its huge tank had filled the *Porcelain* with reaction mass. I moved closer to the vessels to avoid the big ground vehicle. I walked on.

The *Kinsolving* was a sharp-looking vessel of 80 tonnes. A combination of sailors and ground crew were loading sections of three knocked-down featherboats into her central bay. Though equipped with star drive, a 15-tonne featherboat's cramped quarters made it a hellish prison on a long voyage. The little vessels were ideal for short-range exploration from a central base, and they were far handier in an atmosphere than ships of greater size.

What would it be like to stand on a world other than Venus? The open volume of the Betaport storage dock made me uncomfortable. What would it be like to walk under an open sky?

Why in *God's* name was I thinking of doing this?

The last of the expedition's four vessels was the 80-tonne *Mizpah*, also in a transport cradle. She was much older than the *Porcelain* and the *Kinsolving*. Clearly—even to a layman like me—the *Mizpah* wasn't in peak condition.

The *Mizpah*'s main lock and boarding ramp amidships couldn't be used because of the transport cradle, but her personnel hatch forward stood open. On the hatch's inner surface, safe from reentry friction and corrosive atmospheres, were the painted blazons of her co-owners: the pearl roundel of Governor Halys, and the bright orange banderol—the oriflamme—of Councilor Frederic Duneen.

The *Mizpah* wasn't an impressive ship in many ways, but she brought with her the overt support of the two most important investors on the planet. If nothing else, the *Mizpah*'s participation meant the survivors wouldn't be hanged as pirates when they returned to Venus.

If anyone survived. When I eavesdropped on the private discussion between Ricimer and Gregg, I'd heard enough to frighten off anyone sane.

Thomas Hawtry—Factor Hawtry of Hawtry—stepped from the *Mizpah*'s personnel hatch. Two generations before, Hawtry had been a name to reckon with. Thomas, active and ambitious to a fault, had mortgaged what remained of the estate in an attempt to recoup his family's influence by attaching himself to the great of the present day.

He was a man I wanted to meet as little as I did any human being on Venus.

Hawtry was large and floridly handsome, dressed now in a tunic of electric blue with silver lame trousers and calf-high boots to match the tunic. On his collar was a tiny oriflamme to indicate his membership in Councilor Duneen's household.

Hawtry's belt and holster were plated. The pistol was for show, but I didn't doubt that it was functional nonetheless.

"Moore!" Hawtry cried, framed by the hatch coaming two paces away. Hawtry's face was blank for an instant as the brain worked behind it. The Factor of Hawtry was a thorough politician; though not, in my opinion, subtle enough to be a very effective one.

"Jeremy!" Hawtry decided aloud, reforming his visage in a smile. "Say, I haven't had an opportunity to thank you for the way you covered me in the little awkwardness with Lady Melinda."

He stepped close and punched me playfully on the shoulder, a pair of ladies' men sharing a risque memory. "Could have been *ve*-ry difficult for me. Say, I told my steward to pass you a little something to take the sting out. Did he . . . ?"

Lady Melinda was an attractive widow of 29 who lived with her brother—Councilor Duneen. Hawtry'd thought to use me as his go-between in the lady's seduction. I, on the other hand—

I would never have claimed I was perfect, but I liked women too much to lure one into the clutches of Thomas Hawtry. And as it turned out, I liked the Lady Melinda a great deal more than was sensible for a destitute member of the lesser gentry.

"Regrettably, I *didn't* hear from your steward, Thom," I said. No point in missing a target of opportunity. "And you know, I'm feeling a bit of a pinch right now. If—"

Not much of a target. "Aren't we all, Jeremy, aren't we all!" Hawtry boomed. "After I bring my expedition back, though, *all* my friends will live like kings! Say, you know about the so-called 'asteroids expedition,' don't you?"

He waved an arm toward the docked ships. A hydraulic pump began to squeal as it shifted the *Absalom 231* in its cradle.

"Captain Ricimer's . . ." I said, hiding my puzzlement.

"*And* mine," said Hawtry, tapping himself on the breast significantly. "I'm co-leader, though we're keeping it quiet for the time being. A very political matter, someone of my stature in charge of a voyage like this."

Hawtry linked his arm familiarly with mine and began pacing back along the line of expedition vessels. His friendliness wasn't sincere. In the ten months I knew Hawtry intimately in the Duneen household, the man had never been sincere about anything except his ambition and his self-love.

But neither did Hawtry seem to be dissembling the hatred I'd expected. Irritated at his go-between's lack of progress and very drunk, Hawtry had forced the Lady Melinda's door on a night when her brother was out of the house. The racket brought the servants to the scene in numbers.

I, the gentleman who *was* sharing the lady's bed that night, escaped in the confusion—but my presence hadn't gone unremarked. The greater scandal saved Hawtry from the consequences of his brutal folly, but I scarcely expected the fellow to feel grateful. Apparently Hawtry's embarrassment was so great that he'd recast the incident completely in his own mind.

"I'm going to take the war to the Federation," Hawtry said, speaking loudly to be heard over the noise in the storage dock. He accompanied the words with broad gestures of his free hand. "And it *is* a war, you know. Nothing less than that!"

A dozen common sailors examined the *Porcelain*'s hull and thruster nozzles, shouting comments to one another. The men weren't on duty; several of them carried liquor bottles in pockets of their loose garments. They might simply be spectators. Ricimer's flagship was an unusual vessel, and the expedition had been the only subject of conversation in Betaport for a standard month.

"Asteroids!" Hawtry snorted. "The Feds bring their microchips and pre-Collapse artifacts into the system in powerful convoys, Jeremy . . . but *I'm* going to hit them where they aren't prepared for it. They don't defend the ports on the other side of the Mirror where the wealth is gathered. I'll go through the Breach and take them unawares!"

Hawtry wasn't drunk, and he didn't have a hidden reason to blurt this secret plan. Because I was a gentleman of sorts and an acquaintance, I was someone for Hawtry to brag to; it was as simple as that.

Of course, the proposal was so unlikely that I would have discounted it completely if I hadn't heard Ricimer and Gregg discussing the same thing.

"I didn't think it was practical to transit the Breach," I said truthfully. "Landolph got through with only one ship of seven, and nobody has succeeded again in the past eighty years. It's simpler to voyage the long way, even though that's a year and a half either way."

Interstellar travel involved slipping from the sidereal universe into other bubbles of sponge space where the constants for matter and energy differed. Because a vessel which crossed a dimensional membrane retained its relative motion, acceleration under varied constants translated into great changes in speed and distance when the vessel returned to the human universe.

No other bubble universe was habitable or even contained matter as humans understood the term. The sidereal universe itself had partially mitosed during the process of creation, however, and it was along that boundary—the Mirror—that the most valuable pre-Collapse remains were to be found.

Populations across the Mirror had still been small when the Revolt smashed the delicate fabric of civilization. Often a colony's death throes weren't massive enough to complete the destruction of the automated factories, as had happened on the larger outworlds and in the Solar System itself.

For the most part the Mirror was permeable only to objects of less than about a hundred kilograms. Three generations before, Landolph had found a point at which it was possible to transit the Mirror through sponge space.

Landolph's Breach wasn't of practical value, since energy gradients between the bubble universes were higher than ships could easily withstand. Perhaps it had been different for navigators of the civilization before the Collapse.

"Oh, the Breach," Hawtry said dismissively. "Say, that's a matter for sailors. Our Venus lads can do things that cowards from Earth never dreamed of. If they were real men, they wouldn't kiss the feet of a tyrant like Pleyal!"

"I see," I said in a neutral voice.

I supposed there was truth in what Hawtry said. The ships of today were more rugged than Landolph's, and if half of Captain Ricimer's reputation was founded on fact, he was a sailor like no one born to woman before him. But the notion that a snap of the fingers would send a squadron through the Breach was—

Well, Hawtry's reality testing had always been notable for its absence. His notion of using the Lady Melinda as a shortcut to power, for example . . .

The *Porcelain*'s crew was shifting the first of the plasma cannon from the lowboy. A crane lifted the gun tube onto a trolley in the hold, but from there on the weapon would be manhandled into position.

The *Porcelain*'s ceramic hull was pierced with more than a score of shuttered gunports, but like most vessels she carried only one gun for every four or more ports. The crew would shift the weapons according to need.

"They'll get their use soon!" Hawtry said, eyeing the guns with smirking enthusiasm. "And when I come back, well—it'll be Councilor Hawtry, see if it isn't, Moore. Say, there'll be nothing too good for the leader of the Breach Expedition!"

I felt the way I had the night I let the spacers inveigle me into the crooked card game, where there was a great deal to gain and my life to lose. I said, "I can see that you and Captain Ricimer—"

"Ricimer!" Hawtry snorted. "That man, that artisan's son? Surely you don't think that a project of this magnitude wouldn't have a gentleman as its real head!"

"There's Mister Stephen Gregg, of course," I said judiciously.

"The younger son of a smallholder in the Atalanta Plains!" Hawtry said. "Good God, man! As well have you commander of the expedition as that yokel!"

"I take your point," I said. "Well, I have to get back now, Thom. Need to dress for dinner, you see."

"Yes, say, look me up when I return, Moore," Hawtry said. "I'll be expanding my household, and I shouldn't wonder that I'd have a place for a clever bugger like you."

Hawtry turned and stared at the ships which he claimed to command. He stood arms akimbo and with his feet spread wide, a bold and possessive posture.

I walked on quickly, more to escape Hawtry than for any need of haste. Dinner was part of Eloise's agenda, though dressing was not. Quite the contrary.

In an odd way, the conversation had helped settle my mind. I wasn't a spacer: I couldn't judge the risks of this expedition.

But I could judge men.

Hawtry was a fool if he thought he could brush aside Piet Ricimer. And if Hawtry thought he could ride roughshod over Stephen Gregg, he was a dead man.

BETAPORT, VENUS

The Night Before Sailing

Three sailors guarded the city side of Dock 22. Two of the men carried powered cutting bars. The third had stuck forty centimeters of high-pressure tubing under his belt, and a double-barreled shotgun leaned against the wall behind him.

On the other side of the airlock, a tubular personnel bridge stretched to the *Porcelain*'s hatch. Though Dock 22 was closed and the interior had been purged, too much of the hellish Venerian atmosphere leaked past the domed clamshell doors for the dock to be open onto the city proper.

Traffic on Dock Street was sparse at this hour. The airlock guards watched me with mild interest. That turned to sharp concern when they realized that I was guiding directly toward them the drunk I supported. The sailor with the length of tubing closed the pocket Bible he'd been reading and threw his shoulders back twice to loosen the muscles.

"My name doesn't matter," I said. "But I've an important message for Mister Gregg. I need to see him in person."

"Piss off," said one of the sailors. He touched the trigger of his cutting bar. The ceramic teeth whined a bitter sneer.

"This the *Bahia*?" mumbled the drunk.

I held a flask to the lips of the man draped against me. "Here you go, my friend," I said reassuringly. "We'll be aboard shortly."

"Gotta lift ship . . ." the drunk said. He began to cough rackingly.

"I wouldn't mind a sip of that," said one of the guards.

"Shut up, Pinter," said the man with the tubing. "You know better than that."

He turned his attention to me and my charge. "No one boards the *Porcelain* now, sir," he said. "Why don't you and your friend go about your business?"

"This is our business," I said. "Call Mister Gregg. Tell him there's a man here with information necessary to the success of the expedition."

Pinter frowned, leaned forward, and sniffed at the neck of the open flask. "*Hey,* buddy," he said. "What d'ye have in that bottle, anyhow?"

"You wouldn't like the vintage," I said. "Call Mister Gregg now. We need to get this gentleman in a bunk as soon as possible."

The sailor who'd initially ordered me away looked uncertain. "What's going on, Lightbody?" he asked the man with the tubing. "He's a gentleman, isn't he?"

"All right, Pinter," Lightbody said in sudden decision. He gestured to the wired communicator which was built into the personnel bridge. "Call him."

He smiled with a grim sort of humor. "Nobody asks for Mister Gregg because they want to waste his time."

Gregg arrived less than two minutes after the summons. His blue trousers and blue-gray tunic were old and worn. Both garments were of heavy cloth and fitted with many pockets.

Gregg didn't wear a protective suit, though the air that puffed out when he opened the lock was hot and stank of hellfire. He didn't carry a weapon, either; but Stephen Gregg was a weapon.

Sulphurous gases leaking into the personnel bridge had brought tears to Gregg's eyes. He blinked to control them. "Mister Jeremy Moore," he said softly. The catch in his voice might also have been a result of the corrosive atmosphere.

I lifted the face of the man I supported so that the light fell fully on it. "I'm bringing Captain Macquerie aboard," I said. "We're together. I, ah, thought it would be wise not to trouble the general commander."

"Where's 'a *Bahia*?" Macquerie mumbled. "Gotta lift tonight . . ."

"Ah," said Gregg. I couldn't see any change in his expression; the three common sailors, who knew Gregg better, visibly relaxed. "Yes, that was good of you. Piet's resting now. The two of us can get our pilot aboard quietly, I think."

He lifted the shanghaied captain out of my grip. "Piet's too good a man for this existence, I sometimes think. But he's got friends."

Gregg cycled the airlock open. The inner chamber was large enough to hold six men in hard suits. He paused. "Lightbody? Pinter and Davies, all of you. You did well here, but don't report the—arrival—until after we've lifted in the morning. Do you understand?"

"Whatever you say, Mister Gregg," Lightbody replied; the other two sailors nodded agreement. The men treated Gregg with respect due to affection, but they were also quite clearly afraid of him.

As the airlock's outer door closed behind us, Gregg looked over the head of the slumping Macquerie and said, "You say you want to come with us, Moore. I'd rather pay you. I've got more money than I know what to do with, now."

The inner door undogged and began to open even as the outer panel latched. The atmosphere of the personnel bridge struck me like the heart of a furnace.

The bridge was a 3-meter tube of flexible material, stiffened by a helix of glass fiber which also acted as a light guide. The reinforcement was a green spiral spinning dizzily outward until the arc of the sagging bridge began to rise again. A meter-wide floor provided a flat walkway.

I sneezed violently. My nose began to run. I rubbed it angrily with the back of my hand.

"I'll come, thank you," I said. My voice was already hoarse from the harshness of the air. "I'll find my own wealth in the Reaches, where you found yours."

"Oh, you're a smart one, aren't you?" Gregg said harshly. "You think you know where we're really going . . . and perhaps you do, Mister Moore, perhaps you do. But you don't know what it is that the Reaches cost. Take the money. I'll give you three hundred Mapleleaf dollars for this night's work."

The big man paced himself to walk along the bridge beside me.

The walkway was barely wide enough for two, but Gregg held Macquerie out to the side where the tube's bulge provided room.

"I'm not afraid," I said. I was terribly afraid. The personnel bridge quivered sickeningly underfoot, and the air that filled it was a foretaste of Hell. "I'm a gentleman of Venus. I'll willing to take risks to liberate the outworlds from President Pleyal's tyranny!"

The effect of my words was like triggering a detonator. Stephen Gregg turned *fast* and gripped me by the throat with his free left hand. He lifted me and slammed me against the side of the bridge.

"I wasn't much for social graces even before I shipped out to the Reaches for the first time," Gregg said softly. "And I never liked worms taking me for a fool."

The wall of the bridge seared my back through the clothing. The spiral of reinforcing fiber felt like a white slash against the general scarlet pain.

Macquerie, somnolent from the drugged liquor, dangled limply from Gregg's right arm. "Now," Gregg said in the same quiet, terrible voice. "This expedition is important to my friend Piet, do you understand? Perhaps to Venus, perhaps to mankind, perhaps to God—but certainly to my friend."

I nodded. I wasn't sure I could speak. Gregg wasn't deliberately choking me, but the grip required to keep my feet above the walkway also cut off most of my air.

"I don't especially want to kill you right now," Gregg continued. "But I certainly feel no need to let you live. Why do you insist on coming with us, Mister Moore?"

"You can let me down now," I croaked.

The words were an inaudible rasp. Gregg either read my lips or took the meaning from my expression. He lowered me to the walkway and released me.

I shrugged my shoulders. I didn't reach up to rub my throat. I am a gentleman!

"I—" I said. I paused, not because I was afraid to go on, but because I'd never articulated the reason driving me. Not even to myself, in the dead of night.

"I have a talent for electronics," I continued. I fought the need to blink, lest Gregg think I was afraid to meet his gaze. "I couldn't work at that, of course. Only artisans work with their hands. And there was no money; the Moores have never really had money."

"Go on," Gregg said. He wiped the palm of his left hand on the breast of his tunic.

"So I've had to find ways to live," I continued, "and I've done so. Mostly women. And the problem with that is that when I found a woman I really cared about—there was no place the relationship could go except the way they've all gone, to bed and then nowhere. Because there's no me! Doesn't that make you want to laugh, Mister Gregg?"

"I'm not judging you, Moore," Gregg said. He shifted Macquerie, not for his own comfort but for that of the snoring captain. Gregg's effortless strength would have been the most striking thing about him, were it not for his eyes.

"I'm twenty-seven," I said. My bitterness surprised me. "I want to put myself in a place where I *have* to play the man. I pretended it was the money that was pulling me, but that was a lie. A lie for myself."

"Let's walk on," Gregg said, suiting his action to his words. "The air in this tube isn't the worst I've breathed, but that's not a reason to hang around out here either."

I managed a half smile as I fell into step beside the bigger man. Now I massaged the bruises on my throat.

"You don't have to play the man when you're out beyond Pluto, Moore," Gregg said reflectively. "You can become a beast—or die. Plenty do. But if you're determined to come, I won't stop you."

He looked over his shoulder at me. His expression could be called a smile. "Besides, you might be useful."

The *Porcelain*'s airlock was directly ahead of us. I dropped back a step to let Gregg open the hatch.

I thought about the cold emptiness of Stephen Gregg's eyes. I had an idea now what Gregg meant when he spoke of what the Reaches cost.

VENUS ORBIT

Day 1

I'd never been weightless before. My stomach was already queasy from the shaking the *Porcelain* took from the 500 kph winds of the upper Venerian atmosphere. I hadn't eaten since early the night before, but I wasn't sure that would keep me from spewing yellow bile across the men working nonchalantly around me.

I clung to the tubular railing around the attitude-control console. The starship's three navigational consoles were in the extreme bow; the heavy plasma cannon was shipped in traveling position between the consoles and the attitude controls.

Guillermo was at the right-hand console. Ricimer, Hawtry, and the vessel's navigator, Salomon, stood behind the Molt, discussing the course.

"We need to blood the force, *blood* it," Hawtry said. He was the only member of the group speaking loudly enough for me to hear.

Hawtry wore a rubidium-plated revolver and the silver brassard which identified him as an officer in the Governor's Squadron. He had at least enough naval experience to keep his place without clutching desperately at a support the way I did.

A sailor carrying a tool kit slid along the axis of the ship, dabbing effortlessly at stanchions for control. "Careful, sir!" he warned in a bored voice before he batted my legs—which had drifted upward—out of his way.

Because the sailor balanced his motion by swinging the heavy tools, his course didn't change. My feet hit the shell locker and rebounded in a wild arc.

Stephen Gregg stood in the center of the three-faced attitude-control console. He reached out a long arm over Lightbody, reading placidly in one of the bays, caught my ankle, and tugged. I released my own grip and thumped to the deck beside Gregg.

Gregg's right boot was thrust under one of three 20-cm staples in the deck. I hooked my toes through both of the others. My hands hurt from the force with which I'd been holding on since liftoff.

"Want to go home now, Moore?" Gregg asked dryly.

"Would it matter if I did?" I said. The spacer who'd pushed past me was working on the Long Tom's traversing mechanism. A hydraulic fitting spit tiny iridescent drops which would shortly settle and spread over the *Porcelain*'s inner bulkheads.

"Not in the least," said Gregg. His voice was calm, but his head turned as he spoke and his gaze rippled across everything, *everything* in his field of view.

"Then I'm happy where I am," I said. I glanced, then stared, at the controls around me. "These are fully automated units," I said in surprise. "Is that normal?"

"It will be," Gregg said, "if Piet has his way—and if we start bringing back enough chips from the outworlds to make the price more attractive than paying sailors to do the work."

"What we *should* be doing," I said bitterly, "is setting up large-scale microchip production ourselves."

Gregg looked at me. "Perhaps," he said. "But that's a long-term proposition. For now it's cheaper to use the stockpiles—and the operating factories, there are some—on the outworlds. And it's important that men return to the stars, too, Piet thinks."

In a normal starship installation, there was a three-man console for each band of attitude jets—up to six bands in a particularly large vessel. The crewmen fired the jets on command to change the ship's heading and attitude, while the main thrusters, plasma motors, supplied power for propulsion.

On the *Porcelain*, a separate artificial intelligence controlled the jets. The AI's direction was both faster and more subtle than that of even the best-trained crew—but spacers are conservative men, those who survive, and they tend to confuse purpose-built attitude AIs with attitude control through the main navigational unit.

The latter could be rough because the equipment wasn't configured for the purpose. Even so, I believed machine control was better nine times out of ten than anything humans could manage.

"You do know something about electronics, then," Gregg said, though he wasn't looking at me when he spoke.

"Do people often lie to you?" I snapped.

"Not often, no," the bigger man agreed, unperturbed.

"Usually there's an officer to command each control bank," Gregg continued mildly. "Here, I'm just to keep the crew from being bothered by—gentlemen who feel a need to give orders. Lightbody, Jeude, Dole."

The sailors looked up as Gregg called their names.

"Dole's our bosun," Gregg said. "These three have been with Piet since before I met him, when he had a little intrasystem trader. He put them on the controls because they can be trusted not to get in the way of the electronics."

Jeude, a baby-faced man (and he certainly wasn't very old to begin with), wore a blue-and-white striped stocking cap. He doffed it in an ironic salute.

"Boys, meet Mister Jeremy Moore," Gregg went on. "I think you'll find him a resourceful gentleman."

"A friend of yours, Mister Gregg?" Jeude asked.

Gregg snorted. Instead of answering the question, he said, "Do you have any friends, Moore?"

"A few women, I suppose," I said. "Not like he means, no."

My guts no longer roiled, but they'd knotted themselves tightly in my lower abdomen. I focused my eyes on the viewscreen above the navigational console. Half the field was bright with stars, two of which were circled with blue overlays. A three-quarter view of Venus, opalescent with the dense, bubbling atmosphere, filled the rest of the screen.

"That's a very high resolution unit," I said aloud. "I'm amazed at the clarity."

"Piet doesn't skimp on the tools he needs," Gregg said. "It's a perfect view of the hell that wraps the world that bore us, that's certainly true."

He paused, staring at the lustrous, lethal surface of gas. "Does your family have records from the Collapse, Moore?" he asked.

"No," I said, "no. My grandfather sold the factory ninety years ago and moved to Ishtar City. If there were any records, they were lost then."

"My family does," Gregg said. "The histories say it was the atmosphere that protected Venus during the Revolt, you know. Outworld raiders knew that our defenses wouldn't stop them, but they couldn't escape our winds. The Hadley Cells take control from any unfamiliar pilot and fling his ship as apt as not into the ground. The raiders learned to hit softer targets that only *men* protected."

"Isn't it true, then?" I said, responding to the bitterness in Gregg's voice. "That's how I'd already heard it."

"Oh, the atmosphere saved us from the rebels, that much was true," Gregg said. "But when the histories go on, 'Many died because off-planet trade was disrupted . . .' *That's* not the same as reading your own ancestors' chronicle of those days. Venus produced twenty percent of its own food before the Collapse. Afterwards, well, the food supply couldn't expand that fast, so the population dropped. Since the distribution system was disrupted also, the drop was closer to nine in ten than eight in ten."

"We're past that now," I said. "That was a thousand years ago. A thousand *Earth* years."

A third spark in a blue highlight snapped into place on the star chart. "The *Kinsolving*," said Dole, ostensibly to the sailors to either side of him at the console. "And about fucking time."

Lightbody sniffed.

Piet Ricimer raised a handset and began speaking into it, his eyes fixed on a separate navigational tank beneath the viewscreen.

"Bet they just now got around to turning on their locator beacon," Jeude said. "Though they'll claim it was equipment failure."

"Right," said Gregg, his eyes so fixedly on the pearly orb of Venus that they drew my gaze with them. "At Eryx, that's the family seat, there was a pilot hydroponics farm. They figured what the yield would support and drew lots for those who could enter the section of the factory where the farm was."

Gregg's face lost all expression. "The others . . ." he continued. "Some of the others tried to break into the farm and get their share of the food. My ancestor's younger brother led a team of volunteers that held off the mob as long as they could. When they were out of ammunition, they checked the door seals and then blew the roof of their own tunnel open to the surface. That's what the atmosphere of Venus means to me."

"It was worse on Earth," I said. "When the centralized production plants were disrupted, only one person in a thousand survived. There were billions of people on Earth before the Revolt, but they almost all died."

Gregg rubbed his face hard with both hands, as if he were massaging life back into his features. He looked at me and smiled. "As you say, a thousand years," he said. "But in all that time, the Greggs of Eryx have always named the second son Stephen. In memory of the brother who didn't leave descendants."

"That was the past," I said. "There's enough in the future to worry about."

"You'll get along well with Piet," Gregg said. His voice was half-mocking, but only half. "You're right, of course. I shouldn't think about the past the way I do."

It occurred to me that Gregg wasn't only referring to the early history of Eryx Hold.

The bisected viewscreen above Ricimer shivered into three parts, each the face of a ship's captain: Blakey of the *Mizpah;* Winter of the *Kinsolving;* and Moschelitz, the bovine man who oversaw *Absalom 231*'s six crewmen and automated systems.

Blakey's features had a glassy, simplified sheen which I diagnosed as a result of the *Mizpah*'s transmission being static-laden to the point of unintelligibility. The AI controlling the *Porcelain*'s first-rate electronics processed both the audio and visual portions of the signal into a false clarity. The image of Blakey's black-mustached face was in effect the icon of a virtual reality.

Ricimer raised the handset again. Guillermo switched a setting on the control console. The Molt's wrists couldn't rotate, but each limb had two more offset joints than a human's, permitting the alien the same range of movement.

"Gentlemen," Ricimer said. "Fellow venturers. You're all brave men, or you wouldn't have joined me, and all God-fearing and patriots or I wouldn't have chosen you."

The general commander's words boomed through the tannoy in the ceiling above the attitude-control console; muted echoes rustled through the open hatchways to compartments farther aft. No doubt the transmission was being piped through the other vessels as well, though I wondered whether anybody aboard the *Mizpah* would be able to understand the words over the static.

"I regret," Ricimer continued, "that I could not tell you all our real destination before we lifted off, though I don't suppose many of you—or many of President Pleyal's spies—will have thought we were setting out for the asteroids. The first stop on our mission to free Venus and mankind from Federation tyranny will be Decades."

"We'll make men out of you there!" Hawtry said in guttural glee. The pickup on Ricimer's handset was either highly directional or keyed to his voice alone. Not a whisper of Hawtry's words was broadcast.

"A Fed watering station six days out," Jeude said, speaking to me. As an obvious landsman, I was a perfect recipient for the sort of information that every specialist loves to retail.

"They wouldn't need a landfall so close if their ships were better found," Dole put in. "Fed ships leak like sieves."

On the screen, Captain Winter's lips formed an angry protest which I thought contained the word " . . . piracy?"

This was Ricimer's moment; the equipment Guillermo controlled brooked no interruption. Blakey tugged at his mustache worriedly— he looked to be a man who would worry about the color of his socks in the morning—while Moschelitz couldn't have been more stolid in his sleep.

"Our endeavors, with the help of the Lord," Ricimer continued, "will decide the fate of Venus and of mankind." He seemed to grow as he spoke, or—it was as if Piet Ricimer were the only spot of color in existence. His enthusiasm, his *belief,* turned everything around him gray.

"We must be resolute," he said. His eyes swept those of us watching him in the flagship's bow compartment, but the faces on the viewscreen also stiffened. Though his back was toward the images, Ricimer was looking straight into the camera feeding his transmission.

"I expect the company of every vessel in the expedition to serve God once a day with its prayers," Ricimer said. "Love one another: we are few against the might of tyranny. Preserve your supplies, and make all efforts to keep the squadron together throughout the voyage."

The general commander stared out at his dream for a future in which mankind populated all the universe under God. Even Thomas Hawtry looked muted by the blazing personality of the man beside whom he stood.

"In the name of God, sirs, do your duty!"

ABOVE DECADES

Day 7

The *Porcelain* made nineteen individual transits in the final approach series; that is, she slipped nineteen times in rapid succession from the sidereal universe to another bubble of sponge space and back.

At each transit, as during every transit of the past seven days, my stomach knotted and flapped inside out. I clung to the staple in the attitude-control station, holding a sponge across my open mouth and wishing I were dead. Or perhaps I *was* dead, and this was the Hell to which so many people over the years had consigned me . . .

"Oh, God," I moaned into the sponge. My eyes were shut. "Oh, God, please save me." I hadn't prayed in real earnest since the night I found myself trapped in Melinda's room.

The transit series ended. Only the vibration of the vessel's plasma motors maintaining a normal 1-g acceleration indicated that I wasn't standing on solid ground. I opened my eyes.

A planet, gray beneath a cloud-streaked atmosphere, filled the forward viewscreen. "Most times the Feds've got women on the staff," Jeude was saying as he and his fellows at the console eyed Decades for the first time. "And they aren't all of them *that* hostile."

I released the staple I was holding and rose to my feet. I smiled ruefully at Gregg and said, "I'll get used to it, I suppose."

Gregg's mouth quirked. "For your sake I hope so," he said. "But I haven't, and I've been doing this for some years now."

Besides the ship's officers, the forward compartment was crowded by Hawtry and the nine gentlemen-adventurers who, like him, stood fully equipped with firearms and body armor.

The ceramic chestplates added considerably to the men's bulk and awkwardness. Many of them had personal blazons painted on their armor. Hawtry's own chestplate bore a gryphon, the marking of his house, and on the upper right clamp the oriflamme of the Duneens.

"Now that's navigation!" said Captain—former captain—Macquerie with enthusiasm. "We can orbit without needing to transit again."

It had taken Macquerie a few days to come to terms with his situation, but since then he'd been an asset to the project. Macquerie was too good a sailor not to be pleased with a ship as fine as the *Porcelain* and a commander as famous as Piet Ricimer.

"The *Kinsolving*'s nowhere to be seen," said Salomon as he leaned toward the three-dimensional navigation tank. "As usual. The *Mizpah* can keep station, the *cargo* hulk can keep station, more or less. Winter couldn't find his ass with both hands."

"There they are," Ricimer said mildly. He pointed to something in the tank that I couldn't see from where I stood. It probably wouldn't have meant anything to me anyway. "One, maybe two transits out. It's my fault for not making sure the *Kinsolving*'s equipment was calibrated to the same standards as the rest of ours."

"If the *Absalom* can keep station," Salomon muttered, "so could the *Kinsolving*—if she had a navigator aboard."

"Enough of this nonsense," said Thomas Hawtry. Several of the gentlemen about him looked as green as I felt, but Hawtry was clearly unaffected by the multiple eversions of transit. "We don't need a third vessel anyway. Lay us alongside the *Mizpah*, Ricimer, so that I can go aboard and take charge."

Guillermo looked up from his console. "The cutter should be launched in the next three minutes," he said to Ricimer in his mechanically perfect speech. "Otherwise we'll need to brake now rather than proceeding directly into planetary orbit."

"You'd best get aft to Hold Two, Mister Hawtry," Ricimer said. If he'd reacted to the gentleman's peremptory tone, there was no sign of it in his voice. "The cutter is standing by with two men to ferry you."

Hawtry grunted. "Come along, men," he ordered as he led his fellows shuffling sternward. Watching the sicker-looking of the gentlemen helped to settle my stomach.

"Sure you don't want to go with them?" Gregg said archly. "When they transfer to the *Mizpah,* there won't be any proper gentlemen aboard. Just spacers."

"I'm a proper gentleman," I snapped. "I just have little interest in weapons and no training whatever with them. If you please, I'll stay close to you and Mister Ricimer and do what you direct me."

"Mister Hawtry?" Ricimer called as the last of Hawtry's contingent were ducking through the hatchway to the central compartment. "Please remember: there'll be no fighting if things go as they should. We'll simply march on the base from opposite directions and summon them to surrender."

Hawtry's response was a muted grunt.

Salomon and Macquerie lowered their heads over the navigation tank and murmured to one another. The Molt Guillermo touched a control. His viewscreen split again: the right half retaining the orb of Decades, three-quarters in sunlight, while the left jumped by logarithmic magnifications down onto the planetary surface.

A fenced rectangle enclosed a mixture of green foliage and soil baked to brick by the exhaust of starships landing. In close-up, the natural vegetation beyond the perimeter had the iridescence of oil on water.

There were two ships with bright metal hulls in the landing area, and a scatter of buildings against the opposite fence. The morning sun slanted across the Federation base. Obvious gun towers threw stark, black shadows from the corners and from the center of both long sides.

I licked my lips. I didn't know what I was supposed to do. The *Porcelain* shuddered like a dog drying itself. Lights on the attitude-control panels pulsed in near unison, balancing the shock. The three sailors looked alert but not concerned.

"That's the cutter with Hawtry aboard casting off," Gregg said.

He glanced at the bosun. "How long before we begin atmospheric braking, Dole?" he asked.

Dole, a stocky, dark man with a beard trimmed to three centimeters, pursed his lips as he considered the images on the viewscreen. "About two hours, sir," he said.

Jeude, beside him, nodded agreement. "We could go into orbit quicker," he said, "but it'll take them that long to transfer the fine gentlemen to the *Mizpah*—good riddance to them."

"Watch your tongue, Aaron Jeude," the bosun said.

Jeude's smile flashed toward Gregg, taking in me beside the bigger man as well.

"What do we do, Gregg?" I asked. My voice was colorless because of my effort to conceal my fear of the unfamiliar.

"We wait," Gregg said. "Ten minutes before landing, we'll put our equipment on. And then we'll march a klick through what Macquerie says is swamp, even on the relative highlands where the Feds built their base."

"I don't have any equipment," I said. "If you mean weapons."

"We'll find you something," Gregg said. "Never fear." He spoke quietly, but there was a disconcerting lilt to his tone.

Six sailors under Stampfer, the *Porcelain*'s master gunner, bustled around the Long Tom, opening hydraulic valves and locking down the seats attached to the carriage. They were readying the big weapon for action.

"Will there be fighting, then, Gregg?" I asked, sounding even to myself as cool as the sweat trickling down the middle of my back.

"At Decades, I don't know," Gregg said. "Not if they have any sense. But before this voyage is over—yes, Mister Moore. There will be war."

The *Porcelain*'s two cargo holds were on the underside of the vessel, bracketed between the pairs of plasma motors fore and aft, and the quartet of similar thrusters amidships. Number Two, the after hold, had been half-emptied when the cutter launched. Now it was filled by a party of twenty men waiting for action, and it stank.

"You bloody toad, Easton!" a sailor said to the man beside him. "That warn't no fart. You've shit yourself!"

My nose agreed. Several of the men had vomited from tension

and atmospheric buffeting as the ship descended, and we were all of us pretty ripe after a week on shipboard. I clutched the cutting bar Gregg had handed me from the arms locker and hoped that I wouldn't be the next to spew my guts up.

The *Porcelain*'s descent slowed to a near-hover. The rapid pulsing of her motors doubled into a roar. "Surface effect!" Gregg said. "Thrust reflected from the ground. We'll be touching down—"

The big gentleman wore back-and-breast armor—the torso of a hard suit that doubled as protection from vacuum and lethal atmospheres—with the helmet locked in place, though his visor was raised for the moment. In his arms was a flashgun, a cassegrain laser which would pulse the entire wattage of the battery in its stock out through a stubby ceramic barrel. Gregg was shouting, but I needed cues from his mouth to make out the words.

The last word was probably "soon," but it was lost in still greater cacophony. The starship touched its port outrigger, hesitated, and settled fully to the ground with a crash of parts reaching equilibrium with gravity instead of thrust.

I relaxed. "Now what?" I asked.

"We wait a few minutes for the ground to cool," Gregg explained. "There was standing water, so the heat ought to dissipate pretty quickly. Sufficient heat."

It seemed like ten minutes but was probably two before a sailor spun the undogging controls at a nod from Gregg. The hatch, a section of hull the full length of Hold Two, cammed downward to form a ramp. Through the opening rushed wan sunshine and a gush of steam evaporated from the soil by the plasma motors.

It was the first time I'd been on a planet besides Venus.

"Let's go!" boomed Stephen Gregg in the sudden dampening of the hold's echoes. He strode down the ramp, a massive figure in his armor. "Keep close, but form a cordon at the edge of the cleared area."

I tried to stay near Gregg, but a dozen sailors elbowed me aside to exit from the center of the ramp. I realized why when I followed them. Though the hatchway was a full ten meters wide, the starship's plasma motors had raised the ground beneath to oven heat. The center of the ramp, farthest from where the exhaust of stripped ions struck, was the least uncomfortable place to depart the recently-landed vessel.

I stumbled on the lip at the end of the ramp. The surroundings steamed like a suburb of Sheol, and the seared native vegetation gave off a bitter reek.

The foliage beyond the exhaust-burned area was tissue-thin and stiffened with vesicles of gas rather than cellulose. The veins were of saturated color, with reds, blues, and purples predominating. Those hues merged with the general pale yellow of leaf surfaces to create the appearance of gray when viewed from a distance.

I wore a neck scarf. I put it to my mouth and breathed through it. It probably didn't filter any of the sharp poisons from the air, but at least it gave me the illusion that I was doing something useful.

Sailors clumped together at the margin of the ravaged zone instead of spreading out. The forward ramp was lowered also, but men were filtering slowly down it because Hold One was still packed with supplies and equipment.

"Stephen," called the man stepping from the forward ramp. "I'll take the lead, if you'll make sure that no one straggles from the rear of the line."

The speaker wore brilliant, gilded body armor over a tunic with puffed magenta sleeves. The receiver of his repeating rifle was also gold-washed. Because the garb was unfamiliar and the man's face was in shadow, it was by his voice that I identified him as Piet Ricimer.

Gregg broke off in the middle of an order to a pair of grizzled sailors. "Piet, you're not to do this!" he said. "We talked—"

"You talked, Stephen," Ricimer interrupted with the crisp tone of the man who *was* general commander of the expedition. "I said I'd decide when the time came. Shall we proceed?"

Forty-odd men of the *Porcelain*'s complement of eighty now milled in the burned-off area. About seventy-five percent of us had firearms. Most of the rest carried cutting bars like mine, but there were two flashguns besides Gregg's own. Flashguns were heavy, unpleasant to shoot because they scattered actinics, and were certain to attract enemy fire. I found it instructive that Stephen Gregg would carry such a weapon.

The sky over the Federation base to the south suddenly rippled with spaced rainbow flashes. Four seconds later, the rumble of plasma cannon discharging shook the swamp about the *Porcelain*.

A ship that must have been the *Mizpah* dropped out of the sky. The sun-hot blaze of her thrusters was veiled by the ionized glow of their exhaust. Plasma drifted up and back from the vessel like the train of a lady in court dress.

"The stupid *whoreson!*" said Stephen Gregg. "They were to land together with us, not five minutes later!"

Ricimer jumped quickly to the ground and trotted toward Gregg. "Stephen," he said, "you'd best join me in the lead. I think it's more important that we reach the base as quickly as possible than that the whole body arrives together. I'm very much afraid that Blakey is trying to land directly on the objective."

As the *Mizpah* lurched downward at a rate much faster than that of the *Porcelain* before her, a throbbing pulse of yellow light from the ground licked her lower hull. From where I jogged along a step behind Ricimer and Gregg, the starship was barely in sight above the low vegetation, but she must have been fifty or more meters above the ground.

The plume of exhaust dissipated in a shock wave. Seconds later, we could hear a report duller than that of the *Mizpah's* cannon but equally loud.

Ricimer held a gyro compass in his left hand. "This way," he directed. Twenty meters into the forest, the *Porcelain* was out of sight.

"The bloody whoreson!" Gregg repeated as he jogged along beside his friend and leader.

"How . . ." I said. My voice was a croaking whisper. I couldn't see for sweat between the angry passes I made across my eyes with my sopping kerchief.

" . . . do you stand this?" I finished, concluding on a rising note that suggested panic even to me. I deliberately lowered my voice to add, "You're wearing armor, I mean."

Piet Ricimer squeezed my shoulder. Ricimer's face was red, and the sleeves of his gorgeous tunic were as wet as my kerchief. "You'll harden to it, Moore," he said. He spoke in gasps. "A kilometer isn't far. Once you're used to, you know. It."

"The men won't follow . . ." Gregg said. He was a pace ahead of us, setting the trail through the flimsy, clinging vegetation. He didn't look back over his shoulder as he spoke. "Unless the leaders lead. So we have to."

"A little to the right, Stephen," Ricimer wheezed. "I think we're drifting." Then in near anger he added, "Macquerie says the base was set on the firmest ground of the continent. What must the rest be like?"

Each of my boots carried what felt like ten kilos of mud. The hilt of the cutting bar had a textured surface, but despite that the weapon kept trying to slide out of my grip. I was sure that if I had to use the bar, it would squirt into the hands of my opponent.

The assault force straggled behind the three of us. How far behind was anybody's guess. About a dozen crewmen, laden with weapons and bandoliers of ammunition, slogged along immediately in back of me. They were making heavy going of it. The mud had stilled their initial chatter, but they were obviously determined to keep up or die.

Three of the spacers were the regular watch from the attitude-control consoles. I suspected the others were among Ricimer's longtime followers also. With their share of the wealth from previous voyages, why in God's name were they undergoing this punishment and danger?

And why had Jeremy Moore made the same choice? The day before sailing, Eloise had made it clear that there was a permanent place for me. On her terms, of course, but they weren't such terrible terms.

The only thing that kept me up with the leaders was that I *was* with the leaders. I was with two undeniable heroes; staggering along, but present.

"If she'd really crashed," Ricimer said, "we'd have—she'd shake the ground. The *Mizpah*."

"Fired off all ten guns descending," Gregg muttered. There was a streak of blood on his right hand and forearm, and his sleeve was ripped. "Means they landed with them empty. Feds may be cutting all their throats before we come up. Stupid whoresons."

Then, in a coldly calm voice, he added, "Stop here. We've reached it."

I knelt at the base of a spray of huge, rubbery leaves. My knees sank into the muck, but I didn't think I could've remained upright without the effort of walking to steady me. Ricimer halted with his left hand on Gregg's shoulder blade. Sailors, puffing and blowing as though they were coming up after deep dives, spread out to either side of the trail we had blazed.

The native vegetation had been burned away from a hundred-meter band surrounding the Federation base. Water gleamed in pools and sluggish rivulets across the scabrous wasteland. The natural landscape was inhuman and oppressive; this defensive barrier was as ugly as a cinder.

The perimeter fence was of loose mesh four meters high. Judging from the insulators the fence was electrified, but it didn't provide visual screening. Trees heavy with citrus fruit grew within the enclosure.

In the center of the fenceline were a gate and a guard tower, at present unoccupied. Two men were strolling toward the tower up a lane through the trees. They were laughing; one carried a bottle. Both had rifles slung.

Gregg aimed his flashgun from the concealment of a plantainlike growth with blue leaves the size of blankets.

"Wait, Stephen," Ricimer ordered. He took off his gilt-braided beret, wiped his face in the crook of his arm, and put the beret on again. "Mister Sahagun!" he called, stepping out into the cleared area. "Mister Coos!"

At the words, I recognized the pair as two of the gentlemen who'd transferred to the *Mizpah*. They'd taken off their heavy armor. I'd thought they were Federation soldiers whose bullets might kill me in the next seconds.

Sahagun groped in startlement for his slung weapon before he recognized the speaker. "Ricimer, is that you?" he called. "Say, we're supposed to bring you in, but I just see that this bloody gate is locked. We'll—"

Gregg had shifted infinitesimally when Sahagun touched his rifle. Now he moved an equally slight amount. His flashgun fired, a pulse of light so intense that the native foliage wilted from the side-scatter. Great leaves sagged away, fluttering in the echoes of the laser's miniature thunder.

I tried to jump to my feet. I slipped and would have fallen except that a sailor I didn't know by name caught my arm.

The bolt hit the crossbar where it intersected the left gatepost. Metal exploded in radiant fireballs which trailed smoke as they arced away. Coos and Sahagun fell flat on ground as wet as that through which we'd been tramping.

"That's all right," Gregg called as he switched the battery in his weapon's stock for a fresh one. As with his friend and leader, there was no hint of exhaustion in his voice now. "We'll open it ourselves."

"I think," said Piet Ricimer softly, "that we'll wait till our whole force has come up before any of us enter the base."

There was nothing menacing in his words or tone, but I felt myself shiver.

"Ah, glad you've made it, Ricimer," said Thomas Hawtry as he rose from the porch of the operations building. A score of men stood about him. Many of them were frightened-looking and dressed in rags of white Federation uniforms. "I've got some very valuable information here, *very* valuable!"

Hawtry spoke with an enthusiasm that showed he understood how chancy the next moments were likely to be. Like the others of the *Mizpah's* gentlemen, he'd put aside his breastplate and rifle.

"In a moment, Mister Hawtry," said Piet Ricimer. He wiped his face again with his sleeve. "Captain Blakey. Present yourself at once!"

The *Mizpah* had come down within a hundred and fifty meters of the administration buildings and base housing, blowing sod and shrubbery out in a shallow crater. The multitube laser that slashed the descending vessel from a guard tower had shattered a port thruster nozzle.

Yawing into the start of a tumble, the *Mizpah* had struck hard. The port outrigger fractured, though the vessel's hull appeared undamaged. Our men and Molts from the base labor force now surveyed the damage.

I bubbled with relief at having gotten this far. Clouds scudded across the pale sky. It felt odd to know that there was no solid roof above, but it didn't bother me the way I'd been warned it might.

I wondered where I could find a hose to clean my boots. I glanced down. My legs. They were covered in mud from mid-thigh.

Blakey broke away from the group beside the *Mizpah* and trotted toward Ricimer. The *Mizpah's* plasma cannon were still run out through the horizontal bank of gunports. To fire paired broadsides into the Federation base as the ship descended, Blakey must have rolled the *Mizpah* on her axis, then counter-rolled.

"There's a treasure right here on Decades," Hawtry said, pretending that he didn't realize he was being ignored, "and I've located it. The Feds here are too cowardly to grab it up themselves!"

A freighter was docked at the far edge of the perimeter, nearly a kilometer from the administration building. That ship had taken much of the *Mizpah* gunners' attention. One blast of charged particles had struck her squarely, vaporizing a huge hole. The shock of exploding metal dished in the light-metal hull for half its length and set fire to the vessel's interior. Dirty smoke billowed from the wreck and drifted through the nearby fenceline.

I couldn't imagine any purpose in shooting at the freighter beyond a general desire to terrorize the defenders. In all likelihood, the Feds stationed here wouldn't have been aroused to defense except for the sudden blaze of cannonfire.

Blakey whipped off the broad-brimmed hat which he, like many experienced Venerian travelers, wore under an open sky. "Mister Ricimer," he blurted, "I didn't have any choice. It was Mister Hawtry who—"

"May I remind you that I gave you specific direction to land a kilometer north of the Federation compound, Captain Blakey?" Ricimer said in a knife-edged voice. "No one but the Lord God Almighty takes precedence to the orders I give on this expedition!"

"No sir, no sir," Blakey mumbled, wringing his hat up in a tight double roll. The spacer's hair was solidly dark, but there was a salting of white hair in his beard and mustache.

"Now, wait a minute, Ricimer," Hawtry said. He remained on the porch, ten meters away. The Federation personnel about him were easing away, leaving the gentlemen exposed like spines of basalt weathered out of softer stone.

"The *Mizpah*'s condition?" Ricimer snapped.

"We'll jack up the port side to repair the outrigger," Blakey said. He grimaced at his crumpled hat. "Then we'll switch the thruster nozzle, we've spares aboard, it's no—"

"You lost only one thruster?" Ricimer demanded, his tongue sharp as the blade of a microtome.

"Well, maybe shock cooling from the soil took another," Blakey admitted miserably. "We won't know till we get her up, but it's no more than three days' work with the locals to help."

I noticed that one of the Federation personnel was a petite woman who'd cropped her brunette hair short. She nervously watched the byplay among her captors, gripping her opposite shoulders with her well-formed hands.

I wondered if we'd be on Decades longer than three days. Although a great deal could happen in three days.

"Look here, Ricimer!" boomed Hawtry as he stepped off the porch in a determination to use bluster where camaraderie had failed. "The Molts that have escaped from here, they loot the ships that crash into the swamps. There've been *hundreds,* over the years, and the Molts have all the treasure cached in one place. That's the real value of Decades!"

Ricimer turned his head to look at Hawtry. I couldn't see his eyes, but the six gentlemen stepping from the porch to follow lurched to a halt.

"The real value of Decades, Mister Hawtry," Ricimer said in a tone without overt emotion, "was to be the training it gave our personnel in discipline and obedience to orders."

Ricimer turned to the men who'd accompanied him from the flagship. "Dole," he said mildly, "find the communications center here and inform the *Absalom* and *Kinsolving* to land within the perimeter. Oh—and see if you can raise Guillermo aboard the *Porcelain* to tell them that we're in control of the base."

"I'll go with him," I volunteered in a light voice. "I, I'm good with electronics."

"Yes," Ricimer said. "Do it."

Dole didn't move. I started toward the administration building as an obvious place to look for the radios. Stephen Gregg laid a hand on the top of my shoulder without looking away from Ricimer and the gentlemen beyond. I stopped and swallowed.

Ricimer swiveled back to the *Mizpah*'s captain. "Mister Blakey," he said. "You'll leave repairs to the *Mizpah* in the charge of your navigator. You'll proceed immediately to the *Porcelain*, in company with Mister Hawtry and the other gentlemen adventurers who were aboard the *Mizpah* when you decided to ignore my orders."

"Lord take you for a fool, Ricimer!" Hawtry said. "If you think I'm going to rot in a swamp when—"

Gregg locked down his helmet visor with a sharp *clack*. The flashgun's discharge was liable to blind anyone using it without filters to protect his eyes. Dole snicked the bolt of his rifle back far enough to check the load, then closed it again. Others of Ricimer's longtime crewmen stood braced with ready weapons. A cutting bar whined as somebody made sure it was in good order.

"There'll be no blasphemy in a force under my command, Mister Hawtry," Ricimer said. Though his voice seemed calm, his face was pale with anger. "This time I will overlook it; and we'll hope the

Lord, Who is our only hope for the success of these endeavors, will overlook it as well."

Hawtry stepped backward, chewing on his lower lip. He wasn't a coward, but the muzzle of Gregg's weapon was only two meters from his chest. A bolt at that range would spray his torso over hectares of swamp.

Ricimer's posture eased slightly. He reached into his belt pouch, handed Blakey the compass from it, and resumed. "You will find the *Porcelain* on a reciprocal of this course. Tell Mister Salomon that your party will guard the vessel until we're ready to depart. The crew will be more comfortable here at the base, I'm sure."

Hawtry let out a long, shuddering breath. "We'll need men to deal with the menial work," he said.

Ricimer nodded. "If you care to pay sailors extra to act as servants," he said, "that's between you and them."

Hawtry glanced over his shoulder at the accompanying gentlemen. Without speaking further, the group sidled away in the direction of the *Mizpah* and the gear they'd left aboard her.

Gregg opened his visor. His face had no expression.

Dole plucked at my sleeve. "Let's get along and find the radio room, sir," the bosun said. "You know, I thought things were going to get interesting for a moment there."

I tried to smile but couldn't. I supposed I should be thankful that I could walk normally.

DECADES

Day 8

I turned at the console to look out the window of the commo room. Halfway across the compound, male prisoners from the Decades garrison and the damaged freighter were unloading spoiled stores from the *Absalom 231*. With my left hand I picked a section from the half orange while my right fingers typed code into the numeric keypad.

"That's it!" said Lavonne. She'd been Officer III (Communications) Cartier when Decades Station was under Federation control. "You've got the signal, Jeremy!"

"Thanks to you and this wonderful equipment," I added warmly, patting my hand toward Lavonne without quite touching her. I pursed my lips as I looked over the console display. "Now if only the *Mizpah*'s hardware weren't a generation past the time it should've been scrapped . . ."

The console showed the crew emptying the hulk, from the viewpoint of the port-side optical sensors in the *Mizpah*'s hull. Occasionally some of the Venerians and Molts replacing the *Mizpah*'s damaged thrusters came in sight at the lower edge of the display, oblivious of the fact they were being electronically observed. Because the *Mizpah*'s sensors only updated the image six times a second, the picture was grainy and figures moved in jerks.

Lavonne stripped the fascia from one of the orange sections I'd handed her, using her fingers and the tip of a small screwdriver. "Why, we could connect all the tower optics with this!" she said in pleased wonder. "Superintendent Burr keeps worrying that one day the Molts on guard will decide to let in the wild tribes from the swamp. But someone could watch what's going on in the towers from here."

Several people came up the stairs from the lower level of the admin building, talking among themselves. I'd left the commo room's door ajar, though I'd made sure the panel could be locked if matters with Lavonne proceeded faster than I expected.

"Ah—it's Molts that you're afraid of," I said, "and you use Molts for *guards*?"

"Well, the ones who've been trained to work for humans are trustworthy, I suppose," the woman said defensively. "Freshly caught ones used to escape from the holding pens while the ships carrying them laid over here."

She bent past me to tap the screen where a corner of the inner compound was visible past the cargo hulk. Electrified wire surrounded thatch-roofed wooden racks. If it hadn't been for the voices in the hallway, I'd have taken up the offer implicit in Lavonne's posture.

"That was years ago," she added, straightening. "They can't get out of the station now that the perimeter's fenced too."

The door opened. Piet Ricimer stepped in, his head turned to catch Gregg's voice: " . . . who on Duneen's staff was paid to load us with *garbage* in place of the first-quality stores we were charged for."

I jumped to my feet, knocking my knees on the console. Macquerie and Guillermo entered behind Ricimer and his aide. I'd learned to recognize Guillermo from the yellowish highlights of his chitin and his comparatively narrow face. It was odd to think of the aliens as having personalities, though.

"I've, ah, been connecting the squadron's optics through the console, here, Ricimer," I said. "Ah—save for the *Porcelain;* I'd have to be aboard her to set the handshake."

I was nervous. What I'd done here had been at my own whim; and there was the matter of Lavonne, not that things there had come to fruition. Birth in a factorial family made me the social superior of the general commander, but I hadn't needed Hawtry's humiliation to teach me that the reality here was something else again.

Ricimer glanced at the display. "From the *Mizpah*?" he said. "I'm delighted, Moore."

Gregg offered me a bleak grin over the general commander's shoulder. Lavonne, who'd moved toward a corner when the command group entered, eyed the big man speculatively. There were things about women that I would *never* understand.

"I was surprised to find you aboard after we lifted off," Ricimer commented. "Stephen explained, though; and I can see that you'd be an asset in any case."

"I, ah, regret the inconvenience I've caused," I said. I nodded to the pilot. I'd tried to avoid Macquerie thus far during the voyage, but a starship was close confinement for all those aboard her. If there was going to be trouble between us, best it happen under the eyes of Ricimer—and more particularly Gregg.

Macquerie smiled wryly. "My own fault not to wonder why somebody was buying me drinks, Mister Moore," he said. Unlike the others, Macquerie respected me for my birth. "Anyway, Captain Ricimer says he'll put me down on Os Sertoes with my in-laws."

A white asterisk pulsed at the upper corner of the screen as Macquerie spoke. I noticed it from the corner of my eye. The icon might have been there for some while, and I didn't have any notion of what it meant.

I opened my mouth to call a question to Lavonne. Before I spoke, Guillermo reached an oddly-jointed arm past me and touched a sequence of keys. Captain Blakey, his image streaked by static, snarled, "Come *in*, somebody, isn't there anybody on watch on this God *damned* planet?"

Piet Ricimer put his left hand on my shoulder, guiding me out of the way so that he could take over the console. The general commander's grip was like iron. If I'd hesitated, he would have flung me across the radio room.

"I'm here, Captain Blakey," Ricimer said.

The static thinned visibly with each passing moment. I recognized the pattern. Thrusters expelled plasma, atoms stripped of part or all of their electron charge. The exhaust radiated across the entire radio frequency spectrum, with harmonics as it reabsorbed electrons from the surrounding atmosphere. A thruster was firing in the vicinity of the *Porcelain* . . .

"Mister Hawtry's taken the cutter!" Blakey said. "He and the others, they're sure they know where Molt treasure is and they've gone off to get it. They have a map!"

"Do you know where—" Ricimer began.

Blakey cut him off. "I don't know where they're going," he blurted. "I wouldn't go, sir, I refused! But they got two of the sailors to fly the cutter for them, and now there's nobody aboard the ship but me and the other four sailors they brought. I tried to stop them, but they wouldn't even let me to the radio to warn you, sir."

"We can't call the cutter while its thruster's operating," Gregg said. "Not that the damned fools would listen to us."

"Outside of the plateau the station's on . . ." Captain Macquerie said grimly. "I know, you think it's a swamp, but it's the only solid ground on the continent. Five klicks in any direction from the station, it's soup. It maybe won't swallow them, but they'll play hell unclogging their nozzles to lift off again."

My face grew still as glass; my mind considered the capabilities of the console built to the standards of the chip-rich North American Federation. The cutter's motor created RF hash that would smother normal attempts at communication, but that meant the thruster itself was a signal generator.

"The superintendent got the map years ago from an old drunk in the maintenance section," Lavonne volunteered. "He really believes it, Burr does. But even if it was real, it'd be suicide to go so far outside the base."

I changed displays to a menu, then changed screens again. A jagged line drew itself across a display gridded with kilometer squares and compass points. "There's a range and vector," I said to the room in general. "I don't have terrain data to underlay."

The track quivered into a tight half-circle and stopped. The thruster had been shut off. The terminus was a little over ten kilometers from the screen's reference point—the console itself.

Ricimer nodded and said crisply to Guillermo, "Alarm?"

The Molt entered a four-stroke command without bothering to call up a menu. One of Guillermo's ancestors, perhaps more than a thousand years before, had been trained to use a console of similar design. That experience, genetically imbedded, permitted the Molt to use equipment that he himself had never seen before. A four-throated horn in the roof of the admin building began to whoop *Hoo-Hee! Hoo-Hee!*

So long as men depended on Molts and pre-Collapse factories

to provide their electronics, there would be no advance on the standards of that distant past. I was one of the few people—even on Venus—who believed there *could* be improvement on the designs of those bygone demigods.

I reached between Ricimer and Guillermo to key a series of commands through the link I had added to the system. The *Kinsolving*'s siren and the klaxon on the *Mizpah* added their tones to the Fed hooter. *Absalom 231* didn't have an alarm, or much of anything else.

Ricimer flashed me a smile of appreciation and amusement. Stephen Gregg's mouth quirked slightly also, but the big gentleman's face was settling into planes of muscle over bone, and his eyes—

I looked away.

When Ricimer nodded to Guillermo, the Molt entered fresh commands into the console. The hooter and klaxon shut off, and the *Kinsolving*'s siren began to wind down.

"This is the general commander," Ricimer said. His voice boomed from the alarm horns; the tannoys of the three Venerian ships should be repeating the words as well. "All Porcelains report armed to the cargo hulk. Captain Winter, march your Kinsolvings at once to the flagship. Other personnel, guard the station here and await further orders."

Ricimer rose from the console in a smooth motion and swept me with him toward the door. Gregg was in the lead, Guillermo and Macquerie bringing up the rear. Lavonne gaped at us. Her confusion was no greater than my own.

"But the *Absalom*. Captain?" Macquerie said. "Surely . . ."

"The *Mizpah* can't lift, the *Kinsolving* with the featherboats aboard won't hold but thirty or forty men," said Stephen Gregg in a voice as high and thin as a contrail in the stratosphere. His boots crashed on the stair treads. "The hulk's half empty. This is a job for troops, not cannon. If it's a job for anyone at all."

"We can't abandon them, Stephen," Piet Ricimer said, snatching up his breastplate from the array in the building's entrance hall.

The others, all but the Molt, were grabbing their own arms and equipment. I supposed my cutting bar was somewhere in the hardware, but I didn't have any recollection of putting it in a particular place. Guillermo wore a holstered pistol on his pink sash, but the weapon was merely a symbol.

"Can't we, Piet?" Gregg said as he settled the visored helmet over his head. "Well, it doesn't matter to me."

I thought I understood the implications of Gregg's words; and if I did, they were as bleak and terrible as the big gunman's eyes.

"Stand by!" Piet Ricimer called from the control bench of the *Absalom 231.*

"Stand by!" Dole shouted through a bullhorn as he stood at the hatch in the cockpit/hold bulkhead. The bosun braced his boots and his free hand against the hatch coaming. A short rifle was slung across his back.

Most of the eighty-odd spacers aboard the hulk were packed into the hold, standing beside or on the pallets of stores that hadn't yet been dumped. At least half the food we'd loaded at Betaport was moldy or contaminated. Fortunately, the warehouses at Decades were stocked in quantities to supply fleets of the 500-tonne vessels which carried the Federation's cargoes.

I was crowded into the small crew cabin with about a dozen other men. I gripped the frame of the bunk folded against the bulkhead behind me. I had to hold the cutting bar between my knees, because its belt clip was broken.

The hulk's thrusters lit at half throttle, three nozzles and then all four together. The moment of unbalanced thrust made the shoddy vessel lurch into a violent yaw which corrected as Ricimer's fingers moved on the controls.

"If he hadn't shut off the autopilot," Jeude grumbled to my right, "the jets'd have switched on about quick enough to flip us like a pancake. Which is what we'd all be when this pig hit."

"If he hadn't shut off the autopilot," said Lightbody to my left, "he wouldn't be our Mister Ricimer. He'll get us out of this."

The tone of the final sentence was more pious than optimistic.

The *Absalom 231* lifted from its hobbling hover to become fully airborne. The roar of the motors within the single-hulled vessel deafened me, but flight was much smoother than the liftoff had been.

"Say, sir," Jeude said to me, "wouldn't you like a rifle, sir? Or maybe a flashgun like your friend Mister Gregg?"

"I've never fired a gun," I shouted in reply to the solicitous spacer. *Your friend Mister Gregg.* Did Gregg and I have friends, either one of us?

"I thought all you gentlemen trained for the militia," Lightbody said with a doubtful frown. He held a double-barreled shotgun, perhaps the one he'd had when guarding access to the *Porcelain.* Bandoliers of shells in individual loops crossed his chest.

"Well, don't worry about it, Mister Moore," Jeude said cheerfully. "A bar's really better for a close-in dustup anyway."

Someone in the hold—most of them, it must be to be heard in the cabin—was singing. " . . . is our God, a bulwark never failing."

Macquerie and Guillermo peered from either side over Ricimer's shoulders to see the hulk's rudimentary navigational display. The Molt had downloaded data from the base unit to the Absalom 231 before leaving the commo room. I couldn't guess how fast we were traveling. The hulk wallowed around its long axis. No starship was meant for atmospheric flight, and this flimsy can less than most.

Gregg stood behind the general commander, but he didn't appear interested in the display. He glanced back, his face framed by his helmet, and noticed me. Gregg bent down and touched the sliding switch on the hilt of my cutting bar.

"That's the power switch," Gregg said, speaking with exaggerated lip movements instead of bellowing the words. "Click it forward to arm the trigger."

I laid my thumb on the switch. "Thank you," I said. My mouth was dry.

Gregg shrugged and straightened again.

"There it is!" Macquerie shouted. "There it is, a pentagon, and there's the cutter!"

"Stand by!" Dole cried, his amplified voice a dim shadow as thruster noise doubled by reflection from the ground. The men in the hold couldn't hear the bosun's warning, but the changed exhaust note was as much notice as veteran spacers needed.

The Absalom 231 lurched, wobbled, and swung an unexpected 30° on its vertical axis. Jeude grabbed me as centrifugal force threw me forward.

The hulk hit with a sucking crash. My shoulders banged into the bed frame behind me, but I didn't knock my head.

More people than me had trouble with the landing. Two of the sailors in the cockpit lost their footing, and the clangor of equipment flying in the hold sounded like someone was flinging garbage cans.

"Move! Move! Move!" Dole shouted. Gregg was at the cockpit's external hatch, spinning the manual undogging wheel more powerfully than a hydraulic pump could have done the job.

My bar had spun away at the landing. Lightbody retrieved the weapon as Jeude hustled me forward with a hand on my elbow.

"Think that was bad," Jeude remarked, "you'll appreciate it when you ride in a hulk with anybody else piloting."

Gregg jumped out the hatch, his shoulders hunched and the flashgun cradled in both hands. Piet Ricimer followed, wearing a beret and carrying a repeating carbine. "For God and Venus!" he cried. Guillermo leaped clumsily next, half pushed by a sailor named Easton who followed him.

Lightbody cleared the hatchway, his shotgun at high port. The opening was before me. The ground was meters below; I couldn't tell precisely how far. The vegetation was similar to what we'd seen on the trek from the *Porcelain* to the Federation base, but it seemed lusher. Huge leaves waved in the near distance, hiding the figures who brushed their supporting trunks.

I jumped with my eyes closed. A leaf slapped my face and tore like wet paper.

I landed and fell over when my right leg sank to the knee in soupy mud. I could see for five meters or so between the stems in most directions, though the broad leaves were a low ceiling overhead. The trees rose from pads of surface roots. Between the roots, standing water alternated with patches of algae as colorful as an oil slick.

I struggled upright. My left boot was on firmer ground than the right, though I couldn't tell the difference visually. I saw a group of figures ahead and struggled toward them. Jeude hit with a muddy splash and a curse.

"Easton, what's the line?" Piet Ricimer demanded. The pudgy sailor bent over an inertial compass the size of his hand.

The swamp was alive with chirps and whooping. I hadn't noticed anything like the volume of sound nearer the base. I sank into a pool hidden by orange weed floating in a mat on its surface. Lightbody reached back and grabbed me.

A lid lifted from the ground at Easton's feet. The underside of the lid had a soft, pearly sheen like the inner membrane of an egg; the hole beyond was covered with a similar coating to keep the wet soil from collapsing. The Molt in the spiderhole rammed a spear up into Easton's abdomen.

The fat Venerian screamed and dropped the compass. Gregg shot the Molt at point-blank range with his flashgun. The alien's plastron disintegrated in a white glare and a shock wave that jolted me a step backward. Shards of chitin stripped surrounding leaves to the bare veins.

Easton lurched three steps forward until the spear protruding from his belly tripped him. He fell on his face, his legs thrashing against the soft dirt.

Jeude turned and fired. I couldn't see his target, if there was one. Screams and shots came from the direction of the hulk's rear loading ramp.

Piet Ricimer picked up the compass, wiped its face on his sleeve, and checked a line.

Gregg slung his flashgun. He hadn't had time to lower the filtering visor, so he must have closed his eyes to avoid being blinded by his own bolt. Easton carried a rifle. Gregg pulled it and the bandolier of ammunition from the body which still trembled with a semblance of life.

"Guillermo," Ricimer ordered coolly as he dropped the compass in his purse, "go back to the ship and sound recall with the bullhorn. The rest of you, follow me to the cutter!"

He swung the barrel of his carbine forward, pointing the way for his rush. Another spiderhole gaped beside him. Lightbody and Gregg fired simultaneously, ripping the Molt with buckshot and a bullet before the creature was halfway into its upward lunge.

Ricimer vanished beyond a veil of dropping leaves. The others were following him. I stumbled forward, terrified of being left behind. The only thing I was conscious of was Gregg's back, two meters in front of me. Guns fired and I heard the whine of a cutting bar, but the foliage baffled sound into a directionless ambience.

I burst out of the trees. A swath of bare soil bubbled and stank where the cutter's motor had cleared it while landing.

The boat itself lay at a skew angle five meters away. A human, one of the sailors who'd accompanied the gentlemen exiled to the *Porcelain,* lay beside the vessel. A Molt of olive coloration leaned from the cutter's dorsal hatch, pointing a rifle.

Ricimer shot the Molt and worked the underlever of his repeater. Ten more aliens with spears and metal clubs rushed us from the opposite side of the clearing. I was the man closest to them.

"Watch it!" somebody shouted. A rifle slammed, but none of the Molts went down.

I swept my bar around in the desperation of a man trying to bat away a stinging insect. I tugged at the trigger but the blade didn't spin. The ceramic edge clinked on the shaft of a mace hammered from the alloy hull of a starship. Another Molt thrust a metal-tipped spear at my crotch.

"The power switch, you whore's cunt!" Stephen Gregg bellowed as he butt-stroked the Molt spearman, then thrust the blunt muzzle of his rifle into the wedge-shaped skull of the alien with the mace. A ruptured cartridge gleamed partway out of the rifle's chamber, jamming Gregg's weapon until there was time to pick the case out with a knifepoint.

Lightbody fired. Jeude was reloading his rifle; Ricimer had dropped to one knee, pumping rounds into Molts who were too close to miss.

I found the power switch and thumbed it violently. My index finger still tugged on the trigger. The torque of the live blade almost snatched the weapon from my grasp.

One of the aliens was twice the size of the others. He shambled forward with an axe in either hand. Bullets smashed two, then three dribbling holes in his chest.

Gregg clubbed another spearman. He held his rifle by one hand on the barrel while he tried to untangle the flashgun's sling with the other. The big Molt lunged close to Gregg and brought an axe down.

I stepped forward, focused on what I was doing and suddenly oblivious of the chaos around me. My cutting bar screamed through the steel axe-helve in a shower of sparks.

Somebody fired so close that the muzzle flash scorched my sleeve. I ignored it, continuing the stroke. The blade's spin carried it through the Molt's triangular head and into the torso. Brownish ichor sprayed from the wound.

Motion, more Molts beyond the toppling body of the giant. I couldn't see out of my left eye. I stepped over the Molt thrashing in front of me and cut at the next without letting up on the bar's trigger. The Molt tried to club me, but I was within the stroke. The shaft, not the studded tip, of the club gashed my forehead.

The Molt's head and club arm fell to one side while the remainder of the corpse toppled the other way. I followed the cutting bar's edge toward another alien, but that one was already flailing, its plastron shattered by a charge of buckshot.

I turned, looking for Molts. They were all down. I hacked at the alien giant, tearing a wide gouge down his carapace. Nerve trauma sent the creature into another series of convulsions.

Somebody grabbed me from behind. I twisted to bring my howling bar back over my head. A hand closed over mine. Gregg's thumb switched off the cutting bar.

"I've got him!" Gregg said. "It's all right, Moore."

Ricimer wiped my face with a swatch torn from the tail of his own red plush tunic. I could see again; I'd been blinded by fluids from the Molt I'd cut apart.

Jeude looked all right. Lightbody was breathing hard. He'd opened the breeches of his shotgun, but he hadn't inserted the reloads ready between the fingers of his left hand. There was a bloody tear in his tunic.

"Into the cutter, *now!*" Ricimer ordered as he jogged drunkenly toward the small vessel.

"All personnel return to the ship!" crackled an amplified voice. Through the bullhorn, Guillermo's mechanically precise tones were indistinguishable from the voice of a human speaker. "All Porcelains return to the ship!"

"Piet, watch—" Gregg shouted as Ricimer gripped the coaming of the cutter's dorsal hatch with his left hand and leaped upward. Ricimer held the repeater like a pistol in his right hand, aiming it ahead of him as he swung into the hatchway. The *wham* of the rifleshot within the cabin was duller but hugely amplified compared to the blast it made in the open air. Ricimer dropped into the vessel.

"Get him!" Gregg ordered as he bent to pick up the rifle dropped by the Molt shot in the cutter.

I didn't realize I was "him" until Dole and Jeude gripped me by opposite arms and half hoisted, half heaved me into the cutter's roof hatch. I grabbed the coaming as I went over so that at least I didn't hit like a sack of grain.

Ricimer was in the seat forward. Two Molts and a human lay dead in the cabin. The human had been gutted like a trout.

Jeude, Lightbody, and Dole leaped into the cabin in quick succession. Three of the attitude jets snarled, rocking the cutter to starboard. Lightbody sprawled against the side of the cabin. His eyes were open but not animated. I wondered if the spacer's wound was more serious than the surface gash it appeared to be.

Ricimer glanced over his shoulder as Gregg boarded, his breastplate crashing against the coaming. The cutter's single plasma motor lighted with a bang and a spray of mud in all directions from the hull.

The vessel hopped forward from the initial pulse, then lifted in true flight as Ricimer relit the thruster. The initial cough of plasma had cleared mud from the nozzle so that the motor could develop full power without exploding.

Stephen Gregg braced his legs wide, leaning outward from the dorsal hatch. His rifle's muzzle lifted in a puff of white propellant gases. The blast was lost in the roar of the thruster.

Gregg dropped the rifle back into the cabin behind him without looking; Dole slapped the grip of his own weapon into Gregg's open hand. The big gunman aimed again. Jeude reached forward to take Ricimer's repeater and five cartridges from a pocket of the bandolier the general commander wore over his body armor.

I stood beside Gregg, gripping the coaming with my free hand to keep from being flung away by the cutter's violent maneuvering. I still held the cutting bar. The ichor sliming the blade had dried to a saffron hue.

Gregg fired. A Molt twisting through shrubbery forty meters away toppled on its face.

The Molt was visible because Ricimer reined the cutter in tight circles only five meters above the soggy ground. The thruster's plasma exhaust devoured plants directly below the nozzle and wilted the foliage of those ten meters to either side.

Ricimer dropped the little vessel almost to the soil. A dozen puffs of vapor fountained from the surrounding vegetation, some of them forty meters away. The nearer plumes were iridescent plasma, the more distant ones steam. Piet had set down directly on a spiderhole. The exhaust blasted through all the passages connected with the initial target. Molts anywhere in that portion of the tunnel system were incinerated.

Gregg shot, using Ricimer's repeater. He shifted as he worked the lever action, never taking the butt from his shoulder, and fired again.

The cutter rotated vertiginously as well as porpoising up and down. I couldn't see the Molts in the foliage until Gregg's bullets slapped them into their death throes, but the gunman didn't appear to waste a shot.

A gray streak splashed itself on the yellowed ceramic hull near where I stood. I gaped at it for a moment before I realized a bullet had struck and ricocheted harmlessly.

The goal that drew Hawtry and his fellows was a stone platform less than five meters across. Foliage curtained all but the center of the structure. Macquerie must have been looking at a radar image to tell that it was a pentagon.

Ricimer swept the cutter at a walking pace along the side away from the *Absalom 231,* fifty meters distant. He was avoiding men from the group in the hold who might have fought their way toward the target. Searing exhaust wilted enough vegetation to show a doorway in one face of the building. A Molt flopped in tetanic convulsions nearby, its carapace the deep red of a boiled lobster.

Ricimer set the cutter down on ground which plasma had baked on an earlier pass. He jumped up from the controls, shouting, "Dole, radio the hulk and bring the men back!"

Ricimer snatched a rifle the bosun had just reloaded. Gregg hoisted his buttocks onto the hatch coaming, swung his legs over and dropped, ignoring the steps and handholds formed into the outer hull.

I tried to follow and instead tumbled sideways. The ground was still spongy enough to cushion my landing.

Thomas Hawtry stepped out of the stone structure, holding a rifle. He'd lost his helmet, and a powerful blow had crazed the surface of his breastplate.

"We've found the treasure, Ricimer!" Hawtry called in attempted triumph. His face was white and his voice cracked in mid-sentence. "And an idol that we'll destroy in the Lord's name!"

"You others, keep guard," Ricimer ordered curtly as he strode toward the Molt temple. Coos came through the doorway behind Hawtry. Ricimer pushed him aside and went within.

Gregg followed Ricimer; I followed Gregg. I walked almost without volition, drifting after the leaders as thistledown trails a moving body.

The temple's floor was set three steps below the ground surface. The walls were corbeled inward, enclosing a greater volume than I'd expected from the size of the roof.

A Venerian battery lamp illuminated the interior. A spindle of meteoritic iron, twenty kilos or so in weight, rested on a stone pedestal in the center. Microchips—sacked, boxed, and loose—were piled in profusion on low benches along the walls. A silver starburst marked some of the containers, indicating the chips within were purpose-built: new production from pre-Collapse factories operating under Federation control.

Six gentlemen stared at us, their saviors. Sahagun clasped his hands together in prayer; Delray's face was as pale as ivory. Four were seriously wounded. The three missing men must be dead, unless they'd had sense enough to stay aboard the *Porcelain*.

A Molt in a loose caftan lay face-up on the stone floor. I didn't remember having previously seen a Molt wearing more than a sash. The alien had been shot at least a dozen times. Judging from the smell, someone had then urinated on the body.

Salomon appeared at the door to the temple, holding a cutting bar. "I left Macquerie in charge aboard the ship," he said. "Say, there *is* a fortune here!"

"We'll need stretchers," said Piet Ricimer. His voice was color-less.

"I've got blankets coming," the navigator said. "We can use rifles for poles. Any Molts left are keeping out of the way for now."

Salomon's bright tones grated on my consciousness. I suddenly realized that I wasn't the man I'd been ten minutes before. Ten minutes . . .

Piet Ricimer lurched toward the doorway without speaking fur-ther. Gregg jumped up the steps to precede his commander. He'd unslung the flashgun and held it ready for use. Salomon back-pedaled quickly to get out of their way. I followed the others, swaying slightly.

"Mister Salomon," Ricimer said in a cold, clear voice in the day-light. "See to it that the chips are loaded as quickly as possible. If the *Absalom*'s hoses will stretch, we'll refill the cutter's tank. I ran her out of reaction mass. If they won't reach, we'll blow the cutter in place. I'm not staying in a place so dangerous any longer than necessary. We'd best call the *Porcelain* into the fenced perim-eter as well."

"We'll take the idol," Hawtry said. "We can't leave the bugs to their idol. It's an affront to the Lord!"

Men from the *Absalom*'s hold stared about the steaming dev-astation, holding their weapons ready. Many of them had fresh wounds. Dole was already organizing carrying parties to load the captured chips.

"Yes, Mister Hawtry," Ricimer said in a voice as bleak as the rav-aged surface of Venus. "It is an affront to the Lord."

DECADES

Day 11

The garrison of Decades Station had mobile floodlights to illuminate threatened portions of the perimeter if the wild Molts
should attack. Two banks of them threw a white glare over the
Porcelain's gathered crew. I stood at the rear of the assembly, feeling
dissociated from my body.

"By the grace of God, we have come this far," Piet Ricimer said.
He spoke without amplification from the flagship's ramp. His clear,
vibrant voice carried through the soft breeze and the chugging of
the prime movers that powered the lights. "The coordinates of our
next layover have been distributed to every captain and navigator. We won't have settled facilities there, so be sure to complete
any maintenance requiring equipment we don't carry."

The next layover would be Mocha, one of the Breach worlds.
The Southerns occasionally laid over on Mocha, but there was
no colony. Mocha's only permanent inhabitants were a handful
of so-called Rabbits: hunter-gatherers descended from pre-Collapse
settlers. Though remnant populations like Mocha's were scattered
across the former human sphere, none of them had risen to the
level of barbarism.

"We've gained a small success," Ricimer said. Stephen Gregg was a bulky shadow in the hold behind the general commander, out of the light. Dole and others of Ricimer's longtime followers stood at the foot of the ramp. Not a bodyguard, precisely, but—there.

"We have also had losses," Ricimer said, "some of them unnecessary. Remember that success is with the Lord, but that we owe to Him and to our fellows discipline as well as courage."

Federation prisoners listened to the general commander's address from beyond the pool of light. We'd left them unguarded since the day we landed. When we lifted off in the morning, the Feds could carry on as they had before.

I wondered if Lavonne was listening. After the hulk returned to the base, she'd been very . . . "understanding" would be the wrong word; Lavonne hadn't in the least understood my desperate need to return to *life*. But she'd done what she could, as much as anyone could who hadn't been there, and I thought it had been enough.

I prayed it had been enough.

"There'll be one personnel change on the next stage of the voyage," Ricimer said. "I'm transferring Mister Hawtry to the *Absalom*—"

"You'll do *what*, you little clown?" Thomas Hawtry bellowed as he pushed his way onto the loading ramp. He'd been standing in the middle of his coterie of gentlemen. He stepped forward alone.

"Mister Hawtry—" Ricimer said. Behind him, Stephen Gregg moved into the light, tall and as straight as a knifeblade.

"If you were a gentleman and not a potter's whelp," Hawtry cried, "I'd call you out!"

I slid forward through the crowd. My hands were flexing.

Gregg stepped in front of the general commander. He held a rifle muzzle-down along his right thigh. His face had no expression at all. "I'm a gentleman, Mister Hawtry," he said.

Hawtry stopped, his right foot resting on the ramp.

Gregg pointed his left index finger at Hawtry. "And take your hat off when you address the general commander," Gregg said. His voice had a fluting lightness, terrible to hear. "As a mark of respect."

"Stephen," Ricimer said. He lifted a hand toward Gregg's shoulder but didn't touch the bigger man. "I'll handle this."

"Mister Hawtry," Gregg said. He didn't shout, but his tone pierced the night like an awl. "I won't warn you again."

I reached the front of the assembly. Easy to do, since men were edging back and to either side. Ricimer's veterans formed a tight block in the center.

Hawtry wasn't a coward, I knew that. Hawtry stared at Gregg, and at Ricimer's tense face beyond that of the gunman. Hawtry could obey or die. It was as simple as that. As well argue with an avalanche as Gregg in this mood.

Hawtry snatched off his cap, an affair of scarlet and gold lacework. He crushed it in his hands. "Your pardon, Mister Ricimer," he said. The words rubbed each other like gravel tumbling.

Gregg stepped aside. He looked bored, but there was a sheen of sweat on his forehead.

"There will be no duels during this expedition," Piet Ricimer said. His tone was fiery, but his eyes were focused on the far distance rather than the assembly before him. "We are on the Lord's business, reopening the stars to His service. If anyone fights a duel—"

Ricimer put his hand on Gregg's shoulder and turned the bigger man to face him. Gregg was the dull wax of a candle, and his friend was a flame.

"If anyone fights a duel," Ricimer said. "Is that understood?"

Gregg dropped to one knee before the general commander. He rotated his right wrist so that the rifle was behind him, pointing harmlessly into the flagship's hold.

Ricimer lifted him. Gregg stepped back into the shadows again. "If anyone fights a duel," Ricimer repeated, but the fierceness was gone from his voice, "then the surviving parties will be left at the landfall where the offense against the Lord occurred. There will be no exceptions."

He looked out over us. The assembly gave a collective sigh.

Ricimer knelt down. "Let us pray," he said, tenting his hands before him.

Decades Station had barracks to accommodate more transients than the whole of the Venerian force. One of the blocks was brightly illuminated. In it, spacers with a flute, a tambourine, and some kind of plucked string instrument were playing to a crowd.

I sat on the porch of the administration building across the way, wondering if any of the Federation women were inside with our men.

Lavonne would be waiting for me in her quarters. I'd go to her soon. As soon as I calmed down.

" . . . could stick them all in the hulk," said a voice from the darkness. Footsteps crunched along the path. Two sailors were sauntering toward the party. "None of them gentlemen's worth a flying fuck."

"Well, they're not much good for real work," said a second voice, which I thought might be Jeude's. "Get into a fight, though, they can be something else again."

"Gregg?" said the first voice. "I give you that."

"I swear the new fellow, Moore, he's as bad," replied might-be-Jeude. The pair were past the porch now, continuing up the path. "Straight into a dozen Molts, *no* armor, nothing but a bar."

"Likes to get close, huh?"

"He didn't even stop when they were dead!" the second man said, his voice growing fainter with increasing distance. "I swear, Dorsey, you never saw anything like it in your life."

My eyes were closed and I was shivering. After a time, I'm not sure how long, I stood shakily and began to walk toward the station's staff quarters.

MOCHA

Day 37

The mid-afternoon sun was so wan that stars were already out on the western horizon. At night they formed a sky-filling haze, too dense to be called constellations. The wind that swept across the ankle-high tundra was dank and chill.

"There's one of them," I said. I started to raise my hand to point at the Rabbit sidling down the slope a kilometer away.

The native didn't seem to be walking directly toward the ships on the shallow valley's floor. His track would bring him there nonetheless, as a moth spirals in on a flame.

Piet Ricimer caught my arm before it lifted. "He'll think you're trying to shoot him," Ricimer said.

"Yeah," Macquerie agreed. "No point in putting the wind up the little beasts. They can fling stones farther than you'd believe."

A pump chuffed as it filled the *Kinsolving* with reaction mass from a Southern well we'd reopened the night before. The Southerns had also left a score of low shelters whose walls were made of the turf lifted when the interior was cut into the soil. The dwellings crawled with lice, so today some of our people were building similar huts at a distance from the originals.

"There were a dozen Rabbits in the old Southern camp when we landed," Gregg muttered. "Where did they go?"

Macquerie shrugged. "Mostly they sleep in little trenches without top cover," he said. "Hard to see unless you step in one. Anyway, if they're gone, they aren't pilfering from us."

"They can't take enough to harm us seriously," Ricimer said. "They're men like us. I won't have them treated as animals."

Macquerie sniffed and said, softly enough to be ignored, "Hard to tell the difference, *I'd* say."

Ricimer resumed walking toward the top of the slope. Distances were deceptively great on Mocha's treeless landscape. The surface rippled in shallow valleys separated by low ridges. Rare but violent storms cut raw gullies before the torrents drained to impermeable rock layers from which the vegetation would in time lift the water again.

"There's nothing on the other side different from here, you know," Macquerie said. He was breathing harshly by now.

"I need the exercise," Ricimer said. He paused again and looked back. "Was this where Landolph landed, then?" he asked.

Macquerie and the general commander were unarmed. Gregg cradled his flashgun; the weight of the weapon and its satchel of spare batteries wasn't excessive to a man as strong as he was.

I carried a cutting bar. I'd known to pick one with a belt clip this time.

"Yes, that's right," Macquerie agreed. "Since then, nobody touches down on Mocha unless there's a problem with the gradients into Os Sertoes. Once or twice a year, that can happen."

The *Kinsolving*'s crew had off-loaded a featherboat and were assembling it. Ricimer planned to use the light craft to probe the Breach without stressing one of the expedition's larger vessels.

"Three more of them," I said. "Rabbits, I mean." I lifted my chin in a quick nod toward mid-slope in the direction of the camp.

The four of us must have passed within a few meters of where the natives had appeared. The Rabbits slouched along, apparently oblivious of the starships scattered in line for half a kilometer across the valley floor. One Rabbit wore a belt twisted from the hides of burrowing animals; another carried a throwing stick. Mocha's winds limited the growth of plants above ground, but the vegetation had sizable root systems.

"Some of them know Trade English," Macquerie said.

"From before the Collapse?" Gregg asked. I noticed that the big man continued to scan the ridgeline above us while we others were focused on the Rabbits.

Macquerie shrugged. "I don't have any idea," he said.

Piet Ricimer wore a cape of naturally-patterned wool. He threw the wings back over his shoulders. The wind was behind him now, though it was still cold enough for me. "That's why what we're doing is important," Ricimer said. "Those people."

"You're risking your life for the Rabbits?" Macquerie said in amazement.

"For mankind, Captain," Ricimer said. His voice was rich, his face exalted. "If man is to survive, as I believe the Lord means him to, then we have to settle a thousand Earths, a hundred thousand. There'll always be wars and disasters. If we're confined to one star, to one planet really—when the next Collapse comes, it'll be for all mankind, and forever."

"Earth has returned to the stars," I said. "The Feds and the Southerns are out on hundreds of worlds between them. They have no right to bar Venus from space—"

"Nor will they," Gregg said. His voice was as gray and hard as an iron casting.

"—but they're *there*," I continued. "Mankind is."

"No," said Ricimer, speaking with the certainty of one to whom the truth has been revealed. "What they're doing is mining the stars and the past to feed the present whims of tyrants. None of the settlements founded by the Federation and the Southern Cross is as solid as the colony on Mocha was before the Collapse. The destiny of mankind isn't to scuttle and starve in a ditch on a hillside!"

Captain Macquerie cleared his throat doubtfully. "Do you want to go on up the hill?" he asked.

Ricimer laughed. "I suppose we've seen what we needed to see here," he said. The power informing his tones of a moment before had vanished, replaced with a light cheerfulness. "And had our exercise."

The distance back to the *Porcelain* looked farther than the ridge—still above them—had seemed from the vessel's ramp. "We're not here to found colonies," I said.

"Ah, we're here to bait the whole of mankind out to the stars by bringing back treasure," Ricimer said.

He strung his laughter across the breeze like quicksilver on a glass table. "To break Earth's monopoly, so that there won't be another revolt of outworlds against the home system, another Collapse . . . And quite incidentally, my friends, to make ourselves very wealthy indeed."

The trio of Rabbits glanced around, their attention drawn by the chime of distant laughter.

MOCHA

Day 38

I lounged at the flagship's main display, watching an image of the floodlit featherboat transmitted from the *Kinsolving*'s optics. A six-man crew had finished fitting the featherboat's single thruster. Guillermo was still inside the little vessel, setting up the electronics suite. Ricimer intended to take the vessel off exploring tomorrow or the next day.

Trench-and-wall barracks had sprouted beside each of our ships. Plastic sheeting weighted with rocks formed the roofs and sealed walls against the wind. The turf-and-stone dwellings weren't much roomier than the ships, but they were a change after a long transit.

I was alone aboard the *Porcelain*. I'd volunteered for communications watch, and I hoped to tie the featherboat—Ricimer had named it the *Nathan*—into the remote viewing net I'd created. No reason, really. Something to do that only Jeremy Moore could do. The audio link was complete, but the Molt was still enabling the featherboat's external optics.

I had one orange left from the bags of citrus fruit we'd loaded on Decades. It'd taste good now, and oranges don't keep forever . . .

Boots scuffed in the amidships section. Somebody—several

somebodies, from the sound of it—had entered via the loading ramp to the hold.

Crewmen returning for personal items, I supposed. I was bored, but I didn't particularly want to chat with spacers who'd never read a book or a circuit diagram.

The hatch between the midships section and me in the bow was closed but not dogged. It opened for Thomas Hawtry, followed by Delray and Sahagun. I got up from the console.

"We brought you some cheer, Jeremy," Hawtry said as he walked past the 17-cm cannon, locked in traveling position on its cradle. He was smiling brightly.

Sahagun carried a square green bottle without a label. Delray held a repeating carbine; uncharacteristic for him to be armed, but perhaps they were worried about Rabbits in the starlit night.

Hawtry held out his hand for me to shake. Holding—not quite seizing—my hand, Hawtry guided me away from the console. Delray stepped between me and the controls. The other four surviving gentlemen of Hawtry's coterie entered the bow section.

Hawtry patted the back of my hand with his left fingertips, then released me. "Sorry for the little deception, Jeremy," he said. His tone was full and greasy. "Didn't want to have an accident with you bumping the alarm button, because then something awkward would happen. That's it there, isn't it?"

Hawtry nodded toward the console.

"Yes," I said. "The red button at the top center."

Coos wiggled the cage over the large button to make sure it was clipped in place. He and Farquhar carried rifles also. Levenger and Teague wore holstered pistols like Hawtry's own, but those could pass simply as items of dress for a gentleman.

When I came back to the *Porcelain* from our hike, I'd returned my cutting bar to the arms locker in the main hold. *A bar's really better for a close-in dustup,* Jeude had said on Decades, but there were seven of them here . . .

"We're here to save the expedition, Jeremy," Hawtry said. "And our lives as well, I shouldn't wonder. You've seen how that potter's whelp Ricimer hates gentlemen? You've been spared the worst of the insults, but that will change."

He lowered himself into the seat I'd vacated. Coos and Sahagun stepped to either side so that Hawtry could still view me directly.

"So you're planning to kill the general commander and replace him?" I said baldly. I crossed my hands behind my back.

Delray and Teague looked uncomfortable. "Say, now, fellow," Hawtry said with a frown. "Nobody spoke of killing, not in the least. But if we—the better class of men—don't act quickly, Ricimer will abandon us here on Mocha. He as good as stated his plans when he put me, *me,* aboard the *Absalom.* A hulk can't transit the Breach, anyone can see that!"

"Go on, then," I said. My voice was calm. I watched the unfolding scene from outside my body, quietly amazed at the tableau. "If you're not going to kill General Commander Ricimer, what?"

Sahagun glanced at Hawtry and held the bottle forward a few centimeters to call attention to it.

"Say, I'm the real commander of the expedition anyway," Hawtry said. He looked away and rubbed the side of his nose. "By Councilor Duneen's orders, and I shouldn't wonder the governor's directly. If it should be necessary to take over, and it is."

"Thomas, what are you going to do?" I said, with gentle emphasis on the final word.

"A drink so that that psychotic bastard Gregg goes to sleep," Hawtry said, rubbing his nose. "That—that one, he won't listen to reason, that's obvious."

Sahagun lifted the green bottle again. The liquor sloshed. The container was full, but the wax seal around the stopper had been broken. Delray grimaced and turned his back on the proceedings.

"Ricimer, he's not a problem without Gregg," Hawtry continued. "We'll put them on the *Absalom*—and a few sailors for crew, I suppose. There won't be any problem with the men. They'll follow their natural leaders, be *glad* to follow real leaders!"

"But you want me to give Gregg the bottle," I said. I sounded as though I was checking the cargo manifest. "Because he'd wonder if any of you offered it."

"Well, drink with him, jolly him along," Hawtry said. "It won't do you any harm. You'll wake up in the morning without even a headache."

He rubbed his nose again.

"That Gregg's got a hut of his own," Levenger said in a bitter voice. "While the rest of us sleep with common sailors!"

"Gregg doesn't sleep well when he's on the ground," I said. I felt the corners of my mouth lift. Maybe I was smiling. "He doesn't want to distress other people. And there's the embarrassment, I suppose."

Hawtry lifted himself angrily from the seat in which he'd been pretending to relax. "Listen, Moore," he said. "Either you can do this and things'll go peacefully—or I'll *personally* shoot you outside Gregg's door, and when he comes out we'll gun *him* down. He won't have a chance against seven of us."

Not a proposition I'd care to bet my life on, Thomas, I thought. My lips tingled, but I didn't speak aloud.

"We'll kill you as a traitor, and him because he's too damned dangerous to live!" Hawtry said. "So which way will it be?"

"Well, I wouldn't want anyone to think I was a traitor," I said. "But you'll have to wait—"

Hawtry raised his arm to slap me, then caught himself and lowered his hand again. His face was mottled with rage. "There'll be no delays, Moore," he said savagely. "Not if you know what's good for you."

"Gregg knows I'm on watch," I explained in a neutral voice. "If I appear before I've been relieved, he'll be suspicious."

"Oh," said Hawtry. "Oh. How long are you . . ."

I looked at the chronometer on the navigation console set to ship's time. "Oh," I said, "I think ten minutes should do it."

The midships hatch banged violently open. "No time at all, gentlemen," said Stephen Gregg as he stepped through behind the muzzle of his flashgun. His helmet's lowered visor muffled his voice, but the words were as clear as the threat.

Gregg wore body armor. So did Piet Ricimer, who followed with a short-barreled shotgun. Dole and Lightbody were behind the commander with cutting bars. Stampfer, the gunner, carried a heavy single-shot rifle, and Salomon had a repeater. There were more sailors as well, shoving their way into the bow section.

Hawtry dived for the compartment's exterior hatch, an airlock. Perhaps he felt that no one would shoot in a room so crowded.

"Steady," Ricimer murmured.

Hawtry tugged the hatch open. No one tried to stop him. Jeude waited in the airlock with his cutting bar ready. He twitched the blade forward, severing Hawtry's pistol belt and enough flesh to fling the gentleman back screaming.

"Take their weapons," Ricimer said calmly.

"It may interest you *gentlemen* to know," I said, my voice rising an octave as my soul flooded back into my body, "that there was a channel open to Guillermo in the featherboat all the time we were talking. And if there hadn't been, I assure you I would have found another way to stop you traitors!"

"It wasn't me!" Coos cried. He was a tall man, willowy and supercilious at normal times. "It wasn't—"

Lightbody punched Coos in the stomach with the butt of his cutting bar, doubling him up on the deck. Coos began to vomit.

"I'll expect you to have that cleaned up by end of watch, Lightbody," Ricimer said as he uncaged the alarm button.

"Aye-aye, *sir!*" Lightbody said.

The flagship's siren howled a strident summons.

"Listen. Moore," snarled Hawtry's voice through loudspeakers mounted to either side of the main hatch. A spotlight on the *Kinsolving* two hundred meters away was focused on the flagship's hold. "I'll *personally* shoot you outside Gregg's door, and when he comes out we'll gun *him* down."

Wind sighed across the valley, bearing away the murmur of the gathered spacers. Someone called, "Bastard!" in a tone of loud amazement.

"Ricimer, he's not a problem without Gregg," said Hawtry's voice. Guillermo was working the board, mixing the gentleman's words for greatest effect from the recording the Molt had made in the *Nathan.*

Hawtry struggled against his bonds in the center of the hold. Dole had cinched Hawtry's ankles to a staple. The gentleman's wrists were tied in front of him and he was gagged besides. Hawtry's six followers stood at the base of the ramp—disarmed and discreetly guarded by trusted sailors, but not shackled.

"We'll kill you and him!" said Hawtry's voice. You'd have had to hear the original words to realize the speech was edited. At that, Guillermo hadn't distorted the thrust of the gentleman's harangue.

Piet Ricimer stepped forward. "Thomas Hawtry," he said. "You knew that this expedition could succeed only if we all kept our oaths to strive together in brotherhood. Your own words convict you of treason to the state, and of sacrilege against God."

Stephen Gregg, a statue in half armor, stood at the opposite side of the hatch from Ricimer. He hadn't moved since Dole and Jeude fastened the prisoner in front of the assembly.

A kerchief was tied behind Hawtry's head. Ricimer tugged up the knot so that the gentleman could spit out the gag.

Hawtry shook himself violently. "You have no right to try me!" he shouted. "I'm a factor, a *factor*! I need answer to no judge but the Governor's Council."

Unlike Ricimer's, Hawtry's voice wasn't amplified. He sounded thin and desperate to me.

"Under God and Governor Halys," Ricimer said, "I am general commander of this expedition. I and your shipmates will judge you, Thomas Hawtry. How do you plead?"

"It was a joke!" cried Hawtry. He turned from side to side in the glare of lights focused on him. "There was no plot, just a joke, and that whorechaser Moore knew it!"

The crowd buzzed, men talking to their closest companions. Hawtry's coterie stood silent, with gray faces and stiff smiles. Gregg's eyes, the only part of the gunman that moved, drifted from them to the prisoner and back.

Contorting his body, Hawtry rubbed his eyes with his shoulder. He caught sight of me at the front of the assembly. "There he is!" Hawtry shouted, pointing with his bound hands. "There's the Judas Jeremy Moore! He lied me into these bonds!"

I climbed the ramp in three crashing strides. The cutting bar batted against my legs, threatening to trip me. Hawtry straightened as he saw me coming; his eyes grew wary.

A tiny smile played at the corners of Stephen Gregg's mouth.

"Aye, strike a fettered man, Moore," Hawtry said shrilly.

I pulled the square-faced bottle from the pocket of the insulated vest I wore over my tunic. Hawtry's face was hard and pale in the spotlights.

"Here you are, Thomas," I said. A part of my mind noted in surprise that a directional microphone picked up my voice and boomed my words out through the loudspeakers so that everyone in the crowd could hear. "Here's the bottle that you ordered me to drink with Mister Gregg."

Hawtry's chin lifted. He shuffled his boots, but Dole had shackled him straitly.

I twisted out the glass stopper. "Take a good drink of this, Thomas," I said. "And if it only puts you to sleep, then I swear I'll defend your life with my own!"

Hawtry's face suffused with red hatred. He swung his bound

arms and swatted the container away. It clanked twice on the ramp and skidded the rest of the way down without breaking. Snowy gray liquor splashed from the bottle's throat.

"Yes," I said as I backed away. I was centered within myself again. For a moment I'd been . . . "I rather thought that would be your response."

I'd watched in my mind as the bar howled in the hands of my own puppet figure below. It swung in an arc that continued through the spray of blood and the shocked face of Thomas Hawtry sailing free of his body.

Piet Ricimer stepped forward. He took Hawtry's joined hands in his own and said, "Thomas, in the name of the Lord, won't you repent? There's still—"

"No!" said Stephen Gregg thunderously as he strode into the center of the hatchway. The ceramic armor added bulk to the rangy power of his form. "There's been forgiveness aplenty. The next time it'll be your life, Piet, and I'll not have that."

Gregg laid his great left hand over Hawtry's wrists and lifted them away from Ricimer. Gregg raised Hawtry's arms, ignoring the prisoner's attempt to pull free, and shouted to the assembly, "Is this man guilty of treason? Shall he be marooned here as a traitor?"

"Yes!" I screamed. Around me I heard, "Aye!" and "Guilty!" and "Yes!" A murmur of, "No," a man crying, "You have no right!" But those latter were the exceptions to a tide of anger tinged with bloodlust. The sailors were Betaport men, and in Betaport Piet Ricimer sat just below the throne of God.

"No, you can't do this!" Delray shouted angrily. The other gentlemen stood silent, afraid to speak lest Gregg turn the mob on them as well.

Gregg dropped the prisoner's arms. "You didn't want to obey the general commander, Hawtry," he said. "Now you can rule a whole planet by yourself."

Officers of the *Mizpah* and *Kinsolving* stood in a clump at the back of the assembly, muttering and looking concerned. They knew better than the common sailors how much trouble could come from punishing a powerful noble. Blakey was Councilor Duneen's man, while Captain Winter trimmed his behavior to the prevailing winds.

"You can't *do* this!" Delray repeated. The wind toyed with his voice.

Perhaps a third of the assembly could make out his words, while the rest heard only faint desperation. "The Rabbits will kill him!"

The other gentlemen moved away as though Delray was thrashing in a pool of his own vomit. A sailor behind Delray patted a baton of steel tubing against the calluses of the opposite palm, but the gentleman took no notice.

"They'll flay him with sharp stones!" Delray shouted. "You can't do this!"

I didn't know Delray well and hadn't liked what I did know: the third son of Delray of Sunrise, a huge hold in the Aphrodisian Hills. Very rich, very haughty, and even younger than his 19 Earth years.

It struck me that there was a person under Delray's callow exterior who might have been worth knowing after all.

"He's right," Gregg said abruptly. The amplified boom of his voice startled me after an interval of straining to hear Delray's cries. "Dole, cut his feet loose. Hawtry, we'll find a gully out beyond the ships."

I blinked, shocked by a sudden reality that I'd avoided until that moment. It was one thing to eat meat, another to watch the butcher. Dole stepped up the ramp, his bar humming.

"No!" said Ricimer, placing the flat of his hand on Gregg's breastplate. He directed the bigger man back. *Piet's too good a man for this existence,* Gregg had said the last night on Venus.

"Give me a ship!" Hawtry blurted. His face was as white as a bone that dogs were scuffling over. "Give me a featherboat, C-cap-com*man*der Ricimer!"

"Mister Hawtry," Ricimer said, "you cannot pilot a starship, and I will not diminish a force devoted to the Lord's work for the sake of a traitor. But the judgment on your treason was that of the expedition as a whole. Therefore the expedition will carry out the necessary sentence."

Ricimer turned to face the assembly. He didn't squint, though the spotlight was full on his face. He pointed to the front of the crowd, his arm as straight as a gun barrel.

"Coos, Levenger, Teague," he said, clipping out syllables like cartridges shucked from a repeater's magazine. "Farquhar, Sahagun. And Delray. Under the direction of Mister Gregg, you will form a firing party to execute sentence of death on the traitor Thomas Hawtry. Tomorrow at dawn. Do you understand?"

None of the gentlemen spoke. Farquhar covered his face with his hands.

Hawtry shuddered as though the first bullet had struck him. He closed his eyes for a moment. When he reopened them, his expression was calm.

"This assembly is dismissed," the general commander said in a voice without triumph or pity. "And may God have mercy on our souls."

MOCHA

Day 39

Mocha's sun laid a track of yellow light from the eastern horizon. Ricimer and Hawtry stood at the edge of the shallow mere, talking in voices too low to carry twenty meters to where the nearest of the other men waited.

The air was still, for the first time that I could remember since we landed here. I shivered anyway.

A group of sailors commanded by the *Porcelain*'s bosun held single-shot rifles. The men were chatting companionably. Jeude punctuated his comment by raising his left hand in the air and wriggling the fingers. He and the others laughed.

About half the expedition's complement had trekked to the north end of the valley to watch the execution. The remainder stayed with the ships, pretending this was a normal day. Occasionally someone might pause and glance northward, but there would be nothing to see. The irregularity of the valley's floor seemed slight, but it was enough to swallow a man-height figure in half a kilometer.

I didn't know why I was here. I rubbed my hands together and wondered if I should have brought gloves.

The gentlemen of the firing party faced one another in a close circle, shoulders together and their heads bowed. A spacer cried out, "Pretty little chickens got their feathers plucked, didn't they?"

The remark didn't have to be a gibe directed against the gentlemen . . . but it probably was. Delray spun to identify the speaker. The gentleman remembered his present place and subsided in impotent anger.

Stephen Gregg, standing alone as if contemplating the sunrise, turned his head. "Roosen?" he called to the spacer who'd flung the comment. "I'm glad to know you have spirit. I often need a man of spirit to accompany me."

Roosen shrank into himself. His companions of a moment before edged away from him.

I chuckled.

Gregg strolled toward me, holding the flashgun in the crook of his left arm. Gregg wore his helmet and a satchel of batteries, but he didn't have body armor on for the morning's duties.

The big man nodded toward the mere thirty meters away, where Hawtry and the general commander still talked. "So you would have protected Mister Hawtry from me if he'd been willing to drink from your bottle, Moore?" Gregg said in a low, bantering tone.

Sometimes Ricimer's aide looked like an empty sack. Now—there was nothing overtly tense about Gregg, but a black power filled his frame and dominated the world about him.

I shrugged. "Thomas isn't the sort for half measures," I said evenly. "Sleep where death would do, for example. Besides . . . I rather think he resented my—closeness. With Councilor Duneen's sister."

My mouth smiled. "Though to listen to him, he wasn't aware of that. Closeness."

Gregg turned again to face the sunrise. "I was mistaken in my opinion of the man I brought aboard in Betaport, wasn't I? Just who are you, Moore?"

I shrugged again. "I'm damned if I know," I said. Then I said, "I could use a woman right now. The Lord *knows* I could."

Ricimer and Hawtry clasped hands, then embraced. Ricimer walked back to the company. His face was still. The crowd hushed.

Gregg's visage became cold and remote. "Distribute the rifles," he ordered as he strode toward the gentlemen and the sailors waiting to equip them for their task.

Dole muttered a command. He gave a single cartridge and a

rifle, its action open, to Sahagun. That gentleman and the other members of the firing party accepted the weapons with grimaces.

"Take your stand!" Gregg ordered. He placed himself beside and a pace behind the gentlemen. His flashgun was ready but not presented.

"I'll give the commands if you please, Mister Gregg," Thomas Hawtry called in a clear voice. He stood at apparent ease, his limbs free.

Gregg looked at Ricimer. Ricimer nodded agreement.

"May God and you, my fellows, forgive my sins!" Hawtry said. "Gentlemen, load your pieces."

The men of the firing party were mostly experienced marksmen, but they fumbled the cartridges. Coos dropped his. He had to brush grit off the case against his trouser leg. Breeches closed with a variety of clicks and shucking sounds.

Hawtry stood as straight as a sunbeam. His eyes were open. "Aim!" he said.

The gentlemen lifted their rifles to their shoulders. Farquhar jerked his trigger. The shot slammed out toward the horizon. Farquhar shouted in surprise at the accidental discharge.

"Fire!" Hawtry cried. The rest of the party fired. Two bullets punched Hawtry's white tunic, and the bridge of his nose vanished in a splash of blood.

Hawtry crumpled to his knees, then flopped onto his face. There was a hole the size of a fist in the back of his skull. The surface of the water behind him danced as if with rain.

Delray opened the bolt of his rifle to extract the spent case, then flung the weapon itself toward the mere. The rifle landed halfway between him and the corpse twitching spastically on the ground.

Delray stalked away. The remainder of the firing party stood numbly as Dole's team collected the rifles.

Gregg turned and walked back to me. He looked drawn and gray.

"I'm impressed with the way you handled yourself the other night," he said quietly. "And on Decades, of course; but courage in a brawl is more common than the ability to stay calm in a crisis."

I hugged myself and shivered. A spacer had tossed a tarp over Hawtry's body. Two other men were digging a grave nearby.

Piet Ricimer knelt in prayer, his back to the dead man.

Brains and bits of bone, splashing the mere in a wide arc.

"How do you sleep at all, Mister Gregg?" I whispered.

Gregg sniffed. "You can get used to anything, you know," he said. "I suppose that's the worst of it. Even the dreams."

He put a hand on my shoulder and turned me away from the past. "Let's go back to the ship," he said. "I have a bottle. And you may as well call me Stephen, Jeremy."

MOCHA

Day 51

When the alert signal throbbed on the upper right corner of the main screen, I slapped the sidebar control that I'd preselected for potential alarm situations. Salomon dumped the transit solutions he'd been running at the navigation console and echoed all my data on his display.

A grid of dots and numbers replaced the 360° visual panorama I'd been watching for want of anything better to do. Presumably some of the Rabbits were female, but it hadn't come to that yet.

I didn't understand the new display. A pink highlight surrounded one of the dots.

I held the siren switch down briefly to rouse the men sleeping, gambling, or wandering across Mocha's barren landscape. A few seconds could be important, and even a false alarm would give the day some life it otherwise lacked.

"It's the passive optical display," Salomon explained. "An object just dropped into orbit. If it's not a flaw in the scanner, something came out of trans—"

"*Nathan* to squadron," said Piet Ricimer's voice, flattened by the program by which the *Porcelain*'s AI took the static out of the featherboat's transmission. "Respond, squadron. Over."

I switched the transceiver to voice operation while my left hand entered the commands that relayed the conversation through the loudspeakers—tannoys I'd taken from Federation stores on Decades—on poles outside the temporary shelters. It'd been something to do, and the disorganized communications among the ships scattered here had offended my soul.

"Go ahead, Commander," I said before I remembered that Salomon was on watch this morning. "We're on voice."

Handover procedures were cumbersome and basically needless between two parties who knew one another. Without visuals—the featherboat's commo was rudimentary—there was a chance that one speaker's transmission would step on the other's, but that wasn't a serious concern.

"Moore?" Ricimer said. His words blared through the external speakers to the men alerted by the siren. "We've got to leave immediately. Get essential stores out of the *Absalom;* we're leaving her. We'll be abandoning the *Nathan* here too, so that frees up space on the *Kinsolving* for the Decades loot. We'll be coming in on the next orbit—"

The featherboat couldn't communicate through her thruster's discharged ions.

"—and I want to lift off within an hour of when we land. Is that understood?"

"We understand, Commander," I said. I rose from the console. Officers and senior men would be gathering work crews from men more concerned with getting their personal gear back aboard the ships.

"I'll address the squadron when we reach orbit," Ricimer said. The transmission was beginning to break up beyond the AI's capacity to restore it. The caret on the main screen that was the *Nathan* had already slipped beneath the horizon of the display. "Before we negotiate the Breach . . ."

His words died in a burst of static.

"I've got takeoff and initial transit programs loaded," Salomon said to me with a wry smile. Perhaps it was a comment on the way the gentleman had hijacked communications with the general commander.

Men were already crashing aboard the *Porcelain,* shouting to one another in a skein of tangled conversations. I strode for the midships hatch to get through it before the crush arrived in the other direction.

"I'm going to pull the AI from the hulk," I called back to the navigator. "It's not worth much, but it's something . . . and it's the only thing *I* can do now."

MOCHA ORBIT

Day 51

Because of the adrenaline rush of the hastened liftoff, weightlessness didn't make me as queasy as it had on every previous occasion.

"Men of Venus," Piet Ricimer said, standing before the video pickups of the main console.

The general commander's tone and pose were consciously theatrical, but not phony. An unshakable belief in his mission was the core of Ricimer's being. "My fellows. While I was on Os Sertoes, a Southern colony three days transit from here, six Federation warships landed. Their admiral announced that they'd arrived to protect the Breach from Venerian pirates under the command of the notorious Ricimer."

He allowed himself a smile.

The interior of the *Porcelain* looked as if a mob had torn through the vessel. Belongings seemed to expand in the course of a voyage. Objects were never repacked as tightly as they'd been stowed before initial liftoff. Loot, even from a near-wasteland like Mocha, added to the bulk, and the crew's hurried reboarding would at best have created chaos.

The interior of the *Kinsolving,* visible on the split screen past the set face of Captain Winter, was an even more complete image of wreckage. The quality of the *Mizpah*'s transmission was so poor that the flagship's AI painted the field behind Blakey as a blur of color. On all the vessels, items that hadn't been properly stowed before liftoff drifted as the ships hung above Mocha.

"The Feds will be patrolling all the landing sites in the region, I have no doubt," Ricimer said. I could hear the words echoing from tannoys in the compartments sternward. On the *Kinsolving*, sailors listened in the background as tense, dim shapes. "We aren't here to fight the Federation. We're here to take the wealth on which President Pleyal builds his tyranny and turn that wealth to the use of all mankind."

Another small smile. "Ourselves included."

Stephen Gregg stood between a pair of stanchions, doing isometric exercises with his arms. He was too big to be comfortable for any length of time on a featherboat, but not even Piet Ricimer had dared suggest Stephen remain on Mocha during the exploratory run.

"I've set an initial course," Ricimer continued. "The *Nathan* tested the gradients within the throat of the Breach. I won't disguise the fact that the stresses are severe; but not too severe, I believe, for us to achieve our goal."

"It was rough as a cob," Jeude muttered, trying to emasculate his fear by articulating it. "The boat nigh shook herself apart. Mister Ricimer, he kept pushing the gradients and she couldn't *take* it."

I put a hand on the eyebolt which Jeude held. I didn't quite touch the young sailor's hand, but I hoped the near-contact would provide comfort.

Part of my mind was amused that I was trying to reassure someone who understood far better than I did the risks we were about to undergo. There were times that the risks couldn't be allowed to matter. At those times, it was a gentleman's duty to be an example.

"There is one further matter to attend before we proceed," Ricimer continued. "Our flagship has been named the *Porcelain*. I am taking this moment, as we enter a new phase of our endeavors, to rechristen her *Oriflamme*. May she symbolize the banner of the Lord which we are carrying through the Breach!"

He swept off his cap and cried, "In the name of God, gentlemen, let us do our duty!"

"Hurrah!" Salomon cried, so smoothly that I remembered Ricimer's whispered conversation with his navigator before he began his address. Throughout the flagship the *Oriflamme*—and aboard the other vessels, men were shouting, "Hurrah!"

I shouted as well, buoyed by hope and the splendor of the moment. For the first time in my memory, Jeremy Moore was part of a group.

Ricimer shut off the transmission and slipped into his couch to prepare for transit. Guillermo and Salomon watched from the flanking consoles.

I let go my grip and thrust myself across the compartment toward Stephen. My control in weightlessness was getting better— at least I didn't push off with all my strength anymore—but it was short of perfect. Stephen caught me by the hand and pulled me down to share a stanchion.

"You may think you dislike transit now," Stephen said, "but you'll know you do shortly."

"Yes, well, I was going to suggest that I'd get out and walk instead," I said. "Ah—it occurs to me, Stephen, that the oriflamme is the charge of Councilor Duneen's arms."

Stephen nodded. "Yeah," he said. "Piet thinks it may take the Councilor's mind off the fact that we've executed one of his chief clients. Not that Hawtry was any loss, not really; but the Councilor might feel that he needed to . . . react."

"Ah," I said. "It was the general commander's idea?"

"Prepare for transit!" Salomon warned over the PA system.

"Oh, yes," Stephen agreed. "Piet thinks ahead."

I followed Stephen's glance toward the general commander. It struck me that Ricimer was, in his way, just as ruthless as Stephen Gregg.

IN TRANSIT

Day 64

The leg of the attitude-control console nearest me began to quiver with a harmonic as the *Oriflamme*'s thrusters strained. The vessel flip-flopped in and out of transit, again, *again.* The surface of the leg dulled as tiny cracks spread across the surface, metastasizing with each successive vibration.

Life was a gray lump that crushed Jeremy Moore against the decking. My vision was monochrome. Images shifted from positive to negative as the *Oriflamme* left and reentered the sidereal universe, but I was no longer sure which state was which.

The sequence ended. Bits of ceramic crazed from the leg lay on the deck beneath the attitude controls.

Salomon got up from his console. His face looked like a skin of latex stretched over an armature of thin wires. "The charts are wrong!" he shouted. "Landolph lied about coming here, or if he did, it's closed since then. There *is* no Breach!"

Pink light careted a dot on the starscape above Guillermo's console. Either the *Kinsolving* or the *Mizpah* was still in company with the flagship. I didn't care. All that mattered now was the realization that if I was dead, the nausea would be over.

"I'm going to add one transit to the sequence without changing the constants," Piet Ricimer said from the central couch. Above him, the main screen was a mass of skewed lines. "From the tendency of the gradients, I believe we're very close to a gap."

Guillermo's three-fingered hands clicked across his keyboard, transmitting the solution to the accompanying vessel.

Stephen Gregg was curled into a ball on the deck. He'd started out leaning against the attitude-control console, but lateral acceleration during a previous series of transits had toppled him over. He either hadn't wished or hadn't been able to sit up again.

The sailors without immediate duties during transit were comatose or praying under their breath. Perhaps I should have been pleased that experienced spacers were affected as badly as I was.

"The gradients are rising too fast!" Salomon shouted. "The levels are already higher than I've ever seen them, and—"

Lightbody came off his seat at the attitude-control console. The sailor didn't have a weapon, but his long arms were spread like the claws of an assassin bug. Salomon started to turn, shocked from his panic by the palpable destruction lunging toward his throat.

Stephen caught Lightbody's ankle and jerked the sailor to the deck. I leaped onto the man's shoulders.

Lightbody's face was blank. The wild light went out of his eyes, leaving the sailor with a confused expression. "What?" he said. "Wha . . ."

"Sorry, sir," Salomon muttered. He sat down on his couch again.

I rolled away. I had to use both hands to lever myself back to a squat and then rise. The jolting action had settled my mind, but my limbs were terribly weak. I could stand upright, so long as I gripped a stanchion as though the *Oriflamme* was in free fall rather than proceeding under 1-g acceleration.

Lightbody stood, then helped Stephen up as well. Lightbody returned to his seat. I held out a hand to bring Stephen to his stanchion.

"Prepare for transit," Piet Ricimer said. He hadn't risen from his couch or looked back during the altercation.

Light and color. Blankness, blackness, body ripped inside out, soul scraped in a million separate Hells.

Light and color again.

"There," said Piet Ricimer. "As I thought, a star . . . and she has a planet. We will name the planet Respite."

RESPITE

Day 68

The plateau on which the *Oriflamme* and *Mizpah* rested above the jungle was basalt. The fresh ceramic with which teams resealed the vessels' stress-cracked hulls was black, and the sound of grinders processing the dense rock into raw material for the glazing kilns was nerve-wracking and omnipresent.

Stephen checked the weld which belayed the glass-fiber line around a vertical toe of basalt near the plateau's rim. He nodded. I let myself drop over the edge.

The mass of the plateau dulled the bone-jarring sound. My chest muscles relaxed for the first time in the three days since the grinders had started work.

The basalt had formed hexagonal pillars as it cooled from magma in the depths of the earth. Cycles of upthrust and weathering left this mass as a tower hundreds of meters above the surrounding jungle. As the outermost columns crumbled, they created a giant staircase down into the green canopy.

Forty meters below the top of the plateau, my boots touched the layer of dirt covering the sloping top of a broken pillar. I released my harness from the line and stepped away, waving Stephen down in turn.

A pair of arm-long flying creatures paused curiously near Stephen, hovering in the updraft along the plateau's flank. The "birds" were hard-shelled, with four wings and sideways-hung jaws. They were harmless to anything the size of a man and hadn't learned to be wary.

The forest far below was a choir of varied calls. Mist trailed among the treetops, and a plume hectares in area rose a few kilometers away like a stationary cloud. I wondered if a hot spring or a lake of boiling mud broke surface there in the jungle.

Respite's atmosphere had a golden hue. I found I actually liked being under an open sky, unlike most men raised in the tunnels and impervious domes of Venus. It made me tingle with uncertainty, much the way I felt when making my initial approaches to a woman.

The feeling of peace below the rim was relative. The rock vibrated from the teeth of the grinders, felt if not heard. The terrace was a nesting site for a colony of the flying creatures. Hundreds of them stood at the mouths of burrows excavated in the soil, goggling at us with octuple eyes. They clacked the edges of their front and rear pairs of wings together querulously.

Opinions of the flyers' taste among our crew ranged from adequate to delicious: Salomon swore he'd never before eaten anything as good as the sausage of smoked lung tissue and organ meat he'd made from the creatures. In any event, the expedition would leave Respite well stocked with food.

Stephen landed with a grunt. His fingers massaged his opposite shoulders. For this excursion he'd slung a short rifle across his back, rather than the flashgun he favored. "I don't know about you," he said, "but I'm not looking forward to the climb back, ascenders or no. I'm not in shape for this."

"I'm not looking forward to going back to the noise," I said. I felt the strain in my arms and thigh muscles also, but I thought I'd be physically ready before I was mentally ready to return. "I suppose it's better than falling apart in transit, though."

Stephen sniffed. "Worried about the *Kinsolving*?" he said. "Don't be. Winter just didn't have the stomach for this. He's headed back to Venus with the rest of Hawtry's node of vipers. That lot'd make me ashamed to be a gentleman—if I gave a damn myself."

The hexagonal terrace sloped at 30°, enough to tumble a man over the edge if he lost his footing. Each of the basalt columns was about ten meters wide across the flats. I stepped forward carefully. "With the Decades loot besides," I noted.

As I passed close to nesting sites, the creatures drew themselves down as far as they could into their burrows. Because the soil was so shallow, their heads remained above the surface but the clicking of the wings was muted.

"Commander Ricimer," I went on, "thinks they've just missed this landfall and gone on through the Breach. The *Kinsolving.*"

"Piet likes to think the best of people," Stephen said. He walked over to me without apparent caution. The wind from the forest ruffled our cuffs and tunics upward and bathed us in earthy, alien odors.

"And you?" I asked without looking at my companion. Something moved across the distant forest, perhaps a shadow. If the motion had been made by a living creature, it was a huge one.

"Oh, I'd *like* to, sure," Stephen said, adjusting his rifle's sling.

"The loot's the reason I'm not angry," Stephen added. "There's enough value aboard the *Kinsolving* to arouse attention, but not nearly enough to buy Winter's way out of trouble for attacking the colony of a state with whom Venus is at peace. That lot has punished themselves."

I looked at my companion. "Technically at peace," I said.

"Politicians are *very* technical, Jeremy," Stephen said. "Until it's worth the time of somebody in court to cut corners. And the Decades loot won't interest the likes of Councilor Duneen, which is what it'd take to square this one."

I peered over the edge of the terrace. The next step down was within five meters of the outer lip of the one we were on. A pattern of parallel semicircular waves marked the surface of the step, springing out like ripples in a frozen pond from the side of the column on which we stood.

Pits weathered into the rock offered toeholds. I turned and swung my legs over.

"It's a long way down," Stephen warned. "And it's likely to be a longer way back up."

"I want to check something," I said. "You don't have to come."

I clambered my own height down the rock face, then pushed off and landed with my knees flexed. Perhaps Stephen could pull me up with our belts paired into a rope, or—

Stephen slammed down beside me. He'd jumped with the rifle

held out so that it didn't batter him in the side when he hit the ground. He grinned at me.

I shrugged. "It's the pattern here," I said, walking toward the ripples in stone.

Conical nests built up from the surface indicated that flyers of a different species had colonized this step. These were hand-sized and bright yellow in contrast to the dull colors of the larger creatures. Hundreds of them lifted into the air simultaneously, screeching and emitting sprays of mauve feces over the two of us.

I ducked and swore. Stephen began to laugh rackingly. The cloud of flyers sailed away from the plateau, then dived abruptly toward the jungle.

Stephen untied his kerchief, checked for a clean portion of the fabric, and used that to wipe down the rifle's receiver. "I was the smart-ass who decided if you thought you could make it back, I sure could," he explained. "Nobody's choice but mine—which is why I let Piet make the decisions, mostly."

I stepped to the point from which ripples spread from the rock face. As I'd expected, the basalt had been melted away. Because the rock was already fully oxidized, it splashed into waves like those of metal welded in a vacuum.

The cavity so formed was circular and nearly two meters in diameter. It was sealed by a substance as transparent as air—not glass, for it responded with a soft *thock* when I tapped it with my signet ring.

The creature mummified within was the height and shape of a man, but it was covered with fine scales, and its limbs were jointed in the wrong places. At one time the mummy had been clothed, but only shreds of fabric and fittings remained in a litter around the four-toed feet.

"Piet said it looked from the way the rocks were glazed that ships had landed on the plateau in the past," Stephen remarked. "Landolph, he thought. But after he looked closer at the weather cracking, he decided that it must have been millennia ago."

"What does it mean?" I asked.

"To us?" said Stephen. "Nothing. Because our business is with the Federation; and whoever this fellow was, he wasn't from the Federation."

IN TRANSIT

Day 92

The *Oriflamme* came out of transit—out of a universe which had no place for man or even for what man thought were natural laws. This series had been of eighteen insertions. The energy differential, the gradient, between the sidereal universe and the bubbles of variant space-time had risen each time.

I stood with one hand on the attitude-control console, the other poised to steady Dole if the bosun slipped out of his seat again. I hadn't eaten in . . . days, I wasn't sure how long. I hadn't kept anything down for longer yet. Every time the *Oriflamme* switched universes, pain as dull as the back of an axe crushed through my skull and nausea tried to empty my stomach.

Dole had nothing to do unless Piet Ricimer ordered him to override the AI—which would be suicide, given the stresses wracking the *Oriflamme* now. Helping the bosun hold his station, however pointless, gave me reason to live.

Stephen Gregg stood with a hand on Lightbody's shoulder and the other on Jeude's. Stephen was smiling, in a manner of speaking. His face was as gray and lifeless as a bust chipped out of concrete, but he was standing nonetheless.

During insertions, the *Oriflamme*'s thrusters roared at very nearly their maximum output. Winger, the chief of the motor crew, bent over Guillermo's couch. He spoke about the condition of the sternmost nozzles in tones clipped just this side of panic.

A few festoons of meat cured on Respite still hung from wires stretched across the vessel's open areas. We'd been eating the "birds" in preference to stores loaded on Decades, for fear that the flesh—smoked, for the most part—would spoil. There was no assurance we'd reach another food source any time soon.

Salomon's screen was a mass of numbers, Ricimer's a tapestry of shaded colors occasionally spiking into a saturated primary. The two consoles displayed the same data in different forms, digital and analogue: craft and art side by side, and only God to know if either showed a way out of the morass of crushing energies.

The *Mizpah* in close-up filled Guillermo's screen. The gradients themselves threw our two vessels onto congruent courses: the navigational AIs both attempted with electronic desperation to find solutions that would not exceed the starships' moduli of rupture. The range of possibilities was an increasingly narrow one.

"Stand by for transit," Piet Ricimer croaked. "There will be a sequence of f-f-four insertions."

He paused, breathing hard with the exertion. Guillermo compiled the data in a packet and transferred it to the *Mizpah* by laser.

Winger swore and stumbled aft again to his station. He would have walked into the Long Tom in the center of the compartment if I hadn't tugged him into a safer trajectory.

The *Mizpah*'s hull was zebra-striped. The reglazing done on Respite had flaked from the old ship's hull along the lines of maximum stress, leaving streaks of creamy original hull material alternated with broader patches of the black, basalt-based sealant. Leakage of air from the *Mizpah* must be even worse than it was for us, and it was very serious for us.

More pain would come. More pain than anything human could survive and remain human. *Oh God our help in ages past, our hope in years to come . . .*

"We need to get into suits," Salomon said. He lay at the side console like a cadaver on a slab. "They're in suits already on the *Mizpah*." The navigator's eyes were on the screen before him, but he didn't appear to be strong enough to touch the keypad at his fingertips.

A sailor sobbed uncontrollably in his hammock. Stephen's eyes turned toward the sound, only his eyes.

"This sequence will commence in one minute forty seconds," Ricimer said. His words clacked as if spoken by a wood-jawed marionette. "The gradients have ceased to rise. We're. We're . . ."

Stephen didn't turn his head to look at Ricimer, but he said, "You're supposed to tell us that we've seen worse, and we'll come through this too, Piet."

Watching Stephen was like watching a corpse speak.

Ricimer coughed. After a moment, I realized that he was laughing. "If we do come through this, Stephen," Ricimer said, "be assured that I will say that the next time."

"Prepare for t-trans—" Salomon said. He couldn't get the final word out before the fact made it redundant.

My head split in bright skyrockets curving to either side. Guillermo's screen, fed by the external optics, became hash as the *Oriflamme* entered a region alien to the very concept of light as the sidereal universe knew it.

Back a heartbeat later, another blow crushing me into a boneless jelly which throbbed with pain. The gasp that started with the initial insertion was tightening my throat and ribs, or I might have tried to scream.

Half the *Mizpah* hung on the right-hand display. A streak of centimeter-thick black ceramic ringed the stern. Where the bow should have been, I saw only a mass as confused as gravel pouring from a hopper.

Transit. There was a God and He hated mankind with a fury as dense as the heart of a Black Hole. The mills of His wrath ground Jeremy Moore like—

Back, only gravel on Guillermo's screen, dancing with light, and then *nothing* because the *Oriflamme* had cycled into another bubble universe and I wished that I'd been aboard the *Mizpah* because—

The *Oriflamme* crashed into the sidereal universe again and stayed there while I swayed at Dole's station and Stephen Gregg held Jeude's slumping form against the back of his seat. There must have been a fourth insertion and return, but I hadn't felt it. Perhaps I'd blacked out, but I was still standing . . .

"The gradients have dropped to levels normal for intrasystem transits," Ricimer said. He sounded as though he had just been awakened from centuries of sleep. The muscles operating his vocal cords were stiff. "We'll make a further series of seven insertions, and I believe we'll find Landolph's landfall of Pesaltra at the end of them. Gentlemen, we have transited the Breach."

I tried to cheer. I could only manage a gabbling sound. Dole put up a hand to steady me; we clutched one another for a moment.

"We made it," Jeude whispered.

Guillermo's display showed a blank starscape, and there was no pulsing highlight on the main screen to indicate the *Mizpah*.

PESALTRA

Day 94

The ramp lowered with squealing hesitation, further sign that the stress of transiting the Breach had warped the *Oriflamme*'s sturdy hull. Air with the consistency of hot gelatin surged into the hold. I was the only man in the front rank who wasn't wearing body armor. Sweat slicked my palm on the grip of the cutting bar.

"Welcome to the asshole of the universe," muttered a spacer. He spoke for all of us in the assault party.

"Well," said Piet Ricimer as he raised the visor of his helmet. "At least nobody's shooting at us."

Steam still rose from the mudflat that served Pesaltra as a landing field. Nine of the local humans were picking their way toward the *Oriflamme*. Molts—several score and perhaps a hundred of them—stood near the low buildings and the boats drawn up on the shore of the surrounding lagoons. The aliens formed small groups which stared at but didn't approach the vessel.

There were no weapons in sight among the Feds or their slaves.

Finger-length creatures with many legs and no obvious eyes feasted on a blob of protoplasm at the foot of the ramp. They must have risen from burrows deep in the mud, or the thruster exhaust would have broiled them. The creatures were the only example of local animal life that I could see.

"No shooting unless I do," Stephen Gregg said, "and *don't* expect that. Let's go."

He cradled his flashgun and strode forward. Stephen's boots squelched to the ankles when he stepped off the end of the ramp. I sank almost as deep, even though I didn't have the weight of armor and equipment Stephen carried.

The front rank, ten abreast, stamped and sloshed forward. The second rank spread out behind us. The locals wore thigh-length waders of waterproofed fabric. In this heat and saturated humidity, their garments must have been nearly as uncomfortable as our back-and-breast armor.

There were mountains in the western distance, but the Pesaltran terrain here and for kilometers in every direction was of shallow lagoons and mud banks with ribbons and spikes of vegetation. None of the plants were as much as a meter high; many of them sprawled like brush strokes of bright green across the mud.

A bubble burst flatulently in the middle of the nearest channel. I guessed it was the result of bacterial decay, not a larger life-form.

I felt silly holding a cutting bar as a threat against people so obviously crushed by life as the Fed personnel here. How the rest of the assault party must feel with their guns, armor, and bandoliers of ammunition!

Though Stephen Gregg wouldn't care . . . and maybe not the others either. Overwhelming force meant you were ready to overwhelm your enemy. What could possibly be embarrassing about that?

"Ah, sirs?" said one of the locals, a white-haired man with a false eye. "You'd be from the Superintendency of the Outer Ways, I guess?"

He stared at the *Oriflamme* and its heavily-armed crew as if we were monsters belched forth from the quavering earth.

It wasn't practical to carry building materials between stars. The colony's structures were nickel steel processed from local asteroids or concrete fixed with shell lime. Three large barracks housed the Molt labor force; a fourth similar building was subdivided internally for the human staff.

A middle-aged woman stood on the porch with the aid of crutches and leg braces. The door to the room behind her was open. Its furnishings were shoddy extrusions of light metal, neither attractive nor comfortable-looking.

The same could be said for the woman, I thought with a sigh.

Sheet-metal sheds held tools and equipment in obvious disorder. A windowless concrete building looked like a blockhouse, but the sliding door was open, showing the interior to be empty except for a few shimmering bales.

Garbage, including Molt and human excrement, stank in the lagoon at the back of the barracks. The hulls of at least two crashed spaceships and other larger junk had been dragged to the opposite side of the landing site.

Ricimer halted us with a wave of his hand and took another step to make his primacy clear. "I'm Captain Ricimer of the Free State of Venus," he said to the one-eyed man. "We've come through the Breach. We'll expect the full cooperation of everyone here. If we get it, then there'll be no difficulties for yourselves."

The Fed official looked puzzled. The men approaching with him had halted a few paces behind. "No, really," the man said. "I'm Assistant Treasurer Taenia; I'm in charge here. If anyone is. Who are you?"

Dole stepped forward. The butt of his rifle prodded Taenia hard in the stomach. "When Captain Ricimer's present," he said loudly, "nobody else is in charge—and especially not some dog of a Fed! Take your hats off, you lot!"

Only two of the locals wore headgear, a cloth cap on a red-haired man and another fellow with a checked bandanna tied over his scalp. Dole pointed his rifle in the face of the latter. The Fed snatched off the bandanna. He was bald as an egg.

Dole shifted his aim. "No, put that up!" Piet Ricimer snapped, but the second Fed was removing his cap and a third man knelt in the mud with a look of terror on his face.

Taenia straightened up slowly. He blinked, though the lid covering his false eye closed only halfway. "I don't . . ." he said. "I don't . . ."

Ricimer stepped up to the man and took his right hand. "You won't be hurt so long as you and your fellows cooperate fully with us. Are you willing to do that?"

"We'll do anything you say," Taenia said. "Anything at all, of course we will, your excellency!"

Ricimer looked over his shoulder. "Mister Moore," he said.

"When we lift off, I'll want to put a transponder in orbit to inform Captains Winter and Blakey of our course should they pass this way. Can you build such a device with what we have on hand?"

I nodded, flushing with silent pleasure. Ricimer had noticed my facility with electronics and was willing to use it. "Yes, yes, of course," I said. "But I suspect I can use local hardware."

Ricimer smiled at me. "I can understand a man being interested in a challenge," he said. "Though I'm surprised at a man who doesn't find this voyage enough of a challenge already."

Ricimer's face set again; grim, though not angry. There was no headquarters building, so he indicated the human barracks with a nod of his carbine's muzzle. "Let's proceed to the shelter," he said.

"But why in God's name would you want to come *here*!" blurted the Fed wringing his bandanna between his hands.

"That," remarked Stephen Gregg as we twenty Venerians swept past the flabbergasted locals, "is a fair question."

"Well, we don't have anybody to communicate *with*," Schatz, Pesaltra's radio operator, said defensively to me. "They were supposed to send a new set from Osomi with the last ferry, but they must've forgot it. Besides, the ferry comes every six months or a year, and nobody else comes at all. It's not like we've got a lot of landing traffic to control."

Across the double-sized room that served the station's administrative needs, Salomon rose from a desk covered with unfiled invoices. "What do you *mean* you don't have any charts?" he snarled at Taenia. "You've got to have some charts!"

The floor was covered with tracked-in mud so thick that a half-liter liquor bottle was almost submerged in a corner. Paper and general trash were mixed with the dirt, creating a surface similar to wattle-and-daub. I'd dropped a spring fastener when I pulled the back from the nonfunctioning radio. I'd searched the floor vainly for almost a minute, before I realized that the task was vain as well as pointless.

"We're not going anywhere," Taenia said in near echo of Schatz's words a moment before. "What do we need navigational data for?"

"If we were going anyplace," Schatz added with a variation of meaning, "they wouldn't have stuck us on Pesaltra."

"We'll search the files," Piet Ricimer said calmly. He gestured his navigator to the chair at the desk and dragged another over to the opposite side. "Sometimes a routing slip will give coordinates."

"But not *values,*" Salomon moaned. He organized a thatch of hard copy to begin checking nonetheless.

"But how do you communicate across the planet?" I said to Schatz. The sealed board was still warm when I pulled it from the radio, though the Fed claimed it had failed three months before. Schatz hadn't bothered to unplug the set—which had a dead short in its microcircuitry.

Venerians stood in the shade of buildings, staring at a landscape that seemed only marginally more interesting than hard vacuum. The low haze the sun burned off the water blurred the horizon. The glimpse I'd gotten through the *Oriflamme*'s optics during the landing approach convinced me that better viewing conditions wouldn't mean a better view.

"There's nobody . . ." Schatz said. "I mean, there's just us here and the collecting boats, and nobody goes out in the boats but the bugs. So we don't need a radio, I'm telling you."

Three Venerians had boarded one of the light-alloy boats on the lagoon. It was a broad-beamed craft, blunt-ended and about four meters long. A pole rather than oars or a motor propelled the craft. From the raucous struggle the men were having, the water was less than knee-deep.

"Bugs?" I repeated in puzzlement.

"He means the Molts, Jeremy," Stephen Gregg said dryly. "It's a term many of the folk on outworld stations use, so that they can pretend they're better than somebody. Which these scuts obviously are not."

I unhooked my cutting bar. The tool's length made it clumsy for delicate work, but it would open the module.

"There's no call to be insulting," Schatz muttered. He was afraid to look at Stephen. His hand rose reflexively to shield his mouth halfway through the comment.

"Is he helping you, Jeremy?" Stephen asked.

I looked up from the incipient operation with a scowl. "What?" I snapped, then remembered I owed Stephen . . . Well, owed him the chance to be whatever it was I'd become. "Sorry, Stephen. No, he's useless to me."

"Get a shovel and a broom," Stephen ordered Schatz crisply, "and get to work. I expect to see the entire floor of this room in one standard hour."

I triggered my bar and let it settle after the start-up torque. I held the electronics module against the blade with my left hand, rotating the work piece while holding the cutting bar steady.

"But there's bugs—" Schatz said, raising his voice over the keen of the bar's ceramic teeth.

Stephen's face went as blank as a concrete wall. His eyes seemed to sink a little deeper into his skull, and his lips parted minusculely.

Schatz backed a step, backed another—hit the doorjamb, and ducked out into the open air.

I shut off the power switch for safety's sake before I hung the bar back on my belt. I parted the sawn casing with a quick twist.

"Useless," Stephen said in a hoarse voice. "But he *will* clean this room."

"And so's this," I said. "Useless, I mean—fried like an egg."

I dropped the pieces of module back onto the radio's chassis and shook my head. "I'm going out to check the wrecked ships," I said. "Could be something there will help. I doubt this lot is any better at salvage than at anything else."

Stephen's eyes focused again. "Yes, well," he said. "I'll come with you, Jeremy."

He gestured me out the door ahead of him. Schatz stood halfway along the porch, holding a mattock in one hand and arguing with the woman on crutches.

"To keep from doing something you'll regret, you mean," I said over my shoulder to Stephen.

"Not quite," Stephen said. "But I don't want to do something that Piet would regret."

The high scream of my cutting bar ground down into a moan as the battery reached the limits of its charge. I backed away from the twisted nickel-steel pedestal I'd sawn most of the way through. Federation salvagers at the time of the crash had removed the navigational AI from the pedestal's top.

I gasped for breath. My gray tunic and the thighs of my trousers were black with sweat.

Stephen looked down into the freighter's cockpit. The wreck lay on its side, so a rope ladder now dangled from the hatch in the ceiling. The force of the crash had twisted the hatchway into a lozenge shape.

"I repeat," Stephen said. "I could take a shift."

"I know what I'm doing," I snarled, "and you bloody well wouldn't! I haven't put in this much work to have somebody saw through the middle of the board."

I was trembling with fatigue and the heat. I hadn't recovered from the strains my mind had transmitted to my body during the weeks of brutal transit. Maybe I'd never recover. Maybe—

"Come on up and have some water," Stephen said mildly, reaching a hand out to me. "The distillation plant here works, at least."

Stephen's touch settled my flailing mind so that I could climb the ladder. As Stephen lifted, the muscles of my right forearm twisted in a cramp and pulled my hand into a hook. I flopped onto the crumpled hull, cursing under my breath in frustration.

Salomon trudged toward us across the seared mud of the landing field, holding a curved plate of shimmering gray. The object was as large as his chest. Hydraulic fluid from the infrequent ships had painted swatches of ground with a hard iridescence.

Stephen's flashgun was equipped with a folding solar panel to recharge the weapon when time permitted. He had spread the panel as a parasol while I worked in the cabin below.

Stephen had brought a 10-liter waist jug from the *Oriflamme* when I got my tool kit. The curved glass container was cast with a carrying handle and four broad loops for harness attachment. I lifted it with care, letting my left hand support most of the weight.

Stephen took my cutting bar and opened the battery compartment in its grip. He swapped the discharged battery for the one in the flashgun's butt. The charging mechanism whined like a peevish mosquito when the flashgun's prongs made contact.

The jug's contents were flavored with lemon juice, enough to cut the deadness of distilled water. Micropores in the glass lifted water by osmosis to the outer surface, cooling the remaining contents by convection. The drink was startlingly refreshing.

"Thought I'd join you," Salomon said. He lifted the object he held, the headshield of some large creature, to Stephen to free his hands.

The Federation freighter was a flimsy construction built mostly of light alloys on this side of the Mirror. It had touched down too hard, ramming a thruster nozzle deep into the mud as the motors were shutting down. The final pulse of plasma blew the vessel into a cartwheel and ripped its belly open.

The crew may have survived with no worse than bruises, but the ship itself was a total loss. The hull had crumpled into a useful series of steps, though you had to watch the places where metal bent beyond its strength had ripped jaggedly.

"There's no information at all," the navigator complained bitterly. I offered him the heavy jug, but he waved it away. "We'll have to coast the gradients, looking for the next landfall, and there's no guarantee that'll have navigational control either. Osomi sounds like another cesspool, sure, maybe a bit shallower."

"If Landolph could do it, Piet can," Stephen said calmly. He tapped the plate of chitin. "What's this?"

"The values aren't even the same on this side of the Mirror!" Salomon said. "The people here live like animals, drinking piss they brew for a couple months after the ferry from Osomi drops off supplies. Then they run out of dried fruit and don't even have that!"

"It's from a local animal, not a Molt, I suppose?" I asked. By helping Stephen break the navigator's mind out of its tail-chasing cycle of frustration, I found I was calming myself. I smiled internally.

Salomon shrugged. "It's a sea scorpion," he said. "They live in the lagoons. The head armor fluoresces, so it's used for jewelry this side of the Mirror. That's the only reason anybody lives here— if you call this living!"

Stephen looked at his arm through the chitin. The shield was nearly transparent, but sunlight gave it a rich luster that was more than a color.

"Pretty," I said. I liked it. "How big is the whole animal?"

"Three, four meters," Salomon said. He reached for the jug, then grimaced and withdrew his hand. "I've got a bottle back on the ship," he said. "I was going to celebrate when we transited the Breach, but when the time came, I didn't feel much like it."

He glared at the surrounding terrain. "We've come through the Breach, we've lost most of the squadron—"

His head snapped toward Stephen and me. "You know that the *Kinsolving* and *Mizpah* aren't going to show up, don't you?" Salomon demanded.

"Yes," said Stephen evenly. "But we're going to leave a transponder here anyway."

Salomon shuddered. "And what we've got for it is a mud bank—and a bale of crab shells that wouldn't be worth a three-day voyage, much less what *we've* gone through!"

"They'll be trading material," Stephen said. "We'll need food as we go on, and sticking a gun in somebody's face isn't always the best way to bargain."

I grinned at him. "Though it works," I said.

"It's not a magic wand, Jeremy," Stephen said. "It depends on the people at either end of the gun, you see."

Stephen's voice dropped and he rasped the last few syllables quietly. I felt sobered by the results of my quip. I put my hand over his and drew the gunman back to the present.

"You know," Stephen resumed with a dreamy softness, "Pesaltra is actually a pretty place in its way. Water and land stitched together by the plants, and the mist to soften the lines."

Salomon knew Stephen well enough to fear him in a killing mood. He nodded with approval that we'd stepped back from an unexpected precipice. "They catch the scorpions in traps, Taenia says," he said. "It's dangerous. Every year they lose a few boats and half a dozen Molts running the trapline."

"We're not doing it for the shell," Stephen said. He wasn't angry, any more than a storm is angry, but his tone brooked as little argument as a thunderbolt does. "We're not doing it for the wealth, either, though we'll have that by and by."

In a way, it wasn't Stephen Gregg speaking, but rather Piet Ricimer wearing Stephen's hollow soul. There was fiery power in the words, but they were spoken by someone who knew he had nothing of his own except the Hell of his dreams. "We're doing it for all men, on Venus and Earth and the Rabbits, bringing them a universe they can *be* men in!"

Stephen's big frame shuddered. After a moment, in a changed voice, he added, "Not that we'll live to see it. But we'll have the wealth."

I flexed my hands and found they worked again, though my right arm had twinges. "I'm going to finish down below," I said.

"Let me take a look," Stephen said. He furled the charging panel and collapsed its support wand so that he could bring the flashgun with him into the wreck.

Inside the cockpit, we stood on what had been the outer bulkhead. The freighter was a single-hulled vessel, shoddier by far than the hulk we'd abandoned on Mocha. The navigational pedestal stuck out horizontally from the nearly vertical deck. I'd sawn more than three-quarters of the way around its base.

"You know," said Salomon reflectively from the hatchway, "we might do best to wait for the Osomi ferry to come for the shell. They'll have at least local charts. Though it may be ten months, from what Taenia says, and I'm not sure I'd last four."

"We'll last if we have to," Stephen said calmly. His fingertips explored the pedestal and ran the edges of my careful cut. He unslung the flashgun and handed it to me. "Though I doubt that's what Piet has in mind."

"Give me a little room, Jeremy," he said as he gripped the flanges which once held the AI module. Even as Stephen spoke, the huge muscles in his back rippled. The unsawn portion of the base sheared with a sharp crack.

Stephen had twisted the pedestal rather than simply levering it down with his weight. He set it before me, fractured end forward. "Satisfactory?"

I wiggled the data module which the Feds hadn't bothered to remove after the crash. They couldn't lift it from the top because the pedestal was warped. The bayonet contacts were corroded, but they released on the third tug and the unit slid out.

"Lord Jesus Christ," Salomon said in startled hope. "Do you suppose . . ."

I touched the probes of my testing device to the bank's contacts. Numbers scrolled across the miniature screen. The data couldn't be decoded without a proper AI, and they wouldn't have meant anything to me anyway; but the data were present.

"I think," I said as I folded the probes back into my testing device, "that we've got a course for Osomi."

TEMPLETON

Day 101

The planet's visible hemisphere was half water, half land covered by green vegetation. A single large moon peeked from beyond the daylit side of the disk.

"That's not Osomi," Salomon said. He'd pitched his voice to suggest he was willing to be proven wrong.

"No, that's Templeton," Piet Ricimer agreed with obvious relish. "Mister Moore? Is Jeremy here forward?"

"Shutting off power in forty-three seconds," Guillermo warned over the tannoys.

"I'm here," I said as I tried to get to the bow.

The *Oriflamme* was at action stations, so we were all wearing hard suits. That made me clumsier than usual after transit. Besides, each crewman took up significantly more room than he would under normal conditions.

I knocked the attitude controls with my right knee, then my hip bumped Stampfer at the sights mounted on the turntable with the Long Tom. I was in a hurry because for the next few seconds, the thrusters were braking the *Oriflamme* into orbit. I knew I wouldn't be able to control my movements at all without that semblance of gravity.

The only thing we'd known about the destination in the salvaged module was that we were headed for a Federation planet—*if* scrambled data hadn't sent the *Oriflamme* to the back of beyond. Our five plasma cannon were manned, but the gunports were still sealed. We'd have to lock our helmet visors if the guns were run out.

I caught the side of the general commander's couch just as the thrusters shut off. An attitude control fired briefly. My legs started to drift out from under me. I managed to clamp them hard against the deck. "Yes, sir?" I said.

Piet Ricimer turned from adjustments he was making in the external optics. The lower quadrant of the main screen held an expanded view of a settlement of some size on the margins of a lake. It was after nightfall on the ground, but a program in the display turned the faint glimmers which charge-coupled devices drew from the scene into a full schematic.

"You did better than you knew, Jeremy," Ricimer said. "Templeton is the center for the entire district. This may be exactly where we needed to be."

I smiled mechanically. I was glad the general commander was pleased, but it didn't seem to me that arriving at a Federation center was good luck.

"How do you know—" Salomon said from the side couch. He remembered where he was and smoothed the stressed brittleness of his voice. He resumed, "Captain, how do you know it's—any particular place? Our charts don't . . ."

Templeton's day side flared under the *Oriflamme*'s orbit, though the screen insert continued to show the settlement. The Feds had graded a peninsula for use as a spaceport. Forty-odd ships stood on the lakeshore where they could draw reaction mass directly. The number surprised me, but not all the vessels were necessarily starships.

"I talked to the personnel on Pesaltra," Ricimer explained. "They weren't a prepossessing lot or they wouldn't have been shipped to such a dead end. But they'd all been at other ports in the past, and they were glad to have somebody to talk to. They weren't navigators, but they knew other things. Taenia was a paymaster on Templeton until his accounts came up short last year."

Ricimer manipulated his display into a plot of the planet/satellite system. "The district superintendent is on the moon," he continued, nodding to include me. "Rabbits have attacked the Templeton settlement several times, so there's a strong garrison—but the garrison has mutinied twice as well. The superintendent feels safer on the moon, where he's got plasma cannon to protect him. The chips are warehoused there too until the arrival of the ship detailed to carry them to Umber."

Men in the forward section craned their necks to hear Ricimer's explanation. He noticed them and switched on the vessel's public address system.

"What about the garrison?" Stephen Gregg asked. His voice was strong and his face had some color. The prospect of action had brought Stephen through in better condition than I'd seen him after most transit sequences.

"We need air and reaction mass," Ricimer said through the shivering echo of the tannoys. "Our hull was seriously weakened when we crossed the Breach, and the rate of loss will be a problem until we're able to effect dockyard repairs."

I frowned. *Surely we wouldn't see a dockyard until we'd returned to Venus? And that meant a second passage through the Breach . . .*

Salomon noticed my expression. He lifted his eyebrows in the equivalent of a shrug—his shoulders were hidden beneath the rigid ceramic of his suit.

"We have to land somewhere soon to restock," Ricimer continued, "but we need to gather intelligence and navigational data also. Templeton is the place to do that. We'll go in quietly, get what we need, and leave at once. We won't have to fight."

"I've plotted a descent to the port," Salomon said. "Will you want to go in on the next orbit or wait, sir?"

Piet Ricimer's smile swept the nearest of the men who followed him. "I think we'll go in now, Mister Salomon," he said. "I think now."

We'd been down for twenty minutes.

Trusted sailors watched panoramas of the *Oriflamme*'s surroundings on the upper half of the three bow displays. On the lower half, Guillermo planned liftoff curves while Salomon ran transit solutions. We didn't have another plotted destination, but if necessary the officers could coast the energy gradients between bubble universes until a radical change in values indicated the presence of a star in the sidereal universe.

Piet Ricimer was considering other ships in port with us. I

watched him expand images one at a time, letting the AI program fill in details which were a few pixels of real data. Some of the ships were tugs and orbital ferries, obvious even to my untrained eyes. None of them seemed to be warships.

Our hull pinged as it continued to cool from the friction of its descent. I unlatched the back-and-breast armor, the last remaining portion of my hard suit. Stripping the ceramic armor had been a ten-minute job for fingers unfamiliar with the process. It would take me longer yet to put the suit back on if I had to.

Most of us had doffed only the arm and leg pieces. To me armor was crushing, psychologically crushing. I felt as though I was drowning every time I put the suit on.

Stephen grinned harshly at me. "You'll wish you hadn't done that if we lift under fire in the next ten seconds," he observed.

Piet Ricimer turned his head. "If that happens," he said, "*I'll* certainly regret it, Stephen. There don't appear to be plasma cannon protecting the port, but there are at least a dozen multitube lasers on the settlement's perimeter. I suspect they'd do nearly as well against us as they would a Rabbit assault."

"There's a car coming!" called Fahey, watching the sector northward, toward the port buildings. "Straight to us!"

Ricimer stood up. All eyes were on him.

"I think we'll admit them by the cockpit hatch," he said calmly, "since the assault squad's drawn up in the hold. Remember, if we're to succeed, we'll do it without trouble."

Stephen took a cutting bar from the forward arms locker. "Without noise, at any rate," he said.

The forward hatch was a chambered airlock; Ricimer cycled the inner and outer valves together. I felt heat from the plasma-cooked ground radiate through the opening in pulses.

Piet stepped to one side of the hatchway with Guillermo beside him. I hesitated a moment, but Stephen guided me to stand across from the general commander. My body was a screen of sorts for Stephen's threatening bulk.

The Federation car pulled up before the cockpit stairs. The lightly built vehicle had four open seats and rode on flotation tires; the port area flooded on a regular basis.

The driver was a Molt wearing a red sash. Two more Molts were in back, and a small man with a high forehead and a gray pencil mustache rode in the forward passenger seat.

The human got out and straightened his white uniform as if he didn't see us watching him from the ship. A Molt handed him a briefcase. He tucked the case under his arm, took three brisk strides to the steps, and climbed them with a *click-whisk* sound of his soles on the nonskid surface. The driver remained in the vehicle, but the other Molts followed. The aliens walked with a sway because of their cross-jointed limbs.

The little man glared from me to Ricimer. Close up, the Fed's uniform was threadbare, and the one and a half blue bars on the collar implied no high rank. "I'm Collector Heimond," he said, "and I want to know why you landed without authorization! I'm the officer in charge, you know!"

"If you're in charge," Ricimer snapped in return, "then maybe you can tell me why our request for landing instructions was ignored for two orbits! We need to replenish our air tanks after a run from Riel, and I wasn't about to wait till tomorrow noon when some of you dirtside clowns decided to switch on your radios!"

"Oh!" said Heimond. "Ah. From Riel . . ."

We hadn't—of course—signaled the port control before braking in, but Federation standards were such that nobody on the ground was going to be sure of that. Even if the radio watch happened to be awake, the set might have failed—again—for lack of proper care.

Heimond's eyes took in the 17-cm plasma cannon which dominated the *Oriflamme*'s forward section. "Oh!" he said in a brighter tone. He glared at Ricimer, sure this time he held the high ground. "You're the escort, then? Where have you been? She's already left a week ago without you!"

"*She* left?" Ricimer said. He sounded puzzled but nonchalant. Maybe he was.

"*Our Lady of Montreal!*" Heimond snapped. "The treasure ship! You're the *Parliament*, aren't you? You should have been here weeks ago!"

"Yes, that's right, but we were delayed," Ricimer agreed easily. "We'll just catch up with her. You'll have her course plan on file at port control?"

"Yes, yes," Heimond said, "but I don't see why nobody's able to do anything when it's supposed to be—"

One of the Molts flanking Heimond said, "This ship isn't made of metal."

The cockpit stairs were four steps high. I jumped straight to the ground. Though the surface was originally gravel, repeated baths in plasma had pulverized it and glazed the silica. I felt the residual heat from our landing through my bootsoles, but the breeze off the lake was refreshingly cool.

I got into the vehicle and thumbed the power switch of my cutting bar. "Please wait here quietly," I said to the driver.

"Or you will kill me?" the driver asked in a rusty voice. His chitin had a dark, almost purple cast in the light above the hatchway. The Molts who'd gone aboard with Heimond were lighter and tinged with olive, complexions rather like Guillermo's.

"I think my friend aiming a laser from the hatchway will kill you," I said. I didn't bother to look at Stephen. I *knew* what he would be doing. "I'm here to warn you so that he doesn't have to do that."

"All right," the Molt said. His belly segments began to rub together in alternate pairs. The sound had three distinct tones, all of them gratingly unpleasant.

"What are you doing?" I snapped, raising the cutting bar.

"I am laughing, master," the Molt said. "Collector Heimond will not be pleased."

My subconscious had been aware of the light of a new star. Distance-muffled thrusters began to whisper from the night sky. Another ship was on its landing approach.

The *Oriflamme*'s main ramp shrieked and jolted its way open. Stephen swung from the hatch with Piet behind him. Following them, protesting desperately, was Collector Heimond in the arms of Jeude and Lightbody.

Stephen gestured to the Molt and ordered, "Get aboard the ship for now. We'll release you when we lift."

"Yes, master," the Molt said. He got out of the vehicle and climbed the stairs. Dole watched from the hatchway with a rifle. The Molt was slowed by spasms of grating laughter.

Ricimer slid into the driver's seat. "We're going to the port office," he said to me. He had to shout to be heard over the roar of the starship landing. "Heimond's going to find the *Montreal*'s course for us. She took on board six months' accumulation of chips, most of them purpose-built in the factory still working on Vaughan."

The four others, one of them Stephen in his half armor,

clambered into the back. It was really a storage compartment with a pair of jump seats. The car sagged till the frame and axles touched.

"Let me bring my kit and I can get more than the one course," I said. I lifted my leg out of the car. "I'll dump all the core memory!"

Stephen's big arm blocked me like an I-beam. "I have your kit, Jeremy," he shouted as Ricimer put the overloaded vehicle in gear. Behind us, the *Oriflamme*'s crewmen were dragging hoses to the lake to top off our reaction mass.

The incoming ship set down at a slip on the other side of the peninsula, much closer to the buildings on the mainland. Silence crashed over the night, followed by a final burp of plasma.

"Tell us about the *Montreal*, Heimond," Ricimer ordered. He drove at the speed of a man jogging. Faster would have been brutal punishment. The surface of the quay was rough, and the weight the car carried had collapsed the springs.

"Last year President Pleyal ordered that only armed ships could carry more than a hundred kilos of chips," the Fed official said. "We'd never worried about that before. It makes routing much more difficult, you see—and then an escort vessel besides!"

He sounded shell-shocked. It didn't seem to occur to him that present events proved that Pleyal had been right to worry about treasure shipments even among the Back Worlds.

Some of the ships we passed had exterior lights on. Occasional human sailors watched our car out of boredom. Most of the crews were Molts who continued shambling along at whatever task had been set them. If I hadn't heard the driver laugh, I might have thought the aliens were unemotional automata.

"How many guns does the *Montreal* carry?" Ricimer asked calmly. His eyes flicked in short arcs that covered everything to our front; the men behind him would be watching the rear. Despite the rough road, Piet's hands made only minuscule corrections on the steering yoke.

"How would I know?" Heimond snapped. "It's none of my business, and it's a damned waste of capacity if you ask me!"

He drew in a breath that ended with a sob. I looked back at Heimond as we passed a ship whose thruster nozzles were being replaced under a bank of floodlights. The port official's cheeks glistened with tears. He was looking straight ahead, but I didn't think he was really seeing anything.

"*Our Lady of Montreal* is rated at five hundred tonnes," Heimond said softly. "I think she has about a dozen guns. I don't think they're very big, but I don't know for sure. I don't know even if you kill me!"

A wave of dry heat washed us. The ship that landed after ours had baked the ground we were crossing. She was a largish vessel, several hundred tonnes. Her exterior lights were on, but she hadn't opened her hatches yet.

"We're not going to kill anybody, Mister Heimond," Piet Ricimer said. "You're going to get us the information we need, and then we'll leave peacefully. Don't worry at all."

Port control was a one-story, five-by-twenty-meter building of rough-cast concrete at the head of the peninsula. A man sat on a corner of the roof with his legs crossed and his back to an antenna tower, playing an ocarina. He ignored us as we pulled up in front.

"Here," Stephen said in a husky voice, handing my electronics kit forward. Stephen's face was still, his soul withdrawn behind walls of preparation that armored him from humanity. He took Heimond's collar in his free hand.

The control building, a line of repair shops, and a three-story barracks that stank of Molt excrement separated the peninsula from the rest of Templeton City, though there was no fenced reservation. The dives fronting the port were brilliantly illuminated.

I could see at least a dozen lighted compounds on the hills overlooking the main part of the city. That's where the wealthy would live.

Woven-wire screens instead of glass covered the front windows of the port control building. Lights were on above the doorway and within. A Molt stood behind the counter that ran the length of the anteroom.

Stephen pushed Heimond ahead of him into the building; the rest of us followed as we could. I was clumsy. My kit and the cutting bar in my other hand split my mind with competing reflexes.

"Don't do anything, Pierrot!" Heimond called desperately to the Molt. "Don't!"

Only the Molt's eyes had moved since the car pulled up anyway. The creature looked as placid as a tree.

"The data bank is in back?" Ricimer said, striding toward the gate in the counter.

A truck returning from the city with a leave party drove past port control. The diesel engine was unmuffled. The sudden *Blat!Blat!Blat!* as the vehicle came around the corner of the building spun us all.

Heimond cried out in fear. A drunken Fed flung a bottle. It bounced off the screen and shattered in front of the building. Lightbody raised his carbine to his shoulder.

"No!" Ricimer shouted. Stephen lifted the carbine's muzzle toward the ceiling.

"Let's get into the back," Stephen ordered. He gestured the Molt to join us.

Heimond found the switch for the lights in the rear of the building. The data bank stood in the center of a bullpen. There were six screen-and-keyboard positions on either side, with long benches for Molt clerks. The human staff had three separate desks and a private office in the back, but I didn't care about those.

I sat on a bench and opened my kit beside me. The bank had both plug and induction ports. I preferred the hard connection. The plug was one of the three varieties standard before the Collapse.

Jeude bent to look into my kit. "What—" he said.

"No!" ordered Piet, placing his left hand under the young sailor's chin and lifting him away from me. I appreciated the thought, but Jeude wouldn't have bothered me. I lose all track of my surroundings when I'm working on something complex.

I attached the partner to the data port and matched parameters. The five-by-five-by-ten-centimeter box hummed as it started to copy all the information within the Fed data bank.

The job would have taken a man months or years. I'd designed the partner to emulate the internal data transfer operations of whatever unit I attached it to. It was an extremely simple piece of hardware—but as with the larva of an insect, that simplicity made it wonderfully efficient at its single task of swallowing.

The partner couldn't do anything with data except absorb it. Sorting the glut of information would be an enormous job, but one the *Oriflamme*'s AI could handle with the same ease that it processed transit calculations.

Plasma motors coughed, shaking the ground and casting rainbow flickers through the bullpen's grimy side windows. Heimond sat at a desk with his head in his hands. Stephen and Piet interrogated him, pulling out responses with the relentless efficiency of a mill grinding corn. I couldn't hear either side of the conversation.

The partner clucked. A pathway query replaced the activity graph on the little screen. So far as I could tell, neither supplemental cache was terribly important. One held the operating system, while the other was probably either backup files or mere ash and trash. I cued the second option, though maybe we ought to—

I rose, drawing the others' eyes. The thruster snarled again, raggedly. Some ship was testing its propulsion system.

"I think I've got everything important," I said. I'd been hunched over the partner for long enough to become stiff, though it hadn't seemed more than a minute or two. "This is—"

A Fed in a blue uniform with a gold fourragère from the left shoulder strode through the door from the anteroom. "Hey!" he shouted. Jeude shot him in the chest, knocking him back against the jamb.

There were half a dozen other Feds in the anteroom. They wore flat caps with PARLIAMENT in gold letters above the brim. One of them grabbed at his holstered pistol. Stephen shot him with the flashgun from less than five meters away.

The laser sent dazzling reflections from the room's brightwork as it heated the air into a thunderclap. The Fed's chest exploded in a gout of steam and blood, knocking down the men to either side of him.

I keyed shutdown instructions into the partner's miniature pad. If I disconnected the unit mechanically first, the surge might cost us the data we'd risked our lives for.

I glanced over my shoulder. Jeude fired the other barrel of his shotgun at a woman running for the outside door. He missed low and chewed a palm-sized hole in the counter instead. Ricimer hit the running woman. She slammed full tilt against the window screen and bounced back onto the floor. A pair of Fed sailors made it out the door despite Lightbody's shot and two more rounds from the commander's carbine.

The partner chirped to me. I jerked it free and slammed the lid of the kit down over it. "I'm coming!" I shouted, because by now I was the last Venerian left in the building.

Heimond was hiding under his desk and the Molt clerk stood

like a grotesque statue in one corner. The first Fed victim sat upright in the doorway. His legs were splayed and his face wore a dazed expression. Jeude's buckshot had hit him squarely at the top of the breastbone, but he was still—for the moment—alive.

Which is all any of us can say, I thought as I jumped his legs. My boots skidded on the remains of the man Stephen's bolt had eviscerated. I caught the counter with my free hand and swung myself through the gate. I'd left my cutting bar behind. There was more shooting outside the building.

The room stank worse than a slaughterhouse. Ozone, powder smoke, and cooked meat added their distinctive smells to the pong of fresh-ripped human guts. The woman Ricimer shot was huddled beside the outer door. She'd smeared a trail of blood across the floor to where she lay.

Heimond's car pulled a hard turn as I ran out the front door. Ricimer was driving again. Stephen stood on the passenger seat. He'd slung the flashgun and instead held Piet's repeating carbine.

The man on the roof now lay full length on his back. I don't know if he'd been killed or had passed out from drink.

I jumped into the back with Lightbody and Jeude. The car hadn't slowed, and I'm not sure anybody realized I wasn't already on board. Jeude fired again. The flash from the shotgun's muzzle was red and bottle-shaped.

"Shut that popgun down until there's a target in range, you whore's turd!" Stephen snarled in a voice with more hatred than you'd find in a regiment of Inquisitors.

Stephen swayed as the car jounced. I grabbed his belt so that if he fell he wouldn't be thrown out. He poised the butt of the carbine to crush my skull, but his conscious mind overrode reflex at the last moment.

I sucked breaths through my mouth. I was dizzy, and nothing around me seemed real.

The car had a quartet of headlights above the hood, but only the pair in the center worked. They threw a long shadow past a bareheaded man in blue running down the track a hundred meters ahead of us.

Stephen fired once. The man pitched forward with one arm flung out and the other covering his eyes. We jolted past the body at the car's best speed, 50 kph or so. There was no sign of the other Feds who'd escaped from port control with that one.

"Stephen, sit down!" Piet Ricimer ordered. Gregg ignored him.

The boarding ramps of the ship that landed after ours were down, and the vessel was lighted like a Christmas star. Molts and humans in blue uniforms stood on the ramps and at a distance from the vessel: the ground directly underneath would still be at close to 100°C from the ship's exhaust.

A man on the vessel's forward ramp pointed toward our swaying vehicle and shouted orders through a bullhorn. "The fucking *Parliament!*" Jeude snarled. "The real fucking escort, and why she couldn't have showed up tomor—"

A uniformed woman ran into our path, waving her arms over her head. Piet swerved violently. Stephen fired, a quick stab of yellow flame. The Fed toppled under our right front wheel.

We lurched but the wheels were mounted on half-axles and had a wide track. Stephen flailed, completely off balance. The car didn't go over. By bracing my leg against the side of the compartment I kept Stephen from falling out as well.

Lightbody cried, "Lord God of hosts!" as he fired toward the *Parliament,* and Jeude's shotgun boomed again despite the fact that I was sprawled half across him as I clung desperately to Stephen. The car's frame swayed upward as the heavy front wheel slammed down. The rear wheel hit the woman's body, and Stephen shot the blue-sashed Molt who tried to leap over the hood at Ricimer.

A ship down the line lit her thrusters. A bubble of rainbow fire lifted and cooled to a ghostly skeleton of itself before vanishing entirely. The *Parliament* was a dedicated warship. I'd seen three rectangular gunports gape open in succession in my last glimpse of her, but now we were past.

Stephen got his legs straight and sat down. His carbine's bolt was open. He opened a pocket of Piet's bandolier and took out a handful of cartridges. The *Parliament's* siren howled and a bell on the Molt barracks clanged a twice-a-second tocsin.

A ship tested her thrusters again. This time the vessel lifted slightly from her berth and settled again ten meters out in the roadway. She was the *Oriflamme.* The 20-cm hoses with which she'd been drawing reaction mass dangled from her open holds.

Glowing exhaust backlit us. I stared stupidly at the spray of dust ahead of our right front wheel. "There's a truck following—" Jeude shouted.

Maybe he meant to say more, but three violent hammer blows

shook our vehicle. Stephen pitched forward, the severed tags of his flashgun's sling flapping. A palm-sized asterisk of lead smeared his backplate; the ceramic was cracked in a pattern of radial lines. My face stung, my hands bled where bits of bullet jacket had splashed them, and I still didn't realize the Feds were shooting at us.

I twisted to look back the way we'd come. A slope-fronted truck bounced down the road in a huge plume of dust. It was moving twice as fast as we could. Red flame winked from the framework on top of the vehicle. The Feds had welded dozens of rifle barrels together like an array of organ pipes.

Bits of rubber flew off our left rear tire, though it didn't go flat. Because of Rabbit attacks, the garrison of Templeton had a mobile reaction force. It was too mobile for us.

Stephen leaned across the back of his seat and rested his left elbow on my shoulder. It was like having a building fall on me. I had just enough awareness of what was happening to close my eyes. The flashgun drove its dazzling light through the tight-clenched eyelids, shocking the retinas into multiple afterimages when I looked up again.

The laser mechanism keened as it cooled beside my ear. Stephen tilted the weapon and slapped a fresh battery into the butt compartment. The flashgun wasn't going to do any good; even I could see that.

The truck was armored. The metal shutter over the windshield glowed white, but the driver behind it was unharmed. Flashgun bolts delivered enormous amounts of energy, but a monopulse laser has virtually no penetration. Even a hit on the driver's periscope might be useless, since properly designed optics would shatter instead of transmitting a dangerous amount of energy.

"Bail out!" I shouted. I squirmed to the side of the compartment. Jeude wasn't moving; Lightbody thumbed a cartridge into the breech of his rifle.

"Jump!" I shouted, but as I poised Lightbody fired again and Stephen leaned forward against the butt of his squat laser.

A bullet hit our right rear wheel and this time the tire did blow. The car fishtailed, flinging me against the seats. The sky ripped in a star-hot flare. Concussion pushed the car's suspension down to the stops, then lifted us off the ground when the pressure wave passed.

The *Oriflamme* had fired one of her 15-cm broadside guns. The truck was a geyser of flame. Fuel, ammunition, and the metal armor burned when the slug of ions hit the vehicle.

Ricimer crossed his wrists on the yoke, countersteering to bring us straight. The wheel rim dragged a trail of sparks across the gravel.

"Salomon shouldn't have risked running out—" Ricimer cried.

Another of the *Oriflamme*'s cannon recoiled into its gunport behind a raging hell of stripped atomic nuclei.

The facade of the Molt barracks caved in. The interior of the three-story building erupted into flame as everything that could burn ignited simultaneously.

Wreckage spewed outward like the evanescent fabric of a bubble popping. Shattered concrete and viscous flame wrapped port control and the maintenance shop on the barracks' other side.

Ricimer stood on the car's brakes. Because of the blown tire we spun 180° and nearly hopped broadside into the lip of the *Oriflamme*'s stern ramp. Stephen rose in his seat and poised like a statue aiming the flashgun. I tried to raise Jeude one-handed—I'd clung to my electronics kit since the moment I slammed it over the data we'd come to get. Lightbody bent to help me.

Stephen fired. A secondary explosion erupted with red flame.

Piet grabbed Jeude's legs. He and I and Lightbody lifted Jeude out. The smooth surface of Jeude's body armor slipped out of my hand, but Lightbody's arms were spread beneath the wounded man's torso.

Beneath the torso of the dead man. A bullet had struck Jeude under the right eye socket and exited through the back of his neck. Strands of his blond hair were plastered to the wounds, but his heart no longer pumped blood.

A thumping shock wave followed several seconds after Stephen fired. He'd managed to do effective damage with the flashgun instead of leaving the fight to the thunderous clamor of plasma cannon.

We ran up the ramp, carrying Jeude among us. The air shimmered from the hop that had lifted the *Oriflamme* into firing position. Salomon poured full power through the thrusters. Heat battered me from all sides. I would have screamed but my lips and eyelids were squeezed tight against the ions that flayed them like an acid bath.

I fell down, feeling the shock as the third of our big guns fired. Acceleration squeezed me to the deck as the jets hammered at maximum output. I was blind and suffocating and at last I did scream but the fire didn't scour my lungs.

I thrashed upright. The crewman spraying me with a hose shut it off when he saw I was choking for breath. I was wrapped in a soaking blanket. So were the others who'd staggered aboard with me.

Dole knelt and held Piet's hands with a look of fear for his commander on his face. Stephen checked the bore of his flashgun and Lightbody was trying to unlatch his body armor. The fifth blanket must cover Jeude, because it didn't move.

Our ramp was still rising. Through the crack I could see waves on the lake fifty meters below, quivering in the icteric light of a laser aimed at us from the Templeton defenses. Something hit the hull with a sound more like a scream than a crash. Our last broadside gun slammed as the ramp closed against its jamb.

Piet got to his feet. Dole tried to hold him. Piet pushed past and staggered toward the companionway to the *Oriflamme*'s working deck. His face was fiery red under the lights of the hold. Stephen walked behind Piet like a giant shadow.

I stood up. Pain stabbed from my knuckles when I tried to push off with my free hand. My face was swelling, so that I seemed to be looking through tubes of flesh. Soon I wouldn't be able to see at all.

I stumbled to the companionway, swinging my arm to clear startled crewmen from my path.

I had to get to the bridge. *My* partner held the course we would follow until we won free or died.

INTERSTELLAR SPACE

Day 102

"Sir, *please* leave the dressing in place," begged Rakoscy, the ship's surgeon. "I can't answer for what will happen to your eyes if you don't keep them covered for the next twenty-four hours at least."

"It's under control, Piet," Stephen said, taking Piet's hands in his own. He pulled them down from Piet's eye bandage with as much gentle force as was necessary. "There's nothing to see anyway. Salomon'll tell us when the data's been analyzed."

Dressings muffled both men's hands into mittens. The visored helmet Stephen wore because of the flashgun's glare had protected his face.

Lightbody moaned in a hammock against the cross-bulkhead, drugged comatose but not at peace. He'd come through the night better than the rest of us physically, but I was worried about his state of mind.

I hadn't thought of Lightbody and Jeude as being close friends. I don't suppose they were friends in the usual sense, a deeply religious man and an irreverent fellow who talked of little but the women and brawls he'd been involved with between voyages. But they'd been together for many years and much danger.

I could see again. Shots had shrunk the tissues of my face

enough for me to look out of my eye sockets, and Rakoscy had left openings in the swaths of medicated dressings that covered the skin exposed to the plasma exhaust. I felt as though a crew had been pounding on my body with mauls, but Rakoscy assured me there'd be no permanent injury.

It was good to worry about Lightbody's state of mind, because then I didn't have to consider my own.

Salomon turned his couch and said, "Sir, Guillermo and I have a course to propose."

Rakoscy led Piet by the hands to the center console. I suppose it would have made better sense for Salomon to use Piet's couch under these circumstances. The same AI drove all three consoles, but the main screen was capable of more discriminating display because it had four times the area of the others.

Salomon hadn't suggested he take over, much less make the decision without asking. Logic wasn't the governing factor here. It rarely is in human affairs.

Stephen moved nearer to me and hesitated. I'm not sure whether or not he knew I could see.

"That seemed close," I said quietly. "Or is it something I'll get used to after the fiftieth time?"

Stephen gave a minuscule smile. "No," he said, "that was pretty near-run, all right. If it hadn't been for Salomon taking the initiative, it would've been a lot too close."

He coughed. "You're all right?"

"Yeah," I said. "I don't have much color vision at the moment, that's all."

He looked hard at me, but he didn't push for answers to the real questions. *Why had God saved me and taken Jeude beside me? If there was a God.*

Piet settled onto his couch and sighed audibly. Fans, thrusters, and the noise of the ship herself working filled the *Oriflamme* with a constant rumble. With time, that drifted below the consciousness.

There were no human sounds aboard now. The crew in the forward section had fallen tensely and completely silent.

Piet switched on the public address system by feel. "Go ahead," he said.

"Trehinga is about six days transit from Templeton," Salomon said. "Seven, according to Federation charts, but I'm sure we can do it in six."

The navigator had shown himself to be able and quick-thinking. As Stephen said, he'd saved us on Templeton. Salomon ran out the big guns against orders when he heard the landed *Parliament* identify herself as a presidential vessel—a dedicated warship—over the radio. The Feds we met were a party sent by the *Parliament*'s captain to port control when nobody replied to the radio.

Despite his proven ability, Salomon licked his lips from nervousness as he proposed a solution based on information that the general commander couldn't see. Alone of us aboard the *Oriflamme*, Salomon was afraid that his responsibilities were beyond him.

"It has dock facilities," he continued. "We've lost two attitude jets, and the upper stern quarter of the hull was crazed by laser fire as we escaped. But there shouldn't be much traffic."

"Trehinga grows grain for the region," Guillermo put in from the opposite console. "There are no pre-Collapse vestiges, and therefore little traffic or defenses."

Salomon nodded, gaining animation as he spoke. "The port's supposed to have a company of human soldiers," he said, "but Mister Gregg says he doubts that." He looked up at Stephen.

Piet nodded agreement. "A few dozen militia, counting Molts with spears and cutting bars," he said. "Unless the Back Worlds are much better staffed than the Reaches in general."

"Of course, Templeton was no joke," Stephen said. The lack of concern in his voice wasn't as reassuring as it might have been if a less fatalistic man were speaking.

"Templeton was a treasure port," Piet said briskly. "Go on, Mister Salomon. What about the risk of pursuit from Templeton?"

"The bloody *Parliament* isn't pursuing anybody till they build her a new bow, sir," Stampfer said. "Since me and the boys on Gun Three blew the old one fucking off as we lifted."

The satisfaction in the master gunner's voice was as obvious as it was deserved.

Piet nodded again in approval. "And there wasn't anything docked on Templeton when we arrived that would be a threat," he said. "Nevertheless, we'll need to take some precautions if we're going to do extensive repairs."

Piet turned his head—"looked," but of course he couldn't see—from Salomon to Guillermo and back. "Are we ready to go, then?"

he asked. The infectious enthusiasm of his tone helped me forget how much I hurt. Piet had been burned at least as badly.

"The first sequence of the course is loaded," Guillermo said. Salomon glanced up in surprise, but the Molt knew Piet Ricimer.

"Then let's go," Piet said. "Gentlemen, prepare for transit!"

TREHINGA

Day 109

The cutter touched bow-high. Piet cut the motor and we skipped forward on momentum, crashing down on the skids about the boat's own length ahead of its thruster's final pulse. It was a jolting landing compared to Piet's usual, but I understood why he wouldn't take chances with plasma for a while.

Lightbody and Kiley had undogged the dorsal hatch when we dropped below three thousand meters. They and the four other sailors packed beneath the hatch slid it open, but Stephen was first out of the vessel and I managed not to be far behind. I was more mobile than the men in half armor and bandoliers of ammunition.

A featherboat with room for twenty men and a small plasma cannon would have been better for this assault, but that option had gone missing with the *Kinsolving*. Twelve of us were squeezed into the cutter. Four spacers would cover the pair of grain freighters on the landing field, while we others "captured" the settlement of New Troy: a two-story Commandatura with bay windows and a copper-sheathed front door, and fifty squalid commercial and residential buildings.

The landing field was adobe clay, flat and featureless. Dust puffed under my boots. The sun was near zenith, but the air felt pleasantly cool.

The *Oriflamme* roared down from orbit above us. Salomon would be on the ground in three minutes, but it would be at least five minutes more before anyone left the ship safely except wearing a full hard suit. The flagship could dominate the community by her presence and the threat of her heavy guns, but a quick assault required a lighter vessel.

The Commandatura was fifty meters from where we'd landed. People watched us from its windows and the doorways of other buildings.

According to the database I'd copied on Templeton, Trehinga was fairly well populated, but most of that population lived on latifundia placed along the great river systems of the north continent. New Troy was the planet's administrative capital and starport, but it was in no sense a cultural center.

Still, some of the people watching were women.

A pair of men in white tunics, one of them wearing a saucer hat with gold braid on the brim, walked out of the Commandatura. Stephen and I started toward them. Dole was beside me, carrying a rifle as well as a cutting bar, and the other sailors fanned out to the sides. Piet ran to join us, last out of the cutter because he'd been piloting it.

The Fed officials paused at the base of the three steps to the Commandatura's front door. They stared at us, all armed and most of us wearing body armor.

"Raiders!" the older man shouted.

Stephen pointed his flashgun.

"Don't anyone shoot!" Piet cried as he aimed his own carbine toward the Feds. "And you, wait where you are!"

"Raiders!" the Fed repeated. He turned and took the four steps in two strides. His companion raised his hands and closed his eyes. The onlookers of a moment before vanished, though eyes still peeked from the corners of windows.

I ran toward the Commandatura, holding my cutting bar in both hands to keep it from flailing. The others followed me as quickly as their equipment allowed.

"You won't be harmed!" Piet said.

The Fed official grabbed the long vertical handhold and started to pull the door open. Piet fired. His bullet whacked the door near the transom, jolting the panel out of the Fed's hand. The Fed ran into the edge of the door instead of slipping between it and the jamb. The impact knocked him back down the steps, scattering blood from a pressure cut over his right eye.

I ran past the man. He moaned and squeezed his forehead with his palms stacked one on the other. I tugged at the door with my left hand. Piet's bullet had split the wood of the heavy panel, wedging it tighter against the jamb. Stephen jerked the door open but I eeled into the reception area ahead of him.

There were offices to right and left behind latticework partitions. Either half held a dozen Molts and a few humans among the counters and desks. A man in his fifties had crawled under his desk. The opening faced the front door, so he was perfectly visible.

Two rifles lay on the wooden floor of the anteroom. Men in white Federation military tunics stood in the office to the left, with the lattice between them and their weapons. Their hands were raised, but from the looks on their faces they expected to be killed anyway.

I started up the central staircase to the second story, taking the steps two at a time. Behind me Piet ordered, "Get them all in the left room. Loomis and Baer to guard them!"

Heavier boots crashed on the stairs behind me. Stephen breathed in gasps. Dole whuffed, "Christ's *blood*!" as his boot slipped. Armor and equipment slammed down loudly on the hardwood treads. *I could be shot from behind by accident,* I realized, but the thought didn't touch the part of me that was in control.

As fast as we'd arrived, the personnel of New Troy had found time to respond. The folk downstairs reacted by hiding and dissociating themselves from their weapons, but that might not be everyone's choice.

To the right of the stair head was an openwork gate of cast bronze. The workmanship was excellent. The pattern was based on pentacles, like that of the Molts' own architecture. The gate was locked. Somebody inside had tried to draw a curtain for visual privacy, but he/she had torn the fabric in panic. The room beyond had thick rugs and a good deal of plush furniture, though I couldn't see any people in the glance I spared it.

The door to the left was thick, ajar, and carried the legend in letters cut from copper sheet-stock GUARDS OF THE REPUBLIC. I rammed it fully open with my shoulder.

The interior was dim because the space was partitioned into smaller rectangular chambers. A man stood at the end of the central hallway, trying to step into his trousers one-handed. He saw me and straightened, aiming his rifle.

I lunged toward him. He flung away the rifle and screamed, "No, don't shoot!" He crossed his arms in front of his face.

"Watch the other doors!" Stephen ordered behind me, the fat muzzle of his flashgun pointed at the Fed soldier. The partition walls didn't reach the high ceiling. Dole, Lightbody, and I kicked open doors.

Two men came out with their hands raised. One of them snarled, "Traitor!" He must have thought we were mutineers from a Back Worlds garrison. Dole knocked the man down with his rifle butt, then gave him a boot in the stomach.

There were ten cubicles in all, each with a bunk, a table, and a freestanding wardrobe. Others had been occupied recently, but the three men who'd surrendered were the only ones present now.

"Maher, take them down with the rest," said Piet. He'd waited at the stair head until he was sure there'd been no trouble in the guards' dormitory.

"I'll—" Stephen said.

Piet turned and smashed the gate open with the heel of his right boot. He strode into the room beyond with his carbine slanted across his body—ready for trouble but not expecting it. I was the last man to follow him.

Four Molt servants huddled at the rear corner of the room, out of sight from the doorway. French windows opened onto a balcony overlooking the walled garden behind the Commandatura. A narrow staircase led from the balcony to the garden.

A Molt was pruning Terran roses, apparently oblivious of the commotion going on around him. There was a shed against the back wall, and a small but ornate residential outbuilding at the end of the pathway through the center of the garden. The outbuilding's door closed as I watched.

"Where's the commander?" Piet said, pointing his left hand imperiously at the cowering Molts. Piet held his carbine muzzle-up in his right hand; the butt rested in the crook of his elbow.

One of the Molts gestured toward a heap of large, embroidered pillows along the sidewall. "Masters," the Molt said, "none of us know where Secretary Duquesne might be."

Dole groped in the pile of pillows, found something, and jerked a fat man in loose trousers and an open-throated shirt into view. "Wakey, wakey," the bosun said, laying the muzzle of his rifle on the bridge of Secretary Duquesne's nose.

"Please!" Duquesne squealed. "Please!"

"Let him up," Piet said, obviously relaxing. "I don't think he'll be any difficulty."

"Piet, there's somebody in the building behind this," I said, nodding toward the French windows.

The *Oriflamme* touched down. While the thrusters' roar reflected from the ground, the doubled noise rattling the window casements made further speech impossible, Piet gestured first to me, then to Lightbody, and last toward the outside stairway. Stephen nodded the ceramic barrel of his flashgun and stepped to a window from which he could command the whole back of the garden.

I'd reached the midway landing when Salomon shut off the *Oriflamme*'s motors. The sudden silence released a vise the noise had clamped around my chest. I wasn't aware of the pressure until it stopped.

"Sir?" said Lightbody. I glanced over my shoulder. "Will there be treasure in there?" He nodded down the path ahead of us.

"In a manner of speaking," I said, because I had a notion as to just who might be housed in the cottage. "Not that'll make us rich, though."

I wondered if Piet had the same suspicions I did; and if so, what he'd meant by sending me to investigate.

The gardener continued spraying his roses with a can designed for a Molt's three-fingered hands. He crooned in a grating voice as we passed, but it wasn't us he was speaking to.

The *Oriflamme*'s ramp began to lower with a loud squeal. The ship was going to need a lot of work. I didn't believe she could ever be reconditioned to the point she could pass the Breach a second time.

The curtain on the window to the left of the door fluttered as we approached. I paused to hang the cutting bar from my belt . . . though of course, she could be guarded, probably *would* be guarded. The place had blue trim and white stucco walls, though both were flaking to a degree.

"Open in the name of the Free State of Venus," I said, pitching my voice to command rather than threaten.

Nothing happened. I tried the latch. It was locked.

"This is absurd," I muttered.

Lightbody stuck the muzzle of his shotgun into the six-pane window casement and swept the barrel sideways, shattering half the glass and snatching the curtain aside. There were two women within. I'd expected only one, and these were both tough-looking. They wore the white jackets of the Federation military.

"Open the door, then!" Lightbody said. His face grew red and his voice sank into a growl. "You whores!"

"We're not armed!" snarled the 40-year-old woman with light brown hair. The name tag over her left pocket read VANTINE. She might have been handsome at one time, but not since the scar drew up the left side of her mouth.

Lightbody kicked the center panel out of the bottom of the doorframe. He was furious. "Easy . . ." I warned, but his bootheel smashed the central crossbrace from the door, flinging jagged fragments into the room. Vantine jumped back from the latch when she realized that we were in no mood to play games.

"Lightbody!" I said, but I might as well have been in Betaport for the effect I had. He half turned, then lunged against the remnants of the door. The back of his armored shoulder hit the top panel. It splintered also as Lightbody spun into the small living room. The furniture—a couch, two chairs, and an end table—was of local wood with lacework coverings. The oval area rug was patterned in small pentagons of gray, pink, and white thread.

The two women backed toward the couch, keeping their hands plainly in sight.

I stepped between them and Lightbody. "Where's the person who lives here?" I asked. The cottage had two more rooms, a kitchen and—through a bead curtain—a bedroom.

"We live here," said the second woman, whose black hair was shot with gray. Her name tag read PATTEN and her face was less attractive than Dole's. "We're not billeted with the other soldiers because we're women, can't you see?"

"You're whores!" Lightbody shouted. "Soldiers of Hell, most like! Prancing about as if you was men!"

He swung his shotgun toward Patten. I grabbed it with both hands. He was bigger than me and stronger for his size. He forced me back.

I snatched the cutting bar from my belt. "Lightbody!" I shouted.

I thumbed on the power and triggered the bar. "If you won't obey me, then by God you'll obey this!"

I don't think it was the threat that brought Lightbody to his senses so much as having my face pressed into his above the crossways shotgun. He slumped back.

"Sorry, sir," he muttered. He turned his face aside and wiped it with his callused right palm. "It's against God and nature to see women pretending to be men."

I let go of him. I was trembling. The bar shook as much with my finger off the trigger as it had the moment before. "We're not here for that," I said. My voice shivered too.

I turned. The women watched with a mixture of anger and loathing. Patten wore a crucifix around her neck. I jerked it with my left hand, breaking the thin silver chain. "We're not mutineers," I said, "we're from Venus. And we're Christians."

I'd spent more time in the Governor's Palace than I had in a church, and I'd only been to the palace twice.

I slapped the crucifix into Patten's hand. "Keep your idols out of sight, or I won't answer for the consequences."

The bead curtain rattled as I walked into the bedroom. The chance that either Patten or Vantine was the secretary's mistress was less than that of Piet swearing allegiance to President Pleyal.

I opened the large freestanding wardrobe beside the door. The clothes within were gauzy and many-layered, decorated with lace and ribbons. Shades of blue predominated. The bottom of the wardrobe held shoes in ranks; no one was hiding there.

The wood above me thumped. I backed a step and looked up. A flaring cornice ornamented the wardrobe's top. The hollow behind the cornice was about twenty centimeters deep. A blond woman, gagged and with furious blue eyes, peered over the edge at me.

I tossed my cutting bar onto the bed to free both hands. "Lightbody, watch that pair of yours!" I warned.

I got extra height by hopping onto the wardrobe's bottom shelf, scattering delicate shoes. The woman squirmed completely over the cornice, trusting me to take her. Her weight was no problem.

Her wrists were tied, first behind her back, then to her ankles. Patten and Vantine had been busy in the minutes they'd had since we landed. They'd used filmy stockings for the bonds; not Terran silk, but something at least as strong. I ripped my bar's ceramic teeth across the fabric with the power off.

The captive pulled the gag out of her mouth when I'd freed her hands. She was in her mid-twenties and far, far too supple and beautiful to be wasted on a pig like Secretary Duquesne . . .

Well, that was true of a lot of women, and no few men.

"Thank you, sir," she said as she got to her feet in a motion as smooth as that of smoke rising. "My name is Alicia."

She walked into the living room without looking back at me. I suppose she was used to having men follow her without question.

Alicia's dress was pale orange. The soft fabric fit loosely and had no particular shape of its own. She moved like a puff of flame.

Lightbody faced the two soldiers, holding his shotgun at low port. His eyelids flicked in surprise when he saw Alicia. Patten and Vantine glared at her with molten hatred. My thumb slid the bar's power switch forward.

"Sergeant Vantine here . . ." Alicia said coldly. She stepped to the soldier's side without coming between Vantine and Lightbody's shotgun, then reached under the tail of Vantine's tunic.

" . . . has a gun," Alicia continued. Vantine moved minusculely. I reached over Alicia's shoulder and touched the tip of the bar to Vantine's right ear.

Alicia pulled a small revolver from Vantine's waistband. "I know about it," she went on in the same distant voice, "because the sergeant—"

Her face suddenly broke into planes like those of an ice carving, inhuman and terrible though still beautiful. Alicia backhanded Vantine across the jaw with the butt of the revolver. Vantine staggered.

Alicia hit her again, this time on the forehead. Vantine's head jerked back. There was an oval red splotch above her left eye.

I closed my left hand over Alicia's on the gun. She relaxed with a great shudder, leaning against me and closing her eyes. "Because the sergeant put it *into* me," Alicia said softly. "And she told me to be a good girl and stay quiet like Ducky wanted, or she'd shovel hot coals there instead."

I dropped the revolver into my pocket. It was surprisingly heavy for something so small. Patten held Vantine by the shoulder and elbow, helping her stay upright. Alicia straightened and stepped to the side. She watched the proceedings regally.

"Strip," I said to the soldiers. Lightbody looked at me oddly, Patten with fear.

"Oh, don't worry about your virtue, ladies, not from me," I said. "You'll strip to make sure you've no more toys hidden. We'll tie your hands with our belts, and then Lightbody'll march you to the Molt pen where you and your friends will stay until we lift."

My voice caught repeatedly on images my mind threw up; Vantine and Patten, and the bound girl between them. Secretary Duquesne had acted quickly to keep his mistress safe when raiders landed. Safe in his terms, safe from other *men*.

The Fed soldiers only stared at me. I touched Vantine's tunic with the tip of my cutting bar, then triggered it. White fluff spun up from the whine.

"Don't worry about your virtue, ladies," I repeated. My voice quivered like the cutting bar's blade. "But your lives, now, that could very easily be a different matter."

TREHINGA

Day 111

The Federation freighter C^*, renamed the *Iola* after Salomon's mother and for the next few days a Venerian warship, lifted thunderously from New Troy. The freshly-cut gunports in her hold gaped like tooth cavities when the rest of the bare metal hull reflected sunlight. The *Iola* was 15° nose-down; she rotated slowly around her vertical axis because the thrusters weren't aligned squarely.

"I thought you said automated ships were safer on liftoff than landing?" I said to Piet, moderating my voice as the *Iola* climbed high enough to muffle her exhaust roar.

Piet quirked a smile at me. "The concept of automation isn't a problem," he said. "Just the cheap execution. Besides, it's safe enough."

"Or you'd be taking her up yourself," Stephen said in a tone of mild reproof. Alicia heard enough in the gunman's voice to look sharply at him. She'd known a lot of men in her 25 standard years, but none like Piet or Stephen Gregg.

She'd known men like me. I didn't doubt that.

The *Iola* had risen to a dot of brilliant light in the stratosphere. The sound of saws and the rock crusher became loudly audible again, now that the thrusters were gone.

The Federation laser battery that hit us as we escaped from Templeton had crazed several hull laminations as well as taking out two attitude jets. The shock of repeated transits flaked the damaged sheathing off in a five-meter gouge.

The crew was sandblasting the fractured edges just as a surgeon would debride a wound in flesh before closing it. When they finished the prep, they'd flux the boundaries and layer on ceramic again. I suspected Piet would oversee that final process himself. Hawtry was right when he claimed Piet's father was a craftsman rather than a gentleman.

Another team removed attitude jets from the second Federation freighter, the *Penobscot*. We carried spare jets in the *Oriflamme*, but all the original nozzles were badly worn from the long voyage. Jets from the ships and stores here would replace our spares.

Dole had muttered to me that he'd rather use burnt-out ceramic than trust Fed metalwork, but Piet seemed to think the tungsten nozzles would be adequate. Sailors as a class were conservative: "unfamiliar" was too often a synonym for "lethal." The general commander of an expedition through the Breach had to be able to assess options on the basis of fact, though, not tradition.

Alicia raised a slim hand toward where the *Iola* had vanished. "But *where* are you sending the ship?" she asked.

It didn't seem to occur to her that anybody might think she was asking out of more than curiosity. Stephen and I exchanged glances: mine concerned, his clearly amused.

Piet, with an innocence as complete as I'm sure Alicia's was, answered, "We're just putting her in orbit with two guns, Mistress Leeman. The *Oriflamme* can't lift while we're working on her hull, and there's the risk that a Federation warship will arrive while we're disabled."

As he spoke, Piet began walking down Water Street. New Troy stretched along a broad estuary. It had a surfaced road along the water and a parallel road separating the buildings from the field where starships landed. A dozen barges were moored to quays behind the grain elevators.

"Warships here?" Alicia said. "Don't worry about that. I haven't seen one in . . ." She shivered. "Nine months, I've been here. Earth months. I was born in Montreal."

There was more to the last statement than information. I wasn't sure whether she meant it as a challenge or an admission, though.

"Still, it's better not to run a risk," Piet said mildly. "We'll reship the guns to the *Oriflamme* in orbit, I think. Since, as Jeremy points out, the C^* is worse maintained than I'd thought from viewing her."

He tipped me a nod.

"Dole takes a crew up in the cutter to replace Salomon tomorrow?" Stephen asked.

Piet shook his head. "Guillermo tomorrow, Dole the following day. Stampfer asked for a watch, but I don't trust his shiphandling, even with automated systems."

He glanced at me. "I wouldn't put it so bluntly to Stampfer, you know, Jeremy," he said.

I shrugged. "He's a gunner," I said. "One man can't do everything."

Though maybe Piet could. Being around him gave you the feeling that he walked on water when nobody was watching.

The pen for Molts being transshipped was adjacent to the Commandatura. There'd been a dozen aliens behind the strands of electrified razor ribbon when we landed. Neither the C^* nor the *Penobscot* was a dedicated slaver, but both vessels carried a handful of Molts as part of their general cargo.

We'd turned the Molts loose. Half of them still wandered about New Troy, looking bewildered and clustering when we distributed rations from the Fed warehouse. Secretary Duquesne, his seven soldiers, and three of the officials who'd been cheeky enough to sound dangerous had replaced the slaves in the pen.

For the most part, the humans—residents as well as transients from the barges and two starships—seemed willing to do business on normal terms and otherwise keep out of our way. The local Molts were no problem without human leaders. Stephen, Piet, and a sailor who'd been to the Reaches with them had separately warned me that Molts *would* fight for human masters, even masters who treated them as badly as the Feds generally did. It was a matter of clan identification among the aliens.

Duquesne trembled with anger as he watched the four of us saunter by the pen. He touched the razor ribbon, forgetting that the metal was charged. A blue spark popped and threw him back. Patten and a male soldier heard the secretary bellow and ran to help.

"Run toward the wire," I ordered Alicia in a low voice.

"Ducky!" she cried.

I let her go two steps and grabbed her roughly around the neck. "Get back here or you'll be in there with him!" I shouted as I swung her between me and Piet.

Stephen faced the pen and raised the flashgun's butt toward— not quite to—his shoulder in warning. Duquesne and his henchmen scurried out of sight within the wooden shed meant to shelter slaves.

We walked on. "That was a good thought, Jeremy," Piet said.

I shrugged. "Maybe it'll help," I said. I didn't suggest we hang Duquesne and the two women who'd been so enthusiastic to carry out his orders. Piet wouldn't go along with the idea, and I've got better things to do than waste my breath.

We passed one of the hotels/boardinghouses for human transients. Men watched from chairs on the lower-level stoop. Stephen eyed them, shifting slightly the way he carried the flashgun. The captain of the *Penobscot* banged his chair's front legs back down on the deck and threw us a salute.

Piet had addressed the population of New Troy the night we arrived, promising that we would deal fairly with them as individuals, paying for whatever merchandise or services we required. Our quarrel was with President Pleyal and his attempt to dictate to all mankind.

When Piet was done, Stephen added a few words: if there was trouble, the colony would pay for it. If one of our men was killed, there would be no colony when we left. The next visitors would find the bones of the present inhabitants in the ashes of their buildings.

There was a line of men—our men—reaching out the door of the next building, a brothel. There were three girls, though Dole said the fiftyish madame had turned tricks as well during the crush the night before.

The waiting spacers grew silent and looked away. Piet turned his head in the direction of the river and said to Alicia, "Do the landowners have guards on their estates, Mistress Leeman?"

Alicia sniffed. "They arm trusties to track Molts who run away," she said. "None of the landowners are going to risk their life or property to help the secretary, though."

We were past the brothel. Piet didn't approve of whoring or drunkenness, but he didn't order his crew to remain chaste and sober while on leave. A cynic would say Piet was too smart to give orders he knew would be ignored . . . but I'm not sure most of this crew would ignore an order of his, even an order that went so clearly against their view of nature.

Sunset painted clouds in the eastern sky, while veils of heat lightning shimmered behind them. We might have a storm before morning. I doubted the shed in the Molt pen was waterproof.

The combination saloon and general merchandise store next to the brothel was owned by Federation Associates—President Pleyal himself, in his private capacity. The facade sagged, and I could see through the grime of the display windows that the roof leaked badly. The store had twenty meters of frontage, but the shelves within were dingy and almost empty. A Molt clerk stared back at us, as motionless as a display mannequin.

Boards filled the lower three-quarters of the saloon's window frames, leaving only a single row of glass panes for illumination. A drunk lay in the street. Two men arguing in front of the door stepped inside when they saw who we were.

"This is why we have to bring Venus to the stars," Piet said. "New Troy, a thousand New Troys—this can't be allowed to continue as man's face to the universe."

"Commander," I said, "it's a frontier. You can't expect polish on a frontier."

Piet stood arms akimbo in the middle of the street. Tracked-on clay covered the plasticized surface. The adobe would be slick as grease in a rainstorm.

Three grain elevators marked the boundary of the human community of New Troy. Beyond were pentagonal towers the Molt labor force had built for itself. Their upper floors were served by outside staircases. Though constructed from scrap material by slaves, the towers had a neat unity that the human buildings lacked.

"Let's go back," Piet said. He turned up the broad passage beside the saloon and the nearest elevator. After a moment, he went on, "It's not a frontier, Jeremy. It's a dumping ground, a midden. Pleyal is mining the universe for his personal benefit, not mankind's."

His voice was rising. The louvered shutters of most of the windows on this side of the saloon were swung back from unglazed casements. A barge crewman at a table followed us with his eyes as we passed.

"The only kind of men who'll come to the stars to serve a tyrant are the trash, or men as grasping and shortsighted as their master is," Piet said. "The few of a better sort sink into the mire because they're almost alone. This isn't a frontier where hardship makes men hard, it's a cesspool where filth makes men filthy! And it will *not* change until the claim of Pleyal to own the universe beyond Pluto is disproved. At the point of a gun if necessary!"

The fronts of commercial buildings on the starport side duplicated those on Water Street. The saloon's facade had one fully-glazed sash window. The bartender was a Molt. A dozen men sat inside, drinking from 100-ml metal tumblers.

None of the clientele was from the *Oriflamme.* Our men had taken over a saloon at the other end of town by arrangement between Dole and local businessmen. Nobody wanted the sort of trouble that could explode when violent enemies got drunk together.

"One ship won't bring down the North American Federation," Alicia said. This evening she wore a frock of translucent layers. The undermost was patterned with Terran roses which seemed to climb through a dense fog of overlying fabric.

"Our success will bring other ships, Mistress Leeman," Piet said. "Raids on the Federation Reaches have already increased twentyfold in the two years since, since *we*—"

He gripped Stephen's right hand, though he continued to look toward Alicia on his other side.

"—came back with more microchips than had been seen on Venus since the Collapse."

"It's not just the wealth for Venus," Stephen said. "It's the wealth that doesn't go to Earth to help President Pleyal strangle everyone but Pleyal."

There was no line on the starport side of the brothel. A lone Federation spacer glanced at us from the doorway. A pink-shaded lamp inside was lighted. I stepped into a pothole that the sky's afterglow hadn't shown me.

Alicia lifted her chin in a taut nod. "So you'll replace bums with pirates? That's your plan?" She paused. "Bums and whores!"

"We'll break the present system, mistress," Piet said, "because it can't be reformed. With the help of God we'll do that. Then there'll be room for men—from Earth, from Venus, from the Moon colony and Mars, perhaps—to expand in however many ways they find. Rather than as a tyrant demands, in a fashion that will come crashing down when the tyranny does—as it must!—in a second Collapse that would be forever."

The last words were a trumpet call, not a shout. Another man would have blazed them out with anger, but Piet's transfiguring vision was a joyous thing. Though even I'd seen how harsh the execution would be.

"I went to the Reaches to trade," Stephen said in the thin, lilting voice I'd heard him use before. "I wonder what would have happened if we'd been left to trade in peace, hey?"

He laughed. Alicia shut her eyes and missed a step. She squeezed against me instinctively.

"Maybe I'd sleep at night, do you think?" Stephen went on in the same terrible voice. Piet took his friend's hand again.

The slave pen was unlighted. Figures moved around a lantern at the Water Street end. It was about time for the prisoners to get their rations.

Floodlights gleamed on the *Oriflamme*. Half a dozen crewmen continued to work on the hull. "If I thought we had time," Piet said, "I'd grind off the repairs we made on Respite and reglaze from the original. I don't think the basalt bonded well, despite the surface crazing."

"There'll be time for that after we've taken the *Montreal*," Stephen said. "Or it won't matter."

Piet gave a nonchalant shrug. "We'll take her," he said. "And return home, with the help of God."

He looked at Alicia, smiled, and bowed slightly. "I think I'll go aboard and see how the repairs are coming," he said. "Mistress Leeman, I've appreciated your company."

"I'll go along with you, Piet," Stephen said. "Maybe I'll bunk in the ship tonight."

He gave me a wan smile. The two of them walked in step toward the *Oriflamme*, though I'm sure neither was attempting to match strides. They were as different as an oyster and its shell; and as much akin.

I opened the wicket into the Commandatura garden for Alicia.

"Captain Ricimer really believes in what you're doing," she said softly. Roses perfumed the air. There were lights in the far wing of the building, but the garden seemed to be empty. "But Mister Gregg doesn't."

"I think Stephen believes the same things as Piet does," I said. "I just don't think he cares very much."

"He frightens me," she said.

Stephen would never kill anyone by accident, I thought; but Alicia understood too much for that to sound reassuring to her. "He's a good friend to Commander Ricimer," I said. "Not a very good friend to himself, though."

I paused to twist off a rose. Its deep pink glowed like a diamond's heart with the last of the sunset. I broke the thorns off sideways with the tip of my thumb, then handed the flower to Alicia.

She giggled and put the stem behind her ear. Flying creatures as big as gulls swooped and climbed over the river. Their calls were surprisingly musical.

Alicia turned at her cottage's new door—a panel of raw wood that Molt workmen had fitted the evening before. "You're a very gentlemanly pirate, aren't you?" she said. "You could easily have forced me to—whatever you chose."

I shrugged. My skin was tingling. "I respect you too much for that," I said. *I respect myself too much.* Again, though I don't lie when I can avoid it, one chooses the particular truth he speaks aloud.

"A girl doesn't always want to be respected quite so much," Alicia said. My arms were around her by the middle of the sentence, and my lips muffled the final word.

Near morning, as I was starting to dress to be gone before dawn, Alicia told me about Secretary Duquesne's personal cache of chips in a pit beneath the floor of the garden shed.

TREHINGA

Day 114

"Here's the whores you wanted, Mister Moore," Lightbody said in a tone that could have been forged on an anvil. He gestured Patten and Vantine into the walled office I'd taken for this interview. Baer stood behind the women with a cutting bar.

Because the Federation soldiers wore trousers and had hired on to fight, Lightbody called them whores, *thought* of them as whores. He treated Alicia with the deference due a lady; and she was a lady, as surely as I was a gentleman, but the twists of Lightbody's mind disturbed me at a basic level nonetheless.

The *Oriflamme* fired a matched pair of attitude jets in the field outside. The hull repairs were complete. Piet and Guillermo were doing the final workup. We'd lift by evening, so it was time for me to act.

"You can take their hands loose, Lightbody," I said. The women were filthy. Facilities in the slave pen were limited to a trough, buckets, and mud. Twice so far we'd had rain before dawn, and the yellow adobe clay was everything I'd expected it to be.

Were conditions reversed, Secretary Duquesne would have us hanged out of hand—unless he directed Patten and Vantine to torture us to death instead. I didn't think of this pair as whores. More like vicious dogs, to be trusted only in their malice.

Lightbody looked doubtful, but he opened the knots on the women's wrists with the spike of his clasp knife. He held his shotgun out to the side where the prisoners couldn't easily grab it. "You'll want us to stay in here with you then, sir?" he suggested.

I shook my head. "No," I said, "I want to have a friendly talk in private. Close the door and wait outside."

The two sailors obeyed, but I could tell they didn't think much of the idea. To reassure them, I laid my cutting bar on top of the desk I was using, with its grip ready for my hand.

I'd chosen the office of the Clerk of Customs because the room was private and it had a large window. I wanted the light behind me for this interview. The clerk—the older of the pair who'd come out to the cutter initially—had decorated the walls with wood carvings. Molt workmanship, I supposed. The pieces were intricate, but I didn't find them attractive.

The women glared at me with caged fury. Their white tunics were sallow with dried mud, and their faces weren't much cleaner.

I waited for the next pair of jets to finish their screaming test, then said, "You can sit down." I gestured to the chairs against the wall behind the women.

"What do you want from us?" Vantine demanded in a voice which broke with anger.

"Help," I said. "For which I'm willing to pay."

They were making it easy for me, though I'd have carried through in any case. I'd seen this pair in action the morning we arrived. No amount of feigned contrition now would have changed the decision I'd made.

"And if we don't agree, you're going to threaten us with that toy?" Patten said, nodding toward my cutting bar. "I ought to feed it to you!"

"No threat," I said. I picked up the bar and waited a moment. If Lightbody and Baer heard the blade whine, they'd burst in on us.

The *Oriflamme* fired two more attitude jets. I triggered the bar and shaved the corner off the desk. I laid the weapon down again.

"This is so that you won't make the mistake of attacking me," I said. "If you did, I'd—"

Another part of my mind started to fog my conscious intelligence. My voice was husky and very soft.

"—cut you into so many pieces that they'd have to fill your coffins by weight." I swallowed. "And I don't want that, I want a friendly conversation, that's all."

The part of me that hid behind the red fog, the part that had been in control at the Molt temple and was almost in control just a moment before—that part very much wanted another chance to kill.

The women had straightened as I spoke. Their faces were expressionless, and the earlier bluster was gone.

"What do you want?" Vantine repeated quietly.

"We'll be lifting for Quincy soon," I said. I was all right again, though my hands still trembled. "We're hoping to meet *Our Lady of Montreal* there." I smiled. "If not there, then we'll catch her farther on. It depends on how long she lays over on Fleur de Lys. But before we leave Trehinga, I'd like to find the treasure stored here."

The women looked at one another cautiously, then back to me. Patten massaged her right thigh through her dirty trousers.

"There's no chips, no artifacts here," Vantine said. She was more afraid of keeping silent than of speaking. "Trehinga wasn't settled before the Collapse. There's nothing but wheat."

"I can't imagine that a man like Secretary Duquesne doesn't have a private hoard," I said. "I don't know what sort of favors he's trading to the ships' captains who land here, but there'll be something. He'll be building up a store so that when he retires to Earth he has something better than a Federation pension to support him. Chips are the most likely, but maybe pre-Collapse artifacts smuggled from other planets, sure."

"We don't," Vantine said very carefully, "know anything about that." She watched me the way a rabbit watches a snake.

Attitude jets—the last pair of the morning, unless Piet saw a need to retest—fired. The sound wasn't so loud that I couldn't have talked over it, but the three-second pause was useful.

"I'd pay you each a hundred Mapleleafs if you showed me where the cache was," I said. I held up a pair of twelve-sided coins bearing President Pleyal's face toward the women.

The paymaster's safe on the opposite side of the Commandatura contained a fair amount of currency. As Piet had promised, we weren't robbing the businessfolk of Trehinga, but the Federation government was another matter.

The women stared at me. Patten began to laugh. "Are you crazy?" she said. She regained her composure. "Do you think *we're* crazy? We lead you to Duquesne's personal stash, and then you go off and leave us here? Do you have any idea what he'd do to us then?"

I shrugged. "I've got a notion, yeah," I said. "Open the door, would you please?"

Vantine obeyed. Her companion's laughter was half bravado, but Vantine was clearly terrified. She'd sensed . . . not, I think, what was about to happen, but that *something* was about to happen.

Lightbody raised his shotgun's muzzles when he saw everything was calm. "Baer," I said, "go out and gather as many of our off-duty people as you can in five minutes. Into the garden. And tell the locals to come, too. There'll be some entertainment."

"What are you doing, sir?" Lightbody said as Baer ran down the corridor shouting.

"For the moment," I said, "you and I wait here with the ladies. Then we'll go out to the garden too."

I put my hand on the cutting bar. I was shaking so badly that the blade rattled on the desk and I had to put it down. Patten was silent, and Vantine was as gray as if someone was nailing her wrists to a cross.

There were easily a hundred people in the garden when we came out—me in front, the prisoners behind, and last of all Lightbody with the shotgun. I'd had him tie Patten's right wrist to Vantine's left while we waited. They couldn't escape, but it was important that they not be seen to try. "Hey, Mister Moore!" Kiley called from the crowd. "Do they take their clothes off now?"

I waved with a grin; but the joke made me think of Jeude, and the grin congealed.

The Molt gardener stood on one leg, rasping the other one nervously against his carapace as he watched people brush his precious roses. Because of the thorns, the bushes weren't likely to be trampled; but sure, some sailor might clear more room with his cutting bar.

Funny to think of a Molt worrying about Terran roses on one of the Back Worlds. In those terms, most of life seemed pretty silly, though. I suppose that's where religion comes in, for those who can believe in a god.

I waved my bar ahead of me to make a path. A lot of those

present were locals, as I'd hoped, but they kept to the edges of
the courtyard. The central walkway and an arc facing the back of
the Commandatura were filled with Venerians. More spectators
streamed in through the wickets beside the building and the larger
gate onto Water Street.

Baer had done a good job, though I wasn't quite sure how he'd
managed it so quickly. I'd wanted a big enough gathering that word
would spread at once throughout the community, but this was
ideal.

Alicia's jalousies were lowered; she would be watching from
behind them. I'd told her she should at all costs stay hidden this
morning.

"What are we doing?" Vantine asked over the chatter of the
crowd.

"Keep moving, whore!" Lightbody snapped. I suspected he prodded Vantine with the gun as he spoke.

"None of that!" I ordered. "The ladies are helping us."

As I turned my head to speak, I saw that Piet and Stephen
had come out the back of the Commandatura. They were following us.

The storage shed was padlocked. I sheared the hasp off in twinkling sparks. A bit remained hanging from the staple. I flicked it
away with the tip of the cutting bar: the steel would be just below
red heat from friction.

Stephen reached past and slid the door open. He grinned in a
way that was becoming familiar, but he didn't ask any questions.

The shed's floor was wooden and raised a few centimeters from
the ground. Tools optimized for Molt hands, crates, a coil of
fencing, and other impedimenta were stacked around the walls,
but the two square meters in the center of the shed were clear.

There'd be a catch hidden somewhere, but I wasn't going to hunt
for it. I swept my bar in an arc through the flooring. Nails *pinged*
bitterly within the cloud of sawdust; the head of one bounced from
my shin.

I stepped forward, turned, and drew the reverse arc. The crowd
outside was pushing for a better view, but Stephen planted himself in the doorway to keep people out of my blade's way. Patten
and Vantine watched in dawning awareness.

Stringers gave. The rough circle of floor fell with a crackle under
my weight. I kicked the fragments of lumber aside.

A rectangular steel door measuring a meter by eighty centimeters was set in concrete where there should have been bare soil. I gripped my bar with both hands.

"Jeremy?" Piet Ricimer called.

I looked up. Piet handed Stephen the white silk kerchief he'd worn around his neck. "Cover Jeremy's eyes," he said.

Stephen knotted the silk behind my head. I saw through a white haze. The doorplate had no keyhole, but the hinges were external.

"We didn't—" Patten shouted at the top of her voice, but the scream of my bar cutting metal drowned her out.

A rooster tail of white sparks cascaded to either side of the bar's tip, pricking my bare hands and charring trails of smoke from the wood they landed on. A chip of steel flicked my forehead. Momentary pain, gone almost as soon as I jerked my head.

"Step back, Jeremy," Stephen ordered. His arm kept me from stumbling on the wood floor that I'd forgotten.

I was shaking with effort and my tunic was soaked. I'd been holding the cutting bar as though it supported me over a chasm. I pulled the kerchief off so that I could breathe freely, then mopped my face with it.

There were three black-edged holes in the silk. *I* wouldn't have thought of covering my eyes.

Stephen kicked the door with his bootheel, aiming for the concealed lock. The plate rang. This wasn't a real safe, just a protected hiding place. The second time Stephen stamped down, the back of the lid where I'd sheared the hinges sprang up.

The lid was more than two centimeters thick. Stephen lifted it by the edges with his fingertips. He tossed it past me into a corner of the shed.

"We didn't have anything to do with this!" Patten cried. Vantine hugged herself, shaking as if in a cold wind.

Stephen reached into the opened stash. He came up with a mesh bag of microchips in one hand and what looked like the core of a navigational AI in the other.

He walked out into the sunlight. "There's fifty kilos of chips here!" he shouted to the crowd. There were shouts of awe and surprise, some of them from the local spectators.

I came out with Stephen. "Lightbody," I called loudly, "release these women at once."

Patten tried to hit me. I stepped close and embraced her. I caught a handful of her short hair to keep her from biting my ear in the moment before I backed clear again. Lightbody still didn't understand, but Piet held both women's free elbows from behind so that they couldn't move.

I waved the hundred-Mapleleaf coins so that they caught the sunlight. Vantine was numb. Patten spat at me, but nobody at any distance could see that. Certainly not the locals at the back of the crowd.

"And here's your pay," I said, dropping both coins into Vantine's breast pocket.

There was sick horror in Vantine's eyes. I didn't much like myself, but I'd done what I'd needed to.

At least the pay was fair. The Sanhedrin had only paid thirty pieces of silver to finger a victim for crucifixion.

"Everybody's aboard, sir," Dole called over the clamor of men claiming bits of shipboard territory after days of freedom to move around. "Smetana was sleeping it off behind Gun One so I didn't see him."

Piet nodded to me. I ran two seconds of feedback through the tannoys as an attention signal, then announced, "Five minutes to liftoff."

I'd told Stephen he should take the right-hand couch since Guillermo was in the *Iola*, but he'd insisted I sit there instead. At least I could work the commo as well as the Molt could, and it wasn't as though the process of lifting to orbit required a third astrogator.

Piet's screen echoed the settings that Salomon had programmed. Salomon flipped to an alternate value, then flopped back to the original, all the time watching Piet.

"Either," Piet said with a smile. "But yes, the first, I think, given the *Iola*'s present orbit."

The *Oriflamme*'s displays were razor-sharp, though the lower third of my screen was offset a pixel from the remainder ever since we'd come through the Breach. The population of New Troy watched from buildings and the road.

I could have expanded any individual face to fill the entire screen. That probably wouldn't be a good idea.

Stephen knelt beside my couch. "Have they let Duquesne out of his cage yet?" he asked.

I shook my head. "I don't see any of that lot," I said. I slewed and expanded the slave pen in the field. The prisoners were still there behind razor ribbon. "Maybe the locals are afraid that he'll start shooting and we'll flatten the town."

"Maybe they just don't like the bastard," Stephen replied. He laced his fingers and forced them against the backs of his hands. His face was empty; that of a man you saw sprawled in a gutter. "Lightbody says the pair of women you released stole a boat and headed upriver."

He raised an eyebrow. I shrugged.

Piet leaned toward me. "We've made a preliminary examination of the database you found, Jeremy," he said.

I turned away from Stephen. "Was it valuable?" I asked. "I don't see why it was part of Duquesne's stash."

"Valuable, though perhaps not in market terms," Piet said. "It's a courier chart. It has full navigational data for the Back Worlds and the longer route to the Solar System. The value to us is . . ."

He smiled like an angel. "Perhaps our lives."

"Shall I initiate, sir?" Salomon asked sharply.

Piet's attention returned to the business of planning liftoff. "One minute!" I warned over the PA system.

I swung the magnified view on my screen sideways a touch, focusing on the woman at the wicket beside the Commandatura.

"We couldn't bring her along, you know," Stephen said in a low voice. "Anyone female."

"She didn't ask, did she?" I said. I didn't realize how angry I was until I heard my tone. I started to blank the display, then instead expanded it further. The discontinuity fell just at the point of Alicia's chin.

"It wasn't a clever plan, Stephen," I said softly. "I didn't ask her about anything. She volunteered . . . She volunteered everything that she gave me."

Stephen put his hand on my arm. "Best I get to my hammock," he said as he rose.

Salomon engaged the AI. Our roaring thrusters drew a curtain of rainbow fire across the face of a woman I would never see again.

ABOVE QUINCY

Day 127

Men in hard suits were around us in the forward hold, though our cutter's optics were so grainy they suggested rather than showed the figures. Clanks against our hull were probably restraints closing; chances were the ramp had locked shut since I didn't feel the vibration of the closing mechanism anymore.

"All right, you lot," Lightbody ordered as he lifted himself from the pilot's couch. "Open her up! Ah—"

He remembered I was alone in the back of the cutter, "Ah—sir!"

Baer rose from the attitude controls. I'd already freed the undogging wheel by bracing my boots against thwarts and slamming a spoke with the shoulder of my hard suit. I spun the wheel fully open, then let Baer help me slide the hatch back over the dorsal hull.

The two sailors Piet gave me to crew the cutter were solid men, either of them capable of piloting the vessel alone in a pinch. Lightbody wasn't used to thinking of a landing party as two sailors and a gentleman, though.

The crew of the *Oriflamme* was at action stations. I'd been sent down to the settlement on Quincy to gather information. I could be spared if *Our Lady of Montreal* appeared while the cutter was on the surface.

I floated out of the cutter's bay. Maher, one of the sailors who'd locked us into the hold, grabbed me with one hand as he hinged up his visor with the other.

"Captain Ricimer's waiting on you forward, sir," he said. He aimed me toward the companionway, then shoved me off like a medicine ball. A sailor waiting there absorbed my momentum and redirected me up the tube.

Dole hugged me to him as I drifted into the forward compartment. He kicked off, carrying us both to the navigation consoles—skirting the 17-cm plasma cannon with a neat carom from the ceiling gunport, still for the moment closed.

I didn't know whether the men were obeying Piet's orders or if they'd simply decided on their own that Mister Moore in free fall was clumsy as a hog on ice. Maybe the process was demeaning, but it'd halved the time I would've taken to negotiate the distance on my own.

I gripped Piet's couch to stay in place. I'd expected to see Stephen, but I realized he would be with the assault party in the after hold.

Piet's screen and that of Salomon to his left were filled with navigational data in schematic and digital form. Guillermo's display showed the world we were orbiting. Quincy was ninety percent water, with strings of small volcanic islands and one modest continent—for the moment on the opposite hemisphere. Ivestown, the planet's sole settlement, was on the continent's north coast. Farms nearby provided garden truck and fruit for starships which stopped over to load reaction mass, but there was no large-scale agriculture and nothing of interest in Ivestown save the pair of brothels.

Piet turned the PA system on to echo my words. He lifted himself on his left arm to face me directly, since the hard suit prevented him from twisting his torso in normal fashion. We'd radioed from Ivestown before lifting off to return, but face-to-face communication was far better than depending on RF transmissions through Quincy's active ionosphere.

"The *Montreal* hasn't arrived yet," I explained. "Nobody down there is even expecting her."

I shook my head in renewed wonder. "It's like talking to a herd of sheep. There's eighteen, twenty humans in Ivestown, and about all they're interested in is scraping local algae off the rocks and eating it. It turns their teeth brown. I suppose there's a drug in it."

"They could be lying," Salomon said. "To keep us here instead of following the *Montreal.*"

"No," I said. "No. Lightbody checked the field. He says there hasn't been a ship landed at Ivestown in weeks. Sure, the *Montreal* could land anywhere on the planet, but they wouldn't have. And— you'd have to see the people down there. They don't *care.*"

I suppose all four of the colony's women worked in the brothels when a ship was in; maybe some of the men did too. I'd have found coring a watermelon a more satisfying alternative. Piet couldn't have asked a better proof of Fed colonies being garbage dumps rather than frontiers.

Salomon sighed and relaxed his grip on the arm of his couch. Because the navigator had unlatched his restraints to look at me, his armored body began to rise. "It might be weeks before the *Montreal* arrives," he said. "We might have to wait for months. *Months.*"

Piet looked toward the screen before him. I don't know whether he was actually viewing the course equations displayed there or letting his mind expand through a range of possibilities as vast as the universes themselves.

"We've waited months already," Piet replied. His voice was soft, but the PA system's software corrected to boom the words at full audible level from the tannoys in all the compartments.

Salomon looked at me for support. I wanted desperately to be back in a gravity well. My hard suit's rigid presence constricted my mind. We hadn't stayed long enough on the ground for me to take the armor off. I said nothing.

"If we land . . ." Salomon said. The prospect of an indefinite stay in weightless conditions was horrifying to veteran spacers as well as to me, but Salomon still wasn't willing to complete the suggestion. He knew it was a bad one, knew that landing would jeopardize the whole expedition.

"If we land," Piet said with his usual quiet certainty, "then we have to hope that the *Montreal* sets down without first determining who we are. If instead she transits immediately, we won't be able—"

"The Feds are too sloppy to worry about a ship on the ground," Salomon said. His voice didn't have enough energy to be argumentative. "Especially on the Back Worlds."

"We've risked a great deal," Piet replied. "Many of our friends have died. Many others as well, and they're also human beings. We aren't going to cut corners now."

He tapped his armored fingertip twice on the audio pickup as a formal attention signal. "Gentlemen," he said, "you may stand down for the moment. Don't take off your hard suits. I regret this, but we have to be ready to open the gunports at a moment's notice."

I nodded within the tight confines of the helmet sealed to my torso armor by a lobstertail gorget. My eyes were closed. I'd like to have been able to pray for mercy.

"Men," Piet said. "Comrades, *friends*. With the Lord's help, we'll prevail. But it's up to us to endure."

The tannoys chirped as Piet switched off the PA system.

We would endure.

ABOVE QUINCY

Day 129

I unlatched the waste cassette—the shit pan—of Stephen's hard suit. You can change your own, but you're likely to slosh the contents when you reach beneath your fanny with arms encased in rigid armor.

This cassette leaked anyway. Stephen made a quick snatch with a rag. A few droplets of urine escaped despite that. Because we were in free fall, the drops would spread themselves across the first surface they touched, probably a bulkhead.

That wouldn't make much difference, because the *Oriflamme* already stank like a sewer from similar accidents. What bothered me worse was the way my body itched from constant contact with my suit's interior.

"If I ever have a chance to bathe again," I said softly, "all that's left of me is going to melt and run down the drain like the rest of the dirt."

The *Oriflamme*'s crew hung in various postures within the compartment. The only comfortable part of free fall was that any of the surfaces within the vessel could serve as a "floor." Piet lay on his couch, apparently drowsing. Dole was on lookout at the left console. Guillermo's usual position was empty. The Molt had gone into suspended animation and was bundled against the forward bulkhead in a cargo net.

The displays were set for blink comparison. Images of the stars surrounding the *Oriflamme* flashed against images taken at the same point in the previous orbit. The AI corrected for the vessel's frictional slippage and highlighted anomalies for human examination. In two days of waiting, we had the start of a catalog of comets circling Quincy's sun,

Kiley held open the clear bag so that I could add my cassette to the dozen already there. A detail of sailors would open the after hold and steam the day's accumulation, but there were limits to the cleaning you could do in free fall and vacuum.

Stephen slapped an empty cassette into the well of his suit. "You've never been on a slaving voyage, with Molts packed into the holds and all the air cycled through them before it gets to you," he said. "Though we didn't have to stay suited up that time, that's true."

I looked at him. "I didn't know that you'd been a slaver," I said.

Stephen turned his palms up in the equivalent of a shrug. "Back when we were trying to trade with Fed colonies," he said. "The only merchandise they wanted were Molt slaves. Piet wasn't in charge."

He smiled. "Neither was I, for that matter, but it didn't bother me a lot." There would have been as much humor in the *snick* of a rifle's breech opening. "And that was back when some things did bother me, you know."

"Hey?" said Dole. Piet, who I'd thought was dozing—and maybe he was—snapped upright and expanded by three orders of magnitude a portion of the starfield blinking on his display. Dole was still reaching for the keypad.

The magnified object was a globular starship. We had no way of judging size without scale, but I'd never heard of anything under 300 tonnes burden being built on a spherical design. Plasma wreathed the vessel. Her thrusters were firing to bring her into orbit around Quincy.

Piet wound the siren for two seconds. The impellers couldn't reach anything like full volume in that time, but the moan rising toward a howl was clearly different from all the normal sounds of the *Oriflamme* in free fall.

"General quarters," Piet ordered crisply. "Assault party, remain in the main hull for the moment."

He paused, his armored fingers dancing across his console with tiny clicks. "My friends," Piet added, "I believe this is the moment we've prepared and suffered for."

Stephen checked the satchel which held charged batteries to reload his flashgun. I bent and held him steady with both hands to get a close look at his waste cassette. It was latched properly.

When the *Oriflamme*'s gunports opened, we'd be in hard vacuum. That was the wrong time to have the pressure within somebody's suit blow his waste cassette across the compartment, leaving a two-by-ten-centimeter hole to void the rest of his air.

Lightbody unbound Guillermo and pumped his arms to break him out of his trance. The Molt was a doubly grotesque figure in the ceramic armor built for his inhuman limbs.

Salomon slid into his console as Dole propelled himself clear. The bosun could land the vessel manually and run the AI during normal operations, but he lacked the specialized training to match courses with a ship trying to run from us. With a competent navigator like Salomon backing Piet Ricimer at the controls, the Federation vessel didn't have a prayer of escaping either in the sidereal universe or through transit.

I'd hung a cutting bar from one of my hard suit's waist-level equipment studs. I unclipped it. There was no need to, but it gave me something to do with my hands. Catching our quarry was only the first part of the business.

"Prepare for power!" Salomon warned. Veteran sailors had already made sure their boots were anchored on the deck, "down" as soon as the thrusters fired.

A 1-g thrust simulated gravity. I was at an angle, because my right foot bounced from the deck. Stephen kept me from falling.

The Fed vessel's image filled the main screen. That was another jump in magnification, though I supposed we were closing with them in real terms. Some of her plating had been replaced, speckling the spherical hull with bright squares. Her lower hemisphere was crinkly with punishment from atmospheric friction and the bath of plasma exhaust during braking.

Everyone in our forward compartment stared at the screen. The men amidships and in the stern cabin could only guess at what was happening, since the navigation staff was too busy to offer a commentary.

Our quarry's hatches would lower like sections of orange peel. There was an inlay of contrasting metal set beside one of them.

I couldn't read the lettering, but I made out the figure of a woman with her hand outstretched.

"See the Virgin?" I said to Stephen. "I think she's the *Montreal*."

"Half the Feds' shipping is our lady of this or that," Stephen said. His voice was that of a machine again. "But if not this time, then another. And we'll be ready."

As Stephen spoke, his hands moved as delicately as butterfly wings across the stock and receiver of his flashgun. He'd folded the trigger guard forward so that he could use the weapon with gauntlets on.

"Unidentified vessel," crackled the tannoys. Piet had set them to repeat outside signals. This must have been from a communications laser since our thrusters and those of our quarry were snarling across the RF spectrum. "Sheer off at once. This is the Presidential vessel *Montreal*. If you endanger us you'll all be sent to some mud hole for the rest of your life!"

"Gentlemen," Piet ordered, "seal your suits."

He snapped his visor closed. I tried to obey. The cutting bar clacked against my helmet. I'd forgotten I was holding it. I couldn't feel it in my hand because of the gauntlets.

Our commo system switched to vacuum mode instead of depending on atmospheric transmission. Piet's voice, blurred almost beyond understanding, growled through the deckplates and the structure of my hard suit. "Run out the guns."

We dipped lower into orbit around Quincy, losing velocity from atmospheric friction as well as from our main motors. The *Oriflamme* began to vibrate fiercely. The *Montreal*'s image trailed a shroud of excited atoms.

The gunport in the starboard bulkhead swung inward, glowing with plasma from our own exhaust. The *Oriflamme*'s out-rushing atmosphere buffeted us and carried small objects—a glove, a sheet of paper, even a knife—with it.

Ambient light vanished because there were no longer enough molecules of gas to scatter it. All illumination became direct, turning armored men into outlines lit by the gunport. When hydraulic rams advanced the muzzle of the Long Tom through the opening, we became a ship of ghosts and softly gleaming highlights.

The image of the *Montreal* on our main screen took on a slickness that no working starship could have in reality. The tornado of exhaust and roaring atmosphere degraded the data from our optical pickups. The screen's AI enhanced the image in keeping with an electronic ideal, substituting one falsehood for another.

Three gunports slid open along the midline of the *Montreal's* hull.

Our hard suits didn't have individual laser commo units, though a few of the helmets could be hardwired into the navigational consoles. Radio was useless while the main engines were firing anyway. I touched my helmet to Stephen's and shouted, "Why don't we shoot?"

The muzzles of plasma cannon emerged from the *Montreal's* gunports, setting up violent eddies in the flow of exhaust back over the globular hull. The guns looked very small, but the lack of scale could be deceiving me. Unlike us, the Federation crew wouldn't have been waiting in hard suits. A handful of gunners must have suited up hastily while the bulk of the personnel aboard prayed the gun compartments would remain sealed from the remainder of the vessel.

"If we disabled them now"—Stephen's voice rang through the clamor shaking our hull—"they'd crash and we'd have only a crater for our pains. Of course, they aren't under the same con—"

The *Montreal's* guns recoiled into the hull behind streaks of plasma. The *Oriflamme* grunted, shoved by atmosphere heated from a near miss.

"—straints," Stephen concluded.

"Assault party to the aft hold," a voice buzzed. The order could have been a figment of my imagination. Dole and Stephen were moving, as well as other figures anonymous in their armor.

I'm going to die in this damned hard suit, and I can't even scratch. I started to laugh, glad no one could hear me.

Our four 15-cm cannon amidships were trained to starboard like the Long Tom. Wisps of our thrusters' plasma exhaust wreathed the weapons through the gap between the ports and the guntubes.

Stampfer sat at a flip-down console against the opposite bulkhead. The 15-cm magazines to either side of him were locked shut for safety. I wondered how long that precaution would be followed during the stress of combat. If a bolt hit an open magazine, the *Oriflamme's* hull might survive. I doubted that any of the crew would, hard suits or no.

I glanced over the gunner's shoulder as we passed. *Our Lady of Montreal* was centered on the director screen, but several phantoms overlaid the main image. The console was calculating the effect of atmospheric turbulence, our exhaust, and the target's own exhaust. Because a plasma bolt is by definition a charged mass, contrasting charges could affect it more than they would a bullet or other kinetic-energy projectile.

I was halfway down the companionway when a shock jolted my grip loose from the ladder. I fell the rest of the way into the after hold, landing like a ton of old iron on Stephen's shoulders.

I managed to keep a grip on my cutting bar. I had only an instant to feel foolish before the next man fell on top of me.

Stephen helped me up. Armored men staggered into line like trolls. Stephen and I took our places in the front rank, facing the bulkhead that would pivot down into a boarding ramp.

The *Oriflamme* had dived deep enough into the atmosphere that the interior lighting appeared normal again. I took a chance and raised my visor. Stephen did the same. The air was hot and tasted burned because of traces of thruster exhaust.

"The *Montreal* doesn't mount heavy guns," Stephen said. "They won't be able to do us serious damage in the time they'll have before we land."

His face was quietly composed, and his eyes still looked human. There was nothing to do until the ramp opened, so Stephen's mind hadn't yet reentered the place that it went when he killed.

The man beside us bobbed his face forward to look through his open faceshield. It was Dole. There were twelve of us in the front rank this time, packed so tight that the bosun couldn't turn to face us he normally would while suited up. "Bastards did good to hit us the once," he shouted. "Don't worry about them getting home again, sir."

"Don't discount the Fed gunners," Stephen said calmly. "They may have somebody as good as Stampfer. It only takes one if they have director control."

"I'm not worried," I said. I stood in the body of a man about to charge through a haze of sun-hot plasma toward a ship weighing hundreds of tonnes and crewed by anything up to a thousand enemy personnel. I wasn't a part of that suicidal mission, I was just observing.

The siren sounded, warning that we were about to touch down. Stephen and I linked arms and braced one boot each against the ramp. I felt a sailor in the second rank clasp my shoulder. There were no individual gripping points within the hold, but if we locked ourselves together, I figured the whole assault party would be able to stay upright.

Our rate of descent was much higher than Piet's normal gentle landings because we had to remain parallel with *Our Lady of Montreal*. She was dropping like a brick, either from panic, general incompetence, or as a calculated attempt by the Fed captain to get an angle from which he could send a bolt into the thruster nozzles on our underside.

Braked momentum slammed down on me at 6 g's. I thought we'd hit the surface, but Piet had instead opened the throttles at the last instant. The ground effect of our rebounding exhaust rocked the *Oriflamme* violently from side to side. *Then* our extended skids hit the surface.

Everybody in the hold fell down like pieces of a matchstick house. I was under at least two men. Somebody's gauntlet was across my visor. I supposed I should be thankful that he'd forced the visor shut instead of ramming his armored fingers directly into my eyes.

I'd thought we could remain standing no matter how hard we hit. Man proposes, God disposes . . .

The men on top of me got up. One of them was Stephen, identifiable because he carried both his flashgun and a rifle. Somebody else tried to step across my body. I pushed him back as I lurched to a squat. I found my cutting bar beside me and stood up with it. I clipped the weapon to an equipment stud again. I should have left it there until it was time to use the blade.

The hatch unsealed. Air charged by our exhaust swirled around the edges of the ramp in a radiant veil. As the lip lowered, I saw *Our Lady of Montreal* looming like a vast curved wall before us. She was at least fifty meters tall through her vertical axis, and no farther than that from us. The hatches that could open out from the great sphere's base were closed, but I saw unshuttered gun ports on the lower curve.

A 15-cm plasma cannon fired directly overhead. Its brilliance was so dazzling that it rocked me back against the men behind. My faceshield reacted instantly, saving my vision by filtering black everything except the ionized track itself. Even combed by the filter, the bolt was bright enough to turn the massive shock wave five milliseconds later into anticlimax.

A fireball shrouded *Our Lady of Montreal*. Her own vaporized hull metal had exploded into white flame.

The bubble of light lifted away on the gases expanding it. Our bolt had punched a hole a meter in diameter in the *Montreal*'s lower quarter. The edges of the gap glowed for a moment; then the *Oriflamme*'s second gun blew a similar blazing hole beside the first.

Stampfer was firing our battery with a two-second pause between bolts—time to dissipate the ionized haze which would lessen the effect of an instantly following round. The *Oriflamme* rocked at each discharge. The recoil of a few grams of ions accelerated to light speed was enough to shake even a starship's hundred tonnes.

The Long Tom fired. Its discharge was heavier than the midships guns' by an order of magnitude. The *Oriflamme*'s bow shifted a centimeter on the landing outriggers.

The lower quarter of the Federation vessel was a fiery cavity. The hatch had been blown completely away, but the mist of burning metal beyond was as palpable as marble.

The end of our ramp was still a meter and a half in the air. The blast of the main guns had deafened me. I couldn't even hear my own voice shouting, "God and Venus!" as I leaped to the ground.

I crashed down on my face. The plasma cannon firing from the *Montreal* hit the sailor behind me instead and blew him to vapor. Bits of his ceramic armor scattered like grenade fragments.

I got to my feet. Stephen aimed his flashgun up at a 45° angle. His laser bolt, so bright under most conditions, was lost in the greater brilliance of the plasma weapons moments before.

I stumbled toward the cavity Stampfer's guns had blasted for our entry. It roiled with ionized residues of the cannonfire and the ordinary conflagrations which the bolts had ignited in the compartments beyond. With my visor down, I was breathing from the suit's oxygen bottle.

An explosion above us almost knocked me down again. Stephen's bolt had punched into the cannon's 5-cm bore, damaging the nearly spherical array of lasers within the chambered round. The lasers were meant to implode a deuterium pellet at the shell's heart and direct the resulting plasma down a pinhole pathway aligned with the axis of the gun barrel.

Instead, the cannon's breech ruptured. The blast was more violent than the one which killed the man behind me, and I doubted whether Federation armor was as good as our Venerian ceramic.

The rocky soil beneath the *Montreal* was glazed by exhaust and our heavy cannon. The hatch had been wrenched away, but the lintel was square and a meter and a half above ground level. Stalactites of nickel-steel plating hung from the lower edge of the wound.

The white glare of the vessel's interior had dulled to a deep red. Fluid dribbling from the ruptured hydraulic lines burned with dark, smoky flames.

I gripped the lower lip of the opening and kicked myself upward. To my amazement, I wobbled into the hold despite thirty kilos of hard suit and weakness from the days we'd spent in free fall.

The vessel's cylindrical core held tanks of reaction mass and liquefied air behind plating as thick as that of the external hull. Shock waves had started a few of the seams, but the structure in general was still solid. Dual companionways to the higher decks were built into the core structure.

The horizontal deck was 1-cm steel. Blasts generated by our plasma bolts had hammered the surface downward as much as twenty centimeters between frames. The hold's internal bulkheads were flattened, and the hatches that should have closed the companionways had been blown askew.

Five Federation crewmen in the lower hold were in metal hard suits when our first 15-cm bolt penetrated the hull. The suits remained, crushed and disarticulated. From the top of a thigh guard stuck the remains of a femur burned to charcoal. That bone was the only sign of the people who'd been wearing the suits.

I looked behind me. Several men in armor were trying to clamber up with one hand hampered by weapons. I clasped the nearest man under the right shoulder and heaved. His face was down, so I don't know who he was. He skidded aboard, got to his feet, and clumped toward a companionway.

Half the assault party still straggled between the *Oriflamme* and the Federation vessel. We'd landed on an expanse of stony desert, well inland of Ivestown. I doubt the *Montreal*'s captain had chosen the site deliberately, but at least we weren't going to fry the colonists and their hundred or so Molt slaves as a byproduct of the fighting.

Stephen, his flashgun slung over the rifle on his left shoulder, heaved himself upward. I grabbed him and brought him the rest of the way. Other sailors were pairing, one to form a stirrup for the foot of the second. A plasma cannon, too light to be one of ours, fired. I saw the reflected flash but not the point of impact.

A bullet whanged down a companionway and ricocheted from the deck. I reached the helical stairs ahead of Stephen. He grabbed my shoulder to stop me, then stuck his flashgun up the vertical passage. I unclipped my cutting bar and switched it on.

Stephen fired. Sparks of metal clipped by the laser pulse spat down the shaft in reply. The bolt wasn't likely to have hit anybody, but it might clear the companionway for a few seconds. Stephen clapped me forward. His gauntlet cracked like gunfire on my backplate. I started up the steps.

The hatch to the next deck upward had either been open or blown open by gouts of plasma belching up the companionway every time our cannon hammered the hold. The compartment beyond, once an accommodation area, was a smoky inferno.

Plastic and fabrics of all sorts burned in the air the fire sucked from the companionway. The atmosphere of the sealed deck must have been exhausted within a few minutes of the moment our cannon flash-ignited everything flammable.

I could have charged into the blaze, protected by my hard suit, but there was nothing there for us. The fires would destroy all life and objects of value before they burned themselves out. If the *Montreal*'s decks were pierced by too many conduits and water lines, the blaze here was likely to involve the whole ship.

The hatch to the third level was closed. I passed it by and continued climbing. The gunports were higher on the hull. We had to silence the *Montreal*'s plasma cannon.

A bare-chested man with a short rifle stuck his head from the next hatchway, saw me three rungs below him, and ducked back. A Molt with a cutting bar lunged out instead. I slashed through his legs between the upper and lower knee joints. He fell backward in a spray of brown ichor. I crushed his weapon hand against the flooring, then stepped over him into the cargo deck beyond.

The *Montreal*'s fourth deck was stacked with bales and crated goods within woven-wire restraint cages. There were no internal bulkheads. At the end of an aisle between ranks of cargo were three Molts wearing oxygen masks and padded garments of asbestos or glass fiber. They were trying to pivot a light plasma cannon away from the gunport so that it could bear on me.

The man with the rifle leaned over a row of crates and fired. His bullet hit me in the center of the chest and splashed upward, staggering me. I recovered and charged the Molts at a shambling run.

One of them swung at me with the kind of long forceps the

Feds use to load their solid-breech plasma cannon. My bar screamed through the levers in a shower of sparks.

The alien scrambled away. I chopped the back of a Molt's head, then reversed my stroke through the right arm and into the chest of his fellow who was tugging on the gun's tiller.

The surviving Molt flung the handles of his forceps at me. They bounced off my helmet. I cut him in half. My bar's vibration slowed momentarily, then spun up again through a spray of body fluids.

The human stepped around a row of cargo and aimed at me. The butt of Stephen's flashgun crushed his skull from behind.

The cannon that'd exploded was ten meters farther along the curve of the hull. The blast had crushed the stacks of cargo outward in a wide circle. The feet of three Molts and another human were carbonized onto the deck near the gun's swivel, but nothing above the ankles remained of the crewmen.

I couldn't see any other Feds in the jumble of cargo. My whole body was on fire. I lifted my faceshield to take an unconstricted breath.

Stephen slammed my visor back down. He reached past me to tilt the plasma cannon toward the ceiling a meter above our heads.

I turned away. The world went white with a blast that spread-eagled me on the deck. Stephen was still standing, I don't know how.

I pushed myself to a crouch, then stood in a fog of swirling metal vapors. The point-blank charge of plasma had blown a two-meter hole into the level above. Fires burned there and among the cargo around us.

Stephen restacked one crate on another beneath the hole. A Molt fell through from the deck above. A bubble of vaporized metal had seared the creature's thorax white.

I wasn't sure I could lift Stephen, so I hopped onto the crates and raised my right foot. Stephen made a step of his hands. His powerful thrust popped me through onto the deck above.

The large compartment was Molt accommodations. I guessed the aliens were crew rather than cargo. Though the facilities were spartan, there were hammock hooks and cages for the Molts' personal belongings.

The plasma bolt had blown out half the lights. I couldn't see more than twenty Molts huddled in space meant to quarter a hundred.

I reached for Stephen with my left hand. I had to jab the tip of my bar down like a cane to keep from overbalancing. Every heartbeat swelled me tighter against the oven of my armor.

Stephen crashed upward. I staggered toward the single hatch out of the compartment. My vision was so focused that I didn't know whether Stephen was behind or beside me. Molts had squeezed against the internal bulkhead when the deck burst in a fireball near the curve of the hull. They scattered to either side of my advance like chickens running from the axe.

I pushed at the hatch. It didn't move. I raised my bar to cut through. Stephen reached past me and pulled the handle open.

I lurched into a corridor ten meters long. It was full of Fed personnel, human and Molt. A four-barreled cannon on a wheeled carriage faced one companionway; a tripod-mounted laser whose separate power pack must weigh fifty kilos was aimed at the open hatch of the other.

An officer wearing gold-chased body armor turned and pointed his gun at me. The weapon had a thick barrel with only a tiny hole in the middle of it, and the stock fitted into a special rest on the breastplate.

I swung my bar at the Fed. He was too far away for me to reach before he fired. A starship hit and spun me around. I bounced onto the floor on my back. My faceshield was unlatched, but the helmet had rotated sideways 20° to cut off part of my vision.

Stephen stepped across my body with his flashgun raised. I threw my left arm across my eyes. Side-scatter from Stephen's bolt glared off the corridor's dingy white walls. A crate of shells for the cannon blew up like so many grenades. Stephen fell over me.

I twisted out from under his legs. The blast had knocked down the nearest Feds as well, though the crew of the laser five meters away at the opposite end of the corridor was trying to swing its weapon onto us. The cable to the power pack wasn't flexible enough for them to change front without repositioning all their equipment.

I jerked off my helmet and flung it at the Feds. The four Molts gripping the power pack's carrying handles continued stolidly to walk it around.

I could see again and I could breathe. The officer's projectile had hit the top of my breastplate at a flat angle. It shattered the plate and tore loose the clamps holding plastron, gorget, and helmet together.

Half my breastplate flopped from the waist latches. Ceramic

continued to crumble away in bits from the broken edge, because the shock had completely shattered the plate's internal structure. Breath was a sharp pain. I didn't know whether the chest muscles were bruised or if cracked ribs were ripping my lungs every time I moved.

I walked toward the laser. I would have run, but my backplate clanked behind me like a ceramic cape and caught my heels.

A human sailor with a full mustache and sideburns that swept up to bright chestnut hair gaped at me. He was wearing padded protective gear like that of the gunners on the deck below. He dropped his side of the laser and sprang toward the companionway hatch.

His human officer shot him in the back with her double-barreled pistol. She aimed at me past the power supply. Her head jerked back, and she fired the pistol into the ceiling as her nerves spasmed.

Her body toppled forward. There was a bullet hole over her right eye, and her brains splashed the bulkhead behind her.

I hacked at a Molt. He staggered back, bleeding from the stump of an arm and the deep cut in his carapace.

The nearest Molt wrapped his hard-surfaced arms around me while the others scrambled toward the cross-corridor at the end of the main one. They kept the power pack between me and them. Stephen fired his rifle again, but not in my direction. I cut awkwardly at the Molt's back. My limbs were still in their jointed ceramic cylinders, and the damned backplate dragged at me like an anchor.

The Molt moaned through the breathing holes along his lateral lines. My bar wouldn't bite—the battery was drained. I screamed in frustration, pounding the Molt with the pommel. He slipped down under the impacts, but his arms wouldn't release. His skull was a mush of fluids and broken chitin, but he wouldn't let go.

Stephen grabbed the Molt's shoulder with his left gauntlet and flung the corpse away from me. I staggered against the jamb of the hatchway. I wanted to get rid of the backplate, but I couldn't turn the studs behind me. I stripped off my right gauntlet instead as Stephen closed the firing contacts of the Federation laser and hosed its throbbing light across the other gun crew.

Stephen's flashgun was a monopulse weapon. This tripod-mounted unit had two separate tubes. It sequenced its output through them in turn to avoid the downrange vapor attenuation that reduced continuous-beam lasers' effectiveness.

The Fed officer who'd shot me was loading another fat cartridge into the breech of his weapon. The beam glanced from his polished breastplate in dazzling highlights, then hit him in the neck and decapitated him.

I flung away my left gauntlet. My hands curled with pleasure at being free. The backplate latches turned easily.

Two Molts were starting to rise. Their thoraces burst soggily as the beam vaporized soft parts within the chitin shell.

A man in Venerian armor with his chest burned out lay just within the companionway hatch. He was probably the fellow who'd gone on while I helped Stephen into the hold. He held a rifle, and a cutting bar was clipped to his armor.

Exploding ammunition had knocked the multibarrel cannon sideways in the corridor. Stephen concentrated his flux on the breechblocks. The laser's feedline was beginning to smoke. The unit should have been allowed to cool every few seconds between bursts. Stephen was deliberately destroying both the weapons that could endanger a man in a Venerian hard suit.

Shells in the four cannon barrels cooked off in quick succession. Three of the weakened breeches failed, flinging fragments of jagged tool steel across the corridor and shredding two of the Molts who'd been crippled by the initial blast. There had been another human gunner also, but she must have run down the end corridor.

I took the cutting bar from the dead Venerian's waist stud and started up the companionway. My armored boots clanged on the slotted metal treads. I hadn't had time to take off the leg pieces.

The important thing was that my face and chest were free. The weight didn't matter so much, but days of constriction had driven me almost mad.

Or beyond almost.

The companionway was full of smoke from the fire on the lower deck, but because the air wasn't circulating the conditions weren't as bad as I'd thought they would be. I wished I'd thought to detach the oxygen bottle from my suit; but I hadn't, and anyway the projectile that smashed the breastplate had likely damaged the regulator as well.

Shots and screams echoed up the tube. Some of what sounded like human agony probably came from machines. I wondered if other members of the assault party had climbed this high. Movement in hard suits was brutally exhausting, and other men hadn't had Stephen to help them forward.

The hatch onto the next deck was closed but not dogged tight. I could hear people raggedly singing a hymn on the other side. The leader was a female, and hers was the only voice that didn't sound terrified. I passed the hatch by and turned up the final angle of the companionway to the highest deck.

The hatch was sealed. I tugged at an arm of the central wheel. They'd locked it from the inside. I paused, thinking about the hatches I'd seen on the *Montreal*'s lower decks.

A bullet howled up the companionway. It or a bit of it dropped at my feet, a silvery gleam, before it rattled its way back down through the stair treads.

The locks were electrical, activated by a button in the center on the inner dogging wheel. The powerline ran through the upper hinge.

I set my bar's tip on the hatch side of the hinge and squeezed the trigger. Nothing happened. I was dizzy from smoke and fatigue. I'd forgotten that the dead man wouldn't have slung his bar with the power switch on.

I thumbed the slide and tried again. The blade screamed angrily and sank into the tough steel. Chips, yellow and blazing white, spewed from the cut. The severed power cable shorted through the hatch metal in a brief halo of blue sparks.

I tugged again on the wheel. This time it spun freely, three full turns to withdraw the bolts which clamped the hatch to its jamb. I grasped the vertical handhold, pulled the hatch toward me, and charged onto the bridge of *Our Lady of Montreal*.

I thought they'd be waiting for me, alerted by my bar's shriek and the inner wheel spinning as I undogged the hatch. I'd forgotten how much else was going on. There were six humans and maybe ten Molts in the domed circular chamber. They turned and stared at me as if they'd just watched the Red Death take off his mask.

I suppose they were right.

Nearest to me were a pair of humans in white tunics. I thrust rather than slashing at the face of the woman who held a cutting bar. She staggered backward. The man tried to point his rifle but I grabbed it by the fore-end and twisted the muzzle upward. He shrieked and pulled away, but I held him by the weapon he didn't think to drop. My bar cut spine-deep in his neck, drowning his cry in his own blood.

The bridge instrumentation was a ring of waist-high, double-facing consoles. The three human officers in the center of the ring wore metal helmets and gleaming back-and-breast armor. One of them shouted an order.

Molts sitting at the outer positions lurched toward me from seats configured to their alien torsos. None of them had weapons, though one Molt picked up a portable communicator and threw it at my head.

I chopped a Molt's skull, then backhanded a deep gouge across the belly plates of another. I watched my body in amazement. The animal controlling me moved with the relentless fury of a storm against cliffs.

I still held the rifle like an oar in my left hand. I jolted a Molt back with the butt, then sawed through his ankles with a stroke that buried my bar momentarily in the pelvis of the creature who'd grabbed my forearm. I kicked the Molt free with an armored boot.

A bullet hit the back of the Molt toppling beside the cut-off feet. One of the officers was shooting at me with a handgun. His two fellows had ducked behind the ring of consoles. When he saw me turn toward him, he dropped flat also.

The screen of the nearest console showed a real-time image of the *Oriflamme*. Our five big plasma cannon had cooled enough to be reloaded and run out, but Stampfer hadn't fired again for fear of hitting those of us aboard the *Montreal*.

Additional men in ceramic armor trudged across the fused plain toward the Federation vessel. They looked pathetically small compared to the *Oriflamme*, much less the *Montreal*.

Molts threw themselves on me from right and left. I twisted my arm to saw the carapace of one with the back of my bar. The Molt's hard thorax jolted against me as a gun fired and an awl of red pain stabbed through my upper abdomen. The Fed soldier with his back to the other hatch had fired his shotgun.

I punched the Molt holding my right arm with the cutting bar's pommel. I broke the chitin, making the creature move back enough that I could draw the blade down through his right thigh.

Two of the Fed officers rose from behind the consoles again. My legs were mired in thrashing Molts whose muscles contracted as they died. I dropped the cutting bar and brought the butt of the rifle I'd grabbed around to my right shoulder.

The woman fired her pistol at me from three meters away and missed. The man who'd shot at me before gripped his pistol with both hands as he pointed it. I thrust the muzzle of my rifle in his direction and jerked the trigger.

My bullet blew apart the screen of the console a meter to the right of him. The woman behind that console gasped and doubled up, clutching her groin. Instead of shooting me, the man threw himself under cover again.

I couldn't move my legs. The soldier with the shotgun closed the breech over a fresh cartridge and raised his weapon again. My rifle had a tube under the barrel so it was probably a repeater, but I didn't know how to chamber a new round. I threw it at the soldier and missed. The Fed ducked for an instant anyway.

I squatted on the pile of spasming Molts, trying to find my cutting bar or some other weapon. The Fed soldier dropped his shotgun and raised his hands over his head.

Stephen and Piet Ricimer stepped past me. They still wore their hard suits, but their visors were raised. Stephen deliberately fired into the curving outer bulkhead to ricochet a bullet behind the ring of consoles. A Molt hiding there jumped up. A charge of buckshot from Piet's shotgun knocked the Molt back with a ragged hole in his plastron.

The officer with the handgun raised his head to see what was happening. The second bullet from Stephen's revolving-chamber rifle hit the man in the forehead and spun his helmet into the air in a splash of brains.

The Fed sprang fully upright, his arms flailing. Stephen shot him again, this time through the upper chest, but when the man turned and fell we could see his skull had already been opened like a soft-boiled egg.

The *Montreal*'s bridge was thick with gunsmoke and blood. I was beginning to lose color vision, and I didn't seem to be able to stand up even though the Molts had finally become shudderingly flaccid.

"I surrender!" a man screamed from within the ring of consoles. I remembered that there had been three officers there when I burst into the compartment. "In the name of Christ, have mercy!"

"Stand with your hands raised, then!" Piet ordered with his shotgun still butted on his shoulder. He stepped aside, putting his back to a bulkhead rather than the open hatchway.

Stephen knelt beside me. His rifle gestured the Fed soldier farther away from the shotgun the man had dropped. Somebody hammered on the sealed hatch. They'd pay hell trying to break in like that.

The third Fed officer rose from his hiding place. He peered from behind the helmet he'd taken off to hold in front of his face. There was a pistol holstered at his side, but I'm sure he'd forgotten it was there.

Stephen traded the rifle for his flashgun. He nodded toward the hatch. "Open it," he said to the captured soldier. Stephen was ready, just in case whoever was on the other side came in wearing metal rather than ceramic armor.

"Order your men to stop fighting," Piet said to the captured officer. The Fed was the youngest of the three on the bridge. He was pudgy, and his hair was so fine and blond that his pink scalp showed through it. "There's no need for more deaths."

"How bad are you hit?" Stephen asked, his eyes focused on the hatch the prisoner was undogging.

"I'm just tired," I said. "None of this is my blood."

Dole stamped through the hatchway with a cutting bar and a chrome-plated rifle. The gun's muzzle had been sheared off at an angle, but I supposed it would still shoot at the ranges we'd been fighting here.

The stink of opened bodies was making me dizzy. I had to get out of the stench, but I was too dizzy to stand.

"The hell it's not," Stephen said. "Dole, come here and give me a hand. We need to get him back to Rakoscy."

His gauntleted fingers tore the side of my tunic the rest of the way open. There were two puckered, purple holes on the side just below my rib cage. The Molt hadn't shielded me completely from the shotgun pellets after all.

"Surrender!" the Federation officer called into a microphone flexed to his side of a console. "Captain Alfegor is dead! Surrender! Surrender! They'll kill us all!"

Echoes of his voice rumbled up the companionways. I could still hear shots, though.

"Didn't know where you'd gone to," Stephen said quietly. He reached around my back and under my knees. Dole knelt to link arms with him. "Had a dozen of them charge around the back corridor just when I'd drained that damned laser. Could have been a problem if Piet hadn't come up the companionway about the same time."

"I know how you felt," I said; or I tried to, because about that time the stink of death swelled over the last of my consciousness in a thick purple fog.

NEW VENUS

Day 140

The planet was uncharted. Piet had located it at a good time. The last day of the run, we'd used personal oxygen bottles because a patch had cracked badly.

I didn't have enough energy to run out with the others as soon as the ramp lowered. I sat in the hold on a pallet of chips, far enough back that the heat still radiating from the glazed soil didn't bother me. The naming ceremony on the lakeside was over, and the crowd of relaxed sailors was breaking up.

At the base of the ramp, ten men under Salomon argued bitterly among themselves about the hoses we'd taken from *Our Lady of Montreal* to replace the set damaged when we fled Templeton. The Federation equipment was the correct diameter, but both ends of the hoses had male connectors—as did the fittings of our water tanks. We'd have to make couplers to use the hoses. That job could have been done during the long run from Quincy if anybody'd noticed the problem before.

I got up very carefully and walked down the ramp. I'd be in the way if I stayed in the hold. Salomon would have enough problems doing shop work without offloading the treasure first.

The chips had come cheap enough, I suppose. Three dead, only

434

two wounded. The Feds hadn't been equipped to deal with our hard suits. Smetana had lost his leg—stupidly—by getting it caught in the mechanism of the *Montreal*'s cargo lift. My wound was pretty stupid too.

The men fell silent as I walked past them. "Good to see you, Mister Moore," Salomon said formally. I gave him a deliberate nod. The story'd gotten around. More than the story, the way it usually happens. The men seemed to think I was a hero. *I* thought—

The soldier's face dissolving in a red spray as I rammed my bar through her teeth and palate, then jerked the blade sideways.

I tried not to think at all, and it didn't help.

Piet, Stephen, and Guillermo were chatting at the lakeside. I joined them. Nearby, men had started laying out the temporary houses they'd live in while we were on New Venus.

"Feeling better, Jeremy?" Stephen asked to welcome my presence.

"I'm all right," I said. "Just tired. You know, the bruises I got from the back of my breastplate when the bullet hit me are worse than the little shot holes."

I waggled my left hand in the direction of where Rakoscy had removed the buckshot. I could move my arms well enough, but it still hurt to twist my torso.

"And if Rakoscy hadn't clamped off the vein those shots punctured," Piet said with a cold smile, "you wouldn't have felt any pain at all from your ribs. I hope the next time you'll remember you have nothing to prove. Nor did you on Quincy."

I shook my head. Shrugging was another thing I had to avoid. "It just happened," I said. "I wasn't trying . . ."

I wasn't human when it happened. I didn't want to say that. "The ground cover doesn't have a root structure to bind turf," I said. I pointed to the men surveying the ground beside the *Oriflamme*. "How are they going to make houses?"

"Oh," said Piet, "a frame of brush, then a spray glaze to seal and stabilize it. We won't be here but a week at the most."

He looked back at the *Oriflamme* and frowned. "The patch that failed could have killed us. It was my fault."

"Piet," Stephen said forcefully, "the only way we could've checked the substructure—which is what failed, not the patch—is to have removed the inner hull in sections. Which would've taken us three months, sitting on the ground beside the *Montreal* and wondering when the next Fed ship'd pass by and snap us up. I *still* don't

believe that a fifty-millimeter Fed popgun cracked a frame member
that way."

"Well, it was probably the strain of the Breach," Piet said. "I
know, I know . . . But not only can't we afford mistakes, we can't
afford bad luck."

"I'd say our luck had been fine," I said. "At least half the
Montreal's cargo was of current production chips, not pre-Collapse
stock. There's enough wealth to . . ."

The value was incalculable. I would have shrugged. I turned my
palms up instead.

"The value is roughly that of the gross domestic product of the
Free State of Venus," Stephen said quietly.

I looked at him: the scarred gunman, the consummate killer.
It was easy to forget that Stephen Gregg had once been in the
service of his uncle, a shipping magnate. I suspected that he'd been
good at those duties too.

Piet grinned, his normal bright self again. "I think I'll cast a
plaque claiming the world for Governor Halys," he added. "Do it
myself, I mean. We can weld it to one of those rocks."

He pointed. Three natives—Rabbits—who certainly hadn't been
on the clump of boulders twenty meters away when Piet started
speaking took off running in the opposite direction. The two males
were nude except for body paint. The female wore a skirt of veins
combed from the sword-shaped leaves of a common local plant.
Her flaccid breasts flopped almost to her waist.

Piet and Stephen darted to the side so that they could watch
the Rabbits past the boulders. Guillermo and I followed slowly.
It hurt me to move, and I doubt the Molt saw any reason for
haste.

Several of the crewmen noticed the fugitives as well. Kiley
shouted and started to run, though he didn't have a prayer of
catching them.

"Let them go!" Piet ordered. I was always surprised how loud
his voice could be when it had to.

Brush grew down to the lakeshore a little north of where we'd
landed. The Rabbits vanished into it.

"I thought I'd seen a village in that direction while we were making our approach," Piet said.

"There are no industrial sites on this world," Guillermo said.
If he'd been human, his voice would have sounded surprised. "I

examined infrared scans. Even overgrown, the lines of human constructions would show up."

Stephen looked at him. "You do that regularly?" he asked. "Check on IR while we're orbiting?"

"Yes," the Molt said simply.

Piet shrugged. "This world isn't in the chart Jeremy found for us," he said. "Even though the Federation cartographers had access to pre-Collapse data."

Stephen was the only one of us who was armed. He'd unslung his flashgun when the Rabbits appeared, though he'd kept the muzzle high. Instead of reslinging the weapon, he cradled it in his arms.

"During the Collapse," he said, "colonies pretty much destroyed themselves. It wasn't Terran attacks, certainly not here on the Back Worlds. Maybe their ancestors—"

He nodded in the direction the Rabbits had fled.

"—came from Templeton or the like as things were breaking down there. Trying to preserve civilization."

Piet sighed. "Yes," he said. "That could be. But you don't preserve civilization by running from chaos."

He glanced back at the ship. Dole headed a crew working on the section damaged by the *Montreal*'s plasma cannon, and Salomon's men had already stretched the hoses to the lake.

"I think we can be spared to visit the native village," he said, smiling again. "They don't appear dangerous."

Stephen shrugged. "If we go," he said, "we'll go armed."

He glanced at me, I guess for support. My mind was lost in the maze of how you preserve civilization by cutting apart the face of a woman you hadn't even seen five seconds before.

"The *Montreal* carried a couple of autogyros," Stephen said as we broke out of the path through the brush. "You know, one of those would have made scouting around our landing sites a lot simpler."

The Rabbit village was in sight beneath trees that stood like miniature thunderheads. Up to a dozen separate trunks supported each broad canopy.

"Woof!" said Maher, the last of the six in our party. "'Bout time we got clear of that!" Not only was Maher overweight, he'd decided to wear crossed bandoliers of shotgun shells and to carry a cutting bar. His gear caught at every step along a track worn by naked savages.

"You were going to fly the autogyro, Stephen?" Piet asked mildly. "Or perhaps we should have brought along one of the Federation pilots to do our scouting for us."

The Rabbits lived in a dozen or so rounded domes of wattle-and-daub. There were no windows, and they'd have to crawl on hands and knees to get in through the low doors. I wondered whether they had fire.

Stephen laughed. "Well, they're supposed to be easy to fly," he said. "Not that we had room to stow another pair of socks, the way we're loaded with chips."

Rabbits began to congregate in front of the huts as we approached. There were more of them than I'd expected from the number of dwellings, perhaps two hundred. The adult males carried throwing sticks, shell-tipped spears, and what were probably planting dibbles, though they would serve as weapons.

"Open out," Piet ordered in an even voice. "*Don't* point a weapon."

We fell into line abreast as we continued to saunter at the pace Piet set toward the village. He and Maher carried shotguns. Loomis had a rifle, Stephen his flashgun, and even Guillermo wore a holstered pistol, though I doubt he'd have been much use with it.

I held a cutting bar in both hands like a baton. Even its modest weight strained my abdomen if it hung from one side or the other.

"Stephen," I said. "Will you teach me to shoot?"

"Yes," he said, the syllable pale with lack of affect.

"We won't need weapons now," Piet said briskly. "Wait here."

He strode ahead of the rest of us with his right hand raised palm-outward. "We are peaceful travelers in your land," he called in Trade English. "We offer you presents and our friendship."

Piet was still ten meters from the Rabbits when they threw themselves to the ground. The men lashed themselves with their own weapons; the women tore their skirts into tufts and tossed them in the air with handfuls of dirt. Small children ran screaming from one adult to another, demanding reassurance which wasn't to be found.

"Wait!" Piet boomed in horror as he sprang forward. "We aren't gods to be worshipped, we're men!"

He forcibly dragged upright a Rabbit who was drawing a barbed spearhead across his forearm. "Stop that! It's blasphemy!"

Stephen pushed his way against Piet's side, though if the Rabbits had turned on us, there wasn't a lot he could have done. I'd have been even more useless, but I stood to Piet's right and grabbed the polished throwing stick that a Rabbit was beating himself across the back with. I wasn't about to try lifting anybody in my present condition, but the Rabbit didn't fight me for the stick. It was a beautifully curved piece. The wood was dense and had a fine, dark grain.

"Stop!" Piet thundered again.

This time the Rabbits obeyed, though for the most part they huddled on the ground at our feet. The children's shrieks seemed louder now that the adults weren't drowning them out.

An old woman came from a hut, leaning on the arm of a young man. She wore a pectoral and tiara made from strings of colored shells.

The youth supporting her was nude except for a genital cup, like most other males. A middle-aged man walked a step behind and to the right of the woman. He wore a translucent vest of fish or reptile skin. I could see the impressions the scales had left after they were removed.

The ordinary villagers edged back. They crawled until they'd gotten a few meters away, then rose to a crouch. Except for the man in the vest, the villagers looked ill-nourished. That fellow wasn't fat, but he had a solid, husky build. He stepped ahead of the old woman, keeping enough to the side that he didn't block our view of her.

We shook ourselves straight again. I still held the throwing stick. I stuck my cutting bar under the front of my belt to have it out of the way.

The two sailors ostentatiously ported their guns. I'd been too busy to look, but I'd bet they'd been aiming into the crowd and now hoped Piet hadn't seen them. Piet probably *had* seen them, the way he seemed to see everything going on, but he didn't choose to comment. Could be he thought Loomis and Maher showed better judgment than the rest of us had.

The old woman stretched out both arms and began speaking in a cracked voice. Her words were in no language I'd ever heard before. She paused after each phrase, and the man in the vest thundered what seemed to be the same words. They didn't make any more sense the second time at ten times the volume.

Maher looked at me and frowned. I nodded the throwing stick as a shrug. I didn't know how long this was going to go on either. At least it wasn't an attack.

After ten minutes of stop-and-go harangue, the old woman started to cough. The youth tried to help her, but she swatted at him angrily. The man in the vest looked back in concern.

The woman got control of her paroxysm, though she swayed as she lifted the clicking pectoral off. She handed it to the youth, mumbled an order, and then removed the tiara as well. It had been fastened to her thinning hair with bone pins.

The youth walked to Piet, holding the objects at arm's length. The Rabbit was shivering. His knees bent farther with every step, so that when he'd reached Piet he was almost kneeling.

"We thank you in the name of our governor," Piet said as he took the gifts. "We accept the objects as offered by one ruler to another, not as the homage owed only to God."

He turned his head and hissed, "Loomis? The cloth."

Loomis hastily pulled a bolt of red fabric out of his pack. He'd forgotten—so had I—the gift we'd brought. The cloth came from the Commandatura on Trehinga, but it might well be Terran silk. Stephen had suggested it would be useful for trading to Rabbits and free Molts.

Piet held the bolt out to the youth. The youth turned his head away. The man in the vest snarled an order. The youth took the cloth. He stumbled back from Piet, crying bitterly.

Piet's mouth worked as though he'd been sucking a lemon. "Well," he said. He turned and nodded back the way we'd come. "Well, I think we've done all we can here."

That was true enough. Though I for one wasn't about to bet on what we *had* done.

NEW VENUS

Day 143

The moon was up, so I hadn't bothered to take a light when I went walking. The satellite was huge, looking almost the size of Earth from Luna, though it had no atmosphere and its specific gravity was only slightly above that of water.

The four crewmen's lodges were laid out as sides of a square. A bonfire leaped high in the middle and a fiddler played dance music. Repairs to the *Oriflamme*'s hull were complete, or as complete as possible. Liquor acquired on Trehinga and Templeton competed with slash the motor crewmen brewed from rations.

Being able to walk for the past three days had loosened up my chest muscles. I still got twinges if I turned too suddenly, and when I woke up in the morning my lower abdomen ached as though I'd been kicked the night before; but my body was healing fine.

I was returning to the *Oriflamme*. I'd continued to bunk aboard her. The minimal interior illumination hid rather than revealed the ground beneath the starship, but the moon was so bright that I noticed the hunching figure while I was still fifty meters away.

"Hey!" I shouted. I wasn't carrying a weapon. I ran toward the figure anyway. Adrenaline made me forget the shape my body was in as well as damping the pain that might have reminded me. "Hey!"

The figure sprang to its feet and sprinted away. When it was out of the *Oriflamme*'s shadow I could see that it was a Rabbit— a female, judging from the skirt.

Piet opened the forward hatch holding a powerful light in his left hand and a double-barreled shotgun by the pistol grip in his right. The light blazed onto the Rabbit and stayed there despite her attempts to dart and twist out of the beam. Furrows dribbling fresh blood striped her back.

The Rabbit finally vanished into the brush. None of the men celebrating at the shelters had taken notice of my shout or the Rabbit.

Running—jogging clumsily—actually felt good to me, though I didn't have any wind left. The short spurt to the ramp left me puffing and blowing.

I knelt beneath the ship where the Rabbit had hidden. She'd dropped or thrown away something as she fled. I doubted it was a bomb—fire was high technology for these savages—but I wasn't taking chances.

Piet flared his lens to wide beam. "Anything?" he asked as he hopped down beside me.

"This," I said, picking up the handle of a giant comb: a carding comb for stripping leaf fibers so they could be woven into cloth. The teeth were long triangles of shell mounted edgewise so that they wouldn't snap when drawn through tough leaves.

The teeth were smeared a finger's breadth deep with blood so fresh it still dripped. Piet switched off the handlight. I crawled carefully from beneath the *Oriflamme*; it'd be several minutes before I had my night vision back, and I didn't want to knock myself silly on a landing strut.

"Perhaps we should set guards," Piet said. "Of course, we'll be leaving tomorrow. If all goes as planned."

I flung the comb in the direction of the village a kilometer away. There were drops of blood on the glazed soil where the Rabbit had hidden for her ceremony. I sat down on the ramp. I felt sick. Part of it was probably the exertion.

Piet sat beside me. "You wouldn't have had to go as far as the village to find a woman for your desires," he said. "You could just have waited here."

There was nothing in his tone, and his face—softened by the moonlight—was as calm as that of a statue of Justice. The fact that he'd spoken *those* words meant the incident had bothered him as much as it did me. Wine let the truth out of some men; but for others it was stress that made them say the things that would otherwise have been hidden forever in their hearts.

"I was just walking, Piet," I said quietly. "There's some of the men gone up to the Rabbit village, I believe; but I was just working the stitches out of my side."

He nodded curtly. "It doesn't matter," he said. "That sort of thing is between you and the Lord."

I got up and raised my face to the moon. "I haven't lied to anybody since I came aboard the *Porcelain*, Piet," I said. My voice shuddered with anger. *With all the things I'd done, before and especially after I met Piet Ricimer, to be accused of this—*

I thought about what I'd just said, and about the cloak of moral outrage I'd dressed myself in. I started to laugh. Some of my chest muscles thought I shouldn't have, but it was out of their control and mine.

Piet stood with a worried look on his face. Maybe he thought I'd snapped, gone mad in delayed reaction to . . . to too many things.

"No," I gasped, "I'm all right. I was just going to say, I haven't been lying to anybody except maybe myself. And I'm getting better about that, you see?"

We sat down again. "Jeremy," he said, "I'm sorry. I shouldn't have spoken."

I shrugged. I could do that again. "If you hadn't," I said, "you'd have gone the rest of your life thinking that's what I was doing out there tonight. When I was just going for a walk."

Fifty meters away in the temporary accommodations, the fiddler was taking a break. A chorus of sailors filled in *a cappella*, "A mighty fortress is our God, a bulwark never failing . . ."

They might as easily have swung into *The Harlot of Jerusalem*. I started to laugh again. This time my ribs forestalled me.

"I'm fine," I repeated. I was beginning to wonder, though, and it wasn't my body that caused me the concern.

"If President Pleyal establishes the rule he wants over all mankind," Piet said, "his fall will be a collapse worse than the Collapse. Because we don't have the margin for survival that men had risen to a thousand years ago. Folk like these—"

He waggled a finger northward.

"—mistaking men for gods, they'll be all that remains of humanity. We *have* to succeed, Jeremy."

"I'll be glad when we lift," I said. I looked at Piet, leaning back with his arms braced on the ramp. "Because you're wrong, you know. It's not gods they think we are. They're not worshipping, they're trying to placate demons."

I shuddered, closed my eyes, and opened them again on the vast, raddled face of the moon. "Which is why," I went on, "that quite apart from standards of hygiene, the women here are in no danger from me. I'm not interested in a woman who thinks she's being raped."

I clasped my hands together to keep them from shaking. "Particularly one who thinks she's being raped by a minion of Satan."

And if God was Peace, then she would surely be correct.

DUNEEN

Day 155

My rifle roared, lifting the muzzle in a blast of gray smoke. I now knew to hold the weapon tight against me. The first time I'd instinctively kept the buttplate a finger's breadth out from my shoulder. The rifle had recoiled separately and *fast*. Instead of pushing my torso back, it whacked me a hammerblow.

"Did I hit it?" I asked, peering toward the target—a meter-square frame of boards twenty meters away. The aiming point was a circle of black paint. My bullet holes spread around it in a shotgun pattern against the rough-sawn yellow wood.

"You hit it," Stephen said. "Reload and hit it again. Remember you want to be solid, not tense. You're using a tool."

I cocked the rifle, then thumbed the breech cam open and extracted the spent cartridge for reloading. "It'd be easier if all our guns were the same kind, wouldn't it?" I said. I nodded toward the revolving rifle in the crook of Stephen's left elbow.

"All machine work instead of craftwork?" Stephen said. "Where that thinking ends is another Collapse—a system of automatic factories so complex that a few hit-and-run attacks bring the whole thing down. Everybody starves or freezes."

I pulled a cartridge from my belt loop but held it in my hand instead of loading. "That's superstition," I said, more forcefully than I usually spoke to Stephen. This was important to me. "Civilization isn't going to fall because every gunsmith on Venus bores his rifle barrels to the same dimensions."

If man was ever really to advance, we had to design and build our own electronics instead of depending on the leavings of pre-Collapse civilization. That required something more structured than individual craftsmen like Piet's father casting thruster nozzles.

Stephen shrugged. I couldn't tell how much it mattered to him. "It isn't the individual aspect," he said. "It's the whole mind-set. On Earth they're setting up assembly lines again."

"But for now . . ." I said as I slid the loaded round into the chamber sized to it and not—quite—to that of any other rifle aboard the *Oriflamme,* "I'll learn how to use whatever comes to hand."

During the voyage from New Venus, Stephen had showed me how to load and strip each of our twenty-odd varieties of firearm. It gave us both something to concentrate on between the hideous bouts of transit. This was the first time I'd fired a rifle.

I thought of the officer on the *Montreal*'s bridge clutching the hole in her groin as she fell. The first time I'd practiced with a rifle.

One of the local herbivores blundered into the clearing. A peck of fronds was disappearing into its mouth. Spores, unexpectedly golden, showered the beast's forequarters and the air above it.

The creature saw us. The barrel-shaped body froze, but the jaws continued to masticate food in a fore-and-aft motion. My shots hadn't alerted the creature to our presence. The local animals didn't seem to have any hearing whatever.

"We have plenty of meat," Stephen said. "Let it go."

The creature turned 270° and crashed away through the vegetation. I could track its progress for some distance by the spores rising like a dust cloud.

I glanced down at my rifle. "I wasn't going to shoot it," I said.

I meant I wasn't going to try. The board target was considerably larger than the man-sized herbivore. The skill I'd demonstrated thus far wasn't overwhelmingly high.

"It gets easy to kill," Stephen said. His voice was slipping out of focus. "Don't let it. Don't ever let that happen."

"One more!" I said loudly. I closed the breech with a distinct *cluck,* seating the cartridge, and raised the butt to my shoulder again.

Concentrate on the foresight. The barrel wobbled around the target, let alone the bull's-eye. *Squeeze the trigger, don't jerk it.* My whole right hand tightened.

I tried to hold the rifle as I had the cutting bar as we sawed boards for the target, firmly but without the feeling of desperate control that the firearm brought out. I wasn't making something happen. I was easing the trigger back against the rough metal-to-metal contact points of a mechanism made by a journeyman rather than a master.

The muzzle blast surprised me the way Stephen said it was supposed to. Splinters flew from a hole a few centimeters left of the bull's-eye.

"Yeah," Stephen said. "You're beginning to get it. In another day or two, you'll be as good as half the crew."

He shook his head disgustedly. "They think they can shoot, but even when they practice, they plink at rocks or ration cartons. If they miss, they don't have a clue why. They'll make the same damned mistake the next time, like enough."

I extracted the empty case. Powder gases streamed through the open breech. "What does it take to get as good as you are, Stephen?" I asked, careful not to meet his eyes.

"Nothing you can learn," he said. He sat down on the trunk of a fallen tree with bark like diamond scales. "And it's not something you'd think was worth the price, I suspect."

I sat beside him. I couldn't hear the *Oriflamme*'s pumps anymore. They must have completed filling our water tanks. "Do you know how long Piet intends to lay over here?" I asked. "It seems a comfortable place, if you don't mind muggy."

I flapped the front of my tunic, sopping from the wet heat.

"The only thing that worries me is the Avoid notation in the database you found for us," Stephen said. He half cocked his rifle and began to rotate its five-shot cylinder with his fingertips, checking the cartridge heads. The pawl clicked lightly over the star gear. "There's nothing wrong with the air or the biosphere, so why avoid it?"

"There's a hundred charted worlds with that marker," I said. "Maybe Pleyal woke up on the wrong side of the bed the morning the list was handed him."

"Come on back and we'll clean your weapon," Stephen said as he rose. "Don't leave that to somebody else to—"

I was staring skyward. Stephen followed my eyes to the glare of bright exhaust. "God *damn* it," he said softly. "It's a starship landing, and it sure isn't from Venus."

We ran through the forest as the *Oriflamme*'s siren sounded.

The strange vessel drifted down like a dead leaf. Starships—the starships I'd seen landing—tended to do so in a controlled crash because the forces being balanced were so enormous. This ship must have a remarkably high power-to-weight ratio, even though its exhaust flames were the bright blue-white of oxyhydrogen motors rather than the familiar flaring iridescence of plasma.

Dole was leading a party of twenty men from the main hatch into the forest. "Mister Gregg, do you want to take over?" the bosun shouted when he saw us. All the men were armed, but several of them hadn't waited to pull on their tunics when the alarm sounded.

"No, go ahead," Stephen ordered as he sprang up the steps to the cockpit airlock.

Dole's section would hide in the forest so that we weren't all bottled in the *Oriflamme* if shooting started. It would take anything from ten minutes to half an hour for the ship to lift. In the meanwhile, the *Oriflamme* was a target for anybody in orbit who wanted to bombard us.

To a degree that worked both ways. The *Oriflamme*'s gunports were open, though of course our guns couldn't sweep as wide a zone as could those of an orbiting vessel able to change its attitude. Stampfer was raising the 17-cm gun into firing position. The violent blasphemy he snarled during the process, only a meter from Piet's couch, showed how nervous the gunner was.

Stephen grabbed the flashgun slung from the same hook as his rolled hammock. I think if he'd had his favored weapon, he would have stayed with Dole outside. Stephen took a repeating rifle with him when we left the ship because the dog-sized local predators hunted in packs of three or more.

Piet glanced aside from his console. "They've announced they're friendly," he said. "And I presume they are or we'd know it by now, but . . ."

Because the strangers didn't use plasma motors, they could communicate by radio even while they were landing. That didn't seem

a sufficient trade-off for the greater power of fusion over chemical energy, but it had its advantages.

Stephen donned his helmet as he stepped out the airlock again.
Piet smiled and returned to his plot.

I followed Stephen. I still carried the slung rifle. I'd picked up
my cutting bar also, as much for the way it focused me as for any
good I'd be able to do with it against a starship.

The strange vessel was no bigger than a featherboat, though it
was shorter and thicker than the *Nathan,* say, had been. It settled
only twenty meters from the *Oriflamme,* bow to bow. Its combustion engines were loud by absolute standards, but they whispered
in comparison to those of a normal starship. Plasma thrusters
mixed low-frequency pulses with the *hiss* of ions recombining
across and beyond the upper auditory band, creating a snarl more
penetrating and unpleasant than I could have imagined before I
heard it myself.

The ship's four stubby legs seemed to be integral rather than
extended for landing. Portions of the scaly brown hull were charred
from heat stress during reentry, but the material didn't look like
the ablative coatings I was familiar with. It looked like tree bark.

The strange vessel had no visible gunports or hull openings of
any kind. I walked toward it; either leading Stephen or following
him, it was hard to say. A spot grew in the mid-hull. At first I
thought a fire smoldered on the coating, but it was a knot opening
as it spun slowly outward.

The hole froze when it reached man-size. The figure that stepped
out of the ship was humanoid but certainly not human, though
most of its body was covered with a hooded cape of translucent
fabric. It had reptilian limbs and a face covered with patterned
nodules like those of a lizard's skin. The jaw was undershot, the
eyes pivoted individually, and the hands gripped a stocked weapon
with a ten-liter pressure tank.

"I'd worry," Stephen murmured, "if they weren't armed." His
voice was in the husky, dissociated mode in which I knew he didn't
worry at all; only planned whom to kill first.

The second person out of the ship was a human, though he wore
a flowing cape like that of the guard who preceded him. Tiny flowers filled the socket of his left eye like a miniature rock garden,
and his right leg beneath the cape's hem was of dark wood with
a golden grain. When the cape blew close to his body, I could see

a handgun of some sort tucked against the front of his right shoulder.

"Hello, Gregg," the man said. It was hard to think of someone with flowers growing from his face as being human, and the fellow's rusty voice didn't help the impression. "I thought the Feds had killed you on Biruta."

Two more reptiles, armed as the first had been, got out of the strange ship. Their capes were a uniform dull gray, but the human's had underlayers which returned sunlight in shimmers across the whole optical spectrum.

"Hello, Cseka," Stephen said. "They tried, but we got away."

Cseka glanced beyond us. Piet stood in the cockpit hatch. "Ricimer too, eh?" Cseka said. "Well, I didn't get away. They caught me on Biruta and they made me a slave. How long's it been, anyway? Standard years, I mean."

"Five years, Captain," Piet said. "Would you come aboard the *Oriflamme*? Your friends, too, if they care to."

"Aye, we'll do that," Cseka said. He spoke a few throaty words to his guards and stumped forward. "These are the Chay," he said, again in Trade English. "And I'm no longer a captain, Ricimer, I'm chief adviser to the Council of On Chay."

Cseka walked with a stiffness that the false leg didn't fully explain. I wondered what other injuries the cape concealed.

"And I'm the worst enemy Pleyal and his bastard Federation will ever have," Cseka added as he climbed the cockpit ladder. He spoke quietly, but his voice squealed like chalk on slate.

The Chay walked with quick, mincing steps, though there was nothing birdlike about their erect bodies. Their bulging eyes swept at least 240° even when they faced front, and they continually rotated their heads to cover the remaining arc.

"The mummy on Respite," I murmured to Stephen as we followed the guards back aboard the *Oriflamme*.

"I was thinking that," he said. "And now I really wonder how long ago he was buried."

Stephen was still distant from his surroundings. Perhaps it was mention of Biruta, where Pleyal's men had treacherously massacred Venerian traders. For reasons of state, there was still formal peace between the Free State of Venus and the North American Federation; but because of Biruta, there was open war beyond Pluto, and survivors like Piet and Stephen were the shock troops of that war.

Piet and Stephen and Captain, now Chief Adviser, Cseka.

The Long Tom was aligned with the bow port—and the Chay vessel—but not run forward to battery. Stampfer was still with the gun, but he'd sent his crew aft so that only he and the navigation officers waited for us in the bow compartment. Piet had dropped the table which hung on lines from the ceiling. Men watched through the hatch and from an arc outside the cockpit.

"Five years," Cseka said. "You lose track. Five years."

He took the tumbler of cloudy liquor Piet offered him: slash distilled from algae. This was a bottle we'd brought from Venus rather than what the motor crews brewed whenever we landed, but there wasn't a lot of difference.

"We have, ah, wines and such," Piet said. "Loot, of course."

Cseka drained his tumbler in three wracking gulps. Slash proved anywhere from fifty to eighty percent ethanol. "A taste of home, by God," he muttered. "The Chay, they can do anything with plants, but they can't make slash that's real slash."

"Perhaps they're too skillful," Stephen said. I don't know whether he was joking. "Slash doesn't permit subtlety."

"I was their slave for . . ." Cseka said. He frowned and refilled his tumbler. "Years. You can't measure it. Pleyal's slave, bossing gangs of Molt slaves all across the Back Worlds. The eye, that was from Biruta. They took my leg off on a place that hasn't any name. Pleyal doesn't waste medicines on slaves when amputation will do."

He swallowed another three fingers of slash. Cseka's eye was fixed on the bottle, but I can't guess what his mind saw.

"And then the Chay raided the plantation I was running on Rosary." Cseka gave us all a broad, mad grin. The tiny flowers wobbled in his eye socket as he turned his head. "I escaped with them. They might have killed me before they understood. That would have been all right, I'd still have been free of Pleyal."

The Chay had a sweetish odor like that of overripe fruit. I couldn't tell whether it was their breath or their bodies. They looked silently around the compartment. One of them reached toward the 17-cm cannon, but his long-fingered hand withdrew before it quite touched the gun. Stampfer, squat and glowering, relaxed minusculely.

"I've been guiding On Chay ever since," Cseka said. "Not leading—the Council leads. But I know the Feds, and I help the Chay fight them. The *bastards*."

"We came through the Breach," Piet said, "but we'll have to return the long way to Venus. We'll carry you back with us and give you a full share of—"

"No!" Cseka shouted. His hand closed on the neck of the bottle. I thumbed the power switch of my cutting bar and opened my left hand to grab the nearest Chay's weapon before he could—

Cseka relaxed and beamed his clownface grin at us again. "No, I'm where I belong," he said. He spoke now in a cracked lilt. "Killing Feds. Killing all the Feds, every one of the bastards, every one."

He poured more slash. Stephen almost hadn't moved, but "almost" was the amount he'd tucked the flashgun into his side to have a full stroke when he swept the butt across the heads of Cseka and the guard nearest him. Piet had reached across the back of his couch, where a double-barreled shotgun hung by its sling, and the lever from the plasma cannon's collimator was in Stampfer's hand.

"I want you to come back to On Chay with me," Cseka said, sipping this time instead of tossing the liquor off. "I told our scouts to look for ceramic-hulled ships, you know. To report to me at once and not to attack. And here you appear in *this* system."

He seemed to be oblivious of what had almost happened. Perhaps he didn't remember. The Chay hadn't moved, but their facial skin had shifted from green/brown to mauve.

"We appreciate the offer . . ." Piet said. "But—"

"No, it's not out of your way," Cseka said with a dismissive wave of his hand. "The fourth planet here."

"That's a gas giant," Salomon said sharply from his console.

"Yes, the second moon out," Cseka agreed. He was all sweet reason now. The sharpness was gone, but his voice still sing-songed. "It'll be worth your time. The Chay grow tubular fullerenes, *grow* them, any length you want. Kilo for kilo, they're worth more than new-run chips."

Piet's face grew blankly quiet. He wasn't looking at anyone. We all waited for him to speak. The *Oriflamme* wasn't a democracy.

He smiled dazzlingly. "Yes, all right," he said to Cseka. "We'll follow you, then?"

Cseka nodded, the flowers bobbing in his eye socket. "Yes, yes, that's what we'll do," he said. Suddenly, fiercely he added, "I knew there'd be ships from Venus sooner or later. Between us, we'll kill them all!"

He turned and slammed out through the open airlock without further comment. The three guards exchanged glances, only their eyes moving, before they strutted after their human leader.

Stephen relaxed slightly. "Cseka was always a bit of a hothead," he said in an emotionless voice.

Piet watched the castaway climb back aboard the vessel in which he had arrived. "That was a different man, the one we knew," he said.

"You trust him, then?" I said. I switched off the cutting bar and hung it, so that I could work life back into the hand with which I'd been gripping the weapon.

"No," said Piet. The port of the Chay vessel began to rotate closed before the last of the guards hopped through. "He's obviously insane. But he's different from the man Stephen and I knew."

He pushed the button controlling the *Oriflamme*'s siren, calling the men aboard for liftoff.

I dropped my rifle and ammo satchel on the deck. "I'm going with them," I said. I jumped from the airlock instead of using the steps. Over my shoulder I called, "We need to know more about the Chay than we do now!"

Men piling aboard via the ramp looked in surprise as I sprinted to the alien vessel. Nobody tried to call me back from the bridge. Piet and Stephen weren't the sort to waste their breath.

"Cseka!" I shouted. "Open up! Let me ride with you!"

The port continued to spin slowly closed. It had shrunk to the size of my head. I stuck the blade of my unpowered cutting bar into the opening.

The port stopped closing. I waited. The Chay vessel's hull pulsed slowly as I stood beside it with my hand on the grip of my bar.

After a minute or so, the knot rotated the other way again. When the opening was large enough, I climbed aboard.

ON CHAY

Day 156

The engines' firing level reduced gradually, as though someone was shutting down the fuel valves by micro-adjustments as we settled toward the moon's inhabited surface. Some *thing* was, but not a person, unless the Chay vessel herself had personality as well as life.

One of the reptiles chewed a banana-shaped fruit that dribbled purple juice down his jaw and the front of his cape. It seemed to have a narcotic effect. The Chay's eyes hadn't moved since he began eating; translucent lids slipped back and forth across them at intervals.

Cseka lay on his back, staring at the frameless screen that covered the cabin ceiling. Instead of a real-time scan, adjusted images swept over the display area at one- or two-second intervals.

None of the vessel's crew was anywhere near the controls aft. The ship was landing itself.

"Are those irrigated lands?" I asked, gesturing toward a swatch of blue-green on the surface swelling toward us. It could as easily have been a lake. I wasn't sure whether the patterns I saw in the colored area were real or an artifact of the unfamiliar optical apparatus.

"We live on mats of vegetation," Cseka said in a drugged voice. He didn't look at me when he spoke. "On Chay has too many

454

earthquakes to live directly on the ground. The mats slide when the earth shakes, you see."

"Life couldn't arise on a planet—'moon'—so unstable," I said, speaking the thought I'd had ever since I connected the Chay with the mummy on Respite. "It must have been colonized from somewhere else. Perhaps in the far past."

"Yeah, that's probably so," Cseka agreed without interest. "There's maybe a hundred Chay worlds. They all call themselves On Chay. I suppose the Chay had a Collapse too."

Translucent circles like strings of frog eggs clung to one another within the mat we were approaching. Elsewhere, larger circles differed in hue from the neighboring vegetation. The primary lowered in the sky above us, a turgid purple mass shot with blues and yellow.

The controls spoke in a guttural, blurry voice. The two sober Chay looked around. Cseka roused himself from his couch and growled toward the controls.

The engines fired at high output. We accelerated sideways, and I fell against a bulkhead. The resilient surface cushioned me, then formed into a grip for my furious hand.

"I'm to guide your friends down outside the city," Cseka grumbled. "I forgot the way plasma thrusters tear up everything around."

The Chay vessel was smaller inside than I'd expected. The thick hull contained everything necessary for the starship's operation and the well-being of the crew, but it didn't leave much internal volume.

"The *Oriflamme* is already in orbit?" I asked.

Cseka looked at me as if he were trying to remember where I'd come from. I hadn't noticed anything odd when I ate rations prepared for Cseka—none of the food was meat, according to him, though I'd have sworn otherwise. Most likely, the castaway's problems had nothing to do with his present diet.

"You said we were guiding my friends down," I prodded. "So they were waiting for us?"

"Yeah, sure," Cseka said with an angry frown. "Look, we got here, didn't we? Our ships don't process course equations as fast as the Feds do, maybe, but they don't come down sideways because a cosmic ray punched the artificial intelligence at the wrong time."

We'd transited from above Duneen almost as soon as we reached orbit. A human vessel—even the *Oriflamme* with Piet running the boards—would have taken at least half an hour to calibrate.

The next transit, from a point so removed that the system's sun was only a bright star when it rotated across the ceiling screen, had taken what I think was the better part of a day. I was used to transits in quick series, several to several score insertions in sequence, followed by periods of an hour or more to recalculate. Chay vessels used a completely different system.

The advantage—it minimized the horrible sickness of transiting through nonsidereal universes—was balanced by the fact that the Chay didn't continue accelerating during calibration. We were in free fall all the time we waited for the brain built into the vessel's hull to prepare for the next transit. Combustion rockets weren't as fuel-efficient as plasma thrusters, and the navigational system obviously didn't cope with small, sudden changes as well as humans' silicon-based microprocessors did.

"They were met in orbit," Cseka murmured, settling back onto his couch. "But they didn't want to land until we'd arrived. You had."

The ceiling visuals were more like mural paintings than the screens I was used to. The mat of vegetation covered the bow third of the image. There were circular fields of varying size within the general blue-green mass. Occasional bright, straight lines suggested metalwork. From what Cseka had told me about Chay culture, I assumed they were biologically formed as well.

I'd thought the castaway would be babblingly glad of human company after his years among aliens. Instead, Cseka remained in his own world throughout the voyage. He gave verbal orders to the controls when the ship demanded them. My questions were answered in monosyllables or brief phrases, the way a busy leader snaps at an importunate underling; responses only in the technical sense, which in no way attempted to give me the understanding I'd requested.

Despite that, I'd learned a great deal about the Chay to guide Piet when he dealt with the race. A day's discomfort was nothing compared to what we'd been through already; and the risk—

I'd made that decision when I came aboard the *Porcelain*. So had we all.

The vessel was settling to the west of the mat. As we neared the ground I realized that resolution of the Chay optics was amazingly good, more like still photographs than the scanned images I was used to. The visuals were real, too, not data cleaned up by an enhancement program. The surface had all the warts and blemishes of a natural landscape.

The soil beneath us was russet, yellow, and gray. There were dips and outcrops, but no significant hills. Frequent cracks jagged across the surface, often streaming sulphurous gases. Vegetation outside the large mats was limited to clumps and rings. None of it was high enough to cast a shadow from the primary on the eastern horizon.

"Is it breathable?" I asked as I watched a fumarole just upwind of where we trembled in a near-hover. "The air."

"What?" Cseka said. He blinked, then frowned. "Of course it's breathable. A little high in carbon dioxide, that's all. These—"

He plucked the cowl of his cape. It stretched across his face as a veil.

"—filter it. I'll have some brought to your ship."

He spoke to the vessel's controls again. We resumed our descent at less than three meters a second.

"The Chay wear them also," I said. We would land in a shallow depression hundreds of meters in diameter, half a klick from the inhabited vegetation. Atmosphere vessels—platforms supported by three or more translucent gas bags—drifted from the city toward the spot.

"When they're out of their domes, yes," Cseka said.

I squatted against the bulkhead's lower curve, not that we were going to land hard enough to require my caution. If the Chay couldn't breathe the atmosphere of On Chay without artificial aids, there was no question at all that they were the relicts of a past civilization rather than autochthons.

The engines roared at higher output and on a distinctly different note. I recalled how the nozzles had dilated as the Chay vessel landed on Duneen. The exhaust spread to reflect from the ground as a cushion against the lower hull.

"Do you have a filter for me?" I asked, pitching my voice to be heard over the engines. How quickly did CO_2 poisoning become dangerous? Could I run to the *Oriflamme* after she landed?

"Christ's blood," said Cseka. He wiped his good eye with the back of his hand, then waved toward the guard whose muscles had frozen while the last of the fruit was a centimeter from his mouth. "Take his!"

Cseka growled a few additional words to the Chay. The mobile guards unfastened their fellow's cape by running a finger down a hidden seam. They pulled the garment away from him as we landed lightly as thought.

One of them handed the cape to me. I wrapped it around my shoulders, avoiding the patch of sticky purple juice. The edges sealed when I pressed them together, though the fabric felt as slick as the surface of the *Oriflamme*'s hull.

The Chay's naked body was skeletally thin. The pebbly frontal skin was light gray-brown, while the sides and back were a darker shade of the same drab combination. The color variations of the face and arms were absent.

The creature wore a net garment similar to a bandeau across its midriff. A few small objects hung from the meshes. I couldn't guess what their human analogs might be.

One of the Chay spoke. It was the first time I'd heard one of their voices. The word or words seemed sharper than those of Cseka speaking the language, but obviously he managed to communicate.

The whorled patch of bulkhead spun slowly outward, opening to a dark sky and the coruscation of the *Oriflamme*'s thrusters descending. I smoothed the sides of my borrowed cape over my nose and mouth, then ducked through the hatchway as soon as it had opened enough to pass me.

The *Oriflamme* dropped in a wide circle of Chay vessels, ten or a dozen of them. These ships were constructs, three to six pods linked by tubes fat enough that a man or Chay could crawl between them.

The individual hulls were similar to the one that had carried me to On Chay. I had a vision of giant pea vines festooned with starships. I suppose that was pretty close to the truth.

The *Oriflamme* wobbled slightly like a man walking on stilts, though anyone who'd seen another starship land would be amazed at how skillfully Piet balanced the thrust of his eight engines. The Chay escort kept formation around him like fish schooling rather than individually-controlled machines. They dropped with less than a quarter of their jets lighted, further proof of how much less massive they were than human vessels.

I'd used my hand to block the glare of the *Oriflamme*'s thrusters. When Cseka got out behind me, he'd sealed the front of his cowl up over his eyes. I tried the same thing. The fabric blocked the high-energy—UV and blue—portion of the exhaust and dimmed the whole output to comfortable levels, without degrading the rest of my vision more than ten or twenty percent. That was about as good as our helmet visors.

The dirigibles I'd seen on our vessel's screen sailed nearer. The supporting gas bags were the size and shape of the starship hulls, though the walls were thin enough to be translucent. Eight to ten meters beneath each set of bags hung a platform, some of which were large enough to hold several score Chay.

The bigger dirigibles mounted a plasma cannon at the bow. The weapons were metal and of small bore, swivel guns like those *Our Lady of Montreal* had carried.

I nudged Cseka. "Where do they get the cannon?" I shouted over the *Oriflamme*'s hammering roar.

"Trade," he said. "For fullerenes. We've got embassies from most of the states of Earth here, but the shipments go through too many hands. That's why we want Venerians. To set up our own foundries."

About half the Chay riding the dirigibles wore plain gray capes like those of Cseka's guards. The remainder were clad in a variety of other metallic hues. Most of these were shades of silver, but cinnabar reds and blues as poisonous as that of copper sulfate were dazzlingly present. A few Chay gleamed with the same gold undertones as Cseka's cape.

A hundred meters up, the Chay vessels increased thrust and hovered while the *Oriflamme* dropped out of their circle. Moving in a single flock, the escorts pulsed sideways through the sky in the direction of the mat of vegetation.

The *Oriflamme* landed nearby in an explosion of dirt. Each of the thruster nozzles acted as a shaped charge blasting straight down. The soil was friable, without enough sand in the mixture to bind it into glass.

I hunched and covered my head with my arms. Cseka remembered to duck a moment later, but the two guards who'd followed us out of the ship continued gaping at the *Oriflamme* until the dirt cascaded over us. It was like being caught in a rugby scrum.

I fell over on my right side. One of the rocks that bounced off my forearm would have knocked me silly if it had hit my head instead. Pebbles settled while the wave of lighter dust traveled outward in an expanding doughnut. A dirigible nosed toward us through the cloud.

I shook the hem of my cape free of the dirt loading it and jogged toward the *Oriflamme*. Cseka shouted something, but I couldn't understand the words. Maybe he was calling to the Chay in their own language.

The forward airlock opened as I neared the *Oriflamme*. Stephen, identifiable even in a hard suit by his size and the slung flashgun, swung down the integral steps and stamped toward me across the glowing crater the plasma motors blew around the vessel.

He raised his visor when he was clear of the throbbing boundary. "I'll carry you," he said.

"I hoped you might," I said, but he didn't hear me because he had to lock his visor down again to draw a breath.

I stepped into his arms and, like Saint Christopher carrying our Lord, Stephen tramped back across the blasted soil and up the steps into the *Oriflamme*. The ground had cooled below the optical range, but radiant heat baked the sweat from my calves and left arm in the few seconds I was exposed.

Both valves of the airlock stood open until Stephen set me down. The forward compartment was closed off from the rest of the ship. Piet and half a dozen senior members of the complement waited for us in oxygen masks.

"This is a filter," I said, plucking the hood down from my eyes. I realized how strange I must look. "How high *is* the carbon dioxide?"

"Five and a half percent," Piet said. The outer door had closed, so he took his mask cautiously away. "I'm surprised the Chay breathe Duneen's atmosphere when their own is so different."

"They're as alien here as we are," I said. "From what I could drag out of Cseka—believe me, he's crazy. It's like his mind was dropped and all the pieces were put together blind."

I hawked to clear my throat. My cape's filter mechanism didn't seem to bind the ozone formed by plasma exhausted into an oxygen atmosphere. On the main screen, three dirigibles moved toward the *Oriflamme*. Cilia on the platforms' undersides rowed the air. They raised some dust from the ground, but less than turbines of similar thrust.

"There's a hundred or so Chay worlds," I resumed. "There's no overall direction—they're as likely to fight with each other as trade."

"How unlike humans," Piet said dryly.

"Some of them do trade with the Feds," I said. "And it sounds like the Feds have taken control of some Chay worlds. Most of the Chay, though—like this system, they're marked 'Avoid' on the pilotry chart because a Fed ship gets handed its head if it messes with the locals."

One of the dirigibles swung broadside to the *Oriflamme;* it hovered with its platform on a level with the cockpit hatch. The six supporting gas bags loomed above us. Their total volume was several times that of the starship. Low-ranking Chay stood near bales of gray capes like those they themselves wore, waiting for our hatch to open.

"I didn't see a single piece of metalwork, much less ceramic, on the ship," I said. I nodded toward the image of the armed dirigible. "They've got cannon—"

"Southern Cross work," said Stephen without bothering to look again at the weapon he'd already assessed. "And about as dangerous at one end as the other, I'd judge."

"They can do anything with plants," I said. "They can sequester lanthanides in fullerene tubes a meter long, Cseka swears."

"What good is that?" Stephen asked.

"On Earth, they're starting to use them to replace damaged nerves," I replied. "Cseka wants us to set up a cannon foundry here. In exchange, they'll provide either biological products or the plant stocks that make them. He's serious, but—"

"*Us*, to set up a foundry?" said Piet. "Or Venus?"

I nodded with my lips pursed. "Yeah, that's the thing. I think maybe he means us. We could convince him that we don't have the expertise ourselves, but—"

"Unless he remembers what my father does for a living," Piet said with a smile.

"We can't train this cack-handed lot to cast cannon!" I snapped. "Any more than I could teach them to build silicon AIs. Or breathe water! But I don't know how well Cseka is going to hear anything that doesn't agree with what he wants to hear."

Piet nodded. "Not a unique problem," he said. "Though I think we'd better meet with his leaders. Compressed fullerenes are what give our hulls—"

He tapped Stephen's breastplate affectionately.

"—and armor hardness that Terran metallurgists can't equal. If the Chay are so much better at creating fullerenes than we are with our sputtering techniques—"

Piet smiled.

"—then we owe it to Venus to learn what we can."

He fitted the mask back over his face. "Our hosts have waited long enough," he said. "I'll take a few men and some gifts to meet with them. And we'll see what we see."

Stephen frowned at "*I'll* take"; but as I'd noticed before, he didn't waste his breath in futile argument. "I'm one of the men," he said.

"And I'm another," I added.

"Yeah, those are food crops," Cseka agreed, peering over the edge of the platform at the brown and ocher vegetation twenty meters below. "The inside stems and the leaves both. You wouldn't know it was the same plant."

The platform didn't have a guardrail, but Piet seemed equally nonchalant as he leaned forward to view the fields. Chay agriculture was labor-intensive: at least a hundred gray-clad figures stooped over the sinuous crop, pruning and cultivating. The vines were as big around as my thighs, but the relatively small leaves looked more like fur than foliage.

Stephen and I stayed back a step from the edge. He grimaced every time Piet overhung the platform, and his free hand—the one not on the grip of his flashgun—was poised to snatch his friend back if a jolt sent him toppling.

However, the dirigible rode as solidly as a rock. The platform was suspended on hoselike tubes that stretched and compressed as the gas bags lifted or fell in the breeze. The deck undulated only slightly as cilia beneath stroked us forward.

We slid between two brown-tinged domes together covering nearly a hectare. "Workers' housing," Cseka volunteered, gesturing with his elbow toward the dome on our side of the platform. I could see the dim outlines of tiered buildings under the curving surface. Cseka had spoken more during the ride from the *Oriflamme*'s landing site a kilometer away than he did during the day's voyage from Duneen.

I carried a flashgun too, but just as a gift to the council. Our ceramic cassegrain lasers were far superior to the nearest Terran equivalents, though not many Venerians cared to use weapons so heavy and unpleasant for the shooter. I sometimes wondered whether Stephen carried a flashgun because each round was so effective, or if a part of him liked the punishment.

A clear dome far larger than those housing the Chay workers loomed before us. The structures inside looked like mushrooms with multiple caps one above another on a single central shaft. Those near the middle of the enclosure had eight or nine layers.

Our dirigible settled to the ground. Rather, settled onto a living surface of hair-fine leaves woven as tightly as carpeting. The arched opening in the dome was big enough for three or four people to walk abreast. The passage writhed like an intestine instead of going straight through to the interior.

"Come," said Cseka. "The council will be waiting for us."

He stepped from the platform to the carpet of vegetation. Stephen and Piet fell in to either side of the castaway, while the three of us carrying presents—Dole and Lightbody with me—followed closely behind. Chay on the dirigibles wheezed a fanfare on horns several meters long driven by four musicians squeezing bellows simultaneously.

There wasn't a door at either end of the tunnel, but its walls were lined with fine hairs that greatly increased the surface area. That and the winding course—the dome's wall was only three meters through even here where it was thickened, but the passage was a good twenty—served to filter the carbon dioxide down to levels the Chay found comfortable.

A crowd of Chay with their cowls thrown back lined both sides of the route inside the dome. At least half of them wore the colored garments I'd come to associate with higher ranks. As we six humans entered the enclosed area, the spectators began to stamp their feet in a slow rhythm. The flooring was as hard and dense-grained as a nutshell, and the dome reverberated.

We walked along a boulevard a hundred meters wide, thronged with stamping Chay. Musicians from the dirigibles followed us, wheezing on their horns. Additional spectators leaned from the upper stories of buildings.

"Do they have radio, do you suppose?" I said. I was speaking mostly to myself at first, but I added loudly enough to be heard by the men ahead of me, "Captain Cseka, do the Chay have radio?"

A party in silvery capes marched to meet us. They played instruments a meter and a half long; bangles on either end clattered like the beads of an abacus when the musician plucked his one string. These strings, the bellows trumpets, and the stamping crowd each kept an individual rhythm. Only the cacophony aboard *Absalom 231* in the atmosphere of Decades approached the result.

Cseka turned his head. "Only to talk to human ships," he shouted. "We use beans that vibrate the same as others from the same pod instead."

He shrugged. "The range is only a few light-seconds and they aren't faster than light, nothing like that. But they work."

The string players reversed course to precede us down the boulevard. The towers were arranged in three rings of increasing height. At the center of the enclosure, a low building sat in a circular court several hundred meters across.

Near the entrance to the central structure was a cage, grown rather than woven in a lattice with about a hundred millimeters across openings. The two lines of string players parted around it. A man—a human being in the remnants of a Federation uniform—clutched the bars to hold his torso upright.

There were—three at least, maybe more—human corpses in the cage with the living man. One of them had been dead long enough that the flesh had sloughed to bare his ribs. The stench of death and rotting waste was a barrier so real that I stumbled three steps away.

Piet stopped and touched his hand to Cseka's arm. "What's this?" Piet asked, exaggerating his lip movements to be understood without bellowing.

"Sometimes we take Feds alive," Cseka said nonchalantly. "They're brought here for entertainment."

His right hand came out from beneath his cape with the handweapon I'd seen outlined there. Grip, receiver, and barrel were one piece of dark brown, black-grained wood. A lanyard growing from the butt quivered back in a springy coil which held the pistol out of the way when it wasn't in use.

Cseka fired. A snap of steam lifted the gun muzzle. The prisoner screamed and arched convulsively. He skidded on his back, thrashing across a floor slippery with filth.

Cseka held his weapon up for us to see. "Darts," he said. "They're not fatal, not usually. But they drop a fellow quicker than bullets. And they—"

He aimed again toward the prisoner. The procession halted when we did, but the wracking music continued.

Piet put two fingers under the barrel of the dart gun and lifted it away. "Please don't," he said. "The things we have to do in war are terrible enough."

"Nothing could be enough!" Cseka shouted. He raised the pistol and brought it down in a slashing stroke at Piet's head. Stephen blocked the blow with his left forearm, catching Cseka's wrist numbingly. The pistol flew loose and slithered back under the cape.

Cseka began to giggle. "Nothing could be enough," he repeated. "Some day we'll have them all here, with your help."

He strode around the left side of the cage. We five Oriflammes scrambled to catch up, but the Chay in the procession resumed marching without missing a step.

The Chay hadn't reacted to the momentary human conflict. The Fed prisoner lay quiescent. His eyes were open, and his chest trembled like that of a dog panting.

"Our rifles throw fireballs a hundred meters," Cseka said, his voice raised only to be heard over the background noise. The maniacal rage switched itself off and on in an eyeblink. He tapped the barrel of Stephen's flashgun. "Within their range, they're better than this."

"Within their range," Stephen repeated. There was nothing in his tone to suggest he believed the Chay shoulder weapons—they certainly weren't rifled—were really as effective as his laser at any range.

The string players flared to either side of the central building. The structure was nearly cylindrical, as if a balloon had been inflated in a tube. The walls slanted slightly inward and the roof edge was a radiused curve instead of square.

We walked into the building. The single chamber held several score Chay in golden capes and at least a dozen humans. Like us, the humans wore the gray local garment, but their hats were of a number of Terran styles. I recognized a pair of Southerns, a large man in a kepi with United Europe military insignia, and a pair of women from the Independent Coastal Republic. Their state had been fighting for thirty years against Pleyal's federated *remainder* of North America.

There was an open aisle down the center of the room. Cseka led us toward the empty dais at the end. The music and stamping outside stopped, but the chamber sighed with the spectators' breathing. The walls were lighted from within, giving the effect of translucence which the black exterior belied.

We halted two paces from the dais, as close as any of the spectators stood. A human leaned close to me and said in Trade English, "You're from Venus, is it not so? You're bringing arms to trade?"

"We're passing through," I replied; in a whisper, though the questioner had spoken normally. I think he was a European. United Europe had no extra-solar colonies, but several of its states engaged in trade beyond Pluto.

He sniffed. "There's nothing they want but arms, cannon especially," he said. "Well, there's enough for all."

The wall behind the dais rotated open like the port in the Chay starship. Ten Chay carried through three others on a litter whose wooden surface gleamed like polished bronze.

The trio were completely naked and very old. They hunched like dogs sitting up. Their skins were nearly white. Their three tails twisted together and appeared to have fused into one flesh.

The silver-caped porters lowered the trio to the dais. The spectators shouted. The voices of the Chay were more or less in unison though of course unintelligible. The humans—the man next to me, at least—cried, "Hail, the all-powerful council!"

The trio's mouths opened as one. "Greetings to this worshipful assembly," boomed the front wall of the chamber while the two side walls were snarling something in the language of the Chay themselves. The Trade English words seemed synchronized with the lipless mouth of the center councilor.

The room stilled. The walls had been suffused with amber light. The floor level was now emerald green, and the hue was slipping upward as if by osmosis. The councilors focused their independently-rotating eyes on us.

"We have discussed you with Lord Cseka," said the center figure. His voice through the front wall was understandable despite the sidewalls' accompanying harsh gutturals. "Your enemies are our enemies. Together we will drive the Federation pirates out of existence except as our slaves and your slaves."

The trio paused. The councilors were as thin as mummies, pebbly skin sunken drumhead-tight over an armature of bone. Their ribs fluttered when they breathed.

Piet lifted his arms forward to call attention to himself without advancing into the cleared zone before the dais. "All-powerful council!" he said in a voice pitched to be heard in a larger arena than this one. "We bring you the greetings of Venus and our ruler, Governor Halys. We ourselves are but chance travelers, but permit us to offer a few trifles as a foretaste of the trade the future will bring between your people and ours."

He twisted his head back toward me. "Jere—" he murmured. I gave him the flashgun before he finished the request.

"A laser with a range of kilometers," Piet called. The weapon weighed nearly twenty kilos, as I well knew, but he balanced it on the palm of one hand so that he could deploy the charging parasol from the butt with the other.

"In good light, you can fire every three minutes at full power!" he added. We weren't providing spare batteries as a part of this gift. "Your enemies and ours of the Federation have no hand-weapons so effective."

A porter took the gift from Piet and set it on the dais beside the council. Lightbody held his load out. Piet shook his head curtly and gestured to Dole instead.

Dole handed forward a round bowl a meter in diameter. Piet raised it overhead and turned it so that all the assembly could see Governor Halys' gray pearl charge on a field of creamy translucence.

"As your folk with plants, so ours with ceramics," Piet said. "This is merely a symbol of—"

He flung the bowl down on the floor as hard as he could. It bounced back into his hands with the deep, throbbing note of a jade gong. The assembly, Chay and humans alike, gasped with surprise.

"—the skill with which our experts, experts whom I can encourage to journey here from Venus, cast plasma cannon!"

The sidewalls rumbled phrases in the local tongue, though the councilors weren't speaking. Chay spectators whispered among themselves. The human ambassadors eyed us with speculation and some disquiet.

"One last thing," Piet said as a porter took away the undam-aged bowl. He was emphasizing that we were geese who would lay golden eggs, a prize for what we would bring rather than what we were. "Like the others, this is only a symbol of the trade that will start upon our return to Venus."

Piet took from Lightbody the navigational computer we'd stripped out of one of the Federation ships captured on Trehinga. I'd have reduced the simple unit to components for ease of stor-age, but Piet stopped me for reasons I now understood.

"In order to capture a vessel in transit," Piet said, "your AI must solve the same equations the other vessel's does. We of Venus will supply you with electronic artificial intelligences that will allow you to track Federation ships across the bubble universes instead of being limited to attacking those you find grounded or in orbit. There will be no safety for the enemies of On Chay and Venus!"

This time the Chay spectators stamped their feet as the trans-lation boomed to them from the sidewalls. It was almost a minute after a porter took the—crude—AI that the chamber quieted again.

The walls replied in the councilors' three voices, "Men of Venus, our folk are already delivering to your vessel phials of drugs, fabrics, and the tubular fullerenes we know your folk especially prize. Trade for the future, yes . . . But we will propose to you other arrangements as well. Go now, and tomorrow we will meet with you again."

Piet bowed low. I knelt and tugged Dole and Lightbody down with me. The aisle through the assembly had closed, but the spectators squeezed aside again to let us pass. The Chay were stamping their enthusiasm.

I was in the lead of our party, walking with the steady arrogance that befitted a gentleman of Venus. I'd never before in my life wanted so badly to get out of anything as I did that drumming council chamber.

"I wonder if this balloon can go faster than it has so far?" Piet said, looking over the fittings of the dirigible carrying us back to the *Oriflamme.* We were traveling at about 20 kph, the speed of a man jogging.

He raised an eyebrow in question as he swept his glance over the airship's crew. The dozen Chay present on the return journey wore the gray of common laborers. They continued to ignore Piet and the rest of us.

"The big ones with guns," Dole said, answering the surface question. "They've got more legs on the bottom than these do." He thumped his bootheel on the platform.

"They might speak English anyway," I said.

"My thought as well," Piet agreed in a satisfied tone. This was no place to discuss our real intentions.

The primary was past mid-sky, flooding the land with soft blue light. On Chay was a warm world for all its distance from the sun. The planet it circled was nearly a star in its own right, and vulcanism spurred by the gas giant's gravity warmed the satellite significantly.

Another pair of small dirigibles passed ours on their way back to the city. Tents of thin sheeting had sprung up around the *Oriflamme* during our absence, and bales of unfamiliar material were stacked near the main hatch. The council had been as good as its word when it promised gifts.

"They really want to be our friends," I said. Even if the Chay understood English, they weren't going to pick up my undertone of concern.

"On their terms," Stephen said, "they certainly do."

Men wearing Chay capes moved out of the way so that the dirigible could land beside the open forward airlock. The ground had cooled, so we didn't have to hop from the platform to the ship in reverse of the way we had disembarked.

The first thing I noticed when I stepped down was that the ground wasn't still. Microshocks made the surface tremble like the deck of a starship under way.

Dole must have thought the same thing. He nodded to the tents crewmen were building from fabric the Chay had brought and said, "Even if we get a big one and they come down, it's not going to hurt nobody."

I nodded agreement, then grinned. A seasoned spacer adapted to local conditions; the landsman I'd been six months ago would have been terrified. On Venus, ground shocks might rupture the overburden and let in the hell-brewed atmosphere.

"Guillermo?" Piet called to the Molt who'd been directing outside operations during our absence. "Turn things over to Dole and join us on the bridge, please."

The Chay crew paid us no attention. They backed the dirigible from the *Oriflamme* before turning its prow toward the city. Again I noticed the delicacy of the driving cilia. Mechanical propellers or turbines would have scattered the tents our crew had just constructed.

Salomon waited for us alone in the forward section, though as we entered a pair of sailors carried bedrolls toward the main hatch while discussing the potential of converting Chay foodstocks into brandy.

"I've run initial calculations for an empty world twenty days from here," the navigator said. "We'll have to refine them in orbit, of course."

"I don't know that it's come to that, exactly," Piet said cautiously. I'm sure he would have started the calculations himself if Salomon hadn't already done so.

"Cseka scares the hell out of me," I said. "The Chay scare me even worse. They—"

"They're friendly," Piet said.

"They're not *human*," I said. "An earthquake may not hurt you, but it isn't your friend. There's nothing I saw in there today—"

I waved in the direction of the city.

"—that convinces me they won't decide to eat us because, because Stampfer's got red hair."

"I haven't had a chance to look over the goods they've brought us . . ." Stephen said. He took off his helmet and kneaded his scalp with his left hand. "But I don't think there's much doubt that trade—in techniques, at least, given the distance—could be valuable."

He gave us a humorless grin. "Of course, that's only if the Chay decide to let us go. Jeremy's right, there."

Guillermo had said nothing since he entered behind us. He was seated at his usual console. His digits were entering what even I recognized as a sequence to lift us to orbit.

Piet laughed briefly. "So you all think we should take off as soon as possible," he said. "Even though Chay knowledge could give Venus an advantage greater than all the chips the Federation brings back from the Reaches?"

"What we think, Piet," Stephen said, "is that you're in charge. We'll follow whatever course you determine."

"I'm not a tyrant!" Piet snapped. "I'm not President Pleyal, 'Do *this* because it's my whim!' "

I swallowed and said, "Somebody has to make decisions. Here it's you. Besides, you're better at it than the rest of us. Not that that matters."

I grinned at Stephen. His words hadn't been a threat, because the big gunman accepted that all the rest of us knew the commander's decision was the law of this expedition. As surely as I knew that Stephen would destroy anything or anyone who tried to block Piet's decision.

"Yes," said Piet. He sat down at his console and checked a status display. "Air and reaction mass will be at capacity within the hour. We'll check the gifts, see what's worth taking and what's not, but we'll leave the bales where they are for the time being. We don't want to give the impression that we're stowing them for departure."

He looked up at the rest of us and smiled brilliantly. "Primary set is in six hours. An hour after that, we'll inform the crew to begin loading operations. When they're complete—another hour?— we'll close the hatches and lift."

Piet rubbed his forehead. "I didn't," he added as if idly, "much care for the way our hosts treat their prisoners."

The *Oriflamme* shuddered as another shock rippled through the soil beneath us.

✧   ✧   ✧

The primary was just below the horizon. The sun at zenith in the clear sky was only a blue-white star, though it cast a shadow if you looked carefully.

Three dirigibles rested outside the entrance to the domed city, their partially deflated gas bags sagging. The airships and their crews were armed, but the Chay all wore gray. None of their officers were present, and the guards themselves didn't bother to look at me as I walked into the dome.

Half a dozen Chay in orange and pastel blue capes preceded me by twenty meters. A group of gray-clad laborers followed at a similar distance, chattering among themselves. Like me, some of the laborers left their cowls up and the veils over their faces even after they entered the dome.

I hadn't done a more pointlessly risky thing since the night I went aboard the *Porcelain*. Though . . .

Boarding the *Porcelain* hadn't made me a man, perhaps, but it had made me a man I like better than the fellow who'd lived on Venus until then. I wasn't going to leave a human prisoner here to be tortured to death.

The hard floor of the dome was a contrast to the springy surface of the mat on which it rode. The cape hung low enough to cover my feet, but I was afraid somebody would notice that the sound of my boots differed from the clicking the locals made when they walked. I took deliberately quick, mincing steps.

There were hundreds of pedestrians out, but the broad boulevard seemed deserted by comparison with what I'd seen in the afternoon. Though the dome was clear, it darkened the sky into a rich blue that concealed all the stars except the sun itself. The walls of overhanging apartments wicked soft light from within, but even the lower levels weren't bright enough to illuminate the street.

I could see the cage ahead of me. I gripped the cutting bar beneath my cape to keep it from swinging and calling attention to itself; and because I was afraid.

I could claim to be looking around; but the Chay would want to carry me back to the *Oriflamme*, and if they did that they'd see we were loading the ship to escape. To save the others, I'd have to insist on staying overnight in the city. What would the Chay do with me when the *Oriflamme* lifted?

Lord God of hosts, be with Your servant. Though I'd been no servant

of His; a self-willed fool, and a greater fool now because I wouldn't
leave an enemy of mine to die at the hands of enemies of his.

I'd slipped away from the *Oriflamme* without causing comment.
I told Dole I was going for a walk to calm my nerves. I didn't
want my shipmates to worry if they noticed I was gone.

It didn't seem likely they would notice, what with the work of
preparing for departure. I was only in the way.

There were no guards around the Council Hall or the cage in
front of it. Occasional Chay strode across the court, on their way
from one boulevard to another, but they didn't linger. Even those
in bright garb were hard to see. My gray cape would be a shadow
among shadows.

A Chay in silvery fabric walked out of the Council Hall carrying a bundle. I paused beside a tower, close against the wall. If
the fellow had been a moment slower, I'd have been crossing to
the cage myself. The grip of my bar was slick with sweat.

The Chay thrust his bundle into the cage. He had to wiggle it
to work it through the mesh. It fell with a slapping sound to the
floor within. The Chay called something obviously derisory in his
own language, then went back the way he'd come.

Feeding time at the zoo. The prisoner didn't move. I couldn't
even be sure which of the still forms within the lattice was the
living man.

There wouldn't be a better time. I walked to the cage, keeping my
steps short. Out of the corner of my eye I saw a Chay laborer start
across the courtyard. I continued forward, my heart in my throat.
The Chay disappeared past or into a neighboring residential tower.

I took the cage in my left hand and shook it to test the structure. The bars were grown as a unit, not tied together where they
crossed. They were finger-thick, hard and obviously tough; but my
bar would go through them like light through a window.

"Ho! Federation dog!" I snarled. I pitched my voice low though
loud enough for the prisoner to hear. I could still brazen out my
presence if I had to. "Come close to me or it'll be the worse for you!"

"I don't think he can move, Jeremy," Piet said from behind me.
"We'll have to carry him."

I turned, my mouth open and the tip of the bar sliding from
beneath my cape. Piet was indistinguishable from a Chay in his
gray cape, but his voice was unmistakable.

"Yeah, well," I said. I switched my bar on. "I'll drag him out, then."

The blade *zinged* across the bars. I cut up, across and down, then bent to slash through the base of the opening. I wondered how the Chay had created the cage to begin with, since it didn't appear to have a door anywhere. I couldn't believe they'd simply grown it around their prisoners.

Piet caught the section as it started to fall. He held a cape to me as I hung my bar. I'd brought an extra garment myself, so Piet tossed his spare onto the cage floor to be rid of it.

My boot skidded on the slimy surface. I had to grab the frame to keep from falling. One of the prostrate figures moaned softly. I raised his torso, tugged the cape around him, and lifted him in a packstrap carry.

The cut section now hung from the hinge of tape Piet had wrapped around it. When I ducked out, he taped the other side so that our entry wasn't obvious.

The prisoner was a dead weight, though a modest one. It was like carrying an articulated skeleton, more awkward than heavy. Piet took the man's other arm and we strode back the way we'd come.

"Do Chay get drunk, do you suppose?" I said.

"Let's hope so," Piet said. "We're a couple of fools to do this."

The few remaining pedestrians scurried along with their heads down. "If the Chay have a curfew . . ." Piet said, speaking my thought.

"The dome wall isn't very thick except where the door is," I replied. "I can cut a way out if the gate's closed. We can."

The tunnel was open. A Chay in a violet garment entered as we neared it. We passed him in the other direction. He called out in his language. We ignored him. I walked on my toes to approximate the mincing Chay gait until we were around the first bend in the gateway.

The sunlight outside was as faint as my hope of salvation. I drew a great breath through my filter and said, "So far, so good."

The crews of the airships on guard didn't challenge us. Some of the Chay were eating beneath their veils. The mat of vegetation rolled underfoot, absorbing high-frequency ground shocks and smoothing them into gentle swells.

A tall figure strode toward us from the shadow of a translucent brown dome. "I'll carry him, if you like," Stephen offered in a low voice.

"He's not heavy," Piet said.

We walked on. Stephen fell into step behind us and a little to Piet's left, where he could watch our front as well as guarding the rear. This final part of the route was over an organic causeway crossing scores of circular fields only ten or twenty meters in diameter.

The ground rumbled. A line of dust lifted in the distance, kicked into motion by the quake. The causeway swayed gently. Beneath us, plants waved their zebra-striped foliage at us.

"I hadn't expected that the two of you would do this together," Stephen said in a pale voice. We hadn't spoken during the trek, but we could see that now there were no Chay between us and the edge of the mat.

"We weren't, Stephen," Piet said. "Jeremy made a foolish decision quite independently of me."

"I jumped out of a year's growth when he spoke to me," I said.

My voice sounded almost normal. That surprised me. I'd just learned that Stephen thought I'd supplanted him in Piet Ricimer's friendship. I'd known there were a lot of ways this jaunt could get me killed, but that one hadn't occurred to me.

"Tsk," said Stephen. "I don't lose control of myself, Jeremy."

I stumbled, then stared at him past the sunken form of the man we carried. "Do you read minds?" I demanded.

"No," said Piet. "But he's very smart."

"And a good shot," Stephen said with a throaty chuckle.

I laughed too. "Well, nobody sane would be doing this," I said aloud.

Though the mat felt like a closely woven carpet to walk on, it was actually several meters thick. The edge was a sagging tangle of stems, interlaced and spiky. There were no steps nor ramp off the island of vegetation; the Chay never walked on bare soil. The ground beyond bounced the way tremors shake the chest of a sleeping dog.

Stephen hopped down ahead of us. "Drop him to me," he said, raising his arms. "I'll take him from here."

I looked at Piet. He nodded. "On three," he said. "One, two, *three*—"

Together we tossed the moaning prisoner past the border. Stephen caught him, pivoting to lessen the shock to the Fed's weakened frame. The landscape heaved violently. Stephen dropped to his knees, but he didn't let his charge touch the ground.

My cape tore half away on brambles as I clambered down, baring my legs to the knee. There was no longer need for concealment, only speed.

Stephen strode onward with the Fed held lengthways across his shoulders like a yoke. Small shocks were incessant now. I had to pause at each pulse to keep from falling when the ground shifted height and angle.

"I should have allowed more time," I muttered. The *Oriflamme* was still out of sight beyond the rim of the bowl in which we'd landed.

"You were there before I was," Piet reminded me.

"Don't worry," Stephen said. "They aren't going to leave without us."

Piet laughed. "I suppose not," he agreed.

"I'd thought . . ." I said. "Maybe I'd just put him out of his misery. But I couldn't do that."

Stephen gave an icy chuckle. "We've brought him this far," he said. "We may as well take him the rest of the way."

We reached the lip of the bowl. The center of the depression was only twenty meters or so lower than the rolling plain around it, but that was still enough to conceal a starship. Sight of the *Oriflamme* warmed my heart like the smile of a beautiful woman.

A squeal similar to that of steam escaping from a huge boiler sounded behind us. It was more penetrating than a siren and so loud that it would be dangerous to humans any closer than we were.

I turned. Three cannon-armed dirigibles lifted above the city.

"Here," said Stephen, swinging his burden to Piet as if the Fed were a bundle of old clothes. "I'll watch the rear."

He locked a separate visor down to protect his eyes. A full helmet would have been obvious even under his cowl. Stephen parted his cape and threw the wings back over his shoulders, clearing his flashgun and the satchel of reloads slung on his left side.

I seized the Fed's right arm. "Run," Piet said, and we started running.

The *Oriflamme* was three hundred yards ahead of us. The ground had been still for a moment. Now On Chay shook itself violently. I stumbled but caught myself. The prisoner's legs swung like a pendulum to trip Piet and send him sprawling.

As Piet picked himself up, I glanced over my shoulder. The Chay dirigibles were a hundred meters high. Stephen walked sedately twenty meters behind us, watching our pursuers over his shoulder. The alarm still screamed from the Chay city.

Piet and I ran on. We'd taken only three strides when the bolt from a plasma cannon lit the soil immediately behind us into the heart of a sun.

The shock wave flung us apart. I smashed into a waist-high bush that might have been the ancestor of the mat on which the city was built. It clawed my chest and my legs as I tore myself free.

The cannon that had fired was a bright white glow in the bow of the center dirigible. Stephen swung his own weapon to his shoulder. A meters-long oval of soil blazed between him and us where the slug of plasma struck.

Stephen fired. The bolt from his laser was a needle of light against retinas already shocked by the plasma discharge.

The underside of a gas bag supporting the right-hand dirigible ruptured in a veil of thin blue flames. The Chay used hydrogen to support their craft. The fire spread with the deliberation of a flower opening, licking the sides of the bags adjacent to the one the bolt had ignited. The craft sank out of sight. The crew was trying desperately to land before the conflagration devoured them as well as their vehicle.

Piet stumbled forward alone with the prisoner. I grabbed the Fed's free arm and shouted, "D'ye have a gun?"

"Only a bar!" Piet said. "I didn't *want* to hurt the Chay, just free this poor wretch."

A laser pulse plowed glassy sparkles across the ground ahead of us. The bastards were shooting at us with the flashgun we'd given them that morning!

Stephen fired. A microsecond following the *snap* of his bolt, our world erupted in another plasma discharge.

The shock threw Piet and me sprawling, but this time the cannoneers were aiming at Stephen. Dirt fused into shrapnel and blew outward in a fireball which kicked Stephen sideways with his cape afire.

Fifty meters from us, Salomon or Guillermo lit the *Oriflamme*'s thrusters momentarily to check the fuel feeds. Bright exhaust puffed across the encampment, blowing down tents and disturbing the piles of Chay goods we were abandoning. Grit sprayed the back of my neck.

We had no secrets now. Stampfer would be screaming curses as he tried to rerig the Long Tom for combat, but that would take minutes with the *Oriflamme* laden as heavily as she was now.

I started toward Stephen. His flashgun had ignited a bag of the left-hand dirigible an instant before its plasma cannon fired. Blue hydrogen flames, hotter than Hell's hinges for all their seeming delicacy, wrapped the mid-line gas bag and involved the sides of the bags adjacent to it.

I'd seen Stephen shoot before. If he hadn't hit the Chay gunner, even at five hundred meters, it was because he didn't choose to kill even at this juncture.

The dirigible's crew dumped their remaining lift to escape. The platform dipped out of sight, taking with it the white glare of the plasma cannon's stellite bore. Only the center vehicle was still aloft; its cannon would be too hot to reload for some minutes yet.

Stephen rolled to his feet before I could reach him. His fingers inserted a charged battery in the butt of his flashgun and snapped the chamber closed over it before he tore away the blazing remnants of his cape. The rocky soil still glowed from the second plasma discharge, and a nearby bush was a torch of crackling orange flames.

I turned again. Piet was beside me. The Fed had managed to lift his torso off the ground. We snatched him up again and bolted for the *Oriflamme*'s ramp, dragging the fellow's feet. Stephen staggered behind us like a drunk running.

Twenty men spilled out of the *Oriflamme*'s main hatch. Those with rifles banged at the dirigible. Given the range and light conditions, I doubt any of them were more effective than I would have been.

"Get aboard!" Piet screamed. Kiley and Loomis each took the prisoner in one hand and one of us in the other, as if they were loading sacks of grain. "Don't shoot at the Chay, they're—"

The sky behind us exploded. A sheet of fire flashed as bright for a moment as if the primary had risen. I looked back. Bits of the last dirigible cascaded in a red-orange shower while hydrogen flames lifted like a curtain rising.

A Chay plasma cannon would cool very slowly because of its closed breech and the high specific heat of the metal from which it was cast. The gunners had tried to reload theirs too soon, and the round cooked off before it was seated. The thermonuclear explosion shattered the platform, rupturing all six hydrogen cells simultaneously.

Parts of the fiery debris were the bodies of the dirigible's crew.

We tumbled together in the forward hold. The ramp began to rise. Dole was shouting out the names of crewmen present. I hoped nobody'd gone so far from the hatch that he was still outside.

The *Oriflamme* lifted before the hatch sealed. Reflected exhaust was a saturated aurora crowning the upper seam.

Men of the support party disappeared up the ladderway in obedience to the bosun's snarled orders. I lay on my back, too wrung out to move or even rise. Piet bent over the rescued prisoner, so Piet at least was all right. Rakoscy ripped away Stephen's smoldering trousers with a scalpel.

I rolled over, but my stomach heaved and I could barely lift my face from the deck. Molten rock had burned savage ulcers into Stephen's calves above the boot tops. Bloody serum oozed as Rakoscy started to clean the wounds. Stephen rested on one elbow, holding his flashgun muzzle high so that the hot barrel wouldn't crack from contact with the cooler deck.

"Christ's blood, I shouldn't have gone back to the city!" I said. Piet was there to free the prisoner also, but that didn't change my responsibility. "Now I've made the Chay enemies for all their soldiers we killed."

"Dole," Piet ordered, "send this man up to the forward cabin and get some fluids in him. We don't want him to die on us now."

"We didn't kill anybody, Jeremy," Stephen said. He wasn't looking at me. He wasn't looking at anything, though his eyes were open.

"Ferris and Lightbody!" Dole snapped. "You heard the captain. And a bath wouldn't hurt him, neither."

I managed to sit upright. I didn't speak. Maybe Stephen hadn't seen the third dirigible explode, hadn't seen the Chay bodies trace blazing pinwheels toward the ground . . .

"As for what the plasma cannon did . . ." Stephen continued in an emotionless voice. "I'll take responsibility for my own actions, Jeremy, but not for what others choose to do."

"Here, I've got your flashgun, Stephen," Piet said, gently lifting the weapon from his friend's hand.

"I've got enough company in my dreams as it is," Stephen said as our thrusters hammered us toward orbit.

NEW ERYX

Day 177

The portable kiln chuckled heavily on the far side of the *Oriflamme*, spraying a smooth coat of glass onto the cracks in the hull. The run from On Chay hadn't been unusually stressful, but the *Oriflamme* was no longer the vessel that had lifted in maiden glory from Venus.

The constant drizzle didn't affect the kiln, but I already felt it was going to drive me mad in much less time than the week Piet said we'd need to refit. "Does it ever stop, do you think?" I muttered. "The rain, I mean."

"The globe was almost entirely overcast when we orbited," Piet said mildly. He smoothed the throat closure of a Chay cape. Because of the confusion of loading, we had fifty-odd of the garments aboard. They'd turned out to be waterproof. "There's no pilotry data, of course."

The world he'd named New Eryx—after the factorial hold of Stephen's family on Venus—was uncharted, at least as far as the Federation database went. Piet and Salomon had extrapolated the star's location by examining the listed gradients and found a planet that was technically habitable. Even if it was driving me insane.

"I've never gotten used to a bright sky," Stephen said. "Too much

Venus in my blood, I suppose. I like the overcast, and I don't mind the rain."

Lacaille, the prisoner we'd rescued, came by with a file of sailors who carried the trunk of one of the squat trees growing here in the dim warmth. They didn't notice the three of us sitting on a similar log.

Lacaille had been first officer on a ship in the Earth/Back Worlds trade, a year and a half's voyage in either direction for Federation vessels. Now he was talking cheerfully with men who'd helped kill a hundred like him the day we boarded *Our Lady of Montreal.*

"I'm glad we rescued him," I said. "He's a . . ."

"Human being?" Piet suggested. There was a smile in his voice.

"Whatever," I said. Trees like the one the men with Lacaille carried had a starchy pith that could be eaten—or converted to alcohol. Lacaille said identical trees were common on at least a score of worlds throughout the region. New Eryx wasn't on Federation charts; but somebody'd been here, and a very long time ago.

"He's fitting in well," Stephen said. "Of course, we saved his life. You did."

I snorted. "I can't think of a better way to make a man hate you than to do him a major favor," I said. "Most men. And damned near all women."

Stephen stood and stretched powerfully. He'd slung a repeating carbine over his right shoulder with the muzzle down to keep rain out of the bore. The only animal life we'd seen on New Eryx— if it was either animate or alive—was an occasional streamer of gossamer light which drifted among the trees. It could as easily be phosphorescent gas, a will-o'-the-wisp.

"Think I'll go for a walk," Stephen said without looking back at us. He moved stiffly. The burns on his legs were far from healed.

"Do you have a transponder?" Piet warned.

"I'll be able to home on the kiln," Stephen called, already out of sight. "Low frequencies travel forever."

"Because he seems so strong," Piet said very softly, "it's easy to overlook the degree to which Stephen is in pain. I wish there was something I could do for him."

He turned and gave me a wan smile. "Besides pray, of course. But I wouldn't want him to know that."

"I think," I said carefully, "that Stephen's the bravest man I'll ever know." *Because he gets up in the morning after every scream-ing night, and he doesn't put a gun in his mouth;* but I didn't say that to Piet.

I cleared my throat. "What'll happen with the Chay, do you think?" I said to change the subject.

"There's enough universe for all of us, Chay and Molts and humans," Piet said. "And others we don't know about yet. I wouldn't worry about what happened at On Chay, if that's what you mean. There'll be worse from both sides after we've been in contact longer, but eventually I think we'll all pull together like strands in a cable. Separate, but in concert."

"Optimist," I said. Christ! I sounded bitter.

Piet laughed and put his hand over mine to squeeze it. "Oh, I'm not a wide-eyed dreamer, Jeremy," he said. "We'll fight the Chay, men will, just as we fight each other. And the Chay fight each other, I shouldn't wonder."

His tone sobered as he continued, "The real danger isn't race or religion, you know. It's the attitude that some men, some people—Molts or Chay or men from Earth—have to be controlled from above for their own good. One day I believe the Lord will help us defeat that idea. And the lion will lie down with the lamb, and there will be peace among the nations."

He gave me a smile; half impish, half that of a man worn to the edge of his strength, uncertain whether he'll be able to take one step more.

"Until then," Piet said, "it's as well that the Lord has men like Stephen on His side. Despite what it costs Stephen, and despite what it costs men like you and me."

The kiln chuckled, and I began to laugh as well. Anyone who heard me would have thought I was mad.

UNCHARTED WORLD

Day 232

We touched the surface of the ice with a slight forward way on instead of Piet's normal vertical approach. For this landing, he'd programmed a ball switch on his console to control the dorsal pairs of attitude jets. He rolled the ball upward as his other hand chopped the thrusters.

The three bands of attitude jets fired a half-second pulse. Their balanced lift shifted enough weight off the skids to let inertia drag us forward. Steam from the thrusters' last spurting exhaust before shutdown hung as eight linked columns in the cold air behind us as the *Oriflamme* ground to a halt.

Salomon unlatched his restraints and turned to face Piet's couch. "Sir," he said, "that was brilliant!"

I swung my feet down to the deck. Men with duties during landing had strapped themselves to their workstations. The rest of us were in hammocks on Piet's orders. No matter how good the pilot, a landing on an ice field could turn into disaster.

The reaction-mass tanks were almost empty, though. Our choice had been to load a nitrogen/chlorine mixture from the moon of one of the system's gas giants, or to risk the ice. The gases would have given irregular results in the plasma motors as well as contaminating the next tank or two of water. Nobody had really doubted Piet's ability to bring us down safely.

"Thank you, Mister Salomon," Piet said as he rose from his console. "I'm rather pleased with it myself."

He glanced at the screen, then touched the ramp control. "At least we don't have to wait for the soil to cool," he added.

The center screen was set for a 360° view of our surroundings. There was nothing in that panorama but ice desert picked out by rare outcrops of rock. Irregular fissures streaked the surface like the *Oriflamme*'s hull crazing magnified. The ice crevices weren't dangerously wide. Most of those I could see were filled with refrozen meltwater, clearer and more bluish than the ice surrounding.

"I'll take out a security detail," Stephen said. He clasped a cape of some heavy natural fabric around his throat and cradled his flashgun. I didn't have warm clothing of my own. Maybe two or three of the Chay capes together . . .

"Security from what, Mister Gregg?" Salomon asked in surprise.

"We don't know," Piet said. "We haven't been here before."

I picked up my cutting bar and snatched a pair of capes as I followed Stephen aft. Crew members weren't going to argue the right of a gentleman to appropriate anything that wasn't nailed down. Besides, this wasn't a world that even men who'd been cooped up for seven weeks were in a hurry to step out onto.

The ground beneath the *Oriflamme* collapsed with the roar of breaking ice. We canted to port so violently that I was flung against the bulkhead. Men shouted. Gear we'd unshipped after our safe landing flew about the cabin.

The vessel rocked to a halt. I'd gotten halfway to my feet and now fell down again. The bow was up 15° and the deck yawed to port by almost that much. I was afraid to move for fear the least shift of weight would send the *Oriflamme* down a further precipice.

Piet stood and cycled the inner and outer airlock doors simultaneously from his console. "Mister Salomon, Guillermo," he said formally. "Stay at your controls, please. I'm going to take a look at our situation from outside."

Stephen and I followed Piet through the cockpit hatch. Elsewhere in the ship, men were sorting themselves out. Their comments sounded more disgruntled than afraid.

I was terribly afraid. I'd left the capes somewhere in the cabin, but I held my cutting bar in both hands as I jumped the two meters from the bottom of the hatch ladder to the ground.

The wind was as cold as I'd expected, but the bright sunlight was a surprise. Unless programmed to do otherwise, the *Oriflamme*'s screens optimized light levels on exterior visuals to Earth daytime. This time the real illumination was at least that bright.

The *Oriflamme*'s bow slanted into the air; her stern was below the surface of the shattered ice.

"We're on a tunnel," Stephen said, squatting to peer critically at the ground. "We collapsed part of the roof. Do you suppose the sunlight melts rivers under the ice sheet?"

"Can we take off again?" I asked. The wind was an excuse to shiver.

"Oh, yes," Piet said confidently. "Though we'll all have blisters before we dig her nozzles clear . . ."

LORD'S MERCY

Day 233

The sweat that soaked my tunic froze at the folds of the garment. The mittens I'd borrowed were too large. We'd reeved a rope through the tarp's grommets to serve as handles. It cut off circulation in my fingers even though there were four of us lifting the hundred-kilo loads of ice and scree away from the excavation.

At least we weren't going to be crushed if we slipped. Stampfer headed a crew of ten men, off-loading the broadside guns using sheerlegs and a ramp. If a cannon started to roll, it was kitty bar the door.

We reached the crevice fifty meters from the *Oriflamme*. Maher and Loomis at the front of the makeshift pallet were staggering. Dragging the tarp would have been a lot easier, but the gritty ice would have worn through the fabric in only a trip or two.

"Stand clear," I ordered. The sailors in front dropped their corners. Lightbody and I tried to lift ours to dump the load down the crevice. I could barely *hold* the weight; Lightbody had to manage the job for both of us. Next load Maher and Loomis would have that duty, but the load after that—

"About time for watch change, isn't it, Mister Moore?" Maher asked in a husky whisper.

"One more trip," I muttered. I didn't have any idea how long we'd been working. Blood tacked the mittens to my blistered palms, and I'd never been so cold in my life.

"Yes, *sir!*" said Maher.

We started back to the excavation. I could barely see, but the route was clear of major obstacles.

In the pit, men worked with shovels, levers, and cutting bars to clear the thruster nozzles. The whole plain was patterned with tunnels chewed through the ice by a creature several meters in diameter. It had moved back and forth like a farmer plowing a square field, each swing paralleling without touching the one laid down previously in the opposite direction.

I suppose Piet was right to name the world Lord's Mercy. If we'd set down exactly parallel to the tunnel pattern, the *Oriflamme* might have flipped upside down when the roof collapsed. On the other hand, if we'd landed perpendicular to the tunnels, we might never have known they were there.

The *Oriflamme*'s siren moaned briefly: it was time to change watches after all. We were working two hours on, two hours off. I didn't dare think about how much longer the process would have to go on.

"I'll take it," I said. The men dropped their corners of the emptied tarp; I started to drag it alone toward the excavation.

"Dear *God* I'm tired," I muttered. I didn't know I was speaking aloud.

"You got a right to be, sir," Lightbody called appreciatively as he and the others slanted away toward the hatch.

The common spacers were each of them stronger than me and knew tricks that made their effort more productive besides. I was helping, though, despite being by birth a gentleman. A year ago I'd have found that unthinkable.

"We'll take that now, sir," said Kiley, at the head of the team from the starboard watch replacing mine. I gave him the tarp. Our replacements looked stolid and ready to work, though I knew how little rest you could get in two hours on a ship being stripped of heavy fittings.

I thought of Thomas Hawtry. Would he and his clique have been out working beside the sailors if they'd made it this far on the voyage?

Stephen limped up the ramp from the excavation. He hadn't

been directing the work: Salomon did that. Stephen was moving blocks that only one man at a time could reach, and nobody else on the *Oriflamme* could budge.

I laughed aloud.

"Eh?" Stephen called.

"Just thinking," I said. Oh, yes, Hawtry would have obeyed any order that Stephen Gregg was on hand to enforce.

Stephen sat down on a stack of crates, loot from *Our Lady of Montreal;* for the moment, surplus weight. I sat beside him. "Are you feeling all right?" he asked.

His flashgun was in a nest of the crates, wrapped in a Chay cape to keep blowing ice crystals from forming a rime on it. I'd set my cutting bar there too when Salomon put me on the transport detail. Stephen wore his bar slung. He'd used it in the excavation, so refrozen ice caked the blade.

"I feel like the ship landed straight on top of me," I said. I heard Dole snarling orders to the men in the excavation. "You look a stage worse than that."

"I'll be all right," Stephen said. His voice was colorless with fatigue. "I'll drink something and go back down in a bit. They need me there."

He glanced at the closed forward airlock. Piet hadn't moved from his console since he'd organized the procedures. He even relieved himself in a bucket. If the *Oriflamme* started to shift again, it would be Piet's hand on the controls—balancing risk to the ship and risk to the men outside, where even exhaust from the attitude jets could be lethal.

"They'll need you when the port watch comes back on," I said forcefully. "Until then you're off duty."

I was marginal use to the expedition as a laborer, but I could damned well keep Stephen from burning himself out. Having a real purpose brought me back from the slough of exhaustion where I'd been wallowing the past hour.

Stephen shook his head, but he didn't argue. After a moment, he removed a canteen from the scarf in which he'd wrapped it to his waist cummerbund-fashion. Body heat kept it warm. He offered it to me. I took a swig and coughed. Slash that strong wasn't going to freeze at the temperatures out here in any case.

Stephen drank deep. "There's algae all through this ice," he said, tapping his toe on the ground. "That's why it looks green."

He offered me the canteen; I waved it away. Kiley's men stepped briskly toward the crevice with their first tarpaulin of broken ice. They'd be moving slower by the end of their watch . . .

"There was a lot of rock in some of the loads we brought out," I said. "We're not down to the soil, are we?"

Stephen laughed. He was loosening up, either because of me or the slash. "Frass," he said. "Worm shit. The tunnel was packed solid for a meter or so like a plug. If we'd landed just a little more to the side, the skid would've been on top of it and we might—"

Three hundred meters from where we sat, ice broke upward as if it were being scored by an invisible plow. I jumped to my feet and shouted, "Earthqua—"

It wasn't an earthquake. The head of a huge worm broke surface. The gray body, flattened and unsegmented, continued to stream out of the opening until the creature's whole forty-meter length writhed over the plain.

The transport crewmen dropped their tarp to stare. Diggers climbed from the excavation, summoned by shouts and the sound the worm made breaking out. Stephen had unwrapped his flashgun, but the worm didn't threaten us. It was undulating slightly away from the *Oriflamme.*

"I doubt it even has eyes," I said. "Maybe it hit a dike of rock that it's going to cross on the surface."

"All right, all right," Dole hectored. "You've had your show, now let's get this bitch ready to lift, shall we?"

Something dark green and multilegged climbed out of the opening the worm had made. This creature was about three meters long. Its mandibles projected another meter. They curved outward and back like calipers so that their points met squarely when the jaws closed.

The predator took one jump toward the worm it had been pursuing through the tunnel, then noticed the *Oriflamme* and the men outside her. The beast turned, hunched on three of its six pairs of legs, and leaped toward us.

"Back to the ship!" Dole bellowed. The men of his watch turned as ordered and ran for the excavation.

I unhooked my cutting bar. The main hatch couldn't be closed because of ice wedged into the hinge. There'd seemed no need to clean it while the excavation was still in process . . .

A second beast like the first hopped from the tunnel; a third member of the pack was directly behind the second. The worm wriggled into the distance, perhaps unaware that its pursuers had suddenly turned away.

The leading predator covered ten meters at each hop. Because its legs worked in alternate pairs, the creature no more than touched the ice before it surged forward in another flat arc.

Stephen's flashgun *whacked*. The bright sunlight of Lord's Mercy dimmed the weapon's normally dazzling side-scatter.

The bolt hit the predator's first thoracic segment and shattered the plate in a spray of creamy fluid. The head, the size of a man's torso, flipped onto the creature's back. It was attached by only a tag of chitin. The enormous mandibles scissored open and loudly shut.

A fourth hard-shelled predator crawled from the tunnel. The three living members of the pack hopped toward us, ignoring the thrashing corpse of their fellow.

Either the creatures thought the *Oriflamme* was prey, or they were reacting to us individual humans as interlopers in their hunting territory. Either way, their intentions weren't in doubt.

Stephen clicked up the wand that supported his laser's solar charger, then spread the shimmering film. He hadn't brought spare batteries with him this time.

"I'll draw them away from the hatch," I said. I began walking out onto the ice field. I didn't trust the footing enough to run.

Stephen set his flashgun on the crates with the panel tilted toward the sun. He left it there and strode parallel to me, triggering his cutting bar briefly to spin the blades clear of ice. The predators angled toward us, one after another.

Ice powdered beneath the creatures every time they sprang. The bottoms of their feet were chitin as jagged as the throat of a broken bottle. It gave the beasts good purchase on any surface soft enough for it to bite.

A band of single-lensed eyes gleamed from a ridge curving along the top and front of each predator's headplate. Though the individual eyes didn't move, the array gave the creatures vision over three-quarters of the arc around them.

The nearest creature focused on me. Its mandibles swung a further 30° open, like a hammer rising from half to full cock. Its deliberately short hop put me exactly ten meters away for the final spring.

I threw myself forward, holding my bar vertical in front of me. The predator slammed me down, but I was inside the circuit of its mandibles instead of being pierced through both sides when the tips clashed together.

The knife-edged chitin was thicker than that of a Molt's carapace, but my bar's ceramic teeth could have sheared hardened steel. The blade screamed as I cut the left mandible away. The creature stood above me, ripping my thighs with its front pairs of walking legs.

I held my bar in both hands and cut into the predator's head. Side-hinged jawplates cracked and crumbled on the howling bar.

The creature sprang back. White fluid gushed from the wound in its head. The creature's abdomen was slender and hairy, like that of a robber fly. It twisted around under the thorax as the creature went into convulsions.

Stephen was holding the second predator's mandibles away from his chest with both hands. The beast shook him violently, trying to break his grip. Stephen had dropped his cutting bar. It lay beneath the creature's scrabbling back legs.

I rose and slashed at the base of the right mandible, again using both hands. My feet slid out from under me. I caught the target in the belly of my blade, but my long draw stroke cut into the joint at a flatter angle than I'd intended.

Weakened chitin cracked like a rifle shot. Stephen tossed the mandible away. A ribbon of pale muscle fluttered behind it.

Stephen still had to hold the remaining mandible to prevent it from impaling him. I stood and fell down again immediately. I was slipping on my own blood and fluids from the creatures I'd butchered.

The last predator poised ten meters from Stephen for the leap that would cut him in half. A laser bolt stabbed through its open jaws. The flux lit the creature's exploding head through translucent flesh and chitin.

Piet flung down the flashgun. The solar panel that had recharged it quivered like a parachute. He raised a cutting bar. "Handweapons only!" Piet shouted as he charged the wounded predator. Twenty men carrying tools from the excavation followed him, slipping on the ice.

Stephen let the creature throw him free. It poised to leap onto him again, predator to the last. Piet sawed three of its legs apart in a single swipe. In a few seconds, all the left-side legs were broken or sheared. Men hacked with clumsy enthusiasm into the creature's thorax.

I stood up, then fell over again. Hall and Maher ran to me. Stephen crawled on all fours behind them.

"Rakoscy!" Piet shouted. "Rakoscy, get over here!"

"Christ's blood, his legs've been through a fucking meat grinder!" Dole cried. "Bring that fucking tarp over here! We need to get him into the fucking ship!"

"Mister Moore," somebody said with desperate earnestness. "Please let go of your bar. Please. I'm going to take it out of your hand."

The last voice I heard was Stephen's, snarling in a terrible singsong, "He'll be all *right* and I'll *kill* any whoreson who says he won't!"

WEYSTON

Day 249

Piet lifted the cutter's bow so that we wouldn't stall even though the thruster feed was barely cracked open. The display held a 30° down angle to our axis of flight, paralleling the barren ground a thousand meters below.

"You know . . ." Stephen said, one leg braced against the sidewall and his left hand gripping the central bench on which the two of us sat. "You're going to feel really silly if you have to explain how you got yourself killed on a sandhill like this."

"Tsk, don't call it a sandhill," Piet said cheerfully. "The name honors your uncle, remember. Besides, it's not a stunt, I saw something when I brought the *Oriflamme* in."

"And why shouldn't the officers go on a picnic?" I said. My legs were straight out, but I was trying my best not to let them take any stress. Though the shins were healing well, they hurt as if they were being boiled in oil if I moved the wrong way.

Lightbody's lips moved slowly as he watched the screen from the jump seat and separate attitude controls behind Piet's couch. I think he was murmuring a prayer. From Lightbody, that would be normal behavior rather than a comment on the way the cutter wallowed through the air. I doubt it occurred to Lightbody to worry when Piet was the pilot.

"Found him!" Piet said./"Eleven o'clock!" Stephen said, pointing./"There it is!" I said.

Metallic wreckage was strewn along hundreds of meters of sandy waste, though the ship at the end of the trail looked healthy enough. It was a cheaply-constructed freighter of the sort the Feds built in the Back Worlds to handle local trade.

"They came in on automated approach," Piet guessed aloud. He boosted thrust and gimballed the nozzle nearly vertical. "Hit a tooth of rock, ripped their motors out, and there they sit since. Which may be fifty years."

The cutter dropped like an elevator whose brakes had failed. Piet made a tight one-eighty around the crash site, killing our momentum so that he didn't have to overfly for the horizontal approach normal with a single-engined cutter.

"Not very long," Stephen said. "Light alloys wouldn't be so bright if they'd been open to the atmosphere any length of time."

We crossed the trail of torn metal, then blew out a doughnut of dust as we touched down within twenty meters of the freighter's side hatch.

Piet turned his head and smiled slightly. "If I don't keep my hand in, Stephen," he said, "I won't be able to do it when I have to."

"You could fly a cutter blindfolded on your deathbed, Captain," Lightbody said. "Begging your pardon."

Lightbody squeezed by to undog the hatch. I could have done that job if anybody's life had depended on it, but none of us still aboard the *Oriflamme* needed to prove things to our shipmates.

Weyston's air was thin and sulfurous, unpleasant without being dangerous. The system was charted but unoccupied. Federation cartographers hadn't even bothered to give the place a name, since there was nothing beyond the planet's presence to bring a vessel here.

We needed to reseal the *Oriflamme*'s hull; this was the suitable location closest to Lord's Mercy. We had sufficient reaction mass for some while yet—which was a good thing, because observation supported the note in the pilotry data that the planet had no free water whatever.

I stood deliberately as Lightbody swung himself onto the coaming of the dorsal hatch. "Give you a hand, sir?" he asked, reaching toward me.

"I'm not proud," I said. I clasped the spacer's shoulders and paused, steeling myself to flex my legs and jump.

"I've got him, Lightbody," Stephen said. He clasped me below the rib cage and lifted me like a mannequin onto the cutter's hull.

I laughed. "All right," I said, "you've convinced me I'm bloody useless and a burden to you all. Can we look over the wreck, now?"

Stephen handed Lightbody a rifle and his own flashgun as I slid down the curve of the hull to the ground. This flight was basically recreation, but there was no place on the Back Worlds where we were safe. By now, it didn't strike any of us as silly to go armed on a lifeless world.

There was movement inside the wreck.

"Hello the ship!" Piet called. No one responded. I powered my cutting bar.

A man in gray trousers and a blue tunic hopped from the hatch. Stephen presented his flashgun. "No!" the stranger shouted. "No, you can't shoot me!"

"We don't have any intention of shooting you, sir," Piet said. He crooked his left index finger to call the man closer. The fellow had a sickly look, but he was too plump to be ill fed. "Are there any other survivors?"

"No one, I'm the only one," the Fed said.

I walked around him at two arms' length. I wouldn't have trusted this fellow if he'd said there was a lot of sand hereabouts. He'd been relieving himself out the hatch; and almost out the hatch.

"Anybody aboard?" I called, waiting for my eyes to adapt to the dim interior. The power plant was dead, and with it the cabin lights.

The chamber stank. Blood and brains splashed the forward bulkhead above the simple control station.

I jerked my head back. Piet and Stephen were behind me. The castaway squatted beneath the muzzle of Lightbody's rifle.

"His name's McMaster," Stephen said, nodding toward the Fed. "He was the engineer. Doesn't seem as happy to be rescued as you'd think."

"Let's check the other side," I said, walking toward the freighter's bow. "Is there any cargo?"

The hatch from the cabin to the rear hold had warped in the crash, though there was probably access through the ship's ripped underside.

"Windmills," Stephen said. "They lost the starboard thrusters maybe a month ago on a run from Clapperton to Bumphrey. This was the nearest place to clear the feed line, but the AI wasn't up to the job of landing."

Piet said, "Two Molts and the human captain were killed in the crash. I don't think McMaster is completely . . ."

"Oh, he's crazy," Stephen said. "But he started out a snake or I miss my bet."

The graves were three shallow mounds in the lee of the wreck. I prodded with the blade of my cutting bar and struck mauve chitin ten centimeters below the surface. Stephen dragged the corpse of a Molt out by its arm. The creature's plastron was orange and had a spongy look.

"She hit the bulkhead during the crash," Piet said. "I don't think we need disturb the others."

Together we scooped tawny sand over the corpse again. I used my bar, the others their boots. "Decided where the next landfall is going to be?" Stephen asked.

"Clapperton," said Piet. "There's a sizable Fed colony there, but Lacaille and the pilotry data agree that only one of the major land masses is inhabited. We can fill with water and maybe hunt meat besides."

We had the Molt covered as well as it had been when we started. Stephen stepped back from the grave and surveyed the landscape. "What a hell of place to be buried," he said.

"It's only the body," Piet said in mild reproof.

We all felt it, though. This was a world with no life of its own, that would never have life of its own. Being buried here was like being dumped from the airlock between stars.

Stephen frowned. He stepped to the third mound and pulled something from the sand.

I squinted. "A screwdriver?" I said.

Stephen held it out to us. "That's what it was made for," he said softly.

The shaft was stained brown. Sand clung to the dried fluid. Not blood, but very possibly the copper-based ichor that filled a Molt's circulatory system.

Stephen wagged the tool delicately in the direction of the castaway on the other side of the wreck. "Didn't trust there'd be enough food to last till . . . whenever, do you think?" he said.

"The crash unhinged him," Piet said.

Stephen raised an eyebrow. Piet grimaced and said, "We can't leave a human being here!"

Stephen flung the screwdriver far out in the sand. "Then let's get back," he said mildly. "Only—let's not name this place for Uncle Ben, shall we? He won't know, but I do."

CLAPPERTON

Day 290

Air heavy with moisture and rotting vegetation rolled into the hold as the ramp lowered. Though we'd landed after sunrise so that the glare of our thrusters wouldn't alert distant Fed watchers, the thick canopy filtered light to a green as deep as that reaching the bottom of a pond. Treetops met even over the river by which we'd entered the forest.

We piled out of the vessel. Our exhaust had burned the leaf mold to charcoal traceries which disintegrated when a boot touched them. Black ash spurted to mix with steam and the gray smoke of tree bark so wet that it only smoldered from a bath of plasma.

There were twenty of us to start, though another crew would lay hoses to the river as soon as we were out of the way. Six of the men were armed. The rest of us carried tools and the net which, once we'd hung it properly, would camouflage the *Oriflamme*'s track. Piet had nosed us between a pair of giant trees and almost completely into the forest, but the starship's stern could be seen from an autogyro following the river at canopy height.

"Good *Christ!*" said Stampfer, pointing his rifle with both hands. "What d'ye call *that!*"

Piet had taken the *Oriflamme* straight over the bank at a point that the river kinked. Bobbing belly-up in the slight current at the bend was a creature twenty meters long. Its four short legs stuck up stiffly; the toes were webbed, but the forefeet bore cruel claws as well.

The smooth skin of the creature's back was speckled black over several shades of brown, but the originally white underside now blushed pink. We'd boiled the monster as we coasted over it.

Its head was broad and several meters long. The skull floated lower than the creature's distended belly, but I could see that the long, conical teeth would interlock when the jaws were closed.

"The big predators here live in the water," Lacaille said. He gestured with his three-hooked grapnel. He and I were one of the two teams who'd climb to anchor the top of the net. "That's good that that one's dead. It'll be a month before another big one moves into the territory."

The Federation officer chewed his lower lip. "I didn't know they got *that* big," he said. "They don't around North Island base."

"Let's go, you lazy scuts!" Dole ordered. "Quicker we get this hung, the likelier you are to get home and sling your neighbor off the top of your wife!"

Strictly speaking, the bosun was talking to the men dragging the net out of the hold. Everybody knew that the likely delay was in getting lift points twenty meters up the tree boles, though.

I waved acknowledgment and walked back to the left-hand tree of the pair at the *Oriflamme*'s stern. Stampfer started with us. Stephen called, "I'll keep an eye on this end," and waved the master gunner toward the center of the track.

"Are there many dangerous animals?" I asked Lacaille with a nod toward the predator floating in the shallows. The corpse had bloated noticeably since I'd first seen it.

Unlike McMaster, Lacaille had become a willing shipmate. He was a real ship's officer, not a noble who'd had authority but no skill. I think he was glad to serve with a company of spacers as good as Piet Ricimer's. There wasn't a better crew in the human universe.

"No big carnivores on land," Lacaille said. "There's dangerous animals, sure, and some of the plants are poison. The garrison burns back the jungle for a hundred meters around the base."

He shrugged. "A soldier got bitten on the foot and had his leg swell up till they cut it off. But it could've been a thorn instead of a sting. Liquor's killed twenty-odd that I know of."

We'd told both Federation officers that we'd drop them with their own people when we could. I don't think that affected either Lacaille's helpfulness or McMaster's surly silence. People's dispositions were more important than their attitudes.

The tree Lacaille and I were to climb had shaggy buttress roots that spread its diameter at the base to almost twenty meters. The three of us walked carefully to the far side of the bole where plasma hadn't scoured the hairy surface.

I'd insisted on being one of the climbers, because I needed to convince myself that my shins had healed properly. Maybe Lacaille had something similar in mind. The Chay had certainly handled him worse than the bug on Lord's Mercy had done me.

The *Oriflamme* didn't carry climbing irons, so Lacaille and I wore boots with sharpened hobnails. This tree's shaggy bark and the stilt roots of the giant on the other side of the *Oriflamme* ought to make it easy to get to the height required.

"Trade me for a moment," Stephen said. I didn't know what he meant till he handed me the flashgun and slipped the grapnel and coil from my belt. Stephen stepped back and swung the hooks on a short length of line.

The trunk started to branch just above where the top of the buttress roots faired into the main trunk. Leaves fanned toward the light seeping through the thin canopy over the watercourse. The lower limbs were stubby and not particularly thick, but they'd support a man's weight. Our exhaust had shriveled some of the foliage.

Stephen loosed the grapnel at the top of its arc. The triple hook wobbled upward, stabilized by the line it drew. It curved between the trunk and the upraised tip of a limb. As the line fell back, it caught on rough bark and looped twice around the branch. The hooks swung nervously beneath the limb with the last of their momentum. If the line started to slip under my weight, the points should lift and bite into the wood.

I returned Stephen's flashgun. I hadn't brought a weapon; my cutting bar would just have been in the way as I climbed. The weight of the cassegrain laser felt good. Among the forest sounds were a series of shrill screams that made me think of something huge, toothy, and far more active than the predator now bloating in the river.

Lacaille started up the line ahead of me. *Hey,* I thought, but I didn't say anything. He ought to be leading, because he still had a grapnel to toss to a higher branch.

I followed the Fed, walking up the top of a buttress root like a steep ramp. The 8-mm line was too thin for comfortable climbing. Lacaille and I wore gloves with the fingers cut off, but my palms hurt like blazes whenever I let my weight ride on the line. I used my hands only to steady myself. Fine for the first stage, but there were another ten meters to go.

Lacaille got out of my way by stepping to the next limb, 15° clockwise around the tree bole though only slightly higher. He tried to spin his grapnel the way Stephen had. The hooks snagged my branch.

"Hey!" I shouted—more sharply than I'd have done if I hadn't still been pissed at Lacaille taking the lead. Besides, I was breathing hard from the exertion, and my shins prickled as though crabs were dancing on them.

"Sir!" Lacaille said. "I'm sorry!"

He slacked his line. Weight pulled the hooks loose for Lacaille to haul back to his hand.

"Look," I said, "neither of us is"—I shrugged—"an expert. Just toss the damned thing over a branch a couple meters up. That's all I want to climb at a time on the straight trunk anyway."

I crossed my legs beneath the branch as I worked my own grapnel loose for the next stage. The line had cut a powdery russet groove in the bark. Sticky dust gummed both the line and my fingers.

Lacaille tossed his grapnel, this time with a straight overarm motion. More our speed. He set his hooks in a limb not far above him and scrambled up, panting loudly. That was a three-meter gain, a perfectly respectable portion of the ten we needed.

I stuck the grapnel's shaft under my belt and shifted to the branch Lacaille had just vacated. My line dangled behind me like a long tail. I paused to brush sweat out of my eyes. I saw movement to the side.

Three creatures the size of bandy-legged goats peered down at me from a limb of an adjacent tree. Two were mottled gray; the third was slightly larger. It had a black torso and a scarlet ruff that it spread as I stared at it.

"Holy Jesus!" I shouted. I snatched at my grapnel, the closest thing to a weapon I was carrying.

The trio sprang up the trunk of their tree like giant squirrels. They vanished into the canopy in a handful of jumps. Divots ripped from the bark by their hooked claws pattered down behind them.

"Are you all right?" Stephen shouted. "What's happened?"

"We're all right!" I shouted back. I couldn't see the forest floor, so Stephen couldn't see us, much less the creatures that had startled me. "Local herbivores is all."

That was more than I knew for certain, but I didn't want Stephen to worry.

"There's something sticky here," Lacaille warned. "I think it's from the tree. Sap."

I peered upward to make certain that Lacaille was out of the way before I started to climb. This portion of the trunk was covered with a band of some mossy epiphyte. Tiny pink florets picked out the dark green foliage.

Something was pressed against the bark a few degrees to Lacaille's left and slightly above him. I doubted that he could see the thing from his angle. It eased toward him.

"Freeze, Lacaille!" I shouted.

"What?" he said. "What?" His voice rose an octave on the second syllable. He didn't move, though.

The thing was a dull golden color with blotches of brown. It could almost have been a trickle of sap like the one Lacaille had noticed, thirty million years short of hardening to amber.

Almost. It had been creeping sideways across the bark's corrugations. The creature stopped when Lacaille obeyed my order to freeze.

I drew the grapnel from my belt, then paid the line out in four one-meter loops.

"What's happening, Moore?" Lacaille said. He had his voice under control. He was trying to look down at me without moving anything but his eyes.

"Not yet," I whispered. Lacaille couldn't hear me. I was speaking to calm myself.

I lofted the grapnel with an underhand toss. It sailed as intended through empty air past the creature.

The thing struck like a trap snapping. Its head clanged against the grapnel's slowly rotating hooks and flung them outward—with the creature attached.

"*Watch out below!*" I screamed. The snakelike thing streamed past me, dragged by the weight of steel where it had expected flesh. I let go of the line.

The creature was a good ten meters long, but nowhere thicker than my calf. Tiny hooked legs, hundreds of them, waggled from its underside.

I heard the ensemble crash into the ground. A cutting bar whined. The blades *whanged* momentarily on metal, probably the grapnel's shaft.

"What was it?" Lacaille demanded. "Can I move now? What *was* it?"

"It was a snake," I said. "I think it was a snake."

I wiped my eyes again. "Stephen?" I called. "Tell them to hitch the hawser to Lacaille's line where it is, will you? We've gone as high in this tree as *I* want to go."

"Roger," Stephen said, his voice attenuated by distance and the way the foliage absorbed sound.

I looked at Lacaille. "Yeah, it's all right now," I said. "I hope to God it's all right."

I stepped away from the 2-cm hawser so that Dole and his crew could begin lifting the camouflage net. Lacaille knelt beside the creature a few meters out from the cone of roots. The snake had slid the last stage of its trip to Stephen's cutting bar.

Stephen looked from the creature to me. "Don't touch the damned thing unless you want to get clawed by those feet," he said. "*I* think it's dead, but it has a difference of opinion."

I squatted beside Lacaille. The creature's skull was almost a meter long. Stephen had cut it crosswise, then severed the back half from the long body—which was still twitching, as Stephen had implied.

"I should've taken a bar with me," I said. "I was crazy not to."

"This worked pretty well," Stephen said. "I don't see how you could improve on the results."

He tilted up the front of the creature's skull on his bar. A bony tongue protruded a handbreadth from the circular mouth. The tongue's tip had broken off on the grapnel. The sides of the hollow shaft were barbed and slotted. The tongue was designed to rip deep through the flesh of the creatures it struck, then to suck them dry.

"Wonder if it injects digestive fluids?" Stephen mused aloud.

Lacaille stood, then doubled up and began to vomit.

"Get him back to the ship," Stephen suggested quietly. "Guillermo can find some slash if you can't."

"I can find something," I said. "Come on, Lacaille. I need a drink, and out here is no damned place for anybody who feels as queasy as I do right now."

"I'm all right," Lacaille muttered as he cautiously straightened. He wiped his mouth with the back of his hand before he turned to face me.

"Any one you walk away from, hey?" he said with an embarrassed smile. "I suppose I can walk."

He could. We could. Dole's men were raising one end of the net by the hawser Lacaille and I had drawn into the branches on Lacaille's grapnel line. We'd wired a pulley to the limb as well. It wasn't strictly necessary, but it made the lift a lot easier for the men below.

I was only half kidding about needing a drink. Since the snake stalked us, I'd trembled while we continued to work high in the tree. Seeing the creature close up made the fear worse.

We stepped over the rolled net. The bosun was arguing precedence with Salomon, whose men were laying hoses to the river. Both men paused and nodded to us. Piet, examining the tree that would anchor the other end of the camouflage, waved cheerfully.

"You saved my life," Lacaille said in a low voice.

"That fellow might have decided I looked juicier," I said. "He wasn't anybody's friend."

We had to pick our way carefully across the burned patch surrounding the *Oriflamme*. Dense roots withstood the gush of plasma and lurked within the ash, ready to turn an ankle or worse.

"Look," Lacaille said. He stopped and waited for me to meet his eyes. "I won't fight my own people."

"Nobody asked you to," I said. "Christ's blood, d'ye think we can't do our own fighting?"

Lacaille grimaced and shook his head in frustration. "Look," he said. "McMaster? You should have left him where he was."

"You're not the first to think that," I said slowly. I glanced around. I didn't know where McMaster was. I couldn't find him outside nor among the party shifting gear in the hold ten meters from where Lacaille and I stood. "Piet's . . . soft-hearted, though."

"Tonight," Lacaille said. "When shortwave propagation's good, McMaster's going to signal the North Island base on the backup commo suite aft."

Salomon's men joined Dole's on the 2-cm hawser. It would be easier to slide the hoses under the hem of the camouflage net than to lift the roll, so the teams were combining to do the jobs in sequence.

"He told you?" I asked without emphasis.

"McMaster *brags* about things that nobody would admit!" Lacaille said. "Not just this, terrible things! He's a terrible man."

Piet walked toward us, probably wondering what we were discussing.

"Yeah, I can believe that," I said. It wasn't surprising that a man who'd been swimming for years in the filthy slough of President Pleyal's colonies would be unable to recognize that Lacaille might have feelings of gratitude toward those who'd saved his life. Far more surprising that Lacaille's personal decency *had* survived.

"Ah . . ." I added. "Don't say anything to Piet, though. All right?"

Lacaille nodded in relief. "You'll tell Mister Gregg?" he asked.

"Stephen's got enough on his conscience as it is," I said, putting on a bright smile to greet Piet. "I'll see that this one's handled."

We sat at trestle tables sawn from the local wood with cutting bars. The boards' surface was just as rough as you'd imagine. The afternoon's downpour had driven the ash into the clay substrate in a butter-slick amalgam. We'd spread cover sheets over us, but the rare chinks of evening sky we could see were clear.

"You know . . ." said Dole with a mouth full of tree-hopper, maybe one of the trio that'd startled me. It had peeked down at the commotion, this time where Stephen could see it. "That fellow out in the lake might not have steaked out so bad."

"Not for me, thanks," I said, thinking about the monster's teeth. At the other table they were eating a ragout of the local "snake." I didn't even look in that direction.

"Precooked, even," Piet said with a grin. He looked as relaxed as I'd seen him in a long while. We'd have known by now if a Fed on Clapperton's far side had chanced to notice us sliding into the forest. "Well, we had other things on our mind."

Winger, the chief motor mechanic, said, "I don't like the way the main engine nozzles are getting, sir. We've switched out the spares aboard, and they're getting pretty worn themself."

"Umm," Salomon said. "They wouldn't pass a bottomry

inspection at Betaport, but I don't think we need to worry as yet."

An animal screamed in the near distance. It was probably harmless—and the "snake" couldn't have made a sound if it had wanted to—but my shoulders shrank together every time I heard the thing.

The local equivalent of insects swarmed around the hooded lights we'd spiked to tree boles to show us our dinner. The creatures were four-legged. They varied in size from midges to globs with bodies the size of a baseball and wingspans to match. They didn't attack us because of our unfamiliar biochemistry, but I frequently felt a crunch of chitin as I chewed my meat.

"The nearest place that'd stock thruster nozzles is Riel," Lacaille volunteered without looking up from his meal. "But the port gets a lot of traffic, and it's defended."

"Real defenses?" Dole asked, glancing over at Lacaille. "Or a couple guns and nobody manning them?"

"I'd sure rather have warehouse stock than cannibalize a ship," Winger said. "It's a bitch of a job unscrewing burned-in nozzles without cracking them."

The little receiver in my tunic pocket squawked, "Calling North Island Command! Calling North Island Command! This is—"

Everyone in hearing jumped up. The opposite bench tilted and thumped the ground. Lacaille's mouth opened in horror.

"What in the name of Christ is that?" Stephen asked softly. He wasn't looking at me. His eyes roved the forest, and the flashgun was cradled in his arms.

"It's all right!" I said. "Sit down, everybody. It's all right."

"Yes, sit down," Piet decided aloud. He bent to help raise the fallen bench, holding his carbine at the balance so that the muzzle pointed straight up. He'd jacked a round into the chamber, and it would take a moment to clear the weapon safely.

He sat again and looked at me. "*What* is all right?"

"—Venusian pirate ship full of treasure," my pocket crackled. I took the receiver out so that everyone could see it. "Plot this signal and home on it. I don't have the coordinates, but it's somewhere in the opposite hemisphere from the base. Calling—"

I switched the unit off. Dole said, "McMaster!" and stood up again.

"Don't!" I said.

Dole stepped over the bench, unhooking his cutting bar.

"Sit down, Mister Dole," Piet said, his voice ringing like a drop forge.

The bosun's face scrunched up, but he obeyed.

"And the rest of you," Piet said, waving to the men at the other table and the far end of ours. They'd noticed the commotion, though they couldn't tell what was going on.

"I fiddled the backup transmitter," I said in a voice that the immediate circle could hear. "No matter what the dial reads, it's transmitting a quarter-watt UHF. He could be heard farther away if he stood in the hatch and shouted."

Stephen made a sound. I thought he was choking. It was the start of a laugh. His guffaws bellowed out into the night, arousing screamers in the trees around us. After a moment, Stephen got the sound under control, but he still quivered with suppressed paroxysms.

"We still have to do something about the situation, though," Piet said softly.

"No," I said. From the corner of my eye, I noticed a shadow slip from the main hatch and vanish into the forest. "The situation has just taken care of itself."

A smile of sorts played with Piet's mouth. "Yes," he said. "I see what you mean. He doesn't want to be aboard the target his friends are going to blast."

He turned his head. "Mister Dole," he said crisply, "we'll have the net down at first light. The voyage isn't over, and we may need it another time. I expect to lift fifteen minutes after you start the task."

"Aye aye, *sir!*" the bosun said.

"I suppose it'll be weeks before another big gulper takes over this stretch of the river," Lacaille said.

"Maybe not so long," Stephen said. He got up and stretched the big muscles of his shoulders. "And anyway, I'm sure there are more snakes and suchlike folk than the one you and Jeremy met."

He chuckled again. The sound was as bleak as the ice of Lord's Mercy.

ABOVE RIEL

Day 311

Guillermo's screen showed the world we circled in a ninety-four-minute orbit. The central display was a frozen schematic of Corpus Christi, Riel's spaceport, based on pilotry data, Lacaille's recollections, and images recorded during the *Oriflamme*'s first pass overhead.

"There are fourteen vessels in port that probably have thruster nozzles of the correct size," Piet said, sitting on the edge of his couch. Thirty of us were crowded into the forward compartment, and his words echoed on the tannoys to the remainder of the crew. "Besides those, there's a number of smaller vessels on the ground and a very large freighter in orbit."

"Freighter or not . . ." Kiley murmured, "anything that weighs two kilotonnes gets *my* respect."

"Two of the ships are water buffalos without transit capability," Piet continued. "We'll have to carry our prize off to an uninhabited system to strip it, so they're out. Likewise, a number of the ships are probably unserviceable, though we don't know which ones for sure. Finally, there's a Federation warship in port, the *Yellowknife*."

There was a low murmur from the men. Somebody said, "*Shit*," in a quiet but distinct voice.

"Yes," Piet said. "That complicates matters, but two of our nozzles have cracked. Maybe they just got knocked around when we tipped on Lord's Mercy, but it's equally possible that the other six are about to fail the same way. This will be risky, but we have no options."

"Hey, sir," Stampfer said. "We'll fucking handle it. You just tell us what to do."

That wasn't bravado. Stampfer and everybody else in the *Oriflamme*'s crew believed that Captain Ricimer would bring us all home somehow. Emotionally, I believed that myself. Intellectually, I knew that if I hadn't stumbled as I ran toward the *Montreal*, the Fed plasma bolt would have killed me instead of the man a step behind.

"For ease of drawing reaction mass," Piet said, "the port is in the bend of a river, the Sangre Christi. It's a swampy area and unhealthy, since Terran mosquitoes and mosquito-borne diseases have colonized the planet along with humans."

Men glanced at one another in puzzlement. Malaria didn't seem a serious risk compared to the others we'd be chancing on a raid like this.

A slight smile played across Piet's mouth. "As a result," he explained, "the governor and officers of the garrison and ships in port stay in houses on the bluffs overlooking the river."

His index finger swept an arc across the display. "That should slow down any response to our actions."

Piet sobered. "I'll take the cutter down at twilight, that's at midnight ship's time, with fourteen men aboard," he said. "A party of six will secure the Commandatura and port control—they're together."

"I'll take care of that," Stephen said.

Piet's grin flickered again. "Yes," he said. "I hoped you would."

He looked at me. "There are four gunpits with laser arrays. The fire control system and the town's general communications both need to be disabled. You can handle that, Jeremy?"

"Sure," I said. The task was a little more complicated than it might have sounded to a layman. You have to identify the critical parts in order to cut off their power, blow them up, whatever. But I shouldn't have any difficulty.

"Or Guillermo could," Stephen said, scratching the side of his neck and looking at nothing in particular.

"*I'll* do it!" I said.

"I'll need Guillermo for the other phase of the operation," Piet said. "I don't expect any trouble about landing a cutter without authorization, but I personally can't go around asking which of the ships ready to lift have thruster nozzles in good condition. Guillermo can speak to Molt laborers and identify a suitable prize without arousing suspicion."

He glanced down at the navigator in the couch to his left. "Mister Salomon, you'll command the *Oriflamme* in my absence. We'll rendezvous, the *Oriflamme* and my prize, at St. Lawrence. I don't believe there's any reason to proceed there in company."

Salomon nodded. Men were tugging their beards, rubbing palms together—a score of individual tricks for dealing with tension. I kept clearing my throat, trying not to make a noise that would disturb the others.

"All right," said Piet. "Stephen, you and I will get together and decide on personnel. When we've done that, then we'll go over tactics. I'd like the rest of you to vacate the compartment for a time, please, so that we can organize the raid."

His eyes met mine. "Not the people already told off for the mission, of course."

Crewmen drifted toward the passageway aft. Dole and Stampfer waited grimly. They obviously weren't about to leave unless they got a direct personal order to do so. I doubted Piet would push the point. You want your most aggressive men on a project like this.

I shoved off carefully and caught the stanchion to which Stephen was anchored. "Didn't want me along?" I said very softly.

Stephen shrugged. He didn't look at me. "I don't much want Piet risking his neck by leading this one," he said in a similar voice. "But there wasn't a prayer he'd listen if I said that."

He gave me a broad smile. "I'm responsible for you, Jeremy," he said in a bantering tone. "I brought you aboard."

"Then remember I'm a member of this crew," I said. "And a gentleman of Venus!"

The compartment had cleared except for the officers and two petty officers. "Stephen?" Piet called. "Jeremy?"

"Oh, I won't forget that, Jeremy," Stephen said. He directed himself with an index finger toward the consoles at the bow. "Nor, I think, will our enemies, hey?"

RIEL

Day 312

Our outer hull pinged as it slowly cooled. The pilot's screen was coarse-grained and only hinted at our surroundings. Besides, with fourteen men packed onto a cutter, there were too many heads and torsos in the way for me to see more than an occasional corner.

"Hell," said Winger. "With all the chips we're carrying, it'd be easier to buy the engine hardware."

"This'll be easy enough," Stephen replied in his chilling singsong. "It always has been in the past. Dead easy."

No one spoke for a moment. Our harsh breathing sounded like static on a radio tuned to open air.

"All right," Piet said decisively. "Commandatura team and Guillermo first, we others wait five minutes. I don't want anyone to notice just how full this cutter is."

Dole and Lightbody undogged the hatch, though the bosun would go with Piet to capture the ship that Guillermo picked. Fourteen men weren't many to operate a starship of a hundred tonnes or more, so Piet had picked the most efficient members of the *Oriflamme*'s crew.

Stephen was the first out, jumping lightly to the ground. Under ordinary circumstances, Stephen seemed a little clumsy.

Now, and at previous times like this, he moved with a dancer's grace.

"Hand me the crate," he ordered bleakly. Lightbody and I, seated on the hatch coaming, swung the chest of weapons into Stephen's waiting hands. He didn't appear to notice weight that had made the pair of us grunt.

I hadn't missed anything for being unable to see the vision screen. Piet had brought us down at the north end of the field, some distance from the river. The cutter was tucked in between a freighter that was either deadlined or abandoned—several of her hull plates were missing—and a water buffalo, a tanker that hauled air and reaction mass to orbiting vessels too large or ill-found to land normally.

Neither of our neighbors was lighted. There was no likelihood of anybody noticing that the cutter's sheen was that of hard-used ceramic, not metal.

We hopped down from the hatch. Guillermo was the last out. A Molt who disembarked from a Fed vessel ahead of humans would be whipped to death for his presumption.

Guillermo skulked away from us, heading toward a large freighter in the second row back from the river. A gang of Molt laborers was carrying cargo aboard from high-wheeled hand trucks.

"Take it easy, stay together, and ignore the other people out on the streets tonight," Stephen said. His eyes passed over us, but they didn't appear to light anywhere. "If we do our jobs, there won't be a bit of excitement. That's the way we want it."

A dead man wouldn't have spoken with less emotion.

We set off toward the Commandatura, three short blocks beyond the inland side of the field. Kiley and Lightbody carried the packing crate. We wore a mix of garments picked up on Federation planets, exactly like the crews of ships in Back Worlds' trade. None of the men or Molts on errands about nearby vessels gave us more than a passing glance.

The port was fenced off from the town of Corpus Christi. The pivoting gate was open, and the Molts in the guard shack were eating some stringy form of rations. Nearby was a gunpit. The multitube laser there was also crewed by Molts.

The street cutting the chord of the riverbend was paved. We sprinted to avoid a truck whose howling turbogenerator powered hub-center electric motors in all six wheels. A Molt drove the vehicle, but he was obviously under the direction of the man on the seat beside him. The human waved a bottle out his side window and jeered us.

"Wait a little, buddy," Kiley said. He was breathing hard because of the load of weapons. "Just you wait . . ."

The street leading directly to the Commandatura was paved also and lighted. Stephen, walking with the stiff-legged gait of a big dog on unfamiliar territory, led us down one of the parallel alleys instead.

Buildings in this part of Corpus Christi were wooden and raised a meter above the ground on stilts. Individual structures had porches, but they weren't connected into a continuous boardwalk between adjacent buildings. We walked in the street itself, one more group among the sailors and garrison personnel.

If the town had a sewer system, it'd backed up during some recent high water. Enough light came from the signs and screened windows of the taverns for us to avoid large chunks of rubbish. Vehicular traffic disposed of most of the waste by grinding it into the mud in a fetid, gooey mass. The air was hot and still, and insects whined.

A flung chair tore through the screen of a building we'd passed. Inside, a shot thumped. My right hand reached for the cutting bar that I didn't have.

"Keep moving!" Stephen ordered without raising his voice.

"Yellowknife! Yellowknife!" men shouted in unison above a rumble of generalized rage. Crewmen from the warship were fighting with port personnel, nothing for us to worry about.

My right hand clenched and unclenched in sweaty desperation. Bells rang. A van tore past, towing a trailer with barred sides and top. We walked on.

The Commandatura was a two-story masonry building with an arching facade that added another half story. It stood on a low mound, but floodwater had risen a meter up the stonework at some point in the past. A double staircase led to the lighted front door on the second story. CONSTABULARY was painted in large letters on the wall above the street-level entrance on the side.

There were twenty steps from the street to the Commandatura's front door. Originally there'd been a park in front of the building, but it was full of rubbish now. The governor and folk of quality wouldn't spend enough time here to make the effort of beautifying it worthwhile.

The door was unlocked. Stephen entered. I gestured Kiley and Lightbody in ahead of me, then helped them snatch open the lid of the crate of weapons. The feel of my cutting bar was like a drink of water in a desert.

No one was at the counter on the left side of the anteroom. The plaque on the door to the right read COMMUNICATIONS. A hallway ran past that room toward the back of the building. The door beside the commo room was steel with the stenciled legend KEEP LOCKED AT ALL TIMES. Other doors were wooden panels, some of them ajar.

Stephen signaled Kiley and Maher to watch the hall, then tapped his own chest before pointing to the commo room. Lightbody gripped the door handle and rotated it minusculely to be sure that it wasn't locked.

He nodded. The rest of us poised. Stephen lunged in behind the opening door.

No one was inside the windowless room. The atmosphere was stifling and at least 10° C above the muggy heat outside. The air-conditioning vents in the floor and ceiling were silent; banks of electronics clicked and muttered among themselves.

"I've got it," I whispered, stepping to the box that controlled the building's own alarm system.

"Just because you can breathe the muck here," Loomis said in genuine indignation, "that's no cause to let your air-handling system go like this. What kind of people are these?"

On Venus, as surely as in interstellar space, a breakdown in the air system meant the end of life. Loomis' father supervised a public works crew in Betaport, but I think we all felt a degree of the same outrage.

"Lightbody, watch Jeremy's back," Stephen said. "The rest of you come along. There's somebody supposed to be on duty, and they may not have gone far."

The job centered me so completely that I wasn't conscious of setting the cutting bar down to open my tool kit. After I disconnected the alarms, I went to work on the port's defenses.

A vehicle clanging its alarm bell pulled up beside the building. My hand moved for the cutting bar as I looked at Lightbody in the hallway.

He nodded and stepped out of my angle of vision. I heard the front door open, then close. Lightbody was back. "It's all right, sir," he whispered. "It's the Black Maria bringing a load of drunks to the lockup down below."

I went back to work. A fire director in the southern gunpit controlled the four laser batteries. I couldn't touch the director itself, but its data came from the port radar and optical sensors. I switched them off, then used the tip of my bar to cut the power cable to their console. Sparks snapped angrily between strands of wire and the chassis, but the tool's ceramic blades insulated me.

I heard steps in the hallway. "It's Kiley," Lightbody said.

"There's four guys in the lounge," Kiley said as he joined Lightbody in the hall. "We're tying them up. Mister Gregg didn't want you to worry, sir."

I nodded. I'd found the circuitry powering Corpus Christi's landline telephones. I could shut the system down, but I wasn't sure I wanted to. If the phones went out, people all over the community would run around looking for the cause of the problem. Some of them would come here.

The steel door clanked. Somebody had rested his hand against the other side as he worked the lock. I moved to the commo room doorway with my cutting bar; Kiley and Lightbody flattened themselves on either side of the steel door.

The panel swung inward. A Fed in a gray tunic and CONSTABULARY brassards on both arms stepped through. He had a cut on his forehead and an angry look on his face.

"Hey!" he snarled. "If you fuckers can't get the air-conditioning fixed, we're going to have somebody croak in the cells down there!"

He glared at us momentarily. Concrete steps led down behind him to a room full of echoing metal and alcoholic vomit. I grabbed his throat in my left hand and jerked him forward. Lightbody clubbed the Fed behind the ear as Kiley pulled the door closed.

I let the Fed fall as a dead weight. I drew a deep breath. Lightbody took the man's wrist and pulled him into the commo room.

"I think he's still alive, sir," Lightbody said. He poised the buttplate of his carbine over the man's temple. "Do you want me to . . ."

"Yes, tie him," I said. I was pretty sure that wouldn't have been Lightbody's first suggestion. Lightbody shrugged and undid the Fed's belt for the purpose.

"Here's the others coming," Kiley murmured.

"Come on," I heard Stephen's muffled voice say. "We'll head back to the cutter."

I went to the console and dumped the phones after all. The more confusion, the better . . .

"Wouldn't it be better to go to the new ship?" Loomis asked.

"Only if we knew which it was," Stephen replied in a tone so emotionless that I shivered.

I opened the unit's front access plate. There were three circuit cards behind it. I pulled them.

Stephen stuck his head into the commo room. "Trouble?" he said, glancing at the unconscious Fed.

"No sir, not so's you'd mention it," Lightbody said.

The unlocked stairwell door swung open. Stephen turned. Loomis tried to point his shotgun but the steel panel banged closed again, knocking the gun barrel up.

"Grubbies!" shrieked a voice attenuated by the armored door.

"Outside!" I shouted as I zipped my kit closed over a jumbled handful of tools.

Stephen pushed the door open and fired his flashgun down the stairs one-handed. Metal in the cells below vaporized, then burned in a white flash. Stephen clanged the door shut again.

We bolted out the front of the Commandatura, carrying our weapons openly. Lightbody jumped aside to let me lead.

The van towing the cage was pulled up to the side door. Nobody was inside the vehicle, but the diesel engine was running. A Fed ran out the constabulary door. Kiley fired, knocking the man's legs out from under him with a charge of buckshot in the thighs.

The constabulary door banged against its jamb and bounced a few centimeters open. Stephen's laser spiked at a nearly recipro-cal angle to that of his first bolt. Men screamed as more burn-ing metal sprayed.

I'd never seen controls laid out like those of the van. The steering wheel was in the center of the front compartment. There were hand controls to either side of the wheel, but no foot pedals.

"I'll drive, sir!" Loomis cried, handing me his shotgun. I slid across the bench seat as the others piled in.

Loomis twisted the left handgrip and let a return spring slide it to the dash panel, then pulled the right grip out to its stop. The diesel lugged momentarily before it roared, chirping the tires. We pulled away from the Commandatura. The door of the trailer for prisoners wasn't latched. It swung open and shut, ringing loudly each time.

Loomis turned us and headed up the paved street directly toward the gate. The trailer oscillated from side to side. It swiped a stand of pickled produce, hurling brine and glass shards across the front of the nearest building, then swung the other way and hit a cursing pedestrian who'd managed to dodge the careening van.

A siren sounded from the spaceport. It can't have had anything to do with us, there wasn't time. Stephen reached past Loomis from the other side and flicked a dash control. Our bell began to clang.

Three Molts were swinging a gate of heavy steel tubing across the port entrance. Their officer, a human wearing a gray tunic, saw our van coming. He waved his rifle to halt us.

The four Molts who crewed the port-defense laser were watching the commotion among the ships on the field. The siren came from the *Yellowknife*. All the Fed warship's external lights were on, flooding her surroundings with white glare.

Loomis steered for the narrowing gap between the gate and its concrete post. The Molts continued to trudge forward. The officer threw his rifle to his shoulder and aimed. Stephen's flashgun stabbed. The Fed's chest exploded.

Our left fender scraped the gatepost. My door screeched back in an accordion pleat. The right-side wheels rode over the bottom bar of the gate. The second and third bars bent down but the sturdy framework as a whole didn't flatten.

The van tilted sideways to 45°, then flipped over onto its roof in sparks and shrieking.

I was in the backseat, tangled with Tuching and Kiley. Lightbody had wound up in front. Stephen was kicking open the door on his side and Loomis lay halfway through the shattered windshield. The van's wheels spun above us till Lightbody had the presence of mind to rotate a handgrip and disengage the transmission.

One of the Molts lay pinned between the pavement and the twisted gate. He moaned in gasping sobs that pulsed across his entire body.

The gatepost had stripped off the sliding door in back before we went over. I crawled out. The gunpit crew were running to their multitube laser.

The leading Molt wore a white sash-of-office. Stephen shot him. The bolt hit the right edge of the alien's carapace, spinning the corpse sideways in a blast of steam to trip another member of the gun crew. Stephen bent and snatched the carbine which Lightbody had thrust through the window as he started to wriggle from the van.

I still held Loomis' shotgun. I raised it, aiming for the Molt climbing into the seat on the left side of the gun carriage.

My target was ten meters away. Stephen had taught me that a shotgun wasn't an area weapon: it had to be aimed to be effective. The Molt's mauve plastron wobbled, but not too much, over the trough between the side-by-side barrels. The charge of shot would kick the gunner out of his seat, his chest shattered in a splash of brown ichor. All I had to do was pull the trigger.

I couldn't pull the trigger. I couldn't kill anything *this way,* in the dispassion that distance brought. Not even though the laser's six-tube circular array depressed and traversed toward me at the Molt's direction.

Stephen shot the gunner in the head. The Molt went into spastic motion as if he was trying to swim but his limbs belonged to four different individuals.

Another Molt jumped into the right-hand seat. Stephen worked the bolt of his rifle without taking the butt from his shoulder and blew the back off the second gunner's triangular skull also. The last member of the crew disentangled himself from his dead leader, stood, and immediately fell flailing.

"Come on!" Stephen shouted. He set the carbine on the pavement beside him and braced his hands against the van's quarter-panel. "We'll tilt this back on its wheels!"

I handed the shotgun to Lightbody and ran toward the gunpit. Loomis pulled himself the rest of the way through the windshield and rested on all fours in front of the van. His palms left bloody prints on the concrete, but if he could move, he was in better condition than I'd feared.

A 300-tonne freighter midway in the second row fluffed her thrusters. The plume of bright plasma wobbled toward the town as it cooled, borne on the evening breeze from the river. The engine test would go unremarked by Feds in the port area in the present confusion, but for us it identified the vessel Piet and his men had captured.

The dead Molts had fallen from the gun's turntable. I sat in the left seat and checked the control layout: heel-and-toe pedals for elevation and traverse, a keyboard for the square 20-cm display tilted up from between my knees.

The laser hummed in readiness beside me. The tubes were pumped by a fusion bottle at the back of the pit. One such unit could have driven all four guns, but the Fed planners had gone to the extra expense of running each laser array off a dedicated power source.

If there'd been a common power plant, I could probably have shut it down from the Commandatura. At the time that would have seemed like a good idea, but I'd have regretted it now.

Gunports fell open along the *Yellowknife*'s centerline, black rectangles against the gleaming metal hull. The muzzle of a plasma cannon slid out. The gunners began to slew their weapon to bear on the captured freighter.

Loomis knelt with his hands pressed to his face. Stephen and the other three crew members rocked the van sideways, then pulled it back and gathered their strength for a final push. Either they'd unhitched the trailer, or the crash had broken its tongue.

My targeting screen set a square green frame over the bow of the *Yellowknife*. I keyed a 1 mil/second clockwise traverse into the turntable control. A hydraulic motor whined beneath me.

The van rolled onto its right side in a crunch of glass, then up on its wheels again as my friends shouted their triumph. The motor was still snorting. The diesel must have been a two-stroke or it would have seized by now for being run upside down.

The manual firing switch was a red handle mounted on the gun carriage itself, rather than part of the keyboard. I threw it home against a strong spring, then locked it in place with the sliding bolt.

Flux hundreds of times more concentrated than that of Stephen's flashgun pulsed from the six barrels in turn as the array slowly rotated its fury along the *Yellowknife*'s hull. I jumped from the gun carriage and ran to the van as Stephen tossed Loomis into the back. He piled in beside Lightbody in the driver's seat.

Metal curled from the *Yellowknife* in dazzling white streamers. The pulses hammering the hull would make her interior ring like a bell.

The laser array was a defense against the organic vessels of the Chay. No hostile human ship would dare land with its thrusters exposed to the port's fire, but the *Yellowknife* was too solidly constructed for the flux to penetrate her broadside.

The line of blazing metal slid a handbreadth beneath the open gunports instead of through them. I'd aimed too hastily or the Fed gunners hadn't properly bore-sighted their weapon.

We accelerated toward the captured freighter. A wheel was badly out of alignment. The studded tire screamed against its fender, throwing sparks out behind us. Another ship lit its thrusters to the north edge of the field.

The *Yellowknife* fired a plasma cannon. The intense rainbow flash shadowed my bones through the flesh of my hand. The laser array erupted in white fire. The fusion plant continued to discharge in a blue corona from the fused power cable.

Part of the slug of charged particles missed the gun mechanism and blew out the walls of a building across the street. The wooden roof collapsed on the wreckage and began to burn.

A cutter—*our* cutter—lifted from the edge of the field. It sailed toward the *Yellowknife* at the speed of a man running. Loomis screamed in terror as he realized the vessel was in an arc only five meters high at the point it would intersect our track.

Stephen grabbed the steering wheel with his left hand and spun it clockwise. The van skidded in a right-hand turn. The rubbing tire blew and we fishtailed.

The cutter passed ahead of us in the iridescent glare of its thruster. Its skids touched the concrete and bounced the vessel up again. A human figure leaped from the dorsal hatch, tumbling like a rag doll.

Riflemen in the *Yellowknife*'s open hatch shot vainly at the oncoming cutter. The siren continued to scream. A plasma cannon fired, but the weapon didn't bear on anything: the bolt punished the sky with a flood of ravening ions.

Stephen thrust his flashgun into the backseat. I grabbed it. He opened his door and hung out, gripping the frame with his huge left hand as Lightbody fought to brake the van.

Stephen straightened, jerking Piet off the pavement and into the van with us by the belt of his trousers. A wisp of exhaust had singed Piet's tunic as he bailed out.

The cutter slanted into the bow of the *Yellowknife*. The light ceramic hull shattered like the shell of an egg flung to the ground, but the Federation warship rocked back on its landing skids from the impact. Steam gushed from gunports and a started seam, enveloping the *Yellowknife*'s stern.

"A feedline broke!" Tuching, an engine crewman, shouted.

Lightbody steered toward the captured freighter again. He had to struggle with the shredded tire and Piet squirming to sit up on Stephen's lap beside him.

The wreckage of the cutter fell back from the *Yellowknife*. The warship's bow was dished in and blackened; smoky flames shot from an open gunport.

A green-white flash lifted the *Yellowknife*'s stern centimeters off the ground. The *CRACK!* of the explosion was lightning-sharp and as loud as the end of the world. The van spun a three-sixty, either from the shock wave or because Lightbody twitched convulsively in surprise.

We straightened and wobbled the last hundred meters to the freighter waiting for us with the main hatch open. "*Not* a feedline," Piet said in rich satisfaction. "An injector came adrift and they tried to run their auxiliary power plant without cooling. They'll play hell getting *that* ship in shape to chase us!"

I suppose Guillermo was at the controls of the captured vessel, for she started to lift while Piet and the rest of us were still in the entry hold.

If the three remaining laser batteries had human crews, they might have shot us out of the sky. Molts didn't assume in a crisis that anything moving was an enemy.

Therefore we survived.

ST. LAWRENCE

Day 319

We watched the double line of prisoners dragging the thruster nozzle on a sledge from the captured freighter, the *17 Abraxis*, to the gully where Salomon had landed the *Oriflamme*. The Molts—there were thirty-one of them—chanted a tuneless, rhythmic phrase.

Two of the freighter's human crew had been wounded during the capture. The remaining ten were silent, but they at least gave the impression of putting their weight against the ropes. Lightbody and Loomis, watching with shotguns, wouldn't have killed a captured Fed for slacking; but at least in Lightbody's case, that's because Piet had given strict orders about how to treat the prisoners.

Lightbody's perfect universe would contain no living idolaters; Jeude's death had made him even less tolerant than he was at the start of the voyage. The Fed captives were wise not to try his forbearance.

"Rakoscy says the communications officer is going to pull through," Piet remarked. "I was worried about that."

"That Fed worried me about other things than him taking a bullet through the chest," I said. I wasn't angry—or frightened, *now*. Neither had I forgotten driving across the spaceport under

520

fire because the commo officer of *17 Abraxis* had gotten off an alarm message before Dole shot him out of his console.

The gully contained vegetation and a little standing water, and the defilade location saved the *Oriflamme* from exhaust battering when Piet brought our prize in close by. Though the air was only warm, the sun was a huge red curtain on the eastern sky. That sight wouldn't change until the stellar corona engulfed St. Lawrence: the planet had stopped rotating on its axis millions of years before.

"He was doing his job," Stephen said mildly. "Pretty good at it, too. There aren't so many men like that around that I'd want to lose one more."

"Fortunately," Piet added with a smile, "the staff of the *Yellowknife* hadn't plotted the vessels on the ground at Corpus Christi, so they didn't have any idea which ship was under attack."

We were in the permanent shade of four stone pillars, the fossilized thighbones of a creature that must in life have weighed twenty tonnes if not twice that. The bones had weathered out of the softer matrix rock, but they too were beginning to crumble away from the top.

I turned my head to gaze at the tower of black stone. "Hard to imagine anything so big roaming this place," I said. Vegetation now grew only in low points like the arroyo, and we hadn't found any animal larger than a fingernail.

"A *long* time ago," Stephen said with emphasis. "Who knows? Maybe they developed space travel and emigrated ten million years back."

"Put your backs in it, you cocksucking whoresons," came the faint fury of Winger's voice from the underside of *17 Abraxis*, "or as Christ is my witness, you'll still be here when your fucking beards are down to your knees!"

Piet frowned at the blasphemy (obscenity didn't bother him), but the men were far enough away that he must have decided he could overlook it. The job of removing thruster nozzles—without dockyard tools—after they'd been torqued into place by use was just as difficult as Winger had grumbled it would be when we were on Clapperton.

"They've got seven," Stephen said quietly. "This last one and we're out of here."

"If we don't take spares," I said, deliberately turning my head toward the *Oriflamme* to avoid Piet's eyes.

He glared at me anyway. "The prisoners can get back to Riel on four out of twelve thrusters," he said. "They *can't* get back on two. We aren't going to leave forty-three men here on the chance that somebody will come by before they all starve."

Twelve humans and thirty-one Molts. All of them "men" to Piet, and you'd best remember it when you spoke in his hearing.

"You could manage on two, Piet," Stephen said with a grin. "I'll bet you could take her home on one, though I guess we'd have to gut the hull to get her out of the gravity well to begin with."

I knew Stephen was joking to take the sting out of Piet's rebuke to me. I'd promised Winger that I'd try to get him a spare nozzle, though.

Piet chuckled and squeezed my hand. "All things are possible with the Lord, Stephen," he said, "but I wouldn't care to put him to *that* test. And, Jeremy—"

He sobered.

"—I appreciate what you've tried to do. I know the motor crew is concerned about the wear we'll get from tungsten, and they have a right to be. But if these nozzles don't last us, we'll find further replacements along the way. We won't leave men to die."

I nodded. I looked up at the femur of a creature more ancient than mankind and just possibly more ancient than Earth. Black stone, waiting for the sun to devour it.

A tiny, intense spark shone in the sky where the thigh pointed. I jumped to my feet.

"There's a—"

"*Incoming* vessel!" Piet bellowed as he rose from a seated position to a dead run in a single fluid motion. "Don't shoot! Don't shoot! If she crashes, it could be anywhere!"

Stephen and I followed at our best speed, but Piet was aboard the *Oriflamme* while we were still meters from the cockpit steps.

"This is close enough," Stephen ordered, dropping into a squat a hundred meters from the strange vessel's starboard side. "This swale doesn't look like much, but it'll deflect their exhaust if they try to fry us. Can't imagine anything else we need to worry about, but don't get cocky."

Piet and the rest of us knelt beside him. Stephen, commander of his county's militia before he ever set foot on a starship, was giving the orders for the moment.

Dole's ten men were still jogging to where they'd have an angle on the stranger's bow. Fifty-tonne freighters built like this one on the Back Worlds weren't likely to have hatches both port and starboard, but we weren't taking the risk.

Stampfer was half a kilometer behind us, aligning the 4-cm plasma weapon *17 Abraxis* carried for use against Chay raiders. The *Oriflamme*'s guns were useless while she was in the gully. Salomon, Winger, and the bulk of the crew weren't going to be ready her to lift for an hour or more despite desperate measures.

"You'd think," I said, "that they'd have signaled they were coming in."

Stephen shrugged. "Maybe they don't have commo," he said. "The Feds'd leave the air tanks off to save money if they could get away with it."

"Southerns, sir," Lightbody said unexpectedly.

Stephen and I looked at him; Piet grinned and continued to watch the strange vessel. "This one's Southern Cross construction, sir," Lightbody amplified. "Not Fed. The pairs of thrusters are too far apart for Feds."

The vessel's hatch clanged twice as those inside jerked it sideways by hand rather than hydraulic pressure. Six figures got out. They jumped as far as they could to clear the patch of thruster-heated ground.

One of the newcomers was a woman; common enough for a Terran crew, though I heard Lightbody growl. None of the strangers was armed, and their assorted clothing was entirely civilian.

Piet got up and strode to meet them.

"Guide a little left, Piet," Stephen said as he trotted to Piet's right side. Stephen's left index finger indicated a 30° angle. I moved over to give Piet room but he ignored the direction.

"Piet," Stephen said calmly, "Stampfer will have that plasma cannon trained on the open hatchway. I trust Stampfer, but I don't much trust junk he crabbed out of a Federation freighter. I'd really rather you didn't take the chance of something unlikely happening."

From the tone of Stephen's voice, he could have been asking where to place a piece of furniture.

Piet clicked his tongue, but he bore to the left as directed. "Where would you be without me to fuss over, Stephen?" he murmured.

Possible answers to that falsely light question rang through my head like hammerblows.

"Sirs?" the leader of the newcomers asked. "Are you from the North American Federation?"

He spoke Trade English with a distinct Southern accent. A good dozen additional people, including a few more women, climbed from the vessel behind him. They moved with greater circumspection than the initial party.

The ten of us spread slightly as we bore down on the strangers. We weren't being deliberately threatening, but a group of grim, armed men must have looked as dangerous as an avalanche.

"We are not," Piet said in a proud, ringing voice. "We are citizens of the Free State of Venus."

"Oh, thank God!" cried the woman at the leader's side. She knelt and kissed a crucifix folded in both her hands.

I grabbed Lightbody by the front collar and jerked him around to face me. "No!" I shouted.

I held the spacer till the light eased back into his eyes and he began to breathe normally again. "Sorry, sir," he muttered, bobbing his head in contrition.

Everyone was staring at us. I flushed and lowered the cutting bar in my right hand. Lightbody hadn't done anything overt.

I think Piet understood. I know Stephen did, because he gave me a slow smile and said, "If you ever change sides, friend, I'm not going to let you get in arm's length alive. Hey?"

In context, that was high praise.

The newcomer's leader embraced Piet. "Sir," he said, "I am Nicolas Rodrigo and these are my people, twenty of us."

I eyed the group quickly. If there were only twenty, then they were all in plain sight by now. There were no Molts in the group, surprisingly.

"Until forty days ago, we maintained the colony on Santos," Rodrigo said. "Then two Federation warships, the *Yellowknife* and *Keys to the Kingdom,* arrived under a beast named Prothero. He—"

The woman had risen again. At Prothero's name, she spat. Our eyes meshed, then slid sideways. Quite an attractive little thing in a plump, dark-haired fashion. Young; 18 or 20 at the outside, as compared with Rodrigo's 35 or so.

"—told us that the Southern Cross had been placed under

President Pleyal's protection, and that he was taking control of Santos on behalf of the Federation. He—"

"What do you have aboard your ship?" Stephen interjected abruptly.

"What?" Rodrigo said. "Nothing, only food. Ah—we took back the *Hercules*, this ship, on Corpus Christi. There was confusion when a freighter crashed into the *Yellowknife*."

Kiley chuckled. "I wonder if them poor bastards'll *ever* figure out quite what happened," he said.

"Come along back to our ships, then," Piet said. "We'll be more comfortable there, and I don't want my men I've left there to be concerned."

The bosun's party was moving toward us, slowed by their weight of weapons and, for a few of them, armor. "Mister Dole?" Piet called. "Set five of your men to secure the ship, if you will."

Stampfer must have realized the situation was peaceful; he tilted the muzzle of the light cannon up like an exclamation point above the hasty barricade of crates across the hold of *17 Abraxis*. Maybe the gesture helped the others relax.

Me, I was still trembling in reaction to a few minutes before, when I stopped Lightbody from blowing a pretty woman's head off.

"Prothero put his own men on Santos as overseers," Rodrigo explained, drinking a thimble glass of slash cut three to one with water. "The plantations are worked by Molts, of course. We don't— we didn't export, we just supplied convoys in the Back Worlds trade stopping over."

The Southerns mixed freely with the *Oriflamme*'s crew. A joint party had gone back to the *Hercules*, for supplies including Santos wine. The Federation prisoners watched sullenly as they resumed hauling heavy thruster nozzles.

Piet, Stephen, Lacaille, and I sat with the Southern leaders at a trestle table on the shaded side of the gully. Rodrigo's wife, Carmen, was at his side across the table, occasionally eyeing me as she raised the glass to her lips. She wasn't actually drinking.

"I know Prothero," Lacaille said. "I don't know anybody who likes or trusts him, but he's ... able enough. In his way."

The Southerns watched the Fed castaway sidelong, uncertain about his status. I guess we all were uncertain, Lacaille himself included.

"The *Hercules* was on Santos when the Federation ships arrived," Rodrigo continued. "Captain Cinpeda commanded."

A short, dark Southern nodded. He'd drunk his slash neat. His eyes never left the carafe I'd deliberately slid out of his reach.

"Prothero filled the *Hercules* with food and put his own crew aboard," Rodrigo said. "It was no more than piracy. But how could we fight with no warships of our own?"

Stephen's lips smiled; his eyes did not. Ships don't fight: men do. And Rodrigo wasn't that sort of man.

"Prothero took us with him on the *Yellowknife*," Rodrigo said. "The *Keys to the Kingdom* was his flagship, but she needed repairs. He left her on Santos while he went ahead to Riel."

"She's a great, cranky tub of eight hundred tonnes, the *Keys*," Lacaille said. "I'm not surprised she broke down. Her water pumps again?"

Cinpeda nodded to Lacaille with respect.

"They can't be depopulating all the Southern colonies," I said. "Can they?"

"I think," Carmen Rodrigo said with her eyes lowered, "that the decision was Commander Prothero's. I believe his intentions toward me were . . . not proper. Though he already has a mistress!"

"Prothero's always operated as though the Middle Ways were his own kingdom," Lacaille said. "I doubt he was acting completely on orders."

"We took our chance when the emergency siren sounded," Rodrigo said. "We thought it was a Chay raid. The prize crew had left the *Hercules,* so we went aboard and lifted as soon as the computer gave us a course."

"To home," Carmen said. "We're going back to Rio. Better Pleyal a continent away than Prothero in the next cabin."

There was an edge in her tone that I thought I understood. Carmen Rodrigo might or might not be a virtuous wife; I had my doubts. But she certainly intended to make any decisions of that sort on her own.

"Why *this* course, to St. Lawrence?" Piet asked suddenly. "It's a week's transit in the wrong direction if you intend to return to the Solar System."

"Reaction mass," Cinpeda grunted. "I wonder, master, could you . . ."

He extended his tiny glass. I filled it from the carafe.

"Ah, thank you, thank you indeed, master," the Southern captain said. He shuddered as he tossed the shot down, but his eyes gained a focus that had been missing a moment before.

"Reaction mass," Cinpeda repeated. "Prothero's crew, they'd refilled the air tanks when they landed on Riel, but they hadn't hooked up to the water yet. Food we had, air we had, but there wasn't water for ten days under power."

"There *is* water here, isn't there?" Rodrigo asked in sudden concern as he gazed around him. The planet must have looked like a desert from orbit, and the slight greenery of this arroyo wasn't much more inviting.

"We've bored a well," Piet said. "You can draw from it, now that we've topped off."

"If you were trying to escape," Stephen asked, "why did you land by us—and without signaling?"

"Fucking collimator's out," Cinpeda said with a scowl. "On the laser communicator. Fucking thing drifts. And the VHF transmitter, it's been wonky since they installed it."

He looked as though he was going to ask for another drink. I shook my head minutely.

"We thought you'd done the same thing we did," Rodrigo said, answering the first part of the question. "Come here to get away from Prothero. We knew other ships escaped when we did."

"Didn't even notice this one before we landed," Cinpeda said with a nod toward the *Oriflamme*. "What is it—don't you reflect radar?"

I shrugged. Ceramic hulls did reflect radar, but not as strongly as a similar expanse of metal. The *Oriflamme* was an outcrop in the gully to a radar operator unless the fellow was actively looking for a Venerian ship here.

"And there was no reason to come to *this* place," Carmen added, "except to avoid being on Riel. So we thought you might be from the Southern Cross too, until we saw your guns."

"Does your vessel carry guns?" Stephen said. There was no challenge in his tone, only the certainty of a man who *will* be answered.

"A small cannon," Rodrigo said. "For the Chay, and perhaps not much use against them. We can't defend ourselves against you, sirs."

Piet stood up with a nod. "Nor do you need to," he said. "We have our own needs and can be of little help to you, but we certainly won't hinder."

"How long will you remain on this planet?" Carmen asked without looking—pointedly without looking—at me.

"No longer than it takes to mount two more thruster nozzles, madam," Piet said with a wry grin. "Which is some hours longer than I wish it would be, now that you've arrived."

"Are we so terrible?" Carmen said in surprise.

"The people who may follow you are," I explained gently. "The Feds know how much reaction mass they left on your ship, and they've got the same pilotry data as you do to pick the possible landfalls."

"But we'll deal with them, if it comes to that," Stephen said, hefting his flashgun. His eyes had no life and no color, and his voice was as dry as the wind.

No Federation force would be half so terrible as we ourselves were.

"Piet?" I said as I stood up. "The *Abraxis* has a first-rate commo suite. If you'll let Guillermo help me, I can swap it into the *Hercules* in less time than it takes Winger to fit the nozzles."

"That leaves the *Abraxis* without . . ." Piet said. He smiled. "Ah. One ship or the other."

"And the choice to the men with the guns," Stephen said. He was smiling also, though his expression and Piet's had little in common. "As usual."

"Yes," Piet said. "Go ahead."

"Guillermo!" I shouted as I ran for the forward hatch and my tool kit. "We've got a job!"

The *Oriflamme*'s siren shut off as Guillermo and I clambered aboard the *17 Abraxis*. Piet had held the switch down for thirty seconds to call the crew aboard. Men were scattered from here to the *Hercules*. Hell, some had probably wandered off in the other direction for reasons best known to themselves.

When the alarm sounded; Fed prisoners returning the sledge to the *17 Abraxis* slacked the drag ropes to see what was happening. The Molts continued to pace forward. Maher, one of the pair on guard this watch, punched a Fed between the shoulder blades with his rifle butt.

The prisoner yelped. He turned. Maher prodded his face with the gun muzzle. The Feds resumed the duties they'd been set.

"We don't want to screw up the navigational equipment when

we lift this," I said to Guillermo as I tapped the freighter's communications module. "Do you know if any of the hardware or software is common?"

"No, Jeremy," the Molt said. "I could build it from parts, of course, since one of my ancestors did that a thousand years ago."

Guillermo's thorax clicked his race's equivalent of laughter. His three-fingered hands played across the navigation console. "What we can do, though, is to bring up the AI and keep it running while we separate the communications module and attempt to run *it*."

"Right," I said. Molts were supposed to operate by rote memory while humans displayed true, innovative intelligence. That's what made us superior to them. You bet.

I bent to check the join between the module and the main console. The speaker snapped, "Presidential—

I jumped upright, grabbing my cutting bar with both hands to unhook it. The only reason I carried the weapon was I hadn't thought to remove it after we returned from the *Hercules*.

"—Vessel *Keys to the Kingdom* calling ships on St. Lawrence! Do not attempt to lift. You will be boarded by Federation personnel. Any attempt at resistance will cause you both to be destroyed by gunfire. Respond at once! Over."

The commo screen was blanked by a nacreous overlay: the caller could, but chose not to, broadcast video.

"Stay in the image!" I said to Guillermo. Venerian ships didn't have Molt crew members.

The voice had said, " . . . you both . . ." The Feds had made the same mistake as Captain Cinpeda: they'd seen the metal-hulled vessels, but they'd missed the *Oriflamme* in her gully.

My fingers clicked over the module's keyboard. It was an excellent unit, far superior to the normal run of commo gear we produced on Venus. I careted a box in the upper left corner of the pearly field for the *Oriflamme*.

Piet looked at me, opening his mouth. I ignored him and said, "Freighter *David* out of Clapperton to Presidential Vessel, we're laid up here replacing a feedline and our consort's commo is screwed up. What the hell's got into you, over?"

Guillermo stood with his plastron bowed outward. He scratched the grooves between belly plates with a finger from either hand. I'd never seen him do anything of the sort before. The activity looked slightly disgusting—and innocent, like a man picking his nose.

"Who are you?" demanded the voice from the module. "Who is this speaking? Over!"

Piet nodded approvingly. At least *he* thought we looked like the sort of folks you'd find on the bridge of a Federation merchantman . . .

"This is Captain Jeremy Moore!" I said, tapping my chest with the point of my thumb. "Who are you, boyo? Some bleeding Molt, or just so pig-faced ugly that you're afraid to let us see you? Over!"

Through the open hatch I saw men staggering aboard the *Oriflamme.* Sailors' lives involved both danger and hard work, but their normal activities didn't prepare them to run half a klick when the alarm sounded.

The sledge sat beside the *17 Abraxis,* ready to receive the eighth and final thruster nozzle. It had taken an hour, minimum, to transport each previous nozzle, and another hour to fit the tungsten forging into place beneath the *Oriflamme.*

Guillermo balanced on one leg and stuck the other in the air. He poked at his crotch. I noticed that he'd dropped his sash onto my cutting bar on the deck, out of the module's camera angle.

The pearl-tinged static dissolved into the face of a man who'd been handsome some twenty years and twenty kilograms ago. At the moment he was mad enough to chew hull plates, exactly what I'd intended. Angry people lose perspective and miss details.

"I'll tell you who I am!" he shouted. "I'm Commodore Richard Prothero, officer commanding the Middle Ways, and I'm going to have your guts for garters, *boyo!* My landing party will be down in twenty minutes. If there's so much as a burp from you, I'll blast a crater so deep it goes right on out the other side of the planet! Do you understand, civilian? Out!"

Prothero's three quarters of the screen blanked—completely, to the black of dead air rather than a carrier wave's pearly luminescence. Piet nodded again and crooked his index finger to Guillermo and me.

I didn't imagine that Prothero could intercept the laser link I'd formed between us and the *Oriflamme,* but we needn't take unnecessary risks. The necessary ones were bad enough.

"You'll need more than your helmet," Stephen said in a voice as if waking from a dream. "Put the rest of your armor on, Jeremy."

"When we lift, I'll put my suit on," I said. I wondered what I sounded like. Nothing human, I supposed. Very little of me was human when I slipped into this state.

"The Federation warship orbiting St. Lawrence is an eight-hundred-tonner mounting twenty carriage guns." Piet's voice rang calmly through the tannoy in the ceiling of the forward hold. "We'll be lifting on seven engines, so we won't be as handy as I'd like. In order to return home, we must engage and destroy this enemy. With the Lord's help, my friends, we *will* destroy them and destroy every enemy of Venus!"

Twelve of us waited in the hold. Kiley, Loomis, and Lightbody carried flashguns, but Stephen alone held his with the ease of a man drawing on an old glove.

We'd had time to rig for action, but it would be tight working the big guns with everybody in hard suits. They were probably cheering Piet in the main hull. None of us did. For myself, I didn't feel much of anything, not even fear.

"They must've landed on Riel just after we left," Maher said. "The *Keys* must. Pity they weren't another month putting their pumps to rights."

"We'll lift as soon as the enemy ship is below the horizon," Piet continued, "and our marksmen have dealt with the Federation cutters. The enemy is in a hundred-and-six-minute orbit, so we'll have sufficient time to reach altitude before joining battle."

Even on seven thrusters? Well, I'd take Piet's word for it. Aloud I said, "Lacaille says that the *Keys* is falling apart. You've seen the sort, older than your gramps and Fed-maintained as well. We'll give her the last push, is all."

"Too right, sir!" Kiley said, nodding enthusiastically. He knew I was just cheering them up before we fought a ship with enough guns, men and tonnage to make six of us. All the sailors knew that—and appreciated it, maybe more than they appreciated me standing beside them now. They expected courage of a gentleman, but not empathy.

Two exhaust flares winked in the sky. I lowered my visor. For the moment, the riflemen and I were present to protect the flashgunners from Feds who managed to get out of the landing vessels. I'd wear my suit when it was that or breathe vacuum; but I wouldn't put on that jointed ceramic coffin before I had to.

"I'll take the right-hand one," Stephen said in a husky, horrid whisper. He clicked his faceshield down. "Wait for me to shoot. If anyone jumps the gun—if you survive the battle, my friend, you won't survive it long. On my oath as a gentleman."

"Almighty God," said Piet. "May Thy hand strengthen ours in Thy service today. Amen."

Lacaille was suited up aboard the *Oriflamme*. He'd repeated that he wouldn't fight his own people; but he'd asked not to be left on the ground, either.

We owed him that much. The prisoners locked for the moment in the hold of the *17 Abraxis* would identify him quickly enough to survivors of the Federation landing party. Besides, Lacaille was one of us now—whatever he said, wherever he was born.

"Easy, gentlemen," Stephen said as he lifted his flashgun to his shoulder.

The Fed boats leveled out from their descent and cruised toward the *17 Abraxis* a hundred meters in the air. They were bigger than our cutter, almost the size of featherboats. They didn't act like they saw us. Small-craft optics are crude, and the Feds weren't expecting to find anything in the shadow of the arroyo.

The nearer vessel slowed to a crawl while five meters in the air. It began to settle beside the freighter. Its plasma exhaust flared in an oval pattern that swept stones as big as my fist from the ground.

Stephen fired. His bolt struck the side of the boat's thruster nozzle, close to the white-hot lip. The exhaust already sublimed tungsten from the nozzle's throat and left a black smear on the ground where the metal redeposited.

The laser pulse heated the point it hit to a fractionally greater degree than the metal casing around it. The nozzle lost cohesion. The side blew toward us in a bubble of green vapor as intense as the plasma that drove it. The *crash!* of metal exploding was more dazzling than the flash.

The vessel rolled clockwise on its axis and nosed in almost upside down. The dorsal hatch flew off. Members of the landing party flew out in a confusion of weapons and white tunics.

The second craft was thirty meters in the air and a hundred meters beyond the first. Our three remaining flashgunners fired in near unison. Two of the bolts glanced from the cutter's hull, leaving deep scars in the metal and puffs of aluminum vapor in the air. The third man aimed better but to even less effect: his flux stabbed toward the nozzle but was smothered in the cloud of ionized exhaust.

The boat rotated toward us. A port in its blunt bow gaped open. The riflemen beside me volleyed at the little vessel, flecking the hull when they hit.

Stephen clacked the battery compartment closed and raised his reloaded flashgun. The muzzle of a twin-tube laser thrust from the Feds' gunport. Even pumped by the thruster, it couldn't seriously damage the *Oriflamme*'s hull; but it could kill all of us in the hold, hard suits or no.

The vessel slid toward us in a shallow dive. Stephen fired.

The thruster nozzle was only a corona beneath the craft's oncoming bow. A cataclysmic green flash lifted the vessel in what would have been a fatal loop if the pilot hadn't been incredibly good or incredibly lucky. The cutter screamed overhead and skidded along the ground on its belly for two hundred meters beyond the arroyo, strewing fragments of hull behind it.

The *Oriflamme*'s engines roared. The deck vibrated fiercely, but it would be a moment before thrust rose beyond equilibrium with our mass and we started to lift. Men started for the companionway to the main deck, cheering and clapping one another's shoulders with their gauntleted hands.

My hard suit waited for me in a corner of the hold. I began to put it on, trying not to get rattled as I performed the unfamiliar, unpleasant task of locking myself into armor. Because Stephen and Lightbody helped me, I was suited up within a minute or two of when the hatch sealed out the buffeting of the atmosphere the *Oriflamme* was fast leaving.

ABOVE ST. LAWRENCE

Day 319

Oriflamme's guns were run out to starboard. Stampfer was amidships with the fire director, but the Long Tom's six-man crew stood close about their massive gun.

Gaiters did a halfhearted job of sealing the gun tube to the inner bulkhead. The pleated barriers kept the cabin air pressure high enough to scatter light and even carry sound, but we were breathing bottled air behind lowered faceshields.

The *Keys to the Kingdom* hung on Guillermo's display. It wasn't a real-time image. We viewed one frozen aspect of the spherical vessel, and even portions of that had the glossiness of an electronic construct rather than the rough, tarnished surfaces of physical reality.

There was nothing for scale in the image, but "800 tonnes" meant something to me now as it had not at the start of this voyage. It meant the *Keys* was significantly larger than *Our Lady of Montreal;* and unlike the *Montreal,* she was first and foremost a warship.

God knew, so was the *Oriflamme,* and we of her crew were men of war.

The *Keys'* bridge, indicated by sensor and antenna concentrations, was in the usual place at the top deck. The generally globular design was flattened on the underside so that the thrusters could be grouped in the same plane.

Ramps on the deck above the thrusters served for loading and unloading the vessel on the ground. Because the *Keys* was so large, she was also configured to load in orbit through large rectangular hatches at her horizontal centerline. Her gun decks, indicated by a line of ports that were still closed when our optics drew the image on display, were above and below the central deck.

About twenty guns, Lacaille had said. They'd be smaller than ours and less efficient; but . . . twenty guns.

The usual digital information filled Salomon's screen. I glanced at Piet's display and found, to my surprise, that I understood its analogue data to a degree.

The gray central ball was St. Lawrence. The bead on the slightly elliptical green line circling the planet was the *Keys to the Kingdom* in orbit, while we were the indigo-to-blue line arcing up the surface. The difference in color indicated relative velocities: the *Keys*, in her higher orbit, moved slower than we did as we circled toward the Feds from below under power.

The image on Guillermo's display suddenly shifted into motion, as though a paused recording had been switched back on. We'd come out of the planet's shadow; our sensors were getting direct images of the *Keys to the Kingdom* again.

Our approach was from the *Keys'* underside. Her twenty-four thruster nozzles were arranged four/six/four/six/four. A faint glow still illuminated their heavy-metal casings.

I put my helmet against Stephen's and said, "Don't they see us?"

Plasma flooded from the *Keys'* thrusters. The cloud expanded to hundreds of times the volume of the starship from which it sprang. A moment later, attitude jets spurted lesser quantities of gas which swiftly dissipated. The sphere shuddered and began to rotate so that its main engines weren't exposed to our fire.

"Now they see us!" Stephen replied. Even thinned by conduction through his helmet and mine, his voice was starkly gleeful.

The bubble of exhaust separated from the *Keys to the Kingdom*. It drifted away, cooling and still expanding until it was only a faint shimmer across the starscape. The Fed commander was putting his ship in a posture of defense, because he'd realized that he couldn't escape us. Even on seven thrusters, the *Oriflamme* had a much higher power-to-mass ratio than the huge *Keys* did. We could literally run circles around the Feds in the sidereal universe. If they attempted to transit, we would jump with them: two AIs with identical parameters would *always* pick the same "best" solution.

And that would be the end of the *Keys to the Kingdom.* Piet would bring us up beneath the Feds at point-blank range—and Stampfer would blow the *Keys'* thrusters out, leaving the vessel to drift powerless in interstellar space.

The need to protect our thrusters was behind Piet's decision to disable the Fed landing boats before we lifted. The *Oriflamme's* hull could take a considerable battering from heavy guns and still be repaired. Laser bolts or light plasma cannon could destroy our main engines, however. We couldn't risk being encircled by three hostile vessels, even if two of them were small by comparison with the *Oriflamme.*

Piet shut off our engines. I grasped a stanchion with my left gauntlet as I started to drift up from the deck. The bead that was the *Oriflamme* drove silently across the main display on a course that would intersect the *Keys to the Kingdom* in two minutes, or at most three. The arc marking our past course was now turquoise.

The carriage of the 17-cm gun crawled slowly sideways, making the deck tremble. The fire director was keeping the muzzle pointed at the target Stampfer had chosen.

"All weapons bear on the enemy, sir!" the master gunner announced over the radio intercom. Motors in the gun training apparatus crackled across Stampfer's voice, but so long as the main engines were shut down the whole crew could hear him over the helmet radios.

"Thank you, Mister Stampfer," Piet said in a tone that was so calm he sounded bored. "I trust your aim, but I think we'll close further so that the charges will dissipate less."

Static roared on the intercom. My hair stood on end from a jolt of static, and the hull beside me rocked to a white-hot hammerblow.

There was enough atmosphere at this altitude to light the tracks of the *Keys'* plasma bolts across our optical screen. The Feds had salveod ten guns. Only one round had hit squarely. It was powerful enough to shatter our tough outer hull and craze the inner one in a meter-diameter circle between the gunport and the navigation consoles.

The *Oriflamme* rocked with the impact of ions moving at light speed. Attitude jets snorted, returning us to our former alignment. The Long Tom's gear motors tracked and tracked back, holding a calculated point of impact.

The *Keys to the Kingdom* filled Guillermo's screen. Our green bead and the chartreuse bead of the Federation vessel were on the verge of contact on the analogue display.

"Fire as you bear, Mist—" Piet's voice ordered before static and the ringing *CRASH!* of five heavy guns recoiling blotted out all other sound.

Two of the directed thermonuclear explosions struck the *Keys'* upper gun deck, two struck the mid-line deck, and the last ripped a collop out of the lower gun deck in a grazing blow. Eight cargo hatches blew out along the centerline. Our plasma charges expanded the deck's atmosphere explosively, pistoning the Fed vessel open from the inside.

Bolts that hit the *Keys'* gun decks ripped huge, glowing ulcers in the hull plating. White-hot metal blew inward, mixed with the residual atmosphere, and burned in secondary pulses. The initial impacts wracked the *Keys'* internal subdivisions. These follow-up blasts penetrated deep into the vessel, spreading pain and panic among those who'd thought themselves out of immediate danger.

Attitude jets puffed, rotating the *Oriflamme* on her axis so that our spine rather than our starboard was presented to our enemy. We'd taken one hit and were likely to take others. Piet was adjusting our aspect so that the Feds couldn't concentrate on the weakened portion of our hull.

The Long Tom had recoiled two meters on its carriage. Efflux from the plasma bolt had blown the gaiters inward so that a rectangle of hard vacuum surrounded the barrel. A crewman spun the locking mechanism and swung the breechblock open.

The thermonuclear explosion had heated the gun's ceramic bore to a throbbing white glow. In the absence of an atmosphere, cooling had to be by radiation rather than convection, but even so an open tube would return to safe temperature much sooner than closed-breech weapons of the sort the Feds used. A few wisps of plasma twinkled within the bore like forlorn will-o'-the-wisps.

I caught a momentary glimpse of a sunlit object through the gunport: the *Keys to the Kingdom*. In astronomical terms, we and our enemies were almost touching, but the human reality was that kilometers separated our vessels. The Fed warship was a glint, not a shape.

A four-man damage-control team covered the crazed portion of our hull with a flexible patch. The men moved smoothly, despite weightlessness and their hard suits. Glue kept the patch in place, though positive internal air pressure would be a more important factor when we really needed it. The refractory fabric didn't provide structural strength, but it would block the influx of friction-heated atmosphere during a fast reentry.

Our thrusters roared for twenty seconds to kick us into a diverging orbit. The Federation vessel rotated slowly on Guillermo's screen. All the *Keys'* mid-line cargo hatches were gone.

Additional gunports swung to bear on us. I expected the Feds to fire, but for now they held their peace. Prothero realized that we could reload faster than his gunners dared to. If the Feds fired their ready guns now, they would have no response if we closed to point-blank range and raked them again.

A figure anonymous in his hard suit came from the midships compartment and pushed by me with as little concern as if I'd been the stanchion I held. I thought it was someone bringing Piet a message that couldn't be trusted to the intercom. Instead the man stooped to view the bore of the Long Tom.

The ceramic was yellow-orange at the breech end. Its color faded through red to a gray at the muzzle which only wriggled slightly to indicate it was still radiating heat.

I saw the man's face as he rose: Stampfer, personally checking the condition of his guns rather than trusting the assessment to men he had trained.

"Sir," he said over the intercom, "the broadside guns are ready any time you want them. The big boy here forward, he'll be another three minutes, I'm sorry but there it fucking is."

"Thank you, Mister Stampfer," Piet said. I watched his hands engage a preset program on his console. He still sounded like he was checking the dinner menu. "We'll hit them with four, I think. Load your guns."

Stampfer swooped through the internal hatch in a single movement, touching nothing in the crowded forward compartment. Our attitude jets burped; I locked my left leg to keep from swinging around the stanchion. The main thrusters fired another short, hammering pulse. The curve our course had drawn across that of the *Keys to the Kingdom* began to reconverge.

Stampfer was a lucky man to have a job to do. The cutting bar trembled vainly in my gauntleted hand.

The Federation vessel grew on Guillermo's screen. Black rectangles where the hatches were missing crossed her mid-line like a belt. Apart from that, her appearance was identical to that of the ship we'd first engaged: the damage we'd done, like the guns that had fired on us, was turned away.

We were already closer than we'd been when the *Keys* loosed her opening broadside. This time she held her fire.

"Come on," somebody muttered over the intercom. "Come on, *come*—"

Guillermo's left hand depressed a switch, cutting off general access to the net. His six digits moved together, reconnecting certain channels—Stampfer, Winger, Dole; the navigation consoles. I could have done that . . .

"It would make our job easier if Commodore Prothero was stupid as well as the brute I'm told he is," Piet announced calmly, "but we'll work with the material the Lord has given us. Mister Stampfer, we'll roll at two degrees per second. Fire when you bear."

Thump of the jets, the torque of my armored body trying to retain its attitude as my grip on the stanchion forces it instead to the ship's rotation . . .

Chaos. The 15-cm guns firing amidships and—so sudden it seemed to be a part of the broadside—the smashing impacts of two, maybe three Federation bolts.

Residual air within the *Oriflamme*'s hull fluoresced a momentary pink. The normal interior lights went out; the constant tremble of pumps and drive motors through the ship's fabric stilled.

The navigation consoles were still lighted. Salomon lifted himself in his couch to look back. Piet did not. His armored fingers touched switches in a precise series, looking for the pattern that would restore control.

The *Oriflamme*'s axial rotation continued, modified by the recoil of our broadside guns and the hits the Feds had scored. What size guns did the *Keys* mount: 10-cm? Perhaps bigger; that last impact rang through our hull as if the *Oriflamme* had been dropped ten meters to the ground.

The attitude jets fired, then fired again in a different sequence.

Piet damped first the planned component of our rotation, then brought the plasma-induced yaw under control.

Red emergency lights came on. Because there wasn't enough atmosphere to diffuse their illumination normally, they merely marked points on the inner hull.

A man bowled forward from amidships: Stampfer again. He snatched a spherical shell from Long Tom's ready magazine and settled it into the weapon's breech, using his fingertips rather than the alignment tool shaped like a long-handled cookie-cutter.

The *Keys to the Kingdom* was turning slowly on at least two axes. Our broadside had struck in a concentrated pattern on the huge vessel's lower gun deck and the deck immediately below that. Three of the bolts had burned a single glowing crater that could have passed a featherboat sideways. The fourth was a close satellite to the merged trio. Vapor spurted from it, indicating that we'd holed either an air or a water tank.

A crewman swung the Long Tom's breech shut and turned the locking wheel. Bracing themselves against the steps cut into the deck for the purpose, the men ran their weapon out. Emergency power wasn't sufficient to operate the hydraulics, but Stampfer's crew knew its job.

The master gunner himself crouched beside the individual gunsight set into the Long Tom's trunnion. He had to edge sideways as his men shifted the gun to battery. The fire director must have gone out. At least one of the Fed bolts hit us amidships. We might have lost a gun or even all the broadside guns.

A team ran cable sternward from a manhole in the deck behind me. The auxiliary power unit was amidships, in the bulkhead between our fore and aft cargo holds. These men were tapping one of the main thrusters for power.

"Steady, Captain!" Stampfer's voice demanded. He sounded like he was trying to pull a planet out of its orbit. Up to now, he'd been speaking on a net limited to his gunners. "Stead—"

The Long Tom flashed its horrid rainbow glare as it recoiled into the compartment. There was no air to compress, but the massive cannon drove back with a crushing psychic ambience.

The 17-cm bolt pierced the blurred crater the triplet of broadside guns had melted in the Federation vessel's hull. Because the *Keys* was slowly rotating, the angle of the impact was different. More important, this bolt released all its energy within the spherical hull instead of on the exterior plating.

Silvery vapor geysered from the *Keys'* lower gun deck: metal heated to gas. It slammed outward at a velocity that chemical explosives couldn't have imparted. In the shock wave tumbled shredded bulkheads, dismounted cannon, and the bodies of personnel stationed on the deck our guns had ravaged.

Our internal lights came on; I felt vibration through the stanchion I held as the great pumps begin to tremble again. Stampfer moved amidships, toward his broadside guns. The Long Tom's bore was a cylinder of hellish white, breech to muzzle.

"Holy Jesus preserve us," Salomon said. I looked around. The digital information on his screen meant nothing to me, but I could understand the third track rising from the planetary surface on Piet's display.

Guillermo split his optical screen, setting the *Keys'* image to the right. On the left half was the *Hercules,* rising to higher orbit to join the battle.

The freighter's hatch was open. The 5-cm plasma cannon we'd left the Southerns was mounted on a swivel in the center of the hatchway. Our optics and the software enhancing them were so good that I could make out at least a dozen armored figures within the freighter's hold.

The Southern refugees didn't have hard suits. The *Hercules* was crewed by survivors from the *Keys'* landing party, and perhaps by prisoners released from *17 Abraxis* as well.

The two Federation ships were the jaws of a nutcracker, and the *Oriflamme* was their nut. One hit, even by the swivel gun, on our thrusters and we would no longer be able to maneuver with the *Keys to the Kingdom.* One hit . . .

"Piet," Stephen said, "bring us in tight to the *Keys.* I'll take a party aboard and we'll clear her."

"Prothero's holding his fire," Piet replied. I didn't know whether Guillermo had included me in the command channel, or if the whole crew was hearing the debate. "He'll salvo into our hold if we come within boarding distance. That's what he wants!"

I couldn't command, I couldn't even talk. I trembled in my hard suit. There was a red haze over my vision and I wanted to kill someone, I wanted to kill more than I'd ever before in my life wanted anything . . .

"Jesus *Christ* will you bring us close?" Stephen shouted. "Will you have those whoresons peck us to death and no answer? Bring us close, damn you, bring us close!"

It wasn't anger in his tone. It was white fluorescent rage, and I knew because the same need surged through me, ruling me, *would I never swing my arm and see faces dissolve in blood again?*

"We—" Piet shouted.

The *Hercules* was on an intersecting but not parallel path to the paired orbits of the *Keys* and the *Oriflamme*. Cinpeda had told us—and would tell anybody at gunpoint—that the reticle of the *Hercules*' laser communicator wasn't aligned properly. The Federation crew had to make a close approach to the *Keys* in order to coordinate their attack on us.

I knew that. Until the *Keys to the Kingdom* fired all her loaded guns into the *Hercules,* it didn't occur to me that Commodore Prothero knew nothing of the sort.

The freighter burst into a ball of opalescent vapor. Her own thrusters ruptured, adding their ionized fury to the directed jolts of the Federation cannon. The *Hercules*' light-alloy hull couldn't contain or even slow the cataclysm.

"All personnel except those with immediate gunnery or engineering tasks, assemble in the holds," Piet ordered in a voice as thin as a child's. "Starboard watch to the forward hold, port watch aft. Over."

I followed Stephen toward the compartment bulkhead. Because we hadn't yet loaded the *17 Abraxis*' cutter to replace the one we'd lost on Riel, there was room in both holds for boarding parties.

I noticed that the Long Tom's crew was headed aft with us. They'd apparently interpreted "immediate tasks" to mean tasks more immediate than the six to eight minutes the 17-cm gun would take to cool for the next shot.

The midships compartment looked like the remains of a lobster dinner. Fragments of flesh and ceramic armor floated in the air. Much of the blood had spread across the bulkheads in viscous blotches. Sufficient droplets, wobbling as they tried to remain spherical, still floated in the compartment to paint the suits of us coming from the bow.

The bolt had entered through Number Two gunport at a severe angle, taking an oval bite from the coaming. The main charge had struck Number Three gun, vaporizing the left side of the carriage, much of the gun tube behind the second reinforce, and parts of—

Three men, maybe five. It was hard to say. There were so many body parts drifting in the compartment, rebounding from the bulkheads in slow curves, that my first reaction was that everyone amidships was dead.

Rakoscy was working on an armless man in a transparent cocoon meant as emergency shelter if the ship lost its atmosphere. The bubble was a tight fit for two men wearing most of their hard suits. Another crewman, anonymous in his armor, stood over the cocoon to illuminate Rakoscy's work with a handlight. There wasn't room for an aide within the distended fabric.

It didn't look to me as if the victim had a prayer. I don't suppose Rakoscy could afford to let himself think that way, though.

The forward hold was crowded. Stephen pushed to the front. A Fed bolt had struck near the cross-bulkhead. It hadn't penetrated, but the upper aft corner of the hatch was fractured in a conchoidal pattern. I wondered if Winger would be able to bring the APU back on line . . .

Dole, his helmet marked with three fluorescent bars, stood beside the hatch controls. Lightbody and Maher were at the arms locker beside the bosun. They gave us room as they recognized Stephen, Stephen and me.

"I'll take the line, Mister Dole," Stephen announced, reaching for the magnetic grapnel in the bosun's left hand. "Gentlemen to the front."

"Yessir," Dole said, giving up the grapnel. "If you'd really rather."

Lightbody hooked the line onto one of Stephen's equipment studs. The grapnel had permanent magnets on its gripping surface, but unless something went wrong, its electromagnets would be powered through the line itself.

There was also an adhesive pad to grip nonferrous surfaces. From the way the *Keys to the Kingdom* had resisted our plasma bolts, there was no doubt that her hull was steel, and thick steel besides.

"I'm next," I said to Lightbody. There was movement in the hold, men entering and shifting position. My eyes were focused on the back of Stephen's helmet, and I wasn't seeing even that.

"Sir, will you take a rifle?" a voice said.

The intercom worked with only the usual amount of static. Neither we nor the Feds were burning thrusters. Occasionally an attitude jet fired. For the most part, being weightless in a windowless hold had the feeling of being motionless.

Someone jogged my left hand. Maher was looking at me, offering a falling-block rifle. The side lever was deliberately oversized so that it was easier for a man wearing gauntlets to work.

"What?" I said. I shook my head. I wasn't sure he could see me behind the reflection from my faceplate. "No. no. I have to get closer to do any good."

I blinked, trying to remember things. "You can give me another bar," I said. "Hang it on my suit opposite the line."

I felt clicks against my hard suit. The suit wasn't trapping me this time. My mind was in a much straiter prison than that of my ceramic armor.

"Prepare to board," a voice ordered. Salomon or Guillermo, I couldn't tell which; not Piet.

Dole turned the control wheel and stepped out of my range of sight as he moved to take his own place on the boarding line. Six of our attitude jets fired together in a ten-second pulse, braking the *Oriflamme*'s momentum with perfect delicacy.

The hatch unlocked and began to lower. The fractured corner in front of me flaked off in a slow-motion snowstorm. Shards glittered as their complex surfaces caught the sunlight.

The *Keys to the Kingdom* hung twenty meters away, filling the sky.

The *Oriflamme* wasn't aligned on quite the same horizontal axis as the Federation vessel. I was staring straight into the *Keys'* upper gun deck, but men at the rear of our aft hold would enter through the Feds' centerline if they boarded directly.

The hatch cammed itself down with gear-driven certainty. Stephen gathered himself to jump. One of our plasma bolts had ripped the *Keys'* hull open between two gunports. The compartment beyond was dark, save for the glint of armored shadows.

Fed gunners thrust main battery guns from the ports to either side of the large hole. The muzzles glowed red; their breeches must be yellow-white. The Fed gunners had taken the desperate chance of reloading their weapons while the barrels still shimmered with the heat of previous discharges; taken the chance and succeeded.

The bore of the gun trained on me looked large enough to swallow a man whole, as the plasma it gouted would surely do.

White light with overtones of green and purple blazed through every opening in the *Keys'* gun deck. The shell in the gun aimed at me had cooked off before it could be triggered in proper sequence. The deuterium pellet fused into helium and a gush of misdirected energy, blowing the cannon's stellite breech across its crew and the Fed personnel nearby.

The second cannon fired normally. The bolt hit the forward edge of our hatch. Dense ceramic shattered in fragments ranging in size from dust motes to glassy spearpoints a meter long. One of the latter gutted the man to my right.

I felt the shock through my boots; a film of grit and ions slapped my armor. Stephen leaped. I leaped behind him.

If the Fed gunners had waited another second or two, their plasma bolt would have loosed its devastation in the packed hold instead of shattering the ramp as it lowered. The slug of ions would have killed a dozen of us, maybe more. That wouldn't have slowed the survivors, nor the men still climbing into the hold to join the boarding party.

Stephen sailed forward, his body as rigid as a statue. I twisted slowly around the line clockwise. In one sense it didn't matter, since the *Keys* wasn't under way. We'd be operating without any formal up or down. I couldn't judge where I was going to land, though.

A group of Feds wrestled a multibarreled weapon on the *Keys'* open cargo deck to bear. The human leader was in metal armor. His five Molt crewmen wore transparent helmets and suits of shiny fabric stiffened at intervals by metal rings.

A jet of plasma from one of our midships ports struck the gun carriage. The bolt was small by the standards of the broadside guns firing moments before, but it and the Feds' own munitions blew the weapon and crew apart.

I'd forgotten about the swivel gun Stampfer took from *17 Abraxis*. Stampfer hadn't forgotten.

Stephen bent as he approached the *Keys to the Kingdom*. He held the grapnel forward in his left hand. His arm compressed, taking the shock.

My left boot struck flat on the hull; my right speared through the crater our guns had torn. Swaths of rust and recrystallized steel vapor overlaid the *Keys'* plating. The light was too flat to wake colors, but reflection gave the surfaces different textures.

I hooked my right foreleg into the hole and unlatched myself from the line. A crewman in metal armor loomed from the darkness within the Fed vessel and fired a shotgun into my chest.

My breastplate survived the shock. The crashing impact blew

me back out of the hole. My leg lost its grip, and my flailing arms touched nothing.

Piet Ricimer caught my right wrist in his left hand. He fired his carbine into the hole. The Fed shotgunner was pirouetting from his weapon's recoil. His breastplate sparked as the rifle bullet dimpled it. The Fed continued to spin slowly, but the shotgun drifted out of his hands and a smoky trail of blood froze in the vacuum around him.

I grabbed the rim of the opening and jerked myself aboard the *Keys to the Kingdom* again. Icicles of refrozen steel broke off in my grip.

The Fed constructors had used light alloys for most of the internal subdivisions. Our fire and the exploding cannon had blown them to tatters, leaving the gun deck open except for throughshafts and a pair of parallel hull-metal bulkheads that supported the upper decks when the vessel was on the ground.

Scores of bodies drifted in light that flickered through the hull openings. Most of the corpses were Molts. Their flexible suits were no protection against plasma or against the fragments of bulk-head, weapons, and bodies which the blasts turned into shrapnel.

Figures moved twenty meters from us, near a companionway shaft. A bolt from Stephen's flashgun sent one corpse toward the far hull, shedding limbs.

That corpse was a Molt. Riflefire winked, puncturing two other Molts whom the laser had lighted. A last Molt and an armored human vanished back into the shaft.

Men sailed toward the companionway from behind me. I headed for the freight elevator near the *Keys'* vertical axis. My initial jump was too high. I had to dab along the deck's scarred ceiling to redirect myself. There were no points for gracefulness today.

The circular shaft was of hull metal, but the outer doors were alloy. Blasts had bowed them into the shaft, springing the junc-ture between the leaves wide enough that I could probably have crawled through it as is.

I thrust my bar into the opening to cut outward and down. The blade almost bound, but I jerked it back across to complete the cut, doubling the size of the gap.

It was the first *action* I'd taken since I'd run from the *17 Abraxis* to the *Oriflamme.*

I didn't know where the elevator cage was. If it was below me, the bulged doors would keep it from rising. If not—I'd take my chances on being able to carve through the cage floor before it crushed me into those same jagged doors.

I was thinking very clearly. I wasn't sane, but that's a different question; and the situation wasn't sane either.

The dim ambience of the elevator shaft helped me when my eyes adapted to it. Actually, the light may not have been that dim. Although my faceshield filtered the quick succession of plasma bolts, they'd leached the visual purple from my retinas.

I rose three decks, using my left gauntlet on one of the elevator cables to control my speed and guide me. The sills and paired shaft doors told me where I was. I was pretty sure that the bridge was a deck or two higher yet, but this was as far as the cargo elevator went.

Holding the upper rim of the shaft opening, I cut an ellipse from the panel's inner sheathing. The pieces drifted away from the bar's last contact, tumbling across the shaft. There was no gravity to make them fall.

I should have brought a light . . . but I didn't have a hand for it, and I couldn't hold it in my teeth with the helmet on. The present illumination was good enough, because I knew what I was looking for.

The shaft doors were locked closed by pins under spring pressure. Electromagnets raised the pins when the cage and safeties were in the proper position. If the power was off—as it seemed to be now—the doors could be unlocked as I did, by pulling the mechanism out from the back.

I could have cut through the doors, but that would have warned the Feds on the other side that I was coming.

I wedged the side of a boot into the door seam, then forced the fingers of my left gauntlet in and levered the valves in opposite directions. Faces looked up in terror as I sailed into what had been a circular lounge giving access to individual suites against the hull.

This deck had atmosphere before it flooded past me and down the elevator shaft. Most of the personnel I saw as the light faded to the flatness of direct illumination wore suits, but their helmets were open. Hands groped to slam faceshields closed instead of swinging weapons toward me.

A team of twenty Molts was hauling a carriage gun across the lounge on four drag ropes. The 10-cm cannon was no less massive for being weightless. It slid on with the certainty of a falling boulder when the crewmen dropped their harness.

I let the impetus of my leap from the shaft take me into the crowd of aliens trying to close their helmets. I swung my cutting bar with no aim but to hit *something*, anything.

Ripping the Molts' fabric suits was good enough for my purposes. The limbs and gouts of fluid sweeping past me on the last of the deck's atmosphere were a bonus.

A rifle fired, its yellow powderflash huge for expanding in near vacuum. I was through the Molts within my immediate reach. I pushed off from the plasma cannon traveling relentlessly past me.

I couldn't have executed so complex a weightless maneuver if I'd practiced for weeks. Chance or murderer's luck took me on a vector to the Fed trying to lever another shell into his rifle's chamber as my bar jerked and sparked through the neck of his armor.

I spun and pushed myself toward the next large concentration of the enemy, the group fronting the companionway hatches. Some of the humans were screaming behind their faceshields. God knows I gave them reason to scream.

I grabbed a woman with my left gauntlet. She pounded the side of her riflebutt on my helmet, then tried to short-grip the weapon to shoot me. Her mass anchored my sweeping right-hand cut through her fellows.

The stiffeners in Molt suits were under tension. When my blade sheared a ring, the severed ends sprang apart and dragged the rip in the fabric wider. A bad design for combat . . .

I cut the line of a backpack laser and a corona of high-amperage blue sparks shorted through the metal armor of the man holding it. The Fed's body should have been insulated from the outer shell, but his liner had worn or frayed. The suit stiffened as his flesh burned, raising the internal pressure to several times normal.

I was shaking the woman in my left hand, but I didn't have time to finish her until I'd taken care of the laser and by then she was limp within her articulated armor. She'd lost her rifle; a bullet hole starred her faceshield.

Someone aiming at me, someone shooting at random; her own bullet, triggered at the wrong instant. I held her close as I scanned for living targets.

The 10-cm cannon continued its course into the partition bulkhead surrounding the lounge. This deck was given over to suites for powerful passengers and the *Keys'* command staff. Nonetheless, the hull was pierced with gunports and a few plasma cannon were placed here for emergencies. I'd interrupted a crew shifting an unfired weapon across the lounge to a compartment from which it bore on the *Oriflamme.*

The cannon's stellite muzzle hit the flimsy bulkhead at a skew angle and ground another meter forward, driven by the inertia of tonnes of metal in the gun and its carriage. The wall split at the point of impact and buckled inward across all four edges.

The door popped open like the cork from an overcharged bottle. The suite had still been under normal air pressure. Two Molts and a female servant spurted into the lounge. The servant tried to scream and she shouldn't have, though it didn't make more than a minute's difference since neither she nor the Molts had breathing apparatus.

The suite's main occupant was a plump woman of fifty, wearing a glittering array of jewelry and light-scattering fabrics cut too tight for her build. A transparent emergency bubble protected her. She stared transfixed at the cloud of lung tissue protruding from her servant's mouth.

Feds edged toward me around the right-hand curve of the lounge. There were half a dozen armored humans and as many Molts in the group. I flung away the corpse to drive me toward them.

The Feds hadn't identified me in the carnage and tricky illumination, but they noticed the movement. Muzzle flashes and the sparks of ricocheting projectiles brightened the lounge. The corpse spun as several rounds hit her, and the bullet that punched through my left shoulderguard flipped me ass over teacup.

My left shoulder was cold. Some of that would be the sealant oozing from between the armor's laminae to close the hole. I tried to wriggle my fingers. I couldn't tell if they moved.

My figure somersaulted five meters from the Feds. The Molts were less awkward in their flexible pressure suits, but only a few of them carried firearms. The humans aimed for another volley, and I couldn't do a *damned* thing but spin since I wasn't touching anything I could push off from.

I hurled my cutting bar at the Fed in a parcel-gilt hard suit pointing a rifle at me. A flashgun pulse flickered through his faceshield and ruptured his skull within. The bolt might have reflected harmlessly if it had struck his metal armor.

I unhooked the spare bar from my waist. Feds turned, flailing and throwing equipment in order to get behind the central shaft again.

Piet floated in the companionway hatch. His knees clasped the coaming to steady him against his carbine's recoil. He stripped a fresh clip into the magazine. Stephen's reloaded flashgun exploded a Molt who came on with a cutting bar when his human officers fled.

I tried to brake myself against the ceiling with my left hand. The arm moved, but not properly. My field of view spread into a line of infinite length and no height or width.

Consuming fire shrank to no more than normal pain. Stephen caught my elbow and pulled me to his side. He'd wedged a boot into the plumbing beneath an ornamental wall fountain.

Piet had backed within the companionway. I heard him on the intercom, calling, "Oriflammes to Deck Eight! Oriflammes to Deck Eight! We hold the stairhead, but they'll regroup in a moment!"

Each deck of the *Keys to the Kingdom* was a Faraday cage. The metal construction acted as a barrier impenetrable to radio propagation. If any Venerians happened to be in the companionway shaft—also a metal enclosure—they could hear Piet's summons. Perhaps they'd even be able to answer it; though not, I thought, in time to make a difference.

"Christ's blood, Jeremy," Stephen said in a tone of laughing wonder. "Did you do all this yourself?"

My vision had wobbled in and out of focus since I tried to use my left arm. Until Stephen spoke, I hadn't really looked at anything. The lounge was—

The lounge was very like what I'd passed through in the *Oriflamme*'s midships compartment a lifetime ago. The bodies floating here were whole, or nearly whole. The head, arm, and torso-with-legs of a Molt had floated back together in a monstrous juxtaposition.

There may have been twenty corpses. It was impossible to be sure. I didn't remember killing that many.

"I suppose," I said.

There was so much blood. I dragged the back of my right

gauntlet across my visor. *Again,* I suppose. I didn't remember doing that before either, though I must have. The ceramic dragged fresh furrows across the brown-red haze that dimmed my sight. I needed a wiping rag.

"Well, it's time to do some more," Stephen said. He aimed his flashgun toward a barricade of mattresses floating around the right-hand curve of the central column.

"That's mine," I said and launched myself toward the Feds.

They were coming from both directions this time. Three Molts wearing breastplates and carrying rifles swept out from the left. The flashgun lit the walls behind me as I slid blade-first toward the bedding from nearby suites.

Out of the corner of my eye I caught Piet's figure diving across the lounge. To get an angle from which to shoot, I supposed, but I had enough to occupy me.

The Feds had stacked three mattresses like a layer cake on end. The spun-cellulose filling wouldn't stop a bullet, but we couldn't see through it and it *would* absorb the bolt of a monopulse laser like Stephen's without any fuss or bother.

I ripped the mattresses and the pair of Molts pushing them with a deliberately shallow stroke. The bedding didn't affect my cutting blade, but it would've bound my arm if I'd let it.

The Molts sprang away. One of them was trying to hold the segments of his plastron together; the other didn't have arms below the second joint.

Two human officers in hard suits, and a gunner wearing quilted asbestos with an air helmet, followed the Molts. They'd been poised for attack over or around their barricade. I came through the middle of it with a backhand stroke and a cloud of severed fiber.

The gunner shot at me and missed, though the muzzle blast punched the side of my helmet. I stabbed him where his collarbone met the breastbone, then cut toward the officer on my right. She got her rifle up to block me. My edge showered sparks from where the barrel mated with the receiver.

The second officer put the muzzle of his rifle to my head. Everything was white light because Piet fired the carriage gun wedged into the bulkhead nearby.

This deck was sealed except for the shafts in the center. If the 10-cm cannon had been fired perpendicularly into the hull at this range, it would have blown a hole in the plating; but the *Keys'* hull was thick, and the gun's muzzle was caught at an acute angle to the curve.

The slug of ions glanced around the inner surface of the hull: expanding, dissipating, and vaporizing everything in its immediate path into a dense, silvery shock wave. None of the internal bulkheads survived. Those closest to the muzzle became a gaseous secondary projectile which flattened partitions farther away.

The cannon wasn't clamped into deck mountings. It recoiled freely against the thrust of ions accelerated to light speed, tumbling muzzle over cascabel to meet the shock wave plasma-driven in the opposite direction.

The barrel finally came to rest not far from where Piet had fired the gun. Bits of the carriage still tumbled in complex trajectories. Dents from the tonnes of stellite pocked the hull plating.

Stephen had dodged back into the armored companionway. He'd lost his flashgun and the satchels of spare batteries he'd worn, but otherwise he was uninjured.

Piet survived because he was as far as possible from the ricocheting course of the plasma slug. The shock wave tumbled him, but the *Oriflamme*'s gunners had taken a worse battering and survived—most of them—when a similar bolt pierced our hull.

And I survived. I was out of the direct line of the plasma and swathed in mattresses besides. Everything went white; then I was drifting free on a deck from which all the internal lighting had been scoured. A Venerian focused a miniflood on me. Piet Ricimer caught me by the ankle and pulled me with him back to the companionway. I hadn't even lost my cutting bar.

I can't imagine the Lord wanted me to survive after what I'd done, but I survived.

Maybe some Feds in full hard suits were still alive. Bulkheads, furniture, weapons, and bodies—all the matter that had existed on Deck Eight was still there in the form of tumbled debris that could conceal a regiment. If there were any survivors, they were too stunned to call attention to themselves.

There were six of us now. Stephen led the way up the helical stairs, holding a cutting bar of Federation manufacture. Strip lights in the shaft still functioned. The sharp shadows they threw without a scattering atmosphere acted as disruptive camouflage.

A fireball burped into the shaft from a lower deck, then vanished as suddenly. Fighting was still going on below.

The companionway opened into a circular room on the bridge deck. There were four shafts in all. A bullet ricocheted up one, hit the domed ceiling, and fell back down another as a shimmer of silver.

Two inward-opening hatches on opposite sides of the antechamber gave onto the bridge proper. Against the bulkhead were lockers and, at the cardinal points between the hatches, communications consoles with meter-square displays.

A sailor pulled open a locker. Emergency stores spilled out: first-aid kits, emergency bubbles, flares.

Dole tried a hatch. It was locked from the other side. The left half of the bosun's armor was dull black, as though the surfaces had been sprayed with soot.

"Jeremy, can you get us through—" Stephen said, bobbing his helmet toward the hatch.

"Yes," I said, kneeling. The bulkhead was of hull metal, not duraluminum, but it couldn't be solid and still contain the necessary conduits.

"Wait," said Piet. He stepped to a console and toggled it live. The screen brightened with a two-level panorama of the circular bridge. Inside—

Four heavily-armed figures sexless in plated armor; five human sailors without weapons, armor, or breathing apparatus; three Molts, also unprotected and seated at navigation consoles; and a startlingly beautiful blond woman in a sweep of fabric patterned like snakeskin, with jeweled combs in her hair.

Piet pressed his faceplate to the console's input microphone. "Commodore Prothero!" he said, shouting to be heard through the jury-rigged vocal pathway. "We're sealing this deck. Put down your weapons and surrender. There's no need for more people to die."

With time I could have linked the console to our intercom channel. There wasn't time; and besides, I couldn't see very well. I tried to wipe my visor again, but neither of my hands moved.

Dole and two other spacers were closing the companionway shafts. The hatches were supposed to rotate out of the deck, but long disuse had warped them into their housings. The bosun cursed and hammered the lip of a panel with his bootheel to free it.

Prothero would be the squat figure in gilded armor. Impervious to laser flux, but Stephen didn't have his flashgun any more. Prothero and his three henchmen spoke among themselves.

They must have been using external speakers instead of radio. We couldn't hear them through the bulkhead, but the blonde screamed and one of the unprotected spacers launched himself at Prothero when he heard the plan.

Prothero clubbed the man aside with a steel forearm. "Get us through!" Piet shouted.

I drew the tip of my bar down the bulkhead, cutting a centimeter deep. The sparkling metal roostertail was heated yellow but unable to oxidize in a vacuum.

Two more Fed spacers grappled with their officers. One of Prothero's henchmen blew them clear of his fellows with shotgun blasts, and Prothero himself pulled open the hatch beside me.

I rose, thrusting. Prothero fired a weapon with a needle bore and a detachable magazine for cartridges the size of bananas. The flechette struck the blade of my cutting bar. Bar and projectile disintegrated in a white-hot osmium/ceramic spray.

I smashed the bar's grip into Prothero's faceshield. Red and saffron muzzle flashes shocked the corners of my vision. I could hear the shots as muffled drumbeats while the atmosphere flooded from the bridge to the open antechamber.

I couldn't hold Prothero with my left hand, but I wrapped my legs around his waist and I kept hitting him, even after the faceshield collapsed and the mist of blood dissipated and nothing was moving but my gauntlet, pumping up and down like the blade of a metronome. They say after that I tried to inflate an emergency bubble around one of the Fed spacers. I couldn't manage that, because my left arm didn't work and anyway, it was too late.

I don't remember that. I don't remember anything but the red mist.

LIMBO

A Place Out of Time

I lay at the edge of existence, and the demons wheeled above my soul.

"The controls weren't damaged," said the first demon. "Guillermo's interviewing the surviving Molts for a support crew. When he's done, I'll set her down on St. Lawrence."

"Rakoscy's on his way over. Stampfer's setting up an infirmary for him on Deck Two," said the second demon. "They're dumping cargo into space to make room." Then he said, "So much blood."

"What we did was necessary!" said the first demon in a voice like trumpets. "If we're to stop tyrants like Pleyal and butchers like his Commodore Prothero, then there was no choice. When the *Oriflamme* gets home, she'll bring freedom a step closer for the whole universe."

"We're not home yet," said the second demon, though he didn't sound as if he cared.

"We'll get back," said the first demon. "It's a long run, another ninety days or more. But there's nothing between here and Betaport to fear, save the will of God."

"I figured we'd seal the prisoners on Deck Six once we've swept it for weapons," the second demon said. "I suppose I ought to go take charge, but I'm so tired."

"Dole has it under control," said the first demon. I felt his shadow pass over me. "I wish Rakoscy would get here. I'm afraid to take his suit off myself."

"There's enough treasure on the *Oriflamme*," said the second demon, "to run the Federation government for a decade. Governor Halys will never give it up . . . but when she doesn't, there'll be all-out war between Venus and the Federation."

"It will be as the Lord wills," said the first demon.

My mind drifted from limbo to absolute blackness. Sinking into the embracing dark, I knew that I'd been listening to Piet and Stephen on the bridge of the ship we'd captured. They were no more demons than I was; and no less.

The black turned red as blood.

BETAPORT, VENUS

122 Days After Landing

"Ah, Cedric," said Councilor Duneen. "Let me introduce you to Jeremy Moore. Moore of Rhadicund. Jeremy, this is Factor Read, a businessman who understands the value of a strong navy."

I shook hands with a man younger than me. His eyes never stopped moving. They flicked over the withered arm strapped to my side, then back to my face without even a pause. Read's grip was firm.

"Jeremy will be marrying my sister Melinda this fall, as you may have heard," Duneen continued. "I've found him a townhouse near ours in the capital."

"The Moore who . . ." Read said, nodding toward the *Oriflamme* in her storage berth. Though he was shouting, I had to watch his lips to be sure of the words. None of the heavy machinery was operating today, but the big dock rang with laughter and hawkers' calls.

"Yes, as it happens," I said. I've seen snakes with more warmth in their eyes than Read had, but if reports were true he was the richest man in the Ishtar Highlands. The sort of fellow I'd need to cultivate in my new position as aide to Councilor Duneen, but for now . . .

"Councilor," I said, "Factor Read? Pardon me if you would, because I see some shipmates."

Duneen clapped me on the shoulder. "You can do anything you like here, my boy. You're the stars here today!"

It was the politic thing for the Councilor to say, since he didn't want a row in front of Read and Read's entourage. I had the feeling that he meant it, though.

There were as many folk around Piet and Stephen as there were with Read and Duneen, but some of those pressing for contact with the General Commander were magnates themselves. Mere money couldn't earn the sort of fawning adulation Piet had now.

Though he had the money as well, of course. The lowliest member of the *Oriflamme*'s crew had enough wealth to amaze, for example, a Betaport ship-chandler in a comfortable way of business.

Folk made way for me. Some of them recognized me—"*Factor Moore*" with a nod; broad, smiling, "*Jeremy,* good *to see you again!*"—and some did not, only knew what they saw on my face, but they all made way.

I came up behind a man named Brush. He controlled his niece's estate until she married; an event he was determined should not be before its time. A court toady, not as young as he wished he was, who pitched schemes to the unwary. "You know, Gregg," he said to Stephen, "a friend of mine has a business opportunity that might be the sort of thing that you want now that, you know, you're back."

Stephen looked past Brush to me, then back to the courtier. "Well, Brush," he said in a bantering voice. "It's like this. I'm young, I'm rich, I'm well born. I can do absolutely anything that I want to do. So that means—"

He smiled. Brush stepped back, then bounced forward from my chest like a steel ball shuttling between electromagnets.

"—that the thing I've been doing *is* what I really want."

Brush vanished into the crowd. I touched Stephen's arm. I've never heard anything more stark than his words of a moment before.

Piet waved himself clear with both hands and a broad grin, turning to us. He was dressed in a suit of crimson silk slashed with a natural fiber from Mantichore. It looked like copper or shimmering gold depending on the angle of the light.

Piet touched the miniature oriflamme on my collar. "Well enough for now," he said with a grin, "but Duneen will be wearing your colors before long, Jeremy."

"The Councilor could do worse," Stephen said in the light tone that made strangers think he was joking. "Jeremy has a way of finding routes through unfamiliar systems."

I've heard Stephen's jokes, and they're not the sort of thing that others smile at.

There was a stir at the entrance to the storage dock. Governor Halys was entering with over a hundred courtiers and attendants. Her spot in the assemblage was marked by six members of the Governor's Guard in black hard suits, though the governor herself was hidden.

"Won't be long now," Piet said. For a moment we three were in a reverie, walled off by memories from the voices clamoring around us, at us.

"Hard to believe the ship made it home," said Stephen. "Or that we did either, of course."

I followed his eyes to the *Oriflamme* and for the first time saw her as she'd become on our voyage. Her bow and stern were twisted onto slightly different axes. I remembered Winger complaining about thruster alignment.

We hadn't replaced the forward ramp. The hull was daubed with a dozen muddy colors, remnants of refurbishing with the materials available on as many worlds. We'd had to recoat completely on St. Lawrence after the battle, but the russet sand hadn't bonded well to some of the earlier patches. On Tres Palmas we'd taken much of the stern down to the frames and tried again.

The *Oriflamme* leaked. Air through the hull, water from two of the reaction-mass tanks. All the living spaces were damp during the last three weeks of the voyage. Winger was afraid to run the nozzles from *17 Abraxis* on more than eighty percent thrust, but they were better than the replacements we found on Fowler, so we switched them back again for the last leg.

I think Piet must have had the same revelation. "To God, all things are possible," he said. "But some aren't—"

He squeezed us by opposite shoulders.

"—as probable as others, I agree."

The Governor's entourage paused while Councilor Duneen and other high dignitaries joined it. When the court resumed its progress, attendants began herding a group of bizarrely-dressed, worried-looking sailors aboard the *Oriflamme*. Money hadn't given them either taste or confidence in a setting like this one.

"I think it's unfair that a mob of *scruffs* should be given places and *I* be refused!" said a slender, perfectly-dressed woman, as straight as a rifle barrel and as gray.

I moved and Stephen grabbed me because he knew what I knew, and what the other sixty-odd survivors knew; and what nobody else in the universe would ever know.

"They were good enough to accompany me through the Breach, madame," Piet said. "They will accompany me now."

He didn't shout, but he spoke in a tone that cut this clamor as it had that of so many battles. Everyone for twenty meters heard, and the woman melted away from his eyes.

Piet laughed. "Stephen, Jeremy," he said. "I need to take my place, I suppose. See you soon."

He arrowed through the mob, heading for the Governor's Guard.

Stephen said, "Piet believes that God is aiding us to do His will. I don't know what God's will is. But I don't suppose what I know matters."

He looked at me and added, "I thought we might see your fiancée here, Jeremy."

I shrugged with adrenaline nervousness and smiled. "No," I said, "no. I asked Melinda not to come. I don't want to connect her— in my mind. With this. I'd as soon the Councilor weren't here, but he had to be, of course."

I smiled again. The lip muscles didn't work any better the second time. I gripped Stephen's shoulder. "Stephen, listen," I said. "It happened, it can't ever *not* have happened now. But it's over. We can go on!"

"I'm glad it's over for you, Jeremy," Stephen said. He plucked gently at my sleeve, filling the fabric he'd crumpled when he kept me from breaking a woman's neck with my one good hand. "I was afraid for a time that you were one of those it wouldn't be over for."

He smiled. "I'm responsible for you, you know."

I blinked so that I wouldn't cry. "Let's get aboard," I said loudly, turning toward the ship.

The crowd cheered as it parted to let us board the *Oriflamme*. There in a few minutes we would watch the governor's investiture of a potter's whelp from Bahama District as Factor Ricimer of Porcelain.

FIRESHIPS

To Carolyn Ross
Who's a long way away, but only physically

ABOVE LILYMEAD

June 1, Year 26 of Governor Halys
1000 hours, Venus time

"We can get one more aboard, Sal," called Tom Harrigan from the hatch of the lighter across the temporary orbital dock from the *Gallant Sallie*.

Captain Sarah—Sal—Blythe checked her vessel's hold and said, "No, let 'em go, Tom. We've got two turbines and the crate of spare rotors left, so there'll be a part-load anyway. Tell them to start bringing the return cargo on the next lift, though. We can have the last of this waiting in the dock and our hold clear by the time they get back up."

The access tube connecting the lighter to the dock was three meters long. The valve at the inner end of the tube opened automatically when the air pressure on both sides was equal. The system formed a simple airlock while the outer end was attached to a ship's pressurized hold or cabin.

Technically the business of shifting cargo after a vessel docked was the responsibility of the planetary staff, but Lilymead wasn't really set up to handle cargoes in orbit. The ships that traded to Near Space colonies like Lilymead put down on the unimproved field and waited for tractors to haul lowboys full of stevedores to them over dirt blasted by the exhaust of other vessels.

The huge freighters in which the North American Federation voyaged to the Reaches touched in Near Space only when leakage and slow progress forced them to resupply their reaction mass and atmosphere. Those monsters rarely dared to land on ports without hardened pads and full facilities. Lilymead had a remotely controlled water buffalo to ferry water and air up to them.

Harrigan—Sal's mate—and the starboard watch of eight crewmen slid from the lighter's hold with the delicacy of men experienced with weightless conditions. The Federation lighter's own crew of two wasn't enough to handle cargo as massive as these turbines, even if Sal had been willing to wait while the locals did the job. The dock was processed cellulose, constructed as cheaply as possible to be abandoned after a single use. Inertia would tear a turbine that got away from its handlers right on through the fuzzily transparent walls.

"Say, what's that?" Harrigan said in astonishment as he saw the featherboat that had grappled to another of the dock's four access tubes while he and his men were striking cargo down in the lighter.

The 30-tonne vessel was too small to have an airlock of its own. As Sal and the mate watched, the dorsal hatch opened. A group of civilians caromed out with the spastic overcorrections of folk who thought of gravity, not inertia, when they moved.

"Some local merchants, they said," Sal explained. "Asked to come aboard. We've got a return cargo, but I didn't see any harm in talking to them." She grimaced. "We could use a little extra profit to cover repairs to the attitude jets."

"Oh, Sallie," Harrigan said uncomfortably. The mate never jibbed at her orders, but he couldn't help treating Sarah Blythe as the captain's daughter rather than as the captain in her own right. Harrigan had always assumed that when Marcus Blythe's arthritis grounded him for good, Thomas Harrigan would marry Sal and captain the *Gallant Sallie* himself—while his wife stayed on Venus and raised children as a woman should. "I don't think that'll be much, just a bad connection somewhere, only . . ."

The *Gallant Sallie*'s three bands of attitude jets kept the vessel aligned with the direction her main thrusters were to drive her. On the voyage out to Lilymead, the jets occasionally failed to fire as programmed. The problem forced Sal to go through the trouble and added expense of lightering down her cargo, rather than landing in the port where two other Venerian vessels took advantage of the relaxing of the Federation's embargo on trade with its Near Space colonies. If the jets—most likely their controls—glitched during transit, the error required recomputation and lengthened the *Gallant Sallie*'s voyage. If the problem occurred during landing, well . . .

Captain Sarah Blythe was rightly proud of her reflexes and piloting ability. Since she had the choice, though, the only landing the *Gallant Sallie* would make this voyage would be back on Venus, where dockyard mechanics could go over the vessel and cure what the crew's repeated attempts had not.

The featherboat's passengers, five men and two women, spun in the slight turbulence as they entered the dock's main chamber. None of the seven was a spacer, though Sal was by no means sure they were all the civilians their clothing proclaimed.

Her eyes narrowed. The dark speckling on one woman's cheek was a powder burn. While the stiff leg of the group's leader could have come from any number of causes, the puckered skin of his right forearm was surely a bullet scar.

"Captain Blythe?" the leader said to Harrigan. "I'm Walter Beck. These are my associates in the trading community here on Lilymead."

The *Gallant Sallie*'s working party watched the Fed delegation with the amusement of spacers for landsmen out of their element. Brantling, a senior man who'd have been bosun except for his jealousy of Harrigan, snickered loudly.

"There's our captain!" Tom Harrigan said, anger at Brantling's laughter turning the words into a snarl. "Deal with her if you've business here."

Beck was holding out a bottle of local liquor. He swung it from Harrigan to Sal at arm's length. The gesture set his whole body pivoting away in reaction. Sal caught Beck's cuff and said, "You're welcome aboard the *Gallant Sallie,* miladies and sirs. Left up the passage from the hold, please. We'll speak in the cabin so that my crew can continue their duties."

Sal's gentle tug sent Beck through the hatch ahead of her. Without needing direction, Harrigan and the rest of the work party caught the other Feds and pushed them after their leader like so many billiard balls into a pocket. A few of the thrusts were more enthusiastic than kindly; Sal, still gripping the coaming, braked those Feds with her free hand. The powder-burned female pinwheeled wildly because she'd swiped at the head of the sailor who pushed her off. Brantling again . . .

"Brantling," Sal ordered. "Put a helmet on and check the nozzles of all twelve attitude jets again. Now!"

"Aye aye, Captain," Brantling said, cheerful despite the unpleasant, dangerous, and (at this point) useless task he'd just been set. Brantling never failed to use Sal's title with due deference, because he believed it irritated the mate to hear her called "Captain."

He was wrong. Tom Harrigan couldn't understand Sal's refusing his hand nor her insistence on sailing as captain in lieu of her father; but he had neither jealousy nor anger toward her. He'd been ship's boy when Marcus Blythe brought his two-year-old infant aboard the *Gallant Sallie* for the first time.

Sal seated herself at the navigation console and hooked a tiedown across her lap to keep her there. "What can I do for you, Master Beck?" she asked.

The *Gallant Sallie* was a freighter of standard Venerian design with a nominal burden of 150 tonnes. She had a main hold aft; it could be pressurized, but the large outer hatch was single-panel, not an airlock. The cabin forward served as crew quarters and control room. There were stanchions to help people direct themselves in weightlessness, but the light screen around the toilet in deference to the captain's sex was the only bulkhead within the compartment. There was an airlock near the navigation console in the nose. Hatches at either end of the two-meter-long passageway between the hold and cabin (through the air and water tanks amidships) turned it into an airlock as well.

The visiting landsmen hovered awkwardly in the cabin, stared at by the off-duty crew members. In weightless conditions, all the compartment's volume was usable; but by the same token, gravity didn't organize the space in an expected fashion. One of the Feds started noticeably when he realized his ear was less than a finger's breadth from the feet of a spacer floating in his sleeping net.

Beck looked around before replying. His eyes lingered on the four 10-cm plasma cannon, dominating the cabin by their mass despite being draped with netted gear at present. Beck still held the liquor bottle. It couldn't be used in orbit without a pressure vessel, which Sal pointedly didn't offer. She'd decided that whatever these folk were about, she wanted no part of it.

"I'm sorry for your engine trouble, Captain," Beck said. There was little distinction between the sexes in Fed service, but a female captain on a Venerian ship was unusual enough to arouse interest. "Are you sure you wouldn't like to land and see if our crews couldn't put it to right? You know how clever some Molts can be, almost as if they were human."

"We'll manage," Sal said curtly. "We've got plenty of reaction mass for the return trip. In Ishtar City the people who installed the system can troubleshoot it."

She didn't like Molts; the chitinous aliens made her skin crawl. There weren't many on Venus, but the North American Federation used Molts as slaves to do much of the labor on their starships and the colonies those ships served. Because Molts had genetic memory, they could operate the machinery remaining across the Reaches where mankind had abandoned it after the Rebellion and the Collapse of civilization a thousand years before.

No denying the Molts' value, but—they stank; the food they ate stank; and so far as Sal was concerned, the Federation that depended on Molt abilities stank also.

"As you please," Beck said with a shrug. He grabbed a bundle of dehydrated food to keep from drifting away. "You know," he added as if it were a new thought, "I see that you've got plasma guns. Our port defenses could do with some improvement. Would you—"

"Not interested," Sal said loudly, awakening two of the crewmen who were still asleep. Brantling, who'd pulled an elastic pressure suit over his coveralls, paused beside the airlock without donning his air helmet.

"We could offer a good price," said the powder-burned Fed. She sounded calm, but the cabin wasn't warm enough to have beaded her forehead with sweat.

"Not interested," Sal repeated sharply. She rose from her seat in obvious dismissal. "You know the old saying: 'There's no law beyond Pluto.' Without the great guns, we'd be prey for any skulking pirate we chanced across."

And for any Federation customs vessel; which she didn't say and didn't need to say. The *Gallant Sallie* was a merchant ship, not a raider; but only a fool would put herself and her crew at the mercy of Federation officials who had been bloodied so often and so badly by the raiding captains of Venus.

"Well, we're only here to offer you the hospitality of Lilymead,"

Beck said. "Now that the embargo for Near Space is lifted, we hope to trade with you and your compatriots often."

He offered the bottle of liquor again. Sal took it. It was some sort of local brew, perhaps of native vegetation. The contents were bright yellow and moved as sluggishly as heavy oil.

"Thank you, Master Beck," Sal replied. "I certainly hope we will." The profits were too good to pass up, but she didn't know if she'd touch down the next time either. Too much about the conditions on Lilymead made her uneasy.

Harrigan came up the passage from the hold. "Tom," Sal said, "help our visitors back to their vessel. I'll bring up the rear."

With the loading done, the starboard watch was returning to the cabin behind Harrigan. The mate didn't bother to send his men back into the hold ahead of the visitors, as Sal had meant he should. The passage was a tight fit for people passing in opposite directions, even when they all were experienced spacers. Sal heard curses. One of her Venerians responded to a bump by kicking a Fed hard down the passage into the woman ahead.

The lighter had already cast off. As Sal entered the dock, she saw the little vessel's thruster fire. The bulkhead's translucence blurred the rainbow haze of plasma exhaust. Lilymead hung overhead, its visible continent a squamous green as distinctly different from that of Terran vegetation as it was from the ruddy yellow cloudscape of Venus.

Tom Harrigan was a tall, rawboned man, bald at age 35 save for a fringe of red hair. He glared as the visitors closed the hatch of their featherboat behind them. "If I never see another Federation toady," he said, "it'll be too soon."

Sal glanced at her mate without expression. She was a short, stocky blonde, 24 years old. Earth years, because the folk living beneath the crust and equally opaque atmosphere of Venus had never measured time by Venus years or the yearlong days of the second planet. "I expect to turn around for Lilymead again as soon as I can get another cargo from home," she said mildly. "There's a good profit on glazing earths."

"Glazing earths!" Harrigan said. "The real profit's in microchips from the Reaches, and President Pleyal claims all those for himself. Why, the only reason the Feds even opened their Near Space colonies to us is that Captain Ricimer's raids made Pleyal be a little more reasonable about trade!"

The featherboat cast off from the dock. It continued to hang alongside while the Molt pilot waited for a reentry window. A few stars were bright enough for Sal to see them through the dock's walls.

"All I know," Sal said, a trifle more crisply than before, "is that there's money to be made hauling manufactures out to Lilymead and glazing earths back. That's the trade the *Gallant Sallie*'s going to carry so long as the embargo's lifted and nothing better offers."

The featherboat's thruster flared. Its iridescent brilliance was brighter than the sun until the vessel dropped well within the ball of the planet.

"I'll tell you though, Tom," Sarah Blythe said in an appraising tone. "If that lot comes back again, see to it that I'm awake and the whole crew is on alert. I'm not sure what they've got in mind is trade."

ABOVE LILYMEAD

June 1, Year 26
1515 hours, Venus time

Sal watched through a magnifier as her fingers fed new coils through the narrow slots of an electric drill's stator. She'd cut and teased out the shorted coils on the previous watch while waiting for the lighter to return; now she was rewiring the unit. When she was done, the drill would work again—and as an activity, it beat recomputing the course back to Venus for the umpteenth time.

Rickalds, on watch at the navigation console, straightened up sharply and said, "Captain, the lighter's on course. They're not two minutes out, I swear,"

"Haven't they heard of radio?" Sal snapped as she struck the repair tools and pieces of drill down in a canvas bag. Otherwise the bits would drift into all corners of the ship while she was away from the task. "See if you can raise port control and see why they didn't warn us!"

"Port watch to the dock to load cargo!" Harrigan called, his voice echoing in the hold and up the passageway to the cabin. Tom must have noticed the lighter's braking flare through the cellulose walls. The lighter wasn't scheduled to return for another twenty minutes; based on past experience with the Lilymead personnel, Sal hadn't *expected* them for an hour at best.

"Captain, it's two ships, I think," Rickalds said. He squinted at the holographic display instead of trying to sharpen the view electronically. Rickalds was alert and a willing worker, but he was ill at ease with any tool more complex than a pry bar.

"I've got the controls, Rickalds," Sal said, pushing the spacer from the console. "Airley," she said to the senior man of the starboard watch, "stand by to take over here."

The *Gallant Sallie*'s optronics were original to the vessel and thus older than Sal herself. As built they hadn't been as clear as one might wish, and it took a practiced hand to bring the best out of their aged chips now.

Sal focused, raised the magnification, and rolled a ball switch with her hand to correct for drift as the console's electronics were unable to do. "Damn their fool souls to *Hell*," she snarled.

"Sir?" said Airley.

"Take over!" she said as she left the console and propelled herself down the passageway in a pair of reflexively precise motions. Two vessels were approaching. The lighter was five hundred meters out, still braking with its thruster to match velocities. The featherboat that had brought Beck in the morning had arrived again also, and it was already coupled to the temporary dock.

Harrigan was organizing his eight cargo handlers in the hold, nearly empty now that the rest of the outbound freight had been shifted to the temporary dock. Sal brought herself up on a stanchion and said, "Tom, keep the men aboard and ready the ship to lift. I'm going to see why Beck's here again. If I don't like his reasons, we're out of here!"

She pushed off, using the hatch coaming to correct and brake her motion. "Sal?" Harrigan called to her back. "If we leave, we miss the return cargo."

"Bugger the return cargo!" Sal said.

If the *Gallant Sallie* cut and ran, Sarah Blythe would spend the voyage home worrying about what she'd say to the noteholder, Ishtar Chandlery. She might even have to decide whether it'd be worse to lose the ship than to call on a noble named Samuel Trafficant and . . . beg his kindness. For the moment, though, her concerns were much more immediate.

The *Gallant Sallie*'s arms locker was strapped to the rear cabin bulkhead. Sal wondered if she should have paused long enough to open the locker and take one of the six rifles or the shotgun inside. At least she should have grabbed one of the powered cutting bars that spacers used for tools or weapons as circumstances dictated. She hadn't thought of that till she noticed how lonely the empty dock seemed.

Sal used the crate of turbine spares to halt her. Its mass didn't visibly move when it stopped her 55 kilograms.

The featherboat's hatch, a two-meter-by-one-meter section of the upper hull, lifted as soon as the dock's attachment lips were clamped around the coaming. Atmosphere from the featherboat filled the access tube. The valve started to open inward, toward Sal.

A dozen figures from the featherboat entered the tube. They were armed. Three of them—Beck and two other of the morning's visitors—wore the white uniforms of Federation officials. Six of the others were Molts, their purplish exoskeletons unclothed save for one draped in a pink sash-of-office.

The other three invaders were human also, but they were garbed in clothing cast off by Federation colonists. These last were obviously Rabbits, the human remnants of Lilymead's pre-Collapse population; sunken to savagery, and now slaves of the Federation like the Molts beside them.

"Harrigan, close the hatch!" Sal shouted in a cold, clear voice. She propelled herself toward the access tube. The valve had sprung open when the featherboat equalized pressure, but perhaps she could jam it—

A Molt caught her wrist with three chitinous fingers. Sal twisted. The Molt wasn't as strong as she was, but he raised the cutting bar in his free hand. The surfaces of his triangular face were expressionless.

"I've got this one, bug!" shouted a pudgy human with customs service in tarnished braid on the collar of his uniform. He socketed the muzzle of a revolver in Sal's left ear.

"Don't you move, bitch, or I'll paint your brains all over the walls!" the Fed added, his face centimeters from hers. His breath stank of fear and unfamiliar spices.

Sal heard shots and a cry of pain from the *Gallant Sallie*'s hatch. Beck, wearing a tunic with gold epaulets and holding a rifle awkwardly, crossed the dock with the aid of two Molts.

The lighter was disgorging more armed Feds up a second access tube to join the force from the featherboat. The two Fed vessels were much of a size, but the lighter had greater internal capacity because it didn't need the equipment and hull strength for interstellar travel. There seemed to have been forty or fifty personnel, mostly Molts and Rabbits, packed into the lighter's hold.

"We are here under a valid contract, approved by the Bureau of Out-System Trade in Montreal!" Sal said. "You'll answer to President Pleyal for this piracy!"

"Shut up!" cried the Fed officer. "We've got orders, and by Mary and the Saints, we've got the power!"

He forced his revolver harder against Sal's ear. The two of them rotated slowly. Sal could now see the backs of the attackers entering the *Gallant Sallie*. A gunshot lighted the hold red. Cutting bars whined. There were several more shots in quick succession, but this time the muzzle flashes were obscured.

A Molt drifted from the hatchway. The creature's head had been dished in. The edges of the wound dripped brown ichor.

The Fed holding Sal gaped. There was a hollow *thoonk*. His face bulged and something sprayed Sal, half blinding her. A bullet had taken the officer in the back of the skull and exited beneath his left eye. The projectile went on out through the wall of the temporary dock, leaving a black void in the center of a 20-centimeter bulge stressed to white opacity.

Sal wiped her eyes. The corpse was floating away from her. She twisted the revolver out of fingers that had clamped when the Fed's brain was destroyed.

The *Gallant Sallie* had a sprinkler system, nozzles in the hold fed directly from the tank of reaction mass behind the midships bulkhead. Somebody opened the valve briefly. An opaque cloud of water vapor filled the hold and gushed from the hatch. It was doubly blinding in the low-pressure atmosphere.

Federation personnel retreated gasping through the gray mass. They collided with the reinforcements continuing to arrive from the lighter. Beck reappeared, shouting an unintelligible order. A woman in Federation uniform bumped him into a somersault as she pushed past.

Another bullet came through the wall of the dock from outside, from vacuum. This round smashed the thigh of a Molt with an impact that spun the creature's legs above its head.

Orbit around Lilymead brought the *Gallant Sallie*'s port side to the sun again. So illuminated, the vessel's ceramic hull was clearly visible through the dulling medium of the cellulose walls.

Everybody in the dock could see a gunport open and the muzzle of one of the 10-cm guns appear.

Sal knew that the cannon couldn't be safely fired before the ship cleared for action; the gun probably wasn't even loaded. The Federation groundlings didn't know that, and the blobs of blood and ichor floating about them had drained their morale anyway. As a mob, they broke and forced their way up the tubes to the vessels that had brought them.

Tom Harrigan appeared in the hatchway, veiled in dissipating water vapor. His forehead was gashed and the pry bar in his right fist was bloody. Nedderington paused beside the mate, fired a shotgun at the backs of the fleeing Feds, and recoiled into the hold.

Sal crouched against the side of the dock, holding herself steady by expert, tiny motions. Brantling, still wearing his pressure suit and helmet, stood in the cabin airlock with a rifle. He fired again, this time killing a Rabbit about to reenter the featherboat. Panicked Feds pressed the corpse aboard with them.

Beck, unable to control his body's spinning, drifted close to Sal. She aimed the revolver at him and tried to fire it. The trigger wouldn't move: the ill-maintained weapon was rusted solid. The Fed leader screamed in terror. Sal grabbed Beck by the collar and used the revolver to clout him twice above the ear. Beck's eyeballs rolled up in their sockets.

The lighter pulled away with a blast of its thruster. The dock jerked before main force broke the seal. The lighter's hatch was open, and there were still people trying to board through it.

The dock's inner door closed. The last of the air in the tube puffed the bodies into hard vacuum, their limbs flailing momentarily.

The featherboat separated also. The Fed pilots were terrified by the plasma cannon, whose blast at this range could turn either vessel into a fireball more gaseous than solid. No one was in the featherboat's access tube, but a uniformed human and two Molts were trapped in the dock as the valve closed,

"Sal, are you all right?" Tom Harrigan said. He launched himself to his captain's side across the blood-spattered dock.

Sal straightened, using Beck's mass to control her motion. The Fed leader was coming around. The other Fed survivors stared at Sal and the weapons in the hands of the Venerians joining her in the dock.

"Cooney, give me a hand with the captain!" Harrigan ordered, taking Sal's silence for proof she'd been incapacitated. "Leave these other bastards here to see how well they breathe vacuum!"

"No!" Sal said. "Bring them aboard. And fast—I want to be out of this system in five minutes!"

Harrigan took her arm anyway. He pushed off the wall of the dock, guiding her as if she was a landsman who couldn't navigate in weightlessness. "I say leave them, Sal," he repeated. "They killed Josselyn, and there's a couple more might not make it home."

"No, don't leave me!" Beck pleaded, trailing behind Sal like a heavy dufflebag. "I'm the Fiscal of Lilymead, the President's representative. I'm an important man!"

They entered the hold. Obedient to Sal's orders, her crewmen had policed up all the Fed survivors and were following with them. She thrust the revolver down the throat of her tunic and caught a stanchion.

"You lying bastard!" Harrigan snarled in Beck's face. "If you're Pleyal's representative, why didn't you honor the safe conduct Pleyal gave us?"

Sal kicked forward, up the passageway and into the cabin. Josselyn floated in midair with his throat cut. Bealzy was trying to stuff a loop of intestine back through the bullet wound in Kokalas' abdomen.

"We had orders from Montreal," Beck whimpered behind her. He patted the pocket of his uniform blouse. Paper crackled. "I'm carrying them right here with me. We're to confiscate all Venerian vessels which arrive, regardless of their safe conducts. President Pleyal needs them to help equip the fleet he's gathering to end the Venus rebellion for once and fox all!"

"Rebellion?" Harrigan said, too amazed at the term for the impact of the whole statement to register. "Why, we're not rebels, we're citizens of the Free State of Venus!"

Sal thrust the Fiscal of Lilymead into a net that still held a day's supply of rations for the crew.

"Stay here, don't move, and you'll live even though you don't deserve to," she ordered savagely. To Harrigan she added, "And I mean it, Tom, I want him to stay alive all the way back. There's a lot of people on Venus who need to hear his story!"

Sal strapped herself to the navigation console. While the hard-used electronics moaned to life, she dabbed absently at the grit on her face.

The main hatch clanged shut. Crewmen called to one another as they seated the manual dogs and completed the other familiar business of liftoff.

The holographic display settled to a creamy saffron, picked out by a few strobing points where a circuit misfired. Very shortly the ready prompt would come up and Sal could initiate the first transit sequence.

She glanced at her hands. What she'd wiped from her face was bits of the skull of the Fed who'd been holding her in the dock. The chips were tacky with a slime of fresh pink brains.

Sal managed to turn her head so that her sudden rush of vomit didn't cover the navigation keyboard.

ISHTAR CITY, VENUS

August 10, Year 26
1642 hours, Venus time

The woman who entered the pantry didn't notice Stephen until she'd closed the door behind her and cut off the burr of voices from the party in the function rooms down the hallway. When she saw the big man in the corner holding a bottle of slash, liquor distilled from algae, her eyes widened in startlement. "You're Stephen Gregg," she said.

Stephen looked at her without expression. "I'm not too drunk to remember my name," he said. His eyes flicked from the woman to the bottle in his hand. The slash was vaguely gray in hue. "In fact I'm not drunk at all, though that's not for lack of trying."

"Do you mind if I . . ." she said. She nodded toward the closed door. "I needed to get away from that. They're all over me like lice, each one trying to get his drop of blood."

Stephen smiled faintly. He recognized the woman as Sarah Blythe, the captain who'd brought to Venus notice of the treachery, the latest treachery, of the North American Federation. Identifying her was no great trick. Though the gathering had a social gloss in a mild attempt to mislead President Pleyal's spies, the attendees were principals and agents only; they'd left their consorts at home. Only a handful of the several score persons present were women.

"I'm not the most social of people myself," Stephen said in smiling understatement. He found a glass on the shelf beside him, started to pour, and paused. "Will you have a drink?" he asked. "I only brought slash with me when I ran the servants out, I'm afraid."

"Slash is fine with me," she said. She wore a pale blue jacket and jumper over a ruffed blouse. The outfit was in unobtrusive good taste. Though it was inexpensive by the standards of the guests in the function rooms, Blythe didn't stand out the way a space captain in the midst of a gathering of magnates could be expected to do. "Ah, I'm Sal Blythe. I apologize for the way I—greeted you."

She wasn't a beautiful woman, but she was interesting in appearance as well as personality. Gregg had the impression that Blythe had started to reach for the bottle to drink from it straight, the way he'd been doing. She took a healthy swig from the tumbler he handed her, grimaced, and said, "Paint thinner. But you know, it was what I grew up with, and nothing else seems like a drink."

She looked at him appraisingly. Not the way a man would have done, because when strange men looked at Stephen Gregg, there was always a touch of fear or challenge in their eyes. Very few people could say honestly that they knew Stephen, but almost every adult on Venus knew *of* him. . . .

"I never thought I'd meet you," Blythe said, drinking more of her slash. "And Captain Ricimer's out there as well." She grinned wryly and added, "I'd say that it was worth being attacked by the Feds, but then there's the rest of the pack. They all want the Commission of Redress they expect I'll be issued for the damage the Feds did me on Lilymead."

Blythe's face lost its chubby softness and became momentarily as hard as her eyes. "They don't seem to hear the word 'no' when a woman's saying it," she said.

"Oh, it's not a word they hear very easily from anyone, some of them," Stephen said with a shrug. He took down another glass for himself. "From those who don't have as much money as they do, at least, but that's most people."

As Stephen poured, the door behind Sarah Blythe opened in a blast of sound. "Go away!" he snarled without looking up.

"Oh!" a male voice said. "Terribly sorry, Mister Gregg!" The last syllable was trimmed by the door's firm closure.

"Who was that?" Blythe asked in surprise. All she would have seen of the intruder was the sleeve of a gorgeous coat.

Stephen grimaced and tossed off his slash. "I'm afraid from the voice it was Blenrott of Laodicea," he said. "Our host. I can't seem to get drunk, and that makes me . . . even less tactful than usual. But there's no excuse for me behaving like a—"

He shook his head and smiled without humor. "Rabid dog, I suppose. Well, I'll make it up to him."

Stephen wondered just what it was that Blythe saw when she looked at him. He was 32 years old, taller than most men, and stronger than almost anyone he was likely to meet. His features were regular, and his short hair was a blond so pale that the long scar on his scalp showed through clearly.

At one time Stephen Gregg had been considered a handsome man, but he couldn't imagine anyone found him so today. He'd lost track of the number of people he'd killed over the past ten years. Hundreds, certainly. He knew there was nothing inside him but a lump of cold gray ice, and he was sure that others had to see through the shell of him to that emptiness as clearly as he did himself.

"I'm going out with the commission myself," Blythe said harshly, hunching over the liquor glass. "It was me the Feds attacked, me and the *Gallant Sallie*. It's us who'll take redress from them, by *God* we will!"

She was embarrassed by the outburst. To cover it with a mask of small talk, Stephen said, "I feel the same way about slash. No other run has quite the taste of Eryx slash, though."

He smiled minusculely and added, "If I didn't think it was too affected for words, I'd have my brother ship me a case every week or so."

"That's your hold, Eryx?" Blythe said. She was watching him over the top of her glass, but he wasn't sure she'd taken another sip.

"The family hold," Stephen said deprecatingly. "My brother Augustus is the factor, and it's a very small place, Eryx is." But with a flush of the pride that never ceased to amaze him, he added, "There've been Greggs of Eryx since the Collapse, though."

"You don't live at the hold, then?" Blythe said. Because she knew she was edging beyond the bounds of proper discussion with a stranger—a famous man, a powerful man—she looked at Stephen's elbow rather than his face as she spoke. Her eyes were pleasantly blue with brown rings about the irises.

"It didn't really work out," Stephen said, pouring more slash. "They were more than kind, but I made the family nervous and that made me, you know, more uncomfortable. I've got two rooms in Betaport. On holidays I make day-trips to Eryx so the kids can climb on their Uncle Stephen. But I don't sleep over."

"Two *rooms?*" Blythe repeated. This run of slash proved on the order of seventy-five-percent ethanol. Whether she was used to the liquor or not, it had stripped some of the subtlety that might otherwise have overlain her question.

Blythe's eyes probed Stephen's clothing again as she considered whether her initial appraisal had been wrong. He was in court dress, suitable for wear at functions in the Governor's Palace. The colors were muted, beige and russet, and the cut of the garments was looser than the mode; but the fabric was Terran silk, and the ensemble had probably cost more than a set of eight thruster nozzles for the *Gallant Sallie.*

Stephen laughed, a harsh sound that he hated to hear. "You think that with my share of the loot we took from Pleyal and his thugs in the Reaches, Piet and I and the rest, I ought to be able to afford a place like this myself?"

He gestured, indicating not the pantry in which the two of them were hiding but the suite of which it was a part. The measure of wealth on Venus was the volume of one's dwelling. There'd been an enormous recent growth of trade, fueled directly and indirectly by the microchips that raiders like Piet Ricimer brought home from the pre-Collapse automated production facilities in the Reaches. Men like Blenrott, who'd invested heavily and been lucky, had huge sums to sink into town houses like this one on the fringes of the capital.

"And so I could," Stephen continued. "But if I wanted to have a lot of people around me, Captain Blythe, I'd be out there in the function rooms, wouldn't I?"

"I, ah," Blythe said. Her glass was empty. Stephen leaned toward her to refill it, but she waved him away. She'd already had more than was probably good for her discretion. "I assumed you had a wife or, ah . . ."

"Are you offering?" Stephen said in a cold, professional tone.

Sarah Blythe set her glass on the terrazzo floor beside her. She could have thrown it without much risk of breakage. Metal-poor Venus had developed ceramics technology to levels undreamed of before the Collapse cut the planet off from Earth and the Asteroid Belt. She straightened, took a step forward, and slapped Stephen as hard as she could.

Stephen let the blow land, though it jolted his head to the side. He'd been hit by men who put less steam into their punches. "I'm sorry," he said. "That was stupid and uncalled for. I'll try to make amends."

Blythe swung again. He stopped the blow with the fingers of his left hand. Her eyes widened when she realized how quick the motion had been. "Captain Blythe," he said with the least tremble of emotion, "I apologize."

She'd had a right to hit him, but the impact had taken Stephen Gregg's mind into another place: the place he tried to forget about by drinking. He could control his actions, but couldn't help the suffusing golden joy at the thought of killing again *soon*.

Blythe stepped back and drew a shuddering breath. "I apologize too, Mister Gregg," she said. She didn't meet his eyes. She massaged her right palm with her left hand. If she'd closed her hand into a fist, she'd have broken at least a knuckle. "My question was improperly pers—"

He held out the bottle.

"No, no," she said. "Not for me. I've obviously had too much already."

"Yes, well, maybe I have too," Stephen said, stoppering the bottle. There wasn't much left in it anyway. "You're owner as well as captain of the ship involved in the incident on Lilymead?"

"The *Gallant Sallie*, yes," Blythe said. "My father's still alive, but he assigned the title to me when he had to retire. So that I could pledge a security interest in the ship during out-system trading."

Stephen nodded his understanding. He'd gone into space as a merchant, a supercargo looking out for the interests of his uncle, Gregg of Weyston, an investor in the voyage. Piet Ricimer was a junior officer on the same ship. Amazing the changes that ten years could bring; good and otherwise.

"Marcus Blythe is my father," Blythe said. Then—perhaps because she'd slapped him and wanted to punish herself for reacting the way she had—she went on crisply, "And he *is* my father, in every way that matters. I was born while Dad was on a two-year voyage to Southern Cross colonies in the Reaches. I'm told my mother saw a lot of Samuel Trafficant during the time Dad was gone, I don't know. But Marcus has always been a father to me!"

Stephen nodded again. "Samuel . . ." he said. "That would be the brother of Trafficant of Trafficant?" He'd met Factor Trafficant once, years ago; a heavyset man with hair the same shade of blond as Sarah Blythe's.

"Uncle of the current factor," Blythe said with a deliberate lack of emotion. "I'm told Samuel controls some of the family investments, but I don't really know."

She looked directly at him. "*I* live in Ishtar City near the Old Port with Dad. My mother died before I was two."

Stephen shrugged away the challenge in the stocky woman's gaze. "What's the burden of your *Gallant Sallie*, then?" he asked. "If you're—"

There was a knock on the pantry door. "Stephen?" called a familiar voice through the panel. "Can you join us for the ceremonies?"

"Of course, Piet," Stephen said. "That's why we're here, after all."

He reached past Sarah Blythe for the latch. It wasn't until the door opened, though, that she realized the plumpish, youngish man whom she faced close enough to kiss was Captain Piet Ricimer, the most famous spacer on Venus—and the man whose name President Pleyal was said to scream in his nightmares. "Oh!" Blythe said.

"Captain Blythe," Stephen said with a bland smile for the humor in the situation, "permit me to introduce you to my friend Factor Ricimer. Piet, this is Sarah Blythe, the captain of the ship which escaped during the incident on Lilymead."

Piet shook Blythe's hand with every sign of approval. Piet Ricimer believed that only idolaters like those of the Federation permitted women to do the work of men, but he was rarely impolite—or impolitic—when he could avoid it. Piet's purpose in life, the return of mankind to the stars in furtherance of God's plan, eclipsed every other belief and feeling within him.

"A very good job, Captain," Piet said. "I've noticed that your report gives the credit to your crew, but they wouldn't have reacted as you describe without proper training and a captain they were willing to fight for."

Behind Piet stood Guillermo, Piet's Molt servant. Referring to
Guillermo as a slave was one of the few things that brought Piet
to instant, open anger. So far as Piet was concerned, Molts were
human and the slavery the Feds practiced in the Reaches was a
sin against God.

Crewmen who'd served with Piet on his long voyages treated
Guillermo as a fellow and a dab hand with a starship's controls,
almost the equal of Captain Ricimer himself. The Molt wasn't much
good in a fight, but that didn't matter. Not in a ship with Mister Gregg aboard, it didn't.

Behind Piet and Guillermo stood a servant in Blenrott's livery,
pale and purple. The houseman watched Stephen in obvious nervousness. Stephen caught Piet's eye and nodded to indicate the
servant.

"Factor Blenrott put him at the door of the pantry with orders
not to permit anyone to disturb you, Stephen," Piet explained dryly.
"That's why I had to come fetch you myself. And speaking of that,
the others are probably waiting for us."

Stephen grimaced with disgust at his own conduct. It doesn't
matter how you feel or why you feel that way, you don't take it
out on innocents. In this respect at least, Kaspar Blenrott was surely
an innocent. "I'll make it up to him," he muttered again.

He fell into step a half pace behind Piet and as much to the
side. In this gathering, there was no need for the shoulders and
grim visage of Stephen Gregg to clear the way.

Guillermo was on Piet's other flank. Stephen, for reasons he
didn't care to examine, gestured Captain Sarah Blythe up between
them so that they walked in clear association into the hushed
assembly room.

ISHTAR CITY, VENUS

August 10, Year 26
1653 hours, Venus time

Sal Blythe was personally acquainted with only a handful of the
folk gathered in the assembly room. Captain Willem Casson was
a contemporary of her father's; not a friend, exactly, but a man
who'd sat with the Blythes in a dockside tavern, speaking of voyages
to the Reaches in which he searched for worlds whose pre-Collapse
wealth was not yet claimed by the Federation or the Southern
Cross.

The other attendees Sal knew to speak with were bankers, every
one of them. People from whom she'd raised—more often tried
to raise—money for this or that requirement of the *Gallant Sallie*
over the years. She wondered if now would be a good time to
broach the subject of the additional loan she'd need to fit the vessel
out to raid Federation shipping under the Commission of Redress
she hoped to be granted.

Piet Ricimer mounted the dais in a light flurry of applause. Sal
knew of the two men already on the dais, though they were too
powerful for her to have had any dealings with. Councilor Duneen
headed the Bureau of External Relations; he was said to be Governor Halys' chief advisor on matters of foreign policy. Duneen

was much of a size with Piet Ricimer and less than a dozen years older. The councilor moved with grace and an easy assurance of his own great power, but there was a fire in the soul of the space captain that the courtier lacked.

Alexi Mostert stood beside Duneen. His brother, Siddons Mostert, was in the front rank below, along with Stephen Gregg and many of the most powerful shipping and financial magnates on Venus. Alexi rated the dais because for the past three years he'd been Chief Constructor of the Fleet, the man primarily responsible for the design and building of state warships.

The Mosterts were able and intelligent men who'd expanded a modest shipping firm into the spearhead of trade from Venus. Alexi's purpose-built warships were handy and powerful, each of them supposedly more than a match for one of the much larger vessels of the North American Federation.

Supposedly: the truth wouldn't be known until the outbreak of open war between Venus and the Federation. That test couldn't be long coming, however, if the result of this gathering was what Sal expected it to be.

Ricimer bowed to Councilor Duneen, then called to the assembly in a ringing voice, "Fellow citizens, fellow patriots—I could tell you how serious a threat the Free State of Venus faces today, but I prefer to yield to a man who can speak far more eloquently. I give you Fiscal Walter Beck, until recently the Federation's chief representative on Lilymead and the man responsible for executing President Pleyal's orders there!"

The curtain behind the dais rustled to pass Beck, flanked by a pair of tough-looking sailors. The guards were a dramatic effect: Beck wasn't a threat to anyone. The fiscal had aged a decade in the days since Sal last saw him. The governor's interrogators didn't appear to have physically harmed him, but his skin was gray and his eyes faced a future in which there was no hope.

"I received orders from Montreal, signed by the president and authenticated with his code," Beck said. His tone was singsong because he'd repeated the story so frequently. "The papers being passed around the room are true copies of those orders. They required me to seize all Venerian vessels which called at Lilymead, despite the announced lifting of the embargo on foreign ships trading with us. The orders stated that the North American Federation had need of Venerian ships and particularly their guns for a Fleet of Retribution that would finally end the rebellion of Venus against the proper rule of President Pleyal."

The words, though familiar by now and spoken without affect, stabbed like cold steel through Sal's chest. The North American Federation, which five years before had incorporated the Southern Cross in a lightning sweep, had twenty times the population of Venus and drew on the resources of a hundred colonial worlds. If that power were focused, how could the Free State of Venus survive?

Beck shuffled away at the end of his practiced spiel and disappeared behind the curtains with his guards. A servant offered Sal a copy of the orders captured with the fiscal on Lilymead. Sal took the sheet absently, though God knew she'd studied the original long enough as the *Gallant Sallie* ran for home.

Councilor Duneen stepped forward with a fierce, solemn expression and said, "Individual citizens of Venus have been harmed by this action of President Pleyal. Two ships were captured on Lilymead, four others have failed to return from similar voyages to Federation colonies in Near Space, and"—he nodded in Sal's direction—"the vessel which escaped to give the alarm was damaged in the Feds' treacherous attack and lost the value of its cargo. In all cases, the interested parties will receive Commissions of Redress by the grace of Governor Halys, authorizing them to recoup their losses from the citizens and facilities of the North American Federation. There is another dimension to this event, however."

The room was tensely still as Duneen gazed around his audience. Many of the folk assembled had spent most of their lives grasping for profit. There was a leavening of sharks like Ricimer, like Casson; men who'd fought the Federation already and whose hope had been open war in which all Venus fought together to smash the tyranny of President Pleyal.

Both groups waited in a hush for the words they'd been assembled to hear. No one who opposed the government's plan had been invited; but, as with guests at a wedding, everyone present knew that the future might bring disaster.

"Governor Halys," Duneen continued, "has determined to send a squadron to retrieve the vessels unlawfully held in Federation ports. She will provide two ships from the State service, but there will be many opportunities for patriotic citizens to join in the expedition for the usual share of any profits accruing from the voyage. I won't discuss the details of the makeup and outfitting. That will be in the hands of the man Governor Halys has appointed as General Commander of the squadron: Captain Piet Ricimer!"

The cheer that greeted the announcement was spontaneous and general. Rather, almost general. Stephen Gregg stood at the base of the dais in part-profile to Sal behind him. Gregg's face was expressionless. Only the one gray eye Sal could see had life, a terrible glee that shocked her more than the muzzle of the Fed's revolver touching her head had done.

"Gentlemen and ladies," Piet Ricimer called, his voice riding with the enthusiasm instead of trying to overshout it, "through the generosity of Factor Blenrott, there are tables against the back wall here and separate rooms for those who would prefer to deal amongst themselves in greater privacy. I suggest we break up now and see how we can best put profit and patriotism at the service of the Lord God Almighty!"

Bowing again to the company, Ricimer strode at a swinging pace toward the table where Guillermo already waited. Stephen and the Mosterts fell in behind him. The gathering broke into a score of discussions milling like eddies of bubbles beneath a flume.

A young man in severely muted tunic and trousers—probably an agent rather than a principal—matched his step to Gregg's and began to talk earnestly. As the fellow spoke, he gestured with a notebook open to a page of numbers in column.

"Yes, but is that FOB Ishtar City, or for orbital loading?" Stephen replied in a coolly precise voice. "If it's orbit then yes, we might well be interested."

He didn't sound like the swashbuckling killer that common report held Stephen Gregg to be. He didn't sound like the tortured man Sal had met in the pantry, either.

If Sal tried to see Councilor Duneen in his palace office, she would have to bribe her way through phalanxes of attendants. Here there were only a few magnates with the councilor. On the strength of Duneen's nod to her in his presentation, Sal decided to ask how and when her Commission of Redress would be issued.

She was a hair too slow to approach the dais. Hollin, Grouse, and Richards, the three most importunate of the folk who'd pestered Sal till she took cover in the pantry, closed about her in a ring as close as minimal politeness permitted.

"I've told all you gentlemen my position," Sal said sharply. "I'm not interested in dealing with you."

"Yes, but there've been developments since then," Hollin said. The trio were money men, not shippers; bankers in a large way and reputed to be well known in the Governor's Palace. "In particular we've made an arrangement among ourselves so that the three of us aren't in competition, so to speak."

"We've also looked into your circumstances in detail, Mistress Blythe," Grouse added. "You can't afford to pay the gift Councilor Duneen will expect to release your commission, much less outfit your ship for a raiding voyage. The commission won't exist unless you see reason and transfer your rights to us—for a very respectable sum. We've agreed to pay you three thousand consols—cash, not discounted bills."

Sal turned angrily. Richards stood in that direction, a disdainful sneer on his lips. She wondered what the banker would do if she slapped him the way she'd slapped Stephen Gregg.

The advantage of a Commission of Redress was that the holder was exempted from the Governor's Fifth, the levy on cargoes brought to Venus from beyond the Solar System. If Sal sold her commission to the consortium surrounding her, they stood to greatly increase the value of prizes awarded to ships they owned in the course of the coming raid. Given the fabulous success of Piet Ricimer's previous expeditions, an extra twenty percent could be worth a fortune. Three thousand Venerian consols was a derisory offer, even if Sal had been willing to deal.

"We've called in some favors, Blythe," Richards said harshly. "You'll get no credit in Ishtar City or any of the other ports. And if you're thinking of raising the money you need from some pawnbroker out in the sticks—forget it! They'd need to pass the loan back to a respondent in Ishtar City, and they'd learn that nobody was willing to negotiate your paper."

Grouse frowned a little at Richards' open threat. He gestured calmingly and said, "There's another matter you should consider, Mistress Blythe. Your vessel operating alone is unlikely to make any significant prizes from the Federation. Probably not even enough to pay the expenses of your voyage. The chance of real profit is with the squadron forming now. I shouldn't have to tell you that General Commander Ricimer is far too good a Christian to permit a ship captained by a woman to serve with him."

Sal jerked upright. She felt suddenly sick with frustration. "Listen, you!" she said. "I'm as good a Christian as any man in this room! Show me where the Bible says a woman can't captain a starship. Show me where it says a woman can't do *any* damned thing!"

"I'm sure President Pleyal and his toadies would agree with you, *Mistress*," Hollin said. "I'm equally sure that Captain Ricimer would not. Now, if you'd like us to take up the outstanding loans on the *Gallant Sallie* and leave you without a ship at all, then—"

"Good afternoon, gentlemen," said Stephen Gregg, looming like a fang of rock behind Richards. "I heard you discussing business with my partner, Captain Blythe, here, so I thought I ought to come join you."

He smiled. If Death had a human face, thought Sarah Blythe, it would wear a very similar expression.

ISHTAR CITY, VENUS

August 10, Year 26
1707 hours, Venus time

"Your *partner*, Mister Gregg?" Hollin said. Richards, who'd jerked around as though he'd been stabbed, said nothing. Grouse twitched backward. His reflex, barely controlled, was to try to vanish into the crowd.

"Why, yes, Factor Hollin," Stephen said. He continued to walk forward in a curving path. His advance forced the bankers to move away from Blythe and, not coincidentally, put Stephen's own back to the wall. There was no physical need for that precaution here, but at the psychic level Stephen felt better for it. *We live in our minds, after all.*

He knew the three bankers better than he liked them. They were the new breed of financier, young men who'd made their mark in the current expansion of commerce. Grouse was of an age with Stephen and Piet, and the other two were only in their forties.

Stephen had heard the trio described as ruthless, but the word means different things to different people. *Ruthless means firing into a compartment full of people because somewhere among the screaming civilians is a Fed soldier with a gun. Ruthless is—*

Stephen focused back on the present, on the three well-dressed men staring at him in horror and the woman with a look of concern. Blythe's left hand was raised to touch him, to call him back from where he'd gone for an instant.

"I was sure there'd been a failure of communication," Stephen said. By the end of the sentence, his voice was back to its normal pleasant tenor, free of the rusty harshness that made the first words sound as though they'd been vocalized by an ill-programmed machine. "None of you gentlemen would have insulted my honor by knowingly trying to undercut my arrangements."

"Good *God,* no, sir!" Richards blurted as he backed away. The banker didn't have a high reputation for honesty, but there was no doubting the simple truth of his words this time.

Stephen smiled at the statement, but the bankers missed the humor of it. They bowed their respects and scuttled into the crowd, avoiding one another as well as their former quarry.

Sarah Blythe still stood beside him. Stephen scanned the assembly, looking over her head instead of at her. Not necessary, but—

"Those three had a good notion of what it costs to outfit a commercial vessel for raiding," Stephen said. "They should, after all, since they've had shares in at least a dozen raiders in the past five years. They work with the Mosterts, often as not. Were they right about your own financial condition?"

Blythe nodded, her expression deliberately blank. "Credit's tight, yes," she said. "Credit *was* tight before I came back from Lilymead with an empty hold, though I thought—I think that I'll be able to raise the necessary on the basis of the Commission of Redress."

She cleared her throat. "I . . ." she said. "Ah, thank you for what you did."

She was looking at him, but he continued to view the room. "My pleasure," he said. He laughed, a sound like that of bricks clinking together. "It's a pity, I suppose, but that's really true."

Blythe cleared her throat. "Well, thank you again. I need to see Councilor Duneen, so—"

"We have business to transact," Stephen said crisply. "If you're amenable, I'll take a silent partnership in your venture. You'll retain full control of the *Gallant Sallie*—captain her, engage the crew, all as you've been doing previously. I'll undertake to outfit the vessel for the voyage at my own sole charge, and to provide expertise."

He gave her a businesslike smile. "You'll need an expert, me or someone like me. I assure you, a raiding voyage is very different from the commercial endeavors in which you've been engaged to present."

She nodded back. "I can see that," she said. She didn't really understand, though. She thought he meant differences in staff and equipment. . . .

"The relative value of the ship's share and the backer's share will be determined by survey of the vessel," Stephen continued, speaking with the seamless precision of a man at one with his subject. "We'll each appoint a surveyor, the pair to choose the third man themselves. Captain's and crew's shares aren't affected, of course."

"I'd want to discuss this with . . ." Blythe said, but she let her voice trail off as she reconsidered. Her father, Stephen assumed, though there might well be a man in her life. There deserved to be.

"Alternatively," he concluded, "I'll put a consol down and you'll double it to me on your return. For honor's sake."

He grinned. Her face lost the thoughtful animation of a moment before and became guarded again.

"I told those three that I was your partner, you see," he explained. "So I need to put something into the expedition."

At the back of the room, Piet shook hands with Kuelow of Thorn, leaning across the table to clap the magnate on the back. Piet's eyes met Stephen's in a quick flicker. Stephen flared the fingers of his left hand in an all's-well signal; Piet nodded and switched the full force of his personality to the next man waiting to talk with him, the agent of a syndicate of Betaport shippers.

They'd been looking out for each other for a decade now, he and Piet. One way and another.

"Why are you making this offer, Mister Gregg?" Sarah Blythe said. She wasn't quite able to hide the unintended challenge.

"My uncle is Benjamin Gregg," Stephen said in a mildly bantering tone. "Gregg of Weyston, Weyston Trading. Uncle Ben would disown me if I turned down a business opportunity like this when it dropped in my lap. And there's also . . ."

Stephen looked at Captain Sarah Blythe, feeling the sadness at what so easily might have been: Stephen Gregg, merchant. Stephen Gregg, managing partner in Weyston Trading by now, though Uncle Ben wasn't the sort to give up titular control while life was in him.

"There's also the fact that I said I'd make amends for my boorishness," he went on, rubbing his cheek where she'd hit him.

Blythe snorted. "I'd say running those three off put the debt on my side of the ledger," she said, nodding dismissively toward Factor Richards, glimpsed across the room.

"I said that was a pleasure," Stephen repeated. "God help me, but it was."

"Very well," Blythe said. "My hand on the bargain then, Mister Gregg."

Her grip was firm, but her palms were sweating. If she had not been nervous, that would have meant she didn't understand what had been going on.

"I'll talk to Calaccio about the survey," she went on. "He's the primary noteholder. Ishtar Chandlery, you know."

Stephen nodded. "I'll get one of Uncle Ben's people and tell him to contact Calaccio," he said. "Oh, and if you'll ask Calaccio to turn over the vessel's full supply and maintenance logs to my representative, I'll get to work at once on my end. And let me take care of Duneen."

"I should hit men more often," Blythe said with a straight face.

"If they behave the way I did, you should indeed," Stephen replied.

Blenrott, beaming with the success of the affair he was hosting, turned from a group of courtiers and caught Stephen's eye. Stephen gave him a full bow.

"On Thursday," Stephen said in a voice that Blythe leaned closer to hear, "I'll attend Factor Blenrott's levee. My presence will make his peers think he stands a meter taller; which is stupid, but it's the truth nonetheless."

"I think my friend Mister Gregg can best supply those estimates," Piet said in tones pitched to carry across the five meters of conversation separating the two of them.

"Duty calls," Stephen said, gesturing with his left hand but looking directly at Blythe for the first time since he'd driven away the bankers. "Blenrott's affair will be excruciatingly dull," he went on in the same soft voice as he'd used when he discussed their host before. "That's good. I believe a person should be punished for acting badly. It makes it unlikely that he'll do that particular thing again."

Stephen bowed to the woman and returned to where Piet needed him for a discussion of share percentages.

ISHTAR CITY, VENUS

August 13, Year 26
0317 hours, Venus time

Marcus Blythe opened the street door cautiously, but he dropped his walking stick with a loud clatter before he managed to close the door behind him. He froze.

"It's all right, Dad," Sal said. "I'm up working, so you haven't bothered me."

"Ah," said Marcus. He turned around and saw his daughter seated at the table in the common room of the suite. He'd thought the light was on merely to guide him back to his bed as usual. "Ah."

"Do you need . . ." Sal asked.

"No, I'm quite all right," Marcus said in a tone of injured innocence. He bent carefully to retrieve his stick, fumbling it several times in the process. That was as much his arthritis-twisted hands as the drink, though. In truth, he wasn't drunk by his standards or those of the Old Port District more generally. "I was out toasting the success of our new venture with a few friends, you see."

He began to tremble. Sal rose quickly from her seat, bumping the table and disarranging the array of small parts on it. "Dad?" she said.

594

"No, I'm all right!" Marcus said with a touch of the fire appropriate to a space captain and shipowner; rarely heard since he became a cripple who spent his time drinking with other has-beens.

Sal put her arms around her father anyway, holding him close. There were tears at the corners of his eyes. Marcus wasn't an old man, but to himself—not to her, never to her—he was a useless one.

"Is it really going to happen, Sallie?" he said.

Sal used the bandanna with which she secured her hair in private to dab at the tears. "I don't think Mister Gregg lies about things, Dad," she said." I don't think he could imagine a reason he'd want to. Now, if you're really all right, why don't you wash up before you go to bed? I've changed your sheets—and not before time."

"Yes, I'll do that," Marcus agreed humbly. He didn't move for a moment. "It . . . Sallie, it's so hard to believe that my own daughter is in partnership with Stephen Gregg. Mister Stephen Gregg!"

"Yeah," Sal said. "It is very hard to believe."

She hadn't let herself feel anything. She didn't know what she even ought to feel. Elation? Fear? There was reason enough for those and any number of other emotions; she just didn't know what was right.

"It means we'll be rich, you know, Sal," he said. "When I was young I thought—well, you're young, you know. But—"

"I don't know that we're going to be rich," Sal said, almost completely concealing her nervous irritation at hearing her father tempt fate. "All we have is a chance, a *chance* to recoup our losses on the last voyage."

"Oh, it's better than that, girl!" Marcus said, irritated in turn at having his hopes discounted. "Why, Gregg is Captain Ricimer's right-hand man! Gregg's cut his way to a dozen fortunes in the Reaches. You think he's not going to make sure this latest investment doesn't turn a profit too? A profit in a rich *gentleman's* terms!"

Sal swallowed. "I know that Mister Gregg is a skillful business-man, Dad," she said. "I just don't want you to get your hopes up. Would you like a hand to the corner?"

The bathhouse was at the junction with the main corridor three doors down.

"And I want you to know," Marcus bumbled on, "that nobody thinks the less of you for . . . what you've done. Your mother was a good woman at heart, a truly loving wife while we were together, and—"

"Dad, shut *up*," Sal said in a voice like a dragon's. "You're drunk and you don't know what you're saying."

She turned her father around in a curt movement better suited for shifting furniture and opened the door for him. Men were shouting at one another in slurred anger somewhere in the night, but they could have been blocks away. When there weren't crowds of pedestrians to absorb sound, it echoed long distances in the underground corridors of the older Venerian settlements.

"I'm not drunk!" Marcus protested feebly. "Sallie, what did I—"

"Sweat *all* the booze out of you before you come back here!" Sal said. "In the future, don't tell foolish *lies* to your drunken friends, and especially don't tell them to me!"

Puzzled, shocked completely sober, Marcus Blythe stumbled into the street. "Sallie, I'm sorry for—" he called.

She slammed the door on the last of his words and stood trembling against the inside of the panel for a moment. Were they all saying that she was Gregg's mistress? If her father said it to her face, then they probably were.

Sal sighed. It didn't matter. Most folk assumed the only use for a woman on a starship was to service the sexual needs of the crew. She'd lived with that all her life, so she could live with this too.

She sat down at the table and began to sort the parts into groups by subassemblies. She'd tacked a high-intensity lamp to the wall to work by. Its glare made her eyes sting; she switched it off and rubbed her forehead, swearing softly at nothing she could put a clear name to.

After a moment Sal turned the light back on. She dipped the copper bristles in solvent and resumed brushing the rust off the sear.

Spread before her on the table was the completely disassembled revolver that she'd pulled from the Federation officer's death grip. After she had it completely cleaned, she would treat the external surfaces with a corrosion-resistant phosphate finish.

When Sarah Blythe went beyond Pluto the next time, she would go armed.

BETAPORT, VENUS

August 14, Year 26
1741 hours, Venus time

Piet Ricimer rose from the table in the back room of the Blue Rose
Tavern and stretched with a groan. "I'm going to complain to the
landlord about how hard the chairs in this room are," he said.

"They were comfortable enough six hours ago," Stephen said.
"Maybe we've just worn them out."

The Blue Rose was on Ship Street, facing the port's transfer
docks. The tavern had been Piet's headquarters from the beginning, long before he'd bought the freehold with a small fraction
of the profits on his most recent raiding voyage.

Business was good tonight. A gust of laughter from the public
bar rumbled its way through the wall. Guillermo was outside, acting
as doorkeeper in case an important message arrived in person
rather than by telephone.

"Six hours?" Piet echoed. "So it is. Shall we take a break?"

"Ten minutes more," Stephen said. He typed a string of commands on the keyboard, then rotated the holographic screen so
that the display faced his companion. "I want to run through the
last of the ships offered to the squadron."

Piet sat down again, his expression neutral. "All right," he said.

In the public bar, three sailors sang in excellent harmony, "*There were ninety and nine who safely lay—*"

"The *Gallant Sallie*," Stephen said. He leaned back in his chair so that his shoulders touched the glazed tiles of the wall behind him. "A well-found vessel of a hundred and fifty tonnes. A crew of sixteen plus the captain and mate. She mounts four ten-centimeter guns, sufficient for the purpose we'd want her for—which I take to be transport rather than combat. She could easily be up-gunned, of course."

"No, we don't need another fighting ship," Piet said. He looked at Stephen rather than the display. "If I recall correctly," he continued evenly, "this vessel's owner and captain is a woman."

Stephen got up, turned to face the corner behind him, and forced his palms hard against both walls of the angle. "Governor Halys is a woman, Piet," he said in a tense, clipped voice. "We serve a woman."

"We serve mankind, Stephen," Piet replied. His arms were spread, his right hand on the console and his left draped with deliberate nonchalance across the back of his chair. "I hope that we serve God as well, by executing His plan to return mankind to the stars. But I take your point."

Piet was speaking softly. His face, no longer neutral, bore a look of concern similar to that of an adult with an injured child.

Stephen sighed, turned, and wrapped his arms around himself. He was trying to find a position that relaxed him. "It's not just Lilymead, Piet," he said without meeting his friend's eyes. "I've looked at the *Gallant Sallie*'s maintenance records. I may not know the first thing about piloting, but I can see from repair invoices whether the captain's been beating a ship around. She's good."

"By now, perhaps the *first* thing," Piet said with a smile.

Stephen laughed, glad of the release. "All right, I'm a gentleman and can't be expected to touch my delicate fingers to a navigation computer," he said.

Piet stood. He put his right hand on the back of Stephen's hand and his left on Stephen's right shoulder. "Are you asking me to do this, Stephen?" he said.

Stephen met his eyes at last. "Yes, I am," he said.

In the public bar, dozens joined the trio to roar, "*Rejoice, for the Shepherd has found His sheep!*"

The *a cappella* rendition ended in a general cheer.

"All right, Stephen," Piet said, sitting down again. "Let's run through the rest of these and get something to eat, shall we?" He grinned. "Perhaps to drink as well."

"That's the last," Stephen said. He breathed out a sigh of relief more intense than anything he'd felt outside of combat. The feeling took him completely by surprise.

He looked at his friend. "Thanks, Piet," he said.

"It's little enough to do for you, Stephen," Piet said. He was dressed in flashy style even now, closeted with a friend doing bookwork. His tunic was black plush crossed by triple gold chevrons, in contrast to Stephen's worn blue garment with one of the buttons missing. "You came out beyond Pluto with me the second time because I needed you. Even though you knew what it would cost."

"No, by then it wouldn't have done me any good to stay home," Stephen said. "That's not, that's nothing for you to worry about. I—"

He glanced toward the door. The voices of sailors beginning "*Three Old Whores from Betaport*" didn't penetrate his consciousness, though his ears filed the information.

He looked down at Piet again and said with lilting simplicity, "Since the first voyage, the only time I'm really alive is when I'm killing something. That's not your doing, Piet. Best I ought to be out in the Reaches where enemies come with proper labels, isn't it? Otherwise—"

Stephen shrugged. His mouth smiled, but he couldn't control what his eyes showed to those who watched him at times like these.

Piet stood up. "We'll get something to eat," he said, gripping his friend's hand. Then he said, "Stephen? Do you know why you want the *Gallant Sallie* in the squadron?"

"Not really," Stephen said. He chuckled. "In my case, introspection isn't a terribly good idea, you know."

He opened the door to the public bar. "Dinner, Guillermo," he said, putting his free hand on the Molt's chitinous shoulder. "Blackie's as usual?"

Sailors cheered and doffed their caps to Captain Ricimer and Mister Gregg. In Betaport, Piet Ricimer stood just below the throne of God—and Mister Stephen Gregg was the angel with the sword.

"I've been checking prices on provisioning the squadron from common stores and deducting the cost from the captains' shares," Stephen said to his companions as they squeezed toward the street door. "I think it's workable. If we leave it to individual captains the usual way, some of them are going to skimp—which hurts us all. . . ."

BETAPORT, VENUS

October 4, Year 26
1404 hours, Venus time

"My friends, my fellows; some of you my comrades of many years," said Piet Ricimer. He spoke in distinct periods so that his amplified voice, echoing across the huge storage dock, was nonetheless clearly audible. "Our purpose today is the same as that of former years, to free the stars from the tyranny of President Pleyal and the North American Federation."

Sal and the crew of the *Gallant Sallie* stood in a tight group in the midst of nearly two thousand sailors. The storage dock held eighteen starships with room for forty or more. On Venus, all starship operations except takeoff and landing took place in vast caverns like this one. Internal cargo was transferred, repairs were carried out, consumables including air and water for reaction mass were loaded—and finally the crew reported on board. Only then was the vessel winched complete along one of the tunnels to a transfer dock whose dome could be opened to the Venerian atmosphere for launch.

The assembly was being held here because a storage dock was the only volume in Betaport sufficient to hold the numbers involved, the crews of all the Betaport vessels that were part of the squadron. Ishtar City was the capital and financial center of the Free State of Venus, but Betaport and the settlements of Beta Regio were the heart of trade to the Reaches—and resistance to the Feds' claim to own everything beyond Pluto. Though ships would lift from Ishtar City to join the squadron in orbit, most of Ricimer's vessels were in this dock.

"With the help of God, we will take prizes on this voyage," General Commander Ricimer said. So that he could be seen by all, he stood in the open hold of the *Wrath*, a purpose-built warship that Governor Halys had provided to the expedition. "This time, however, we voyage not as raiders but as the champions of Venus and mankind. Our purpose is to harm our enemies rather than to enrich ourselves as individuals."

Ricimer wore half armor, the helmet and chestplates of a hard suit. He was under no threat here, but the gleaming metallized surfaces made his floodlit figure splendid.

"What's he mean, then?" Cooney asked in a whisper loud enough to be sure that Sal heard it. "Does he mean we're supposed to get our knackers shot away for bare wages?"

Tom Harrigan clubbed Cooney silent with the side of his knobby fist. If some of the Betaport sailors standing nearby had heard the question/complaint, they might have used a length of pipe instead. In Betaport, you didn't argue with a statement of Piet Ricimer's.

The *Gallant Sallie* was docked in Betaport now because Stephen Gregg chose to have the refit work done by workmen and suppliers who knew him well. The ship had been gutted to the bare hull and built back again with the newest and best equipment. It wasn't just a ploy of the co-owner to run up the assessed value of his share, either. Sal had gone over the figures. She knew that she couldn't have gotten the work done herself for anything close to the amount Stephen claimed to be paying.

"I hope to make you all rich," Ricimer continued, as though he'd been listening to Cooney himself. The general commander had been a sailor all his life, and he knew how his fellows thought. "But nothing can take precedence over the needs of Venus and God on this expedition."

The *Wrath* and most of the squadron's bigger vessels were carrying soldiers, landsmen whose specialty was war instead of being sailors with guns. Stephen Gregg, the expedition's vice commander, was no sailor, but neither was he merely a soldier. Like Piet Ricimer himself, Mister Gregg wasn't merely anything.

Stephen waited in the back of the hold behind his friend and commander now. His head was barely visible from where Sal stood.

"My comrades, my *friends*," Piet Ricimer boomed. "We go out as a flame—a beacon to all friends of freedom, and a torch to the enemies of God! Let us pray for His help in our endeavors!"

As she bowed her head, listening to the deeply felt sincerity of the general commander's words, Sal wondered what it was that Stephen Gregg might pray for.

LILYMEAD

October 10, Year 26
0247 hours, Venus time

The fields to the north and west of the community grew Terran crops irrigated from deep wells, but the street was shaded by local succulents that spread their thick leafless stems in intricate traceries against the sky. To Stephen, it was like walking under cool green nets.

Besides Piet, Stephen, and Guillermo, the Venerian "embassy" consisted of Sarah Blythe—for her local knowledge—and the mates of the other two freighters, comparable to the *Gallant Sallie,* that had set down with the flagship.

Locally, it was mid-morning. Members of the colony's government were drawn up in front of the Commandatura, a modest building distinguished from its neighbors only by having a coat of stucco over the adobe brick.

Close to three hundred people, a good percentage of the town's population, sat or stood in the street beyond. The humans, generally in front, wore their best clothes, an odd assortment of Terran and locally made finery. The Molts were naked except for an occasional sash-of-office. The tone of the aliens' chitin ranged from yellow-brown to near purple.

603

A few Rabbits, human by genetic inheritance, sauntered from alley to doorway or back. Their patent unconcern was in contrast to the sharp tension of the rest of the crowd.

Four of the six Fed officials wore white tunics; only the sixty-ish woman and the much younger man at her side had uniform trousers to match. The five Molts standing behind the humans were probably principal clerks in their departments, since they wore varicolored sashes.

There were no weapons visible.

Stephen grinned with inward humor at the thought: there were no Fed weapons visible. The Venerian contingent was escorted by fifty soldiers and an equal number of armed sailors, the *Wrath*'s B Watch close-combat team. The warship's broadside of 20-cm plasma cannon dominated the community from the nearby spaceport.

"I don't guess they're going to try anything, Mister Gregg," said Dole, who commanded the sailors. He was the *Wrath*'s bosun and a companion of Piet's from the days Piet was the mate of a tiny intrasystem trader.

"Did you think they would?" Stephen said. He scanned the shuttered windows up and down the town's single street. His palms tingled on the grip and fore-end of his flashgun, a heavy monopulse laser.

There'd always been a chance that some fanatic would decide that shooting the devil Piet Ricimer was worth the total destruction of the colony that would surely follow. At the least hint of a threat, Stephen would act, as he'd acted before.

Piet, wearing a complete hard suit except for the gauntlets and lower-leg pieces, faced the uniformed woman and said, "Are you the Fiscal of Lilymead?"

"Ah!" the woman said, blinking in confusion. She was terrified, they were all of them terrified. "I'm, I'm—"

"Factor Ricimer, I'm Fiscal Dimetrio," the young man at her side blurted with an anguished expression, "but Prefect Larsen is in charge. Mister Beck was merely filling in during the vacancy and—and I've been sent to replace *him*."

Larsen bobbed her head in agreement. "There's no quarrel between Lilymead and the Free State of Venus," she said. "The ships that were, ah, detained, they've all been released. The two here and the others elsewhere, I'm told, a week ago. Mister Kansuale here will verify that. He's, he's from Venus too."

"Won't you have some fruit?" said another Fed official. He was a gangling lad who seemed to have outgrown his uniform tunic. He gestured the Molt behind him to come forward with a basket of lemons the size of oranges. "Our Lilymead lemons are exceptionally large and sweet!"

He was more like a puppy than a puppy was. Stephen started to laugh. Everybody looked at him, but he was used to that. Holding his flashgun muzzle-up in one hand, he took a lemon, examined it, and bit one end off to suck some of the juice.

"He's right, Piet," Stephen said. To Prefect Larsen he added, "You know, you folks here ought to stick to agriculture and leave piracy to experts." He smiled. "Like us."

"There was confusion, but it's been resolved, truly," Larsen said, wiping her forehead with her cuff. "Kansuale, tell them. *Tell* them."

Kansuale was stocky, bald, and dressed in civilian clothes of dull blue with patches of electric green. The style had originated on Earth and been picked up by fops on Venus some three years since. Heaven knew how this trader came by it.

Kansuale bowed to Sal, then to Piet, and said, "Captain Blythe, gentlemen. I've been trading on Lilymead for seven years, but I was born and raised in a smallholding at the base of Mount Cypris."

"Can you identify him, Captain?" Piet asked Sal.

She nodded. "By communicator from orbit," she said. "He was my contact. I suppose he arranged for the lighter to transfer cargo." She sniffed. "The old screen wasn't very good, but the voice and the general features are right."

Sal looked uncomfortable in the helmet and breastplate of the hard suit Stephen had insisted she take as part of the *Gallant Sallie*'s refit. In the past, the vessel had carried a single hard suit for operations in heat or corrosive atmospheres. It was a shoddy piece of work as well as being larger than Sal could wear comfortably.

She needed better than that. Especially out beyond Pluto, where bullets were as likely a hazard as the natural ones.

Kansuale had been wary but not frightened the way the Fed officials were. When the trader saw that he wasn't being accepted as an unquestioned friend, his eyes drifted guardedly across the harsh faces before him.

"Yes . . ." he said. "The ships embargoed here, the *Clerambard* and the *Daniel III*, lifted off five days, Earth days, ago. A courier had brought orders from Montreal countermanding the previous orders."

"It was only a clarification," Dimetrio said. "Really, it—"

Dole, acting with the freedom of a man who'd served with Piet Ricimer for fifteen years, tapped his carbine's muzzle on the bridge of the fiscal's nose. "I hear liars' noses grow," Dole said. "I know sometimes they get shot off."

Piet gestured his bosun back with a glance.

"However, the ships had been stripped of their weapons and all spares and tools," Kansuale continued. He'd obviously decided that his safest course lay in telling the full truth in as flat a tone as possible. "Also, three crewmen and the captain of the *Daniel III* had been killed when the ships were captured."

Piet looked at Larsen and raised an eyebrow.

"I understand that's correct," the prefect said miserably. "It was before my arrival, you realize."

"The guns and gear was all sent off to Asuncion before," said an official. The tag over the pocket of his blue tunic read supervisor, but there was enough grease in the fabric and under his fingernails to indicate that he actually worked on ships as well as supervising a crew of Molts. "Then they tell me to put the bitches back the way they were *tout le suite* and send them home—and how am I going to do that, I ask you, when they've taken the gear to Asuncion, huh?"

"How much warning did you have that we were coming?" Stephen asked. There were more spies than honest men in the Governor's Palace.

Stephen held the opened lemon to his lips, squeezing as he sucked in more of the tart, luscious juice. He watched Larsen over his hand and the fruit in it.

"Ten days," she said in a dead voice. She was looking in his direction, but her eyes weren't focused on anything so close. "Send the Venus ships back, get all the other shipping off to Asuncion or Racine where there's defenses. Everybody to scatter from the settlements here and hide out until the, the—"

The struggle in Larsen's mind brought her back to the present. "Your squadron," she said simply, meeting Stephen's gaze. "The pirates. We were to hide in the wild until you were gone and not give you any help. What would that have done? You'd have burned and blasted everything on Lilymead to a crater, that's what it would have done!"

The prefect had gone beyond fear to acceptance of the worst possible event. "Well, maybe you'll do that anyway," she said bitterly to Piet. "But I didn't come to Lilymead to be prefect of craters and burned fields, so you can just go ahead and shoot me before you start!"

Piet smiled and slung the double-barreled shotgun he carried as a personal weapon. "I don't think we'll need to do that," he said mildly. "Prefect Larsen, you'll supply provisions and reaction mass to my squadron at prices I will set after consultation with my officers."

He nodded to Sal Blythe.

"We will pay for these items—" Piet continued.

Fiscal Dimetrio blinked in surprise as great as that of seeing his life hang on Dole's 3-kilogram trigger pull.

"—in Venerian consols, after deductions for damages to the ships detained in violation of your government's safe conduct." His smile hardened momentarily as he added, "These damages will include death benefits for the men who were murdered. Do you understand?"

There was a stir in the crowd of civilians. Those near the front could hear Piet's clear voice. They repeated the words to their fellows farther back, whether or not they believed the statements.

"Yes sir," Prefect Larsen said, though that probably wasn't true. "We'll—may I radio my people? Quite a lot of them are hiding in the bush without proper shelter or provisions."

Piet nodded. "Go about your affairs, all of you. Major Castle," he said to the commander of the contingent of soldiers, "secure the west end of town. There's to be no looting or mistreatment of residents. Dole, you and your men cover the east. Confiscate weapons, but no trouble."

The troops dissolved into half squads under the bawled orders of their officers. Piet entered the Commandatura with the Fed officials. The flaccid remains of the lemon lay in the street. Stephen, his flashgun in ready position again, followed Piet because he couldn't force his way to the front in time. The hallway was frescoed with scenes of the planet's settlement.

"I thought . . ." Sal Blythe said beside him. "I mean, if we're at war . . ."

Piet turned around and gave her his brilliant smile. "We're at war with President Pleyal," he said. "We're at war with a system that strips the Reaches of pre-Collapse remains without building anything new. A colony like Lilymead is just what mankind needs if we're to grow until we're so widely dispersed that there can't be another Collapse, not one that threatened *all* civilization."

"There's the problem with where their orders come from, of course," Stephen said. He instinctively looked in both directions along the corridor. The Commandatura appeared to be empty except for the officials who'd waited outside.

Brave folk. All those who'd stayed were brave folk.

"Oh, we'll take care of that the better way, Stephen," Piet said cheerfully. "You and I and Venus will, with the help of God. We'll cut off the tyranny at its head!"

And if you feel cheated of your chance to see real war, Captain Sarah Blythe, Stephen thought, *then wait till our next landfall on Racine.*

RACINE

November 11, Year 26
0745 hours, Venus time

The *Gallant Sallie*, overfull though not overweighted by her cargo of soldiers, bobbed in the wake of the *Wrath*'s transsonic passage. "Don't touch those controls, you cunt brains!" Sal screamed to Harrigan and the two men with him at the attitude control panel.

The artificial intelligence—the new AI configured for atmospheric control, separate from the navigational unit—brought the ship steady with microburns from the attitude jets. Humans, even the picked men Sal had on the manual boards for backup, would have overcorrected and set the *Gallant Sallie* looping in a yo-yo pattern.

Though the new AI worked perfectly, the quick oscillation at 200 kph was too much for the stomachs of a dozen of the soldiers. One of them slammed his helmet visor closed to avoid spewing across the back of his neighbor; a kindly reflex, but one he was sure to regret until he got to a place where he could hose his suit out.

For that matter, the way the *Gallant Sallie* shuddered was frightening to anybody who knew the starship was roaring toward New Windsor, the planetary capital, at only a hundred meters above the ground. The soldiers packing the hold and too much of the cabin didn't realize the situation, thank God.

Several of the squadron's vessels fired from orbit. Plasma charges wobbled and dispersed in the kilometers of atmosphere. The bolts flickered like heat lightning rather than slashing cataclysmically, searing hectares without destroying any target of metal or masonry.

That sort of bombardment might keep the Feds' heads down or at least draw their attention away from the ships coming in on the deck with companies of soldiers. It wouldn't seriously harm the defenses. The *Wrath* was designed to accept damage to her thrusters without corkscrewing out of control, so Piet Ricimer was taking her point-blank past the starport to deliver smashing blows.

Since the big warship's wake hadn't spun the *Gallant Sallie* into the ground, Sal was glad for the support.

The display Stephen had provided was crystal clear, amazingly clear to somebody who'd been used to optronics from the generation before her own. The AI projected digital information onto rushing terrain. The brown rock slashed with gullies of lush blue-tinged vegetation seemed too real to be an electronic image; but that's what it was, just like the map spread across the display's upper left quadrant.

Sal waited, her hands splayed and ready to take control from the guidance program. The *Gallant Sallie* had been chosen for the assault because of her state-of-the-art electronics, but Captain Ricimer had emphasized that in combat, events couldn't be preprogrammed. Sal's instincts were a necessary part of the operation.

She wondered where Stephen was. Aboard the *Wrath*, or in another of the assault vessels?

The horizon rippled with dazzling saffron brilliance, ten 20-cm plasma bolts fired within a microsecond. Piet Ricimer had to be just as good a pilot as his reputation to achieve what happened next: ten more rounds, nearly instantaneously. He'd let the recoil of the first broadside lift the *Wrath* from an axial tilt to port into a starboard tilt that aligned the other battery with ground targets.

The pulsing map cursor indicating the *Gallant Sallie*'s position slid past the ridgeline of the valley in which New Windsor lay. The city sprang into life on the main screen.

New Windsor was built of stone, dirty-looking volcanic tuff brightened by roofs of red, orange, and yellow sheeting. There were at least a thousand buildings plus corrals for the Molt slaves whose transshipment was a major part of the colony's commerce.

The town had a wall and fence with watchtowers containing plasma cannon and multitube lasers. "Setting down!" Sal shouted as she rotated the thrusters to brake the *Gallant Sallie* fast.

The ship was stubbornly alive in Sal's hands, resisting the change from forward flight to hover the way a gyroscope fights a twisting force. She cued the attitude jets. The AI fired corresponding pairs from the bow and stern rings, swinging the *Gallant Sallie* broadside to her direction of flight.

One person with electronics like these could pilot a starship more precisely than the best-trained crew of a decade ago. Because of the microchips that Venerian raiders had wrenched from Federation hands in the Reaches, and because of the production lines set up on Venus with that loot, ships had become a hundred times safer than the cranky tubs in which mankind first returned to the stars.

The *Gallant Sallie* rotated 30° on her axis, raising her main thrusters to a part-forward attitude. Soldiers had toppled in clattering heaps when the vessel swung. Now they slid toward the starboard bulkhead. Sailors cursed and dodged the landsmen, dangerous weights in their hard suits festooned with weapons.

Sal doubled the thruster output momentarily. Precisely metered thrust balanced momentum. The *Gallant Sallie* halted fifty meters in the air.

The moment before the ship's vertical axis rotated back to normal was when the city defenses were most dangerous. The weapons on the guard towers were relatively light, intended for use against men and gangs of escaped Molts. They could damage a starship's hull badly enough to require later repairs, but they couldn't blast the *Gallant Sallie* out of the air. A hit on a thruster exposed as the vessel maneuvered, however, would shatter the nozzle. At this low altitude, the skewed thrust would drive the *Gallant Sallie* into the ground like the spud of a rototiller.

The Feds didn't fire. The starship settled gently against decreasing thrust, touching the volcanic soil so gently that Sal barely felt the outrigger struts compress.

That sort of control was possible because men like Piet Ricimer had a dream, and because men like Stephen Gregg were willing to pay the price of that dream.

Sal shut down the thrusters. She felt hydraulics whine as Rickalds in the hold raised the main hatch. Brantling beside her swung clear the outer cabin lock; the inner valve had been open since the *Gallant Sallie* had hit the atmosphere minutes before at the start of her low-level run toward New Windsor.

Heat from the rocks and wisps of the plasma exhaust that had seared those rocks to a glow entered the cabin. Soldiers trotted down the boarding ramp. Their hard suits protected them against the conditions of landing as against enemy fire that didn't come. The sailors were used to the heat and ozone, though Brantling sneezed and Sal's vision blurred as her eyes watered.

Another Venerian freighter screamed in low and disappeared into the smoke rising from north of the city. An explosion near the starport made the rocks quiver palpable seconds before the airborne shockwave reached the *Gallant Sallie*. A column of black debris twisted upward a thousand meters before it belled over and rained bits of itself over a wide area.

There was still no shooting from the walls six hundred meters way. Officers had sorted the soldiers from the *Gallant Sallie* into a line. They began to advance toward the city. Sal's crewmen were looking at her, but she didn't know any more than they did. Radio was useless for communications because the ions jumping from so many plasma engines were broadcasting across the RF spectrum. Nobody was bothering to direct a tight-beam commo laser toward the *Gallant Sallie*.

Sal rose from the console. "Clear our guns!" she ordered. The 10-cm cannon were in their traveling position. They couldn't have been used while the cabin was packed with soldiers. Run out there'd have been more room in the cabin, but opening the ports while the *Gallant Sallie* was making her approach would have created worse turbulence and an atmosphere sharp with exhaust ions.

As Sal spoke, the air began to shudder from the vibration of powerful thrusters. The *Wrath*, bathed in rainbow veils of her own exhaust, was settling into the starport. Her active thrusters were at full power, because half the warship's nozzles were cold and shrouded by blow-off screens. They would only be lit in case of damage to the operating units. The *Wrath*'s guns were out and ready to fire, but they remained silent.

"The city's been abandoned!" an unfamiliar voice announced from the console speaker. The *Gallant Sallie*'s contingent of soldiers had reached the walls. Some of them were waving their arms and one, standing on a guard tower, had thought to inform the ship with a modulated laser. "There's no troops, and there's nobody moving!"

"Tom, relay that to the ships in orbit," Sal ordered. Her legs trembled, and she had to grab the back of the seat to keep from falling.

"We've won!" Brantling cried loudly. "The Feds are too scared of us to even stand and fight! By God, we'll run them out of space before this voyage is over!"

Her men were cheering. *It was all so easy,* thought Sarah Blythe. *But so is falling, until you hit the ground.*

NEW WINDSOR, RACINE

November 12, Year 26
1244 hours, Venus time

There were more than five hundred Molts in the pen. They pressed forward, making a groaning sound by rubbing their belly plates together. The noise was horrible, like that of rocks shearing in a landslip.

Soldiers with linked arms formed an aisle from the gate to troughs of water and tables of food overseen by Molts released earlier. The troops wore hard suits for protection. They didn't carry weapons, lest a Molt grab a gun or cutting bar and use it in starving desperation. Without the soldiers to stem and direct the flow of ravenous aliens, the feeding operation would turn into a feeding frenzy.

Guillermo and a Molt whose chitin showed the silvery patina of age stood near the gate, calling what Stephen assumed were words of calm and encouragement to the released slaves. There were humans who claimed to understand the aliens' own clicking speech, but Stephen wasn't one of them. There was usually at least one Molt in a group who spoke Trade English; and besides, diplomacy was somebody else's job.

One of the last of the squadron's ships was coming down with a great roar of thrusters on the city side of the field. New Windsor's port could comfortably handle a larger number of vessels than those comprising the Venerian squadron, but the later-landed crews were expected to walk some distance across the baked and blasted field. This captain—the ship was a large one of the old spherical style, so it was probably Captain Casson's *Freedom*—was setting down near the city, despite the danger to other vessels and people moving to and from them.

Starships weren't Stephen's area of responsibility either, but his face was hard behind his filtered visor as he watched the *Freedom* settle. Piet's lips pursed also, but if he said anything it would be to Casson in private. The first time, at least.

A soldier raised his armored fist to punch a Molt who'd shoved hard against him. Major Foster, commanding the company involved, rapped the back of the soldier's gauntlet with his swagger stick and shouted, "None of that! Move them on, that's all!"

Foster stepped back to Piet, with whom he'd been watching the proceedings. This was the last of the six pens, all of them full of slaves captured on worlds in which Molt culture survived though the human colonists vanished after the Collapse.

Racine, a Near Space planet with a relatively easy passage to the Reaches, was a convenient nexus for the slave trade. Most of the Molt-occupied planets were found in Near Space. The greatest need for slaves was on the planets of the Reaches where automated factories had built up huge stockpiles of microchips immediately after the Collapse, and where a few of the production lines were still operable, capable of turning out chips optimized for specialized needs. Because of the Molts' genetic memory, the Feds could use the superb ancient facilities without having the least understanding of them.

"Mind, I don't blame him," Foster said, shouting to be heard over the Molts' chitinous moans. "The way these filthy animals fight and shove when we're only trying to help them would try the patience of a saint, and I don't claim sainthood for my boys."

"The slaves were grabbed up from maybe twenty worlds," Stephen said, a fraction of a second before he consciously knew he was going to speak. "All their normal clan and rank gradations were erased with their capture. They were brought here, packed in the holds of freighters with no light and too little to eat, shifted into these pens—which broke up any status relationships that might have started to form during the voyage—"

Stephen was speaking loudly of necessity; but though he didn't really intend it, he knew his voice had a mocking lilt sure to put the back up of anybody toward whom it was directed.

"—and then not fed at all for three days," he continued, "because the guards went haring off into the hills when they heard the pirates were coming. You know, if that happened to me, I might not be at my most civilized either."

"The only thing I would add to that, Stephen," Piet said, stepping between his friend and Major Foster, "is that the Molts are free now, not slaves. Before we leave Racine, they'll have weapons and a rudimentary social structure."

Piet smiled. "Quite apart from the justice of the matter," he added, "I think this will prove a better way to disrupt an evil Federation commerce than burning the city down would be."

The newly freed Molts spread to either side around the provisions. Most of them drank first, ducking their triangular heads into the troughs, then moved to the piles of foul-smelling yeast cakes to snatch food into their mouths. The aliens' metabolism was lower than that of similar-sized human beings, but their exoskeletal bodies didn't have a layer of subcutaneous fat for energy storage. Three days was very close to the point at which the slaves would have begun dying of hunger.

"I meant no disrespect to you, Mister Gregg," Major Foster said stiffly. His face was mottled with tight-held emotions. Like Piet, he wore only a helmet. Stephen's half armor increased his already considerable superiority in size. "If you'd care to treat the matter as one requiring satisfaction between gentlemen, however—"

"I wouldn't," Stephen said. He stepped sideways so that he could take Foster's right hand without pushing Piet out of the way. "I apologize, Major Foster. For my tone and for any negative implication that could have been drawn from my words."

The Molts ate with a clicking buzz like a whispered version of their speech. The sound was much slighter than that of the moans that preceded it. The relative silence was equivalent to that of drips falling from trees in the minutes following the passage of a deafening rainstorm.

Foster let his breath out with a rush. "That's very handsome of you, Mister Gregg," he said. "But there's no need for an apology, none at all. I just wanted to be clear that I intended no offense."

Foster had obviously thought he was about to be challenged to a duel by Mister Stephen Gregg, an event Foster expected would be short and fatal for himself. That wouldn't have prevented the soldier from accepting the challenge—he was a gentleman, after all, one of the Fosters of Solange—but the relief he felt at being given his life back was as clear as a desert sunrise.

Stephen shook his head in irritation at his own behavior. "Piet," he said, "we'd better find some Feds who want to fight soon. Or you're going to have to lock me away until we do. I don't—"

He squeezed Foster's hand again and released it. "I haven't been sleeping well, Major," he said. "I'm irritable. But that's no cause to take it out on an officer controlling his men as ably as yourself."

"When we start making sweeps of the surrounding territory, Mister Gregg," Foster said in an attempt to be supportive, "then I'm sure we'll all find our fill of action."

"Have you been to see the *Gallant Sallie* since our landing, Stephen?" Piet asked. His eyes held a friend's concern.

"Thanks, Piet," Stephen said. "But I think if you don't need me here just now, I'll go get myself something to drink."

Quite a lot to drink. Possibly enough that he'd be able to sleep without being awakened every few minutes by the cries of people he'd killed over the years.

RACINE

November 20, Year 26
1214 hours, Venus time

With Sal piloting, Brantling at the attitude-jet controls, and fif-teen soldiers aboard, the cutter was packed and sluggish. Sal spotted the farm in the valley a thousand meters below and started a shallow turn to starboard. Her first concern was not to collide with Tom Harrigan's cutter; her second, not to lose control and spin into the ground. Cutters weren't ideal for use in an atmosphere; they were simply what the squadron had available for the purpose.

If telling the soldiers what was going on had a place in her cal-culations, it was as a bad third. She didn't need Lieutenant Pringle hammering on her shoulder and shouting over the roar of the thruster, "There! Go back now! There's one of their farms!"

"Get back, damn you!" Sal said as she spun the wheel to adjust the nozzle angle. A cutter couldn't hover on its single thruster, but an expert pilot could use a combination of thrust and momen-tum to bring the craft down in light fluttering circles like a leaf falling.

The farm was situated in a swale several kilometers long, nar-row and steep-sided at the top but spreading wide at the shallow lower end. The farm buildings—house, barns, and the pentagonal

Molt quarters, all within a stone-walled courtyard—were at the
upper end. The sharp slope provided more shelter from the fierce
winds that swept Racine in spring and fall.

Sal caught sunlight winking from Harrigan's cutter as it slanted
toward the bare plains above the head of the swale. She hauled
her craft in the direction of the vegetated lower end.

Sal and Tom Harrigan had long experience maneuvering the bigger and equally cranky *Gallant Sallie* in atmospheres. As a result
they were among the pilots chosen for raids beyond New Windsor,
even though the boats and troops involved came from other, larger
vessels of the squadron.

"They're shooting!" Pringle cried. If he'd jogged her shoulder
again, she'd have taken a hand from the thruster's shuddering
control wheel and elbowed him in the throat. "Christ's *blood,* they'll
regret that!"

There were a dozen figures in the farm's courtyard. The cutter's
optics weren't good enough to show weapons, but flashes indicated some of the Feds were indeed shooting at Harrigan's cutter as it circled down nearby.

Sal raised her craft's nose for aerodynamic lift as they thundered
up the swale. Initially the vegetation was of crimson-leafed local
varieties, stunted to the height of moss by the winds of the month
before the squadron arrived. Closer to the buildings were fields
of some thick-stemmed grass, corn or sorghum. The cutter's plasma
exhaust shriveled the crop to either side and gouged a trench
through the soil.

A line of junipers planted along the courtyard wall screened the
buildings from the fields. Sal flared the thruster nozzle and brought
her cutter down just short of the trees. It was a landing any pilot
would have been proud of, given the load the cutter carried, but
soldiers cursed as the impact slammed them into their fellows and
the bulkheads.

The cutter's dorsal hatch had remained open throughout the
flight. The soldiers piled out, chivied by their lieutenant. Pringle,
in the far bow, couldn't reach the hatch until most of his men
had exited. Because they didn't expect serious opposition on patrols
like this, most of the troops wore only their helmets. Full armor
would have made it nearly impossible to board and debark from
a cutter's tight confinement.

Sal heard a soldier cry in pain; he'd probably fallen against a skid. A cutter's single small thruster didn't bake the ground to an oven the way a full-sized starship did, but the outriggers were exposed to the exhaust when the nozzle pivoted forward for landing. The bath of ions didn't damage the ceramic structure, but you didn't want to touch it till it had cooled for an hour, either.

Now that the thrusters were cold, Sal lifted the radio handset. "Cutter Blythe to base," she reported. She craned her neck to the side to shadow her navigational display so that she could read it. Daylight streaming through the open hatch washed out the self-luminous characters. "We and Cutter Harrigan have found Feds at vector three-three-one degrees, nineteen point three klicks from base."

She heard the faint popping of rifles at a distance, from or directed at Tom's men. "There's fighting going on. I don't know how serious it is."

She cleared her throat. Was that a proper report? She wasn't a soldier! "I don't think it's too serious. Out."

Brantling, holding a rifle from the *Gallant Sallie*'s arms locker, hopped to the cutter's upper deck. He shaded his eyes with his left hand to watch. The cutter's optical display showed a blurry image of Pringle and his men waddling toward the junipers.

Sal checked that her revolver was still in the flapped cross-draw holster along her left thigh. She swung herself to the deck just as Brantling jumped onto the ground well beyond the thruster's reach. Sal followed her crewman without letting herself think much about what she was doing.

Walking was harder than she'd expected. The soil was soft, and dark green leaves hid the furrows. Pringle called an order in a high-pitched voice. His soldiers pushed through the juniper hedge but halted at the waist-high wall beyond.

Most of the squadron's landsmen were combat veterans who'd fought against President Pleyal on Earth while serving in the Independent Coastal Republic. Only about half the troops were Venerians. Pringle was from Ishtar City, but from their accent and what she overheard of their conversation, most of the men under him were citizens of United Europe. A few of them shared the hatred of the Federation general among sailors from Venus, but for the most part the troops were fighting for pay and loot.

That was all right, so long as they fought.

Sal reached the wall and knelt between a pair of soldiers. One man rested his rifle on the cement coping; the other carried a

cutting bar and had a short-barreled shotgun dangling on a lanyard looped through his right epaulet. He gave Sal a gap-toothed
grin.

She peered over the wall, breathing hard. Juniper branches had
scratched her face, and her low-sided shipboard slippers were full
of sticky black dirt.

The stone house was forty meters away. A bullet ricocheted from
its roof, passing high overhead with a nervous *bwee-bwee-bwee.*
An unarmed man ran out the back door, followed by half a dozen
women and children. Four men with guns left the building last.

The Feds were looking over their shoulders toward where
Harrigan's cutter had landed. They were nearly to the stone wall
before one of the women looked up, saw the waiting Venerians,
and screamed. Pringle's order was drowned in the blast of shots.

All the Fed males went down, along with several women. Pellets
from the edge of a shotgun's pattern clawed the face of a 6-year-
old. He ran in circles, shrieking and spraying blood.

Pringle and his soldiers jumped over the wall and charged the
buildings. A Molt came out of the nearer barn. Brantling, running with the troops, shot and spun the alien. A shotgun blast from
one of the other cutter's men knocked the Molt sprawling.

Sal was alone in a haze of sweetish smoke. Ceramic cartridge
cases gleamed in the sunlight. The troops hadn't bothered to pick
the hulls up for reloading as they would during target practice.

Someone inside the farther barn screamed, but there were no
more shots. Soldiers from both cutters ran into the buildings. Sal
could glimpse them through the windows of the house.

The survivors of the Feds who'd run toward Pringle's men lay
flat among their dead and wounded. Two soldiers with cutting bars
guarded them. One of the troops had caught the wounded boy
and was applying a pressure bandage; the victim kicked and flailed
his arms in blind terror. Sal stepped over the wall to help. As she
did so, the boy went as flaccid as a half-filled bladder. He'd fainted,
or . . .

Sal jogged past the prisoners and into the house, so that she
wouldn't have to consider the other possibility for the moment.
The holstered revolver slapped her thigh as she moved.

There was a dead man in the kitchen, decapitated by a cutting
bar. Wisps of his white beard, sawn by the same stroke, drifted
in the air. There was blood over everything.

The living room beyond was a tangle of bedding and overturned furniture that several soldiers were searching with their cutting bars. The farm had obviously taken in refugees from New Windsor; maybe relatives, maybe not.

A whining bar slashed a cushion to fuzz. The stroke continued toward Sal's head. She ducked. It looked like simple vandalism to her, but perhaps the soldiers knew what they were doing.

She started up the stairs to get away from the troops' enthusiasm. A plasma thruster blatted unexpectedly. A cutter hopped the wall at low level and landed in the courtyard. Reinforcements sent because of her report, she supposed. There was room for a good pilot to land without hurting anybody on the ground, but he'd better have been good.

A woman screamed in the room at the top of the stairs. The door was ajar. Sal flung it open with her left hand. The panel bounced back from Lieutenant Pringle's shoulder. He stepped aside so that Sal could enter.

She'd tried to draw her revolver. She only managed to get the holster flap unbuttoned before she saw that there was no danger.

Two soldiers held the fully clothed woman they'd dragged from piled bedding in which she'd tried to conceal herself. The captive was about Sal's age, swarthy and terrified. "Not a treasure in chips," Pringle said cheerfully, "but she should provide some entertainment."

The woman's dress was a shiny orange synthetic fabric. One of the soldiers tried to rip it at the neckline and only managed to jerk the captive's head forward. She continued to scream.

"Let her go!" Sal said. She looked at Pringle. "Make them let her go at once!"

The second soldier put his free hand beside his comrade's. They pulled in opposite directions. The dress tore all the way down the front. The bandeau beneath was so loose that one of the woman's full breasts flopped out.

"You needn't watch," Pringle said coolly. "They shot at us, so they ought to know what to expect."

One soldier caught both the woman's wrists in one hand. He flung her backward onto the bed when his partner kicked her legs from beneath her.

"Stop that!" Sal said. Pringle stepped in front of her. She backed and drew the revolver.

"Listen, you whore!" Pringle shouted. "If you don't want to find yourself spread-eagled beside her, you'd better—"

He moved forward. Sal couldn't shoot him in cold blood.

"Tom!" she screamed. She raised the revolver's muzzle and fired three shots into the ceiling as fast as she could pull the trigger. The blasts were deafening in the enclosure. Bits of shattered lath from the ceiling exploded across the room. One of the bullets bounced back from the roof slates and buried itself in the window ledge.

The two soldiers jumped up from their captive. Pringle grabbed Sal's wrist. He punched her in the jaw with his free hand. "Stupid whore!" he shouted.

Sal's world went white and buzzing. She sagged until Pringle let go of her wrist; then she fell to the floor. She could hear voices, but they were ten decibels weaker than they'd been a moment before.

Stephen Gregg stepped into the bedroom. He held his flashgun to his shoulder. Pringle dropped the revolver he'd twisted from Sal's grip.

More men followed Stephen, too many for the available space. "I gave orders against rape," said Piet Ricimer as he knelt beside Sal. "Mister Dole, all three of these men are to be confined in close arrest. I'll try them later this evening."

"Sir, I . . ." Pringle said. "We . . ."

Ricimer put an arm under Sal's shoulders. "Can you move?" he asked.

She could hear normally. When she raised her torso with Ricimer's help, her eyes focused again also. "I'm all right," she said, hating the wobble in her voice.

Stephen said, "Dole? Hold this." He handed his heavy flashgun to the bosun.

"Look!" Pringle said. "This is—"

Stephen slapped him with his open hand. The sound was as loud as a revolver shot. Pringle flew across the room, hit the far wall, and fell onto the bed from which the Fed woman had just risen.

Pringle's cheek was a mass of blood where his teeth had cut him from the inside. His lower jaw hung loose.

Stephen's face was as white as old bone. He took the flashgun back from Dole without looking away from the bleeding officer.

NEW WINDSOR, RACINE

November 25, Year 26

0811 hours, Venus time

The thousands of soldiers and sailors were too many for Commandatura Square in the center of New Windsor, so Piet had decided to use the gate arch of a Molt pen for the gibbet. Stephen stood at Piet's side, looking out at the expressions of the assembled men: some angry, some worried, some obviously drunk. All of them grim, as grim as the task itself.

"We'll make our landfall in the Reaches at Castalia," Piet said quietly. At the other gate support, Pringle was kneeling in prayer with the flagship's chaplain. "It's a Molt world, but the Molts are organized in small bands of migratory hunters, very unusual for them. They're too sparsely settled and too dangerous for the Feds to make slaving expeditions there. I'm not worried about us being discovered, though we'll keep a guardship in orbit at all times."

Dole and a detail of armed sailors guarded the two men taken with Pringle. One of the soldiers had a greenish pallor and looked as though he might faint.

"Rather than directly to Arles?" Stephen said. He didn't really care where they went next. The future was a gray blur, punctuated by flashes of screaming red.

"I'd like to have a base to reconnoiter before we hit Arles," Piet explained. "Besides, it'll be a long voyage. We have to expect it to take twenty days since there's so many ships to keep together, and we certainly won't make it in less than fifteen. The soldiers won't have much stomach left after so many transits."

"The soldiers won't be alone," Stephen said with a wan smile. He could no more learn to be comfortable when his whole body seemed to turn inside out during transit than he could have learned to be comfortable with a sunburn. The experience was simply one to be borne for however long was necessary.

Pringle stood up. His face was pale but composed. Dole looked at Piet. Piet nodded, and the crowd gave a collective sigh.

"Several of the warehouses here are full of the metal ingots the Feds use for trade with the Molts," Piet murmured. He was talking about the future to avoid thinking about the immediate present. "We'll carry a sufficiency of them to buy peace with the Castalian tribes for the short time we'll be staying."

Dole tossed a rope with an ordinary slipknot in the end over the crossbar of the gate. Two of his squad were fitting a canvas hood over Pringle's head. They walked the officer over to Dole. The bosun snugged the loop around Pringle's neck and handed the free end of the rope to the soldiers convicted of attempted rape—and sentenced to execute judgment on the officer who'd egged them on.

Piet took the bullhorn from Guillermo, who stood on his other side. "Men of my command," he said. "Soldiers of God."

He paused. The ships in the spaceport beyond reflected faint echoes of his words.

"We are here to defeat the tyrant Pleyal who sets himself up as a rival to God," Piet said. His voice had the full, rich tone he used to lead assemblies in prayer. "If we act like beasts, then our Lord, in Whose sole help we trust, will desert us and leave us to die like beasts of the field."

The breath of the crowd soughed like a low, sad breeze. Sal Blythe was there somewhere. Stephen couldn't make out her face, and he didn't really want to. Not here, not now.

"I would rather undergo any torture myself than to permit that to happen by my own inaction!" Piet shouted. He threw down the bullhorn and said crisply to the pair of soldiers, "Carry out your duties."

The soldiers pulled on the rope, grunting to lift Pringle hand over hand. Dole hadn't bothered to hang a pulley, so the crossbar's friction was added to the weight of the man gurgling under the hood. A sailor in the front rank of the assembly fell on his face before his neighbors could grab him.

One of the executioners wept as he staggered forward, trying to haul briskly. Both of them had their backs to the man they were strangling. Pringle's legs kicked out wildly. His arms were tied behind his back to prevent him from climbing up the noose.

Dole judged height and distance, shrugged, and tied the rope off to the support beside Piet, Stephen, and Guillermo. "All right," the bosun said gruffly to the executioners. "You two have done your job. Go put something on your hands before the rope burns get infected."

Pringle thrashed. His body spun on the single strand like a fly caught by a jumping spider. Occasionally he was able to draw enough breath to make the hood flutter.

"For *Christ's* sake!" Stephen said. "Doesn't he have any friends? Are they going to leave him to choke for the next five minutes?"

"If he had any friends, Stephen," Piet said in a voice as gray as a millstone, "they'd be afraid of what you might do if they ended this."

"*Christ,*" said Stephen Gregg. The word was as close to a prayer as he'd spoken since he first voyaged to the Reaches.

He stepped forward, caught the hanging man's leg at the knee, and jerked down with all his strength.

Pringle's neck popped like a twig breaking, severing the spinal cord and finishing him without further pain.

CASTALIA

December 15, Year 26
0250 hours, Venus time

The truck Sal had borrowed from the *Wrath* was more of a powered bed frame with an open cab. It lurched as one or more of
the six driven wheels dropped into a hole concealed by vegetation matted by earlier traffic. The jolts weren't dangerous; the truck
was designed to carry heavy loads under much worse conditions.
If a starship had bounced around that way, though, it would be
on the verge of crashing or disintegration. Sal's jaw had been set
and her knuckles white within a minute of when she started driving
toward the *Sandringham* and the guarded trading station on the
edge of the forest beside the vessel.

The savannah's yellowish vegetation grew in flat stems forming coils up to two meters off the ground. The mass looked like
a tangle of razor ribbon but the stems weren't any stronger than
grass blades. A vehicle crushed them down, and a man could force
his way through without a machete or cutting bar if he had to.

Four similar trucks were parked in the clearing that plasma had
seared to the red soil when the starship landed. Sal still couldn't
see the guard post. She stopped beside the *Sandringham* and shut
off her loudly ringing ceramic diesel so that she could hear. Three

sailors who'd watched Sal approach from the starship's hatch said nothing.

"Is Mister Gregg here?" Sal called. "Stephen!"

Captain Wohlman had landed the *Sandringham* on the edge of the forest, almost a klick from the site the general commander designated and several hundred meters from the nearest of the squadron's other vessels. Wohlman wasn't exceptionally skillful even during his intervals of sobriety, and the *Sandringham*'s electronics were in a class with those of the *Gallant Sallie* before her refit.

Piet Ricimer had made virtue of necessity by establishing the *Sandringham* as the contact point with the local Molts. The trading post protected the outlying vessel and made it clear to the aliens that they weren't to approach the rest of the squadron.

Ricimer hadn't chewed Wohlman out for his bad landing, but the captain was by his own action isolated in a dangerous spot. So, of course, were his men. Sal figured they had a right to be surly, but they didn't need to take it out on her.

"I said—" she said, rising in the open cab. Yellow-gray foliage quivered at the corner of her eye. She reached for her revolver. Stephen stepped out, cradling the flashgun he favored.

"Stephen!" Sal cried. "Ah, Mister Gregg."

"Stephen," he said with a smile. He reached into the cab and spun the large wing nut securing the wheel to the steering column. "I don't want this to wander away," he said, pulling the wheel off one-handed. The trucks didn't have starter locks, but there were other basic security arrangements.

Stephen looked up at the three sullen crewmen. He smiled again, a very different expression from the one with which he greeted Sal.

"I wanted to see the forest," she said as she jumped from the truck.

"We've got a party of Molts," Stephen said. He handed her the steering wheel so that he was free to use the flashgun. "You can see them and the forest. And me."

The guard post was a long shed with roof and walls—rolled up, since it wasn't raining—of plastic sheeting, hung on a frame of local wood. The post was only twenty meters from the edge of the oval the *Sandringham*'s exhaust had cleared, but the vegetation had sprung back to hide the path completely.

Fifty or so troops stood nearby. They wore half armor and had their weapons ready, but they didn't appear nervous. Three more landsmen, technicians rather than line soldiers, sat at a humming console beneath the shed. They looked up from their screens, nodded to Stephen—one looked at Sal with speculation—and went back to their duties.

"We can pick up a Molt's footfalls a thousand meters out," Stephen explained in a quiet voice. "Closer in we can vector on airborne noise as well, though—"

He grinned. She didn't remember having seen Stephen so . . . relaxed wasn't the word, but perhaps cheerful.

"—if they come hand over hand through the tree branches, there could be a problem before we sort things out."

Stephen was genuinely glad to see her.

Captain Casson and two of his officers squatted with Guillermo at the tree line, facing four of the local Molts. The locals' exoskeletons were cloudy gray. The color looked sickly to a human, but the soft sheen of wax over the chitin indicated the creatures were in good health. Three-kilo ingots of aluminum and rust-streaked iron were stacked on a pallet behind Casson.

"There's twenty more of them in the forest," Stephen said. "They've got bows with arrows nearly two meters long. I wouldn't think that was practical. According to what the Feds who've landed here report—the survivors report—the Molts know what they're doing well enough."

One of the four Molts visible was easily twice the size of his fellows and weighed at least 150 kilos. The giant held a mace with a triangular stone head, the only weapon visible among the delegation.

"The big one's the chief?" Sal said.

"The chief's companion," Stephen said. "Just a tool, really. I wouldn't want to meet him hand to hand. Though I don't suppose he'd like that either."

His tone was soft. Sal expected his lips to twist into the terrible grin she'd seen there before, but instead Stephen gave the Molt bodyguard a wry but honest smile. "I wonder if they're friends, he and his chief," he said.

Casson handed an ingot to a Molt. The Molt scraped a chitinous fingertip across the soft aluminum, then passed the ingot to one of his fellows.

Trees rose like giant bristles from the margin of the savannah.

Instead of rounded surfaces, the trunks were sharply triangular in cross section as if their growth had been crystalline rather than organic. Limbs spiked out in clusters of three. The boles and branches were gray. The foliage that flared like a pattern of giant fans a hundred meters in the air was a yellow similar to that of the ground cover.

"You slapped Lieutenant Pringle," Sal said in a voice no one but the pair of them could have heard. "Instead of . . ."

Stephen snorted. He wasn't looking at her. "I have better things to do than break my knuckles," he said in a tone as thin as a knifeblade. "Shooting him . . . shooting him would have been murder. You have to have control."

His face was frozen, horrible. "Control is what sets human beings apart from the beasts, you know."

The Molt tribesmen were now examining an iron ingot. Three of them were, that is. The giant's lidless eyes were fixed on Stephen. Just watching.

"Stephen," Sal said. "If there wasn't a war, what would you do?"

In a bleak voice Stephen said, "If I had *no* purpose in life, you mean? Well, I don't think I need to worry about that. There'll never be a time that men exist and there's no war."

"There's more to you than that!" Sal said. Casson looked back with a scowl. She hadn't meant to shout.

She tugged Stephen a few steps down the path to where the vegetation screened them. Soldiers watched sidelong, but none of them were willing to look directly at Stephen at this moment.

"Listen to me!" Sal said in an angry whisper. "You're still human. Just as human as the ones who haven't faced what you've faced. You've got a soul!"

When the muscles of Stephen's cheeks relaxed, he looked like a wholly different person. "You know, Sal," he said liltingly. It was the first time he'd called her "Sal." "Late at night, I believe in God. A just God would put a person who'd done the things I've done in Hell."

Sal wanted to look away from his eyes, but she forced herself to meet them.

"And that's just what He's done," said Stephen Gregg.

CASTALIA

December 18, Year 26
1704 hours, Venus time

Sunrise on Castalia sent streaks of purple and violet streaming out of the clouds on the eastern horizon. Flying creatures mounted in vast spirals from communal burrows in the savannah. The scales on their wings caught light in jeweled splendor as they rose.

Already most of the captains of the twenty vessels on the ground stood with specialists in the flagship's ample port-side boarding hold. Wohlman, red-faced and puffing with exertion, was jogging the last hundred meters to the open hatch.

Stephen had never known Piet to miss consulting his officers on matters of general importance. Neither did he recall a time when Piet failed to make the final decision himself, whatever the sense of the assembly.

"Please, you aren't going to leave me here, are you?" whimpered Bowersock, the captain of the local-area freighter that a squadron featherboat had captured above Arles. "The bugs here are cannibals; they *eat* men."

"Shut up, you!" Dole said. He jerked up on the prisoner's hands, tied behind his back.

Piet, Guillermo, and a technician knelt on the pair of cargo

631

pallets that formed a low dais for the council of war. They were making adjustments to the hologram projector that the Molt would operate while Piet spoke.

"It's no more cannibalism for a Molt to eat you, Bowersock," Stephen said quietly, "than it is for me to eat a crayfish. But if you keep your mouth shut like the bosun says, you'll probably be released in your own ship."

"That slopbucket's not worth us taking, that's for sure, Mister Gregg," Dole agreed with a nod.

Bowersock was present as window dressing. Though he was the titular captain of the prize, he didn't know the landing codes for Arles or the other planets among which his vessel shuttled. Bowersock left that and everything else involved in running the ship to the three Molts of his crew.

One of the Molts spoke Trade English. She'd been more than happy to give the Venerians the information they needed—after Guillermo assured her that she wouldn't be left on Castalia either. Bowersock was right about one thing: the local tribes *were* cannibals. Very likely they were also willing to eat humans they happened to catch.

Sal Blythe sat cross-legged on one of the pistons that raised and lowered the hatch/ramp. She smiled at Stephen in friendly awareness, nothing unprofessional. Sal hadn't come forward to chat when she arrived for the council, the way he'd thought she might.

Stephen smiled back.

Captain Wohlman clomped up the ramp. He'd slept in his uniform, perhaps for several days. Piet turned from the projector and said, "Captain Wohlman, captains all. The featherboat *Praisegod* has returned from Arles with current images and a vessel captured above the planet. I've called you to discuss what these developments mean for our plans."

"Doesn't that mean we've already put the wind up the Feds?" Captain Kotzwinkle demanded. He was one of Casson's cronies, though a generation younger and not nearly so experienced. Not a bad navigator, Piet said; and Piet wasn't a charitable judge of such things.

Salomon of the *Praisegod* bent forward to glare at Kotzwinkle. Before either man could speak, Piet said, "The prize's linear amp is burned out. The Fed captain"—Piet nodded to call attention to Bowersock—"confirms that they hadn't been able to reach port control in three orbits and were about to land without making contact."

Stephen stared over the head of the Fed captain at Kotzwinkle. Salomon had sailed with Piet and Stephen before; had saved their lives and an expedition at least once by his quick action. Kotzwinkle was a pimple to be popped if he became troublesome. . . .

"However, he also says the Feds throughout the Reaches have been warned to expect our squadron," Piet said. Guillermo projected into the air beside Piet a holographic view of a city of several thousand buildings and the adjacent spaceport.

"This is Savoy, the capital of Arles," he continued. "According to Captain Salomon's prisoners, the news had been received three weeks ago when their vessel last touched down there."

"There's treachery on Venus for that to happen!" said a military officer with a guttural European accent.

"Very likely," Piet said, "but that's a matter for the governor and such as Councilor Duneen to attend to. What concerns us is merely the immediate situation."

Guillermo expanded the image of the port, crowding all but the margin of Savoy City out of the frame. Stephen watched intently, though he'd gone over the imagery with Piet in private as soon as the *Praisegod* landed.

For the most part, featherboats had optics as rudimentary as those of cutters. Piet himself owned and had equipped the *Praisegod*, with the plan of using her to scout target sites. This view was as sharp as any image taken through twenty klicks of air could be, and the projector's enhancement program ironed out atmospheric ripples and distortions.

There were forty-three vessels in the port area, none of them large or heavily armed. Piet guessed the assembly was regional shipping, collected here under the guns of the port for protection from the Venerian squadron.

The guns were the main focus of Stephen's consideration. Savoy's Commandatura was on the west side of the port, adjacent to the berm surrounding the reservation. Each of the building's four corners had a turret containing a heavy plasma cannon, 15-cm or better. A second four-gun position stood on the east side of the port, two kilometers from the Commandatura.

All eight guns were run out and elevated when Salomon took the images. That didn't absolutely prove that the weapons were loaded and their crews alert, but any sane attack plan would have to presume so.

"The crew of the prize has provided us with the identification codes for Arles," Piet continued. "God willing, there shouldn't be serious difficulty in landing one of our smaller vessels with troops aboard. We'll have to come in near daybreak or sunset, where the ceramic construction of a Venerian craft won't be evident."

"That's a terrible plan," Captain Casson said bluntly. "It's not a plan at all. There's two forts, don't you see?"

"We can't land two ships together; that'd alert them surer than blowing a siren," Kotzwinkle said.

"This is a job for guns, not men!" Casson said. "For good Venerian ordnance. Land the whole squadron together before they know what's happening, then blow them to splinters with point-blank gunfire!"

"The fighting ships, you mean, Captain Casson," Bowersock said in hopeful clarification.

"The fighting *captains,* Bowersock," Casson thundered. "I wouldn't expect to see the *Sandringham* land till the fight was over."

The council dissolved into a blur of discussions between neighbors and simultaneous attempts to gain the floor. The walls of the boarding hold weren't baffled, so echoes magnified the chaos.

Piet gestured to Guillermo. The Molt's console emitted a *bleep-whoop* attention signal not quite loud enough to be painful. Conversation stopped.

"Mister Gregg," said Piet formally, "would you care to give your view, as the expedition's military chief?"

"Yes, I would," Stephen said, stepping onto the dais. He'd also have liked to see how far he could stuff Casson and Kotzwinkle's heads up one another's ass, but there would be no sign of that in his voice. He would be calm.

"If you'll expand the view of the Commandatura, Guillermo . . ." he said. Before the request was complete, the image of the building's roof and four turrets increased tenfold.

"The defenses are intended for use against ships in the air or in orbit above Savoy," Stephen said. He used his left index finger as a pointer. The air-formed hologram shimmered as his hand interrupted the line of one of the projectors. "The other position is the same. Only the two inner gun turrets can bear on vessels actually on the ground within the port reservation. The inner turrets and the mass of the building itself block the other pairs of guns until a ship is above, say, two hundred meters."

"Just what I said!" Casson said. "When we're on the ground, only half their guns can even bear on us!"

"I don't recall you saying anything so foolish, Captain," Stephen said, his voice an octave lighter and snapping like a whip. "My point, of course, is that we can't fire on four of the Fed guns once we're on the ground. *Those* positions would have to be carried by ground assault. Otherwise they'd quite certainly destroy any ship attempting to take off again."

Stephen tapped the air over the western pair of turrets. The image dissolved, then re-formed as he stepped away. "If I'm going to attack a fortress, I'd rather do it by surprise than after an hour or so of fireworks have alerted the defenders."

Stephen stared at Captain Casson without expression. "I hope nobody feels that makes me a coward."

Casson's face went blotchy red. He took a step forward. Kotzwinkle and two other nearby officers grabbed the old man and dragged him back by main force.

"Hellfire!" Stephen whispered. He shivered in self-loathing for what he'd just tried to precipitate. He'd promised himself that he wouldn't lose control . . .

He hadn't lost control. He coldly and with consideration had done a thing that endangered the expedition more than any action of President Pleyal.

"Casson, I apologize," Stephen said. He looked at Piet. "I apologize," he repeated. "Piet, just put me close to the enemy."

"Captain Casson put his finger on the problem," Piet said smoothly. His voice was slightly louder than before, to drown the heavy breathing of Casson and his fellows. "We can only land one ship without causing alarm, and the forts are widely separated."

Piet and Guillermo had choreographed this part of the presentation. "I believe the way around the problem is to land here," Piet continued, extending an index finger. The eastern edge of the reservation, including the berm and gun tower, appeared just beyond the fingertip.

"We'll use a small freighter, a vessel that won't arouse concern," Piet said. The scale of the image rose to encompass the entire port area again. "The cabin will be packed with troops. The hold will contain a landing barge that's also full of troops. As soon as the freighter touches down, the barge will launch under full power, cross the reservation, and land on the roof of the Commandatura."

The council broke into at least a dozen animated discussions. Stephen heard a military officer say to Captain Salomon, "How many men does a barge hold, anyway? Will that be—"

"I'll be in command of the barge's contingent," Stephen said in a loud, calm voice. "I'm expecting a team of eighteen men in half armor. I believe that will be ample for the purpose."

"May I request to lead the cabin party!" shouted Major Cardiff. He was young for his rank at 25, but from reports he'd seen almost continuous action for the past ten years. Cardiff bowed to Stephen. "Under your overall command, of course, sir," he said.

Stephen looked at Piet and raised an eyebrow in interrogation.

Piet shrugged. "I wouldn't think of interfering with your choice of troops for the operation, Stephen," he said.

"I'd be glad to have you, Major," Stephen said, returning Cardiff's bow. What was it about men that made them crave chances to die?

Sal Blythe dropped her feet firmly to the deck. "The *Gallant Sallie* has a full-length hatch," she said over the buzz of general conversation starting to pick up again. "I'll take the assault force down with her."

There was dead silence.

"Thank you for the offer, Captain," Piet said. "I'd like to discuss the matter with your co-owner before I make a decision, though."

"I am the vessel's captain, with full authority to determine her usage!" Sal said. "Under your overall command, of course, sir."

"Stephen?" Piet said.

Stephen Gregg shook his head in amusement, not denial. He chuckled. The world, the universe, was all mad. "Piet, I don't have anything to tell you about how to deploy ships. Nobody in this room does."

Piet nodded crisply. "Captain Blythe, I have full confidence in your piloting skills. The *Gallant Sallie* is a perfectly suitable choice for the mission."

He bowed to the assembly. "Gentlemen, thank you for your attention and advice. The council is dismissed for now. I expect to summon you in the near future to discuss specific assignments."

Piet waited two beats and added, "Will the three officers directly involved in the assault please join me in my cabin for a moment now?"

Talk and the tramp of boots on the hold's hard deck raised a screen of noise. Kotzwinkle threw a glance over his shoulder as he accompanied Casson out the hatchway, but the old captain himself walked stiff-backed in anger.

Sal and Major Cardiff were making their way forward. Stephen leaned close to Piet's ear and said, "Are you learning to delegate?"

"About not taking the *Gallant Sallie* in myself, you mean?" Piet said with an elfin smile. "Well, I'm an able pilot, Stephen; but I can't very well pilot the freighter and the barge both, can I?"

APPROACHING SAVOY PORT, ARLES

January 1, Year 27
1027 hours, Venus time

Federation vessels tended to land fast and hard. Their thrusters and attitude jets weren't in condition to make the sort of perfectly balanced set-downs a Venus skipper strove for. That was especially true of the shoddy, locally built ships that carried the Feds' cargoes within the Reaches.

"There's no danger," Sal warned, "but stand by for a rough ride!" She signaled Brantling, in the hold wearing a hard suit, by turning the light above his hatch control panel from red to green. After Brantling started the hatch cycle, he'd step into the passage between hold and cabin.

The *Gallant Sallie*'s crew had rigged a pair of loudspeakers in the cabin's back corners. Without amplification, the desperately nervous infantry couldn't have heard Sal's reassurance from the navigation console because of the thrusters and atmospheric hammering.

There were twenty-eight troops in their armor, clinging to heavy fiberglass ropes rigged as temporary stanchions. The interior of the cabin had been gutted to hold the men. The normal stores, gear, and plasma cannon had been transferred to the *Mount Ida* along with most of Sal's crew.

This one was neck or nothing.

To look like local traffic, Sal had to drop the *Gallant Sallie* faster through the dawn than she wanted to do. The slamming deceleration that would come two hundred meters up would flatten the troops, ropes or no. There was always the possibility that somebody would flail his armored fist through the attitude controls for all that Harrigan and his men could do to stop it.

"There's no danger!" Sal repeated. The *Gallant Sallie* bobbled like a float in a waterjet as the cargo hatch started to open.

The hatch had to be raised during approach so that the barge could exit the instant the *Gallant Sallie* touched ground. Sal, Tom Harrigan, and Captain Ricimer himself had viewed the ship, discussed stresses, and designed a thruster program for the AI. They'd made sure the maneuver wouldn't either tear off the hatch in the airstream or flip the ship into the ground upside down.

Stephen had then brought up something that none of the spacers would have thought of: when the hatch opened, the infantry would think the ship was about to come apart.

The troops were all brave men, volunteers for the expedition and picked volunteers to be in this forlorn hope under Major Cardiff; but they were landsmen, and the courage to charge a battery of plasma cannon doesn't necessarily prevent panic at the idea of dropping kilometers after a ceramic ball shatters around you. If the men weren't kept informed, there could be a wild-eyed berserk in the cabin at a delicate time.

Thus the prebriefings, the loudspeakers, and the reassurance. Eventually everything breaks, and it isn't as easy to calculate the stresses on a mind as on a hinge joint.

"We're nearing the ground!" Sal said. "There'll be heavy braking in a moment, but we'll set down gently!"

There were no other ships near the gun tower. Half a dozen vessels—probably scrapped hulls—were clustered in the northeast corner some distance away.

Over the years, several Federation freighters had come down east of the berm and the stabilized soil of the port reservation. Only the upper curves of their hulls were now visible, like whales broaching from the bog. The crew of the gun tower wouldn't like seeing a ship wobble down so close to them, wreathed in the flaring brilliance of her exhaust, but neither would they be surprised.

The Commandatura was three stories high, the tallest building in Savoy. The vertical tubes of the four big guns on its roof gleamed in the dawn like stellite smokestacks.

Full-bore thrust roared from the *Gallant Sallie*'s nozzles. The soldiers remained standing for a moment, braced against one another and the bulkheads as well gripping the cables. Exhaust reflected from the approaching ground caught the hatch like an open flap and jerked the ship violently around its bow-to-stern axis. Everybody went down in a clatter of weapons and ceramic armor.

The *Gallant Sallie*'s outriggers touched raggedly. Her thrust had pitted the ground into dimpled mounds. "We're—" Sal shouted.

Rickalds (who'd fallen also; anybody standing would have fallen) was opening the outer cabin hatch. Armored soldiers got to their feet, aware that they'd reached the ground and now everything was up to them.

The *Gallant Sallie* lurched, her port outrigger coming a handsbreadth off the ground as the blast of a thruster from within her hold lifted her. The barge was away, a blaze of iridescence crosshatched on Sal's screen to save the eyes of the viewer.

Go with God, Stephen.

SAVOY, ARLES

January 1, Year 27
1031 hours, Venus time

The barge wasn't a handy craft, but its full-span dorsal hatch could be removed—had been removed before they shipped the little vessel aboard the *Gallant Sallie*—and both sides flopped down to ease unloading on the ground.

Stephen crouched slightly against the buffeting airstream at the starboard front of the cargo compartment, watching the Commandatura loom over the bow. He'd lowered his helmet visor, and he carried the flashgun beneath the compartment's lip. The wind catching the broad muzzle would try to snatch the weapon out of his hands.

Stephen could have fired his flashgun through the turbulence if he'd had to; fired and hit his target, as he'd done more times than he could remember when he was awake. He'd known for a decade, now, that whatever controlled his muscles when he was killing wasn't human.

They were dropping toward the Commandatura. A long plume of glowing ions and dust lifting from the ground marked their course across the spaceport. The barge's low arc from the freighter's hold peaked fifty meters in the air, halfway to their objective.

Officers on the ships below would be screaming at what they thought was a dangerous stunt . . .

A Molt stood on the building's roof watching them. In a moment the alien would cry an alarm; in another moment the barge would crash down among the gun turrets and it would be too late for any alarm.

The Molt was as good as dead. He'd be shot if he survived the flare of the barge's exhaust. Stephen wouldn't kill him, but one of the men beside him would.

Stephen wouldn't kill the Molt because there was no need. There would be plenty of other killing in the next moments, fully justified by the circumstances.

The barge bucked, lifted. For an instant Stephen thought they'd been hit by some preternaturally alert guard, but it was only Piet raising the bow for aerodynamic braking. A huge doughnut of plasma flared about the lower hull, momentarily concealing the roof to the level of the cannon muzzles. The landing skids hit with a crash—speed over delicacy, and barges *did* handle like pigs, even with Piet Ricimer at the controls.

"Get 'em!" Dole bawled as he dropped the sides of the cargo compartment. The assault force, Mister Stephen Gregg and seventeen members of the *Wrath*'s B Watch close-combat team, were out before the side panels had bounced.

Stephen hit the roof running. His repeating carbine, despite its tight sling, clashed against the left side of his breastplate. The trap door in the middle of the roof was open; so were the side hatches of the three gun positions Stephen could see as he ran for the stairs.

Dole was in command on the roof. There were three men for each gun position, to take them *now* because the first ships of the squadron would be landing within a minute. The job of Mister Stephen Gregg, with Giddings and Lewis to load for him and three men more as a security detail, was to find the fire director somewhere within the building and destroy it. To destroy everything that got in their way.

A man—a human being in white with some gold braid on his shoulders—started out of the trap door just as Stephen reached it. The flashgun wasn't the choice for point-blank, but it was in Stephen's hands and he fired. The laser bolt drained the battery in the gun butt in a single pulse. The Fed's torso absorbed the enormous energy and exploded in the steam of his own blood.

He'd been a young man with a delicate mustache.

Stephen tossed the flashgun behind him. Giddings should be there with a satchel of batteries. If not, there was no time to worry about empty weapons now.

The stairs were steep. Stephen unslung the carbine and was throwing up the visor that had darkened to save his vision from the flashgun's intense glare. He didn't have a hand free for the balustrade. His boots slipped midway in fluids spewed from the corpse, and he bounced down the remainder of the steps on his buttocks, backplate, and helmet.

He didn't lose the carbine, didn't even lose his rough point of aim. A Molt stood in the middle of the hallway, blinking his side-moving eyelids at the sudden events. Stephen shot the creature through the center of the chest by reflex. He didn't have time for decisions now, only points of aim.

There were half a dozen small offices on the left side of the hallway. None of their lights were on. Several doors were ajar the way the staff had left them at the close of the previous workday.

The three offices on the right side were larger. Two were closed and dark save for the warmth of dawn blushing from their outside windows onto the frosted glass doors. The Molt had come from the third, near the main stairs at the far end of the hall.

Shots and the scream of a bar cutting something harder than bone sounded from the roof. Stephen's squad came down the stairs as he had, slipping and crashing. Lightbody fired his shotgun into the hallway ceiling. On a bad day, your own people could be more dangerous than the Feds.

A female Molt—female, because her ovipositor was half extended—stepped from the office doorway and knelt over the stiff body of the male. Stephen grabbed her by the hard-shelled neck and shouted, "Where's the fire director?"

"What is a fire director, master?" the Molt said. Her fingers delicately caressed the bullet hole in the dead alien's carapace.

"The gun controls!" Stephen said. "The guns on the roof!"

Lightbody leaned over the stairwell and fired the second barrel of his shotgun toward a lower floor. Calwell and Brody were knocking open office doors, though what they expected to find there was beyond Stephen.

"Master, the data lines to the cannon on the roof come from

the port operations room in the basement of the building," the Molt said.

"Basement!" Stephen shouted as he let her go.

A bullet from below blew splinters and plaster out of the railing where Lightbody'd fired a moment before. Stephen pivoted onto the top tread. Three white-jacketed Feds stood at the base of the stairs. Two pointed weapons; the third was reloading her rifle.

Stephen shot the man with the shotgun. The second man fired into the railing to Stephen's left and Stephen killed him also, head shots out of habit though these targets weren't wearing body armor; most Feds didn't.

Stephen pumped the lever to shuck another round into his chamber. The head of the empty case cracked, and the carbine jammed. Lightbody smashed the third Fed to the floor with a charge of buckshot, then shot her again as she twitched.

"Rifle!" Stephen shouted as he tossed the carbine back. Lewis thrust forward a loaded weapon. Stephen gripped it like a pistol as he took the stairs three at a time, controlling his descent with his left hand on the balustrade. He couldn't afford to fall on his ass now.

The building's second floor was a bullpen of slanted desks and narrow benches designed for the utility if not comfort of Molt clerks. Several of the aliens stood against the wall at the far end of the room, as motionless as painted targets. Stephen ignored them.

Did Molts cry? Surely they grieved. The Molt he'd killed on the third floor was a motion in a hostile building. There'd been no time for a Stephen Gregg to do other than shoot.

The Commandatura had a small barracks on the ground floor, facing the arched street entrance. The guards were probably more for ceremony than function, but the three who'd run upstairs at the sound of gunfire had been alert if not particularly skillful.

Two rifles fired at Stephen midway down the last flight of stairs. The staircase here was real stone, not paint on lath and plaster. One bullet shattered a bannister into pebbles and dust. The other ricocheted from Stephen's breastplate, knocking him back a step and tearing his left biceps with a spray of impact-melted lead.

"Flashgun!" he shouted, but he had the powerful repeater to his shoulder and was firing already when the bullet hit him. The repeater was a lovely weapon with a slide working a glass-smooth

European action, but when Stephen emptied the rotary magazine
he tossed the weapon behind him to be caught or to fall.

There was no time for tools, only for killing. He took the
reloaded flashgun.

A dead guard lay half out the barracks doorway. The door itself
was metal and thick enough to bounce Lightbody's buckshot off
in a bright smear against the panel. It would probably turn rifle
bullets also, but Calwell and Brody were shooting through the high
ground-floor windows at civilians in the street, and Stephen's own
rounds had all gone through the crack in the door.

Somebody out of sight in the barracks was tugging the corpse
out of the way to close the panel. Stephen flopped down his visor
and fired the flashgun through the opening into the Charge-of-
Quarters' wooden desk.

The desk exploded in a fireball that would have hurled blazing fragments twenty meters in every direction if there'd been
enough open space around it. A Fed ran out of the room screaming. Lightbody killed her before Giddings could slap the carbine,
cleared and reloaded, into Stephen's palm. No one else came out.

As soon as the port defenses were out of action, six transports
would brake from orbit. The squadron's initial wave contained
nearly a thousand troops, enough to secure Savoy no matter how
many of the citizens were willing to die to protect their city. First,
though, the port defenses . . .

The door to the basement was set into the well of the main stairs
and labeled authorized personnel only. It was closed and locked.
Stephen reached for the cutting bar clipped to a stud on his breastplate. A bullet came *in* through a front window and knocked bits
from a ceiling molding.

"I've got it!" said Piet Ricimer, switching on his bar. He leaned
into the tool as its tip howled against the lock plate. Piet didn't
like to wear armor while piloting a vessel. He'd tossed on his back-
and-breast plates before leaving the barge, but he hadn't buckled
them properly. The armor flopped open on the right side in a gap
through which a bullet or stone-sliver could fly.

The lock was sturdy. Sparks flew as the cutting bar ripped metal,
but the bolt didn't part.

A projectile whanged off the staircase a meter above Stephen's
head. He turned. Twenty-odd armed Molts were getting out of a
bus marked PORT CONTROL in big white letters. Brody, Calwell,

and Lightbody were banging away at them. The Molts with guns—most of the aliens carried cutting bars or spiked clubs—were shooting back.

Giddings and Lewis had ducked into the shelter of the stone bannisters instead of firing the weapons they carried for Stephen. It was because he could depend on the pair to carry out his directions *exactly* that he'd detailed them for this dangerous and thankless task.

"Flashgun!" Stephen said. A Molt rose with a rifle from behind the engine compartment of the bus. Stephen punched a carbine bullet through the center of the triangular skull, then traded the light weapon for his flashgun.

"Ready!" Piet said.

"Giddings!" Stephen cried as he shot, closing his eyes against the glare. The vehicle's fuel tank was under the cab, cut out in a step to help the driver enter. The laser bolt struck the black-painted metal at a seam. The tank ruptured in a fountain of blazing fuel. Fire engulfed much of the street. Stephen traded weapons.

Piet pulled the door wide. Stephen went through the opening first by using his bulk and strength to shoulder his friend aside. Somebody'd turned off the lights in the room beneath, but the holographic screens of the three control consoles showed movement—huddling, ghostly figures.

Maybe the flashgun would have been a better choice.

Stephen walked down the steps deliberately, firing as quickly as he could work the lever of his carbine. His muzzle flashes were a continuous red throbbing. A human screamed and a Molt gave a loud, rasping cry of agony.

All eight rounds cycled perfectly through the carbine's action. Stephen saved the final three shots for the consoles themselves. The last shorted into arclight as bright as a flashgun pulse, though nearly as brief.

The overhead lights went on. Piet had found a switch at the top of the stairs. Three Molts and a human female lay dead under the consoles where they'd tried to shelter. Where blood mixed with the pools of ichor leaking from the Molts, it reacted to form a purple colloid.

None of the control room crew was armed. If they'd left the lights on, they might all still be alive.

"Stephen, let's get up to the roof," Piet ordered in a crisp tone. "You've taken care of things here."

He set one of the side latches of his armor and added, "I think it'll be the easiest place to defend until the squadron arrives."

Stephen nodded and turned. He was thumbing cartridges into the carbine's loading tube himself, since Piet was between him and his loaders.

Behind the men a console melted down with a sullen hiss, The corpses sprawled beneath it burned with the mingled odors of pork and shrimp cooking.

SAVOY, ARLES

January 1, Year 27
1042 hours, Venus time

A bright blue rocket streaked from the roof of the Commandatura, signaling that the guns had been put out of action. Smoke rose from a ground-floor window. Sal thought she could see an occasional wink of flame in the room beyond.

"*Gallant Sallie* to *Spirit of Ashdod*," she said into the microphone, watching the fancied flame and wondering what it implied for the men in the Commandatura. The *Ashdod* was in geosynchronous orbit above Savoy, from where it could relay Sal's straight-line laser communications to the rest of the squadron. "The guns have all been captured. You can bring the fleet in."

There *were* flames. "Bring the fleet in fast! Over."

Sal still heard occasional shots from the adjacent gun tower, but Major Cardiff had sent up his green rocket three minutes before. The assault force couldn't trust radio within the port area, nor for communication with the rest of the squadron in orbit where any number of ships might be firing plasma thrusters to hold station.

"Acknowledged, *Gallant Sallie*," replied the *Ashdod*'s communications officer. The light-borne signal was clear, though it wobbled in the lower registers. "I'm relaying your message to the *Freedom*. Out."

Captain Casson was in command of the first landing wave. Sal frowned at the thought, remembering the hostility she'd heard— she'd approved—in Old Port taverns in the years before she dreamed she'd ever meet Piet Ricimer herself.

"To hear that puppy Ricimer talk, nobody ever conned a ship before he came along." A shot of slash down Casson's throat, then a long draught of beer.

"Well, a lot of that's said of him, not by him, you know." Marcus Blythe, not as quick to move as he'd been a decade before, but still a spacer and a man. "The Betaport crowd, they know they're second best. It makes them boast when they've the least excuse."

"What other people are saying are the lies they heard from Ricimer's lips first!" Casson glaring around the booth; all spacers, but none of them his equal. All nodding agreement.

Nobody'd ever suggested Willem Casson was likely to hang back in a fight, though. He was a good choice to lead the transports in, as well as a diplomatic one. Casson would have his ships down as soon as orbital dynamics permitted. Half an hour. Even less with luck.

Rickalds had closed the cockpit hatch when the last of the soldiers lumbered out. The soil, heated white by the *Gallant Sallie's* exhaust, radiated unpleasantly into the cabin otherwise. The troops were in full hard suits not as protection against the defenders' small arms (half armor would have been a better compromise for that purpose) but rather so that they could attack immediately across the plasma-seared terrain.

The area had cooled by now. Sal rose from the navigation console and reopened the hatch so that she could look at the Commandatura directly instead of on the *Gallant Sallie's* screen. While Harrigan and the other men examined damage the barge had caused to the hold, Brantling was alone with her in the cabin. He watched Sal but didn't speak.

Humming like a swarm of hornets, a large aircar driven by pairs of ducted fans bow and stern rose into view beyond the Commandatura. The car mounted a squat weapon behind the pilot's hatch. Troops, most of them Molts, looked out from both sides of the central cargo compartment. There must have been forty of them.

The weapon in the car's bow was a multitube laser. It fired three strobing pulses at the Commandatura. Fed troops in the aircar were shooting also.

The laser disintegrated like a bubble popping with a violet flash. The *snickWhack/snickWhack/snickWhack* of the pulses' slapping impacts on the building arrived a measurable second after the laser's destruction.

Sal couldn't see what was happening on the roof of the Commandatura from her angle. Her heart surged at what the event implied, however: Stephen Gregg was alive, and he still had his flashgun.

The aircar banked, circling a stone's throw from the Commandatura at thirty meters altitude. The roof coping would have protected the Venerians against troops shooting from the ground, but it was less use against rifles fired from above.

Rock dust danced from the side of the building. This time Sal saw the spark of Stephen's flashgun, a saffron needle that ripped a puff of metal from the aircar's bow. The vehicle continued its circle unhindered. Guns banged from the cargo compartment. Distance dulled the reports.

The aircar was a military vehicle. The pilot used remote viewing rather than a clear windscreen, and the polished skin was resistant to if not entirely proof against a flashgun's bolt. The fans and the motors driving them were buried deep in the hull, shielded unless the pilot overflew the shooter.

The troops in the cargo compartment could be hit—one of the Feds dropped in the instant the situation formed in Sal's mind. But there were a lot of them, and the vehicle gave them better protection than Stephen and his fellows had. The squadron wouldn't be down before—

"*Brantling, help me*—" Sal shouted as she turned from the hatch and realized the guns weren't there. The *Gallant Sallie*'s plasma cannon were still in orbit, so Sal couldn't blast the Fed vehicle from the air with them after all.

Sal jumped from the hatch. The ground was still too hot for slippers, but she was three steps around the vessel before she noticed the heat. It wouldn't have mattered anyway.

"Captain?" Brantling called from the hatch with nervous concern in his voice.

"Mind the console!" she shouted back.

The revolver holster slapped her left thigh as she ran for the gun tower. The tower platform was ten meters off the ground, supported on four squat concrete legs. Spiral steps were cast into each leg. There was a hatch into the platform at the top of the helix. Halfway up Sal realized she was mounting the northwest leg while Major Cardiff had led his troops up the southwest stairs.

I should have brought a cutting bar in case the hatch was locked. Sal drew her revolver, though the chance of shooting a metal door open was a lot slimmer than the chance of killing herself with a ricochet.

Harrigan shouted from the ground. Sal ignored him. Gunfire from the Commandatura was a constant muffled rattle, and she tried to ignore that as well. She grabbed the latch lever and turned it. There wasn't a lock mechanism.

Sal jerked the door open. The Fed hiding in the compartment beyond screamed, "*Mother of God!*" and swung a crowbar at her. He hit the low ceiling instead.

Sal shot him in the face. The muzzle flash was a saturated red-orange, so vivid in the dimness that she almost didn't notice the thunderous report.

The Fed flopped backward. His forelock was burning. Sal stepped over the body and lifted the trap door to the gun platform beyond.

A Venerian soldier with his faceshield raised saw her, jumped back, and tried to aim his shotgun. Major Cardiff knocked the weapon aside with a shout of fear and anger.

"Where's the fire director?" Sal demanded as she clambered out. There were a dozen corpses on the platform, most of them Molts. Cardiff's men were dragging more bodies from the four metal turrets. The cannon still pointed skyward.

"Mistress Blythe, you shouldn't have come here!" Cardiff said. "You could have been killed!"

"Where's the fire director, you stupid whoreson?" Sal shouted. "There's men dying at the Commandatura now, and there'll be more unless we get our fingers out of our butts and help them!"

Cardiff's head jerked as he looked toward the Commandatura. He'd been too involved with his own operation to consider what was happening across the spaceport. "Yes, I see," he said.

He glanced across his visible troops. "Davis, Podgorny!" he shouted. "Let's get these guns working!"

The northeast turret was the same diameter as the others but was taller by two meters to add space for equipment. Cardiff ran toward it, sluggish in his hard suit. "They've been gunners," the major added as he saw Sal was keeping pace with him.

The fire director was a Janus-faced console in the center of the room beneath the turret. On one side was a narrow Molt-style bench; integral to the other side was a cushioned human chair. The walls and equipment were splashed with ichor, already crusting in the heat, but the bodies had been removed.

"Get one of these guns to bear on the car that's attacking the Commandatura!" Cardiff said to his men. "Can you do it? And don't on your souls hit the building!"

The major stepped back. Davis and Podgorny—Sal didn't know which was which—stepped gingerly to the console. They took off their gauntlets and tossed them clashing to the floor.

"Tubes are loaded, at least," muttered the soldier with a black mustache flowing into his sideburns. He squinted at the screen's pastel images. "Standard gear, but it's not going to track a car flitting like that."

"Just get moving, wormshit!" Sal said. "If you put a twenty-centimeter bolt through the air beside that car, they aren't going to stick around to see where the next shot goes."

The soldier looked up, startled at the words in a woman's voice. The other man said, "Here, I think I've got a solution. I'm not sure which—"

Gear motors whined in the roof of the control room. A soldier outside shouted, "Hey! The turret's moving!"

"It's all right!" Major Cardiff shouted out the hatchway. "Everybody put your visors down, though!"

Cardiff noticed the forearm of a Molt, severed by a cutting bar. He half scraped, half kicked the limb out onto the platform. Sal heard a nearby rifleshot.

"The concrete's a honeycomb, not solid," Cardiff explained. He raised his voice to be heard over the rumble of the turret mechanism. Tonnes of metal were turning in perfect balance. "The gun crews were living up here. The bugs in the crews, at least. The boys are still flushing some of them out."

Sal nodded to indicate she understood. Her face felt stiff. She moved behind the mustached soldier so that she could view his display. He had to lean over the chair to reach the keyboard, since his hard suit was too bulky for him to sit normally at the console.

The upper left corner of the display read ARMED in scarlet letters and MANUAL below them in blue. At the bottom of the screen was a bar with a mass of data regarding temperature, atmospheric conditions, and other matters of no significance at what was point-blank range for the big cannon.

Four green radial lines at 90° to one another midway on the display implied a centerpoint above the right edge of the Commandatura. A similar set of radii trembled slowly down and across the display from the upper right corner, indicating the cannon's true current boresight.

The fire director was capable of zeroing onto a target through the full depth of a planet's roiling atmosphere. The screen's image of the nearby Commandatura was as sharp as a miniature in a glass case. Sal could see the bodies, one sprawled beside the landing barge and the other at the doorway down to the interior of the building. If she dialed up the magnification, she could probably identify the members of the assault force who'd been killed.

The soldier glanced over his shoulder at her. "The guns won't depress enough to bear on the city," he explained. "There's a lock-out in the gun mechanism itself. Fuckers in that car aren't quite so low, though."

He grinned. His front teeth were missing.

Sal noticed she was still holding her revolver. She tried twice unsuccessfully to slide it into the holster. After the second attempt, she glanced down and realized she needed to lift the holster flap.

The Fed's crowbar had showered sparks as it clanged against the concrete. If it had struck her head . . .

The orange radii crawled toward congruence with the green point of aim. "I have the controls!" warned the soldier on the other side of the console.

The man on Sal's side raised his hands to indicate he wouldn't interfere in his enthusiasm. His armored forearm jolted her.

The radii mated. The paired set became orange and began to pulse. The turret mechanism stopped its rumbling movement.

In the sudden silence, Sal heard three shots and a howling ricochet from the platform. Men shouted together in triumph.

The image of the aircar curved slowly around that of the Commandatura. The pilot was holding his speed and attitude steady to help the gunmen in the cargo compartment. Five muzzle flashes, as regular as metronome strokes, winked from one corner of the roof coping.

The aircar slid into the indicated point of aim. For a moment, the vehicle's motion relative to the plasma cannon was almost nil. The soldier controlling the gun touched a control.

The crash of the cannon made the world jump. A miniature thermonuclear explosion flung the forged stellite gun tube back in recoil. Solid-seeming pearly radiance reflected through the open hatch of the director room.

Sal had never seen so large a plasma cannon before, nor had she ever been around a gun when it was fired in an atmosphere. The shock of light and sound crushed her inward like a mass of bricks. Major Cardiff gasped, "Christ Jesus!" and jumped back from the hatch.

Sal stepped outside, staring across the starport. A cloud of scintillant vapor hung in the air to the right of the Commandatura. Fragments of blazing metal traced arcs of smoke out of the center of the glow. The aircar's thunderous destruction would have been deafening had her ears not already been stunned by the cannon's discharge.

Sal felt a low-pitched rumbling through the soles of her shoes. She looked at the turret to see if it was traversing again. The gun, its muzzle white from the plasma it had channeled downrange, was still. Pastel iridescence quivered on the tube and the turret dome.

Sal turned and looked higher, into the western horizon. Six globs of light, starships gleaming from atmospheric friction and the plasma roaring from their thrusters as they braked, thundered toward Savoy.

"Make the remaining guns safe!" Sal called into the director's room. "We don't want any accidents now that our relief's arrived!"

SAVOY, ARLES

January 1, Year 27
1131 hours, Venus time

"By God, sir, look at them run!" said Lieutenant Lemkin, standing on the roof coping in his hard suit to watch the refugees
through an electronic magnifier. The soldier's perch looked dangerous to Stephen, but that wasn't anything for Stephen Gregg to
get worked up about. "Say, can't one of your ships lift a company
west of the city to cut them off? By *God*, we could cut them off!"

"To what end, Mister Lemkin?" Piet said. "To force them to stand
and fight? And I'll thank you not to take so lightly the name of
God Who gave us this victory."

Suppressed pain wrung Piet's voice dry. Weicker, the *Wrath*'s surgeon, was cleaning the burns on Piet's leg while an assistant probed
bits of metal from Stephen's left arm.

"You should have come sooner, Lemkin," Stephen said. "There
was plenty of fighting for everybody half an hour ago."

He was sick with anger at himself. Giddings was dead. So were
Blaise and Portillo, from Dole's contingent, and there were half
a dozen serious wounds.

Plus the little stuff. Piet had made it all the way through the
fighting uninjured, then been burned by flaming debris from the
aircar. Cheap at the price.

It all was, Stephen supposed.

Lemkin hopped down from the coping and faced Stephen in a stiff brace. "Sir!" he said. "My company relieved the Commandatura as ordered, within three minutes of the time the hatches of the *Freedom* transporting us opened. Are you commenting on my courage?"

"I'm not commenting on anything, soldier," Stephen said. "I'm too tired."

Piet lowered his visor to watch the corkscrew descent of a 300-tonne armed freighter. "Four square kilometers of field and we'll have a collision yet," he muttered. "It was a lot simpler when we had one seventy-tonne ship to worry about."

After the first wave, the ships of the squadron were coming down one at a time. They were supposed to land on the east side of the field where there was more space, but through sheer incompetence several had dropped close enough to the Commandatura that their exhaust wash warmed the command group on the roof.

"I think that's the last of the fragments, sir," the surgeon's assistant said.

He stepped back from Stephen and wiped nervous sweat from his brow. Had the fellow been afraid he was going to poke a nerve and have his head blown off for his mistake?

Stephen stood and shrugged off his back-and-breast armor now that his arm was free. He raised the hem of his sweat-soaked tunic and examined the fist-sized bruise where a bullet had slammed the lower edge of his breastplate into the flesh over his hipbone.

"Let me see that," Weicker said sharply. He knelt before Stephen.

Piet frowned as he watched. He looked uncommonly odd with one pant leg cut off at the knee and the calf below smeared with ointment after it had been debrided.

Weicker drew Stephen's waistband down, then up again. "No penetration," he said, straightening.

Stephen tapped the lip of his breastplate. Lead was a bright splash on the black-finished ceramic.

The surgeon shook his head. "If that bullet had hit lower by as little as half its diameter," he said, "pieces of it would certainly have torn your femoral artery. You're very lucky to be alive, sir!"

Stephen looked at Weicker. "Do you really think so?" he asked in a voice he hadn't meant to use.

Weicker frowned in surprise.

Piet laid a hand on Stephen's shoulder. "I'm lucky you're alive," he said. "Let's go downstairs for a moment. There's something in the foyer that you may not have noticed."

Stephen stared at Savoy City. "Sure," he said.

The squadron's troops were moving cautiously into the city under their own officers. In theory, ground operations were conducted under Stephen's control, but the officers had been fully briefed. Besides, they were more experienced at ordinary military operations than Stephen. This wasn't a one-ship, smash-and-grab raid of the sort that had made Piet Ricimer a byword on Venus and a nightmare to President Pleyal.

Stephen Gregg's real job had been to clear the Commandatura. Stephen Gregg's job was to kill, not to command.

Two soldiers came up through the trap door. They'd discarded the arm pieces and lower-body portions of their armor. "Colonel Gregg?" the first of them said.

"Report to Lieutenant Lemkin," Piet said, pointing to that officer.

The soldier recognized the smaller figure shadowed by Stephen's bulk. "Oh!" he said. "Yes, sir, Factor Ricimer!"

"Your leg all right?" Stephen asked as he led the way down the stairs.

Dole had put the Molts captured alive in the gun turrets—the five uninjured ones—to cleaning up the building. The corpses were gone from the hallway, but the hundreds of bullets fired during repeated Fed assaults had knocked the office partitions to splinters.

"Stiff, nothing serious," Piet said. "I was running for the barge's cockpit when the car blew up. I wasn't expecting that."

The bodies on the second floor had been removed also, along with the grass pads that had cushioned the floor. Blood had soaked through the matting and into the porous concrete.

Four Venerian soldiers were posted at windows from which they could watch the boulevard and the buildings across from the Commandatura. They noticed the squadron's commanders and turned. "Sir?" one asked.

"Carry on with your duties, gentlemen," Piet said.

The soles of Stephen's boots were tacky for the next several steps down to the ground floor.

"It surprised me too, Piet," Stephen said. Conversationally, as if it meant no more to him than the color of the sunrise, he went on, "You know, if I hadn't wrecked the fire director in the basement here, we'd have been able to use our own roof guns to bring down that car. I figure that decision of mine cost us most of our casualties."

The steel door to the guard quarters was now shut, but the foyer's marble floor slopped with water on which floated ash and bits of charred wood. Dole and several sailors watched Molts coil hoses. Savoy's fire company was housed in the building adjacent to the Commandatura. The human officers had fled, but the alien crew had managed to put out the blaze in the guard quarters before it spread to the rest of the building. Stephen hadn't thought that would be possible.

Piet gestured around the sides and front of the entrance hallway in which they stood. Sixty percent of the surface was floor to ceiling windows. Most of the small individual panes had been shot or blown out.

"We couldn't have held the ground floor from so many armed Feds," Piet said. "It was difficult enough with them continuing to charge the roof stairs. And we couldn't *possibly* have hit so maneuverable a craft from one of the turrets here. The only way Cardiff managed it—and I bless him for it—was because the Fed pilot wasn't paying attention to what was happening on the other side of the field."

He's right, but I should have thought *of using the guns.* "It's done now," Stephen said aloud.

The Commandatura's front entrance was a pair of double archways. Piet stopped in front of them. The alcove set between the doors held an idealized holographic portrait of President Pleyal clad in gold robes of state: stern, black-haired, standing arms akimbo. Behind Pleyal was a starscape. The motto below the display read *Non sufficit mundus.*

"I've heard of these shrines, but I'd never seen one before with my own eyes," Piet said.

Stephen noted the delicacy of the holographic resolution and calculated the expense. "Rather a waste of good microchips," he said mildly. "But I suppose we'll find something better to do with them back on Venus."

"Do you see the legend?" Piet said. "That means, 'The universe is not enough!' That's what we're fighting against, Stephen! *That's* why we have to fight."

The bodies carried from the Commandatura had been stacked like cordwood in the street outside. There were about a hundred of them, a score of humans and the rest Molts.

"I'm not fighting against anything, Piet," Stephen said softly. "I'm just fighting."

They stared at the splendid, shimmering portrait of a man who confused himself with God. Piet whispered to Stephen, "I should have taken the barge up to ram the aircar as soon as it appeared. The exhaust wash wasn't as great a danger as the gunmen. . . ."

SAVOY, ARLES

January 3, Year 27
1514 hours, Venus time

Sal heard the thump of an explosion from somewhere in Savoy City. She and several other officers turned around. None of them reacted more quickly than Piet Ricimer himself. There was nothing to see over the spaceport berm.

"It can't be too serious," the general commander said with a faint smile. "Probably somebody blowing up a statue of President Pleyal."

Sal returned her attention to the ship the party of officers was examining. At one time the vessel had been named, perhaps *Maria*. Takeoffs and landings had flaked the letters into ghosts of themselves. Nickel-iron hull, eight thrusters with about half the life span left to their nozzles. A hundred and fifty tonnes burden, or perhaps a trifle more.

"Has the government said anything about ransoming the city, sir?" asked Jankowich. He'd probably started thinking along the same lines Sal had when she heard the explosion. "A place that's built of rock the way this one is won't be a snap to blow up if they refuse to pay."

"I didn't send the envoys out till this morning," Ricimer said. "Three Molt officials from the city administration. They'd have been shot out of sheer jumpiness by one side or the other if they'd gone while it was still dark."

"The streets here don't seem to be paved with microchips, Ricimer," Captain Casson said with gloomy relish. "Let's hope they took the loot with them when they ran."

"Yes, I hope that, Captain," Piet Ricimer said. "But as I warned everyone in Betaport, and again in Venus orbit: we're here for God and for Venus, not simply to line our pockets. Now, this ship would seem to me to be worth taking as a prize instead of destroying."

"Can you trust Molts to deal straight with us?" Captain Boler asked, reverting to the previous subject. "I mean, they were fighting us. Mostly the Feds ran, but their bugs sure didn't."

"Yes, they can be trusted," Guillermo said.

The group surveying the vessels captured in the port consisted of Captain Ricimer, six chosen captains (Sal attributed her inclusion among them to Stephen's influence), and Ricimer's Molt servant. According to Stephen, the alien was a quick, skillful navigator. Guillermo might lack Piet's feel for a ship, but he didn't make mistakes at the controls.

The other captains clearly thought of the Molt as furniture. They were shocked when Guillermo spoke.

"Molts form clans with a strongly hierarchical structure, Captain," Ricimer said. He smiled faintly. "Even more hierarchical than our own. They'll treat humans, no matter how brutal, as clan superiors until the structure is smashed."

"Which you certainly did here, sir," Sal said in a loud voice. Stephen was on the city perimeter, setting up defenses in case the Feds tried to retake Savoy. His presence in the survey group would have changed the tone, not entirely in a bad direction.

"The hull's heavier than ceramic and no stronger," Captain Salomon said. "The navigational AI is all right, but the attitude controls are as basic as a stone axe."

"The controls can be upgraded easily enough if the hull's worth it," Sal said. She'd seen Salomon take off and land often enough to understand why Ricimer had given the man a ship.

"A proper spacer doesn't need a machine to do his thinking for him," Casson rumbled. He glared at Sal. "Or her thinking either."

Ricimer and Salomon both opened their mouths to speak. Sal, feeling suddenly cold inside, spread her left hand to silence them. She said, "I'd think that those of us who learned our skills on older ships, Captain, would be the quickest to appreciate how much better and safer the new electronics are than what we were used to. Certainly I'd feel more comfortable in a fleet this size if I were sure that an AI was landing the ship beside me. Instead of some ham-fisted incompetent who couldn't be trusted to hit the whole of Ishtar City, let alone the dock."

Sal had grown up respecting Willem Casson; first because her father did, then because she'd grown old enough to appreciate the old man's exploits herself. Now—

What Casson had done was still impressive. But he didn't like female captains any better than he liked youths from Betaport who'd been brilliant while Willem Casson had merely been courageous; and for all Casson's skill and experience, the expedition would be better off if he'd stayed on Venus.

Three red signal rockets shot up from the doubly baffled entrance through the berm. The gateway was designed to prevent exhaust wash from flaring beyond the port reservation. A three-axle Venerian truck negotiated it and accelerated toward the group conducting the survey.

"I believe that's Stephen driving," Piet Ricimer said. Then he added, "We'll take up the survey another time, gentlemen and Mistress. Stephen doesn't react at nothing."

The vehicle pulled up beside the survey group. Lightbody, a religious sailor who glowered whenever he saw Sal, was in the open cab with Stephen. In back, three Molts kept a fourth prostrate on a blanket from sliding off the open sides.

Captain Ricimer and three of the younger captains hopped onto the truck bed. Sal stood on the cab's running board, looking into the back. Stephen turned in the seat beside her, face remote.

"These are the envoys, Piet," Stephen said. "I brought them directly to you because there wasn't a lot of time."

Piet knelt by the injured Molt, then looked at Stephen in white fury. "This man should never have been moved!" he said.

"I couldn't hurt him now, Piet," Stephen said. "You needed to see him while he was still alive." Piet's anger streamed through as if Stephen's soul was transparent to it.

"Master," said a Molt who'd earlier been working on casualties from the city's capture, humans and aliens as well. "Kletch-han knows he is dying, but he begs to speak with you first."

Ricimer nodded curtly. He touched the upper carapace of the

injured Molt with his fingertips and said, "Kletch-han, how did this happen?"

The Molt's chitinous exoskeleton had a pearly translucence that Sal had never before noticed. Kletch-han wore a sash-of-office with blue chevrons on white. The fabric had been driven into one of his lower belly plates and left embedded in the blunt puncture wound.

"We drove out the west road in the vehicle you provided us, Master," Kletch-han said. Sal could understand the words, but there was more of a clicking crispness to them than was normal in the speech of Molts in high positions. The three envoys had been principal clerks in the Savoy administration.

"We met a group of soldiers three kilometers from the city," the Molt continued. The brown stain was spreading on his sash. "They were in a brush-filled gully beside the road. The officer wore a naval uniform. I didn't recognize him. I got out of the vehicle, holding the white flag you gave me."

Another of the Molts from the embassy raised the flag to show it to the humans. It was a pillowcase tied to the end of a threaded steel rod a meter and a half long and about a centimeter thick. It had been assembled from what happened to be available when Ricimer sent the envoys out.

The base of the rod a handsbreadth deep was smeared with brown ichor.

"I explained that Captain Ricimer had sent us to Director Eliahu to set up a meeting regarding the ransom of Savoy," Kletch-han said. "The officer said to his men, 'Do they think we're going to treat with bug slaves?' He took the flag from me and struck me as you see. He and his troops took the vehicle and drove west-ward with it. That is all."

"We ran into the brush when Kletch-han was attacked," the third envoy said. "When the soldiers left, we carried Kletch-han back to the city. Master Gregg summoned Dirksahla to treat Kletch-han though we told him that was unnecessary. Then Mister Gregg brought us here."

Stephen's face and whole body were quiescent, waiting for emotion to fill them. He had no more expression than the trigger of his flashgun did.

Captain Ricimer nodded. "Captain Blythe," he said crisply. "Are the reaction mass tanks of your vessel topped off?"

"Yes," Sal said, "and the air tanks have been dumped and refilled."

"We won't be high enough to pressurize," Ricimer said. "Gentlemen, help our Molt friends here lift Kletch-han down gently."

Boler and Salomon slid their arms under the chitinous body. Molts massed somewhat less than humans on average, and both captains were powerful men. As they handed the dying envoy to Jankowich and Casson on the ground, Ricimer said, "Stephen, who's our highest-ranking human captive from Savoy?"

"We've got the head of the Merchants' Guild, Madame Dumesnil," Stephen said in a voice that could have been a machine's. "She was trying to load her whole warehouse onto a truck when some sailors from the *Wrath* arrived."

"Fine; have her at the port entrance on my return," Ricimer said. "She'll take the next message to Director Eliahu. Stephen, swing by the *Wrath* on our way to the *Gallant Sallie*. With full AI controls, Guillermo can handle the attitude board alone, but I'll want a second man with Lightbody watching the water flow to the thrusters."

"I'll take care of that," Sal said. She lifted herself into the back of the vehicle, though she supposed she could have ridden on the running board as easily.

"Mistress Blythe, you will do as I command you!" the general commander said with the same shocking rage that had flared at Stephen a moment before.

"Captain Ricimer," Sal replied, "you will not order me off my own vessel! Besides which, you don't have a man better able to monitor the *Gallant Sallie*'s fuel feeds!"

Stephen put the truck in gear, accelerating smoothly. He made small steering corrections to miss the worst of the craters starships had blasted in the field's surface. It was still a bone-jarring ride.

"She's a stubborn lady, Piet," Stephen called over the rattle of the truck.

"She's also correct," Ricimer said. He reached his right hand across the truck bed, swaying with the vehicle's motion. Guillermo put an arm around Ricimer's waist to brace him. "I've noted your shiphandling with pleasure, Captain Blythe. I'm fortunate to have you in this squadron."

The general commander's handshake was firm and dry. Sal swallowed, stunned at the memory of what she'd just done. "Factor Ricimer," she said. "I—"

"And if you'll call me 'Piet' in private, Mistress, I'll feel a little less like one of the Federation's saints' idols," Ricimer continued.

He smiled wanly. "Too many of the people I respect seem to be afraid of me."

"They're confusing you with me," Stephen said. The truck was nearing the *Gallant Sallie* against the eastern berm. The surface on this side of the reservation was less pitted, and he was getting as much speed from the vehicle as the diesel's governor allowed.

"Do you think that's it?" Ricimer—*Piet*—said. He looked at Sal and, in a voice that neither man in the cab could have heard, said, "I sometimes think Stephen and I are halves of the same soul, Sal. But the division was very unjust to him."

They stopped beside the *Gallant Sallie*, casting a spray of sand in front of the cab. Rickalds and Kubelick, the anchor watch, stared from the cockpit hatch in surprise.

Piet jumped from the vehicle. "Stephen," he said, "drive these men back to the port entrance. Make sure Madame Dumesnil is waiting for me."

Stephen got out, slinging his flashgun. "They can drive themselves," he said. "And Salomon will make sure the lady arrives where you want her. I'm going along."

Sal climbed the three steps extended from the cabin airlock when the *Gallant Sallie* was on the ground. "Kubelick," she said, "drive Rickalds back to the gate. Find Captain Salomon and tell him he's responsible for the general commander's orders regarding the head of the Merchants' Guild."

"Stephen, I'm taking a minimum crew on this," Piet said sharply. "You know absolutely nothing about operating a starship!"

"I know about defending them if they come down some place they shouldn't," Stephen said in the same detached tone he'd used since he arrived with the dying envoy. "Besides, you'll have to shoot me to keep me off."

"Captain?" Rickalds murmured with a worried expression,

"Get this damned truck out of here!" Sal shouted as she bent to switch on the vessel's electronics. "We're lifting as soon as you're clear."

Her men obeyed instantly, though Rickalds frowned and muttered a question to Kubelick. Lightbody, carrying a shotgun, was already aboard. Guillermo followed the sailor and sat at one of the three places around the attitude-control boards. The Molt seemed comfortable on a seat designed for humans.

Sal took the starboard motor panel, across the cabin from

Lightbody. Piet settled himself at the navigation console and made adjustments to the couch. Stephen cycled the outer hatch closed and squatted in the lock, his boots and shoulders braced against opposite sides of the chamber.

"Then again," Piet said as he waited for the hydraulics to build up pressure, "perhaps my trouble is that not enough people are afraid of me."

In a different voice he added, "Crew, prepare for liftoff."

Piet lit the thrusters, then brought the *Gallant Sallie* to a roaring hover about a meter above the ground. His left hand made minuscule adjustments in the flow rate of individual motors. The visual display throbbed with plasma, and the hull shook with the hammering of exhaust reflected from the ground.

Sal gripped the stanchion beside her flop-down seat. She expected the general commander to boost thrust to lift out of the port as soon as he'd dialed in the motors to his own satisfaction. Instead, Piet ran up the flow of reaction mass while simultaneously flaring the nozzles with consequent loss of efficiency. The *Gallant Sallie* continued to bobble in place, rising and falling only a few centimeters despite the variation in control settings.

"Lifting," Piet called. He reduced the nozzle irises to three-quarters power. The *Gallant Sallie* sprang a hundred meters in the air. Piet shifted into forward flight, vectoring the nozzles as smoothly as Sal could have done herself after being raised on the vessel.

Stephen smiled from the airlock in her direction. It was a cool expression, the sort of look a statue might have worn. She wasn't sure it had anything to do with her.

The *Gallant Sallie* left the port reservation to the north and curved around Savoy in a shallow bank instead of overflying the city. The newly installed optics gave Sal a better view from the middle of the cabin than she'd have had in past years from the navigation console itself. Arles in the vicinity of Savoy was covered in tawny shrubbery against which the green of introduced vegetation made a vivid contrast.

The line of the main western highway out of Savoy came into view ahead of them. Piet swung the *Gallant Sallie* parallel to the road and about half a kilometer out from it. He flared the thruster nozzles. The ship dropped mushily and slowed to 50 kph of forward motion. Plasma roiled out to either side and behind the vessel, billowing as far as the highway to port and an equal distance to starboard. The *Gallant Sallie* advanced in a hissing roar, burning the countryside around her as bare as a sheet of fresh lava.

Arles had been a major administrative center early in the Federation's recolonization efforts. Now it was a backwater, a source of grain and oil seed for the Reaches and a center of local trade because of the excellent port facilities remaining from the planet's former glory. Many of the villas along the road had been abandoned a generation before, though refugees from Savoy might have been sheltering in the ruins.

Everything died beneath the plasma scourge. Foliage wilted, then blazed in a faint challenge to the seething iridescence. Tile shattered and stone walls crumbled to gravel as moisture within the pores of the rock flashed to steam.

Flesh would explode and burn also, if there were flesh in the sun-hot plasma below. Perhaps there was no one in the *Gallant Sallie*'s path.

Piet swung the vessel five kilometers from the western edge of the city, crossed the highway, and brought the *Gallant Sallie* back on the south side of the road. With the nozzles flared, the motors consumed reaction mass at more than ten times the normal rate to achieve this modest level of thrust. The waste ions spread in a glowing fog, hiding the *Gallant Sallie* from anyone outside the curtain of death.

And hiding from the humans aboard the sight of just what they were doing.

None of them spoke. Lightbody took a small New Testament from a pocket in his tunic and held it, the metal covers closed, as he watched the feed gauges.

As the *Gallant Sallie* approached Savoy, Piet sphinctered down the nozzles and lifted the vessel a safe hundred meters in the air to curve back to the port. As the *Gallant Sallie* rotated at altitude, Sal glanced at the screen's view of what they'd accomplished. The countryside west of Savoy was a steaming, smoking wasteland. Everything in that broad swath was gray.

It had been a brilliant piece of piloting. Sal knew that with the thrusters operating at low efficiency, the controls felt as if they were rubber. Nothing you did at the console seemed to affect the ship. Piet had followed the terrain, rising and falling to achieve the maximum effect without ever endangering the vessel.

They landed very close to the entrance, searing the finish of a

Federation freighter and Captain Casson's *Freedom* as they did so. Sal cleared her throat. "There's a hard suit aboard, sir," she said. "If you'd like to leave before the ground cools."

Piet looked back at her from the console. "Thank you, Captain," he said quietly. "I can wait five minutes."

When Stephen finally opened the cockpit hatch, the sunlight was a relief to Sal. She'd spent what seemed a lifetime in silence with only her thoughts for company.

All five of them were experienced spacers, but they ran to clear the surface immediately surrounding the vessel. Five minutes wasn't really enough for the plasma-heated ground to cool. . . .

The ends of the berm overlapped at the entrance to the reservation. Smaller mounds on both port and city sides increased the protection. Nearly a hundred Venerian officers and men waited for Piet within the baffles.

Between Captains Casson and Salomon stood an angry, frightened woman in her sixties. She was tall and muscular as well as fat; but fat certainly. She eyed Piet as a rat eyes a ferret.

"This is Madame Dumesnil, sir," Salomon said. Casson prodded the woman a step forward.

"Madame," Piet said with a cold anger very different from the blasts he'd directed at Stephen and Sal in the immediate past. "You will be given a vehicle and sent out the highway to the west. You will find Director Eliahu. You will inform him that at local noon every day I will conduct a similar operation until the man who murdered my previous envoy is surrendered to me."

"What sort of—" Dumesnil said.

"You will see as you drive out of the city," Piet said, "and the director will know very well. Make it clear to him, Madame, that unless he complies every village, every farm, every field on Arles will be burned to the bare rock! If there are any men surviving, they'll hide in the ditches like Rabbits after the Collapse and the Molts will hunt them for food. Tell him!"

Piet's body trembled. He gestured to Salomon and muttered, "Put her on a truck and get her out of here."

Dumesnil didn't understand what she'd been told, but Piet's tone shocked her to silence. Salomon bundled her quickly through the crowd to the vehicle that had brought her.

Casson scowled uncomfortably. "You know, Ricimer," he said, "if a Fed managed to shoot out one of your thruster nozzles while you were mooching along at low altitude, you'd likely dive right into the ground."

"I always appreciate my subordinates' concern for my safety, Captain Casson," Piet said so loudly that most of those watching from the sides and top of the berm could hear him. "No matter how inappropriate that concern might be!"

Piet turned sharply to Sal. His eyes were a brown as hard as agate. "Captain Blythe, please have your vessel refueled immediately. I like the way she handles, and I may need her again tomorrow noon."

SAVOY, ARLES

January 4, Year 27
0613 hours, Venus time

Dawn of the short Arlesian day hinted from the east, but the truck coming up the western highway was in complete darkness. The vehicle proceeded at a walking pace. Its headlights were on, and the Klaxon on the driver's side of the cab sounded constantly. The cab's passenger waved a flag.

"Somebody who appreciates the risk he's taking," Stephen Gregg said. He smiled faintly to Sal, who stood beside him.

Stephen hitched his breastplate a little higher. When it hung in its normal position, the ceramic lip pressed the bruise above his pelvis.

"They also appreciate the risk if they wait and Captain Ricimer decides to make another demonstration earlier than he'd said," Sal said.

Stephen shrugged. "Piet'll keep his word to them," he said. "Either way, he'll keep his word."

This side of the city was given over to human residences. Molts who weren't owned by individual Feds—slaves in the municipal and port administration—had housing adjacent to the noise and drifting ions of the port reservation.

Thousands of Molts, seemingly all those who'd remained in Savoy after the human residents fled, now sat or stood where they could watch the oncoming vehicle. The Molts were careful not to crowd the fifty-man Venerian guard post, and they opened lanes quickly for humans coming from elsewhere in the city. Nonetheless, the heavily armed troops eyed the massed aliens with disquiet.

Sal looked at the Molt faces, as surely expectant as if they were muscle under skin instead of hard chitin. "How do you suppose they knew?" she asked. "They're not telepathic, are they?"

"Not that I've heard," Stephen said. Piet was two meters away, talking quietly to Guillermo and the pair of surviving Molt envoys at the gate in the barricade blocking the road. Piet wore half armor for show, but he wasn't carrying a weapon. This wasn't going to be a battle . . . and besides, he had Stephen.

Lewis stood in back of Sal and Stephen, holding a repeater. He wore bandoliers of ammunition and flashgun batteries. Stephen needed to find a replacement for Giddings. He'd never understood why men would volunteer for the job, but they did.

"Maybe Beverly," he murmured.

"Sorry?" Sal said.

"Didn't realize I'd spoken aloud," he said. "I was wondering who I'd get for a second loader." He nodded to Lewis to show that he wasn't treating the man as a piece of furniture.

"There's going to be fighting now?" Sal asked. Her tone was tense, not anxious.

"I don't think so," Stephen said.

The slowly moving truck entered the pool of light cast by the banks of floods mounted on roofs to either side of the barricade. There were five people on the vehicle: all human, all male, and all wearing Federation uniforms of either military or civil style.

None of them was armed. Stephen felt himself relax, though he hadn't been consciously aware of his tension.

The truck stopped. The man beside the driver stepped down. He still carried the white flag he'd been waving from the open cab. Two of the men in back wrestled out the third, whose arms were pinioned behind his back. All four of them approached the barricade. After a moment, the driver got out and stood beside the cab.

"I'm John McKensie, the Fiscal of Arles," said the man with the flag of truce. He was within the penumbra of the floodlights, blinking and angry with fear. "I've brought Navigator Jenks to the Venerian commander."

Piet opened the gate. Stephen was through it behind him. Sal, Lewis, and—unexpectedly—the surviving Molt envoys followed.

"I'm General Commander Ricimer," Piet said. "Kal-cha, is this man Jenks the one who killed your colleague?"

"Are you questioning the word of a gentleman, Mister Ricimer?" McKensie shouted tremblingly.

"Gentlemen don't need to be told it's wrong to murder an envoy under a flag of truce!" Sal said in a voice of harsh authority.

"This is the man, Master," the Molt wearing the yellow sash said.

Jenks was young, probably still in his teens. He had flowing black hair and a beard that partially hid the bruises on his face.

He was beyond fighting now. Jenks' eyes were dull and he looked ready to faint in the hands of the Feds holding his elbows.

Piet nodded. "Very well, then," he said. "I need to confer for a moment."

He turned his back on the fiscal to talk intently with the Molts. Guillermo and Kal-cha fell into a side discussion of clicks and chittering.

Stephen looked around. More Venerians appeared, on foot or driving. Some of them seemed to think there'd been an attack. Nobody started shooting; not yet, at least. Stephen was half smiling as he returned his attention to McKensie.

"I don't know how God can let people like you exist!" the fiscal said in a hoarse whisper. "You slaughtered innocent women and children, *infants.* You burned them alive!"

Stephen felt his mind sinking into the cold, gray place where only the view through a gunsight had reality. He heard his voice lilt as he said, "You know, it takes a lot to set Piet Ricimer off. He's as kindly a man as ever shipped beyond Pluto."

Stephen smiled. He knew he was smiling because he could feel the muscles of his face shift and could see the horror in McKensie's eyes. "But some of Piet's subordinates aren't like that at all. Some of us could line up every man, woman, and child on this planet and cut their throats, and sleep none the worse for it. Do you understand?"

McKensie said nothing. One of the men holding Jenks turned his head away.

Looking grim, Piet stepped aside so that several Molts could come through the gate. One of the aliens was a squat giant with torso and limbs half again the thickness of the others'. He wore a leather bandolier from which dangled a dozen knives in loops.

Jenks stared at the Molt. "He's the butcher!" he shouted in a cracking voice. "He butchers pigs at the port, I've *seen* him. He's a *butcher!*"

"Are you empowered by Director Eliahu to negotiate a ransom for Savoy, Mister McKensie?" Piet asked.

Jenks tried to kick free. The butcher's two assistants gripped the prisoner's arms. The Fed guards backed away. One of them wiped his hands. Stephen felt Sal stiffen at his side.

"We can't afford much," McKensie said. His face was frozen. He kept his eyes on Piet to avoid looking at anything else. "This is a poor planet, a very poor planet."

"We'll discuss that in due course," Piet said. He gripped the fiscal by the shoulder and forced him to turn.

Jenks was crying in the grip of the two assistants. The hulking butcher stepped behind him. The Molt held a knife with a broad 30-centimeter blade in his right hand. He grabbed a handful of Jenks' long hair with his left hand and drew the man's head back.

The watching Molts gave a collective sigh.

The butcher drew his blade across the prisoner's throat in a long, clean stroke, severing everything but the spinal column. Blood spurted a handsbreadth into the air, drowning Jenks' shout in a gurgle.

The butcher stepped back. His assistants upended the thrashing body so that it would drain properly. As Jenks himself had said, their training had been with hogs.

The Molt spectators began to leave. The sun was fully up. Somebody switched off the floodlights, though Stephen didn't hear the order given.

"We'll take your vehicle to the Commandatura, Mister McKensie," Piet said conversationally, "and perhaps your men should come with us. I want it to be clear to my people that you're all under my protection." He gave the envoy a very hard smile. "So that I don't have to hang any of my own men."

"Dole, take two of our people and ride along with them," Stephen ordered. The bosun nodded to a pair of men from the *Wrath.*

"You're staying here?" Sal asked.

Stephen nodded. "For a while," he said. "If I were running the show for the Federation, this is just when I'd counterattack. Of course, that's if I had troops that were worth piss. Which Eliahu doesn't."

Together they looked out at the bleak landscape the *Gallant Sallie* had scoured. The truck with Piet and the Fed envoys drove past them into the city.

"I'm glad you're not working for President Pleyal," Sal said quietly.

He laughed. "Oh, so am I. I hate to be on the losing side, and nobody's going to beat Piet Ricimer."

Jenks lay on ground black with his blood. The Molts had almost completely dispersed. One of the butcher's assistants finished cleaning the knife with a wad of raw fiber, then handed it back to his master. They left also.

"You were lying when you said . . . what you said to McKensie," Sal said.

"There's lies and lies," Stephen said. For a moment he thought he was going back to that place. He felt someone clutch his hand; Sal touched him, held his hand firmly.

"If they thought doing something like that would bother me," Stephen said, "they might think I wouldn't really do it, and that would be worse than a lie. Piet wouldn't order anything like that. Not unless he really had to."

Sal whispered something. He couldn't be sure of the words. He thought they were, "Oh dear God."

"And anyway," Stephen added, "I don't think I could sleep much worse than I do already."

SAVOY, ARLES

January 10, Year 27
1808 hours, Venus time

The *Gallant Sallie*'s crew had the two lower floors of what had been a rich man's residence in the north suburb of Savoy, but Sal kept the two-room suite and garden on the roof for herself. She and Stephen had just finished dinner—Rickalds had cooked it with surprising talent—in the shade of a potted palm tree when they heard boots on the outside staircase. Stephen lifted and pointed the flashgun waiting muzzle down beside his chair.

"Hello the house!" called Piet Ricimer. "May I come up, or would you rather I check back another time?"

"There's never a time I'd regret seeing you, Piet," Stephen called as he settled the flashgun back. "Though it's not my—"

He glanced at Sal.

"Honored, sir, deeply honored," Sal said as she rose and walked to the stairs. The outside facility was little more than a ladder. There was a more comfortable staircase within the suite, but the owner had obviously wanted a means of private access for himself and his guests.

The general commander, resplendent in maroon velvet with a chain and medallion of massive gold, hopped up and over the

675

waist-high wall into the garden. He looked at Sal, in a black-and-silver dress she'd found here in a closet, looked at Stephen, and gestured to the garden. "You have excellent taste, Sal. In all things."

She forced a smile.

"Stephen," Piet said. He sat near the table, on a bench built around a stand of four-meter-high bamboo. "I think we've achieved all we're going to here, and I'm ready to move on. I'm comfortable with the status of the ships and captains. . . ."

He grinned at Sal. His face lit like a plasma thruster when he wanted it to " . . . some more than others, of course. But I'd like your opinion of the troops."

Stephen nodded twice while he marshaled his thoughts. "They fought well during the initial assault," he said. "I'd have been surprised if they didn't, of course. What's of more importance is that they've kept good watch during the past week when the danger receded. Discipline's been good in general. The men obey their officers, and the officers carry out your orders."

"I haven't noticed the friction between soldiers and sailors that I'd feared," Piet said. "Is that your observation also?"

Stephen nodded. "Healthy arrogance on both sides," he said, "but nothing worse. Seven gunshot wounds since the fighting ended, and one fellow managed to lop off his foot with a cutting bar. But it's all been accidental."

He gave his friend a tight smile. "You'd better get us back into action, Piet," he said, "or drunken foolishness is going to eat us down to a nub."

Piet squeezed the back of Stephen's hand and released it. "I think we can expect action on Berryhill," he said. "There's a military garrison there, and the defenses of St. Mary's Port are too dispersed for us to hope to slip in the way we did here."

"The men hired on to fight, Piet," Stephen said. "They'll do that. And Pleyal doesn't have any force in the Reaches that can stand against us."

It was odd to watch the pair of them this way, acting as if they were the only two people in the universe. No bluster, no hesitation, no beating around the bush. The truth as they saw it, analyzed by minds as fine as Stephen's marksmanship and Piet's touch on a starship's controls.

"Then I'll leave you two to your dinner," Piet said, rising. "I'll have a draft of an operational plan tomorrow for us to go over. Mistress Blythe—Sal—your pardon for the interruption."

He was gone over the wall even as he spoke. His boots clacked on the wooden steps.

"People think Piet takes risks," Stephen said as the footsteps faded. "And he does, of course. But they don't understand that he makes plans that keep the risks to a minimum."

"You take risks," Sal said. "With him."

Stephen gave her a wan smile. "What do I have to lose?" he said softly.

She walked to his chair, knelt, and put her arms around him. His body was as tense as a trigger-spring. It was long seconds before he responded.

She felt Stephen get out of bed at close to local midnight. Arles had three moons, but they were too small to cast noticeable illumination.

She didn't speak until she realized that he was putting his clothes on. "Don't go," she whispered.

He bent and kissed her. Then he was gone, and she heard the outside stairs creak with his solid weight.

Somebody on the ground floor was singing, "*From this valley they say you are leaving...*" She thought the voice was Tom Harrigan's pleasant baritone.

Sal slept fitfully till dawn. Whenever her eyes closed, she saw the face of the Fed in the tower, lighted by the red flash of her revolver.

BERRYHILL

The last of the four transports that had carried the ground forces was the *Mount Maat*, a sphere-built 400-tonner even older than Whitey Wister, her captain. Stephen visored his eyes against the glare as she lifted with a delicacy the operation's two new vessels might have envied.

The *Mount Maat* swept south with less than ten meters between her thrusters and the tidal flats. Her exhaust blasted a trench in the mud, flinging up sand fused into gossamer sheets so fragile that they shattered again before they touched the ground.

The tracks of the other transports were clouds fading above the ocean as the steam of their passage cooled. Liftoffs—and the previous landing approaches—so close to horizontal were dangerous for any but the most skilled pilots. Such maneuvers were less risky than rising high enough for the plasma cannon of St. Mary's Port to bear on the ships, though.

The roar of the *Mount Maat*'s motors faded. The transport began to climb into a sky that retained some color from a sun that had just set at ground level. The *Mount Maat* was still vectored away from the port's guns. Her exhaust licked pearly highlights onto the sullen rollers.

"I shipped with Whitey once," Lewis said to Beverly beside him. "Crackerjack pilot, but he's a bugger. Him and his navigator, they're at it every night in their cabin."

"Bit old for that, I'd think," Beverly replied. "Both of them could be my granddad."

"Don't you believe it," Lewis insisted. "Them buggers, they don't never lose pressure in their hoses the way decent folks does."

Stephen's aide for the operation was a European lieutenant named Vanderdrekkan. When the transport was far enough away that the recombining ions of her exhaust no longer completely smothered the RF spectrum, the delicate-looking blond man resumed his conversation on a portable radio.

Major Cardiff had recommended Vanderdrekkan for the job, saying that he was careful and precise. Brave as well, though that went without saying. Vanderdrekkan's only flaw was that he'd take all night to plan an assault when a quick rush would have been cheaper.

The *Gallant Sallie* had been the first of the four transports to land on Berryhill. Piet had planned to use a larger ship, but he'd accepted Sal's offer when she volunteered. Stephen hadn't said anything. He hadn't known what to wish for, and he knew life too well to want responsibility for unpredictable results.

When Stephen Gregg pulled a trigger, he knew exactly what to expect. That was responsibility enough for anyone.

Vanderdrekkan lowered the radio and said, "Colonel? Seibel says they're making progress, but he's going to have to replace the men clearing the path soon."

Troops filed by in a ragged double column. All of them were in half armor. Besides personal weapons, these men from the *Mount Maat* carried cases of ammunition and replacement batteries slung on poles between each pair of them.

"We've got six hundred men," Beverly muttered, more or less to Lewis. "Guess we can wear out a few cutting trail and still whip Pleyal's ass."

Maybe I should put my loaders in charge of the advance company, Stephen thought.

Lieutenant Vanderdrekkan cleared his throat and looked

embarrassed. "Seibel also says he can see a paved road on the other side of the river."

"Tell Seibel . . ." Stephen said. He paused and smiled grimly. He considered waiting till he saw Seibel. No. "Tell Seibel over the radio that it's only a little less likely that the Feds have defended the highway from the obvious landing spot than that they've defended the spaceport itself. Tell him also that if he has further stupid suggestions, I'll be up with him in a few minutes and he can make them to my face."

Lewis grinned and winked at Beverly. The sailors claimed Mister Gregg as one of theirs when they boasted to the squadron's landsmen. Stephen knew very well that he wasn't anybody's, least of all his own; but it was small enough reward for men willing to walk into Hell at his back.

The tremble as of heat lightning to the north was the squadron in orbit exchanging plasma bolts with the defenses of St. Mary's Port. The demonstration might make the Feds nervous, but they wouldn't neglect the ground defenses. "Let's go," Stephen said to Vanderdrekkan. "All Seibel has to do is keep the river on his left, but that may be beyond his competence."

The aide trotted a few paces ahead, muttering, "Make way for the colonel," to heavily laden troops as he passed them. Stephen swung along the muddy track with his loaders following him closely.

Major Cardiff was in charge of the rear guard. He'd wanted to lead the advance, but Stephen needed somebody he trusted to chivy stragglers forward and make sure none of the inevitable minor casualties were abandoned in the brush. Seibel wouldn't have another significant position in any force Stephen was involved with, but his dithering didn't matter now. Stephen didn't have a high opinion of himself as a commander, but he knew how to lead; and you only lead from the front.

The vegetation covering the thick silt along the river was woody, thumb-thick, and branched into whips reaching as far as five meters in the air. In a few hundred meters the troops would reach the limestone bluff on which St. Mary's Port was built. After the climb, they'd be in the local equivalent of short grass and the going would be easier.

There'd be a realistic danger of ambush too, of course. The Feds had been given more than a month to prepare.

Besides Stephen and his immediate staff, the *Gallant Sallie* had landed fifty sailors and a 10-cm plasma cannon on a ground carriage. The gun was in the care of Stampfer, who'd followed Piet as master gunner through a series of commands. Dole was in charge of the men who dragged the weapon and its attendant paraphernalia along the rugged trail. Most of Dole's party was from his close-combat team. There was no risk of a Fed sortie overrunning the gun.

"That's right, boys, put your backs in it," the bosun called from just ahead in the darkness. "If they don't get out in front better, we'll roll some of these soldiers into the ground, seeing they like dirt so well."

Dole was bantering, not snarling at his men. He knew as Stephen did that pride would take the sailors farther and faster than threats ever could.

The plasma cannon was a dense mass filling the track. Stephen heard cutting bars whine up ahead. Sailors were widening the gap opened by the infantry pioneers now leading the column. The cut brush went to corduroy the muddy surface for the gun's balloon tires.

Stephen touched his aide on the shoulder and said, "I'll lead for a moment, Vanderdrekkan." He broke trail through resisting brush to avoid getting in the way of the crew pushing and pulling the massive cannon.

Dole stepped aside to wait for him. "Going up to sort out these landsmen, sir?" he asked.

"Going to make sure we're pointed in the right direction, at least," Stephen said. "Everything under control here?"

The bosun was a stocky man whose bald spot gleamed on a head of coarse black hair. He carried a carbine and wore back-and-breast armor, though the sailors with the gun had been specifically exempted from the orders requiring half armor for the landing force. At least a third of the sailors sweated in ceramic cuirasses as they dragged their tonnes of ordnance forward.

The armor was bravado. *There's nobody on this planet as tough as we are.* And when veteran troops felt that way, they were very generally correct.

"I sent Lightbody and Tiempro forward to set pulleys for the block and tackle at the top of the rise," Dole said. "We'll have the gun sited and ready before you're halfway to town."

Stampfer came back to join them. He and the six men of his crew each wore a canvas vest holding four dense 10-cm shells. The gunner had decided that was a better way to carry munitions on this trail than a wheeled cart.

"Remember, don't get overanxious," Stephen said. He raised his voice enough to be heard by sailors shuffling past on the drag ropes. There was no chance of Stampfer—or Dole—disclosing the gun position before time, but the common sailors might mutter and complain unless they knew the orders came directly from Mister Gregg. "We won't need you unless they come at us with ships. Then we'll need you bad, and I want your first shot to count."

"Don't bloody fear, sir," Stampfer said in a low rumble. He was a squat troll of a man. Instead of a firearm or a cutting bar, the gunner carried a meter-long trunnion adjustment wrench. He was quite capable of using it on anyone jostling him as he laid a plasma cannon.

"Wish I was going with you, Mister Gregg," Dole said. "But I suppose there'll be another time, won't there?"

Stephen nodded. "There always is," he said. *If you live;* but Stephen didn't have to warn the bosun about danger. It was amazing that Dole had survived after following Captain Ricimer and Mister Gregg so long.

The gun had staggered past as the officers talked. "Well, carry on and don't be greedy," Stephen said to Dole and Stampfer. "These soldiers aren't any more use on a ship than I am, so don't grudge them and me a chance to pretend we're good for something."

He pushed into the brush again. "Let's see what Major Seibel's about, Vanderdrekkan. We're certainly not needed here."

ABOVE BERRYHILL

January 18, Year 27
1629 hours, Venus time

Sarah Blythe's new hard suit fitted so well that in weightless conditions she sometimes forgot she had it on. The extra thirty kilos of mass were still there. She strained her shoulder when she caught a stanchion to halt behind Piet Ricimer's console.

The *Wrath* was under combat regulations: all personnel in armor, and internal pressure low to limit air loss during gunnery. A gunner's mate shrieked in a voice made pale by the thin air, "Mister Stampfer's going to *cry* when he comes back if you fucking whoresons don't train your guns better on the next firing pass! I could piss out a port and hurt the Feds worse!"

Piet wore all but the gauntlets of a gilded hard suit. He was talking into a handset against his left cheek while his right hand manipulated a display filled with numbers. After a decent interval, Sal said, "Captain Blythe reporting as ordered, General Commander!"

"At the very least, Captain Holmberg," Piet said, "your ship may draw a bolt that would otherwise have damaged a useful element of the squadron. Take your place in the rotation, or expect to answer for your cowardice as soon as we're on the ground. Out!"

Piet turned to Sal. The *Wrath* had five navigational consoles—the pair to starboard separated from the other three by a splinterproof bulkhead of clear glass. Guillermo was in the seat beside Piet, and a Betaport navigator Sal recognized but couldn't name was at the remaining console of the main triad.

"Holmberg thinks that because the *Zephyr*'s popguns won't do any damage from orbit, he ought to keep her out of the bombardment chain," Piet said. "He doesn't appreciate that the sheer number of ships involved affects Fed morale."

"Holmberg owns the *Zephyr*," Sal said. She hoped she was offering the statement as information rather than seeming to take the part of an Ishtar City man she knew well enough to detest.

"His heirs will own the *Zephyr* if he plays the coward with me," Piet said in a voice as emotionless as the one Stephen used when he discussed similar things.

Piet wiped his face with a bandanna, said, "Sorry," and then went on. "First, how did the landing go?"

He manipulated the keyboard with his right index finger without bothering to look at it. The numbers vanished like a coin spinning and were replaced by an image of Berryhill. Sal wasn't sure whether the vast turquoise globe was a realtime view or summoned from memory.

"No problems, sir," Sal said. The *Queen of Sheba* had come down too close to the river's edge and flooded her boarding holds when the hatches opened, but Captain Gruen had redeemed himself by rocking the transport free with his attitude jets before lighting his thrusters. Nothing Piet had to learn about officially. "The ground forces were proceeding ahead of schedule when I lifted for orbit."

Piet grinned tightly. "Stephen and I discussed the possibility that the river delta would be defended," he said. "I'm glad it wasn't."

The *Wrath* had just completed a firing pass when Sal came aboard in obedience to the general commander's summons. All the squadron's armed vessels—the four transports had been stripped of guns for the landing—were in a gigantic rotation that took them dipping one at a time into the atmosphere above St. Mary's Port. The Venerian bombardment wasn't likely to damage the defenses, but it was all the ships could safely do to support the ground force.

Under Piet's control, the display focused down in a series of x10 steps. After the last jump, an image of St. Mary's Port filled the holographic screen.

There were six gun positions sited around the large rhomboidal field. The tower holding the four heaviest guns was ten meters high, commanding much of the surrounding countryside.

The city south of the port area had originally been protected against marauding Rabbits by a ditch and berm. As the Federation colony grew, danger from the savage remnants of pre-Collapse society receded. Buildings now spilled beyond the berm to the south and west. The holographic image was sharp enough that Sal could see that alleys and the highway south, crossing the St. Mary's River, were barricaded against the expected Venerian assault.

Piet rolled the ball switch controlling the display's scale and focus and clicked up the scale. As the center of the image area slid upward, the port reservation expanded to fill the screen.

"This is what concerns me," Piet said, "and why I called you here."

There were nearly a hundred ships on the vast field, most of them Reaches-built trash with flimsy hulls and too few thrusters for their mass. Half a dozen had the presence of solider vessels, though these weren't of any great size either.

At the time the image was recorded, probably during a firing pass before nightfall, a pair of cylindrical 200-tonne ships were testing their thrusters. Wisps of iridescence glimmered downwind of the hulls, obvious to a spacer's eye.

Piet increased the scale once more. Guns projected from the side ports of both vessels; ten total on one ship, twelve on the other. The tubes were a motley collection with evident variation in size between adjacent gunports.

"They can't hope to engage the squadron with a pair of merchant ships mounting whatever guns they had in inventory," Sal said. "So they're planning to use them on Stephen as mobile batteries. On the ground forces."

"Stampfer will give a good account of himself," Piet said, "but there's dead ground between where the gun is sited and the outskirts of the city. The Feds will drop into the swale as soon as the first bolt hits them."

Piet's mouth pursed as though he were sucking a lemon. "I thought of taking the *Wrath* in close where our fire could be significant," he said, "but the port defenses are well handled. The risk would be too high."

Piet's smile was cold. "Too high to a ship and crew which Venus

will need in the real struggle which is coming soon. I intend instead
to send down a pair of armed cutters to occupy the attention of
the Fed warships until our troops can get into the town. Are you
willing to pilot one of those cutters, Captain Blythe?"

"Yes, sir," Sal said.

She would have agreed to step into space in her underwear if
Piet said it would help Stephen. The analytical part of her mind
suggested that the one course was about as likely to be survivable as the other.

BERRYHILL

January 18, Year 27
2105 hours, Venus time

Dawn winked on the fuselage and rotating wing of the autogyro in Stephen Gregg's sight picture. The Fed scouts flew over the southern edge of St. Mary's Port at a thousand meters altitude, high enough that they were safe from rifle fire from the Venerian ground troops for whom they were searching.

Stephen let his flashgun swing, tracking the glitter long enough to fall into a rhythm with his target. He didn't feel, he never felt, the gentle increase in the pressure the pad of his index finger was exerting on the trigger. The *whack* of the bolt and the blindness as his faceshield instantly darkened to save his retinas came as the usual surprise.

The six soldiers with flashguns in his lead company fired the moment after Stephen did, aiming at the second of the Federation's airborne scouts. Stephen's protective visor would take nearly a minute to fade to clear again. He flipped it up to survey the effectiveness of the laser pulses.

Stephen had hit the engine compartment of the autogyro he aimed at. The bolt had no penetration, even against an aircraft's light-alloy sheeting, but its enormous flux density converted the target surface into a plasma with a shattering acoustic pulse radiating from the back of the panel.

Steam blasted as the shock ripped away radiator hoses as well as the spark plug wires of the in-line engine. The two-seat autogyro staggered and curved downward, supported by the continuing self-rotation of its wing.

The Fed autogyros Stephen had seen in the past used radial engines. He'd expected his bolt to rupture and ignite a fuel tank ahead of the cockpit. This result would do.

The first hundred Venerian troops moved out of the scrub and into the sorghum fields with a shout, though none of them was really running. The march, much of it uphill, had been brutal, and men so heavily laden with weapons and armor wouldn't have been able to run far even if they'd been fresh.

With the reflex of long practice, Stephen's fingers switched the battery in the butt of his weapon for a fresh one while his eyes scanned to find additional targets. Rifles flashed from the darkened fronts of buildings on the outskirts of St. Mary's Port, but small-arms projectiles were no danger at this range. The Feds rarely used flashguns, though they might have crew-served lasers in their defenses.

Stephen thought for a moment the second autogyro had escaped the volley his men had directed at it. The city was a good kilometer away, and slant distance to the aircraft was still farther; a long shot even for a marksman whose bolt didn't deviate from line of sight.

The autogyro was diving away northward. The pilot probably intended to land in the spaceport, out of the battle, but there was no reason to take chances. Stephen aligned the craft with the fat muzzle of his cassegrain laser. He had an almost zero-deflection shot, just a matter of taking account of the target's rapid descent. . . .

Before Stephen pulled the trigger, the advancing half of the autogyro's wing lifted vertical and flew away from the rest of the vehicle. A bolt had hit the wing near its rotor, and the stress of the dive had snapped the structure at the point of damage.

Tumbling over and over, the autogyro plunged five hundred meters into St. Mary's Port. A deep red fireball rose above the buildings three seconds before the thump of the fuel explosion.

"Let's go," Stephen muttered to his staff as he swung into a jog. His side throbbed when his left boot came down and his breastplate slapped against the bruise. Vanderdrekkan ran alongside him, trying to continue a conversation over the portable radio.

The sorghum was waist-high, completely hiding the ground beneath its broad, dark leaves. The furrows were perpendicular to the Venerians' advance, and you couldn't guess how you were going to step from one stride to the next.

The acreage was cultivated as a single expanse by Molts, to feed themselves and the other slaves of the region. There were no fences or hedgerows, but irrigation canals rising slightly above the tilth ran at fifty-meter intervals down the length of the field. Stephen had ordered the flashgunners—the other flashgunners—to crouch behind the northernmost canal mound to support the assault wave.

Midway across the field, six naked men with guns and bows rose from behind the nearest canal. They aimed at the backs of soldiers who'd just passed them without noticing the lurking enemies.

Stephen was still twenty meters behind the skirmish line proper. He fired at a figure by instinct, closing his eyes at the instant of trigger release. The bolt's intensity would leave purple afterimages drifting across his retinas despite his eyelid's shielding, but waiting to put his visor down first meant a soldier's life.

The attackers were Rabbits, remnants of Berryhill's pre-Collapse society. The Feds treated the savages they found on recolonized planets as vermin or slaves—and Molts made far better slaves. That obviously hadn't kept the government here from hiring or cajoling Rabbits to fight for them.

Die for them. The laser bolt caught a Rabbit in the small of the back. His shotgun fired skyward as his torso exploded in a mist of blood. Soldiers ahead of Stephen turned at the flash and muzzle blast.

An arrow struck a Venerian in the center of the chest, shattering on his ceramic cuirass. The Rabbit archer hadn't allowed for body armor. A charge of shotgun pellets ripped the leg of another soldier, but he stayed upright long enough to shoot his attacker three times in the chest with a pump carbine. Another Rabbit missed a rifleshot from two meters away because instead of aiming he waved his weapon wildly in the direction of his target before jerking the trigger.

All six Rabbits were down before Stephen could aim the repeater Lewis slapped into his hand in exchange for the flashgun. A mercenary from the Coastal Republic was finishing a wounded

ambusher by holding his face in the canal with a cleated boot. The
Rabbit's long hair and beard were as red as the blood on the
soldier's left sleeve, torn by a bullet that had ricocheted from his
titanium breastplate.

Powder smoke, ozone from the laser discharge, and the stink
of opened body cavities hung in the air. Beverly picked up a satchel
of batteries with a look of fascinated horror. A bullet fired by
another member of the assault force had cut the strap without—
quite—piercing Beverly's neck.

Vanderdrekkan had drawn but not fired one of his pair of long-
barreled revolvers. "Three wounded, none of them seriously, sir,"
Vanderdrekkan said. "Holtsinger may not be able to accompany
the rest of the force."

The Venerian with the shotgun wound looked up and snarled,
"I can still fucking march anywhere a European pansy can!"
Another soldier had cut Holtsinger's trousers open and was
applying a field dressing.

Flashes and smoke marked where the Feds were firing from the
city. None of the bullets came close enough to matter, though the
attackers were within possible range by now.

"Keep them moving," Stephen said with a curt nod to his aide.
He took the flashgun and jogged forward, trying to pull his skirmishers back into a straight line. Because the ambush had occurred
in the center of the lead company, the ends had drawn forward
like horns pointing toward St. Mary's Port. The second and third
companies started to move out from the brush where they'd
assembled.

With a roar that drowned the crash of occasional plasma bolts
from the spaceport, a medium-sized starship rose into sight from
the valley of the St. Mary's River. The ship moved with glacial slow-
ness, a single maneuver at a time. Not until the vessel had reached
its intended altitude of about fifty meters did its captain swing
the bow to starboard so that his port broadside bore on the troops
a kilometer away.

The ship seemed to float on a cloud of rainbow exhaust. The
morning was quiet, poised between the land breeze of night and
the wind that the river would funnel from the relatively cool ocean
toward the city in a few hours.

Stephen lowered his visor. At this range, he couldn't punch a
flashgun bolt through the exhaust to shatter a thruster nozzle. The

trick was possible—Stephen had done so more than once—but only if the pilot cooperated by bringing the vessel close enough or high enough to give the flashgunner an opportunity.

Stephen aimed at a gunport, a minuscule target and one where even a hit wouldn't change the course of battle. Still, a target. He squeezed off. A flashgun bolt, not his, lit a stern panel. Vaporized metal combined with atmospheric oxygen in a harmless secondary flare. Many of the soldiers were firing, riflemen as well as flashgunners; even one desperate sod with a shotgun whose pellets couldn't *reach* the starship, much less harm it.

Stephen reloaded with his visor down and his head lowered. The starship fired six plasma cannon together.

The guns ranged from under 10-cm bore to 15-cm at least. They weren't especially well laid, but a single charge incinerated six soldiers as it gouged a long furrow across the field. Carbon in the soil and foliage burned red. A bolt that dug to bedrock blasted quicklime in white splendor.

Recoil from the simultaneous thermonuclear explosions rotated the vessel 20° upward on her axis, bringing the port thrusters into slightly better view. Stephen aimed again, seeing the blaze of the tungsten nozzles as a line of dashes through his darkened faceshield. Before he could fire, Stampfer's plasma cannon hit the forward quartet of thrusters squarely.

The thunder of the starship's guns was still echoing from the buildings of St. Mary's Port when the vessel nosed over and her stern motors drove her into the ground. She was nearly perpendicular when she hit. The bow stabbed meters through the soft limestone before strakes fractured and the rest of the ship crumpled like a melon in a drop forge.

Stephen knelt and covered the back of his neck with his hands. The groundshock threw him forward in a somersault fractionally before the sky-filling crash reached him through the air.

The sound went on for several seconds, punctuated by green flashes and the sharp cracking failure of the four stern thrusters. Normally the nozzles were cooled by reaction mass before it was converted to plasma. When the tanks ruptured, the coolant passages emptied and the thrusters exploded.

The ship excavated a crater fifty meters across and nearly half that in depth. Fragments of hull and shattered bedrock flew in parabolas from the impact. The scattered pieces knocked down buildings that the groundshock had spared, crushing Feds and attackers alike.

Stephen got to his feet. "Let's go!" he croaked. He couldn't see. It was a second or two before he remembered to raise his visor, smeared with dirt even though the filtering tint had started to clear.

Plumes of steam and dense black smoke twisted in a single rope from the crash site. Fires had broken out at a dozen places in the city. Despite the wreckage, a Molt fired from the rubble of a fallen wall. Stephen squinted and squeezed his trigger, flinging the alien back dead despite smoke and airborne debris that attenuated the laser's effect. He reloaded as he moved on.

A hundred meters of waste ground lay between the field and the nearest buildings. Plowed-up rocks were piled at the edge of the cultivated area. A few Fed marksmen had fired from rough stone hangars here. One of them was dead beneath a starship hatch that had tumbled like a flipped coin before pinning her to the ground; the rest had fled. Stephen strode past the body.

Lewis and Vanderdrekkan were still with him. Beverly wasn't. Stephen could see only a dozen other members of the lead company, but the casualties couldn't really be that high. Skirmishers who'd been thrown down or even stunned would get to their feet momentarily; the main body of the attack would follow in a matter of minutes or less, splitting the Fed defenses open from the lodgment Stephen and his handfuls tore in the immediate chaos.

"Rifle!" Stephen shouted, wondering if Lewis could hear him. He carried a cutting bar, but it wasn't his weapon. Even in a hand-to-hand fight at a barricade Stephen preferred a gun butt or the muzzle jabbing like a blunt spear to a bar's twitching edge.

For a moment he thought that the roar he heard was blood racing in his ears. Pearly radiance blazed across the buildings, and he turned his head to the left.

Risen from the riverbed but barely brushing the surface of the ground, a second Federation starship parted the pall marking the destruction of its consort. The vessel was swinging to rake its broadside across the Venerian attack. Stephen snatched back the flashgun from his loader. He aimed, because he had nothing better to do.

BERRYHILL

January 18, Year 27
2138 hours, Venus time

Ditches the transports' exhaust had dug across the St. Mary's delta
had filled with water and looked natural, but the amount of litter the ground force had left behind surprised Sal. Pallets, flexible sheeting, empty boxes, and containers of all kinds; clothing,
pieces of body armor, scattered cartridges; even a rifle broken at
the small of the stock.

A wrench pinged on the head of a bolt, rang from the gun
mount, and dropped into a cutter's cabin to clang loudly on the
deck. Tom Harrigan caught the wrench in the air as it started
another bounce, this time toward the attitude-control panel. He
blinked at the tool in pleased surprise.

"Sorry, sailor," muttered Godden, a gunner's mate from the *Wrath*
and in charge of the weapon and two assistants. Over the intercom
wired to Sal's helmet, Godden went on, "We've got this pig dogged
down, ma'am. Ready any time you are."

It had taken fifteen minutes to mount the six-tube laser at the front
edge of Cutter 725's dorsal hatch. The weapon and the 5-cm plasma
cannon being fitted to Piet's Cutter 551 had to be carried within the
little vessels during reentry. Though a cutter could fly at moderate

speed through an atmosphere with the two-meter-by-one-meter hatch open, it couldn't survive braking from orbital velocity; neither could a weapon stuck out in the turbulent airstream.

"725 to 551," Sal said into her communications handset. The modulated laser was directed at the pickup antenna of the cutter eighty meters away, but she had to hope 551's console speaker was at full volume. Piet and his four subordinates were all visible on the hull or half out the cutter's hatchway, wrestling with a mounting that obviously wasn't going as planned. "We're ready to lift. Over."

725's optics were good for a cutter but not *good*. Piet, recognizable only because of his gilded helmet, waved from 551. Sal heard him shout something but she couldn't make out the words. She started to get up from her couch in the far bow of the little vessel so that she could stick her head out the central hatch.

"Captain says go on without him, ma'am," Godden relayed. "Says there's no time to lose."

"Understood," Sal said. "Prepare to lift." She lit 725's thruster, lifted to balance a moment on a three-meter pillar of flame, and roared north up the channel of the river at 50 kph. It would have been nice to fill the water tank, but the small crew couldn't do that and mount the laser at the same time.

The St. Mary's River drained through what had been a fault in a limestone plate. Friction and acids from rotting vegetation carried by the current had widened the crack to half a kilometer, leaving bluffs a hundred meters high on either side of the channel. Sal didn't have time to be impressed, but she heard Godden mutter, "Holy Jesus!" forgetting the intercom was keyed.

She kept the cutter low, fighting the shockwaves reflected from the surface of the water. The plume of steam behind them warned anyone watching that they were coming, but the thruster's snarl echoing up the channel would do that in any case. They could only hope that the Feds were too busy to worry about 725—or that their shots missed.

Steam was the first sign of their quarry as well. The bluffs ten klicks up the river sloped and were only half the height of those nearer the mouth. From side to side and spilling out of the channel was a white pall from which slowly lifted a starship with its guns run out. Vortices shot horizontally through the fog. The captain was using his attitude jets to bring his broadside to bear on the troops south of the city.

Godden bawled something on the intercom. Sal pulled back her control yoke, lifting the cutter's bow and pointing them more directly toward the Federation vessel; the six-tube laser had only 15° of traverse to either side of center.

"Aim for the attitude jets!" Sal shouted, hoping that Godden heard and understood. Harrigan kept 725 flat in the turn so that banking wouldn't introduce another variable in the gunner's calculations.

The laser fired, sequencing the tubes in microsecond pulses. 725 was flying ten or fifteen meters above the river when the first flash lit the channel and ripped a collop from the target's hull plating. The cutter lost all thrust for the duration of the burst, dropping like an anvil until its belly hit the water. Only the up-angle Sal had dialed in for aiming purposes kept them from drilling into the bottom muck to explode.

"*Holy Jesus!*" the gunner shouted, this time surely a prayer as his thumbs jerked back from the laser's butterfly trigger. The thruster nozzle boomed at full power, lifting the cutter on a huge bubble of live steam.

They—she, Piet, Godden, and Tom Harrigan—had worried about the laser's weight, bulk, and means of mounting. Sal had glanced at the weapon's power requirements, found they were within the excess of the fusion motor's output over what the cutter required to stay airborne, and dismissed the question. The others had probably done the same.

The figures were wrong, and the mistake had almost been fatal.

The laser was powered by a magnetohydrodynamic generator that in turn used the cutter's plasma motor as its prime mover. The generator, drawing from upstream of the thrust nozzle, had absorbed virtually all the motor's output. The trickle of plasma that remained wasn't sufficient to drive the cutter forward. Gravity and inertia took control.

Because the water bath enclosed the exhaust, 725 bounced forty meters into the air at a higher acceleration than Sal would have chosen for a craft so flimsy. The Fed starship had a ragged tear where the laser had struck it, so the weapon was a good choice—if they could use it without killing themselves.

"What happened?" Godden demanded. "What happened?"

"Godden, don't shoot till I tell you!" Sal ordered as she fought her control yoke. She brought the cutter around in a wide arc that took them over the city, climbing as she did.

Troops lay flat or dead on the open ground south of the city. The starship, though not seriously damaged by the laser bolts, grounded momentarily in a geyser of dirt because the clanging impacts startled the people at the controls. The thick hull paneling of another Fed vessel was strewn like tinsel around the hole its crash dug nearby.

"Get ready!" Sal warned. 725 was a kilometer high and a similar distance from the Federation vessel, a metallic cigar gleaming in a setting of iridescent exhaust. The cutter was a possible target for the guns of the port reservation, but if that happened at least it would be sudden.

Sal put the yoke over and dived on the target. "Get 'em, Godden!" she said.

The laser fired, ringing at high frequency through the fabric of the cutter. Sal's screen dulled the sparkle of the bolts, but metal burned from the starship's hull was an opaque white radiance wholly different from the wisps of steam still hanging in the river valley.

Again the thruster lost power, but Harrigan lifted 725's nose by increments, making up for frictional losses that steepened the glide angle. Godden traversed as he fired, drawing his stream of pulses along the target's hull at about the level of the open gunports.

When they'd dropped to a hundred meters above the ground, Sal shouted, "Cease fire!" Godden obeyed, and Sal used the thruster's resurgent power to hop 725 over the starship they couldn't have avoided in any other fashion.

The Feds fired a starboard plasma cannon at the cutter. The bolt came nowhere near a target angling past at more than 100 kph. An instant later the Feds fired their five-gun port broadside uselessly toward the eastern horizon. The vessel had yawed after it touched the ground, throwing the programmed plasma bolts wild.

A second cutter, Piet's 551, screamed past 725 on a nearly reciprocal course less than a hundred meters away. The light cannon mounted on 551's hatch fired a slug of ions into the starship's hull, low enough to threaten the stern thruster nozzles. 551 twisted into a banking turn west of the river.

The Federation captain lifted his ship to gain control. He swung the bow north to bring the remainder of his port broadside to bear on the Venerian infantry. Stampfer center-punched the vessel with a 10-cm bolt, powerful enough to smash through both inner and outer hull.

The starship dipped back over the edge of the bluff. None of the damage it had received was fatal; none of it would have prevented a Venerian captain from continuing to fight.

This captain *wasn't* a Venerian. The vessel wallowed up the river, accelerating from a walk to a run as it proceeded northward. Steam boiled in the vessel's track, filtering the hull to a ghostly outline and effectively armoring the Feds against both laser light and plasma.

A bullet cracked on 725's belly. The projectile didn't—couldn't—penetrate the ceramic plating, but the vicious sound made Sal twitch at the controls. The cutter shuddered under her unintended input.

She climbed to three hundred meters over the spaceport. Sal threw the cutter into a hard, banking turn to head back to the delta. 725 staggered and lost thrust as Godden's laser ripped down into a Fed gun position.

"Hold your fire, you cack-handed fool!" Sal shouted. "We're short on reaction mass and I don't want to waste it fucking—"

The thruster burped and quit. Harrigan brought them level with the attitude jets while Sal fought the yoke. The cutter glided better than a brick, but only slightly better.

The motor found a little more water in the tank. Plasma flared, bringing the nose up. Sal deliberately shut the thruster down, husbanding the last of their reaction mass to cushion the shock of landing. Air swept across the open hatch with a *shoop-shoop-shoop* that sounded painfully loud in the near silence.

There was no point in trying to maneuver. Sal aimed for the largest open space in their direction of movement, the park facing the Commandatura of St. Mary's Port. She'd underestimated the flow when the motor was trying to power both the laser and the thruster nozzle. . . .

At twenty meters she screamed, "Hang on!" and lit the thruster with the nozzle gimballed 60° forward. The water tank gave them a second and a half of burn. It was enough, if you didn't care what you said. Cutter 725 hit and slid forward through flowers and an ornamental hedge. The stern lifted, but they missed doing an endo by 10° and a prayer.

725 slammed back down on the skids. The instruments were black. Another bullet rang from the hull.

With a roar like that of a colossal beehive, Cutter 551 set down beside them under power. Sal felt a surge of relief. Whatever they'd gotten into, Piet Ricimer wasn't going to leave them there alone.

ST. MARY'S PORT, BERRYHILL

January 18, Year 27
2220 hours, Venus time

Stephen Gregg saw movement behind the lace curtain blowing in the window across the street. He fired. A cat yowled briefly, despairingly. Stephen pumped a fresh cartridge into the chamber of his rifle, feeling as though the sky had fallen on him.

Somebody's pet. It could have been their child. It probably has been a child one or more times already today.

"Did you get one, sir?" Beverly asked. The loader wore a swatch from a cloth-of-gold altar hanging across his forehead and right eye. Blood had dried black against the fabric.

"Not this time," Stephen said.

A soldier backed out of a doorway down the street, circling his left thumb and forefinger to indicate all clear. Vanderdrekkan, breathing hard, trotted from the adjacent garden with a galvanized bucket. "Here you go, sir," he gasped. "It's water."

Stephen squatted, resting the rifle across his knees so that he could take the bucket in both hands to gulp from it. Beverly leaned forward and slipped a cartridge into the loading gate without disturbing the way the weapon lay. Lewis was three blocks back, his leg broken not by a bullet but when the stones of a crumpled wall turned under his boot.

Stephen thought the water had a chemical tinge, but that could as easily be the crap he'd been breathing in the past however long. He'd exhausted his four 2-liter canteens by the time he reached the city. Since then there'd been nothing but dust and powdersmoke and the stink of air burned by flashgun discharges. He'd refused to take water from the troops he commanded.

Stephen lowered the bucket and checked the location of the dozen men with him on this street. "Odd numbers!" he ordered, his voice no longer the croak it had been during several previous leapfrog advances. He rose to his feet and jogged deliberately forward, scanning for motion.

Fed resistance had broken almost before Stephen and his troops reached the city proper. There'd been a short struggle among the houses barricaded on the edge of town, but the crash of the first starship had shaken down much of the prepared defense line. When the Feds saw the second vessel flee with its tail between its legs, they'd lost heart. Besides, though the Berryhill defenders were armed better than most Federation troops in the Reaches, they didn't have the body armor that protected the Venerians in a close-range slugfest.

At the head of the street was a park behind a waist-high brick wall. Three Molts and a human in a white jacket knelt on Stephen's side of the wall. They didn't see him coming. Cartridge cases around the Feds indicated they'd been firing through the plasma-seared hedge toward the pair of Venerian cutters in the park. A number of Molts with head wounds sprawled among the survivors.

Stephen fired four times. Some of the men who'd advanced with him, the odd numbers covered by the evens, fired also, but there wasn't need for more bullets than the one Stephen Gregg put through each Federation skull.

He swapped his rifle for the loaded carbine without needing to say anything to Beverly. "Coming through!" Stephen cried. "God for Venus! Coming through!"

He jumped over the wall. The Commandatura on the other side of the park was a mass of flames, as was what looked like a barracks block beside the administrative headquarters. Cutter 551's 5-cm plasma cannon wasn't a powerful weapon for space combat, but its slug of plasma could ignite virtually any structure on the ground.

Piet, wearing a helmet of plain off-white ceramic instead of his usual gilded piece, covered Stephen from the hatch of 551 until he was sure of the identification. More heads lifted from the cutters, two beside Piet and three from the farther vessel. Sal's mate, Harrigan his name was, and—

Sal. Captain Sarah Blythe. Her right cheek was bruised blue, but her eyes focused.

More Venerian troops entered the park from other radial streets. St. Mary's Port was built like the southern half of a wheel, with the Commandatura at the center of the chord and the spaceport directly north of the city. A heavy plasma cannon from a gun tower in the middle distance blasted its charge toward the orbiting squadron. There was no other sign of resistance.

Stephen halted by 551. Piet climbed down wearily, taking the hand his friend offered. "Piet," Stephen said, "the whole rest of the squadron could dive into the sun, and it wouldn't hurt Venus as much as if you'd gotten your head blown off here."

"I was going to pick up the crew of 725," Piet said, avoiding the question and Stephen's eyes. "But I had to use the exhaust to keep the Feds away, and then I didn't trust the reaction mass we had left would be enough to get us to a better spot."

"There's only been sniping since P-p-Captain Ricimer swept the north wall with his thruster," Sal said.

Stephen couldn't look at her. "The second ship, that would have been a problem," he said, facing Piet. "I suspect we'd still have gotten through the cannon fire, but not near so many of us. Thanks."

A plasma cannon fired. Only one gun tower seemed still to be operating. "Follow me!" Stephen said, shambling across the ruined park. It was better to act than to think about what might have happened, and might happen yet.

A brick arch beside the burning Commandatura marked the entrance through the port enclosure. A high-sided truck had driven onto the berm and overturned, blocking the passage for further vehicles trying to escape. They were abandoned in the entrance switchback.

Stephen climbed the sloped turf bank and lay down at the top to view the spaceport proper. Piet was on his left; someone else was on Stephen's right, but he refused to look to be sure.

The gun tower from which occasional bolts ripped skyward was half a klick away. The walls were sheer-sided with no rifle ports, even under examination through the electronic magnifier Piet handed Stephen without comment. The door at the base was metal and solid enough, but it wouldn't withstand more than a minute or two of surgery with cutting bars. The gun mounts were countersunk beneath a deep coping for protection, but that meant the tubes couldn't be depressed to bear on attacking infantry.

The tower had external loudspeakers. Through them blared harmonica music at distorting amplification.

"Let's go," Stephen said as he got to his feet. "But watch out for diehards in the ships on the field."

"Wait," said Piet, tugging Stephen's sleeve. "Listen to the music."

What had been puzzling noise suddenly clicked into place in Stephen's consciousness. His brain filled in the lyrics: . . . *where the dearest and best, for a world of lost sinners was slain.*

"*I will cling to the old rugged cross!*" Beverly sang in a hoarse roar. "Love of God, sir, what Fed would play *that* song?"

The harmonica music cut off. A voice, also distorted, called, "If the Venerian gentlemen would care to approach the fort, a European whom the Feds captured and enslaved on New Bayonne would be delighted to open it to them. And if the gentlemen have a way of opening a door which the Feds locked when they fled, they can shut off the noise of these cannon and their damnable automatic loaders."

"We've won," Sal said.

"In three weeks or a month we'll be back on Venus with all the loot the squadron can carry," Stephen said as he started down the inner slope, reaching for a cutting bar with his left hand.

He wondered if there'd ever been a time he'd believed that the survivors won a battle.

ISHTAR CITY, VENUS

March 4, Year 27
0900 hours, Venus time

The footman swung the door of the private office inward and called, "Factor Ricimer and Mister Stephen Gregg to see you, sir!"

Uncle Ben—Factor Gregg of Weyston—rose behind a clear glass desk with nothing on its shimmering top. He'd redecorated the office since Stephen last saw it. The walls and ceiling were single-sheet mirrors, and there were no shelves nor cabinetry to interfere with the illusion of volume.

"Factor Ricimer, I'm honored," Benjamin Gregg said, extending his hand. "Stephen, I'm pleased you were able to come also. It's been too long."

It'd been longer than Stephen had realized. Uncle Ben looked old. His arm trembled, and there were liver spots on the backs of his hands.

Piet Ricimer had entered this office when he was a brash young space captain with a dream for Venus and mankind. In the decade since, Piet had gained experience and ten kilograms of flesh. The lines of his face were softer, but the spirit still burned as bright as it ever had. Piet hadn't lost his dream or his faith in God.

Stephen forced himself to view his own reflection. He was wearing a new set of court clothes in deference to Uncle Ben's sense of occasion. The fabric was a fine twill whose black-and-white striping looked gleamingly gray from any distance. Occasional silver threads added highlights to the perfectly tailored, obviously expensive ensemble.

Wearing the garments, Stephen Gregg looked like Death. The problem wasn't color. If he'd worn pink, he'd have looked like Death. He was tall, gaunt, and blond, and he looked like what he was.

"Gentlemen, please seat yourselves," Uncle Ben said. He sank gratefully into his own chair. The seats were padded and comfortable, the only elements of substance in the room's design. Piet sat down, but Stephen balanced on the arm of the other chair. He was nervous to have his own reflection looking at him wherever he turned his eyes.

"I won't waste your time on chitchat, Factor Ricimer," Ben said. "You know I've invested in your previous expeditions. I didn't invest in this most recent one."

Piet glanced at Stephen and raised an eyebrow.

Stephen smiled faintly, amused to be Piet's business spokesman again. "We made a paper loss, Uncle Ben," he said. "In fact, none of the backers were really out of pocket, but certainly the expedition wouldn't have repaid the risk. I would have told you as much if you'd asked, but you're too good a businessman to have needed the warning."

"We—Venus, myself, and my captains—gained experience in fleet operations, Factor Gregg," Piet said with quiet intensity. "That was more important than the wealth we brought back. Even more than the harm we did President Pleyal!"

Uncle Ben sniffed in amusement. "You did harm there, true enough," he said. "While your fleet was out, no shipments of chips from the Reaches were sent back to Earth for fear of being intercepted. The Federation's credit collapsed."

He looked at Stephen and went on with hard arrogance, "I'm indeed a businessman, and successful enough at it that I can afford to fund my whims. My pocketbook doesn't make all my decisions. Particularly"—the old man's visage softened minusculely—"when the decision involves you, Stephen."

Stephen sucked in his lower lip in a grimace of apology.

"What I'm afraid of, Factor Ricimer," Uncle Ben said, fully the trading magnate again, "is that if Venus doesn't pull back now from this confrontation, matters will go over the brink. The Federation won't make the first move toward reconciliation. Venus has—*you* have, sir—the initiative. If you keep pushing as in the past, the result will be the disaster of an all-out war that nobody can win."

"Pleyal will never give anyone but those he owns the full access to the stars that all mankind needs to survive, sir," Piet said in growing animation. "Pleyal will die or be overthrown, certainly, but whoever replaces him will be the same sort of autocrat. If the Federation thinks Venus is weaker, they'll stifle us. If they think we're weak enough—and we *would* be weak without the opportunities men like your nephew and yes, myself, have wrenched from Pleyal's grip—then they'll crush us utterly. The only way the Pleyals know to live is with their boot on our neck or our boot on theirs."

Piet stood, facing Uncle Ben stiffly. "And with the help of God, sir, I intend that it be Pleyal's face in the dust!"

Uncle Ben stood also. Ten years dropped away from him as he leaned across the desk. "Where will we be with the whole force of the Federation and the Southern Cross against us, Ricimer? Where will we be with hundreds of warships ringing Venus, bombing down through our clouds until every city has been ripped open to an atmosphere that corrodes and burns? During the Rebellion, Venus was a sideshow for the rebels attacking Earth. *We'll* be the focus the next time!"

"All the more reason to build and train a fleet so that we can not only stop Pleyal, we can forestall him!" Piet replied. The two men weren't violent; there was no risk of a slap or one spitting on the other. They were passionate men, and passionate about the subject at issue.

"A stalemate that wrecks trade, that's your answer?" Uncle Ben demanded. "Listen, boy, it was truly said that there was never a good war or a bad peace!"

Stephen got to his feet. "Gentlemen!" he said. He rapped hard on the glass table with his knuckles. It rang like a jade gong. "Gentlemen."

Piet and Uncle Ben eased back from their confrontation, breathing hard. Both of them looked embarrassed.

"Piet," Stephen said, gesturing his friend to his seat while keeping his eyes on Gregg of Weyston. Piet sat down.

"Uncle Ben," Stephen said, "the war's coming. Plan for it. There's always a way for a man who keeps his head in a crisis to make money."

Uncle Ben opened his mouth to speak. Stephen chopped his right hand in a fierce cutting motion. "*No.* Let me finish. Piet will never let go till he's brought down the Federation. If he did, there'd be a hundred to take his place now that he's shown the way. Pushing until the war comes, no matter what you want or I want or Governor Halys herself wants. Depend on it."

Uncle Ben sighed and relaxed. "You could always see as far into a stone block as the next man, Stephen," he said. "And perhaps I can too. But I thought I ought to try."

He turned to Piet and said, "Factor Ricimer, could I prevail upon you for a moment alone with my nephew? My servants will outdo themselves getting you anything you want in the way of refreshment."

The old man smiled. "I directed them not to make pests of themselves, but I suppose as the most famous man on Venus you must be used to it by now."

"Sir," said Piet, "you're one of the men who've made Venus great. I'm honored to know you." He bowed low, then stepped out the door the footman peering through the crack pushed open for him.

The door closed. Uncle Ben looked at his nephew sadly. "When you first set out on a course of what I viewed as piracy, Stephen," he said, "I was worried that you might lose your life. I should have worried about your soul instead."

Stephen drew up sharply. "We Greggs have never been Bible pounders, Uncle Ben," he said.

The old man shook his head. "I don't care about your faith, Stephen," he said. "Fifty years of trade have scrubbed away any belief in God *I* ever had. But I do care about your soul."

Stephen stepped around the desk and put his arms around his uncle. Standing straight, Gregg of Weyston was the height of his nephew. They might have been father and son; as in a fashion they were.

"Somebody had to do it, Uncle Ben," Stephen said softly. "I'm better at it than most."

"No one ever had to tell a Gregg his duty, boy," Uncle Ben said. "But I wish . . ."

"What's done is done," Stephen said. Again, barely audible, "What's done is done."

BETAPORT, VENUS

March 12, Year 27
0445 hours, Venus time

A rotary sander screamed as it polished a patch on the *Wrath*'s outer hull. The yard was working three shifts to put the big vessel right after the strains of her voyage to the Reaches. Though not so much as a rifle bullet had hit the *Wrath*, the repeated shocks of her own 20-cm plasma cannon firing had chipped gunports and even cracked some frame members.

"She was a little too taut for her own comfort when we left Venus," Piet said in near apology. "You mustn't think these repairs are anything against the design or construction. The *Wrath* handles beautifully. If Venus had fifty like her, we'd never have to fear from the Federation."

Captain Ricimer regularly visited the *Wrath* during the early hours of the morning with his friend Mister Gregg. This time they were accompanied by a middle-sized man in brown whose high collar obscured his face. None of the workmen was likely to recognize the third man as Councilor Duneen, who was having a private meeting in plain view on the bridge of the *Wrath*.

"We won't have fifty when Pleyal sends his fleet against us, as you well know," Duneen said. "Ten, I hope, but the rest of our strength in armed merchantmen as in the past."

For all the time Stephen had spent in the *Wrath* on the voyage just completed, he had no feeling for the vessel. That wouldn't come until he'd fought aboard her the first time.

At present the warship's twenty big guns were landed. Half the main-deck plates had been taken up so that the yard crew could work on the scantlings. Sternward, men with a hand kiln were recoating a beam that had been ground down to remove the surface crazing. The kiln nozzle hissed like an angry cat as it sprayed ceramic at just below the temperature of vaporization.

"We could gain more time if we raided Asuncion and destroyed the Federation fleet before it's fitted out," Piet said, with the force of a man repeating an old argument.

"Ricimer, Governor Halys won't permit the fleet to leave the Solar System," the councilor said flatly. "That decision is between her and the three of us"—he nodded to Stephen—"but it's absolutely final. Not to put too fine a point on it, the governor doesn't want her fleet and her most able captains weeks and perhaps months away when the danger to Venus is so great."

"It's not 'months' to a Near Space world like Asuncion, not even for Federation navigators," Piet said. "The way to scotch, to *end* this threat is—"

"*Final,* I said," Duneen repeated. "And I'm not going to claim that I think she's wrong. Asuncion's orbital forts pose a risk that any sensible man would find daunting."

"I'll be given a squadron for operations within the Solar System?" Piet said with a grin of acquiescence. His expression sobered slightly. "That's how the orders will be phrased, 'within the Solar System'?"

Duneen nodded. "Yes. Much of the materiel with which the Feds are fitting out their fleet comes from Earth. You can interdict that trade."

"Winnipeg is the major port on Earth for supplies being sent to Asuncion," Stephen said. They'd known the governor wouldn't permit a distant operation. The choice of an alternative target was Piet's, but the two of them together had roughed out the plan. All that remained was to sell Councilor Duneen on the idea.

"Good God, man!" the councilor said. "You can't just waltz into Winnipeg. The Feds know the risk, and they've surely increased their defenses over the past year!"

"We'll need current intelligence, that's true," Piet agreed.

Duneen shook his head. "The Feds are limiting the traffic that lands even on the commercial side of Winnipeg Port," he said. "Besides, since your last raid there's almost no direct Venus— Federation trade."

"Stephen here is the owner of a vessel in the regular Earth trade," Piet said. "With the right cargo, she'll be able to land in Winnipeg. Even now."

"What kind of cargo . . ." Duneen asked cautiously.

Piet nodded. "Venerian cannon, cast in Bahama. The arms trade from Venus to the Federation is at least as great as it ever was, because the prices Pleyal is willing to pay for first-quality guns is so high in the crisis. My father can get us a cargo from a firm who's supplied guns in the past."

"Look, Ricimer, you can't expect to spy out the port yourself," the councilor said, concern replacing shock on his face. "You'd be recognized!"

"Not as a common crewman," Piet said with a shrug. "The rest of the crew will be folk who've been with me for a decade, folk I know can keep their mouths shut. If I'm going to plan the operation, I can't trust any other eyes than my own."

"Good God," Duneen said softly. "Well, let's hope the governor doesn't hear about it. She'd flay me alive if she thought I'd let her favorite captain take a risk like that!"

Stephen Gregg thought about the risk to the *Gallant Sallie*'s captain, but he didn't speak. That didn't matter to anyone but himself; therefore it didn't matter at all.

EARTH ORBIT

April 6, Year 27
0520 hours, Venus time

The Federation guardship was a blur with three distinct jags across it where the screen's raster skipped a line. Technicians had degraded the *Gallant Sallie*'s optronics by seventy percent for this part of the operation, so the image was even worse than what Sal would have had to make do with before the recent refit.

The four plasma cannon aimed at the *Gallant Sallie* were sufficiently clear. "Ten-centimeter?" Sal said to break the silence that had fallen over the cabin since suction clamps slapped the Fed boarding bridge over the cockpit hatch.

"About that," Stephen agreed in a tone of dreamy disinterest. He sat on a bunk, his hands in his lap and his eyes unfocused.

The outer airlock door squealed as the Federation inspector started to undog it manually from outside.

"Listen to me," Piet Ricimer said crisply from where he manned the attitude-control panel with Dole and Lightbody. "None of us need love the Feds, but anyone who causes an incident will answer to me afterwards. If we're both alive, that is. Understood?"

"Won't be a problem, sir," Dole said mildly. "Won't nobody make a problem."

"Tom, the hatch," Sal said to Harrigan. Harrigan threw the lever that retracted the dogs of the inner hatch hydraulically.

The hatch opened. The slightly higher pressure in the guardship and boarding tube popped the first of the three Fed inspectors into the cabin like a cork from a champagne bottle. Harrigan tried to grab the man. The Fed batted Harrigan's hand away, spinning himself completely around before he fetched up against supply netting on the opposite bulkhead.

"Don't you stinkballers have a pressure system?" the Fed demanded. "And I'll tell you, if you'd taken one spin more before getting your rotation stopped, we'd have blown you to bits and inspected the pieces!"

All three inspectors were puffy-faced and run-down from too long in weightlessness. That probably accounted for some of their ill temper too, though Sal doubted the cream of the Federation military was assigned duty to the ships guarding the orbital entry windows for Winnipeg.

"Look, it's an old ship," she said in what she hoped was a reasonable tone. "First you make us do a slow three-sixty rotation to check for spy cameras, then you tell us to stand still for a boarding bridge. It's not that easy, you know!"

"Didn't say it was easy," said a second inspector. "Said the next trip back, you better learn to control this pig better or we get some target practice."

"Where's your fucking manifest?" the third inspector, the female, demanded. Tom Harrigan gave her a sheaf of hard copy on a clipboard.

The second inspector drifted over to the navigation console. Sal thought he intended to check the resolution of their screen. Instead the man reached down to pat her breast. She doubled her right leg, then kicked him across the cabin.

The Venerian crew grew very still. The Fed caught himself on a bunk, Stephen's bunk. He laughed. "You know, I thought it was funny you stinkballers would have a woman captain. Guess you're just a man with tits, huh, honey?"

"I own the ship, and I'm carrying you the cargo," Sal said tight-lipped. She had to assume that the inspectors lacked the authority to reject a vessel with a cargo like the *Gallant Sallie*'s, however they might bluster. If Sal didn't behave normally, she'd set off more alarm bells than if she did.

"So I see," said the woman with the manifest. "Six fifteen-centimeter plasma cannon. You know, some of you people would sell their mothers, wouldn't you?"

"Look, we're sailors, we're not politicians," Sal said. "If President Pleyal doesn't want to do business, fine. There's a market for these, believe me,"

The second inspector stared at Stephen beside him. "Hey," the Fed said. "You look like shit. Do you have something contagious, is that it?"

Stephen stared at his fingers interlaced on his lap. "I'm here to watch things for the seller," he said in a dead voice. "I'd never gone through transit, and I swear to God that once I'm back on Venus I never will again. Just do your job so I can stand on firm ground again. All right?"

The female inspector scrawled her initials on the bottom of the manifest. Instead of handing the clipboard back to Harrigan, she flipped it into a corner of the cabin. "Let's get out of this pigsty," she said. "The sulphur stink makes me want to puke."

The Feds bounced out the boarding tube. They moved in weightless conditions with the skill of experience, but there was a porcine sluggishness to them. Sal wondered how long Pleyal kept his guardship crews in orbit. Too long, certainly.

Harrigan shut the airlock hatches together. Probert, a motor specialist, said in an injured tone, "Where'd she get that stuff about sulphur? Our air's as clean as clean!"

Because Piet Ricimer was normally a flashy dresser, he stuck out like a sore thumb to his familiars now that he wore a common spacer's canvas jumpsuit. The Feds hadn't given him a second look, though.

He shrugged cheerfully. "If she hadn't made up a problem," he said, "she might have tried to find a real one. Give thanks for a small blessing, Probert."

The boarding bridge uncoupled from one edge to the other with a peevish squeal. Its asymmetrical pressure started a minute axial rotation in the *Gallant Sallie*.

Sal opened an access port in her console and reengaged the full electronics suite. Every stain on the guardship's plating sprang alive on the screen. An associated recorder was storing the images for later use. Though the Feds had made a production of searching the *Gallant Sallie* for external sensor packs, they hadn't bothered to consider that the vessel's normal electronics might be an order of magnitude better than what they expected of her type. Stephen's improvements to the *Gallant Sallie* had required a dockyard rebuild, not just a blister welded to the hull.

"*Gallant Sallie* requests permission to brake for Winnipeg

landing," Sal said into the modulated laser directed at the guardship's communications antenna. "Over."

"Get your filthy scow out of our sky, stinkballers!" the Fed on commo duty replied.

Sal engaged the timing sequence on her AI. In the interval before the *Gallant Sallie* reached the reentry window, Sal looked over the back of her couch toward the men on the attitude controls. "Remember, we're going in manually so that we look the way the Feds expect us to. That means you guys need to make a few mistakes too. I know perfectly well we could between us set down as neatly as the new hardware could do it, but that's not what's called for today."

Piet laughed heartily. The AI gave a pleasant *bong*. Sal lit the eight thrusters, then ran the throttles forward to sixty percent power. The guardship vanished from the viewscreen. Earth, blue and cold-looking to eyes accustomed to the roiling earth tones of Venus, rotated slowly beneath them.

Atmosphere began to jar against the *Gallant Sallie's* underside. Their exhaust streamed around them in the turbulence. Sal set the screen to discount the veiling and distortion of the plasma englobing the vessel. The planet sharpened in chilly majesty again.

"These guns we're delivering, Captain Ricimer?" Sal said, speaking carefully against the apparent weight of deceleration. "They're flawed, aren't they? They'd burst if the Feds fired them."

"Oh, I assure you, Captain," Piet said, "these are first-quality fifteen-centimeter guns. Nicholas Quintel may be a better merchant than patriot, but not even my father ever faulted the workmanship of the Quintel foundry. They have to be perfect. The Feds will certainly ultrasound the tubes, and they may well test-fire them before acceptance."

"Then we really *are* aiding the Feds?" Tom Harrigan asked, squatting with his back to the hatch and holding a stanchion. "This wasn't a trick?"

Stephen looked at him. "Don't worry, Mister Harrigan," he said. "We'll be paying another visit to Winnipeg before the Feds have a chance to mount or transship these guns. All they're doing is renting warehouse decorations for the next few days."

Beneath the neutral tone of Stephen's words was an edge as stark as honed glass.

WINNIPEG, EARTH

April 6, Year 27
0623 hours, Venus time

The *Gallant Sallie*'s plates pinged and clicked as they cooled nearby. The sky at local noon was a pale blue across which clouds moved at high altitude. In ten years, Stephen Gregg had learned to stand under open skies without cringing, but it wasn't a natural condition to him or to anyone raised in low corridors bored through the bedrock of Venus.

Piet, as though he were reading his friend's mind, said, "We're struggling so that men can live on worlds where they don't have to wear armor to go outside . . . but for myself, home is a room cut in the stone."

He gave Stephen his electric smile. "Or a ship's cabin, of course."

The civil port of Winnipeg didn't have a berm. The city whose houses grew like fungus on the ruins of the pre-Collapse foundations was several klicks to the west at the confluence of two rivers. Presumably the locals felt the distance was adequate protection.

There were seventy-odd ships in the civil port. Two of them were quite large, thousand-tonners in the regular trade to the Reaches. Piet eyed the monsters, far on the other side of the spacious field.

"They're being refitted," he said. "The motors have been pulled from both of them."

"The gun towers are dangerous," Stephen said, standing with his hands in his pockets like a slovenly yokel from Venus viewing a real port for the first time. He didn't point or even nod toward the defenses. "The guns are on disappearing carriages. I'll give any odds that when the mounts are fully raised, they can bear on all parts of this field."

The military installations were north of the civil port. A concrete-faced berm enclosed a slightly trapezoidal field of a square kilometer. Towers mounting heavy plasma cannon, at least 20 cm in bore, stood at both south corners where they commanded the civil field as well.

Within the berm, glimpsed during the *Gallant Sallie*'s descent and recorded with crystalline precision for detailed planning, were six ships. Four were of the older spherical style; the domes of their upper decks were visible over the berm. The other two were new purpose-built warships that copied cylindrical Venerian design. A sphere is a more efficient way to enclose space, but the round-nosed cylinders were handier and could focus their guns on a point in a fashion the older vessels couldn't match.

"The gunpit is new," Piet said. "The civil port didn't have any defenses of its own at the last information we had."

The *Gallant Sallie*'s crew left Piet and Stephen alone on the starboard side of the vessel, standing twenty meters away to be clear of the surface recently heated by the exhaust. Ground personnel hadn't yet arrived to carry the cargo to one of the warehouses lining the south side of the port; in fact, there was no sign of customs officials. Winnipeg was fairly busy, but no ships had landed within the two hours before the *Gallant Sallie*. The delay in processing was as likely to be inefficiency as a deliberate insult to Venerians.

"Hey, you two!" Tom Harrigan bellowed. The mate gestured peremptorily from the main hatchway to Piet and Stephen. "Back here now!"

"A good actor," Stephen said as he started back to the *Gallant Sallie*. Deference or even Captain Blythe's direct interest would imply he and Piet weren't common sailors.

"It might be he's jealous," Piet suggested mildly.

"He . . ." Stephen said. He went on, "I really don't think he is. He doesn't understand; but then, neither do I."

"Captain needs you forward, sirs," Harrigan said as the two men sauntered up the ramp. He eyed them the way a child might view his first butterfly: something wondrous and strange, alien to his previous conceptions.

"I believe you're right," Piet murmured as he tramped through the passage behind his friend.

"There's a problem," Sal said crisply before Piet was wholly into the cabin. "The *Moll Dane* out of Ishtar City's on the ground here with a cargo like ours."

She looked grim and determined. Other crewmen held their tongues as they watched. "Which doesn't surprise me, since Dan Lasky's the owner and captain and he's wormshit."

Sal tapped the communications handset with her fingertip. "He's just called and said he'll be over for a visit, bringing a bottle. I told him not till we'd been through customs, but I can't just tell him to bugger himself or it'll look odd."

She made a moue of distaste. "Since we're both running guns to President Pleyal, you know."

"And he'd recognize Piet," Stephen said. "Well, we needed to talk to the troops at the gunpit in the middle of the field anyway."

Sal's eyes narrowed slightly. "Is that safe?" she asked.

Each man's personal gear was in a short duffel bag tied crossways to the end of a hammock netting: head end for the starboard watch, at the foot for the member of the port watch who shared the berth during alternate periods. Stephen opened his and removed a small parcel wrapped in burlap.

"It's safe if we're trading contraband with them," Stephen said. He tossed the package on the palm of his hand before dropping it into one of the bellows pockets on his tunic.

"That was Stephen's idea," Piet said affectionately. "He's the businessman of the partnership, you see."

"I do see," said Sal to the men's backs as they left the cabin more quickly than they'd come.

The Fed position was the better part of a kilometer away. Stephen felt naked outside the ship. There was nothing abnormal about a pair of sailors scuttling away from a vessel in port, but *he* knew that he was carrying out a military operation against the North American Federation. He had no weapon, no armor; nothing but coveralls and the floppy canvas hat that Venerians regularly wore under a naked sky.

A three-wheeled scooter pulled away from the port administration buildings south of the field. The vehicle carried two white-jacketed humans and a Molt driver.

"Customs is finally recognizing the *Gallant Sallie*," Piet said. In a half-sneering, half-despairing tone he added, "Even on Earth the Feds are learning to depend on Molt slaves."

Because the field was so large, the vessels scattered across it looked as sparse as rocks on a Zen sand sculpture. A spherical 400-tonne merchantman took off from the port's left margin. Stephen felt first the tremble through his bootsoles as the thrusters ran up on static test. A plume of exhaust drifted eastward. Stephen's nose wrinkled with the familiar bite of ozone, though this far downwind the concentration was too slight to be dangerous.

The motors were an audible rumble at first, but when the ship managed to stagger its own height above the ground the blast became oppressively loud. Stephen kept his face turned down and away in what by now was a reflex to avoid damage to his sight. Piet bent their course to the other side of a freighter that showed no sign of life. The hull shadowed them until the rising vessel had reached a good thousand meters and her thruster nozzles no longer outglared the sun.

"There's a number of the ships here armed," Piet said, shouting over the roar of the liftoff. "I don't see that as a risk while we're making our landing approaches—the guns won't be run out, and firing up through the dorsal ports is difficult in a gravity well. But they may engage our ships after they've landed."

"You mean the latecomers may get to see some action too?" Stephen said. "I'd begun to think there was a rule that only the folks on your ship got to do any fighting."

"Captain Lasky would have recognized you too, Stephen," Piet said as if apropos nothing. "You're a more famous man on Venus than you might think."

"I'd trade fame for a night's sleep," Stephen said, marveling to hear himself speak the words. Not that the statement was news to Piet, or to others who'd shared the strait confines of a starship with Mister Stephen Gregg and his nightmares. He swallowed and went on, "They're watching us from the wicket. I'm going to wave."

At some time in the past year, the Winnipeg port authorities had installed two 20-cm plasma cannon on separate armored barbettes in the center of the civil field. To protect the gun position from starship plasma, they'd dug a pit several meters deep. The spoil was heaped in a berm that the Feds had faced with concrete to limit exhaust erosion.

The only entrance to the gunpit was through a steel gate with firing ports and a guard kiosk. The guard, a human, began talking into a handset when the Venerians approached within a hundred meters. One of the ports was initially bright from sunlight behind it, but it darkened like the other three a moment later. None of the watching Feds poked a gun out.

Stephen took the package from his pocket and made a quick gesture in the air with it. The guards wouldn't know what the contents were, but the display was communication enough: this pair of spacers had come to trade.

The gate was three meters wide. It squealed painfully outward, pivoting from the end opposite the kiosk, until there was barely room for a man to slip through the gap. "Come on, Christ's blood!" a woman snarled. "You want some prick in the control tower to report you?"

The gate was 1-cm steel plating on a frame of steel tubes. It was heavy and awkward to move by hand without rollers or frictionless bearings, but it wouldn't stop anything more energetic than a rifle bullet. A flashgun bolt would spall fragments from the back like a grenade going off, and a strong man with a cutting bar could slice through in a straight cut, plate and framework both.

The barbette bases were three meters below the original ground surface; even at 90° elevation, the muzzles of the powerful plasma cannon were protected by the berm around the gunpit. So long as the guns were operable, no hostile ship could safely land at Port Winnipeg. A single 20-cm bolt would do so much damage to thruster nozzles that even the largest vessel would lose control and crash.

Rather than stairs, a slope of earth stabilized with plasticizer ran from the gate to the barbette level. Eight humans and four Molts—the Molts had pushed the gate open; now they pulled it closed again—waited on the ramp head for the Venerians.

"What do you have?" asked the woman who'd ordered Piet and Stephen into the enclosure. She was young and plain. Her hair swirled to the right to conceal the fact she'd lost the lobe of that ear. The epaulets of her gray-blue jacket held gold stars crossed with a double line, but Stephen had never bothered to learn Federation rank insignia. Her name tag read PENGELLEY.

"What are you paying with?" he replied.

"You lot are from Venus," said a black-bearded Fed holding a single-shot rifle. Six humans and two Molts carried firearms, though the guns didn't look modern or particularly well maintained.

"So are the cannon they're unloading from our ship," Piet said, nodding in the direction of the *Gallant Sallie*. "Trade is trade, right?"

The doors to the gunhouses were open. Molts in the hatchways watched the proceedings at the gate. The turret armor was at least 15 centimeters thick, proof against penetration by anything except a heavy plasma charge at short range.

"We've got money, if that's what you mean," Pengelley said.

Stephen sniffed. "Mapleleafs? Right, we're going to try to pass Mapleleaf dollars in Ishtar City, the way they're beating the war drums there!"

"We figured," Piet said, "this being a port for the Reaches' trade, that a crate or two of microchips might have dropped out on the ground while a ship was being unloaded."

"Let's see what you've got to trade, stinkballers," the black-bearded man demanded.

Stephen looked at the fellow, smiled, and pulled the first of six 50-mm cubes from his packet. He handed it to Blackbeard.

"Our goods aren't for women," Piet told Pengelley with a smirk.

"What the hell's this?" Blackbeard said in irritation. He held the cube by the tips of all ten fingers, peering into its gray opacity.

"Warm it in your palms," another Fed soldier said. "I've heard of these."

Blackbeard scowled at his fellow, but he did as the man suggested. The gray suddenly cleared as the crystalline pattern of the cube's outer layer shifted to match polarity with the surface beneath.

"Mary, Mother of God!" Blackbeard said.

As well as being an idolator who worshipped saints' statues, President Pleyal was a sanctimonious prig. Under his rule, licentiousness and bawdiness were rigidly suppressed. Objects like these—cubes in which figures engaged in sexual acrobatics as layers changed state—were therefore worth their weight in microchips in the North American Federation.

"Pass it around, soldier," Piet said smugly. "Your pals want a look too."

Pengelley took the cube from Blackbeard. She watched for a moment, then closed her palms over it. "All right," she said. "What's your offer?"

"Three thousand consols apiece," Stephen said. "You pay in chips at the rate of a hundred and thirty consols per K2B, other chips valued in relation to that baseline."

"If you pay thirty thousand up front," Piet added, "you get the other six that we bring from the ship after we're paid. Deal?"

"That's a dirt poor price on K2Bs!" Blackbeard snapped.

"So?" Piet sneered. "Did you buy them out of Federation stores? Is that where you got your chips?"

"You can move these for five thousand apiece here in Winnipeg," Stephen said, removing the sample from Pengelley's hand after the slightest resistance. "Take them to West Montreal and the sky's the limit. Now, do you want to deal?"

Blackbeard clicked the safety of his rifle off, then on again. Stephen grinned at him. Blackbeard grimaced and looked down.

"All right," Pengelley said. She looked around the human members of her command to make it clear that she was speaking for all of them. "But you have to come back to Winnipeg with us to get paid. We'll be off duty in ten minutes. You can ride in with us on the truck. Understood?"

Stephen looked at Piet. "Understood," Piet said coolly.

The risk was obvious, but it was probably the only way the two of them were going to get out of the gunpit alive. Later . . . Well, somebody would become careless later.

And a close-up view of the gun installation had showed Stephen what he'd needed to know. The gunhouses were virtually impregnable if the hatches were closed, as they surely would be in event of an attack. But the turntables, though armored against fire from above, could very easily be jammed by troops who'd shot their way into the pit.

WINNIPEG, EARTH

April 6, Year 27
0701 hours, Venus time

Dan Lasky was a red-haired man in his fifties: overweight, as many spacers became in the narrow tedium of voyages; flushed and defensive, even though he thought the *Gallant Sallie*'s crew was in the same disreputable trade as he was. He pinged a fingernail against the creamy ceramic muzzle of the 15-cm gun unswathed for inspection in the hold and said, "Well, that's the goods, all right."

He gave Sal a knowing glance. "Bet you had to give 'em your left leg for tubes like these, though, huh?"

"Bet you don't think I'm stupid enough to tell you my business so you can undercut me," she answered coldly.

Sal felt dirty every time Lasky looked at her. It was as though he'd found her working in a brothel. It was all very well to tell herself that she was doing it for the Free State of Venus. The feeling of degradation was still far worse than the undoubted danger.

Lasky chuckled breathily. "Let's go forward and open this," he said, waving the half-liter bottle he'd brought. It held some variety of amber Terran liquor. He looked at the grim-faced men in the hold with him and said, "Harrigan, you want a swig too? Guess it'll stretch that far."

"Don't lower yourself, Lasky," Harrigan said. "I'll make do with slash, I guess, and I'll do it in the company I choose."

The common sailors were Betaport men whom Lasky didn't recognize. Sal and her mate were familiar to him, and he was delighted to see their moral comedown.

"I'll have a drink with you," Sal said, leading the way to the cabin, "and then you can take the rest of the bottle away. The quicker I get this cargo unloaded and me off-planet, the better I'll like it."

She was sure that the liquor was expensive. The mechanical uniformity of mass distillation wasn't a taste one learned on Venus, where most taverns brewed their own beer and every outlying hold distilled its own liquors.

She thought of herself and Stephen drinking slash at the first meeting a lifetime ago. It was hard to recognize the people they'd been as anyone she now knew.

"Christ's blood, I wish *I* was lifting soon," Lasky said. "I got people from the Navy, the Treasury, and the Bureau of the fucking Presidency and they're all arguing about whether they're going to pay my price."

Sal sat at the navigation console, rotating her chair to face her visitor on the end of the nearest bunk. Several of the crew were in the cabin—there was no privacy on a ship this size. Lightbody, seated in the airlock, glowered at Lasky as if considering whether to pull off his limbs one by one.

"You go where money takes you, boyo," Lasky said to him harshly. "You're no better than me!"

"Lightbody, go check nozzle wear," Sal ordered. "They should've cooled enough by now."

She'd been around Lightbody long enough to know that the man was in a way more dangerous than Stephen Gregg, because he didn't have Stephen's control. Lightbody's religion was as deep as that of Captain Ricimer, but the sailor's faith was a stark, gloomy thing instead of being the transfiguring love of God.

Lightbody viewed what they were doing as selling guns to Satan incarnate. Loathing at his own part in the transaction made him more, not less, prone to murderous violence against someone else in the same trade.

"What are you trying to pass off?" Sal asked Lasky. She took the bottle and drank. The liquor tasted thin with an undertone of smoke. "There's supposed to be a Navy agent here in an hour. If he takes our tubes at the customs evaluation, I won't have any complaint."

She'd been drinking a lot lately. Since Arles.

Lasky drank in turn without bothering to wipe the mouth of the bottle. "I'm not asking more than fair," he complained. "Standard stellite poundage value with discounts for wear. Trouble is, the Treasury whoreson claims the Feds already own four of the ten tubes."

He took another, even longer, swallow. "Owns them all, by his lights, but he can't prove that."

"Where did you get stellite guns?" Sal asked sharply.

Venerian plasma cannon were invariably ceramic. After the Collapse, metal-poor Venus had been cut off from off-planet sources of metal. The ceramics technology developing from that necessity was now one of Venus' greatest industries. Other human cultures used tungsten and alloys like stellite from the heavy platinum triad for thruster nozzles and plasma cannon. Venerians were certain their ceramic equivalents wore longer as well as being appreciably lighter.

"Where the hell do you think I got them, lady?" Lasky sneered. He offered Sal the bottle again; the level was already below half. She waved it away curtly. "I bought in a lot of forty-seven tubes that came back from the Reaches with I-Walk-On-Water Ricimer, that's where I got them. For a song, too. Nobody on Venus thinks stellite guns are worth houseroom. But hell, the Feds don't know any better."

"And some of the guns come with Federation markings already," Sal said, understanding at last. "Well, I guess that's your problem, Lasky."

Lasky drank again morosely. "Oh, they'll come around," he muttered. "They will if they want the other thirty-seven tubes, they will. Only it may take a month before we get it all clear."

He thrust the bottle toward Sal. "Here," he said. "Go ahead and kill it. Good stuff, huh?"

Sal shook her head. "I've got paperwork to do even if the Navy assessor doesn't show up soon," she said. "Best you get off to your own people and leave me to it, Lasky."

Lasky stood up slowly, obviously unwilling to go back to the *Moll Dane* and a crew of the sort that would work for captains like him. He paused in the airlock. "Maybe I'll see you again in Winnipeg," he said.

Sal looked at the fat man. Wrapped in red tape, the *Moll Dane* could very well be on the ground in ten days when Piet Ricimer and his squadron called on Winnipeg.

"I hope so, Lasky," Sal said. "I really hope you do."

WINNIPEG, EARTH

April 6, Year 27
1257 hours, Venus time

Stephen stared through the tavern's dingy window toward the twilit city beyond. The drink in his hand was fresh, so he tongued it carefully before he took a sip.

No drugs, no poisons; just cheap white liquor, served straight and warm. The Fed soldiers were buying. The bartender had offered mixers, but Stephen had waved them away. He doubted the Feds would add a Mickey Finn to his drink so long as he kept putting the liquor down at a rate they'd be sure would have him under the table in a few more hours, but there was no point in increasing their chances.

"And then he says, 'I don't know why you're complaining, we're on the ground, ain't we?'" Piet said, "like he couldn't see he was standing on the bulkhead because the ship was lying on her *side!*"

The Feds laughed heartily. Piet's stories of incompetent Venerian officers were all true, and they made him the life of the party. He never pumped the Feds for information, but his stories bred stories, and Piet listened.

Stephen Gregg listened too, as he sat halfway down the bar drinking morosely. The liquor wouldn't make him drunk. It just permitted him to view his life through thick windows that blocked the sharper pains and left him with only a dull, murderous ache.

Pengelley had made a call from the port administration building while the remainder of the gun crew waited with Piet and Stephen in a canvas-covered truck. When the truck dropped them all at a tavern in the heart of the city, a nameless fat civilian was waiting with a briefcase of pre-Collapse microchips.

The civilian's bodyguard was broader than Stephen and almost as tall. Apart from those two and the bartender, no one else was present. The man who loitered outside the tavern door was obviously a guard.

The transaction had gone smoothly. The price for the porno cubes was fair, and the chips the civilian offered in payment were of the quality he claimed. There'd been a delay in getting transport back to the field after the deal was complete, though. The Fed soldiers offered to stand drinks; and more drinks; and more, as the slow spring evening shadowed the sky above the city.

"Freshen your drink, buddy?" the bartender offered. "The sergeant, she's paying." He nodded toward Pengelley.

"Sure," Stephen said. "I'm legless already, so another slug can't hurt. They'll have to carry me when the truck gets here."

He and Piet were going to have to make their move when they next went out the back to piss in the alley behind the tavern. The trouble wouldn't be making a break, but rather how they would get from central Winnipeg to the *Gallant Sallie* kilometers away. There was almost no motor transport in this dismal city. If he and Piet tried to hike up the sole road to the port, the locals—who surely had access to vehicles—would easily relocate them.

Piet and Stephen were perfectly willing to leave the Feds with the chips as well as the cubes, but if the Feds guessed that, they'd wonder what the pair of Venerians had really been up to.

If life were simple, then Venus wouldn't have needed a planner like Piet Ricimer. And Piet wouldn't have needed a killer like Stephen Gregg.

Winnipeg was less a city than a rubbish midden with dwellings on top. The community hadn't been bombed during the Outworld Rebellion a thousand years before. Rather, the walls had been pulled down stone by stone by the starving, desperate population during the ensuing Collapse. Occupation of the site had been continuous, reaching its nadir five hundred years in the past.

By the time technological civilization returned to the region under the guise of the North American Federation, the bricks, beams, and ashlars of pre-Collapse Winnipeg had been mined for multiple reuse. Now the city's tawdry present squatted on its ruined past.

Stephen looked down the bar, careful to avoid eye contact with the fat man's bodyguard. The fellow didn't seem smart enough to tie his own shoes, but he might be able to recognize a threat if one glared at him.

Piet was finishing a complicated story that involved a captain setting down in Betaport instead of Ishtar City, well across the planet, as he'd intended. Stephen waited for the last flourish and laughter, then called, "Hey, Janni! Give me a hand to the jakes. I can't walk by myself."

"Piet" wasn't an uncommon name, but it was the one Venerian name that had a connection for *every* Fed.

Piet looked around. As he did so, Sal, Harrigan, Dole, and three other sailors from the *Gallant Sallie* walked in the front door. The local who'd been posted outside to prevent interruption lay on the ground, moaning and clutching his groin.

"There you stupid scuts are!" Sal shouted. "By God, if I hadn't found you in the next five minutes, you could *swim* back to Venus!"

"Oh, ma'am, we weren't AWOL," Piet whined, snaking down beside his leg the case of microchips from the bartop.

The bodyguard stood in front of Sal. He held a meter-long crowbar across his chest. "This is a private party," he grated. "You buggers aren't wanted."

Stephen, moving before anyone but Piet knew he was going to move, stepped behind the bodyguard and gripped him by the belt and the back of the neck. Pengelley shouted and stumbled out of her chair.

The bodyguard managed only a startled grunt as Stephen half ran, half threw him into the wall at the end of the bar. The bodyguard went headfirst through the paneling and the two studs he hit on the way. Bits of plaster crumbled from the ceiling at the shock.

"Jesus, Mary, and Joseph!" Blackbeard cried as he stared at the destruction. The bartender reached beneath the bar. Dole looked at him. The bartender brought his hands back into sight—empty.

"It's your own damned fault, feeding him booze like that!" Sal snarled at Blackbeard. "Christ's blood, he's not safe to be around sober. Harrigan, get them out of here. We're lifting in an hour."

The table had tipped when Stephen and the bodyguard went past. The fat civilian remained in his chair, sitting exactly as he had before the violence. He watched the Venerians leave, Piet still holding the microchips; but he said nothing and his hands, like the bartender's, were in plain sight.

Lightbody was driving a spaceport truck, obviously rented by means of a bribe to the right official. The guns and cutting bars that the rescue party hadn't wanted to display unless necessary were in the cab with him. Nobody came out of the tavern as the vehicle pulled away.

"Thanks, Sal," Stephen said softly.

"My pleasure," she replied in a neutral voice. "Much more pleasure than dealing with Dan Lasky this afternoon."

The truck jounced over potholes in the dirt street. At every corner hung one or more giant portraits of President Pleyal. Some of the pictures had been defaced with paint.

"Lasky's ship, the *Moll Dane*," Piet said, speaking over the rattle of the truck's suspension. "Is it a well-found vessel, Captain Blythe?"

Sal looked at him. Her face was shadowed, but puzzlement was evident in her voice as she said, "Not particularly. Why?"

"That's good," Piet said. "We don't have the authority to take a Venerian vessel prize when we return here. I certainly don't intend to leave the *Moll Dane* in the present hands, but I'd hate to destroy a really trim ship."

He smiled. For a moment, Stephen felt that he might have been looking into a mirror.

EARTH APPROACHES

April 16, Year 27
0120 hours, Venus time

"God's love, that's a sharp image!" Tom Harrigan said as he hung in the air behind Sal at the navigation console, watching the remote display transmitted from the *New Year's Gift.* "If I was looking out the hatch, it wouldn't be that clear!"

The guardship at the orbital window for Winnipeg grew slowly on the screen as the *New Year's Gift* maneuvered carefully closer to the expectant Feds. The guardship's four cannon were run out, but her crew didn't go through the charade of aiming the guns at yet another intrasystem merchantman with a cargo for Winnipeg.

The squadron had captured the *New Year's Gift* at Berryhill on January 1. The vessel was metal and responded to the guardship's hail as the *Mary* of Vancouver with a cargo of forgings from the Asteroid Belt for Winnipeg. There was nothing about the ship or the situation to rouse the inspectors from their boredom.

"The imagery from when we scouted Winnipeg is still in the database," Sal explained. "The AI uses that data to sharpen the details we get from the *New Year's Gift.* Our optronics now are ... We have as good a system as any ship in the squadron, the *Wrath* included."

She touched a control. The display switched from enhanced visuals of the guardship to a scene including both the guardship and the *New Year's Gift* as the latter approached for inspection. The image of the Venerian vessel was entirely computer-modeled from the *Gallant Sallie*'s database.

Sal's whole crew hung in the cabin, using the freedom of weightlessness to position themselves so that everybody had a view of the display. They could get to their duty stations within five seconds. Unless and until the *New Year's Gift* carried out her mission, the rest of the squadron *had* no duty to perform.

Piet had divided his vessels between the thirteen that would stay in Earth orbit to prevent the Feds from reinforcing Winnipeg from space, and the twelve ships that would actually land in the port. The *Gallant Sallie* was in the latter group, but because of her excellent controls, she would land last.

Piet knew Sal would set down within meters of the planned landing spot—not on top of a ship that had landed a few minutes earlier. Some of the larger freighters might in the confusion come down almost anywhere.

"Amazing," Harrigan whispered.

"Cost more than the hull, I shouldn't doubt," said Godden. He'd been assigned to serve as the *Gallant Sallie*'s gunner during the operation. All the ships landing at Winnipeg carried their regular batteries, despite the fact the guns diminished space that could be given over to loot. Even more than the recent voyage to the Reaches, this raid was a military rather than commercial operation.

"Too right it did," Brantling said. "My cousin's the assistant manager at Torrington's Chandlery. He says because it was Mister Gregg buying, Old Man Torrington did the work at cost. Even then it was more than he'd ever heard being spent on a ship this old."

Sal looked back at Brantling. She hadn't known the details. Stephen had listed the equipment at invoice price rather than at its much higher fair market value.

"Keep your fingers crossed," Tom Harrigan said softly.

The images of the guardship and the *New Year's Gift* were almost touching as they prepared for external inspection. The two oversized gunports in the *Gift*'s cargo bay swung open on the side opposite the guardship.

"The scantlings of a tin can like that'll never take the shock of twenty-centimeter guns," Godden muttered disapprovingly. "They'll shake her apart."

Steam puffed from the attitude jets of the *New Year's Gift*. The vessel began to rotate slowly on her axis.

"She doesn't have to survive any longer than it takes to fire two shots," Sal said. She gripped the edge of her keyboard as if it were all that prevented her from dropping over a chasm. "Or even one, if things work out as they ought."

She touched a control. She'd been tempted to display the view that the guardship's crew would have in their last moments of life: the merchantman turning with a slight wobble on her axis; the meter-square hatches open, nonstandard and puzzling, but not a sign of danger. At the final instant, the devouring flash of a 20-cm plasma charge ripping into the guardship before anyone could send a warning to Earth.

Instead, Sal returned the image to the *Gift*-transmitted realtime view of the guardship. Every seam, every rust stain was evident in the enhanced image.

"Firing without running the guns out . . ." Godden said. The gunner was speaking aloud but to himself. "I know, so the Feds don't see what's coming, but the side-scatter'll blow plates off the hull."

The central half of the guardship exploded in rainbow coruscance. An instant later another heavy plasma bolt vanished into the swelling chaos created by the first. The extreme bow and stern of the guardship spun away from the glowing gas cloud. There could be no one alive in either section.

"Prepare for transit," Sal said in a cool, gray voice. Her crew was already taking its stations.

The *Wrath* transited into the orbital window under Piet Ricimer's usual flawless navigation. The big warship began braking for reentry at once. If all went well, in a matter of minutes Stephen Gregg would be leading his band against the Fed guns.

Sal watched the *Wrath* shrink as the warship dropped away from the *New Year's Gift*. Her heart shrank with the image.

WINNIPEG SPACEPORT, EARTH

April 16, Year 27
0142 hours, Venus time

Because the *Wrath* was designed by men who'd done all the jobs on starships in war and peace, the vessel had visual displays in its boarding holds. On merchant ships used for war service, men waiting in the holds in hard suits to attack were as blind as sausages in a can. They had to guess the ship's status from the shocks and bumps: braking thrust, atmospheric turbulence because the guns had been run out; and always at the backs of their minds was the fear that any particular jolt might have been the plasma bolt that would cause the overstressed hull to crumble about them.

Nobody who'd experienced that blind helplessness thought it was beneficial to men preparing for combat, so the *Wrath* had a medium-resolution visual display in both of her boarding holds. Stephen Gregg, twenty-five soldiers under Major Cardiff as second in command, and half the men of the B Watch close-combat team could watch flat prairie galloping closer through a veil of exhaust plasma and the friction-heated glare of the warship's rapid descent.

Piet brought them down out of the east, just above the risen sun. The guardship hadn't flashed the port a warning, so the ground staff wasn't afraid of hostile forces, but the *Wrath*'s display was thunderous and colorful. It was sure to draw eyes in a port where excitement generally meant that a ship had lost control during her landing approach.

"Bet they're waking the crash crews right now, boys," Stephen shouted over the roaring descent. Sailors laughed and catcalled; soldiers relaxed minusculely in their shells of ceramic or metal.

By choice, Stephen would have been silent before action, but this time he had the responsibilities of command. Few if any of the soldiers had experienced a combat descent. Most of them thought the *Wrath* really was about to crash. Hearing the sailors laugh at the thought was the best tonic Colonel Gregg could offer.

Stephen checked the Fed defenses as their images grew. The gun tower batteries were lowered into their cradles. The guns in the pit were vertical in their equivalent rest position. The tubes were dim blurs at the display's modest resolution because they projected only two meters above the gunhouses, but the long shadows the sun threw from them were clear to a trained eye.

The port's scarred gray surface filled the screen. The *Wrath* sailed at a steep angle past a pair of vessels undergoing maintenance on the ground.

"Get a good grip, boys," Dole bellowed. "Captain Ricimer's the best there is, but inertia's still inertia!"

All sixteen thrusters cut in at full output, slowing the big vessel to the speed of a dropping feather in the last two hundred meters before she touched down. Despite the warning and the stanchions planted thickly in a hold designed for combat, not cargo operations, half the landsmen crashed to the deck under the braking thrust.

Dole had wanted to use only sailors for the operation; but the soldiers had more experience in ground operations, and half a dozen of the landsmen were reasonably expert with the heavy, dangerous flashguns that few sailors cared to use. Life is a trade-off. . . .

Touchdown was so delicate that Stephen noticed not the contact but the cessation of the thrusters' roaring vibration. The hold was configured for rapid assaults: instead of a single hatch across the entire frontage, worked by a screw jack, the hold had six paired clamshell doors that sprang open under the action of powerful hydraulic rams.

Ideally they sprang open. This time the lower trio worked

properly, but the center door of the upper tier jammed half raised to hang like the sole tooth in a gaffer's mouth. Men in the middle of the assault force lurched right or left, fouling their fellows as they charged into the seething hell beyond.

The last of the *Wrath*'s exhaust lifted in a superheated dough-nut as the hatches opened. A blast of incoming cooler air ripped trash and pebbles from the ground. It slammed the troops and staggered them, even the sailors who knew more or less what to expect. The flashgun tugged in Stephen's grasp, though he was barely conscious of the fact.

If Stephen Gregg had an article of faith, it was that his weapon would point where he wanted it to point and would fire when it bore on a target, no matter what the universe did to obstruct him. Other men had warmer, brighter gods; but as the veil of plasma lifted and the enemy's gunpit came in sight—this faith would serve. This would serve very well.

Stephen took three paces forward, breathing bottled air in his sealed hard suit. He couldn't see anything until the roiling air settled, but he knew from the display in the boarding hold and a decade of working with Piet that the *Wrath* had set down where planned, twenty meters or so from the gate to the gunpit. There were men to Stephen's immediate right and left. Major Cardiff in armor yellow-striped for identification pressed forward on the left flank of the assault force.

Rocks and debris pattered from the sky on Stephen and his fellows. He saw the gate clearing from the turbulence. The morning sun backlit the firing slits. One of the horizontal bars darkened. Stephen fired without needing to give a conscious order to his trigger finger.

The laser bolt struck just below the slit. It flash-heated the nickel steel in a yellow patch the size of a soup plate with a blazing white heart. The surface facing Stephen blistered outward, while the back of the plate exploded in ragged flakes. The slit brightened as the Fed who'd stood behind it fell.

Stephen reloaded as he ran forward. He paused at the gate to snatch at the cutting bar clipped to the right hip of his suit. Dole beside him already had his bar ready. The bosun cut down in a single powerful stroke. The blade's hornet whine became momen-tarily deeper where it sheared frame as well as plating. To the left, soldiers were mounting the steep berm. Pairs of armored men knelt to form a stirrup of their hands for a third who vaulted to the top.

A sailor fired both barrels of his shotgun down through the slotted opening of the guard kiosk. That probably wasn't necessary, because the Fed guard hadn't worn a hard suit. It was barely possible that the fellow on duty this morning had survived the *Wrath*'s exhaust, but he certainly wasn't in shape to resist. Better to make sure, though. Always better to kill.

Dole's bar cut to the ground in a last spray of burning steel. Stephen and a dozen sailors hit the gate with their armored shoulders, ramming it backward faster than a Fed crew had ever opened it. The body of a Molt lay where Stephen's bolt had spalled supersonic fragments of steel from the plate to disembowel her.

The hatch of the farther gunhouse was closed. The hatch of the nearer gunhouse was closing. Stephen fired into the crack, blowing a divot of metal from the jamb and perhaps reflecting some of the laser's energy into the gunhouse.

The hatch slammed shut anyway. A dozen Fed crewmen, humans and Molts, were trapped in the pit but closed out of the gunhouses. The humans screamed, raising their hands or dodging to shelter on the other side of the armored houses.

A Molt fired his rifle. The bullet hit Stephen in the center of the chest, knocking him back a pace. Scores of bullets and shotgun charges ripped the trapped Feds, killing all of them.

Stephen strode down the ramp. His chest tingled. He didn't think the bullet had penetrated his hard suit, but he couldn't worry about that now. The gun crew wasn't prepared to fight men in full armor, though they'd reacted pretty well to what must have been a complete surprise.

The nearer barbette began to rotate to face the eastern sky. The gunners were preparing for a target to approach from orbit.

Stephen dropped flat on his belly with his head cocked to the side so that he could see from that position despite the limited width of his faceshield. The gunhouse shaded the barbette's gear train, but he could see the quiver of motion. He aimed the flashgun and fired.

The flash of coherent light ignited an explosive secondary glare as metal burned white. The welded gear bound. The barbette stopped with a squeal.

Soldiers with flashguns knelt or sprawled to fire into the

workings of the other barbette. Bubbles of vaporized metal spurted explosively from beneath the gunhouse. A man stepped past Stephen and held his flashgun almost in contact with the nearer gunhouse's hatch.

"Don't!" Stephen bellowed though his hard suit's external speakers.

The soldier didn't hear or didn't care. His bolt blasted a fist-sized divot of steel from the heavy door, making the gunhouse ring but doing no harm whatever to the Feds within. The vaporized metal blew outward, knocking the shooter across the pit. The shock wave staggered Stephen even though he'd braced himself on all fours when he saw what the foolish whoreson was about to do.

Stephen had lowered his face to the ground. If he'd been turned in the direction of the blast, metal would have redeposited on his visor in an opaque coating.

"Throw something in those gun muzzles!" Stephen ordered as he got up. He tossed his discharged flashgun battery toward the nearer plasma cannon, several meters above him. The battery, a 20-by-6-by-4-centimeter prism, bounced back from the stellite tube.

Other men tried their luck with pebbles and debris; a sailor succeeded in lobbing the broken buttstock of a shotgun up and into the gun tube. Major Cardiff was climbing a ladder welded to the side of the farther gunhouse with a Fed's white jacket in his hand to drape over the muzzle.

What looked like a game was nothing of the sort. A plasma cannon's shell was a spherical array of miniature lasers that, when tripped, compressed a bead of tritium from all points but the one in line with the bore. Plasma propagated from the resulting thermonuclear explosion at light speed, but the ions were themselves of slight mass. The least obstruction within the gun tube would disrupt the stream and reflect enough of the enormous energy backward to destroy the weapon itself.

"Vanderdrekkan!" Stephen called, looking around for his aide with the laser communicator. "Van—"

The European lieutenant was at Stephen's elbow. Their suits clashed together as Stephen turned quickly. "Oh! Get up the ramp—"

Major Cardiff stood on the roof of the gunhouse and tossed the wadded jacket into the 20-centimeter hole.

"—and tell Piet that these guns are—"

The *Wrath*'s main battery let loose in a rippling string. Ten bolts, her port broadside—tearing the sky, shocking the assault force as much by the intensity of light as the crashing thunder of air filling each track superheated to near vacuum by the plasma.

A moment later the starboard guns fired. This time the *Wrath*'s hull muffled the havoc somewhat. The targets, hidden from the assault force by the gunpit and berm, fountained in white coruscance a kilometer high.

Piet had landed the *Wrath* so that Hatch 3 was adjacent to the gunpit gate, *and* so that the vessel's guns (trained as far forward as the ports allowed) bore on the towers of the military port. The gun towers were of sturdy construction with sloped concrete copings to shield the guns at the rest position. It would have required several broadsides to hammer through their protection.

Instead of that, Piet had waited till the Feds raised the guns to engage the invaders who had landed in the civil port. As soon as the Fed weapons appeared over the coping, the *Wrath*'s waiting gunners blew them to shimmering plasma.

The Feds didn't get off a shot. Their own ammunition added to the towers' scintillating destruction.

Stephen cleared his throat. The port-side guns had fired directly over the gunpit. "Tell Piet—" he repeated.

The world went white. Every sensory impression vanished.

Stephen Gregg was lying halfway up the gunpit ramp. He was on his belly, his head pointed toward where the gate had been.

The gate was gone. Stephen didn't have his flashgun, and the two satchels of batteries he'd worn over his shoulders on crossed straps were missing also. The cutting bar was still clipped to his left hip.

Stephen levered himself upright and looked back into the pit. The base of the farther gunhouse was stamped down as if drop-forged over the gearing below. The structure's armor had been 15 centimeters thick on the sides, 20 on the front and probably the top. The lower meter or so of the walls was now splayed out from the base. Everything above that height—the height of the plasma cannon's breech when the weapon fired—had been eroded into the iridescent cloud towering from the blast site into a dumbbell thousands of meters high.

The Feds in the gunhouse had fired their cannon. Either they didn't know the bore was plugged or they'd preferred to die in a

blaze of glory rather than surrender to pirates from Venus. Major
Cardiff had been on top of the thermonuclear explosion. He no
longer existed. Several of his nearer men had been blown to fragments despite their sturdy hard suits. The nearer gunhouse had
shielded Stephen, but if he hadn't moved slightly to give an order
it could have—

It could have meant that he'd have gone to whatever eternity
God keeps for men like Stephen Gregg.

The hatch of the nearer gunhouse unsealed. A Fed officer, waving
his white jacket on a pry bar, babbled, "Don't blow us up! Don't
blow us up! We surrender!"

Several Molts crouched behind him, fear in their carriage though
their exoskeletal faces were impassive. The Feds thought Stephen's
men had vaporized the other gunhouse.

"Vanderdrekkan?" Stephen croaked. His aide was one of the
armored men picking themselves up nearby, but he'd lost his laser
communicator just as Stephen had lost the flashgun in the shock
wave.

Stephen had been close to death before, many times before; but
generally he'd known the danger was present. This time—

The fighting wasn't over, not by hours or maybe days, but the
initial assault was complete. Stephen's troops had carried their
objective without casualties and almost without fighting.

And then the blast that Major Lucas Cardiff hadn't felt, and
Colonel Stephen Gregg wouldn't have felt either if he'd been standing one pace to his right. God's will, Stephen supposed; and therefore unfathomable by human beings, Piet would add. But . . .

*Why Cardiff and not me? Why so many others over so many years,
and not me?*

Stephen started up the ramp to carry the message of success
since he couldn't send it to the *Wrath*. Piet Ricimer in gilded half
armor, carrying a shotgun and a laser communicator, stepped
though the opening from which the gate and gateposts had both
been blown by the explosion.

"Bring the squadron in, Guillermo," Piet ordered into the
communicator's mouthpiece. "The guns have been eliminated."

Stephen flipped up his faceshield. Piet's eyes flicked from the
Fed gun position to the man climbing toward him in a hard suit
blurred by the frosty gray of recondensed metal vapor. "Stephen?
Stephen, are you all right?"

"For *God's* sake, Piet," Stephen Gregg whispered as he embraced his friend. "For God's sake."

All Stephen could think of in that moment was that if Piet had leaped from the *Wrath*'s cockpit hatch a few seconds sooner, the general commander in his half armor would have been ripped to atoms as surely as the gate itself.

And Stephen Gregg would still have been alive with the memory.

WINNIPEG SPACEPORT, EARTH

April 16, Year 27
0257 hours, Venus time

Steam, smoke, or sometimes flame flared from every opening of the 400-tonne Federation freighter across the field from the *Gallant Sallie*. While Sal was still in orbit, she'd watched the destruction on a signal from the *Wrath*.

The Fed crew had run out eight of their moderate-sized plasma cannon as Captain Casson brought the *Freedom* down. The Feds fired three bolts at the *Freedom*. They hit twice but didn't penetrate the big armed merchantman's hull. Before the other Fed guns could fire, the *Wrath* and the *Freedom* together put a dozen rounds of 17-, 20-, and 25-cm cannonfire into the metal-built vessel, turning it into a blazing white inferno.

"I'm going to open the hatches now," Sal said.

"We ought to give the ground another minute—" Tom Harrigan said.

Brantling stepped past the mate and threw the controls for the cockpit hatch. Harrigan grimaced but didn't object. Air, throbbing with the heat of the ground and scores of fires across the spaceport, entered the cabin.

Sal stood up and adjusted her pistol holster to the side now that the navigation console's bucket seat no longer squeezed her hips. She thought of taking a respirator from the locker near the hatch, but she didn't bother. She'd breathed hotter, fiercer air every time she crossed to or from a starship in a transfer dock on Venus. She could take this.

A Venerian 6x6 with fiberglass wheels drove toward the *Gallant Sallie*. The vehicle was moving as fast as the load, two heavy plasma cannon, allowed.

Only one Fed ship had attempted to resist the Venerian assault on Winnipeg. The crews—mostly just anchor watches—of the others abandoned their vessels on foot, trudging toward the edge of the reservation. The risk of another ship landing close by in a crown of lethal exhaust seemed less serious than that of being used for target practice by the invaders.

Sal stood a meter back from the hatch so that the angle through the airlock chamber would trap heat radiating from the ground. There was a good deal of activity around the warehouses and administrative buildings on the port's southern edge. The fighting seemed to be over, though Sal couldn't be sure from a klick away.

She wondered where Stephen was.

"Ma'am?" Godden called. "Captain Blythe, sir?"

Sal turned. "Ma'am?" the gunner repeated. "Can I fire into that freighter that's burning? I'd like to see—"

"Christ's blood, man!" Harrigan shouted. "What d'ye want to be wasting ammunition for? Aren't there fireworks enough for you?"

Godden stiffened. "I'd like to see how a gun handles before I use it for serious, sir," he said. Godden was a rated specialist, not a common sailor, and he'd been posted to the *Gallant Sallie* from the general commander's own ship. "And as for blasphemy—your soul's in your own keeping, Mister Harrigan, but I don't care to be party to terms such as you just used."

The remainder of the crew watched the gunner and their officers. Their faces were in general studiously blank, but Brantling wore a broad grin.

"Tom, see what the truck's doing here," Sal ordered crisply. "Godden, one round, and make damned sure that you don't hit somebody driving past!"

She stepped to the hatch to join Harrigan. She'd extricated the mate from a situation he shouldn't have gotten involved with in the first place. Tom wasn't the *Gallant Sallie*'s captain; but everyone aboard was tense and uncertain right now, in a chaotic, dangerous place and out of communication with the other Venerian ships.

When the truck stopped, the driver in the open cab was only two meters from the airlock hatch. The man wore a full hard suit. He'd thrown open his faceshield, but Sal didn't recognize him.

"*Gallant Sallie?*" the driver called. He jerked an armored thumb toward the two 15-cm plasma cannon in the truck bed. "Captain Ricimer said to bring you these to load soonest, then for me to get back. There's more where these come from, if they can just get them out before the whole warehouse burns."

Sal jumped to the truck bed. "Tom, unlimber the winch and get these aboard!" To the driver she added, "You! Pull around to the main hatch."

The truck's torque converter built to a peevish whine as inertia fought the diesel's rattling surge. The vehicle eased forward to halt again by the hatch as it lowered.

Sal rubbed her hands together. Her throat was dry. She should have grabbed a water bottle.

"Is Mister Gregg with the general commander, then?" she asked the driver. She wished she knew the man's name. She'd seen him aboard the *Wrath,* she was sure.

"Oh, yeah," the driver said cheerfully. He gave Sal a slight smile as he eyed her. "The Feds tried to start something at the arms warehouse, so he was there to sort them out."

"He's all right, though?" Sal asked, her heart as parched as her mouth.

"You needn't worry about him, ma'am," the driver said. "Our Mister Gregg—he's the Angel of Death, he is."

The *Gallant Sallie*'s crane squealed as Brantling ran the hook out the beam positioned over a gun tube. Four crewmen were lifting the fiberglass sashes tied around the heavy weapon.

"Harrigan!" Sal called. "When we've got these guns loaded, take charge of the ship. I'm going back on the truck to—to see what's going on."

WINNIPEG SPACEPORT, EARTH

April 16, Year 27
0345 hours, Venus time

The casters clacked like gunshots at every irregularity in the warehouse floor. The manual dolly tracked straight enough, but as the entrance neared Stephen saw that they weren't going to clear the door, which had jammed only three-quarters open.

Piet, across the dolly from Stephen, leaned hard against the muzzle of the 15-cm gun tube. The dolly continued along an unchanged line. The concrete was sloped, slightly but enough to give the tonnes of plasma cannon a will of its own.

"I'm changing sides," Stephen shouted. The fire at the rear of the big warehouse was bursting containers—clangs, not explosions, but they reverberated loudly within the structure.

The hot, smoky air made Stephen's eyes water and his lungs burn. He'd raised his faceshield because he wanted to save the remaining contents of his air bottle for a real emergency, but he was beginning to think he'd need it before they got out of this *damned* building.

The hard suit chafed Stephen's neck, his hipbone, and his knees. Maybe he should have taken the suit off, but when they entered the warehouse they hadn't been sure how quickly the fire would spread. The armor would have been their only chance of survival if the roof had collapsed . . .

"We'll be all right," Piet gasped. The rhythm of the casters slowed slightly. The four men with Piet and Stephen slacked their efforts as they saw the problem ahead.

Stephen let the dolly rumble past, then walked behind it and around to take his position directly in back of Piet. He'd thought of trotting in front of the gun—and thought of slipping on the concrete, exhausted, and having the dolly upset its load onto him. His hard suit might or might not withstand the shock, but they'd certainly lose the gun tube.

"Easy, now," Piet warned. Stephen settled his weight against the weapon, then put a little more of his strength into the side thrust with every pace. The dolly hesitated, then slanted 15° to the right; enough to miss the door wedged open by a corpse that had fallen into the track. Stephen stepped back, made sure the dolly would hold its new line, and trekked around to the right side again.

The sunlight beyond was a beckoning dazzle. Smoke rising from the fires in the rear of the building filtered the overhead lights into ruddy glows. The ventilation fans in the roof peaks prevented the haze from filling the warehouse, but they also stirred the flames to greater enthusiasm. The Feds hadn't stored fuel or munitions here, but the packing materials themselves were combustible.

"Watch the lip!" Piet warned. The metal threshold plate was a half-centimeter higher than the concrete to which it was bolted. The front casters hit the plate at a skew angle. The dolly rocked, then righted, and rolled out onto the stabilized earth of the space-port proper.

A dozen Venerians, several of them gentlemen wearing enameled and polished half armor, were arguing around the 15-cm gun Piet's team had dumped in front of the warehouse before going back for the next one.

"Well, let me tell you, Blassingame!" an officer shouted. "Even if it had been my men responsible for the fire, I don't have to answer to you about it!"

"Let the whole bloody—" another officer said. The sound of the dolly banging over the threshold made him turn.

"God and His saints!" a sailor who'd sailed with Piet in the past blurted. "It's the captain!"

The truck that had carried the first two guns to the *Gallant Sallie* was coming toward the warehouse again. Because of fatigue and the sweat in his eyes, Stephen at first saw only that there was someone in the cab with Tsarev, the driver.

His vision cleared suddenly; he recognized Sal. He wished she was—home on Venus, in orbit; anywhere but in this dangerous mare's nest. But he was very glad to see her.

"All right," Piet said in a hoarse voice. He loosened the turn-buckles clamping the gun to the dolly. "Everyone on the right side and push."

"The truck's coming back, sir," Vanderdrekkan said. He took his place beside the other five men of Piet's team, however, his gauntlets against the plasma cannon.

"It has the winch and shear legs," Stephen rasped. "It'll lift as well from the ground as from this dolly."

"Together," Piet said. "Push . . ."

The men who'd been gathered in front of the warehouse stepped clear when they saw what was about to happen. A pair of sailors moved to join Piet's team, but they were too late to help and unnecessary anyway. The gun tube rolled off the dolly and crashed to the ground like a meteor impact.

Tsarev pulled the truck around in a U-turn, then backed close to the pair of 15-cm guns. Sal stepped out onto the running board to guide him. She was wearing a helmet but no other protective garb.

"Blassingame," Piet ordered. "Take five of these men and get the remaining gun tubes. They're midway down Aisle Three."

A plasma cannon spoke from far across the field. One of the Venerian ships was shooting at Feds peering over the berm of the military port.

"But it's burning, sir!" Blassingame said in surprise. His family had a small hold in the Maxwell Range, not dissimilar to Eryx where Stephen had been born.

"Then you'd better work fast, hadn't you, man?" Piet said. His tone was even rougher than his throat, very unusual for him. "The Feds will have time to sift the ashes for anything we miss, so I don't intend to leave them guns that won't be harmed by a fire."

Blassingame nodded in puzzled agreement. "Whatever you say, sir," he said.

Blassingame wasn't one of the squadron's brighter lights, but now as in the past he'd proved himself dependable within his capacities. He pointed to a group of men and said, "You five, come along now!" He suited his actions to his words by personally wheeling the dolly around to return.

Vanderdrekkan had hopped into the cab. He was trying to raise someone on the truck's radio. He didn't seem to be having any luck because of the varied forms of interference.

Tsarev, Sal, and the three sailors who'd helped push the guns out of the warehouse were looping sashes beneath a tube for the truck's winch to hook. Stephen checked the sling of the rifle that had replaced the flashgun he lost in the gunpit, then knelt to join them.

"Cherwell," Piet ordered sharply. "You and the rest of these men load the guns. When you've done that, go into the warehouse and help Blassingame."

"At once, sir!" Cherwell said, bracing himself to attention. He glared at the men with him and said, "You heard Factor Ricimer. Get to work!"

"Were your arms amputated, Cherwell?" Stephen heard himself demand in a high, liquid voice. "Or is it that you don't think any-one who works with his hands can be a gentleman?"

The plain finish of Stephen's hard suit was now dirty gray from condensed metal. Save for his size, he was anonymous at a quick glance. Cherwell, a young gentleman, hadn't noticed Stephen until he spoke.

Cherwell bent to put his weight with the others rolling the plasma cannon over the fiberglass sash. "I'm not too proud to serve Venus in whatever fashion Factor Ricimer orders," he said with a simple dignity that raised him several steps in Stephen's estima-tion.

A party of ten or a dozen sailors trotted by a hundred meters away. They carried cutting bars and firearms, but only a few of them were wearing body armor. Piet shouted to the men—whatever they thought they were doing was less important than getting the last pair of guns out of the warehouse. They couldn't hear over the gunfire and engine noise pulsing across the spaceport like chop on a pond.

Stephen looked at Sal, who'd stepped out of the way when Cherwell's men took over from Piet's team. She was fresh, but han-dling tonnes of dense ceramic was a job for bulk and peak strength, not endurance and good will.

"Any trouble landing?" he asked inanely. As he spoke, his eyes continued to check his surroundings, and he shifted on his left heel to scan through the helmet locked to the gorget of his hard suit.

"We—" Sal said. She lifted her helmet to wipe her forehead with a bandanna. A roar building within the military port smothered the rest of her sentence.

Plasma billowed over the berm. A cylindrical starship—a moderate-sized freighter, two or three hundred tonnes burden—lifted into sight some distance within the enclosure. The vessel wobbled a little, but it had no forward way on.

A midships hatch was lifted like a wing. There would be a cutter in the hold, ready to take the skeleton crew to safety once the Feds had locked their controls on course for one of the larger Venerian vessels.

"We're going to have to do something about the military port," Piet said. His voice was clear and calm. Sight of the next task had done more than the few moments of rest to cleanse his body of fatigue.

The featherboat and three large cutters Piet had set to watch for just such an eventuality lifted from the field. Bulging cargo nets on the bows of all four boats were filled with spun-glass matting that would resist the wash of ionized exhaust. The 5-cm cannon in the featherboat's nose was covered by the cushion.

A starship was a potential missile with enormous kinetic energy, even at the relatively low speeds possible immediately after take-off. Concentrated cannonfire could destroy a ship—the freighter blazing in the middle of the field was proof of that—but jolts of ions wouldn't in themselves counteract the momentum of hundreds of tonnes of steel. The Fed vessel's bow might be a white glowing mass when it hit a Venerian ship, but that wouldn't keep the impact from being wholly devastating to the target.

A Venerian cutter, then the other two cutters and the featherboat, edged forward at a walking pace. The small vessels kept as low as possible: Fed vessels within the military port would have their cannon trained over the berm to smash anything that rose high enough to be visible. A ship the size of the Fed freighter could absorb punishment for a minute or two, but a boat of less than 50 tonnes would disintegrate at the first plasma bolt.

The freighter porpoised as it started toward the civil port, dipping and then rising again enough to clear the berm. The featherboat and cutters swung wide, still keeping close to the surface of the field.

The Venerian small craft had expert pilots, briefed for this task. Piet had calculated that by butting gently against the freighter's starboard bow and then boosting their thrusters to maximum output, they could swing the bigger vessel harmlessly off its line and send it off over the hectares of wasteland and farms. If the Feds stayed aboard they could perhaps maneuver into the *Wrath* or another important ship despite the picket boats, but that would be literal suicide for the crew. President Pleyal didn't inspire that degree of loyalty.

"I'll take a company into the military port," Stephen decided aloud. "Fifty or a hundred men ought to be enough to sort things out. I don't imagine the Feds will hold after the first volley."

Vanderdrekkan was at Stephen's side again. "I believe all the troops have been committed, sir," he said. "Do you want me to gather men at random, or did you have a particular contingent in mind?"

"Belay that, Cherwell," Piet ordered, gesturing to the half-raised gun tube. "The guns can stay here for the time being. I'm going to need the truck myself."

The Fed merchantman dipped again as it gathered forward speed. If the Venerian pickets hit the Fed too hard, the freighter's thicker hull would shatter the boats and brush the fragments away. The small craft pogoed nervously as they maneuvered toward contact. The featherboat was slightly larger than the cutters, but it too depended on a single thruster. Not even the most skillful pilot and crew could keep a one-nozzle vessel perfectly stable in a hover.

"The A Watch close-combat team is still aboard the *Wrath* for emergencies," Stephen said to his aide. "The Feds getting their act together across the berm is as close to an emergency as we're likely to have. I want men in full armor because the ships inside'll fire when we cross. The splash from plasma cannon is going to be too hot for anything but hard suits."

He was planning against near misses by the Federation cannoneers. Armor didn't make any difference for the inevitable direct hits, since the heaviest suit a man could carry would burn like a cotton wisp in the direct path of a slug of ions.

The Fed freighter nosed over the berm. Two guns fired from the *Freedom*, against Piet Ricimer's direct orders.

The shock wave from the bolts hitting the freighter rocked the

picket vessels violently. The nearest cutter spun a full 360°, touched
the ground, and bounded a hundred meters in the air. The pilot
got control just in time to dive to safety as a bolt from the military port slashed the air where the cutter had been.

A rainbow fireball engulfed the freighter's bow. The *Freedom*
mounted several 25-cm smashers as part of its heterogeneous battery.
Stampfer, the expert on plasma cannon so far as Stephen was concerned, said that 20-cm guns were superior to the big guns because
they cooled much faster between shots and because 25-cm shells
were so heavy that they led to dangerous accidents as the crews
handled them under the stress of combat.

For all that, 25-cm plasma bolts made an impressive show when
they hit a metal hull in an oxidizing atmosphere. The first round
punched the lower curve of the vessel's bow and vaporized a square
meter of hull plating. The bubble of gaseous steel used the top
of the berm as a fulcrum to lift the freighter.

The second bolt, fired a half-second later—and it was probably
pure chance, but Stephen had known for a decade that in war it
was better to be lucky than skillful—hit the nest of four thrusters under the bow. The tungsten nozzles exploded in green radiance, destroyed as much by the ions they were channeling as by
the cannon bolt that overloaded their outer surfaces.

Inertia kept the vessel moving forward even after the bow thrusters were destroyed, but the nose dipped as gravity pulled it down.
The freighter hit the berm, quenching the white-hot metal as it
plowed through a hundred cubic meters of earth. Sparks flew from
rocks in the dirt. The noise was overwhelming, even in comparison to the *clang* of cannonfire a moment before.

The Fed captain reacted instantly and as well as was possible
under the circumstances. He (or not unlikely she, in Federation
service) chopped the throttles to the quartet of thrusters in the
stern. Their continued thrust would have lifted the freighter onto
its ruined nose, then flipped the vessel over the berm on its back.

With the power off and the bow supported three meters above
the ground by the berm, the stern dropped and hit with a crash.
The freighter bounced, hopped several meters forward, and came
down again to break its back on the berm.

The wreckage lay steaming in a haze of dirt. The vessel's
crumpled bow lay in the civil field, but the stern remained in the
military port.

Almost as an afterthought, the final impact flung the prepared escape boat out of the hold. It hit something within the military port. An orange flash brightened the morning momentarily, followed by the thud of an explosion.

"I'm very glad none of our people were injured by those bolts," Piet said in a voice as neutral as possible, given the need to shout to be heard over the continuing clangor. His face was hard.

Stephen regarded casualties as a fact of war, and it didn't particularly matter to him whether they were caused by the enemy or by a friendly mistake. Dead was dead. But for Piet, a victory had to be without friendly loss to be complete. If Casson had killed Venerian sailors when he disobeyed the general commander's orders, he might have found that Piet Ricimer in a rage was as fearful a thing as his friend Stephen Gregg.

Piet looked at Stephen, smiled slightly, and went on, "We won't cross the berm on foot, Stephen. We'll take the *Moll Dane* in. She's sturdy enough to survive a few shots. The loss among unprotected troops would be higher than I'd care to accept."

The guns of the *Freedom* and several other Venerian ships battered the wreckage of the Fed vessel. Plasma bolts were quick darts of iridescence across the field, followed by balls of opaque white fire as collops of steel burned under the ions' impact. The shots hit like hammers on a huge anvil. Shock waves caused each hull plate to slam against its neighbors, flinging heavy fragments into the air.

"All right," Stephen said. His mind worked in several directions at once. Part of him was planning the operation, pulling up information on how the Fed ships had been arranged within the military port when the *Wrath* descended; part of him noted that he'd be able to get another flashgun from the flagship's armory when he returned to gather the close-combat team.

But Stephen Gregg's main concern at this moment—

"That's a good idea, Piet," he said aloud. Cherwell's crew had loosed the gun tube from the winch; the truck was ready to take Stephen to the *Wrath*. "But you're not coming yourself. You won't wear a hard suit while you're piloting in an atmosphere, and you won't take the time to put one on after we've landed."

"I—" Piet said.

"No!" Stephen said. "You scared me too much at the gunpit, Piet. Half the Fed ships across the berm have probably got their thrusters lit. I'm not going to carry your ashes home, and I'm not going to trust you to put your suit on when I know you'd be lying if you told me you would. I won't!"

"Guillermo will pilot the ship," Piet said. He slapped his trouser leg with a bare hand. "I'll put on the rest of my armor on the *Wrath*."

"I'll pilot the *Moll Dane*," Sal said in a voice as clear and strong as those of the men. "Guillermo can work the attitude-control board with Harrigan and Brantling from my ship. They're current on manual systems, and people from a new warship probably wouldn't be."

Stephen looked at Piet. Piet raised an eyebrow. Stephen nodded, although he felt as if the ground had opened beneath his feet.

Sal wouldn't have any use for him if he didn't treat her as a person in her own right; and he wouldn't have any use for her if she weren't a person.

"Right," Piet said, walking to the truck. Stephen boosted his friend into the back of the vehicle, then stepped onto the middle tire and let Piet's wiry strength help lift his own armored weight.

Sal, settling herself in the cab beside Tsarev, ordered, "Swing by the *Gallant Sallie* on the way to the *Wrath*, sailor. And step on it!"

Stephen felt his lips smile, but his mind was a thousand light-years away.

WINNIPEG SPACEPORT, EARTH

April 16, Year 27
0433 hours, Venus time

The interior of the *Moll Dane* was a pigsty, which neither surprised Sal nor mattered to her. There was also up to 10 millimeters' play in the controls. That was no more surprising than the other, but it could matter very much indeed.

"Ready at the attitude controls?" Sal called. A dozen men in hard suits packed the freighter's cabin. When the armored sailors moved, their suits clashed loudly together. The forty or so in the hold had cleared space for themselves by dumping the *Moll Dane*'s stores and cargo onto the field.

"I hope to God that they work better than they look like they work," Tom Harrigan replied. "But yeah, we're as ready here as we can be."

"The bastard responsible for maintaining these won't leave Earth alive if I catch him!" Brantling added.

In fact, Captain Lasky and his crew had very little chance of surviving if men of the Venerian squadron caught them. Technically, selling cannon to President Pleyal wasn't a violation of Venerian law. The men risking their lives in this attack weren't lawyers but rather patriots; and killers already, the most of them.

The gunrunners knew that. They'd abandoned the *Moll Dane* so quickly that half-eaten rations littered the deck.

The lower two-thirds of the *Moll Dane*'s console display was adequate. The images weren't razor sharp, but they were about as clear as those of the *Gallant Sallie*'s screen before the recent upgrade. The top third of the screen was a murky purple sea in which shadowed objects moved like fish swimming at great depths. Thank God that for this hop, the lower portion was all Sal needed.

Sal lit the thrusters. As the vessel shuddered beneath her, she monitored the fuel flow. All eight motors were within comfortable parameters. A slight taste of burned air made her sneeze.

The *Moll Dane*'s layout was similar to that of the *Gallant Sallie*, but Lasky's ship lacked a separate cabin airlock. All entry and exit was through the hold. The passage through the central water tank acted as the only lock for operations in vacuum or a hostile atmosphere.

At the moment, the outer hatch and passage were both open. The assault force breathed bottled oxygen within its hard suits, enduring the wash of exhaust. Sal and her operational crew were old hands, too hardened to be seriously inconvenienced by the amount of plasma that trailed into the cabin.

"Prepare to lift!" Sal warned. She doubted whether the armored men in the cabin could hear her, but they were veteran sailors who didn't need coddling. She slid the two linked quartets of throttle controls forward, then twisted a separate knob to shrink the nozzle irises.

The *Moll Dane* wobbled nervously as the skids unloaded. The stern lifted first and crawled 10° to starboard. Brantling shouted a curse. Attitude jets fired, and the ship steadied.

Stephen and Piet Ricimer were in the vessel's hold. They would be among the first men out of the *Moll Dane.*

The military port was more than a klick from the *Moll Dane*'s berth near the warehouses. Sal found, somewhat to her surprise, that Lasky's vessel handled well in ground-effect mode; a meter or so above the ground, buoyed on a cushion of exhaust reflected onto the belly plates. Sal kept the *Moll Dane* there instead of rising to twenty meters and sailing toward the berm as she'd intended. She had to hold their forward speed to 10 kph to avoid outrunning the effect, but the loss of a minute or two in transit time was a cheap price to pay for the relative safety and control.

Sal corrected twice to avoid ships studding the big field, first a Fed craft and then the *Cyprian,* an armed merchantman from Betaport. Sailors on the *Cyprian*'s loading ramps waved enthusiastically to the *Moll Dane* scudding past in a cloud of dust and plasma.

Sal guided their course toward a point on the berm a hundred meters to the left of the wrecked Fed freighter. She couldn't see any Feds watching from the top of the concrete-surfaced slope—gunners on grounded Venerian ships were looking for any excuse to fire their cannon—but defenders within the military port would be able to track the approaching vessel by its exhaust plume.

The *Moll Dane*'s hatch was to starboard. Sal came to a halt ten meters from the scarred berm, then swung the *Moll Dane* cautiously on its vertical axis to put the berm on the port side. The skids touched twice, port side and then starboard, as the *Moll Dane* rocked queasily. Thanks to luck and skilled hands at the attitude-control console, the vessel didn't overset.

The guns of the Venerian squadron had fallen silent, *God be praised!* The bolt of a friendly gunner who misjudged Sal's intended course could do worse damage in the open hold than the Feds' fire concentrated on the solid hull.

Sal tightened the nozzle irises with the throttles on sixty percent power. The *Moll Dane* lifted, slightly nose-down, and slid forty meters forward, parallel to the berm. If the Feds had aimed their cannon at the center of the previous exhaust plume, they were going to get a surprise.

When she'd brought her vessel its own length beyond its previous location, Sal touched her skids to the ground again to kill her forward motion. She cocked the nozzles a hair to starboard, then slid the thruster controls up to full output. Roaring like an avalanche, the *Moll Dane* rose over the berm at an angle that became a catenary arc when Sal eased back on the throttles again.

At least twenty plasma cannon fired within the two seconds of the *Moll Dane*'s rise and fall. Most of the Fed guns blasted into the berm or ripped the air just above it at the point where the Venerian ship had first paused.

Three bolts struck the vessel. Two of the impacts were sternward. They made the hull ring and may have penetrated the hold full of assault troops, but they didn't affect Sal's control of the *Moll Dane.*

The third round slammed the hull at midline forward. The plasma itself didn't penetrate the cabin, but it blew a high-voltage power line in the ceiling. The *bang* of the explosion was sharper than lightning. Molten metal gouted through the light headliner, spraying the armored assault party and the crewmen in cabin clothes at the attitude controls.

Sal heard Brantling scream. The vessel twisted as Sal lost half the power to her nozzle-alignment motors. She fought her controls. The cabin was bitterly gray with ozone and burned insulation.

The *Moll Dane*'s roll to port slowed, then reversed. Brantling was batting bare-handed at his smoldering tunic, but Harrigan and Piet's Molt navigator were still at the attitude board despite their burns.

Using both hands on the control yoke, Sal kicked the *Moll Dane*'s stern out to cross the bow of the purpose-built Fed warship they'd otherwise crash into. The Fed vessel—the *Holy Office,* according to the osmium letters inlaid onto the bow—had moved parallel to the berm and within twenty meters of it since the *Gallant Sallie* had viewed the military port during landing.

A collision between the *Moll Dane* and the *Holy Office* would have killed everyone aboard both vessels. No amount of damage to a ship of the North American Federation could have repaid the death of Piet Ricimer.

Because of the violent maneuver, the *Moll Dane* hit so hard that the left landing skid shattered. The cabin lights, normally on whenever the vessel was under way, blew out. The navigation console and apparently the attitude controls still had power.

Sal made as swift and skillful an instinctive decision as she'd ever managed in her life: she chopped one starboard and both port thrusters in each quartet simultaneously, but she didn't shut off the remaining motor to bow and stern for another fraction of a second. The momentary additional output eased the *Moll Dane* down on the starboard skid instead of dropping the ship like 200 tonnes of old junk.

The men in the hold were sailors. They fell down at the shock, but a moment later they were on their feet and clumping out of the hold to attack.

In the middle of the enclosure three hundred meters away, a freighter much like the one the *Freedom*'s guns destroyed was being readied for another ramming attack on the Venerian squadron. Ionized exhaust bathed the vessel; she was already light on her skids.

When the *Moll Dane* hopped over the berm, the ramship's captain shut down his thrusters. The hatches were already open. The crew spilled out of the vessel, abandoning ship in a panic greater than their fear of the throbbing hot ground onto which they were jumping.

There were three Fed warships in the military port with their gunports open, as well as a number of freighters that either were unarmed or didn't have crews aboard to work the guns. The warships' guns weren't visible; they'd recoiled back within the vessel when they salvoed at the *Moll Dane.*

Members of the assault force were still jostling their way out of the cabin through the narrow passage. Sal set her console display for a 360° panorama. Men of the first wave from the hold trotted around the *Moll Dane*'s bow and stern, their weapons ready. A score of Fed soldiers stood in the loading ramp of the spherical warship two hundred meters away, shooting as the Venerians appeared.

Stephen, identifiable from the piebald condition of his hard suit, halted at the *Moll Dane*'s bow. He fired five times. Each time his rifle lifted in recoil, his left hand pumped the slide to chamber a fresh round; and each time, a white-uniformed soldier toppled backward. The Feds were wearing body armor, so Stephen must have been aiming for heads—and hitting them.

Stephen tossed the emptied rifle behind him and took a carbine from one of his loaders. Other members of the assault force jogged by like boulders with limbs. Once Sal saw a Venerian stagger when a Fed bullet ricocheted from his armor, but the man caught his step and continued on.

Sal got up from her console when the cabin emptied enough to give the flight crew some room. She opened the first-aid kit on her belt and took out the jar of salve. Tom Harrigan was daubing Brantling's burns. A huge blister was rising on the mate's bald spot. The fringe of hair still smoldered.

There were just the four of them in the flight crew: motormen to watch the plasma thrusters weren't necessary for a quick up and down, and their presence would have meant one fewer man in the assault force. The odds were in the order of ten to one as it was,

though the Venerians were in full armor and further strengthened
by absolute certainty that they would win. Captain Ricimer and
Mister Gregg always won. . . .

"Guillermo, are you all right?" she asked the Molt. The alien's
carapace was normally a smooth brownish mauve. His exoskeleton
didn't blister like human skin, but spattering copper had burned
off the waxy coat and pitted the chitin beneath.

Guillermo took a wad of tarry substance out of his mouth where
he'd been masticating it. "Yes, Captain," he said. He smeared the
softened goo onto his burns with a three-fingered hand.

Harrigan turned his head at the touch of Sal's fingers on his
scalp. His eyes caught the display behind her. "God help us, Sal!"
he shouted. "We've got to get out of the ship!"

Sal looked around. Unusual for a Federation warship, the *Holy
Office* was of cylindrical rather than spherical layout. During the
past two years, Pleyal's naval architects had started to copy the latest
Venerian design philosophy. A port in the vessel's extreme bow had
opened.

Despite the *Moll Dane*'s fuzzy optics, Sal could see members of
the Fed crew swinging a heavy gun on a traveling mount to bear
on the Venerian ship. At point-blank range, the bolt would turn
the interior of the *Moll Dane*'s weakened hull into an inferno.

"Right, we'll—" Sal started to say.

Stephen Gregg took the flashgun one of his loaders carried for
him. He leaned against the *Moll Dane*'s bow, aiming up at the *Holy
Office*. The laser pulse momentarily lit the muzzle of the big plasma
cannon.

Because of the angle, Stephen couldn't fire directly along the
barrel's axis. The gun bore was highly polished to direct the stream
of plasma with minimum erosion, however. The smooth surface
worked equally well to reflect the bolt down to the shell loaded
in the cannon's breech.

Dirty red smoke engulfed the gunport as the shell detonated
in a low-order explosion. Stephen traded the cassegrain laser for
his slide-action rifle. With his loaders behind him, he stalked up
the forward boarding ramp of the *Holy Office*.

WINNIPEG SPACEPORT, EARTH

April 16, Year 27
0441 hours, Venus time

The *Holy Office* was boarded via through-holds, chambers the width of the vessel with no internal partitions, fore and aft on the lowest level. When both the port and starboard hatches were lowered, as they were now, you could see through the ship to the northern berm of the military port.

A human and a pair of Molts lay beside the hatch control panel set into an alcove in the front of the hold. They'd been shot dead by Venerians who'd rounded the *Moll Dane*'s stern with Piet while Stephen led the other contingent by way of the bow.

The bulkhead separating the bow and stern holds was armored and thick. It contained a separate companionway for either hold. As a safety feature, there was no direct connection between the two holds; though that didn't help now, since the aft hatches were open also. The Feds hadn't expected a shipload of Venerian infantry to be lofted over the berm.

The first troops aboard the *Holy Office* had already fought their way up the companionway. A Fed officer in half armor dangled from the railing, his foot caught between a tread and a stanchion. A shotgun blast had nearly decapitated him. A Venerian lay at the foot of the companionway, his breastplate starred by a bullet that had punched through the center of it. A Fed sailor and the ichor-leaking arm of a Molt littered the steps, crushed by the armored weight of men who'd charged up to the main deck.

Stephen's nasal passages were dry from breathing pure bottled oxygen. As he started for the companionway, he touched his left hand to his helmet to raise his faceshield.

The through-hold exploded in a cataclysm of sparks and clangor. Beverly's body caromed into Stephen and knocked him down. The dangling Fed corpse flew out the starboard hatchway in a mist of blood and pureed flesh, all but the leg that still hung from the railing.

Without rising, Stephen turned his head and torso to see where the shots had come from. His rifle fire had killed or dispersed the troops surprised in the lower hold of the spherical Federation warship two hundred meters away. The crew of that vessel had set up a defensive position on the midline deck with hatches intended for loading in vacuum. Men in armor and Molts in protective suits of quilted rock-wool knelt behind a barricade of crated cargo.

At this range, riflefire wasn't particularly dangerous to troops in ceramic hard suits, but the Feds also had an anti-boarding weapon—a hand-cranked rotary cannon. The five 2-cm rounds the gun spit out before it jammed—solid steel shot with no bursting charge—ricocheted lethally from the bulkhead of the *Holy Office* and penetrated everything else they hit.

Beverly was carrying the flashgun. Stephen grabbed the weapon. The sling was caught on the loader's suit. A shot from the rotary cannon had struck Beverly's left shoulder, crushing the backplate and gorget. The ceramic shards were slippery with blood, but there was no time to worry about that now.

"Philips!" Stephen called. He tugged the flashgun. Beverly thrashed, but the weapon didn't come loose. Stephen tugged again. The fiberglass sling parted, and the universe settled into the glassy calm that Stephen Gregg knew so well.

It was the only time he was at peace.

The rotary cannon stood out in sharp relief in Stephen's mind. Three crewmen bent over the weapon, prying at a burst cartridge case. An officer in polished armor shouted orders as she leaned on the hand crank, backing the barrel cluster to give her crewmen's tools more room.

The marksmen, eight or ten of them rising to fire and then

vanishing again behind the barricade to reload, didn't really figure in Stephen's calculations. They were motions in black and white,
while in his mind the cannon and its crew had color and detail
richer than human eyes could possibly make out at this distance.

Bullets whanged across the boarding hold. They didn't impinge
on Stephen's consciousness, any more than did the back muscle
he'd pulled when Beverly cannoned into him.

A Fed crewman, a Molt, stepped back from the gun, waving a
ruptured case triumphantly in the jaws of his pliers. Stephen's index
finger took up the last pressure on the flashgun's electronic trigger. The bolt hit one of the gun's six barrels at the crank assembly. Ionized steel flashed in a white shock wave that knocked down
the gun captain and the two crewmen standing on the near side
of the weapon.

Stephen reached for the satchel holding fresh batteries. It was
gone, his whole equipment belt shot away by the same burst of
fire that wounded Beverly. He started to turn Beverly over to search
for the spares the loader carried.

Philips, kneeling, waved the battery in his right hand. There were
four more batteries fanned upward from Philips' left gauntlet, ready
for Stephen to snatch as he fired.

Violent fighting was taking place on the gun deck of the *Holy
Office*, directly above the boarding hold. Maybe Piet could use help
there, but the crew of the spherical warship was too alert to be
ignored.

The Fed riflemen had ducked to cover when the rotary cannon
exploded beside them, but now one took a chance of rising to
shoot. Smoke drifted from where the blazing steel had sprayed the
barricade. Without being fully conscious of his decision until he'd
made it, Stephen fired into a wooden packing crate instead of the
face of the Molt rifleman.

The crate erupted as it absorbed the energy of the monopulse
laser. The metal food cans inside were nonflammable, but they were
packed in extruded cellulose that ignited in a red fireball.

Feds jumped up, batting at themselves instinctively even though
most of them wore protective garb. Rifleshots from Venerians still
arriving from the *Moll Dane* knocked several of them over. When
the box of cannon cartridges went off in smoky, rippling flashes
a moment later, the surviving Feds abandoned the position to the
flames.

Stephen got to his feet. "Do what you can for Beverly," he said to Philips in a voice that seemed half human even to his own ears. He'd have slung the flashgun if the sling were whole, but he probably wouldn't need the laser in the tight constraints of a starship's compartments. He dropped the flashgun on the deck and took the pump gun lying beside Philips. He liked the feel of the slide working, and the rifle's powerful cartridges were a better choice than the lighter carbine when so many of the Feds wore armor.

Stephen walked up the companionway, taking the last six steps in three. He burst onto the chaotic gun deck like a float bobbing from the deep sea. As he appeared, a Venerian sailor fired at a Molt near the stern and hit instead the 17-cm plasma cannon behind which the target was sheltering. The bullet ricocheted, clipped the left-side latch of Stephen's faceshield, and fell to the deck without actually harming anyone.

The Molt rose with a flechette gun whose four heavy barrels were welded together into a unit that looked massive enough to be part of a ship's landing gear. Stephen and the alien fired simultaneously.

Stephen's bullet slammed the Molt backward with a hole near the top of the plastron. The flechette gun emitted an orange-red, bottle-shaped muzzleflash and a *crack* so loud that it forged compression bands in the smoky cabin air. The hypervelocity projectile struck the lower lip of the Venerian sailor's breastplate, shattered it, and was deflected straight up the inside of the backplate. Battered but still moving, the flechette exited through the neck opening of the armor and tipped off the sailor's helmet as he fell forward.

A Fed grabbed the flechette gun as it fell from the Molt's hands. Stephen shot the man, then shot the fellow again in the head since he refused to fall to a bullet placed perfectly to wreck the knot of blood vessels above the heart.

A red needle sprang up beside Stephen's rear sight, indicating that the round just fired was the last one in his rifle. Beverly hadn't managed to fully load the weapon before Stephen snatched it back from him the last time.

The shot that carried away his battery satchel hadn't touched his bandolier of rifle and carbine ammunition. He took out a fan of five bottle-necked cartridges and began to load.

The *Holy Office*'s crew still held the sternmost third of the gun deck. Gunsmoke and smudge fires ignited by the battle screened the parties from one another, though there were probably eighty or a hundred men and Molts locked in combat in the confined space.

Most shots were fired by men who poked a weapon up from cover one-handed and loosed blindly in the general direction of the enemy. Venerians advanced crabwise, hopping back and forth across the central aisle because the lines of plasma cannon were offset to give them a greater distance to recoil.

Occasionally somebody would bellow forward with a cutting bar. As shots flashed in both directions along the cabin, sparks and the shriek of teeth shearing armor spewed from a gun bay.

Stampfer, who shouldn't have been in the assault party at all, was ignoring the battle. Piet's gunner struggled alone with a 17-cm cannon of the starboard battery. The gun's power assist was either damaged or disabled from the bridge, so Stampfer was running the massive weapon to firing position by cranking the manual capstan with a come-along. The gunner's backplate was cracked and a charge of buckshot had smeared the side of his helmet, but he kept to his self-appointed task.

"Stephen, help me!" Piet Ricimer called from forward. Even in the present noise and carnage, that voice reached Stephen's directing mind. As he turned, his gauntleted fingers continued to feed cartridges up the loading gate in the rifle's receiver.

The battle for the forward portion of the gun deck was over. At least a score of bodies and partial bodies littered the deck or were draped over the guns. Most of the casualties were from the Fed crew, but the Venerian sprawled on his back with a hole through his thigh armor was certainly dead by now if the femoral artery had been nicked.

There were two more bodies in Venerian hard suits at the head of the cabin. The helmet of one had been topped like a soft-boiled egg; brains were leaking out. Piet, holding a cutting bar, stood between the corpses of his companions.

The situation was easy to read. The control room in the nose of the *Holy Office* was separated from the gun deck by an airlock passage similar to but much wider than that between the *Gallant Sallie*'s hold and cabin. Piet had headed for the control room with the two nearest men, leaving the rest of the assault force to deal with the crew of the *Holy Office*. The Venerians had cut through the hinges of the outward-opening hatch and pried it away from the opening.

A Fed in full armor waited in the passage with a pair of cutting bars. The man was a giant. The surface of his hard suit was silvered to reflect laser beams. Judging by the fresh scars—from bullets and cutting bars both—the plates beneath were exceptionally thick as well.

The Venerians were expecting an empty passage when they cleared the hatch. The Fed guardian fell on them, hacking with both hands and rightly confident that his armor was proof against their panicked response.

Piet had dodged back in time—Stephen had never seen his friend completely surprised by any event—but the sailors with him died beneath the paired cutting bars. The giant then backed up and waited for the next assault, knowing that the passage protected his flanks from the numbers that could otherwise be brought against him.

"Don't bother shooting, Stephen," Piet called without taking his eyes off the giant. "If you block the right-hand bar with your own, I'll block the left and—"

Stephen closed to two meters and tossed his rifle in the giant's face. As the weapon clanged harmlessly off the helmet, Stephen lunged forward like a missile himself. Their breastplates crashed together. Stephen caught the Fed's armored wrists before the bars could scissor together on his helmet.

The howling edges pressed toward Stephen's face despite anything he could do. "Christ Jesus bugger you, you Federation whoreson!" he screamed as he butted the Fed's faceplate. He'd always known there were men stronger than he was, but he didn't meet them often.

This man was strong enough to hand Stephen Gregg his head, literally.

For a moment, Stephen thought the vibration and screaming refractories came from the giant's bars cutting into his helmet. The Fed threw himself backward, pulling Stephen with him. They smashed into the hatch between the passage and the control room. The cutting bar fell from the giant's right hand.

Piet Ricimer gripped the Fed's shoulder with his left gauntlet while he drove the tip of his cutting bar into the man's faceplate. The blade suddenly lurched 15 centimeters inward till the tip shrieked on the back of the giant's helmet from the inside. The giant slumped down against the hatch he'd defended as long as life was in him.

"Stephen, are you all right?" Piet demanded. The bar spun itself clear of bits of bone as he withdrew it. "Did he cut you? Are you all right?"

"I'm not hurt!" Stephen said. "Why do you think—"

As he heard himself speak, he realized for the first time that he was on the floor of the passageway, sprawled across the body of the Fed giant. He'd put every bit of his strength into the fight, and the Fed was still stronger.

"I'm not hurt," Stephen repeated more softly. In a whisper he added, "It's better to have friends than be strong, Piet."

"Venus forward!" Piet shouted. "Wraths to me *now*!"

He took a cutting bar the giant had dropped; the battery of Piet's own must be nearly exhausted from cutting at the airlock, then through the giant's thick faceshield. Piet set the tip of the fresh tool against the 10-by-4-centimeter nickel-steel crossbar that locked the hatch. Leaning his whole weight on the hilt, he worried the cutting bar through in geysers of sparks blazing as the blade flung them into the air.

Stephen got to his feet and unclipped his own bar. It wasn't his weapon of choice, but the rifle was somewhere beneath the giant's body. The bar might do better than a gun in the confined space anyway.

The crossbar fell in pieces. The hatch pivoted inward. Stephen crashed into the control room a step behind Piet.

A Fed sailor threw down her rifle as the armored Venerians burst from the hatchway. An officer struggled up from a console, tangled in the cord of a communications handset while he tried to reach his holstered revolver. He screamed in abject terror as Stephen took two long strides toward him.

Stephen slashed with a skill he probably couldn't have equaled in practice. The cutting bar's tip skidded across the surface of the Fed's breastplate and severed the pistol belt. It didn't touch the man.

The holster clunked to the deck. The Fed leaned forward and began blubbering into his hands.

The bridge crew, six humans and three Molts, made no resistance. The man Stephen had disarmed was the only officer. The

Molts were curled into mauve lumps as if preparing to go into suspended animation. Piet, Stephen, and the six men shouldering into the control room behind them looked as out of place as guns among table settings of silver and crystal.

Piet shoved the Fed officer aside, hastily but without brutality, and seated himself at the command console. The sound of fighting on the gun deck had died away; Fed resistance must have broken suddenly. Piet took his gauntlets off and called up an alphanumeric sidebar on the console's panoramic display. Stephen noticed his friend seemed perfectly comfortable working controls in a hard suit when circumstances demanded it.

Stephen picked up the rifle on the deck, then took the sailor's ammunition too by breaking the buckle of her belt. He stepped to the control room's starboard airlock and activated the control. While he waited for the hatches to cycle, he watched the panoramic display.

Until very recently, Federation optronics had been an order of magnitude better than the best available on Venus. That was no longer true at the high end, because Venerian microchip production—and loot—was catching up with the huge pre-Collapse stockpiles the Feds brought back from the Reaches. Nonetheless, the *Holy Office*'s screens gave a crisp, ground-level view of what was happening in Winnipeg's military port.

The administrative offices and barracks were built into the north wall of the berm. A pole stood before the concrete-pillared entrance, but the flag was a red-and-white tangle on this windless day.

The gunports of the warships that had joined the *Holy Office* in firing on the *Moll Dane* were open but empty at present. Plasma cannon had to cool for several minutes between shots—the interval becoming longer as the bore of the weapon increased. Reloading too quickly risked a detonation of the shell that, because the tritium core wasn't compressed in a programmed sequence, was almost certain to rupture the cannon and kill the crew.

Federation plasma cannon were large-crystal castings of tungsten, stellite, or other heavy metals, and they almost invariably had to be loaded from the muzzle. Venus built ceramic breechloaders that cooled more quickly, particularly in an atmosphere. Although the fighting aboard the *Holy Office* seemed to have gone on forever, the minutes that had actually passed weren't long enough for the Feds to reload their pieces.

In common with most spherical-design vessels, this Fed ship carried the tanks for its reaction mass—water—along the vertical axis. Instead of putting a bolt into the ship's thick hull, Stampfer had aimed the powerful 17-cm gun at the mid-line hatch the Feds had opened as a fighting position. Smoke and sparks erupted from the hatchway, but the water tank took the bolt's main impact. Steam pistoned the incompressible remaining liquid through ruptured seams, then flooded every deck with searing fog.

Piet lit the *Holy Office*'s thrusters. Exhaust curled in through the airlock. Stephen snapped down the faceshield he didn't remember lifting and stepped to the outer hatchway, searching for targets.

Another of the *Holy Office*'s big guns fired. When the assault force no longer had Fed crewmen to fight, they'd joined Stampfer in running out the starboard battery. The high entrance doors of the headquarters bunker exploded in a rainbow flash. The shock wave shattered the pillars, which bowed outward and collapsed, dragging the triangular pediment with them.

Piet's voice snarled from the vessel's PA system, "Abandon ship! This is Captain Ricimer speaking. All men off the vessel now!"

Crewmen staggered out of the steam wreathing the vessel Stampfer hit first. Stephen aimed at a figure who still carried a weapon. His shot blasted concrete dust ten meters beyond the Fed. This rifle shot 20 centimeters wide to the left at this range, but because of the downward angle Stephen could adjust his aim.

He reloaded the turn-bolt single-shot and fired again. The Fed skidded facedown on the concrete.

The Fed warship near the east berm, six hundred meters from the *Holy Office,* fired a pair of light plasma cannon. One of the bolts struck the stern of the *Holy Office.* Three 17-cm guns answered it, their crackling discharges ringing at four-second intervals through the fabric of the captured warship. Stampfer must have laid all the guns himself. Common sailors couldn't have hammered the same point with such precision.

The flash of the first bolt hitting was white and prismatic; superheated hull metal blazed in the atmosphere. The second bolt, striking an instant after the initial fireball had lifted from a basin-sized hole in the hull, spent its energy inside the vessel. Flames—red, orange, and streaked with plumes of white smoke at high pressure—engulfed the warship's second deck level.

If the Feds had had the time and the inclination to set up their vessel's internal compartmentalization, the third round wouldn't have added anything to the damage the immediately previous bolt had caused. People act hastily in crises. Not all the companionway hatches were dogged shut, and few of the floor-to-ceiling baffles had been raised to prevent an explosion from involving an entire deck.

Plasma from the third round blew flaming gas and debris into every chamber of the Federation vessel. Gunports flapped outward, spewing black smoke and occasionally parts of Fed crewmen. A ready-use magazine of plasma shells went off on the midline deck. Iridescent flame gouged away the sides of the openings through which it streamed. The vessel settled slightly as white-hot structural members lost strength.

"Abandon ship!" Piet's voice ordered. "Abandon ship! All Wraths out of the military port now!"

A fourth running figure. Stephen killed him. It was a Molt and unarmed when the hot fog cleared momentarily about the body an instant after the shot. Stephen stepped back from the hatch to draw another cartridge from the ammo belt.

He and Piet were the only Venerians still in the control room. The Fed officer and the three Molts—upright now but motionless— stood against the port bulkhead. Stephen glanced through the passageway aft. As far as he could tell, Stampfer and the rest of the assault force had abandoned ship as ordered.

The thrusters roared at full output, though the flared nozzles spread the ions in a billowing sheet across the ground instead of lifting the *Holy Office*. Exhaust puffed through the open airlock, blinding Stephen momentarily with its brilliance. He backed another step from the hatch.

Piet keyed in a complex series of commands, then rose from the console and drew on his gauntlets. The port airlock started to open, forcing two of the Molts to move.

"Stephen!" Piet said in surprise. "Come on, we've got to get out before the ship lifts. I programmed it to crash into the freighters on the west berm!"

"And them?" Stephen said, waving to the prisoners who hadn't fled aft with their fellows.

"Get out!" Piet shouted. "We're going to crash!"

The three Molts turned and leaped into the sea of radiance, one at a time. Though they jumped as far as they could, they were well within the bath of ions when they hit the ground. The bodies shriveled and burned like figures of straw.

"I'll follow you, Piet," Stephen said. He dropped the rifle and grabbed the Fed officer around the waist.

Piet looked momentarily doubtful, but he latched down his visor and jumped from the hatch. The *Holy Office* shook itself like a dog just risen from the water. The nozzle irises were closing, restricting the flow to boost thrust.

Stephen, clasping the screaming officer tightly, took three running steps and leaped from the lip of the outer hatch. Exhaust pulsed around him. His boots hit the concrete two meters below. He skidded but kept his footing, thrusting the Fed out as a balance weight. He kept running until he hit the inner face of the berm.

The Fed's uniform smoldered and his exposed skin was already beginning to blister, but he was alive. For the moment, he was alive.

Which was the most anyone could say, after all.

WINNIPEG SPACEPORT, EARTH

April 16, Year 27
0453 hours, Venus time

Sal grasped a wrist-thick tree growing between a pair of the concrete slabs covering the berm. She reached down to take Brantling's
good hand, his left, while Tom Harrigan pushed the injured sailor
from below.

The berm sloped at 45°, a steeper climb than Brantling could
handle at the moment. There was a flight of broad steps fifty meters
away, but they were crowded with exhausted men in hard suits
carrying their weapons and their casualties. Sal and her flight crew
would have risked jostling and worse if they'd tried to leave the
military port by that route. The assault force had expended too
much physical and emotional energy in its brief fight to be careful
now.

"Thanks, Cap'n Blythe," Brantling muttered as Sal half helped,
half dragged him past her to get a grip and then a foothold on
the tree. Her breath rasped. Four meters of 1:1 slope didn't seem
especially difficult until you tried to climb it when you were wrung-
out emotionally.

Guillermo perched like a gargoyle on the berm's broad top. He
took Brantling's hand for what help he could offer.

ा stop

The flight crew had been forgotten as soon as the *Moll Dane* landed. Nobody informed them of what was happening, nobody even thought about Sal and her men aboard the crumpled freighter. The assault preparations had been sudden and *ad hoc*. Even Sal hadn't thought about what she was supposed to do when and if she survived landing.

Sal had never before felt so completely abandoned.

The note of the *Holy Office*'s thrusters changed, sharpened. Sal looked over her shoulder as the vessel lifted minusculely from the concrete. The nozzle irises were tightening down. An armored figure leaped from the cockpit airlock, stumbled in the iridescent hellfire, and trotted out of the exhaust corona. A second, heavier figure followed. The *Holy Office* began to skitter forward like a chunk of sodium dropped on a still pond.

"I've got it," Harrigan said, ignoring Sal's offered hand to zig-zag leftward instead. His toes had found purchase between two of the facing slabs. Sal got a foot against the tree trunk and flopped belly-down on top of the berm.

The *Holy Office* gained speed gradually as it crossed the military port in hops of ten, twenty, fifty meters. Each time the unmanned vessel tilted enough to lose ground effect, the skid on the lower side brushed sparklingly along the concrete. The ship lifted again, tacking slightly toward that contact, and touched on the opposite skid. Sarah Blythe had no false modesty regarding her own piloting skills, but she could never have programmed an artificial intelligence to carry out the maneuver she was watching.

Harrigan, thinking the same thing, said, "There's somebody at the controls."

"Captain Ricimer *was* at the controls, Mister Harrigan," Guillermo responded with quiet pride.

Three great spherical freighters from the Reaches trade stood three hundred meters apart along the west edge of the port. The *Holy Office* struck the nearest, an 800-tonner, a glancing blow low on the starboard side. The shrieking contact continued deafeningly for several seconds. The warship caromed off the larger merchant-man and swapped ends twice before it smashed broadside into the 1,200-tonne giant north of the initial target.

This time the noise was like that of planets colliding. Both the *Holy Office* and the merchantman had thick hulls, but the kinetic energy of the impact was of astronomical level. The surfaces of nickel-steel plates vaporized and the frame members behind them compressed like putty.

A plasma motor, its nozzle sealed by the 20 centimeters of tough plating rammed into it, became a fusion bomb. The flash seemed to transfuse solid metal. Remnants of the *Holy Office*, half the stern to one side and fragments that had been part of the bow to the other, blew back in a ravening white glare. The four upper decks of the exploding freighter lifted as a piece, flattening as they rose.

A munitions explosion, slighter than the first but cataclysmic nonetheless, gushed red flame from the center of the inferno. The top of the vessel flipped sideways. It struck the ground and carved a trench twenty meters deep through the concrete, then sheared into the remaining freighter.

The third vessel was pinned between the anvil of the berm and the upper half of the 1,200-tonner, a hammer more massive than the *Holy Office* had been when complete. Steam and fire engulfed the site. Slabs shook from the berm hundreds of meters away, and a pall of dust lifted from the surface of the port.

No skill could have planned a result so destructive. "Maybe God does fight for Venus," Sal whispered, though her mind couldn't find much of God in what she had just watched. She'd spent her life carrying cargoes, and shipwreck was the greatest disaster she could imagine.

Below Sal, two men in hard suits staggered toward the stairway. The gilded armor, now scoured and defaced by the plasma bath, was Piet Ricimer's.

Piet kept his right gauntlet against the berm to guide him where he didn't trust his eyes. His left hand gripped the right gauntlet of the bigger man, who held what looked like a bundle of smoking fabric.

Stephen was still alive, but at this moment Sal had only intellect left to be glad of the fact. The earthshaking thumps of further destruction blurred even that.

"That'll teach them not to mess with Venus, won't it, Mister Harrigan?" Brantling crowed. "We fed them the sharp end this time!"

"Aye, by God we did," Tom Harrigan said in guttural triumph. "We've singed President Pleyal's beard, we have!"

Across the port, three ships that could have supplied a large colony for a year blazed in devouring glory.

ISHTAR CITY, VENUS

June 6, Year 27
0331 hours, Venus time

Sal opened the door with exaggerated care, stepped into the front room of the apartment she shared with her father, and closed the door on her fingers. "Christ's bleeding wounds!" she shouted before she remembered she was trying not to disturb Marcus.

Marcus Blythe lurched upright on the divan where he'd been dozing. "Sal?" he called. He turned up the table lamp from a vague glow to full brightness.

"Sorry, Dad," Sal said. "I didn't mean to . . ."

She shook her head in puzzlement, trying to remember what it was she'd meant to say. "Look, why don't you go off to bed now, Dad?"

"Here, you sit down," Marcus said. He tossed off the sheet covering him, then rose from the divan by shifting his torso forward and catching himself with his cane before he fell back. "I'll scramble some eggs for you. You always liked my eggs, didn't you, Sallie?"

"Dad, I'm not . . ." Sal muttered. *Maybe I'm hungry after all.* Her legs weren't working right, certainly. She flopped into the straight-backed chair by the little table. She teetered for a moment but didn't fall over.

771

"Some food will be good, Sallie," Marcus said as he shuffled into the kitchenette adjacent to the front room. "Don't I know it. I've had my nights out partying too, you know."

Sal moved the lamp, certain that Marcus' bottle was on the other side of it. There was no bottle on the table. She frowned and bent over to see if the liquor was on the floor beside the divan. There wouldn't be much left, of course, but . . .

No bottle on the floor either.

"Ferlinghetti at the Fiddler's Green was saying the Southern ship your squadron captured was as rich a prize as any Captain Ricimer ever brought back," Marcus said. Eggs spattered on hot grease.

"Richer than that," Sal said absently. "Where's your bottle, Dad?"

They'd stumbled into the *Mae do Deus* on Callisto, where the crew had attempted to conceal their 2,000-tonne monster when they heard Piet Ricimer was out with a squadron. The vessel had been one of the largest merchantmen of the Southern Cross before President Pleyal's coup de main six years before absorbed what had been a separate nation into the North American Federation.

"Ah, you know, Sallie dearest, I'm not sure there *is* a bottle in the apartment," her father said in brittle cheeriness. "I'll have to pick something up, won't I?"

"What d'ye mean, there's no bottle?" Sal shouted. She stood halfway up, lost her balance, and sat back down with a crash that jolted her spine all the way to the base of her skull.

Marcus' fork clinked busily against the pan, stirring in the spices and pepper sauce. "Fullerenes from the Mirrorside," he said as if he hadn't heard his daughter. "Worth more than microchips are, Ferlinghetti says."

"You bet," Sal agreed morosely. "A captain's share of what we took from the *Mae* . . . I'm a rich girl, Daddy. Your little Sal is rich, rich, rich."

She reached into the right-hand pocket of her loose tunic and brought out a liter bottle of amber Terran whiskey. It was nearly full. She couldn't remember how it had gotten there.

"*Sing praises to our God and king* . . ." Sal warbled, trying to open the bottle. After three failures, she squinted carefully and saw that the bottle had a screw cap instead of the plug stopper she was used to.

Marcus lifted the pan and scraped eggs onto a serving plate. "Ah, Sal?" he said nervously. "I thought that tonight you might, you know, have something to eat and go to bed. Instead of stay—"

"Who the hell are you to think anything, you damned old drunk?" Sal shouted. She stood up. The chair overset in one direction and the table in another. "I'll go to sleep when I'm damned—"

The lamp with a bubble-thin shade the color of a monarch butterfly's wing was Venerian ceramic. It hit the floor and bounced, chiming in several keys but undamaged. The glass bottle from Earth shattered in a spray of liquor.

"Oh, the bastards," Sal said. Her body swayed. "Oh, the dirty bastards."

Marcus scuffled across the room and embraced her. "Let's have a little something to eat, Sallie my love," he said. "You like my eggs, don't you, dear?"

"It'd be all right if I'd seen his face before I shot him," Sal whispered as she hugged her father.

"Sallie?" Marcus said.

"On Arles," she said, thinking she was explaining. "Every night he comes to me and he's a different face. I could take one, that'd be, that'd be . . . But he's different every night, and then *mush*. Red mush, dad. One after another and then they die."

"Oh, Sallie," Marcus said. "Oh, my little baby girl."

Sal shuddered and drew herself upright. "That's all right, Dad," she said. "I appreciate the trouble you took, but I'm going out for a bit, I think. I'll be back, you know, later."

"Sal, *please* don't go out again tonight," Marcus pleaded.

Captain Sarah Blythe, heroine of Venus' struggle against Federation tyranny, closed the door behind her. The night clerk at the baths usually had a bottle under his counter.

BETAPORT, VENUS

July 1, Year 27
1412 hours, Venus time

"What do you think of them, Gregg?" said Alexi Mostert, gesturing as he shouted over the echoing racket of the New Dock. "All three of them as handy as the *Wrath*, and their scantlings just as sturdy."

"We've spread the nozzle clusters," Siddons Mostert added from Stephen's other side. "Another ten centimeters between adjacent thrusters to improve hover performance."

The vessels in the three nearest cradles were purpose-built warships; like the *Wrath*, as even Stephen could see, but the finer points of construction were as much beyond his capacity to judge as they were outside his interests. It was inconceivable that the Mostert brothers had invited him here to talk about scantlings and hover performance.

"Ships are things that I ride on, gentlemen," Stephen said dryly. "I'm sure Piet would be delighted to discuss the way the *Wrath* handled, if you want to talk with him."

The twenty-odd ships fitting out in the gigantic New Dock were either state-owned or under contract to the governor's forces. Access to the dock was limited for fear of sabotage. A platoon

774

of black-armored Governor's Guards at the entrance checked the sailors, workmen, and carters flowing into New Dock at all hours, and there were parties of armed men aboard each vessel.

Stephen suspected that the guards were a psychological exercise thought up by Councilor Duneen or another of the governor's close advisors rather than a response to real concerns. Through the guards' presence, Governor Halys said to the people of Venus, "The Federation threat is real and imminent, and the sacrifices you will shortly be called on to make are justified."

The governor was right about the threat, at least. Stephen Gregg, who knew as much about sacrifice as the next person, would have been uncomfortable urging it on anyone else.

"Yes, Factor Ricimer is a marvelous sailor, isn't he?" Siddons said. "And marvelously lucky as well. Snapping up the *Mae do Deus* like that!"

Siddons was a tall, slightly hunched man with the solemn mien of a preacher. He was the elder brother by two years and looked considerably older than that, although the close-coupled Alexi had spent far more of his life in the hardships and deprivations of long voyages. Alexi Mostert continued to lead an occasional argosy even now that he'd been appointed Chief Constructor of the Fleet.

"If you call that luck," Stephen said with a cold smile. "Piet interviewed prisoners at Winnipeg and learned the ship was already overdue. He calculated her back-course and plotted the locations where her captain might lay up if he learned the Earth Approaches were too risky."

"Ah," Alexi said, nodding in understanding.

"Very simple in hindsight, isn't it, gentlemen?" Stephen said. "Good preparation often makes a task look easy."

"I think back to the days we were shipmates, Piet and I," Alexi said with forced heartiness. "And you too, Gregg. We paid a price, we did, but it was worth it for Venus' sake! There's bigger things than any one man."

Stephen looked at Mostert and shrugged. Alexi Mostert had lost all his teeth while starving on a hellish voyage back from the Reaches, where the Feds had ambushed what was meant to be a peaceful trading expedition. There'd been fifteen survivors out of more than a hundred men crammed aboard a ship that was damaged escaping.

"I don't know what anything's worth, Mostert," Stephen said.

He realized the statement wasn't true even as the words came out of his mouth. Things were worth what somebody was willing to pay for them. That was the first rule of business. Though . . . Stephen wasn't sure that he, or Alexi, or even Piet had paid the prices they did for anything as abstract as "Venus."

"I was wondering," Siddons Mostert said, pausing to clear his throat. "I was wondering who Factor Ricimer thinks the governor should appoint commander of our fleet when Pleyal attacks. Eh, Gregg?"

"I think you ought to ask Piet about that, Mostert," Stephen said. "If you really think it's any of your business."

He heard the edge in his voice. That shouldn't bother anyone who knew him, though it might worry the Mosterts. Friends knew that Stephen Gregg spoke in a musical lilt when he was determining who to kill first.

An electric-powered tractor, its transmission whining in compound low as it dragged three wagons filled with cannon shells, would pass close enough to brush the trio of men. Stephen walked forward, toward the warship looming in its cradle overhead. The legend inlaid in violet porcelain on her bow was GOVERNOR HALYS. There were at least six state or state-hired vessels named that or simply *Halys*, which would be at best confusing in the fleet actions everyone expected.

"Ah, it could be rather awkward, Gregg," Siddons said. He stood looking up at the *Governor Halys*, his neck at the same angle as Stephen's. "It's possible that the governor might feel that she had to appoint someone of a, an older factorial family to the position. Factor Ricimer might think his merits should overcome any question of his birth. Eh?"

"If the governor wants to know Piet's opinion . . ." Stephen said. His words were ordered as precisely as cartridges in a repeater's magazine. " . . . then she should ask him the next time he visits the mansion. I gather he's invited at least once a week when he's on Venus."

"Yes, but—" Alexi said.

"Listen to me, Mostert," Stephen interrupted. "If you brought me here to ask what Piet's opinion on this thing or that thing might be, then I'm going to go off and get a drink and we can all stop wasting our time."

Alexi Mostert turned sideways to face Stephen squarely. He

crossed his hands behind his back and said, "All right, Gregg. What's your opinion of someone other than Factor Ricimer being appointed Commander of the Fleet?"

Stephen looked at the burly older man. He'd known Alexi Mostert for more than a decade. Stephen had shipped out to the Reaches for the first time aboard a vessel of the Mostert Trading Company. Though acquaintances rather than friends, they'd been through harsh times together just as Alexi said, in battle and in its aftermath.

"This is official business, isn't it?" Stephen said. "Somebody's afraid that I might kill anybody who was put in charge of the fleet over Piet's head? Yes?"

Behind him, Siddons Mostert choked. Alexi, standing with as much stiff dignity as his build and years allowed, said, "Well, since the question's come up, Gregg—how would you answer it?"

Stephen stared at Mostert. The older man, though obviously frightened, met his gaze. On all Venus, there were only a few men— and one woman—who could have ordered the Mostert brothers to ask the question that Alexi had just put.

"Since I'm being consulted as an expert," Stephen said in a cool, businesslike tone, "let's consider the general situation first. The governor *has* to appoint someone whose ancestors were factors back to before the Collapse. Otherwise every gentleman in the fleet will be squabbling over precedence. We'll kill more of ourselves in duels than we will Feds in battle."

Alexi let out a deep breath, nodding approvingly.

"I'm aware of that, and I'm sure Piet's aware of it," Stephen continued. "And I assure you, Piet wants Federation tyranny broken more than he wants honors for himself"—Stephen grinned coldly— "much though he wants honors for himself."

"And has earned them, nobody more," Siddons Mostert said effusively. "I think there may have been concern that political necessities might have been viewed as an insult to Factor Ricimer, when nothing could be farther from the truth."

A crane traveling in a trackway built into the dock's ceiling rumbled slowly past, carrying a tank of reaction mass. Drops of condensate fell from the outside of the tank like a linear rain shower. One of them plucked Stephen's right cuff.

"You asked me here to have this meeting," Stephen said, looking up at the huge water tank, "because of the armed guards, isn't that right? In case I flew hot and decided to kill you."

"It was my idea," Siddons admitted miserably. "Alexi said it wouldn't make any difference if, if you..."

Stephen laughed. "Oh, that's true enough to take to the bank, yes," he said.

Ten meters away, an officer in half armor looked bored. Two sailors chatted with their shotguns leaning against a pile of crates in a cargo net beside them. Stephen could have both guns before the guards realized he was taking them; though it would be much easier to grip a Mostert by the throat in either hand and batter their heads together until there was nothing left to break.

Stephen smiled.

"I've never been unwilling to do my duty to Venus and the governor, Gregg," Alexi Mostert said, standing stiff again. For all the words were as pompous as the old spacer looked in his present pose, they were basically the truth. There'd never been a lack of folk on Venus willing to sacrifice themselves for a cause they thought worthy.

"For what it's worth," Stephen said, nodding to Siddons, "I've never killed anybody just because I was angry. I've killed them for less reason, killed them because they were available and I was putting the fear of God into my general surroundings at the time. But never because I was angry."

"You've always been a loyal citizen of Venus, Mister Gregg," Siddons Mostert said. "Nobody doubts your patriotism."

"I'm not a patriot, Mostert," Stephen said. "Sometimes I've been a friend, though. It can amount to the same thing."

He bowed formally to the brothers. "I'm going to get a drink, since I believe we've covered our business, yes?"

"Yes, that's right," Alexi said. "Ah—we're heading for dinner, Siddons and I. If you'd like to come..."

Stephen shook his head, smiling. "Just a drink," he said. His expression shifted, though it would have been hard to say precisely which muscles tensed or slackened to make such a horrible change. "You know," he said, "sometimes I think the only time I'm alive is when I'm killing somebody. Funny, isn't it?"

Siddons Mostert stood with a frozen smile. Alexi, very slowly, shook his head.

HELDENSBURG

July 4, Year 27
2306 hours, Venus time

The wind across the starport was gusty and strong, but it blew directly from Sal, leaning out of the cabin airlock, to the nearest of the forts. The flag of United Europe, sixteen stars on a green field, was only an occasional flap of bunting from behind the pole.

The fort and the three others like it on the margins of the field each had firing slits and a garrison of fifty or so human soldiers as well as heavy, ship-smashing plasma cannon. The troops looked bored as they watched starships from the walls of the position, but their personal weapons were always nearby.

Those were the sorts of details Sal had learned to consider since she started voyaging beyond Pluto.

"All right, lift her, but *easy!*" Tom Harrigan ordered.

Winches on the *Gallant Sallie* and the port operations lowboy took the first strain together. The ceramic turbine for a city-sized plasma power plant would have been a marginal load for either crane alone, especially at the full extension necessary to transfer it from hold to trailer. When the cables took the weight, the turbine skidded toward the hatchway. Brantling slowly let out slack while the Heldensburg operator reeled the load toward the lowboy at the same rate.

779

Wueppertal, the operations manager assigned to the *Gallant Sallie,* nodded approvingly from beside Harrigan. "Wueppertal?" Sal called. "What's the word on our return cargo?"

The Heldensburg official looked around and walked closer to the hatch. The turbine was balanced now. Brantling paid out more cable, allowing the other operator to draw the load over the bed of the lowboy.

Wueppertal patted the two-way radio hooked to his belt. "They've located the rest of the chips, Captain," he said. "It was an inventory error, somebody entering two crates when it should have been eleven. We'll have them out to you yet this evening, after we've off-loaded the rest of your cargo."

The microchips Sal was contracted to carry back to Paris Ouest on Earth were newly manufactured on a Near Space colony of the Independent Coastal Republic. Heldensburg produced very little itself, but in the past ten years it had become a major transit point for Near Space trade.

Heldensburg's powerful defenses were an important attraction, but it wasn't only captains concerned about Pleyal's claimed monopoly on trade beyond Pluto who called here. The ship nearest to the *Gallant Sallie* was a Federation vessel. Molt crew members had pulled several attitude jets and were polishing them on a workbench under the desultory supervision of a boyish-looking human officer.

"Do you have many Feds here?" Sal asked, trying to keep the disapproval out of her voice.

Wueppertal waved a hand. "About a third of our traffic," he said. "Look, their credit drafts spend just the same as yours. If we didn't have those guns"—a nod toward the nearby fort—"then I'd worry, sure But we do."

"Yes," Sal said She might have let the subject drop, but she hadn't been sleeping well for too long. "Heldensburg's too tough a nut for Pleyal to crack, now. But if it weren't for the trouble Venus has been causing him these past ten years, he'd have crushed you all like bugs before you got properly settled."

The turbine settled onto the lowboy. The trailer's suspension compressed a good 10 centimeters before the winch cables slackened.

A spherical 600-tonne merchantman was discharging grain into a series of hopper cars. From details of its design, Sal guessed the vessel was from the Federation. The Feds were drawn here by the variety of available cargoes, just as the other traders were. The fact that those cargoes depended on plasma cannon to keep President Pleyal's warships away was an irony of human existence.

"Oh, there's something to be said for a guy like Pleyal," Wueppertal said with the same tone of almost-challenge that Sal had heard in her own voice. "He knows what order is and he's not afraid to enforce it. Commandant La Fouche said just last week in staff meeting that there's other places that could use a little discipline of the sort."

"We'll give Pleyal discipline, all right," Tom Harrigan said, wandering over to the forward hatch now that the loading operation was complete. "He'll try to clamp down on Venus, and we'll go through his fleet like shit through a goose."

"You think that?" Wueppertal said. He was a smallish man, dark-haired but with brilliant blue eyes.

"I know that," the mate said. "Why, the man who owns this ship, Mister Gregg—that's *Stephen* Gregg, Wueppertal—"

"Co-owns the *Gallant Sallie*, Harrigan," Sal said in a crisp voice.

"Sure, co-owns," Harrigan agreed. "I've seen him clear a Fed warship single-handed—and that in a Fed port! And brought us back rich, too. Why, there's Dock Street ladies who bought country seats from what they made off sailors come back from Winnipeg and Callisto!"

Sal thought of the slaughter, of the columns of smoke rising from Winnipeg Spaceport as the *Gallant Sallie* lifted. She didn't say anything to the men standing below her.

Wueppertal's eyes narrowed. "You know Colonel Gregg?" he said.

Tom Harrigan nodded. "Let me tell you," he said. "When we hopped the *Moll Dane* into the military port at Winnipeg, Mister Gregg was as close to me as you are now. Captain Blythe was piloting"—Wueppertal's eyes followed Tom's nod under a frown of disbelief—"and Mister Gregg was right there with us, and Factor Ricimer too. Don't I have the scars?"

Harrigan bent his head and ran an index finger over the ridged pink-and-white keloid on his scalp. He straightened and continued forcefully, "Listen! When it comes to real war, we'll whip the Feds right back to Montreal, and we'll do it because God's on our side. Factor Ricimer preaches God like nobody you've heard in chapel of a Sunday, and Mister Gregg—he's the Wrath of God, he is!"

Sal thought of the Stephen Gregg she knew. Her eyes were on the distant horizon, and her expression was as hard as cast iron.

The stevedores had completed tying the turbine firmly onto the trailer bed. One of the men called, "Hey, Hymie!" and waved to Wueppertal. "You want us to go on back now?"

Wueppertal said, "Hang on, I'll ride with you!" To Harrigan and Sal he added, "I'll make sure they've got the chips ready to go. The sort of screwups they got running Warehouse Four, they're as likely to be piling more crates on top of yours as they are to be loading them onto trucks."

Harrigan sat on the topmost of the three steps from the hatch to the ground, watching the tractor and lowboy head toward the complex of low warehouses west of the field. "Paris and then home, Sal?" he asked.

Sal shrugged. The gesture was pointless since the mate wasn't looking at her. "Maybe home," she said. "There may be a load of desalinization equipment ready for carriage to Drottingholm. Europe and the Coasties have set up a joint colony there."

A starship was landing almost precisely in line with the morning sun. Harrigan took a filter from his breast pocket and used it to view the ship through the double glare. "A big one," he remarked idly. "Shouldn't wonder if it was another Fed."

He turned his head to look up at Sal. "We've been lucky with cargoes, you know," he said. "Short layovers and almost never lifting empty. Sure a change from the old days."

"It's a change, but it's not luck," Sal replied sharply. "Mister Gregg's making the arrangements. Balancing cargoes, setting up credit lines—judging who'll need something and who can pay for it."

She flicked an index finger in the direction of the lowboy, now halfway to the warehouses. "These power plants. Stephen—Mister Gregg—he set up the whole deal. All the principals had to do was sign the agreement he offered them! We're getting the haulage fees, but buyer and seller both are gaining a lot more from the deal than we are."

"Who'd have thought it?" Harrigan said. "A man like Mister Gregg, and he's a merchant besides!"

The thrusters of the ship in its landing approach braked at maximum output, bellowing across the starport at a level that forbade speech.

Who would have thought it? Gregg of Weyston was one of the largest intrasystem shippers on Venus. It shouldn't surprise anyone that his nephew would have an equal flair for the complexities of trade.

It wouldn't have surprised those who knew Stephen Gregg before he first voyaged to the Reaches and defeated everything he found there except his own human soul.

And very nearly his soul as well.

BETAPORT, VENUS

July 12, Year 27
1658 hours, Venus time

Originally Dock Street had been the route by which starships were hauled between the transfer docks, whose domes slid open for take-offs and landings, and the storage docks where vessels were refitted between voyages. New routes and docks had been built to suit the ever-larger ships operating from Betaport, but Dock Street remained a broad, high-roofed corridor and the center of nautical affairs in a city built on star travel.

Guild marshals were trying to keep the crowd back from the red carpet laid for the occasion. They had their work cut out for them, especially here near the train station where the dignitaries were gathered. The station itself was ringed by men who were something more than an "honor" guard: the *Wrath's* B Watch close-combat team. Today the Wraths carried batons rather than shotguns and cutting bars, but Dole had told them what they could expect if anybody jostled Commander Bruckshaw.

Dole saw Stephen blocked by a press of citizens who'd overwhelmed the guild marshals. "Make a path for Mister Gregg, you whoresons!" the bosun shouted.

Stephen forced a smile. He was as tense as a trigger with only the last gram of take-up remaining. He'd been raised in Eryx, his family's small keep on the Atalanta Plains. Space was at a premium, but there weren't enough people in the entire community to constitute a crowd by Betaport standards.

Stephen's instincts were all wrong for a mob of people like this. Unless of course the folk around him had been hostile, in which case he could have cleared a path very quickly indeed.

The sailors in the crowd were already dodging away when the *Wrath*'s men strode forward. Some countrymen from the surrounding region, come to town for the event, would be lucky if nothing was dislocated; and the wife of one got a baton where she probably hadn't expected it. Dole waggled a horny fist in salute to Stephen as he passed the gentleman through.

Piet Ricimer had turned from the group of town and guild officials inside the station when he heard the shout. "Stephen?" he said. He blinked in pleased wonder. "Stephen!"

"I went to the tailor my uncle recommended in Ishtar City," Stephen said in embarrassment. "He decided brighter colors would 'soften the image,' as he put it. I feel like an idiot."

Piet laughed melodiously. "Nothing in this world or the next is going to make you look soft, my friend," he said. "But you look very striking indeed."

When Stephen Gregg consulted an expert, he abided by the expert's advice; a courtesy he expected from others when they asked *his* advice. Today he wore crimson tights with canary yellow sleeves, matching yellow boots, and a helmet and breastplate of copper/uranium alloy that shimmered purple.

The only part of the outfit he'd refused was the holstered pistol. "Just for show," the court tailor had explained.

Stephen didn't wear weapons just for show.

Piet squeezed his elbow. "Glad you made it," he said. "I'd hate to greet Councilor Bruckshaw without my right arm present."

Air rammed hissing through the station ahead of the train warned of the Councilor's arrival. Intercommunity travel on Venus had been by subsurface electric trains as far back as the first pre-Collapse colonies.

Within communities—even Ishtar City, the largest by far, with a population climbing above 200,000 souls in the past decade—people walked. Corridors cut with difficulty through the planetary crust were too narrow for vehicular traffic. Wealthy folk who thought to ignore the laws as a form of ostentation found themselves overturned within minutes. The mob accepted class distinctions, but it had a firm grasp also of the distinction between citizen and slave.

The train sighed to a halt, then settled with a *clackclackclack* onto the rail as power to the suspension magnets was cut. The double doors sprang open for Councilor Duneen and Councilor Bruckshaw, Commander of the Fleet, to step onto the platform together.

Staff members, ordered by precedence, walked behind their chiefs in more-than-military order. Each councilor had a good dozen folk in his entourage. The first man out of the train behind Duneen was Jeremy Moore, Factor Moore of Rhadicund, and an old shipmate of Piet and Stephen.

Piet strode forward and made a full bow. "Councilors," he said, "you honor Betaport with your presence. Please permit me and the chief men of our community to guide you to your destination."

With Stephen to his right and the Betaport magnates falling in behind, Piet Ricimer walked out of the train station. Four of the *Wrath*'s men led the procession. Dole and the remainder of the team walked along beside the dignitaries, enfolding them the way a magazine follower does the spring that drives it.

A cheer greeted Piet and Stephen. When the councilors came out of the station a moment later, a claque of carefully briefed sailors bellowed, "*Long life to Commander Bruckshaw! Long life to Commander Bruckshaw!*"

Piet leaned close to Stephen's ear and whispered, "After this, I don't think the commander will doubt the loyal willingness of Betaport to accept the decisions of Governor Halys."

"I don't think he'll doubt the loyalty of Betaport's first citizen, either," Stephen whispered in reply. "How do you like the red carpet?"

"*Long life to Commander Bruckshaw!*" The whole crowd had taken up the chant. The guards from the *Wrath* made sure that each new blockful of spectators knew what to shout as the honored visitors approached.

"Excellent quality," Piet said. "I wasn't expecting anything more than a roll of cloth. How much do I owe you?"

Stephen chuckled. "I pointed out to Haskins of Haskins Furnishings that he could double the new price to every social climber in Beta Regio—and *I* wasn't going to make sure he didn't sell somebody a piece that the governor's closest advisors hadn't really stepped on. The use is free, Piet."

"Where would I be without you, Stephen?" Piet murmured. His smile drooped slightly, unintentionally.

"Long life to Commander Bruckshaw!"

It was seven blocks from the train station to the Blue Rose Tavern across from the transfer docks. The tavern had been Piet Ricimer's unofficial headquarters since the days he was an ambitious teenager, mate on an intrasystem trader.

The first wealth from Piet's successful voyages had bought him a ship of his own, but the next stage of his climb was Betaport real estate. He'd bought the ground lease of the Blue Rose before even buying a house for himself. The front room was still a working tavern, but the back and upper floor of the building had become the center of Betaport's operations against President Pleyal and those who would support his tyranny.

Piet had raised a meter-high temporary dais in front of the Blue Rose. He paused at the steps, bowed again, and gestured the governor's councilors to precede him onto it. The Wraths made sure that none of the Betaport magnates tried to increase their dignity by hopping up with the three principals. As for the councilors' staff members—many of them courtiers of high rank themselves—Stephen Gregg stood at the base of the steps, grinning, and no one at all tried to push past him.

"People of Betaport!" Commander Bruckshaw said. He had a high, reedy voice, which nonetheless carried well across the packed street. "Free citizens of Venus!"

The immediate crowd quieted. The sough of folk more distant, chopped to verbal silage by the twists and corners of the corridors, continued as it always did in the cities of Venus.

"I appreciate the honor her excellency the governor did in appointing me commander of her fleet," Bruckshaw continued, "as I appreciate the honor you have done me on my arrival. I know as well as you do that there's a great deal I have yet to learn about crushing the tyrant Pleyal's minions in space, however."

Bruckshaw had an ascetically handsome face. The commander didn't look to be a terribly dynamic personality, but there was no lack of firmness and authority in his countenance. Not only was he a cousin to Governor Halys, members of Bruckshaw's direct lineage had in their own right been powerful figures on Venus for all the thousand years since the Collapse.

"I know also that there are no folk better able to teach me how to pay out the Federation than the sailors of Betaport can," Bruckshaw said, "and the—"

The roar of bloodthirsty triumph from the crowd drowned even the thought of intelligible speech. Bruckshaw and Duneen smiled; Piet Ricimer beamed like a floodlight on the people of the community that raised him.

Bruckshaw raised both hands for silence, still smiling. When the cheers muted to a dull rumble he resumed. "The sailors of Betaport, and the greatest space captain of all time, Factor Ricimer of Porcelain!"

The roar this time made even the previous cheers seem puny. Only the hoarseness of minutes of unrestrained shouting brought the silence for which the commander gestured again.

"In appreciation of Factor Ricimer's unequaled skills and his former services to the Free State of Venus . . ." Bruckshaw said.

He paused. Councilor Duneen stepped forward, holding a box inlaid with wood and nacre imported to Venus at obvious expense. Duneen opened the case. Bruckshaw removed a necklace from which depended a porcelain medallion in the form of Venus seen in partial eclipse: Governor Halys' crest.

" . . . I have appointed Factor Ricimer as my deputy commander," Bruckshaw said, draping the necklace over Piet's head. "He will be my closest advisor, as he has been for so many years the greatest enemy of Federation tyranny!"

The three men on the dais raised their hands together, Piet between the two councilors. They ducked quickly and slipped into the Blue Rose to plan the defeat of the Federation armada that would surely destroy Venus as a free society if they failed.

As Stephen Gregg followed the chiefs through the familiar door of the Blue Rose, he wondered if President Pleyal's officers had ever heard a sound to compare with the cheering. The walls of living rock trembled to the roar.

BETAPORT, VENUS

July 12, Year 27
1741 hours, Venus time

The upper floor of the Blue Rose had originally been four two-room apartments whose tenants sublet space to sailors in port who could afford better accommodation than a flophouse. Folk on Venus lived tightly together, and starship crews were used to living tighter still.

Piet had knocked out the internal divisions, save for two pillars of living rock where the load-bearing crosswall had been. The area had become working quarters for the part of the Ricimer household whose duties involved the still-undeclared war against President Pleyal, with the desks, files, and communications equipment necessary for that task.

Normally Piet conducted business, including conferences, in the back room of the tavern's lower floor. That comfortable, familiar chamber was full when a dozen men were present and packed by twenty. For this meeting, bringing together Governor Halys' representatives with the most experienced of the captains who would command her fleet, Piet needed the volume of the tavern's upper floor.

Stephen looked around the room with a critical eye and decided that Piet's staff had done a creditable job with the makeover. There hadn't been time to tile the bare rock walls. Instead, tapestries covered the scars and scribbles of centuries of occupation by spacers and leaseholders who were themselves only a handsbreadth above poverty.

The hangings were eclectic in style and materials. Batiks and thickly woven wools imported from Earth hung beside Venerian synthetics, and there were even a few Molt designs identifiable by odd color contrasts and recurrent pentagonal motifs. Piet had scoured the wealthy households of Betaport to meet the sudden requirement for wall coverings.

The melange shouldn't have worked together, but it somehow did. The chamber had a barbaric power that well symbolized the strength of Venus against the imposed uniformity of President Pleyal and his North American Federation.

There were many assembly rooms in Ishtar City that could have contained the gathering without difficulty. Commander Bruckshaw had chosen the Blue Rose Tavern to underline implicitly what he had said from the dais: it was due to Betaport sailors that Venus could claim to be a rival to the North American Federation, rather than merely a backwater to be overwhelmed (as the Southern Cross had been) when it suited Pleyal's whim to extend his tyranny.

Bruckshaw's ability to see and willingness to state that fact spoke well of the governor's choice of a commander for her fleet. Stephen Gregg didn't worry about the possibility of losing—he'd be dead before that happened, so it didn't figure in his personal considerations—but he knew the Free State of Venus couldn't afford internal bickering if it were to survive the Federation onslaught.

The delegation of captains from Ishtar City and the few from lesser ports scattered across the wind-scoured face of Venus were already present in the meeting room. They'd had no part in the arrival ceremony. That was between Betaport and the governor's representatives. Some of the outsiders had been drinking downstairs in the tavern. They watched with a palpable air of dogs in another pack's territory as Betaport captains trooped in behind the high dignitaries.

Alexi Mostert caught Stephen's eye and nodded friendly awareness. Captain Casson was present also, but Stephen noted that he and his clique of three younger men stood separate from most of the Ishtar City captains.

The meeting room's only furniture was a small desk holding a holographic projector beside which Guillermo waited, his face chitinously bland. Chairs and a table would have meant formal order and decisions about precedence. There would have been immediate scuffles and perhaps a dozen duels fought in the next days following. So long as the fifty-odd participants could move around freely, no one need feel honor-bound to claim redress for a slight.

Stephen positioned himself in a corner behind where Piet and the two councilors faced the bulk of the gathering. This assembly was for senior captains to give their opinions. Decisions would be made later by a much smaller group, in which Stephen would be present. He'd gain more by watching the interplays than he could by becoming involved at this stage.

To Stephen's amusement though not surprise, Jeremy Moore was in the opposite corner behind Councilor Duneen. Jeremy caught Stephen's eye and winked. He wore a cream suit trimmed with black lace—handsome, verging on the pudgy, every finger's breadth the courtier.

You had to look carefully to notice that Jeremy's left arm was withered and his hand tucked into the bodice of his blouse. At the back of Jeremy's eyes was another sign that didn't come from his time as Councilor Duneen's brother-in-law and trusted assistant; but you had to know to look for that and to recognize what you saw.

"Gentlemen," Commander Bruckshaw said. "Captains of Venus. We all know that the tyrant Pleyal is on the verge of making a direct attack on Venus. He's failed to choke off our trade, he's failed to defend *his* trade against us. His only remaining option is to put his troops in every community on Venus, enforcing his will, under the threat of blowing those communities open to the atmosphere. I've come before you on behalf of the governor to get expert opinions on how Pleyal may be stopped."

Stephen smiled slightly. The Federation also had the option of making peace with Venus; opening its trade, founding joint colonies, and advancing the cause of all mankind instead of the portion of humanity that bowed to President Pleyal.

Piet presumably believed that someday the lion would lie down with the lamb, though it was hard to see signs of that belief in Piet's actions.

"Stop him before he gets started," said Quigley before other mouths had opened. He was a competent, middle-aged Betaport man who'd captained one of the ships that landed during the Winnipeg raid. "Hit Nuevo Asuncion while the Fed fleet is still on the ground there. Blast it the way we blasted Winnipeg and it'll be ten years before Pleyal *could* gather enough ships to mount a real threat again."

"You're forgetting about the orbital forts guarding Asuncion," Groener said from Captain Casson's flank. "Thirty-centimeter guns that'd turn any of our ships inside out if we were stupid enough to come within range."

"Well, I'm talking about a surprise attack, aren't I?" Quigley snapped. "I know Betaport men can navigate well enough to—"

"Gentlemen!" Piet Ricimer said. His shout cut through the babble an instant before it degenerated into a brawl. A run-up of only thirty seconds to a riot would have been quick work even for Venerian space captains, Stephen thought sardonically.

The courtiers seemed to be taken aback. Meetings of the Governor's Council were acrimonious enough by all reports, but the veneer of civilized discourse was a trifle thicker.

"The skills of the men present are witnessed by the fact the men *are* present," Commander Bruckshaw said in the tense hush. "I do not choose to listen to empty comments on the subject."

"But I'll say," Piet said, eyeing Quigley stiffly, "that I personally don't trust my navigation to the point that I'd transit a ship close enough to an orbital fort to be sure of an instantaneous kill. There are three forts orbiting Nuevo Asuncion."

Quigley scowled at his feet in embarrassment. Despite the sparks, it was a good thing the first man to get out of line was from Betaport. By stepping on Quigley hard, Piet had gained the authority to do the same to Ishtar City captains.

"We could blockade Asuncion, though," Salomon suggested. "Cut the Feds off from the supplies they need to complete outfitting their fleet and let them rust on the ground."

Half a dozen men boomed simultaneous responses. Bruckshaw raised his left hand for silence, then said, "Captain Casson, you had a comment to that suggestion?"

"Sure I've got a comment," Casson growled. "It's crazy, that's my comment. We wear our ships out transiting. Use up our reaction mass so when the Feds do come up, they'll be able to run clear of us. Our men spending weeks, months, maybe years weightless—what are they going to be worth in a fight?"

The buzz of agreement following Casson's remarks was by no means limited to the Ishtar City contingent.

"And I might add, there's the governor's problem of how to pay the wages of a large fleet for an indefinite period," Councilor Duneen added. "Though the suggestion clearly has merit."

"If we're all off to Asuncion," Captain Luzanne said, "then what's to keep the Feds from shipping an army to Venus on intrasystem hulls? They don't need a fleet if our fighting ships are buggering themselves off in Near Space."

"They wouldn't dare do that!" a Betaport man shouted.

The friend beside him said, "I don't know why they wouldn't! We did it at Winnipeg, didn't we?"

The chaotic conversation of the next moments was a discussion, not a series of arguments. Bruckshaw let it go on for more than a minute before he raised his hand and said, "Gentlemen. Gentlemen!" Eyes focused on him.

In the hush, Salomon went on, "The Fed strategy will be to englobe Venus and threaten to bomb through the clouds unless we let them land and plant garrisons in our towns. They don't have good maps of Venus and it's not easy to hit anything through the winds of our upper atmosphere, but they'll do real damage. We've got to stop them, break up their formation, before they reach the Solar System."

"Why, if they sit in Venus orbit, we'll eat them like pieces of popcorn!" Groener said. Even Captain Casson scowled and shook his head at his acolyte.

A single bomb could rupture the covering of any community on Venus, letting in the planet's searing, corrosive atmosphere. No responsible Venerian leader could contemplate a battle fought in Venus orbit, when even a victory could cost higher civilian casualties than the ninety-five percent of the population that had died during the Collapse.

Alexi Mostert strode verbally across the gloom with which the gathering reacted to the truth belying Groener's bravado. "While Pleyal will have more ships than we do," he said in a loud voice, "the best of them won't be able to maneuver with the least of ours. The new ships that our yards are turning out for the governor will dance circles around anything wearing a mapleleaf!"

"The *Wrath* came closer to her programmed positions than any other vessel I've handled," Piet agreed. "That's both in sidereal space and during transit."

"Fads are well enough for those that like them," Casson said, showing nearly the truculence of Quigley at the start of the conference. "All I see nowadays are cylindrical ships that're twice as big as anybody in *my* day would think of building so inefficient a design. Give me a round ship with a thick hull, and you can hang me if she doesn't maneuver well enough to pay out the Feds."

"It's gunnery that'll pay them out," said Blassingame, a young fire-eater from a community near Cybebe so small that it had only a single dock. Ships were stored in the town center in the rare event of a second vessel docking while the first was still on the ground. "Maneuvering just lets us keep off and blast them from where they can't board us."

"That's so," Mostert agreed. "I think we can all agree about that: our hope, the hope of Venus, is to stand back and let our guns do the job for us."

"The Federation vessels will be carrying soldiers," said a courtier Stephen didn't recognize, a member of Duneen's entourage. "Over ten thousand troops have been gathered on Nuevo Asuncion, and our expectation is that most or all of them will embark with the fleet."

The speaker was a man in his sixties, wizened and wearing a beaded cap over what was clearly a bald scalp. It was the first time a member of a councilor's staff had entered the discussion.

"The primary purpose of the troops is to provide initial garrisons for Venus if we open our cities due to the threat of bombing," Councilor Duneen added. "But they'll certainly be prepared to fight in a boarding battle between ships as well."

"There's no need to board," Mostert said. "Not for any of our vessels, certainly not for the new-design ships, which can concentrate their fire as—"

He paused a half-beat to glance, not glare, at Captain Casson.

"—geometry prevents old-style spheres like the *Freedom* from doing, though God Himself were at the controls."

"We've smashed Fed ships to gas and fragments plenty of times," Captain Salomon said. "Because they can't maneuver with us, we'll run past them like they were on the ground. Our big guns will chew them away like files eating down an aluminum bar!"

The assembly growled murderous agreement.

Stephen Gregg's expression looked like a slight smile: approving, to an onlooker eager for approval; neutral, to a neutral observer. Jeremy Moore pursed his lips in Stephen's direction, then raised an eyebrow. Stephen shrugged.

The size of the Federation fleet frightened them all, though few in this room would admit it. No one knew exactly how many ships President Pleyal would be able to gather, but everyone was aware that the resources of the Federation were many times greater than those of Venus. Venus was better able to concentrate what ships and men she had, but when the fleets met, the disparity in numbers as well as in the size of individual ships was certain to be great.

The men here wanted desperately to believe that gunnery was the answer to the Federation threat. Maybe they were right, but Stephen as a matter of policy distrusted "certainties" when the folk proclaiming them thought nothing else stood between them and the abyss. The vision of a Federation fleet melting like salt under a hose as plasma bolts washed their ships was attractive, but that didn't make it true.

The next dozen speakers trampled over the same ground. Stephen waited, his face intent but only the surface level of his mind listening. Venerian ships had better fire control, better guns, more *big* guns, ship-smashing guns. Venerian crews reloaded faster, and their ceramic tubes increased the rate of fire by a good thirty percent over that of the Feds' stellite weapons, even when the Feds were crack personnel.

Each statement was true in itself. Stephen had seen the truth repeatedly demonstrated in blood and flame from Winnipeg to the Reaches. But there was a greater question: "Is this enough to destroy the fleet that will otherwise destroy Venus?" Every one of the captains speaking begged the truth of that question, but for Stephen Gregg it had yet to be proved.

Eventually Piet cleared his throat. Councilor Duneen caught Bruckshaw's eye and nodded.

Commander Bruckshaw said, "Gentlemen? As you know, my final plans will be drawn up in close consultation with Factor Ricimer. I think it might be useful at this juncture for all of us to hear what his current thinking on the matter may be. Sir?"

Piet nodded twice and crossed his hands behind his back. "Commander, gentlemen," he said. "I don't believe Governor Halys will permit any significant portion of her fleet to leave the Solar System at the present juncture—"

He glanced in the direction of Councilor Duneen. Duneen smiled dryly and nodded agreement. What had been true before the Winnipeg raid was even more certain now that full-scale war was inevitable.

"Therefore we'll have to rely on picket vessels to inform us when the Feds leave Asuncion," Piet resumed. "I hope and expect, with God's blessing, that we'll still be able to meet the Feds many days' transit from Venus."

"Nuevo Asuncion *is* only eight days from Venus," Casson interrupted.

Bruckshaw looked at the Ishtar City captain with a gaze Stephen wouldn't have wanted turned on himself. Piet merely smiled agreement and said, "Yes, for us; and probably no more than ten days for an ordinarily well-found Federation ship with a Federation crew. But we're not to forget that the Feds will be traveling as a fleet, a very large fleet. Further, they'll know that their only chance of safety against us will be to hold a tight formation at all times. They'll have to make very short transit series."

Casson shrugged with a black expression. Most of the other captains nodded or murmured assent. Everybody knew that not only did a company of vessels travel at the rate of the one least able to navigate accurately, the difficulties increased almost as the logarithm of the number of ships involved.

Practical interstellar travel required that a vessel transfer from the sidereal universe to a series of other bubble universes. Each cell of the hyperuniversal sponge-space matrix had its own different constants of time and distance. The ship retained momentum from the sidereal universe and from thrust expended within each cell that it transited, but the effect of motion within a cell could exceed by thousands of times that of motion within the sidereal universe.

Distances within the sidereal universe were of no practical significance, because even the stars nearest to the Solar System were too far for trade through normal space. The concepts of Near Space and the Reaches referred to the relative length of voyages to those locations through the enormously complex patterns of sponge space.

The artificial intelligences that calculated transit series were the most sophisticated electronics in the human universe. Because of constant slight changes in the association of bubble universes and in the energy gradients separating one cell from the next, no sidereal distance longer than those within the core of a planetary system could be encompassed by a single transit series.

Ships made a number of gut-wrenching hops back and forth from normal space to cells of sponge space, then paused for hours or days while their AIs compared sidereal reality with the navigators' programmed intent. The process was time-consuming and uncomfortable even for hardened spacers, but it made the stars and their multiplicity of Earthlike planets available to mankind. If transit had been developed ten generations sooner, there would not have been a network of colonies burrowing through the crust of Venus—

And surviving, even when the Outer Planets Rebellion brought human civilization down in crashing horror through a handful of pinprick attacks that a less centralized, less homogeneous, society could have ignored.

No two ships metered thrust or judged angles in quite the same fashion. Since differences were multiplied by scores or thousands during every transit, it was obvious that a large fleet that was required to stay in close formation would have to proceed by brief series with correspondingly long delays to recalibrate for the next hop.

The Federation force would certainly be huge, and neither President Pleyal's vessels nor his captains were of Venerian standard. Normally ships in company proceeded each at its own pace and rendezvoused at the end of each day's voyaging. The Grand Fleet of Retribution had to keep much closer contact, or the individual ships would be gobbled up by Venerians in concert. Bruckshaw would have his own problems, since Venerian ships and navigators were of varying capacities too; but the average capacity was very much higher.

"We can easily calculate the Fed course to Venus from the time they rise from Asuncion," Piet continued. "I would recommend that we meet them at the earliest point along that route in which our force can be complete."

He swept the room with his fiery, brilliant smile. Even after so many years, that smile had the ability to warm Stephen. It wasn't a pretense with Piet: it was his real spirit blazing out on those around him.

"Some of you may remember times I've rushed in when others, wiser folk perhaps, would have waited for more support to arrive," Piet said. "Not this time. If we attack the Feds in penny packets while they keep an ordered formation, we'll waste ammunition that we can't afford as well as the morale advantage we have until they see us fail."

No one understood morale effects better than Piet Ricimer. The Feds who knew *Captain Ricimer* was coming down on them with his undefeated pack of killers would think themselves half beaten no matter how great their numbers in ships and men.

Captain Ricimer and his killers. Stephen rubbed his forehead hard, so that the pain drew him back to the present.

"The Feds will take far longer than us to recalibrate in sidereal space for the next transit series," Piet said. "Their ships will be scattered, with the help of God. Our forces can cruise past Fed ships, always staying under power, and hit them with our heavy guns. They won't be able to reply effectively so long as we stand off and keep under way. And if we always remain at the correct point relative to them in sidereal space, they won't be able to transit directly toward Venus."

"We can keep them wandering like Israel in the wilderness!" Salomon said.

Piet nodded assent as solemn as "Amen" to close a prayer. He faced toward Commander Bruckshaw and bowed, turning the meeting back to him.

Bruckshaw cleared his throat. His visage hardened very slightly, an unconscious preparation for his next words. He said, "Gentlemen and captains, you've heard Factor Ricimer's opinion based on his own experience and what has been said in this room. Under God and Governor Halys, I and no other command the fleet of Venus."

He looked around the room, his eyes lighting last of all on Stephen Gregg. Stephen nodded acknowledgment.

"However," the commander continued in a lighter tone, "I'm not a man to overrule experts for the sake of proving my authority. If anyone questions that authority, I'll remove him as I would swat a fly; but with that understood, I will tell you here and now that Factor Ricimer can expect my fullest cooperation in the ordering of the fleet according to expert judgment. My cooperation will extend to the corridors of the palace where perhaps the recommendations of a space captain, even the greatest of space captains, haven't till now been accepted as quickly as the present crisis requires."

Bruckshaw turned and clasped Piet by both hands, raising them into the air as he looked at the assembled captains. The cheering was general and heartfelt; even, Stephen thought, the grudging nod of Captain Casson.

But would it be enough?

BETAPORT, VENUS

July 12, Year 27
1903 hours, Venus time

When the cheers died away, Piet Ricimer rang a ceramic bell shaped like a rose blooming from the end of a baton. The outer doors opened; servants hired for the purpose carried in narrow tables already set with covered dishes and an array of liquors.

"I hope you'll all be able to join me in a buffet," Piet said, "where we can discuss details informally."

The manners of men who lived no more than arm's length from their fellows during long voyages were less fastidious than those of the governor's court. Space captains began lifting lids and—especially—snatching bottles before the tables were even in place against the back wall. Members of the councilors' staffs gaped in horrified surprise, though Bruckshaw's expression was politely bland and Councilor Duneen seemed rather amused.

Stephen wanted a drink, but not particularly in this company. As he considered alternatives, Jeremy Moore walked over to him and said, "I was thinking of taking a turn down Dock Street for old times' sake, Stephen. Care to come?"

Stephen chuckled. "With me looking like the biggest parrot on Venus, and you not exactly dressed like a sailor yourself? The mob's had its entertainment today. Why don't you and I go below, pick up a bottle in the tavern, and chat in Piet's office? It'll be empty, or we can empty it."

"You country boys," Jeremy said with a smile that shimmered over tension. He and Stephen had been shipmates on one voyage, a very long voyage. They'd gotten to know and respect one another; and between them, they'd killed more people than anyone around had time to count. "Afraid of a few people bumping you. But sure, let's do that."

Piet and Councilor Duneen had already gathered clots of people offering ideas or making requests. Stephen made a slight gesture when Piet's eye brushed him; Piet nodded minuscule. To Stephen's amusement, he noticed that Jeremy took leave of Councilor Duneen in precisely the same way.

Jeremy slipped between the servants coming up the narrow stairs before they were fully aware that he was moving past them. He'd always been good at finding paths to a destination, Jeremy had. Stephen followed swiftly, because servants flattened against the stair-well wall at his presence. They would have done the same for any guest; but perhaps without the slight glint of fear at being so close to Colonel Gregg, the killer.

They should have seen Jeremy Moore with a cutting bar on the blood-splashed bridge of the *Keys to the Kingdom.*

Moore was Factor of Rhadicund, a title his ancestors in direct line had held ever since the Collapse. His grandfather had sold up the small keep and moved to Ishtar City to swim—and promptly sink—in the politics of the Governor's Palace.

Jeremy had survived, barely, through his status as a gentleman, on his wizardry with electronics—and because he liked women almost as much as women liked him. He'd joined Captain Ricimer to escape what he was as well as to make himself something better.

"Better" was a word that depended on what you saw to judge; but certainly the Jeremy Moore who returned to Venus had become Councilor Duneen's top aide.

The Blue Rose was crowded with locals who elbowed sightseers hoping for another glimpse of the dignitaries meeting upstairs. Jeremy worked through them with surprisingly little contact. He'd grown up in Ishtar City's Old Town, where the corridors were rarely less crowded than this tavern at present.

"Todd, a bottle of slash," Stephen called through the clamor. His path to the bar cleared when other drinkers recognized his voice. "What would you like, Jeremy? Todd has most anything you'd care for nowadays."

The folk visiting Piet Ricimer's headquarters were a cosmopolitan lot. Todd, who sublet the Blue Rose from Piet and ran the tavern with his family, had found the profit in exotic liquors far exceeded the trouble of keeping them on hand; though for lack of storage space, tuns of beer were delivered every half hour at busy times.

"A carafe of citrus juice if you've got it," Jeremy said, "because I'm really dry. But ice water would be fine."

"Always glad to oblige a gentleman, sir," Todd said. He handed Stephen a square-faced bottle of Eryx slash and the pitcher of orange juice from the refrigerator beneath the bar. He whispered to a child, probably his granddaughter since she couldn't have been older than eight. She scuttled out of the tavern and down the corridor in search of more juice.

Jeremy opened the door to the office, what had been the tavern's private room before Piet acquired the leasehold, and bowed Stephen inside. Stephen glanced at the electronic lock and said, "Was that open?"

Jeremy displayed the little device he wore on his right index finger like a downturned ring. He grinned. "Just to keep my hand in," he said. He closed the door behind them.

Stephen set the pitcher and bottle on the black glass table in the center of the room. The bases rocked slightly because the tabletop was a sheet of obsidian left in its natural state, rather than something cast and polished in a foundry.

"So, Jeremy . . ." Stephen said as he took tumblers from the cabinet in the corner. "Will you be coming out with us this time?"

Jeremy snorted. He lifted the pitcher in his good hand and drank from the side of it. "You won't need a crippled close-combat man, Stephen," he said. "It's going to be a gunnery battle. I heard all those experienced captains say so, one after the other."

Stephen took a swig straight from the bottle of slash. The algal liquor was harsh and warming. "Yeah," he said, his voice deeper than it had been a moment earlier. "I'm worried about the same thing. Maybe they're right, though. Maybe it's just that nobody likes to believe that what he does isn't needed any more."

"What I used to do," Jeremy said softly. The juice trembled in his hand. He slurped more, then put the pitcher down.

Stephen settled himself onto a chair. Jeremy took another on the same side of the table, turning so that he faced Stephen.

"I hear it's you we have to thank for the fact Venus has a single communications net," Stephen said. "Identical codes and everything tied together. I never thought I'd live long enough to see that."

"Ninety-eight percent of Venus tied together," Jeremy said with a reminiscent smile. "You and I may *not* be alive by the time the rest gets linked. But it's really due to Councilor Duneen—and President Pleyal, believe it or not. We need the net for trade, but the council would have bickered till the equator froze except that the councilor convinced Governor Halys that universal communications were a defense necessity."

"I don't doubt your patron's political skill," Stephen said as he savored the cloying, half-rotted aftertaste of slash from his family's keep. "But in my own life, I haven't noticed that a job magically does itself because the man on top gives an order."

Jeremy laughed heartily. "Oh, Stephen," he said, "I've been called names the Feds never thought of! By people who thought there was money to be made and too little of it was coming their way, and by other folks who thought, quite correctly, that I was trampling the right of themselves and their community to be pointlessly unique. I don't know how many times somebody shouted, 'Moore, you don't understand!' When the problem was that I did understand, and that absolutely nothing was going to stop me from doing what was necessary for Venus."

Stephen drank. He saw in his mind's eye the Jeremy Moore of a few years earlier, swinging a cutting bar for as long as there was an enemy standing; and when the last Fed had fallen, he'd hacked corpses in his unslaked bloodlust.

Jeremy chuckled. "Mind," he said, "there *was* a lot of money to be made. But not by pricks. I believe Weyston Trading was the prime contractor for the Atalanta Plains?"

"My uncle thanks you," Stephen agreed. "And I don't think my brother Augustus ever really looked up to me before he learned that the assessment on Eryx Keep had been waived because he was my relative. It's funny. I could have paid the charges easily enough, but that just would have meant I was rich. That Factor Moore had the charges waived—that made me somebody."

He drank again. The level in the bottle had gone down more than he felt as if it should have.

Jeremy stared at his fist on the table and said, very softly, "I'd rather die than wrap my hand around the grip of a cutting bar again."

He looked at his friend and went on. "How are you sleeping, Stephen?"

Stephen shrugged. "Hasn't been a lot of change there," he said with a slight smile directed at the liquor bottle. "It's not the thing I do best."

He looked up. "How about you, Jeremy?"

"Better than it was," Jeremy said. "I don't scare my wife anymore."

He forced a smile, but the expression died on the underlying tension. "It was my own fault, Stephen. I kept trying to explain things that Melinda didn't have the vocabulary to understand. She tried, she really did, but she could only hear words. They didn't mean what they did to me. To us."

Jeremy drained all the juice from the pitcher. Staring at the empty container as he set it on the table, he went on, "And I had to stop drinking. I thought it helped—and it did, it helped me sleep, *you* know what I mean."

Stephen nodded. His big hands were laced around the slash bottle. "More juice?" he asked. "Todd will have some by now."

"I'm all right," Jeremy said. He took a deep breath. "It helped me sleep," he went on, "but I don't have your control, Stephen. I was at a party. It was more of a family thing than politics, though of course with the councilor everything is politics. I'd had a few, no more than usual. Talk got around to our heroes out in the Reaches."

He grimaced. "I shouldn't have—you can't explain, *you* know that. But I said it wasn't heroes out beyond Pluto, it was nothing but blood and waste. And somebody I hadn't met. He told me I ought to keep my mouth shut. When I didn't know what I was talking about. He knew what it was like. His nephew had sailed with Captain Ricimer."

Jeremy's voice quivered. He'd pressed his palm flat against the tabletop, but his forearm trembled. "*Christ*, this is stupid!" he said. "No control, Stephen. No control at all."

"More control than I've got," Stephen said, laying his right hand over Jeremy's. "You got out."

"Stephen, I almost killed him," Jeremy said with his eyes bright.

"It took four men to pull me off." He smiled wanly. "They say it did. God knows I don't remember."

"I decided a long time ago that there were too many fools for me to kill them all," Stephen said. "But it's a temptation, I know."

"There wasn't any problem about it," Jeremy said, his voice stronger and nearly normal again. "Turned out the fellow was a second cousin who'd barely scraped onto the guest list. He came to my office the next afternoon and apologized on his knees. He hadn't known he was speaking to the Factor of Rhadicund."

Stephen laughed with as much humor as his laugh usually held. "He *wasn't* speaking to the Factor of Rhadicund," he said. "He was talking to the fellow who led Piet Ricimer's boarding crew."

Stephen stood up. He looked at the bottle in his hands, then flung it with all his strength at the wall. A tile shattered, but the bottle bounced spraying liquor three times before it caught an angle wrong and disintegrated into tiny crystal shards. Good Venerian material, able to withstand enormous stresses before at last it broke.

"*Christ,* I'm glad you got out, Jeremy," Stephen said to the wall in a husky voice.

Jeremy was standing beside him. "I'm told you've formed a partnership with a Captain Blythe, Stephen," he said mildly.

Stephen looked at him in amazement.

"Well, my job's communications, Stephen," Jeremy said with a tinge of embarrassment. "I don't spy on my friends, but if I hear something, I . . ."

Stephen nodded and turned his head again. "She's a good person, Jeremy. Too good a person to—"

He looked at the table and didn't slam his fist against it after all. Throwing the bottle had reminded him that he didn't dare blame things outside himself for problems that were solely in his mind.

"You know what I'm like, Jeremy," he said. "It's not fair to use a decent person to keep from . . . Anyway, there's slash. Sal and I own a ship together, but there's no need for us to meet. I'd decided that before Winnipeg."

Stephen attempted a smile, decided it worked, and faced his friend again.

"Stephen," Jeremy said softly. "It's none of my business, but listen anyway. She's not a thing, she's a person. If she's willing, then don't keep away from her for her sake. That's *her* choice. All the liquor does is put another shovel of dirt on what's down there. There's not enough liquor in all the world to keep it down forever, so you may as well have a woman help you face it."

Jeremy laughed suddenly. He wiped his sweaty palm on a handkerchief he snaked from the opening in his jacket that held his left forearm, withered by a Federation bullet in the shoulder joint. "Women are," he said in a light tone, "one of my areas of expertise."

Stephen sighed. "Oh, I'll be all right, Jeremy," he said. "Seeing an old friend . . ."

He paused. "You give me hope, Jeremy. Maybe that's what I'm really afraid of. Hope."

"We'd best get back upstairs," Jeremy said. "Making our principals look important is part of the job too, after all."

He swallowed, touched his tongue to his lips, and said, "Stephen? Do you think Piet really will need boarding crews when the Feds come this time?"

Stephen shrugged. Jeremy gripped the bigger man's arm and turned him so that they were face to face. "*Tell* me. Stephen," he said.

"Not as much as Venus needs heroes on the ground here, Jeremy," Stephen said. "War's easy. *You* know that. Making life worth something—that's a lot harder."

Factor Moore of Rhadicund nodded and opened the door to the excited bustle of the Blue Rose Tavern.

BETAPORT, VENUS

July 19, Year 27
1351 hours, Venus time

Hergesheimer Dock was one of Betaport's oldest storage docks. The vessel nearest the entrance was dollied up for movement but the tractor operator, the ship's officers, and an official or two representing the dock were arguing beside the tractor. Everyone involved shouted at the top of his voice, but the volume drank all but a susurrus of echoes.

"There we go," Sal said. "Cradle Eight, not Cradle Three. I got out in the transfer dock when we brought her from Ishtar City, and handwriting isn't Harrigan's strong suit. The *Clarence*, formerly the *Maid of Bellemont*, formerly the *Grace*. Not a new ship, but I've gone up and down in her and she's well-found at the core."

Stephen crossed his hands behind the small of his back and wondered what it was he was supposed to be seeing in the utterly nondescript vessel before them. From any distance the *Clarence* could have passed as a twin to the *Gallant Sallie*.

Sal had asked Stephen to come here with her. He'd been planning to see her ever since he talked to Jeremy Moore, but he hadn't been sure how he was going to make the contact.

He didn't have a clue as to why Sal had brought him here, though.

"The main thing was that she could be had for a song," Sal continued. "The widow wasn't interested in keeping anything that reminded her of her husband—he died in a brothel, not a shipping accident—and the electronics were going to have to be replaced. That doesn't matter for our purposes, of course."

"You bought her?" Stephen said, a light dawning. Sal needed a loan to—

"*You* bought her," Sal said crisply. "To be precise, I bought her on your behalf, using the commercial letter of credit with which you'd provided me."

Stephen grew very still. "The letter of credit was to cover trading opportunities for the *Gallant Sallie* at times when I was unavailable," he said without affect.

"Was it?" Sal said, her chin sticking out in determination. "That's not what the document says. You can rescind it, but the purchase transaction is valid."

"I accept that," said Stephen. He hadn't seen Sarah Blythe in person since the squadron lifted from Winnipeg. . . . "Go on."

"I have a list of captains who I think will work the *Clarence* for quarter shares," Sal said. "That's after you upgrade the electronics to *Gallant Sallie* standards, of course. They're all solid men, but I haven't discussed the matter in case you might have a personal problem with one of them."

She handed Stephen a list printed on flimsy paper. He crumpled it into his palm. "I don't have personal problems with people," he said. He smiled like black ice over lava. "Not long term."

Sal nodded, her face tightly emotionless. "Actually, I think you'll be able to hire—take as partners—all six of them before too long. There are a lot of ships like the *Clarence,* like the *Gallant Sallie* was. They need upgrades. Most people haven't appreciated that the expansion of trade going on right now makes it cost-effective to upgrade even hulls as old as these."

"Sal," Stephen said, "if I wanted to be in the shipping business, I'd be managing Weyston Trading for my uncle right now. I—"

"No!" Sal said. She turned abruptly away and wiped her eyes. "No, Stephen," she said. "Weyston Trading's an established intrasystem operation. I could run it, Tom *Harrigan* could run it. What Venus needs—"

She looked at Stephen fiercely again, pretending to ignore the tears on her cheeks. "What Venus needs is trade, *real* trade, to Near Space and the Reaches. That's going to take somebody with imagination to lead the way, to show other people how much profit there is to be made there. *Everybody* will gain."

"I'm not—" Stephen said.

"You are!" Sal said. "You owe it to Venus and you owe it to yourself!"

Stephen looked at her for some moments without speaking. At last he said, "A strictly business operation, I take it?"

She blinked. "Of course."

He nodded. "All right," he said. "We'll incorporate as Blythe Spirits. You'll be managing director with a fifty percent share of the profits. Oh, and put yourself down for a five percent finder's fee on ships bought for the corporation."

"I—" Sal said. "That isn't . . ."

Stephen smoothed the piece of flimsy so that he could read the names. He squinted. The illumination of Hergesheimer Dock had been marginal even when twice as many of the overhead lights worked. "Tell me about Captain Lou Montrose," he said.

"Stephen, I'm not a manager," Sal whispered.

"We're all learning new things, aren't we?" Stephen Gregg replied with a crooked smile. "We owe it to Venus or some such thing, I'm told."

Looking toward the flimsy, he went on, "What are you doing for dinner tonight?"

The tractor operator finally put his vehicle into gear. The joints of the dolly clanged, echoing through the dock like the bells of a great temple.

BETAPORT, VENUS

September 24, Year 27
2122 hours, Venus time

Sal heard the commotion outside the Blue Rose, but because she wasn't a Betaport native she couldn't judge how unusual it was. Nobody else in the tavern seemed to care.

Stephen threw his last dart into the rim. The ships' officers crowding the taproom groaned or hooted, depending on how their side bets lay.

Sal put her hand on Stephen's shoulder and said, "Some marksman you are!"

"Find me a board that throws back and see how I do," Stephen called, loud enough to be heard generally.

Guillermo stepped from Piet's office behind the taproom. At the same instant the door to Dock Street flew open and a sailor shouted, "Sir! Captain Ricimer! The *Oriflamme*'s in from Asuncion and the Feds are coming out!"

Sal felt her rib muscles tighten. Her mind wasn't ready to consider what the news meant, but her body was already reacting.

All the light went out of Stephen Gregg's expression. He folded his retrieved darts into a strip of soft leather with the economical motions of a man whose fingers had reloaded any number of weapons, and who would shortly be reloading more.

Sound erupted, then ceased like a bubble that rose to the surface of a swamp and plopped into nonexistence. Faces turned toward the messenger in the doorway rotated as suddenly toward Piet Ricimer.

"Guillermo?" Piet said. He sounded nonchalant.

"Ishtar City and the other defense ports have been alerted, Captain," the Molt said. One of Piet's trusted subordinates had been on communications watch in the office every day for the past six. Because ships couldn't communicate with the ground through the charged, turbulent Venerian atmosphere, information would have been carried by land line from the transfer dock to the office at the same time as the dock's external speakers shouted the news to those passing by in the street. "Ships in Betaport intended for the squadron have been informed also."

Sal had seen Guillermo's three-fingered hands working a keyboard intended for humans. The Molt was at least as quick as a human operator because he never, absolutely never, made a false movement. He'd transmitted the alert to all necessary recipients of the information, and he'd still entered the taproom in no more time than it had taken a sailor to run across the street.

Men shoved toward the door in a group just short of a mob. Virtually everyone in the Blue Rose had duties on one of Venus' fighting ships.

"One moment, gentlemen!" Piet Ricimer said, slicing the chaos like a shovel through gravel. Everyone stopped and turned again.

"Guillermo, what is the status of the transfer docks?" Piet asked.

"There are six vessels in orbit queued to land, Captain," Guillermo said. "The docks won't be clear for another three hours at best."

"Much as I thought," Piet said. He beamed to the men around him. "I believe the *Wrath*'s duty officer and anchor watch can receive the reporting crewmen for the next ten minutes without me. That should give us time to finish our game. Captain Salomon, I recall it being your throw."

Stephen Gregg began to laugh the way he had on Lilymead, great, booming gusts of laughter. He bent over, supporting himself in part by resting his empty right hand on his thigh. Men looked at the big man as if he were a ticking bomb.

"Your throw, Mister Salomon," Piet prodded gently.

Salomon swallowed and stepped to the scratch. His darts flew wild, in sharp contrast to earlier in the evening when his mechanical precision had put him and Todarov, his partner, well ahead.

More men entered from Dock Street. Each newcomer started to shout the news, then was hushed by those in the taproom already.

"May God bless our enterprise," said Piet Ricimer in a calm voice. He threw. Each of his darts landed within a millimeter of his point of aim, putting the game to bed.

Stephen enfolded Sal in his arms, squeezed and released her, and strode to the door ahead of Piet; Colonel Gregg preceded Deputy Commander Ricimer through a crowd of their subordinates.

But Stephen was still laughing.

BETAPORT, VENUS

September 25, Year 27
1013 hours, Venus time

"*There were ninety and nine—*" sang six crewmen near Stephen as they gripped the stanchions around the *Wrath*'s Number One gun. They were supernumeraries for takeoff and landing, as were most members of the vessel's complement. "*—who safely lay—*"

"The dome is opening, Captain," Guillermo reported from the leftmost of the three primary navigation consoles. The Molt always sounded prim. His enunciation was perfect, but the hard edges of his triangular jaws clipped words as a matter of physical necessity.

"*—in the* shel-*ter of the fold,*" the singers continued. Perhaps it was their way of dealing with the nervousness on takeoff that was normal even among spacers. Perhaps they just liked to sing hymns.

The great screen before Piet at the center console boiled a smoky yellow-red. The Venerian atmosphere poured down on the *Wrath* as soon as the clamshell lids of the transfer dock began to draw back.

At ground level the air was almost still, but in the topmost of the three bands of convection cells, sulphurous winds of over 400 kph buffeted vessels. The atmosphere had been the Venus colony's greatest protection from out-planet raiders during the Rebellion, but it had devoured a thousand ships and their unskillful or unlucky crews in the millennium since.

"*But one was out on the—*"

"Will you shut the bloody noise off, you bloody widdiful!" Philips said in a shout that was nearly a scream.

The leader of the singers, a gunner's mate, looked around with a sneer on his lips and a snarl on the tip of his tongue. His face cleared and he swallowed the words when he saw that Philips squatted beside Mister Gregg in back of the navigation consoles. Philips might have been speaking on the gentleman's behalf; and anyway, the men who loaded for Mister Gregg had a certain status on the *Wrath*.

"Sorry, sir," the gunner's mate muttered to Stephen, hushing his fellows with a hand.

"You may light the thrusters, Mister Simms," Piet said to the navigator at the console to his immediate right. Simms touched a key.

The vessel came alive. Even on minimum flow the plasma motors gave the *Wrath* a vibrant feel far different from the solemn throb of the auxiliary power unit and the varied shrillness of pumps and fans throughout the hull.

"Sorry, sir," Philips muttered to Stephen. "Seems to me they're singing for fun, not like it was a Christian thing to do now. And it's not right, with our people back home and only us to stop the Feds."

The *Wrath* had thirty-two separate plasma motors, giving the warship a greater delicacy of maneuver than a freighter of similar size could achieve with thrust channeled through eight or perhaps a dozen nozzles. Piet ran their power up and down, four thrusters at a time, as the dock's lid continued to edge sideways above them. On the screen, exhaust added brilliance to an atmosphere lit by a bloody, sullen sun.

"Sir?" Philips asked. He was a solid sailor, a motorman's mate of 25. He retained his ordinary shipboard duties after he volunteered to load for Stephen, though Mister Gregg's convenience became paramount. "What will happen if we don't . . . What if the Feds do reach Venus, sir?"

"The dock is fully open, Captain," Guillermo said. Desire to get the entire squadron into Venus orbit wouldn't affect Piet's normal—nonemergency—start-up routine.

"They'll orbit," Stephen said with deliberate calm. Philips' first child, a girl, had been born three days before. She and the mother were in Betaport, sure to be the second target of Pleyal's forces if not their first. "They'll demand landing clearance under threat of bombing, and they'll get it. Nobody on Venus is going to have cities ripped open."

"They'll put down soldiers, then?" Philips said.

"Garrisons, yes," Stephen agreed. "Enough to show that they're in charge, but not a fighting army it wouldn't be. Maybe five or ten thousand troops, spread out all over the planet. It won't be pleasant. They'll desecrate churches, putting up their idols. And I'm sure folk in the government will be arrested. But not so very terrible for ordinary people, I shouldn't think."

"I guess with their own soldiers in cities, it'll be safer," Philips suggested hopefully. "They won't blow the roof in with their own people there."

"Prepare for liftoff!" Piet announced, his voice ringing through the *Wrath*'s tannoys. The thrusters ran up to full output, their irises still dilated.

Stephen thumped his loader in friendly fashion with his left hand; his right gripped the stanchion against which both men braced themselves. "I don't expect to lose, though, Philips," he shouted over the roar as thruster nozzles shrank down.

Nor did Stephen Gregg expect to survive a defeat himself. But Philips was very naive if he thought President Pleyal would bomb a riotous city any less quickly for the fact a few hundred Federation troops would burn in the corrosive atmosphere with the tens of thousands of Venerian civilians—like Philips' wife and child.

ABOARD THE *WRATH*

September 29, Year 27
0847 hours, Venus time

"Holy Jesus Christ our lord and savior," somebody said in a hushed voice. Stephen realized his eyes were closed. He opened them carefully and saw the fleet of the North American Federation.

The *Wrath* was four days out from Venus. The transit series just concluded had been of twenty-seven separate exits from and reentries to the sidereal universe. Each one had hooked a needle through Stephen's soul and drawn another stitch stranglingly tight.

For ten years, transit had been a regular part of Stephen Gregg's existence. Each new experience was exactly like the last. Sometimes his eyes welled tears; always the pain in his skull made his stomach try to turn itself inside out.

Stephen would rather have had his teeth pulled without anesthetic than undergo transit. Dentistry wouldn't take him across interstellar space to where he had a job to do, so transit it was.

He understood why first sight of the enemy had brought the amazed prayer—it really had been a prayer—from Simms, who'd recovered fractionally quicker than Stephen had. The navigator's pride at meeting the enemy across trackless light-years was muted by realization of what they'd caught.

The Federation fleet was awesome. The number of ships, well over a hundred, wasn't unexpected, though seeing them had an emotional impact on even a prepared mind. What Stephen found shocking was the regularity of the Feds' formation.

He rose to his feet. The *Wrath* was under power, a standard 1-g acceleration for comfort's sake. Piet felt or saw the movement at the back of his console and turned. "That was the last transit series for some hours, I think, Stephen," he said. "How do you feel?"

"I'll live," Stephen said. He quirked a smile, knowing that between them "whether I like it or not" was understood to close the sentence. "I don't want to bother you if you . . ." He shrugged and flicked a finger toward the display.

"Nothing until the commander and the rest of the fleet arrives," Piet said. Ninety percent of Simms' screen was given over to alphanumeric data, but a visual sidebar in the lower right corner showed Venerian dispositions. Three more beads winked into sight simultaneously, bringing the total to ten.

"They're doing a good job of holding together," Stephen said, his eyes on the Federation fleet. The Feds were in a tight globe. Most of the ships were large, and some were very large. The vessels in the interior of the formation, like the stone in a peach, didn't have guns to run out when the Venerians appeared. Those would be the stores ships and probably troopers; not fighting vessels, though their size and added numbers couldn't fail to have a morale effect on their opponents.

The outer sphere was of warships, arrayed with fields of fire interlocked like the spines of a bramble bush. There were at least eighty of them, twice as many as the heavy vessels of the Venerian fleet.

"They've got more experience in fleet operations than we do," Piet said simply. "I'm surprised to see how well they're keeping formation, though. Their captains and commander are both smarter and more skillful than I'd thought they would be."

Guillermo turned from his adjacent console. "I have been listening to the talk within the Federation fleet, Captain," he said.

"How are you doing that?" Stephen asked in surprise. Modulated laser was the only practical means of communication between starships, since plasma thrusters acted as omniband radio-frequency transmitters. Unlike radio, laser communicators were tight-beam devices that had to be carefully aimed to be heard even by the intended recipient.

Guillermo made a grating motion with his belly plates, the Molt equivalent of laughter. "Their communication beams reflect from their hulls, Colonel," he said. "I directed the *Wrath*'s fine sensors to pick up the reflected light, and her fine computers to analyze and enhance the glimmers. As no doubt an ancestor of mine was taught to do before the Collapse."

There were folk who denied that Molts had real intelligence. They claimed the aliens were merely bundles of genetic memory, operating like machines according to programmed pathways. Those folk—bigots, fools, and very often grasping pinchfarts to whom the profit in trading Molt slaves was all the justification neces-sary—hadn't worked *with* Molts the way Piet and Stephen had done in the past decade.

The navigator's sidebar now showed nearly forty ships, though there was no way of telling from the schematic how many of them were the fleet's accompanying light vessels—couriers and rescue craft—without combat value.

"What are they saying, Guillermo?" Simms demanded. "Are they going to attack us?"

"The Federation officers are terrified, Navigator Simms," Guillermo said. "They thought it was impossible that we would locate them before they had reached the Solar System."

Stephen chuckled. The prospect of action was doing more for his transit-induced queasiness than the solid deck alone could have managed. "The other guy's always three meters tall," he said. "We need to remember that to the Feds, we're the other guy."

An attention signal chimed through the *Wrath*. An image of Commander Bruckshaw formed on the upper left corner of the main display. Piet touched a control, reversing the images so that the enemy fleet was a miniature and the commander's huge vis-age looked sternly across the cockpit and from all the flagship's displays slaved to the main screen.

Stephen straightened to parade rest, feet spread and his hands crossed behind his back. Bruckshaw's screen displayed a montage of images from all the vessels linked to his flagship, the *Venus*—probably all the vessels in the fleet at this moment. The view trans-mitted from the optronics of some of the older ships would be at best a fuzzy blur, but Bruckshaw would be well able to see

Stephen if he cared to look. It didn't matter, but the principle of disciplined readiness mattered.

"Gentlemen and sailors of Venus," Bruckshaw said. "This is the day we have prayed for: the day that God may, with His blessing, give the Federation into our hands and free Venus from the threat of tyranny forever."

He gestured. Transmission parameters shrank and stripped the commander's voice, but the *Wrath*'s AI swelled it again to more than fullness. Bruckshaw had a good oral style, and to his words' enhanced majesty he added the bedrock of utter sincerity.

"Our foes are numerous, as we knew they would be," Bruckshaw continued. "The formation they keep looks impressive, but a formation doesn't fight battles—men fight battles, and the men with courage and God on their side win those battles! We will take thirty minutes to prepare ourselves. Then we will all attack. Captains, ready your ships for action!"

The shrilling Action Stations alert stepped on the chime closing the transmission over the command channel. A view of the Federation fleet against an alien starscape replaced Commander Bruckshaw's face again.

"Let's get our suits on, Philips," Stephen said. "I'll want you and Hadley each carrying an extra flashgun as well as rifles this time, I think."

ABOARD THE *WRATH*

September 29, Year 27
0932 hours, Venus time

Piet Ricimer raised a gauntlet to pat Stephen's, gripping the stanchion behind Piet's console. Then he said, "Prepare for action," in a calm, clear voice through the *Wrath*'s PA system.

Piet pressed a key with an index finger, enabling the manual controls. His touch on the yoke was smooth and delicate despite his hard suit. Stephen felt angled thrust send the *Wrath* toward the Federation's defensive globe like a shark easing toward prey.

Stephen's faceshield was raised. Pumps had lowered the *Wrath*'s internal air pressure to half Earth normal at sea level before the ventilation system shut down as a preliminary to action, but the crew wouldn't need to switch to their suits' air bottles until the guns began firing.

The worst disadvantage of operations in near vacuum was that ordinary speech required an atmosphere to carry sound. Stephen's helmet, like those of other key personnel—gunner's mates, damage control teams, motormen—was equipped with a modulated infrared intercom, but for many of the *Wrath*'s crew the later stages of the battle would be fought in silence save for terrifying shocks ringing through their bootsoles.

Flexible gaiters sealed the cannon barrels to the inner hull so that air didn't escape—quickly—when the gunports opened; the temporary splinter shields erected like transparent booths around each gun position were nominally airtight also. The recoil and backblast of the first plasma discharge would start seams in both protective devices, draining the vessel's atmosphere within the minutes of even a short action.

Aboard the *Wrath* everyone wore his hard suit, Guillermo included. The Molt looked odd because the armor was relatively bulky on his narrow limbs. The officers of Federation vessels wore hard suits, but the most part of even the gunnery crews made do with breathing apparatus and quilted asbestos clothing. Many of those aboard, especially the soldiers embarked for this expedition, would have no protection but sealed compartments and a prayer that no Venerian bolt would puncture their section of the hull.

But the Feds had a very great number of ships. President Pleyal wouldn't notice personnel casualties, particularly among Molt slaves, if his fleet crushed or brushed aside the ships defending Venus this day.

"Starboard guns are prepared to fire," Stampfer said. The master gunner made no pretense of aristocratic coolness. If his crews and equipment weren't perfect on the verge of action—and what human endeavor was perfect?—those around him knew it. At the moment Stampfer sounded angry enough to chew a hole through the *Wrath*'s double hull. "Port guns are on twenty-second standby."

The *Wrath*'s gunners manned half the plasma cannon at a time. Because of the time gun tubes took to cool before they could be safely reloaded, full crews for all the guns would have been a waste of the space the men and their subsistence required. Besides the savings in volume, by rotating on her long axis the *Wrath* displayed a fresh expanse of hull to an enemy whose return fire might have damaged the surface initially exposed.

Stampfer was at a mobile fire director plugged into jacks on the gun deck, not at the position provided for him here on the bridge. He wanted—needed—to be in position to aim his cannon by eye if the fire-direction optronics failed in action. Stephen had seen Stampfer running from tube to tube in the past, his crews poised to act exactly as their master gunner ordered. If all the ships in the present fleet hit as hard and as accurately as Stampfer's guns had done in those less sophisticated days, the Feds were in for a long day and a short war.

The main display before Piet was a maze of colored jack-straws—the courses, past and calculated, of all vessels in both fleets. Each ship was a different hue, though with over a hundred and fifty individuals to track some variations were extremely slight. Simms' screen was a mass of alphanumeric data, while Guillermo viewed the fleets as beads rather than vectors and had a numeric sidebar.

None of the navigation displays meant a lot to Stephen, but he could see through the transparent blast wall to the gunnery console. Though the position was unmanned, its screen was slaved to the mobile director Stampfer was using on the gun deck.

A spherical Federation warship swelled on the display, rotating slowly around its axis of motion. Stephen had no certain scale to judge by, but the ship's nine full decks implied it was large—probably upward of a 1,000 tonnes' burden.

The Fed vessel's gunports were open and the guns already run out. She carried more than thirty tubes, but as the image grew Stephen saw to his amazement that the weapons on the midline weren't plasma cannon. The Feds had welded projectile weapons on ground carriages to the deck of the hold.

Given the speeds at which starships traveled, projectiles fired at only a thousand meters per second were unlikely to hit any target that wasn't matching velocities alongside. Projectile cannon had some use in a boarding battle, but not enough to justify their weight and bulk. The Feds must be desperately short of naval ordnance if they were arming vessels with ground weapons.

For safety, the *Wrath*'s ports opened to receive the guns only moments before the weapons fired. A bolt that struck the warship's thick hull might not penetrate, but even a small slug of plasma lucky enough to enter through an open port could wreak terrible damage in the interior.

"Fire as you bear!" Piet ordered.

The *Wrath* shuddered as hydraulic rams slid her ten starboard guns to battery. Internal pressure dropped noticeably. Stephen slapped his faceshield down.

The 20-cm cannon fired a rippling salvo at the Fed a kilometer distant. The gun across the blast wall from Stephen recoiled violently in a haze of plasma. The muzzle and the whole bore glowed white as the gunner's mate opened the breech. The six men of the crew sprang out the rear hatch of their splinter shield, ran around the end of the blast wall, and took their station at the port-side gun.

The shock of the discharges vibrated through the warship's fabric for thirty seconds before it finally damped to a mere lively trembling. Piet gripped a T-handled lever with his left hand, drew it to its lower stop, and then centered it again. A third of the *Wrath*'s attitude jets fired. Another third fired seconds later to balance the initial impulse. The ship rotated 180° on its long axis, bringing its port battery toward the enemy.

The image on the gunnery display didn't change during the *Wrath*'s maneuvers. Four and maybe a fifth of Stampfer's bolts had slammed the Fed's hull. Vaporized metal streamed back like spindrift. Because the Fed was rotating at a meter per second at its midline, no two of the *Wrath*'s bolts struck exactly the same point. One round nonetheless pierced the Fed's hull. A plume of air vented a large compartment.

Sparks flashed across the image; Fed guns recoiled into their ports. They were firing also, but Stephen didn't feel an impact. The spinning vessel was difficult to damage, but it made an almost impossible aiming platform for its own gunners.

"Fire as you bear!" Piet ordered. The port-side guns skreeled forward, blasted back from their ports at one-second intervals bow to stern, and stood in a mist of glowing ions as their crews scampered to the starboard battery again.

Three bolts from the second broadside struck the Federation vessel. One blew gas and fragments in a perfect circle from the midline deck where the shell guns were mounted. The vessel was a converted merchantman. The central hold, intended for easy cargo operations in orbit, was completely open. The 20-cm bolt had struck the deck at a flat angle, disintegrating the partition walls the Feds had erected to subdivide the hold.

The *Wrath*'s shooting had been remarkably accurate, causing casualties and discomfort aboard one of the Feds' larger vessels. Despite that, the damage wasn't serious. Stephen, balancing the hits against the *Wrath*'s load of twenty-five shells per 20-cm gun at the start of the action, didn't believe Stampfer *could* do serious damage to the Fed ship at this rate.

The Fed vanished from the targeting display. Stephen turned— at the waist, because the gorget locked his helmet to his thorax armor—and saw that the entire Federation fleet had transited. Most of the vectors calculated on Piet's display were truncated at point of transit, though the predicted courses of Venerian ships still wove wildly across the screen. The attack had been as uncoordinated as that of bees swarming at a hive robber.

The *Wrath* transited, a sickening lurch from reality that bothered Stephen less than it would have if he'd been expecting it. Navigational parameters were so extraordinarily complex that there was effectively only one solution to a given problem. The *Wrath*'s AI and the artificial intelligences of the other Venerian ships reached the same navigational result as their Federation prey by virtue of knowing the precise instant at which the Fed fleet transited.

Flop. Back to the sidereal universe, a microsecond of ship's time after exit and untold light-years distant from the previous location. The Fed formation hung on the display, distorted like a smoke ring starting to drift. The Feds were gone and the *Wrath* was gone, plunged into a bubble universe with no light or life or existence in human terms, then—

Flop. Stephen's soul turning inside out, but it wasn't really so very terrible, not as bad as it usually was for him. There was an enemy in sight, and it if wasn't a target for the flashgun slung from his right shoulder—that would come. That would surely come.

The Fed formation looked like a melon rupturing at the impact of a high-velocity bullet. Some ships had scattered a considerable distance from the defensive array while others clumped too closely together for safety.

Transit *in* to gray Hell. Moments alone with only the past, with only the dead, and in a blaze of white light Sal with her hand outstretched and a smile.

Flop. The Fed fleet straggled like froth on a beer mug. The captain of the bridge gun crew sprayed the bore of his gun with compressed gas to allow convection cooling. The loader waited with the chunky near-sphere of the shell in his hands, ready to ease it into the breech on command.

Stephen's guts tightened for another transit. The Feds remained in normal space. Had Pleyal's forces not been under pressure by the Venerian fleet, they might have extended the series farther, but already the outlying ships were in danger of being enveloped by their enemy.

A large vessel could accept a great deal of hull damage and

remain a fighting unit, but a bolt or two in the thruster nozzles would leave it helpless. The Feds had to reform their defensive array, or the more maneuverable Venerian ships would attack from "below" and disable them one by one.

"Mister Stampfer?" Piet's voice demanded through the excited shouts cluttering the intercom system.

"Gunners, load your fucking tubes!" Stampfer roared. "And if they fucking blow, it's too fucking bad! Load your tubes!"

The loader of the bridge crew handed his shell into the breech with his captain watching intently. The munition's narrow flats fit the bore with a mirror's precision. The captain closed and locked the breechblock home.

"Prepare for action!"

A pair of Federation vessels collided. Stephen didn't notice the vectors merge, but Piet keyed in a series of quick left-handed commands. An image of the collision filled half of his display.

The ships were both of spherical plan. One was good-sized but the other was much larger—easily 1,200 tonnes. The *Wrath*'s optronics were so sharp that Stephen could read the name inlaid around the seated figure on the giant's extreme bow: SAVIOR ENTHRONED.

The contact had been glancing, but considerable debris sprayed from the point of intersection. The smaller vessel had torn away at least half of the *Savior Enthroned*'s thruster nozzles.

Piet switched back to a full navigational display. With the control yoke he varied the angle and, very slightly, the amount of thrust from the *Wrath*'s nozzles.

Stephen half expected the *Savior Enthroned* to flash onto the gunnery screen. Instead, a cylindrical Federation warship appeared and began to grow. The damaged vessel was in the heart of the Fed formation, protected by the same crush that had caused the collision. Piet had chosen a more practical target.

"Mister Stampfer," Piet ordered, "fire as you—"

A plasma bolt struck the *Wrath*. The lights, already flat because they lacked air to scatter their illumination normally, flickered, then returned.

"—bear."

The 20-cm guns rumbled forward on their tracks, then recoiled in quick succession. The slam of the *Wrath*'s own guns firing was greater than that of the bolt that had hit her.

Three iridescent flashes lit the hull of the Fed vessel. One round may have penetrated: in addition to the plumes of hull metal, Stephen thought he saw light flicker simultaneously from a line of gunports shocked open by a 20-cm bolt. The Fed vessel continued under power, rotating slowly as it drew away.

"Attitude jet S14's running thirty percent down!" reported a voice Stephen didn't recognize. "I think the throat's choked by trash, not damaged. Do you want us to clear it?"

"Absolutely not!" Piet snapped in reply. "No one is to go out onto the hull unless I tell you that the safety of the ship depends on it!"

Piet adjusted his intercom's filter to narrow his next words to a single recipient. "Stephen," he said without turning his armored body to face his friend, "what do you think of the battle?"

Stephen eyed the navigation display as he coded his IR sender to Piet alone. Lines marking the course of Venerian ships curved toward and away from the stolid Federation fleet. For all that, the Feds were reforming the globe from which they'd begun their transit series. In a little while, an hour or so, their AIs would have calculated the next series; then the next, and the next.

The present Venerian attack was less frantic than the first. The most aggressive captains had fired all their heavy guns on the first pass. Gas cooling could speed the recovery of half the battery, albeit at the risk of cracked tubes, but the rate of fire even in the best-conducted vessels was relatively low.

The only Federation ship in serious difficulties was the *Savior Enthroned*—which had not, so far as Stephen could tell, been touched by hostile gunfire. Three featherboats had gone to the big vessel's aid, and a medium-sized freighter was standing by. The damaged ship would be under way by the time the navigational computers had recalibrated, though it was possible that the smaller freighter would attach tow cables to aid maneuvering.

"They can't hurt us, Piet," Stephen said. Piet switched the left half of his display to a close-up of the *Savior Enthroned*. The image looked glossy because computer enhancement invented details that increasing distance prevented the actual optics from viewing.

Stephen shrugged inside his hard suit and continued, "There isn't much better of a chance that we'll hurt them bad enough that they'll really feel. Not if they hold their formation, and especially not if we stand off the way we're doing."

"I'm concerned somewhat about morale," Piet said. "Ours and theirs both, if we're seen to be unable to destroy their ships."

"Can you put the *Wrath* alongside the damaged ship?" Stephen asked.

On the display, the ragged Venerian attacks had almost ceased while ships cooled their guns. The Fed formation was nearly perfect again. At this rate of travel it would take them a month to reach Venus; but they *would* reach Venus.

"Yes," said Piet. "That was my thought also. Both broadsides at very short range might be enough. With the help of God I can transit the *Wrath* into the formation, though we'll be hammered getting off again in normal space."

"No, not that," said Stephen with a faint smile. His mind stared at alternate futures, events that might or might not happen. "They've got their hatches open for repair crews. Get me close enough with fifty men and we'll board and take her."

"That's . . ." Piet said. "Very risky."

"The risk's in getting close, Piet," Stephen said. "I don't know what twenty rounds will do to a ship that big. Remember, we don't have an atmosphere to ignite the interior even if the hull's pierced. I do know what me and a close-combat team will do."

He laughed harshly. "It's all I'm good for, Piet," he added. "You may as well use me."

"It's not all you're good for, Stephen," Piet said. "But God gave us all skills to use in His service, and no one could question your skills. I'll program the transit."

Stephen rotated the dial of his intercom to the *Wrath*'s general command coding. "This is Mister Gregg speaking," he said. "B Watch close-combat team to Hold One. Make sure you've got lots of ammunition, boys, because there'll be God's own plenty of targets where we're going next!"

ABOARD THE *WRATH*

September 29, Year 27
1215 hours, Venus time

Stephen Gregg had never before faced raw vacuum during transit. The clamshell hatches of Hold 1 were open to save fifteen seconds. Stephen, his loaders, and the B Watch close-combat team gripped stanchions and waited.

The starscape vanished. All that existed were random purple flares as a few of Stephen's own optical nerves fired.

Starlight again, though the edge of a different galaxy and both of them indescribably far from the Milky Way in the sidereal universe. For a fraction of a second, Stephen's being regrouped, took stock of itself. The sensation of transit in nothingness was oddly—

Transit. Instead of being locked in his own soul, Stephen was momentarily a part of a universe that was alien but not hostile.

—less disquieting than what engulfed him while traveling in a ship's cabin under normal conditions.

The stars were back but against them was a tiara too dense for a star cluster, too regular for a random distribution of gases. He was seeing the Federation fleet, its nearest components only a few kilometers away—so close that they had shape rather than merely glinting reflection.

Transit. Unexpected, slicing short a calculation of what a flashgun bolt could be expected to do to a Federation warship across three klicks of vacuum. Stephen Gregg merged with a universe as warped and alien as his image of his own soul.

The sidereal universe was a starship's hatch gaping twenty meters away. The *Wrath* and the *Savior Enthroned* both coasted weightless. In the Fed vessel's midships through-hold, a team of Molts in flexible vacuum suits maneuvered a three-head laser cutter and the MHD generator that powered it. Other workmen, most of them aliens, were bringing tools and materials from elevators in the center of the hold.

A featherboat stood a hundred meters off. Four humans, one of them wearing a hard suit, smoothed kinks from a safety net that the featherboat was stretching from the top edge of the *Savior Enthroned*'s hatch.

None of the Feds was armed. Dole sprang for the *Savior Enthroned,* carrying a magnetic grapnel. He didn't bother to use the hydrogen peroxide motor in the grapnel's head. Half a dozen other veteran spacers jumped only fractionally later, each carrying his own line and grapnel.

Before following Dole, Stephen shot the Molt at the controls of the nearer elevator. The laser pierced the Molt's rubberized suit, flinging the body against the back of the cage on the pressure of escaping gases and the creature's ruptured internal organs.

Stephen thrust the flashgun behind him with his index finger raised. Philips exchanged it for the pump-action rifle as Stephen pushed off, the boarding line in the crook of his left arm.

Dole clamped the grapnel to the deck of the vast hold. A Molt swung awkwardly at the bosun with a massive hydraulic wrench. Dole stuck the muzzle of his shotgun against the Molt's chest and fired.

Though Dole gripped the line to keep from being hurled back through the hatchway, recoil spun his body around the grapnel like an armored pinwheel. The shot charge folded the alien's corpse into the appearance of a squid jetting away, leaving a bloom of bodily fluids behind to confuse pursuit.

Dole launched himself toward the elevator with the expertise of a man who had spent almost thirty years in space. Stephen's hard suit clanged hard against the deck and grapnel: he *wasn't* a spacer, not really, and the flat illumination between the stars made it difficult to judge distance. He snubbed the line around his left forearm and fired five times at the Feds in the elevator cage. He hit each of the four Molts in the chest. The human might have been wearing armor so Stephen aimed at her hip joint, a weak point and almost as disabling as a heart shot anyway.

Bodies tumbled wildly, spun by the projectiles' momentum and gases voiding the suits through bullet holes. Materials being brought from other decks for the repair work bounced and floated with the Fed corpses.

Light and shadows shifted. Stephen traded the rifle for Hadley's— two fingers raised—flashgun. Now that Hold 1 was empty, the *Wrath*'s loadmasters had cast off the boarding lines and the warship was moving away under the impulse of her attitude jets only. Her gunports were closed and the protective shutters sealed all thirty-two thruster nozzles.

A plasma bolt bathed the *Wrath* with brilliant coruscation. The *Savior Enthroned* wasn't firing. She was a transport, and the few light guns she carried hadn't even been run out of their ports. The gunners of a Fed warship that had come within half a klick of the damaged vessel reacted swiftly and accurately, though accuracy was easier because there was no relative motion between ships coasting on stored momentum.

Slugs of ions missing to punch through vacuum forever at light speed flickered at the edge of Stephen's vision. Two more rounds hit, lighting the *Wrath*'s hull. A third bolt made the fabric of the *Savior Enthroned* ring like a gong through Stephen's bootsoles.

The *Wrath* shrank without apparently moving. Several more bolts dazzlingly lit her. Ships on all sides of the tight Federation array were firing at the intruder. A Fed passed so close to the glint marking the *Wrath* that Stephen thought the two would collide. The Fed vessel fired and braked with its thrusters.

Piet didn't permit his gunners to respond. The *Wrath*'s best hope of survival was to stay buttoned up and pray that the hull withstood Fed battering. The damage Stampfer and his crews could do wouldn't repay the loss of one of Venus' first-line warships if a bolt entered a gunport at the wrong angle.

Before giving the *Savior Enthroned* his full attention, Stephen fired his flashgun into the cold thruster of the nearby featherboat. Tungsten puffed away in a green flash.

The crew who'd been positioning the safety net had vanished

within the little vessel's cabin. If they knew what they were doing—and it was suicide to assume your enemy *didn't* know what he was doing—they could have taken the featherboat into the through-hold to cleanse it with their exhaust. Now that a dollop had been ripped from the nozzle, asymmetrical heating would rupture it at the first moment of use.

Dole and ten or a dozen boarders had cleared bodies and trash from the elevator so that the doors would close. The cage began to rise, carrying the boarders to the next deck to continue the attack. The working party in the farther elevator had taken their cage down before Venerians could reach it. The shaft still provided passage, but boarders would have to cut their way through heavy doors and alerted defenders.

There was a better way.

The Molts who'd been moving the laser cutter were all dead with their human officer, literally hacked apart by a pair of boarders with cutting bars. The device, five hundred kilos of machinery under 1 g and no less massive for being weightless at the moment, had been tethered by a long cable to a ringbolt on the deck to prevent it from getting away from the crew as they shifted it.

The cutter had struck the deck when the Feds released it and was bouncing lazily upward. Stephen braced one boot against the magnetic grapnel and took the cutter's wheelbarrowlike handles. At first all he could do was to slow the device's rotation around its center of mass. Philips and Hadley joined him, one on either handle.

Neither man was as strong as Stephen, but they were sailors with far greater experience handling massive objects in zero gravity. The weapons and ammunition belts festooning them drifted in all directions as if the loaders were hoop dancers performing, but they anchored the tool firmly. Stephen lifted the cutting heads to the deck above and switched the cutter on.

The generator roared, making the whole apparatus vibrate through the flexible cable. The three-laser head sprayed luminescent vapor from the nickel-steel plating. Pressure of the gas thrust against Stephen's grip, but because of the cutter's size his feet were planted firmly against the deck beneath him. Superheated steel lit the through-deck in a huge flare. The cutters had penetrated to the compartment above and let the atmosphere out to ignite the gaseous metal.

With his loaders steadying him, Stephen swept the cutter in a long circular cut that ended when a two meter disk of steel spun upward, driven by the pressure of its own dissolution. Stephen switched off the tool and gave it a push to send it through into the compartment it had opened. He followed it with a carbine in his hands.

The compartment had been a living and storage volume for fifty or sixty Federation soldiers. Most of them were still in the room, killed when the laser cutter detonated a large ammunition chest strapped to the deck. Shreds of flesh and fabric, equipment and blood, drifted in startling profusion. The laser cutter sailed in slow majesty through the carnage it had achieved.

Stephen ignored the bodies. Only a few of the Feds had been wearing breathing apparatus. Those without would have died when the compartment vented, even if the blast spared them. The hatch on the straight bulkhead, opposite the curve of the outer hull, was fitted with a rail around the jamb for use in weightless conditions. Stephen launched himself toward it, pushing aside floating debris.

Philips reached the hatch ahead of Stephen. He hooked the rail with a finger of the hand holding a flashgun and poised his free hand on the latch. Hadley gripped the other side and braced his boots on the deck so that Stephen could use him as a launching block.

Stephen poised the carbine and raised his left thumb. Philips jerked open the hatch. Stephen stepped through into the corridor beyond.

To the right, three Molts were clamping a net filled with storage drums to the bulkheads in order to barricade the passage. A dozen Fed troops with rifles and shotguns crouched farther on, looking toward the corridor that T-ed into theirs. Bullets from that direction splattered on the cross bulkhead.

To the left more Federation soldiers, all of them human, were bringing up a ten-barrel projectile weapon. Breathing apparatus dangled from their necks, but the corridor was still pressurized so they weren't wearing the masks.

They were landsmen and uncomfortable in weightlessness. The heavy gun had touched the right-hand bulkhead and would shortly spin from the upper deck despite the troops' efforts.

A Fed officer in full armor had his faceshield raised so that he could use the communications panel in a corridor alcove. He goggled at Stephen, hesitating between slamming his visor down and raising the fat-barreled flechette gun slung to his left arm. Stephen shot him in the face—the light carbine bullet probably wouldn't have penetrated a hard suit—and shot the nearest of the white-jacketed soldiers to the right as the recoil twisted him.

Stephen had nothing to anchor him. He fired three times as quickly as he could lever rounds into the chamber. Each shot rotated him faster.

One of the Molts had a cutting bar. He lunged for Stephen as the gunman tried to twist the carbine to bear. Philips put the flashgun against the Molt's chest. The creature's thorax segment disintegrated in a bright flash, but the laser's cassegrain mirrors shattered also.

The hatch slammed shut behind Hadley when sensors told the mechanism that air was escaping through it. Stephen hooked his boot toe through the railing on the corridor side of the jamb and killed the crew of the multibarrel cannon with his last four rounds. Their blood-splotched bodies drifted in cartwheels compounded of their own dying spasms and the momentum of the bullet into each soldier's upper chest.

The heavy gun continued to trundle down the corridor. It brushed Stephen and would have crushed his thigh against the bulkhead despite the hard suit if the impact had been a little more direct.

Shooting and the momentary drop in air pressure warned the Feds on the other side of the barricade. One of them ran down the corridor in panic, forgetting the Venerian troops in the elevator at the other end of the intersecting passage. A bullet splashed her brains against the wall.

A projectile slammed Stephen just over the top of his breastbone. His gorget shattered and he couldn't see for an instant. The breastplate itself withstood the impact.

Hadley tried to hand him a rifle. Stephen grabbed the flashgun instead, still slung to the loader's arm.

The multibarrel cannon drifted into the barricade. One of the bulkhead tie-downs broke. The whole mass, weapon and cargo drums caught in the net, swung majestically around the remaining tie-down and toward the intersection. Fed soldiers, crouching behind the barricade, backed away or tried to stop the cannon's slow progress.

Stephen fired the flashgun point-blank into the ammunition locker fixed to the cannon's trail. Over a hundred 2-cm cartridges went off with a red flash in the middle of the defenders, flinging bodies away. The blast would have sent Stephen down the corridor also, but Hadley was gripping a tie-down like an experienced sailor, and the flashgun's sling held. Dirty smoke bulged out on the shock wave.

Six men in ceramic hard suits sailed from the intersecting corridor to finish the slaughter. Dole was in the lead with a shotgun in one hand and in the other a cutting bar, still triggered and spitting blood from its edges.

A score of Fed soldiers came down the corridor in the direction the ten-barrel cannon had been traveling. Dole pointed his shotgun one-handed and fired. The charge of buckshot hit a bulkhead twenty meters away and ricocheted into the Feds in a cloud of paint chips. The soldiers hadn't expected to meet an enemy so suddenly. Only a few of them wore back-and-breast armor.

Six or eight more men in ceramic hard suits arrived from the elevator to add their fire to the volleys directed at the Feds. Stephen traded the carbine for the pump gun Hadley'd offered him earlier, but by the time he raised the weapon the Feds had vanished back the way they'd come. Eight casualties, some of them still moving, floated in a fog of blood.

"Lightbody, Jones!" Dole shouted through his helmet speaker. "Secure the back way. The rest of you whoresons follow me!"

"Stand where you are!" Stephen Gregg bellowed. "We're not going to kill them by love taps, we're going to tear their bloody throats out if they don't surrender. Guard the corridors while I talk to their captain! And Dole, there's a laser cutter in the hull-side compartment. Put a crew on it."

Stephen snapped up his faceshield and used the rifle butt to pole himself gently into the communications alcove. The Fed officer still gripped the handset in a gauntlet as he floated with a bullet hole between his startled eyes. The panel had a flat-plate vision screen. An officer in a blue jacket watched in horror at the carnage that drifted past the pickup lens at the base of the display.

Stephen ignored the handset and switched the panel to speakerphone. "Do you recognize me?" he shouted to the Fed officer. "I'm Stephen Gregg. Put your captain on and maybe you'll live through the rest of this day. Soonest!"

A sailor fired twice. One of the bullets struck the bulkhead at the end of the passage and ricocheted back, whanging several times on the upper and lower deckplates. Another sailor shouted a curse.

An older female officer took the place of the first at the commo unit. This officer's cap and left lapel were both gold. "Colonel Gregg," she said in a taut voice. "Your ship has been driven away and your small group will inevitably be wiped out unless you surrender. I have eight hundred heavily armed soldiers aboard. Do you yield?"

"You've got a hundred less than you had when I started, missy!" Stephen snarled. "Listen! I've got a laser cutter and all the other tools you were using for repair work. Unless you surrender *now* I'll punch a hole in every compartment of this ship and void it to vacuum. I've already started, missy! I'm Stephen Gregg and I'd as soon kill you all as take your surrender. By God I would!"

A body with no face drifted past the alcove, trailing five meters of intestine through what had been a white uniform. The captain of the *Savior Enthroned* saw the corpse and stiffened. Stephen laughed savagely at her expression.

"The lives of my crew and the troops in my care," the Fed captain said, her voice three tones higher than when she first spoke. "Honorable captivity for the officers and exchange if that . . . if that becomes possible. Yes?"

An explosion or a high-velocity projectile made the giant vessel's hull ring. Some other portion of the boarding party was in a vicious fight.

"Accepted," Stephen said. "But any of your people who're still fighting in three minutes had better be able to breathe vacuum. On my word as a gentleman of Venus!"

The Fed captain grimaced and nodded. She turned a rotary switch and began to speak. Loudspeakers in every corridor and compartment of the *Savior Enthroned* crackled out her orders to surrender the vessel.

ABOARD THE *GALLANT SALLIE*

October 1, Year 27
1554 hours, Venus time

"Three minutes to transit," Harrigan warned from the *Gallant Sallie*'s navigation console. "Lighting thrusters."

Sal drew Stephen's armored form firmly down onto the deckplate so that the 1-g acceleration wouldn't slam him there. His faceshield was raised, but his eyes focused a thousand meters out.

The boarding party had made a single transit jump to get the captured vessel clear before the Feds attempted to retake her. The Federation commander's draconian threats to any captain who failed to hold the preset order had stifled the individual initiative that might have overcome the attack on the *Savior Enthroned*.

The huge globular form of the *Savior Enthroned* drifted in a cloud of debris against an alien starscape. While they waited for a ship—the *Gallant Sallie*, as it chanced—to arrive with navigators and additional flight crew, Stephen's men had voided the trash of battle. If Sal looked closely, she could see that many of the objects floating around the captured ship were mangled bodies, Molt and human both.

The *Gallant Sallie*'s thrusters fired. Apparent weight returned; the deck was downward again. Objects ignored because there'd been forty extra sailors packed into the vessel now settled abruptly. The *Savior Enthroned*'s image became a diminishing ball in the center of the display.

Sal began undoing the clamps that held Stephen's hard suit together. Half the front of the gorget was gone. The sealant repairing the crazed remnant clung to the latch until Sal scraped a knifeblade through it.

Stephen suddenly looked at her. "Lord!" he said. "Sorry, I was a long way . . ."

He glanced wonderingly around the *Gallant Sallie*'s cabin. Sal lifted his helmet off, then the gorget.

"I don't remember coming aboard," Stephen said. He started to take off his own gauntlets, so Sal unlocked the three pieces that covered each arm. "I didn't realize your ship was the one that was going to pick us up."

"We'd ferried a load of ammunition from the Ishtar City Arsenal," Sal said. "Piet thought we'd be a good choice to take your wounded off. And bring you back particularly, Stephen. Piet was concerned that you might be carried to Venus inadvertently."

Stephen laughed harshly. "At least one of Pleyal's ships is going to reach Venus," he said.

"Venus orbit," Sal said. "I don't think there's a transfer dock on the planet that could take her. I . . . It's incredible that you captured her, Stephen."

The boarding party's ten wounded men were on stretchers in the hold with the *Wrath*'s own surgeon and one of his mates. Stephen and his two loaders had come across with their wounded by the same lines that guided the additional prize crew to the *Savior Enthroned*. Dole had come as well. The bosun was keeping himself as inconspicuous as possible because Captain Ricimer's orders had directed him to help take the prize to Venus.

"The Fed medics did a good job with their wounded," Stephen said. He'd forgotten that he'd been removing his hard suit. Sal unlatched the leg pieces. "With guns to their heads. It wasn't necessary, but I didn't try to stop it."

"Prepare for transit," Harrigan warned. Except for the mate, all the *Gallant Sallie*'s crewmen were watching Sal and Stephen out of the corner of their eyes. Nobody was going to say anything—probably nobody cared—but Sal didn't need others to tell her that a captain's place was at the controls during transit.

Human beings had duties also. When they conflicted with the governance of a starship, well, sometimes the starship had to wait.

Transit. Bleakness, grayness, nothingness. *Back,* and she was holding Stephen Gregg's hands though she didn't remember taking them in hers. Transit.

The series was of eight in-and-out jumps, a thirty-second pause to calibrate for the observed position of the straggling Venerian fleet, and a final ninth transit pair to bring the *Gallant Sallie* within a kilometer of the *Wrath.* It was a clean piece of navigation. Sal had had plenty of time to program a back-course to the fleet while the *Gallant Sallie* waited, its hatch open, to receive the party from the captured vessel.

She hadn't known that Stephen was still alive until Dole raised the faceshield of the figure floating beside him like an empty suit of armor.

Attitude jets puffed, rotating the *Gallant Sallie* so that Harrigan could brake the freighter's slight velocity relative to the deputy command vessel. The *Wrath*'s image was the background to the mask of alphanumeric calculations filling the display. Patches of odd-colored ceramic covered battle damage. A crew was at work on the outer hull.

Stephen closed his eyes and took off the linked back-and-breast pieces of his hard suit. There was a huge bruise visible through the sweat-soaked tunic he wore beneath the armor. "Has anything happened with the fleets?" he asked without emotion.

"A lot of shooting," Sal said. "Less damage, and none of it serious. One of the Fed ships blew up all by itself, but you've won our only victory so far, Stephen."

He looked at her, really *at* her. Sal was lifting away the hinged groin and thigh pieces. Stephen put the tips of his fingers on the backs of her hands to hold her attention.

"Sal," he said, "the Feds surrendered because they thought I'd tear the whole ship open and leave even the crew to suffocate when their oxygen bottles ran out."

Sal nodded. "I'm glad they surrendered," she said carefully. "That saved many lives."

Perhaps yours among them, my friend. My love.

"They were right, Sal," Stephen said. "I told them that I'd as soon kill them as not, and that was as true as if I'd sworn by a

God I believed in. I was ready to kill the whole thousand or more of them."

"You didn't, though," she said.

"No, they surrendered," Stephen said—not agreeing.

"Stephen, if it bothers you so much when you think of what might have happened . . ." she said. She paused, wondering if she was willing to go on. "Then the next time, don't do it. But it didn't *happen*."

"I'd have killed them all," he whispered.

Sal turned her hands to grip Stephen's as hard as she could. Part of her prayed that she wouldn't start to cry; but the tears would have been for both of them, herself and the man she held who couldn't weep for the soul he thought he'd lost.

ABOARD THE *WRATH*

October 1, Year 27
1847 hours, Venus time

Piet saw Stephen's approaching figure reflected in the brightwork of his console. He spun the couch with a smile of greeting that hardened minutely as he rose to his feet. "I didn't know you'd been wounded, Stephen," he said.

"It's a bruise, Piet," Stephen said. Maybe he ought to wear something high-necked—though he really didn't want even cloth in contact with the swollen, purple-black flesh over his breastbone. "You should see the other guy."

Piet *had* seen the other guy, many times over a decade. The mangled bodies floating through the compartments of a captured starship were all the same, except perhaps to God.

"Glad you're safe, Colonel Gregg," Simms said quietly. The navigator turned back to his console immediately, as though he were afraid of the reaction.

It always puzzled Stephen that people really did seem to like him. Even people who knew what he was.

"Come view what's happened while you were gone," Piet said. He drew his friend down beside him on the couch turned crossways in respect to the three-dimensional display. "I'd like to get your opinion, and it'll be another hour yet before the Feds complete their calculations."

He touched a control. The blotchy appearance of the enemy after a transit series replaced a real-time image of the Federation globe reformed. The Venerian ships converged on their enemy in a speeded-up review of the battle. Vector lines careted six Venerian vessels moving in line ahead toward a gap in the Fed formation. A sidebar along the top of the display strung database close-ups of Captain Casson's *Freedom* and five similar vessels: spherical armed merchantmen, among the largest ships in the Venerian fleet.

The globe began to collapse on Casson's squadron like an amoeba ingesting prey. Four vessels from the Federation rear guard closed, maneuvering with surprising agility. Stephen frowned. Piet nodded, pleased that his friend had noticed. He touched another control. At the bottom of the display appeared an oddly angular vessel, a dodecahedron rather than a sphere.

"The Feds have brought four orbital monitors with them," Piet said. "The living conditions aboard on a voyage of this length must be indescribable, but—"

The monitors were designed for weightless conditions rather than to operate at most times with the apparent gravity of 1-g acceleration. Their decks were onionskins around a central core instead of perpendicular to the main thrust axis like those of spherical-plan long-voyage vessels.

For all their light frames and the discomfort of their crews, the monitors were dangerous opponents for Casson's self-surrounded squadron. The Fed vessels had many times the usual number of attitude jets to provide the agility Stephen watched on the display, and eleven of twelve facets mounted a powerful gun.

The remainder of the Venerian fleet swept down with unexpected coordination on the "east" quadrant of the Federation globe. Feds closing on Casson turned to meet the new threat. Cracks opened in what had almost become a crushing vise. Casson's squadron eased out of the trap.

Stephen looked at Piet with a faint smile. "Your idea?" he said. "Organizing the rescue instead of letting it turn into a mare's nest as usual?"

Piet shrugged, almost hiding his own smile. "I signaled—Guillermo signaled, of course—all vessels to conform to the *Wrath*'s movements. There wasn't time to do more . . . and somewhat to my surprise, most of the others did as I asked."

He looked at Stephen and shrugged. "We aren't as tightly disciplined as the Feds, Stephen."

Stephen shrugged back. "Tyranny has certain advantages in the strictly military sphere," he said.

Piet's smile became broad and as hard as a gun muzzle. "Tell that to the captain of the *Savior Enthroned*," he said. "You might get an argument."

He returned the display to real-time images and pointed. Barges carried supplies and munitions from the Fed transports to the war vessels on the outer face of the globe.

"We can listen to their intership communications and know they're frightened," Piet said quietly. Guillermo and Simms were absorbed in their work; no one else was close enough to overhear. "Short transit series are a terrible strain. Metal doesn't craze the way our ceramic hulls do, but their seams are working badly and many of their ships have gunfire damage."

He looked at the friend beside him and went on, "Only sometimes I think—if we run out of ammunition before we break the Fed formation, what happens then?"

"Then you put us alongside them, one ship at a time," Stephen said. "And we board them. If that's what it takes."

"The commander acknowledges your communication, Deputy Commander," Guillermo said. The Molt raised his voice but didn't turn his triangular head lest he seem to be intruding his personality into a private conversation. "He is relaying it to the remainder of the fleet for action."

Stephen raised an eyebrow. Piet smiled with slight warmth. "We're three transits from a junction that will carry us to within half an AU of Venus, sixty-five million kilometers," he explained. "The Feds will certainly attempt that route. If we calculate our speed and position correctly, though, we can prevent them from taking the third jump unless they're willing to turn their thrusters directly toward our guns at a few hundred meters range. I suggested such a plan to Commander Bruckshaw."

"If they don't make that junction, then what?" Stephen asked.

Piet laughed. "More of the same, my friend," he said. "At least until we run out of ammunition. Then we'll see."

He preserved a light tone up to the final sentence. On the display beside him, the Fed formation looked as perfect as a poised axe.

ABOARD THE *GALLANT SALLIE*

October 2, Year 27
0813 hours, Venus time

Sal finished her calculations, finished checking the AI's calculations, really. The display reverted from alphanumeric to its previous setting: a view of the Federation globe and, fifty kilometers to one side, the straggling Venerian formation.

Sal lay back on the couch with a sigh. A circle of white light marked the *Wrath*, otherwise an indistinguishable dot at this scale.

"So, Captain . . ." Brantling said from a seat at the attitude-control board. "We're headed back for home, then?"

Sal scowled and for a moment continued to face the display. She realized that she had to tell her crew sometime, and they deserved better than the back of her head when she did so. She got up and faced her men. The whole crew was in the cabin.

"I've decided that we'll hold position with the fleet for a time," she said as professionally as she could manage. "Although we—"

The cheers of her crew interrupted her. Brantling clapped Harrigan on the shoulder and cried, "Hey, I told you she had too much guts to run off when there was a fight coming!"

Kokalas clapped his hands with enthusiasm and said, "We're going to pay them bastards back for Josselyn, we are."

Nedderington, who'd learned everything he could from Godden when the gunner's mate was aboard, rose from the locker holding the *Gallant Sallie*'s meager store of 10-cm rounds and opened the lid.

"No!" said Sal. "No, we're not going in as a fighting ship. Christ's blood! we don't have but two hard suits aboard and one only fits me. All we're going to do is—"

Watch and pray.

"—render assistance to damaged vessels if necessary, and to carry out any other tasks the commander, the *commanders* may set us."

"We'll be following the fleet's transits, Sal?" Tom Harrigan asked. "Or . . ."

"We've got the course plots, transmitted from the *Venus* and the *Wrath* both," Sal said. "We aren't . . ." She paused, wondering how to phrase the description. "We haven't been ordered to accompany the fleet, but we aren't acting against the commanders' wishes, either."

"Captain?" Brantling said, pointing over Sal's shoulder.

She spun. The Federation globe was dissolving in sequential transit. The *Wrath* vanished, then a dozen more of the largest and best-crewed Venerian ships.

"Stand by to transit," Sal said as she dropped back into the navigation console, engaging the AI. An orange border surrounded the display. Five seconds later, the *Gallant Sallie*—

Transit. Sal saw the cabin as a black-and-white negative, but that was only the construct her mind built of familiar surroundings to steady itself.

Starscape. The *Gallant Sallie*'s display was set for real visuals, not icons representing the confronting fleets, but at the previous range there was little visible difference. Ships had been glimmers in starlight, varying by albedo rather than absolute size.

Now the fleets and the *Gallant Sallie* with them had closed considerably. In the fraction of a second after Sal's eyes adjusted to the sidereal universe again, she could see the *Wrath* as an object, blotched from previous damage. Two of the starboard gunports were open because the lids had jammed or were shattered by fire.

Transit. Sarah Blythe had made her first transit when she was two years old. The feeling had never really disturbed her the way she knew it did others.

Starscape. The two fleets on the display were nearly a single mass.

The Federation globe very nearly rested on a lumpy plain of Venerian ships. At this moment Federation AIs would be screaming collision warnings.

The Fed captains knew the real threat was not impact with the tightly controlled first line of the Venerian fleet. They had the choice of overriding the next programmed transit or having their thrusters ripped out by point-blank plasma bolts. Some of the Federation officers were experienced enough to have expected this result as soon as they saw how much more maneuverable their opponents were. Their commander was sure to have a planned response.

The squished and gaping Fed formation vanished raggedly. The Venerian fleet didn't move. Sal disconnected the sequencer.

The *Gallant Sallie*'s AI was very nearly as powerful as those of the *Wrath* and her sister ships, let alone the armed merchantmen that made up the bulk of the Venerian force. Sal would have a solution within a few minutes, whether or not one was relayed from the dedicated warships.

"What's happening?" Rickalds said, panic growing with each syllable. "Ma'am, they're getting away!"

"They're not getting nowhere!" Tom Harrigan snarled contemptuously. "They're running with their tails between their legs 'cause we cut them off. As soon as the computer tells us where they ran to, why, we'll jump right after them. And I shouldn't wonder if we had 'em right by the balls, as strung out as they're going to be!"

The artificial intelligence bordered the screen with blue and threw up a blue sidebar. The complex calculations of the latter were too minute to read.

Sal didn't need to know where the course would take them. All that was important was that it would take them in pursuit of the Feds, in company with the men who would crush the tyrant's force or die.

"Prepare for transit!" she ordered, engaging the sequencer.

"Course received from the *Wrath*, ma'am!" Cooney called from the adjunct communications module at the back of the cabin.

"We've got our own course!" Sal said. The screen's border went orange.

Transit.

Starscape. She couldn't see the Federation fleet. The Feds had a lead of the minutes it took the *Gallant Sallie* to compute their course. A Venerian ship was present, though: the *Wrath. A* dozen more, a score more, Venerian vessels winked into sight.

Transit.

Starscape.

Transit. Brantling's reversed image stared tensely from Sal's mind, though she hadn't been looking at him or even toward the back of the cabin.

Starscape, but partly masked by a planet looming across the sky. The Federation ships were in orbit or already beginning landing approaches.

"Bloody hell!" Tom Harrigan said as he made the identification a fraction of a second before Sal herself did. "That's Heldensburg! The port governor's letting the Feds land on Heldensburg!"

Venerian warships appeared and immediately accelerated through sidereal space toward the scattered Feds. The intended attacks were unplanned and thus far uncoordinated.

"The governor, La Fouche, he's a fan of Pleyal's," Sal remarked. "I remember what the cargo supervisor told us."

Her fingers set the AI to determine a course that would hold the *Gallant Sallie* stationary in respect to the planet below. "I wonder—"

One of Heldensburg's 30-cm cannon sent a bolt across the *Wrath*'s bow. The round probably wasn't aimed to hit. It was simply a warning that a Venerian attempt to interfere with the Feds here would have Heldensburg's ship-smashing port defenses to contend with. The *Wrath* drew away from its target, a big Fed vessel braking from orbit.

The Venerians no longer had to wonder how Port Governor La Fouche would interpret his nation's neutrality in a war between Venus and the North American Federation.

ABOVE HELDENSBURG

October 2, Year 27
1333 hours, Venus time

"Oh, this is too bad!" Commander Bruckshaw said, glaring at the hundreds of ships indicated on the display in the conference room of the *Venus*. "Why, this should never have been permitted to happen!"

Stephen was more amused than not by the sight of so many private vessels, probably everything on Venus capable of the short journey to Heldensburg. The ships had come from every port on the planet as soon as a courier brought word home that the Feds had gone to ground on Heldensburg.

Some of the ships carried supplies and munitions, the way the *Gallant Sallie* had done a few days before, but many captains were motivated simply by a desire to get in a blow of their own against the Federation. The light guns the merchantmen mounted made them as useless in a real battle as their hulls were vulnerable.

The multitude of small vessels could get in the way, true; but so far as Stephen could tell, Bruckshaw's irritation was mostly because the newcomers weren't under his control and hadn't come at his request. The mass of ships was sure to have a psychological effect on the Feds, despite their knowing the influx had little military value.

"I believe most of the captains are here, Commander," Piet said, gently prodding Bruckshaw back to the real matter at hand. This was a live rather than video conference, because if Guillermo could eavesdrop on Federation intership communications, then the Feds—or their Molt slaves—could listen to the Venerian fleet.

Stephen grinned sardonically at Sarah Blythe beside him. She was too tautly professional to meet his eyes. Sal was present because Mister Gregg had brought her to the command group meeting. Stephen knew he was throwing his weight around to bring a friend into a conference called only for the captains of fighting ships; but he had the weight. A score of the gentlemen accompanying Bruckshaw on his flagship crowded the room with even less reason.

"Yes, I see that," the commander said sharply.

Bruckshaw had had a frustrating time. Though he'd closed with the enemy whenever possible, he knew the *Venus* hadn't done any marked damage. On a strategic level, the Federation fleet was unbroken and now in the process of refitting beyond his reach.

Besides those military considerations, the commander had to be galled to know that the only Federation ship captured had been taken by his famous deputy, Captain Ricimer. Bruckshaw had deferred to Piet's experience just as he'd promised he would, but—Bruckshaw was the governor's cousin, and Piet was a potter's son. Though the commander was a decent and intelligent man, he was human.

He grimaced and said in apology, "Factor Ricimer, would you please outline the situation for the assembly?"

Piet bowed to his superior and turned to the company. "We've tried everything we know to get the port commandant, La Fouche, to stop sheltering the Feds," he said in a pleasant voice. "Commander Bruckshaw has sent couriers both to Venus and to Avignon to get the decision reversed through La Fouche's superiors. At best that will take a week—as much time as the Feds need to refit."

A branch of opinion in United Europe held that alliance with President Pleyal was a better choice than the present climate of low-level hostility toward the North American Federation. La Fouche might well be carrying out the policy of his government under cover of personal whim.

"I'm convinced that to attempt to land in Heldensburg with the defenses alerted would be suicidal, not a matter of military consideration," Bruckshaw interjected. "I will not countenance such a waste of the state's limited resources."

Several of the veterans relaxed noticeably. There was murmuring among the gentlemen—stilled instantly when the commander glared at them. Were it not for Bruckshaw's birth status, someone was sure to have suggested a head-on assault and damned as cowardly anybody who caviled. The commander had quashed that wrangle with a combination of good judgment and the courage to voice an unpalatable truth.

"Yes," said Piet. "Venus has no lack of men ready to charge thirty-centimeter guns. My friend Mister Gregg, for example"— he nodded, smiling faintly—"and many others in this room, I'm sure. But the Lord gave us courage to be steadfast in His service, not to throw ourselves away."

"If we wait till the Feds refill their tanks and repair their damage—and Heldensburg has a first-rate maintenance facility as I well know . . ." said Willem Casson. The old man wore a mauve velvet suit and the jeweled awards three trading associations had given him for his explorations on their behalf. "*And* refill their ammunition lockers too, I shouldn't wonder, if there's any shells down there of the right sizes—well, then, what do we do? Use up our air and reaction mass stooging around out of range, then hope we can break their fleet refitted when we couldn't do it before?"

Casson glared at Piet and added, "Because some folk don't have the guts to carry the fight *to* the Feds!"

Sal stiffened. If Piet had taken more than a fraction of a second to reply, there would have been a brawl between his supporters and Casson's.

With his smile still broader, Piet said in a soothing voice, "I didn't mean to impugn the courage or judgment of anyone in this room, Captain. Your point is well taken: we can't afford to permit the Feds to regroup at leisure. Though we can't force them up from Heldensburg with ordinary warships, I believe launching unmanned vessels into the port will send them flying in panic."

"The heavy guns can destroy a ship *as* a ship," Salomon put in, "but it's still a couple hundred tonnes of hardware following a ballistic course. A thirty-centimeter bolt doesn't make a ship vanish."

"You talked about suicide," said Captain Montero. His fists were unconsciously pressed together in front of his chest. "If a ship isn't controlled down to twenty klicks altitude, it's not going to come close enough to scare anybody but farmers in the next province, we all know that."

He looked around challengingly. Montero wasn't a member of one clique or another, just an experienced captain stating a well-grounded opinion. "Coming that close, especially in the sort of junker you'd throw into the ground that way, well, the port guns are going to smash it to bits before the crew can get out."

"Not a ship with a modern navigational system," Sal said loudly, perhaps louder than she'd intended. Men craned their necks to see who'd spoken. The room was full, and Sal was shorter than most of the others present.

Stephen turned his head in unspoken challenge. Men who met his eyes nodded, smiled stiffly, or simply looked away.

"I can program the *Gallant Sallie* to land itself from orbit," Sal continued. She smiled tightly. There was sweat at her hairline, though her voice didn't sound nervous. "It won't be a soft landing, but that's not what we need here. I volunteer my ship for the mission."

"One ship won't do it," said Salomon. "It'll take half a dozen, and I'm not talking featherboats, either. At least a hundred tonnes."

Everyone spoke at once, to the assembly or to a neighbor. Bruckshaw and Piet leaned their heads together for a whispered conversation.

Bruckshaw straightened and said, "A moment!" interrupting the brief pandemonium. "A moment, gentlemen and captains. I've discussed this possibility with Factor Ricimer. We agree that we'll need six ships of at least a hundred tonnes burden to be sure of success."

Piet winced. Bruckshaw caught the expression and added, "With the blessing of God, that is. The Free State of Venus will purchase the vessels involved at a price set after survey by a board of senior captains, chosen and presided over by Factor Ricimer. Let me say that no shipowner will be the loser financially from his patriotism."

He smiled faintly and added, "We appear to have most of the merchant fleet of Venus to pick from, after all."

"Say, I've got a ship you can have!" Captain Groener said from Casson's side. "Assuming the survey covers stores at listed value?"

"Captain Casson?" Piet called. "Captain Salomon? I'd be honored if the two of you would serve with me on the survey board. Will those present who own ships they'd like to volunteer please join us now? We won't go outside this group unless we have to."

There was a surge toward Piet. Most of the fleet's captains themselves owned one or more ships, part of the cloud of light vessels clogging the starscape about Heldensburg. With the survey done the way Bruckshaw implied it would be, this could be a very profitable way to sell a vessel that needed a total rebuild.

Sal shivered. She started to put her arm around Stephen for support but caught herself before the motion was complete. "I should have asked you," she said. "I'm sorry."

"You're the managing director," Stephen said. "And a very good business decision you've made. Go talk to Piet."

He nodded Sal forward. "I wouldn't argue with a choice you had a right to make," Stephen added softly, "any more than I'd expect one of my men to tell me who to kill next."

ABOARD THE *GALLANT SALLIE*

October 3, Year 27
1027 hours, Venus time

"They're clear!" Brantling announced. He was in the cutter in the *Gallant Sallie*'s hold, speaking over the hardwired intercom rigged for the mission.

On the display, Sal could see the barge pulling away with most of the *Gallant Sallie*'s crew and personal effects. Tom Harrigan watched tensely from the attitude-control boards. He, Sal, and Brantling were all the personnel the old vessel had on her last voyage.

Ships didn't have souls; and even if they did, there were humans dying in this war also.

"All right, we're going in," Sal said. She pushed the execute key to start the program. Even that simple movement felt awkward in a hard suit.

Harrigan wore the *Gallant Sallie*'s general-purpose suit. He looked even more clumsy and uncomfortable than Sal felt. Stephen had offered to find armor for Brantling, but the sailor had refused. He waited at the cutter's controls in a helmet, a breathing mask, and a flexible bodysuit.

The attitude jets fired, then counterfired. The thrusters lit with a shudder, returning the vessel to an apparent 1 g of acceleration toward Heldensburg.

Words in white letters crawled across the bottom of the display. The message had been sent on the command channel, overriding the lock Sal had placed on the commo gear.

"*Wrath* sends, 'Our prayers go with you,'" Sal relayed to her fellows. The transmission was slugged "Piet," not "*Wrath*," but she would have felt awkward saying that.

Heldensburg was an ugly planet, yellow beneath the misty blue scattering of its atmosphere. Sal hadn't realized quite how ugly the place was on previous landings here. A turgid pimple, swelling on the display.

Two specks swung toward the *Gallant Sallie*. Sal highlighted and expanded the images.

"I see them! I see the Feds!" Brantling cried.

"Brantling, keep off the intercom!" Sal snapped.

Because the hatch remained open, Brantling had been able to glimpse either the featherboat or the armed barge trying desperately to match courses. The Feds had a number of light vessels in orbit to prevent what the *Gallant Sallie* was about to do.

The thrusters cut out momentarily. The AI used the attitude jets to rotate the *Gallant Sallie*, then fired the thrusters again at an initial 3 g's. They were coming in very hard and fast. A technical expert from the *Wrath* had reprogrammed the artificial intelligence to permit it to execute maneuvers well beyond safety parameters.

Sal checked their heading. The point of impact was drifting west, though for the moment it was still predicted to be within the port reservation. She adjusted the program. Execution was in the AI's electronic hands, but Sal felt the ship quiver minusculely as altitude jets burped moments after she'd entered the correction.

Heldensburg filled the display, as vapid as an ingenue's smile. The port was on the opposite side of the planet. Sal angrily hit keys preset to a series, then another set. A corner of the display—an eighth of the total—became a close-up of the port, a real-time view as relayed from another Venerian ship. On the opposite corner, a Fed featherboat with a light plasma cannon protruding from the bow port accelerated to come up with the *Gallant Sallie*.

The number of Federation vessels crowded even the vast Heldensburg spaceport. From a score of locations, plasma exhaust bloomed like flowers opening. To react so quickly, the Feds must have been expecting, dreading, exactly what was about to happen. The *Gallant Sallie* and her consorts couldn't expect to destroy a significant proportion of Pleyal's fleet, but they could very easily induce a wild panic that threw the Feds into the arms of sharks like Piet Ricimer and his *Wrath.* . . .

Sal rechecked their heading. Below them, clouds swept swiftly eastward as the *Gallant Sallie* cut against the grain of Heldensburg's rotation. The predicted landing—impact—site still drifted west, but less swiftly. With Sal's correction, the ship would hit close to the center of the target.

The atmosphere was beginning to buffet the ship. Even though thrust had dropped to little more than 1 g, movement was difficult.

"Let's—" Sal said as she rose from the console.

The featherboat fired its plasma cannon. A bright ionized track showed on the display because the Feds as well had dipped into the atmosphere in pursuit. The bolt missed closely enough that hair on the back of Sal's arms rose.

"—go!"

Tom Harrigan grabbed Sal and flung her bodily down the passage ahead of him. The ship staggered like a drunken sailor, but Sal had a lifetime's experience on jumping decks.

She caught the lip of the cutter's dorsal hatch and hoisted herself into the cabin. She turned to help Harrigan, but the mate had paused to throw the hatch-closing switch.

Brantling lit the thruster. Plasma smothered the hold in a brilliant fog. The cutter lurched even though the nozzle was irised wide. Sal saw Harrigan's gauntlet flail through the iridescence. She grabbed him and pulled. Harrigan came aboard just as Brantling took the cutter out of the *Gallant Sallie,* ticking on the way against the slowly closing hatch.

Sal pressed her helmet against the mate's and shouted, "You idiot!"

"Sal," Harrigan said, his voice a buzz through the ceramic of his helmet and hers, "I was afraid the open hatch'd throw the AI off in the lower atmosphere."

The *Gallant Sallie* glowed across a broad segment of sky, plunging toward Heldensburg. Brantling was trying to climb out of the atmosphere, but the featherboat now kept company with them less than a kilometer out. Another gleaming reflection, probably the armed barge, was closing as well.

One moment the *Gallant Sallie* was a white-hot comet trailing a cone of superheated atmosphere. In the next the ship disintegrated as a rainbow flash, hit squarely by one of Heldensburg's 30-cm guns. The bolt was powerful enough to destroy the hull's structural integrity; friction and inertia did the rest.

Sal watched transfixed. They'd removed the cutter's hatch before the mission so that nothing would slow her and Tom when they boarded at the last instant. The cutter's attitude as Brantling braked the momentum transferred during the *Gallant Sallie*'s dive gave Sal and Harrigan a perfect view of the port.

The *Gallant Sallie* had broken into three large pieces, plus a score of smaller ones that were refractory enough to survive their bath in the atmosphere. Most of the smaller chunks were separated nozzles and plasma motors, each describing a slightly different trajectory toward the ground. The general effect was that of a shotgun charge, but the smallest of these missiles weighed a hundred kilos and travelled at orbital velocity.

A dozen Federation vessels were already climbing skyward, corkscrewing wildly because their officers hadn't taken the time to balance thrust. Two ships touched in a grazing collision. One continued to climb but the other, an orbital monitor with a lighter hull than the long-haul vessel, caromed out of the port reservation and dropped. The monitor came down in a swamp, only marginally under control.

The barge moved alongside Sal's cutter. The Feds mounted a twin-tube laser on a pintle in the open cabin. A man in metal armor and two Molts with asbestos padding over flexible vacuum suits swiveled the weapon to bear on the cutter.

Sal waved her hand. Harrigan clamped her thigh so that she could raise the other as well. The Fed pilot was probably using a laser communicator to order Brantling to hold station, but Sal didn't want the gunners to doubt her willingness to surrender.

Fifty tonnes or more of the *Gallant Sallie*'s stern hit near the center of the spaceport, narrowly missing a 1000-tonne giant just lifting from the ground. The shock wave sent ripples of dust across the surface.

A plasma motor ripped through the heart of a moderate-sized freighter half a klick away. The victim's thrusters were already lit. Kinetic and thermonuclear energy combined in a stunning fireball, dazzling even against the sunwashed expanse of the port.

Every ship in Heldensburg was attempting to lift. Two more unmanned Venerian vessels dived toward the port, though Sal was sure that at least one of them would miss by several klicks.

The barge edged within twenty meters, seesawing as the pilot tried to match velocity. One of the Molts flung a line belayed to a staple on the barge's hatch coaming. The throw missed ahead, but Sal managed to catch the line as the Fed overcorrected and the barge slipped behind the cutter.

She'd thought the Feds might kill them out of hand, but apparently the crews of the screening force wanted proof that they had done *something* to prevent the disaster taking place beneath them.

Sal gestured Harrigan, then Brantling, ahead of her. From reflex she held the line instead of tying it, since there'd be no one remaining aboard the cutter to cast it off.

Brantling paused at the hatch coaming with a reckless smile on his face. He pointed to the legend on the bow of the barge: A311, and below it in smaller letters ST. LAWRENCE. He touched his helmet to Sal's and said, "Look, Captain! That's their flagship. Only the best for Mister Gregg's friends, hey?"

A 30-cm bolt lit the sky beneath the barge with the iridescent, vain destruction of another incoming Venerian missile.

ABOARD THE *WRATH*

October 3, Year 27
1104 hours, Venus time

The purpose-built Fed warship closing to point-blank range was slightly larger than the *Wrath,* The name blazoned on her bows was *St. Lawrence.* She was the flagship of the tyrant's fleet, and her captain was putting her in the path of the Venerian vessel that had already ripped the thrusters out of three armed Federation merchantmen.

Stephen Gregg watched with professional approval as the *St. Lawrence* grew on the gunnery screen. Courage was easy enough to come by. The Feds aboard the vessels wallowing powerless— one of them dropping back toward Heldensburg with fatal inevitability—were probably brave enough. They'd just lacked the skill to deal with an expert like Piet Ricimer maneuvering beneath the stern of their ship and loosing a salvo into the most vulnerable point. This fellow knew his duty to the ships under his command, and he was able enough to at least make a stab at carrying out that duty.

He was a brave man also, for he surely knew he was about to engage Piet Ricimer, the terrible pirate conqueror.

Both ships were coasting on inertia, their thrusters shut down and shielded against hostile fire. Attitude jets puffed, changing the *Wrath*'s alignment slightly.

"Mister Stampfer," Piet announced over the intercom, "you may fire as you—"

The starboard gunport across the bridge cantilevered open. Stephen had known that the *Wrath* and *St. Lawrence* were on parallel courses; and known also that the two ships were close together.

Until the port lid lifted and he saw nothing but the Fed's scarred, curving hull plates, Stephen hadn't appreciated how *very* close the ships were.

"—bear!"

The 20-cm gun fired, started to recoil, and shattered in brilliance. A plasma bolt had struck at the edge of the port and on the muzzle of the Venerian cannon, blowing glassy shards of both in all directions. The splinter cage vanished. The gun to the trunnions and three crewmen above the waist were missing. The remainder of each was vaporized or scoured away by ceramic shocked into high-velocity sand.

The blast wall partitioning the bridge held, though flying debris scored it foggy. The tube Stephen gripped broke, and he flew across the bridge.

There were dozens of nearly simultaneous shocks, cannon recoiling and plasma bolts hitting the *Wrath* in turn. Vaporized metal from the hull of the *St. Lawrence* spurted, still white-hot and glowing, through the blasted gunport.

The cabin lights were out, but holographic displays cast a pastel glow across the interior surfaces. Stephen scuttled around the blast wall, dabbing with all four limbs. He expected the *Wrath* to swap ends and pour her remaining broadside into the *St. Lawrence*. Instead, the ships continued their matched courses, hurtling through nothingness a hundred thousand kilometers above Heldensburg. Piet had lifted the access plate of his console and was aiming a handlight into the interior.

Stephen braced one boot on the remnants of the 20-cm gun and locked the other armored knee on the hull where the gunport had been. The present hole was easily large enough to pass his body. He leaned out, aiming his flashgun.

Great gaps glowed in the flank of the *St. Lawrence*. The blue-white light winking through a jammed gunport was clearly an electrical fire. Only the fact that the battle was being fought in vacuum kept the entire gun deck from turning into an inferno.

The Fed warship had lower-level boarding holds like those of the *Wrath*, though they were split fore-and-aft instead of being full-length on either side. The hatches were open. Half a dozen Molts wearing padding over pressure suits leaped toward the *Wrath*. Sixty to eighty human soldiers in full or half armor waited to cross on the lines the Molts were carrying.

Stephen shot instinctively. The nearest Molt veered upward, driven by the pressure of gas spurting from his ruptured air pack. Others aboard the *Wrath* fired also. A second Molt tumbled under the impact of a bullet; a third separated from his line, dead though undeflected, and bounced from the *Wrath*'s hull. The remaining Molts set their adhesive grapnels against Venerian ceramic before they could be stopped.

There was a three-meter hole in the *Wrath*'s midships hull, perhaps blasted by a 20-cm gun exploding. The Fed boarding party scrambled toward the opening, guiding themselves by the lines.

Stephen slung his reloaded flashgun and launched himself toward the *St. Lawrence*. If he'd had time to think, he would have been frightened. For all his years in space, Stephen Gregg was as much a landsman as the Fed soldiers creeping gingerly across the boarding lines aft.

The quickest way to stop the boarders was to sever the lines aboard the Federation vessel. That wasn't something to think about, only to execute.

Stephen hadn't judged well the angle at which he'd pushed off. He drifted high. A Federation soldier tugging himself toward the *Wrath* hand over hand looked up and goggled. Stephen shot the man through the faceshield and threw the flashgun away to change course. The cast made him tumble, but the weapon wasn't quite massive enough to bring Stephen in contact with the *St. Lawrence*'s hull.

Beneath Stephen sailed a man in a ceramic hard suit, moving faster and at a flatter angle. He grabbed the lip of the open boarding hatch with one hand and turned to snatch Stephen's boot. He was Hadley, festooned with weapons and ammunition. Philips crossed only a few meters behind. The loaders, both of them accomplished sailors, had followed their principal—and done so with a great deal more skill than that principal had showed.

Stephen gripped a rifle floating from Hadley. Hadley slipped the sling as he cast Stephen into the hold, among the dozen or so Fed soldiers still waiting to cross the lines. Some of the Feds didn't realize a Venerian had boarded, but an officer fired a charge of buckshot into Stephen's right hip. The impact flung him against the forward bulkhead. He shot as he rebounded, starring the Fed's visor behind a gush of escaping air.

Recoil kicked Stephen back into the bulkhead. He pinned himself there deliberately by emptying the magazine into the nearest Feds. An officer's breastplate withstood the bullet that spun the man out of the hatch. His arms and legs windmilled; his mouth was open in a useless scream.

A light plasma cannon, a boat gun rigged as an antiboarding weapon, fired from the *Wrath* into the *St. Lawrence*'s aft hold. Bodies flew out with the debris. More Venerian sailors were crossing to the *St. Lawrence,* using the Feds' own lines or throwing themselves unaided across the ten-meter gap. Muzzle flashes, huge for being unconfined by atmospheric pressure, fluttered within the *Wrath.* The fight on the gun deck wasn't over.

Stephen unclipped his cutting bar and pushed off. He couldn't find his loaders without more effort than he had time for, and the bar was the better tool for the moment anyway.

A Fed stood at the ringbolt to which a pair of boarding lines were snubbed, aiming a rifle at Stephen. The man wore full armor. His face through his visor was white because of the strain with which he pulled at the trigger. The rifle didn't fire. Empty, still on safe, simply broken—it didn't matter. Anything could happen in the panicked confusion of a battle.

Stephen slashed through the lines and continued his stroke upward. The bar's teeth spun sparks from the surface of the Fed breastplate, but they sheared in satisfactory fashion through the rifle's receiver and the thinner armor of the gauntlets holding the weapon. Air and blood sprayed from the cut.

Dole with his white-chevroned helmet sailed into the hold. Six more sailors followed him. The *Wrath* had been short-handed since she took the *Savior Enthroned.* Casualties from the gunnery fight and now the lack of these men would leave Piet with a corporal's guard to conn and fight his ship; but he'd manage, as Stephen Gregg would manage, or die trying.

The hold was empty of living Fed soldiers. The deck shuddered.

The *Wrath* had at last begun to rotate on her long axis, tugging the Fed vessel by the line still attached in the aft hold.

Stephen jumped from the ringbolt to the companionway up from the hold. The pressure door wouldn't open. The hold brightened by perceptible degrees. Stephen turned his body to look.

Dole was spinning the power-assisted wheel on the bulkhead between the fore and aft holds. The clamshell hatches were closing, so the hold's overhead illumination reflected from their inner surfaces.

The *St. Lawrence* rocked from six hammer blows, then a seventh. What remained of the *Wrath*'s port battery had been brought to bear. Ions glared through the crack still open between the mating hatches.

Hadley used the carbine to pole himself to Stephen's side. Instead of offering to trade weapons, the loader undogged the hatch with an easy spin. Air rushing from the companionway shook both men. Vents in the ceiling of the hold opened also to restore pressure.

A shock heavier than that of a 20-cm bolt whipped the vessel's hull visibly. Apparent gravity returned as the *St. Lawrence* got under way.

Stephen took the carbine. Dole jumped to his side.

"Feds have a lot of safety muck, sir," the bosun said. The partial atmosphere made his amplified voice sound like that of a child squeaking. "You can't open the companionway with the hold opened to space, that's all."

"Let's go," Stephen said. Hadley pulled the hatch fully back for the gunman to lead.

There was no one in the companionway. Like the *Wrath,* the Federation warship was built with holds and plasma motors on the lower level and all living and fighting volumes on the single deck above.

The companionway's upper hatch was closed. Stephen expected it to be locked or even welded, but the wheel turned easily in his hand. He gestured behind him.

A sailor stepped by on the narrow landing and pushed the hatch open so hard that he fell partway out into the corridor. Three half-kilogram shots slammed through his helmet and threw neon sparks across the armored hatch. The sailor's legs thrashed, tangling Stephen and dropping him into a squat on the landing.

Stephen fired twice, angling his shots to ricochet bullets down the corridor. The carbine's operating lever broke because of his hasty strength. Dole dragged the dead man back.

Something hit a huge ringing blow on the corridor side of the hatch, knocking it nearly closed. As Dole reached up to pull the valve the rest of the way home, a crew-served laser burned across the lip and coaming, missing the bosun's arm by the thickness of the dust on his armor.

"Rifle," Stephen said, dropping the useless carbine.

Open the hatch again and charge. The Feds might panic; the hatch itself was protection from whatever weapon they'd set up on the hinge side of the valve. Shoot a few, shoot at least *one;* and die, as the men with him would die if they followed, but that was their choice.

Stephen wondered where Philips was. Chances were that he and his loader would be together again in a few seconds, though Philips deserved a cooler part of Hell.

"Sir!" Dole said. "Please—let's go this way."

Dole had dropped his shotgun. He thrust the tip of his cutting bar against the ceiling panel with both hands. The decks were minimum clearance, two meters, so he had good leverage.

The ceiling was nickel-steel like the rest of the ship's fabric, but the plates were only a centimeter thick instead of the 10 centimeters of companionway armor. The cutting bar sliced through with a bloodthirsty howl. White sparks blazed as they fell.

Holds and power plant on the lower level. Living quarters on the main deck. And in the upper curve of the cylindrical hull, the mechanical spaces. Tanks of air and reaction mass, and the pumps that circulated both throughout the *St. Lawrence.* Oh, yes. There was another way to deal with this one.

The Feds could hear the cutting bar's scream. Somebody must have understood what it meant, because a moment later the hatch opened from the corridor side. Stephen blew the head off the Molt that was half lunging, half being pushed toward the companionway.

Stephen continued to pump and fire the powerful rifle. Two other sailors were shooting. Hadley thrust Dole's shotgun between Stephen's legs and loosed both barrels under the valve, into the ankles of the man who'd pulled it open. The Feds still aboard the *St. Lawrence* were crewmen, sailors. They didn't have the armor of the soldiers who'd boarded the *Wrath.*

The Feds couldn't use their heavy weapons while the corridor was choked with their own people. The armored Venerians couldn't miss and couldn't be harmed in the packed chaos. Stephen closed the hatch again.

The hatch didn't lock from this side. The Feds would bring up their laser to face the opening and try again. They were already too late, because a square meter of the ceiling clanged from Dole's shoulders to the landing.

A sailor formed a stirrup of his hands and launched Dole into the mechanical spaces. Another sailor started to follow. Stephen pushed the man aside and put his own boot onto the linked gauntlets. "Hadley, you next," he ordered as he rose through the hole with a great thrust of his arms.

The space above was an unlighted warren of pipes and flocking-insulated panels. Stephen saw the treads of Dole's boots as the bosun crawled down a channel. Dole couldn't possibly see where he was going, but he'd worked the guts of starships enough years to have an instinct for their layout.

Hadley came through the hole gripping a handlight. Stephen took it, hesitated, and switched it on. Fed crewmen might have entered the mechanical spaces through an access port by now, but he'd rather take that chance than remain blind.

With the lamp's aid, Stephen wormed his way up to where Dole squatted in a meter-by-two-meter alcove sculpted in the side of a huge tank. Three arm-thick pipes fed into an armored regulator and out again through a multibranched manifold. Dole set his cutting bar against the regulator. The bar groaned and died. Dole had exhausted the battery in slicing through the ceiling plates.

"Gimmie your bar, sir!" the bosun demanded. "If we open this up, the ship's whole oxygen supply vents. We can take the barge in the aft hold and be long gone by the time the Feds realize they're all dead!"

Stephen set his rifle down to unclip the bar from his armor. He froze.

If you couldn't sleep with it afterwards, then don't do it.

"Dole, can you shut off the water to their thrusters from up here?" Stephen demanded.

"Huh?" the bosun said. His face went momentarily blank. "Yeah, I suppose. Give me the light."

More sailors had crawled into the mechanical spaces. "There's a feed trunk here, Mister Dole!" a man shouted. "But there'll be another to starboard, like enough."

"Cut that trunk and the rest of you guard it!" Stephen ordered. "Dole, Hadley, and me are going to take care of the other half of the system!"

It was three hours before Admiral Jean King, Commander of the Grand Fleet of Retribution, gave up. During that time the *St. Lawrence* drifted with only auxiliary power. Her tanks of reaction mass were draining into the belly of the ship via every crack and passage through the inner hull.

Crewmen making desperate attempts to retake the mechanical spaces failed bloodily. Federation personnel didn't dare use flashguns or even projectile weapons against enemies lurking amid the high-pressure oxygen pipes. The Venerians felt no such compunction.

When King saw a pair of Venerian warships easing closer to his own disabled vessel, he decided to surrender instead to the leader of the boarding party that had actually accomplished his destruction. To carry his offer, King sent one of the Venerian prisoners the *St. Lawrence*'s barge had brought aboard when the *St. Lawrence* reached orbit.

He sent Captain Sarah Blythe.

BETAPORT, VENUS

October 14, Year 27
2217 hours, Venus time

The *Wrath* began to vibrate from the torque of the tractor motors transmitted through the drawbar. When at last the cradle wheels turned, the warship's massive whole rumbled from Transfer Dock 14 into the tunnel leading to the Halys Yard where she would be repaired.

Sal touched Stephen's upper arm. It took the big man's mind a moment to register the contact. When his eyes blinked back to the present and focused on her, the slabs of his facial muscles loosened slightly.

Even before the *Wrath* moved her own length forward, the tractor slowed. The driver had switched its motor to alternator mode to drink the warship's momentum. The cradle's ceramic disc brakes squealed as they heated and finally, white-hot, bit. Dock 14's huge inner doors thundered like the start of a volcanic eruption as they closed behind the halted *Wrath*.

"You know," said Dole in a conversational voice, "there was times I really didn't think I'd be back to see this again."

The bosun threw the switch controlling the doors of the starboard boarding hold. All six segments sprang open as they were

865

designed to do. The wrenching the *Wrath* took from short-series transits and Federation guns had loosened her hull, sometimes in desirable fashions.

The crowd roared. The banks of additional lighting set up in the tunnel shivered to the echoing cheers.

It had been Piet's idea. There would be a formal service of welcome and thanksgiving at the Governor's Palace in three days time; but Piet Ricimer, his crew, and the *Wrath* itself were from Betaport. This was Betaport's celebration.

Stephen had been the one to suggest that the crew be locked through with the ship rather than enter the town in the usual way, by the personnel hatch on Dock Street. The ship tunnel was more spacious, and the patches on the vessel's hull were a more vivid witness to the battle than anything the surviving crew could say.

"God has blessed Venus!" Piet Ricimer cried from the front of the ship's company. "May we always be worthy of His care!"

Guillermo stood at an audio board in the rear of the hold. The Molt kept the directional microphone on the upper hatch aimed at Piet's lips, sending his voice through the *Wrath*'s powerful outside speakers. Even so, the words were a descant to the cheering.

Piet stepped forward, gesturing the crew with him. The crowd surged toward them through the marshals, meeting and mixing on the boarding ramp. Betaport dignitaries in finery more often gorgeous than tasteful mobbed Piet.

Stephen didn't move from the rear bulkhead, but Sal saw his mouth quirk in a smile. Piet wore his half armor for show, though the gold finish was pitted from when he and Stampfer alone crewed a 20-cm gun whose hydraulics had failed. At least the back-and-breast would keep him from being crushed by well-wishers.

Sal stayed beside Stephen. Betaport wasn't her town. Harrigan and Brantling had transferred to the *Freedom* and were probably in Ishtar City now. Sal would see her father and childhood friends in three days, at the formal service.

Floral wreaths and bottles of liquor greeted the crewmen. The marshals had given wives and girlfriends places near the front, though there was no lack of freelances to cherish men who'd returned unattached.

Twice Sal saw *both* a wife and a girlfriend greet the same sailor. Those weren't the only tears shed in the general joy. Piet had listed the butcher's bill and the *Wrath*'s remaining complement in the same couriered dispatch that announced the victory. There were women, one of them with a newborn infant at her breast, who'd refused to believe until the hatch opened and they saw the pitiful few within the *Wrath*'s hold.

Not all those missing were dead. Many were in prize crews, and there were a dozen wounded who ought to survive (though not always with the original number of limbs).

But there were also the men *listed* as missing. In a spaceman's town like Betaport, everyone knew "missing" generally meant drifting in vacuum somewhere more distant than light could reach in a million years.

As the crowd milled beside the *Wrath* in the greatest festival the port would ever see, Stephen turned to Sal with an expression she didn't recognize and said, "I almost killed you on the *St. Lawrence*. I wasn't sure I was going to tell you that."

He had to speak loudly to be heard, even though they stood together.

Sal put her arm around his waist, shrugged, and smiled. His muscles were as taut as a starship's tow cable. "Well, there's risk in anything," she said, "but I agreed with King that I should take the surrender offer instead of him sending one of his officers. You'd have thought that was a trick."

"Not that," Stephen said. "We were about to dump the main oxygen supply, but I didn't. I—we, I didn't know which pipe was which. We cut off reaction mass to the thrusters instead. Because I decided I didn't want to kill a thousand people."

His voice was trembling. Sal tried to hug herself against his chest, but Stephen held her apart and tilted her face so that she met his eyes.

"Another thousand people," he said. Only then did he draw her close.

The expression Sal hadn't been able to recognize was hope.

"Stephen," she said. "Let me stay with you. All night."

"No," he murmured gently. "That—"

"*Please*, Stephen, for God's sake!" she said.

"Sal, it's not you, it's me," he said with his lips to her ear. "On the ground, I don't sleep well. I don't really sleep. I appreciate what you're trying to do, but I don't want anybody around me when . . . Not even servants. Especially not somebody I care about."

Sal drew away and looked into his eyes again. "You don't

understand, Stephen. If it's not you, it'll be the man I killed on
Arles. The liquor helped for a while, but I can't drink enough anymore. If you won't hold me, I . . ."

She flung her head forward and blotted her tears on Stephen's
worn brown doublet. "I don't know what I'll do. I don't know what
I'll do."

He stroked her back with fingers that could bend steel of their
own thickness. "You need *me,* Sal?" he said. "You need me?"

"On my life I do, Stephen," she said. She choked; she didn't know
if he could hear her words or not. "On my very life."

"Christ's blood, what a pair of cripples we are!" he said.

Stephen lifted Sal into the air so that her short blond hair brushed
the ceiling plates. "But you ought to see the other guy," he added
with a wry smile. "And after all, I *didn't* kill you, did I?"

Stephen swung her in a circle around him as though she were
a child rather than a solidly built adult. Piet Ricimer looked up
from the crowd pressing him. Sal caught a glimpse of a beaming
smile replacing the amazement that had flashed across Piet's face.

"I warn you," Stephen said, suddenly serious as he put her down.
"I've got two rooms with nothing but a bed, a wardrobe, and a
lot of slash bottles. There won't be anything else available with
this crowd in town."

"We'll manage," Sal said. She hugged him close again. "We've
managed everything so far."

BETAPORT, VENUS

March 15, Year 28
1455 hours, Venus time

"I am pleased to see you again, Colonel," Guillermo said as he bowed Stephen into Piet's private office.

The Molt was the only one authorized to open the door nowadays. The door *keeper,* on the other hand, was Dole or another trusted sailor who'd been with Captain Ricimer too long to care who a would-be intruder might be. If somebody tried to push into the captain's office, he got knocked down—and lucky if he didn't get a boot in the ribs besides.

Of course, Mister Gregg wanting to see the captain—that was something else again. There weren't appointments between old shipmates.

Piet was hunched over a desk covered with shiny glassine printouts, trying to find a datum as he talked on the phone. He raised three fingers when he heard the door open, but he didn't look up from his search. Stephen moved a stack of flimsies and a sample case—microchips, of recent European manufacture from the look of them—off the chair and sat down.

Piet caught the motion from the corner of his eye. He glanced at Stephen, grinned with enthusiasm, and said, "I'm very sorry, Factor, but something's come up. I'll get back to you."

He hung up the phone and switched it mute. "Stephen!" he said, rising from his chair. "My goodness, I'm afraid I've been as busy as I hear you are yourself!"

"I came by with a business proposition, Piet," Stephen said as they shook hands above the cluttered desk. Piet looked like he'd gained five kilos in the months since the *Wrath* came home, but the fire of his countenance burned just as bright as it ever had.

"I've got something I'd like you to look at too, Stephen," Piet said as they both sat down. "But you first, please. After all, you came to me when I haven't managed to get out to see anybody in far too long."

"Blythe Spirits Limited has six ships, now, Piet," Stephen said, leaning back deliberately in the chair. He'd learned that by feigning ease he could sometimes induce the actual feeling. "They're all of them ships taken in the sweep of Fed shipping we made after the Grand Fleet of Retribution came apart."

He made a face at Pleyal's grandiose title. "They can be had for a song, though the navigational upgrades are a significant factor."

Piet chuckled, then sobered. "Metal hulls aren't as strong as good ceramic, Stephen," he said. "Not that I'm trying to tell you or Captain Blythe your business, but . . ."

Stephen nodded. "Right, but metal degrades instead of failing abruptly the way overstressed ceramic's been known to do."

He smiled grimly. They'd seen it happen to a consort of their own vessel: what had been a ship after one transit disintegrated to a sleet of gravel during the next. There'd been no survivors, and no chance of survivors.

"At the point Sal no longer thinks the hulls are safe," Stephen continued, "we'll strip the electronics and scrap the rest. They're *very* cheap, Piet."

"I wouldn't venture to make business decisions for you, Stephen," Piet said with a reminiscent smile. They'd seen a lot of things together, Piet and he.

Outside the door a cultured, angry voice said, "I have an appointment with the factor, my good man, an appointment!"

Lightbody was on duty with Guillermo. Stephen heard the sailor's reply only as a truculent rumble, but he was willing to bet Lightbody slapped his truncheon of high-pressure tubing into his palm as he spoke.

"Cargoes are going begging," Stephen explained. "The Fed

colonies don't make any complaint about trading with us no matter what Pleyal says back in Montreal. For a lot of them it's us or starve, and they know it. And I'm not talking short-term profits, either. The shippers who make contacts now will have a foundation to build on as the colonies grow."

He leaned forward and stretched his hand across the desk. "Piet," he said, "you and I started out to be traders. Pleyal's beaten. Come on into Blythe Spirits with us."

Piet laughed brightly. Only someone who knew him very well would have heard the slight tension in the note. "All right," he said. He placed his hand over his friend's. "How much would you like from me?"

"Not your money, Piet," Stephen said. "I want you, doing the same thing Sal's doing in Ishtar City. Picking captains who'll get so rich on quarter shares that they'll buy their own ships and make everybody—themselves and Venus and the colonies they serve—that much the richer. Equal partners, Piet. The three of us."

Piet tilted back in his chair and laced his fingers behind his head. "Fernando Comaguena, the Hidalgo of the Southern Cross—the pretender, Pleyal would say—is in Ishtar City now. There's some suggestion the governor might permit him to recruit help on Venus to regain his rightful position in Buenos Aires."

He raised an eyebrow.

Stephen got up and stretched. "Not for me, thank you, Piet," he said. He smiled, wondering if the expression looked as sad as he felt. Though it wasn't a surprise . . . "The Federation's been beaten. Pleyal and his successors can never be a threat to Venus again. They'll never be able to dictate who goes to the stars."

Piet lowered his hands slowly to the desk and stared at them. "It's a little hard to be sure where to draw the line, Stephen," he said.

"Then draw it here!" Stephen said with a passion that surprised them both. "Piet, there'll never be perfect peace while there are men. But there can be peace for *some* men."

Piet pushed his chair back and stood. "Do you have peace, Stephen?" he asked softly.

"Sometimes," Stephen said. He felt the corners of his mouth lift in a wan smile. "More than I did. You know, sometimes I think that eventually I may be able to sleep a whole night through without, without . . ."

Piet walked around the desk.

"Piet, I never knew how important it was to be needed," Stephen whispered.

Piet took Stephen's hands in his. "I need you, Stephen," he said.

"You needed somebody *like* me, Piet," Stephen said harshly. "You don't need me if you're going to put the hidalgo back on his throne—if that's even possible."

"I need a friend, Stephen," Piet said simply.

"Then listen to me, Piet!" Stephen said. "The best thing a friend can tell you is to get out now. Leave the wars to other people and invest in the stars instead. God knows they've cost us enough already, you and me."

He put his arms around the smaller man. They hugged like lovers.

"*God* knows what they've cost," one of the men repeated; but not even an observer in the room would have been sure who spoke.

AUTHOR'S NOTES

1) Readers may notice that the plot of FIRESHIPS is based largely on events in the life of Sir Francis Drake. I therefore think I ought to mention that Sir Francis wasn't an ancestor of mine, and I can prove it.

The Drakes from whom I'm descended (through, let me add, a long line of dirt farmers in the years since they emigrated to the American colonies) are the Drakes of Ashe, a very old and thoroughly undistinguished family of Devonshire gentry. The height of their achievement arrived when a member of the family became Sheriff of Devon; however their—our—coat of arms, a wyvern (a two-legged dragon) displayed, is attested back to 1307.

Francis Drake was the son of a shipwright and lay preacher. He grew up in a hulk in the mud of the Medway, where his father was employed in the dockyard.

When Francis rose to prominence, entirely through his own efforts, he began to use our coat of arms. One of my ancestors promptly complained to the College of Heralds and quashed this mere *mechanick's* claim to kinship—thus depriving the Drakes of Ashe of our one chance to embrace somebody important in our number.

The story doesn't end quite there, however. Francis Drake went from success to success. He was knighted and gained the right to his own coat of arms. The first, extremely ornate, design Sir Francis submitted to the College of Heralds had as its crest a full-rigged ship.

Caught in the rigging, dangling head down and helpless, was a wyvern . . .

2) I wasn't sure I was going to mention this further aspect of FIRESHIPS, but I think I should. When I decided to do a series of novels using the Age of Discovery for plot paradigms, I didn't intend the matter of what wars cost the people who fight them to be a major theme. I'm not a writer who claims his characters get away from him: mine don't. But this aspect of the three novels grew unexpectedly from the subject matter.

I've learned that the people who haven't been there themselves really aren't going to understand what I'm trying to tell them, but to be very explicit: it isn't the things that were done to you that are hardest to live with afterwards. It's what you became and the things you did to survive, one way and another.

For the folks who have been there—you've got friends, you've got people who understand *even if you haven't met them.* It's not just you. You're not alone.

We're not alone.

Dave Drake
Chatham Country, NC